Silent Music

Silent Music

Jane Hawking

ALMA BOOKS

ALMA BOOKS LTD
3 Castle Yard
Richmond
Surrey TW10 6TF
United Kingdom
www.almabooks.com

First published by Alma Books Ltd in 2016

© Jane Hawking, 2016

Cover design: Jem Butcher

Jane Hawking asserts her moral right to be identified as the author of this work in accordance with the Copyright, Designs and Patents Act 1988

Printed in Great Britain by CPI Group (UK) Ltd, Croydon CR0 4YY

ISBN: 978-1-84688-412-2
EBOOK: 978-1-84688-418-4

This is a work of fiction. Names, characters, places and incidents either are products of the author's imagination or are used fictitiously. Any resemblance to persons, living or dead, is entirely coincidental.

Silent Music

FOR JONATHAN

PART ONE

1

As the long fingers of encroaching night crept into the stuffy little bedroom, the small figure on the bed would have been all but invisible had her tossing movements not disturbed the darkness with glimmering reflections of the dying light. Still wide awake, she kicked off the covers and, stretching her legs until they touched the hard end of the bed, strained not only her ears but every muscle in her body to catch the rise and fall of the argument which filtered up through the floorboards and through the open windows from the room below. She would have preferred not to hear her mother's outbursts, but an irresistible compulsion prevented her from pulling the bedclothes over her head and closing her ears and her mind to the domestic drama being enacted downstairs. Every word of her mother's studied performance was clearly audible, but the low, moderate tones of her father's replies as he repeated the same words over and again were more difficult to grasp. She could imagine him shaking his head in anxious uncertainty as he spoke: "I really can't see how we can manage it, I can't see at all."

Shirley, her mother, the author of the outbursts, interrupted her husband in rhythmic crescendos of hysteria. Ruth, the silent audience of her parents' disagreement, alone in the blackness of the little back bedroom, winced at the injustice of the accusations bombarding her father.

"Well, come on, John! Here am I offering to work all the hours in the day, doing something I know I can do, to give us a decent income, and all you can say is 'I can't see how we can manage it'," shouted Shirley, mimicking his hesitant speech with caustic sarcasm.

He replied calmly, stoically hiding his distress, choosing his words carefully in an attempt to avoid further outbursts or provoke his wife even more. "I don't want you to have to work all the hours in the day. In fact, I don't think you should have to work at all: it's not right."

"But I worked in the War, harder than you will ever know!" was her immediate, defiant retort. "It was all right for women to work then – they had to – so why shouldn't they work now? Other women work even now, so why shouldn't I?"

Searching for inspiration, she quickly stumbled on a wider cause, the truth of which was irrefutable, and she went triumphantly into the attack: "Men are afraid, that's why; men are afraid of losing their power if women can do everything they can do. They're afraid their supper won't be ready for them in the evening and their shirts won't be ironed. Well, I've had enough of that." Ruth imagined Shirley flouncing round the table, doubtless hobbling with that strange limp of hers, pulling the cloth off and throwing it into a corner in a symbolic gesture of disgust.

John disregarded this latest challenge with its wide-ranging sociological implications as, perhaps unwisely, he was still concentrating on the previous, more personal, issue. "Anyhow, my pay is not that bad since I was promoted," he volunteered quietly after some consideration. "Don't forget I am the Deputy Manager of the office now and that means something!"

"Your pay means something! It's not that bad!" she exclaimed, her resentment whipped again into a dramatic frenzy. "What do you mean 'not that bad'? What does it mean? We haven't got a car, we haven't got a fridge, we haven't got a television, and here we are in this pokey little house with no garden and neighbours on all sides."

She stopped to draw breath and then raised her voice even higher, as if deliberately addressing the neighbours. "I bet they're all listening, with their ears glued to the walls!" she shouted more loudly, as if inviting the said audience to listen in. She considered her next move, and in an adroit change of tactics and with an impeccable sense of timing, her voice faded in a plaintive diminuendo, as she moaned quietly in self-pity. Forgetting her anger she assumed the role of the tragic heroine.

"To think that people always said I was bound to be a ballerina or a film star!" Suddenly she raised her voice again. "You said so too, don't you remember? And just look how I have ended up!" Having reached its highest pitch of pathos, her anger dissolved in convulsive sobbing, lending true drama to the awful tragedy of her plight.

Ruth heaved a sad sigh in the darkened room. This was not a sigh of sympathy for Shirley's misfortune, so poignantly expressed downstairs, but a sigh of despair for her father's predicament. Although the entire neighbourhood might well have heard what was going on, without having to glue their ears to the walls, such rows were not of resounding interest because, whatever the cause, they always assumed the same predictable pattern, though this one was definitely the worst in a very long time. For Ruth, on the other hand, their impact never ceased to be harrowing. She wanted to rush to her father's defence against her mother; she would shout back at her that there was no reason to attack Dad so viciously. He was kind and gentle, and it was obvious that he tried very hard to do his best for them. For all her problems, Shirley was spoilt and selfish. If only he would make a stand, put her in her place. Ruth wanted to run downstairs and hug him protectively, but she did not dare for fear of making matters worse.

On this particular occasion she had wanted to warn her father of the danger signals when he first set foot in the door that evening. As usual, there had been not the slightest opportunity to give him so much as a word of warning or even a signal to put him on his guard, so her good intentions had remained unfulfilled and this row was the result. In contrast to her father, who needed to have every nuance explained to him in fine detail, Ruth, with the instinct of a small animal, had perceived from the very moment she came home from school that the atmosphere was charged with an electrical excitement. As past experience suggested, this was sure to explode over her father's head at supper time, as indeed it had.

Shirley had been involved in an animated discussion with Mr Farjeon, the elderly man from the newspaper shop, whom they all called "Old Fargone". The compulsive chatter was all about premises and rents, quotas and reps, licences and wholesaling, terms which meant nothing to Ruth and, since Shirley (she did not like to be called "Mummy" or "Mum" and certainly not "Mother") had scarcely acknowledged her daughter's arrival, Ruth had deemed it wisest to run straight through the house out to the little backyard, collecting a glass of orange squash and a biscuit on the way. Wondering what was happening, but mindful of Shirley's dangerously tense excitement and conscious that her presence would not be welcome, she sat herself down on the back doorstep with her knees clasped to her chest and gazed up at the grimy London sky, relieved only by an apologetic hint of distant blue, a faint acknowledgement that somewhere far away the summer sun was shining brightly.

Noises assailed her from all sides as she sat puzzling over how best to warn her father of the build-up to the inevitable approaching explosion. He, poor thing, was so innocent he would be bound to provoke it – he always did – and there would be nothing that she could do to help him. One might have suspected that he had a blind spot for these crises, because he had never learnt to judge the emotional temperature or the state of Shirley's moods any more than he could anticipate or dominate her bouts of manic tension, even when they had been building up for some weeks.

Sometimes she maintained control over these periods herself, but when they raged out of control, as was happening now, the outcome would be a tempestuous session possibly followed by a fall into the depths of depression, and then he would nurse her like a child with untiring love and patience. Tonight the storm would rage for hours, and in the end Shirley would be certain to get her own way; that was the time-honoured conclusion. At first she would rant and rave, then she would wheedle and cajole until Dad (at least Ruth had one parent who did not mind being addressed as such) was completely disarmed, his powers of resistance depleted, his mental faculties drained and his generous nature exploited.

So seriously was Ruth absorbed in these considerations that, for once, she scarcely noticed the invasive clamour of human and animal activity from the neighbouring houses: it ricocheted off the three tight walls of the little yard and the back wall of the house, adults scolding, children whining, wirelesses blaring, dogs barking, all against the incessant hum of the capital city. Suddenly a familiar and welcome sound sent a thrill through her hunched frame, interrupting her musings, leaving them momentarily suspended in empty space and drowning out all other noises. The sound was none other than the majestic panting of an express train, perhaps even the Flying Scotsman, as it ponderously heaved its way out of Euston station, echoing among the narrow lines of houses. It drew closer, gathering speed and whistling as it passed through the cutting at the end of the street, only half a dozen houses away.

Closing her eyes and holding out her arms in rapture, Ruth stood up to immerse herself in the clouds of warm, gritty smoke which filled the yard in a dense comforting fog, opening her mouth to gulp the sticky black smuts. They smelt and tasted of tar and coal, like that yellow soap that was Grandpa's favourite, and they conjured up powerful images of independence, of travel, of escape, of green fields and countryside, of the sea and of summer holidays. They brought visions of those carefree days when Dad and Shirley would talk happily to each other, laughing as they walked arm in arm along the promenade or the pier, while Ruth played on the beach and Nan, who always came to join them for that week, dozed in her deckchair in the sun.

Those times were a fleeting glimpse of the real life, of life as it should be lived. They happened only once a year, for only one brief week, but that week was the most important of the whole twelve months. In that week Shirley seemed to escape from a wicked spell: miraculously, she would suddenly try to be nice to everyone – to Dad, to Ruth herself, and even to Nan. You might almost believe that she did in fact possess some qualities of human kindness after all, even if at other times they were only occasionally perceptible.

She would laugh and cheer at the performances at the Pier Theatre, and afterwards, on the way back to the hotel, she would cling to Dad's arm, whispering and giggling in his ear and caressing his cheek till she brought a broad smile to his lips. She would even patiently spend ages before dinner trying to fix a bow to Ruth's slippery brown hair, and then, standing back to admire the finished effect, would remark, "You know, Ruth, one day you might be quite pretty after all." This concession was usually accompanied by a cuddle which, as they descended the stairs to dinner, made them appear to be the closest of mothers and daughters.

On holiday, Shirley would make a conspicuous effort to be civil to Nan; she would chat to her occasionally about nothing in particular, and had been known to give her a helping hand up steps. No one would ever think that a month or two earlier she had been fretting and complaining explosively about taking Nan on holiday, although it had been her idea in the first place. "It's my only week by the sea, and I have to spend it with your mother!" she would exclaim to Dad, stressing the "your" with recriminatory indignation, sometimes, if the situation got out of hand, even insisting that he should tell his mother not to come. Usually by the next morning the upset would have subsided and nothing more was said, so Nan came on holiday as usual, unaware that her impending presence had been the cause of a domestic disturbance.

As the clouds of smoke from the passing train began to disperse, Ruth was about to resume her seat on the back doorstep when, out of the corner of her eye, she glimpsed the flash of red claw-like nails, reaching out to grab her from behind. She ducked out of the way and escaped the claws but did not avoid the impact of Shirley's knife-edged tongue. "You naughty girl! What do you think you are doing out there in all that smoke? How many times do I have to tell you not to stand in the yard when a train is passing? That makes more washing! Don't you think I've got better things to do? Go up to your room at once!" Without daring to point out that Shirley did not actually do the washing because Ruth and her father did it themselves on

Saturdays, Ruth obeyed meekly, thankful to be out of reach of the red claws, but no sooner had she gone upstairs than she was called down again to lay the table for supper.

Shirley was busy clearing piles of official-looking papers away and taking them into her private domain, the front room, from which Ruth was excluded except on special occasions. Every shelf, nook and cranny in that room was full of Shirley's treasures – porcelain shepherdesses, china horses, glass swans and plaster geese, all conspiring to create so many hazards that Ruth was positively glad to be kept out. There Shirley entertained her friends, or rather held court, for it was generally accepted in the neighbourhood that with her blonde hair, her good looks, her slim, striking figure and her high heels, she was a cut above the rest of the street and, far from feeling resentful, her neighbours regarded it as an honour to be invited in for coffee and a smoke.

They doubtless still hung on to the faint hope, as she did, that she was a star waiting to be discovered. Perhaps they were secretly expecting their patience to be rewarded when, at some undefined future date, they would be there on the spot, ready to reap the benefits of a fortunate acquaintance. Though now, with the advancing years and little sign of any progress, they could be forgiven for having some misgivings as to the likelihood of these ambitions ever being fulfilled. Usually, by the time they left, there was little to choose in terms of tar content between Shirley's parlour and the backyard when a train was passing through the cutting. Ruth had also learnt the folly of attempting to point out that particular comparison.

Shirley retreated into the front room, leaving Ruth to assemble the usual Monday supper of cold meat, bread and pickles in the kitchen. With any luck she would be able to warn her dad that something was afoot as soon as he entered the house. Alas, the mere sound of his key in the lock of the front door was enough to bring Shirley bounding out of her lair, like a wild animal ready to pounce, bursting with pride at the ingenuity of the scheme she was devising. A swift glance from the kitchen told Ruth that her father was weary and hungry. His face was sallow, beaded with sweat in the heat. He searched in confusion for an appropriate answer to Shirley's impetuous "You'll never guess what has happened!"

Predictably, his answer, when it came, did not in any way satisfy her expectations. "Let me take my jacket off and have a wash, love," he said, kissing her on the cheek. "It's been such a hot day and so stuffy in the office." He worked in the Rates Office at the local borough council.

This simple request was immediately interpreted by Shirley as a rebuff. Wiping the perfunctory but sweaty kiss from her cheek with the back of her hand in disgust, she glared at her husband, but summoned the reluctant grace to wait till he sat down before proceeding. "Might you take a little interest in what I have to tell you?" she enquired, her voice already hard and laden with scorn. Ruth, seated between the two contenders like an umpire at a tennis match, watched and listened with bated breath. "Of course, love; go on, tell me," John replied.

He then made the unfortunate mistake of tucking with ill-concealed relish into his supper, not giving his impatient wife the full and undivided attention that she required. Consequently, instead of suggesting proposals for mutual consideration as had been her intention, Shirley indignantly presented him with a *fait accompli*, which indeed had the required effect of interrupting his meal in an astounding fashion. He sat staring at her, his mouth open, his fork waving in the air, when she baldly announced, "We're going to move; we're going to buy or rent the newsagent's and set up in business." She smirked defiantly before continuing: "Old Fargone is retiring, and he has agreed either to sell or, for the time being until we can raise the money, to let it to us."

At last Ruth understood why Shirley had been so busy and preoccupied, not only this afternoon but every afternoon for the past two or three weeks. She had been preparing a major upheaval in their lives, and this was evidently the first that Dad had heard about it. She, Ruth, did not count; she did not expect to hear about things, holidays, moves and such, until they happened, but she was cross that her dad had not been consulted earlier over such an important matter. Naturally there would be an almighty row. Shirley would feel slighted at having her plans questioned, for this was tantamount to doubting her ability: after all, as they and anyone else who cared to listen were frequently reminded, *she* was the daughter of a successful newsagent and knew all there was to know about the business. Dad, on the other hand, initially dumbstruck at the full seriousness of the situation, would want much more information, facts and figures, and time to investigate the pros and cons before coming to any decision. Shirley would be unable to restrain her impatience and Dad would retreat unhappily into himself. The forthcoming row was as easy to anticipate as night following day, but this one was different in that it was going to hinge on a question of considerable significance to them all.

Ruth ate her supper hurriedly while her parents glared in dull hostility at each other, each anticipating the other's reactions and preparing to counter them. As she finished her bread and butter, her father turned to her, his face a picture of doleful resignation, and said, "Ruthie, I think you had better go upstairs."

"Yes," Shirley snapped, in a deceptive display of agreement with her spouse. "You can forget about the washing-up and go to bed early tonight. it'll do you good."

The row which had been going on for hours down below was finally waning now that Shirley's well-rehearsed repertoire was finally exhausted. They had been through the gamut of her life history: her early artistic talent, the hopes of her devoted father, his paper shop, her successes at the dance school, the promise of a fantastic career which was certain to bring her fame, wealth and glamour, the experiences of the War – all frustrated in a dead-end marriage which brought her drudgery and poverty in a London backstreet. Dad had heard it all often enough, so had Ruth: he was entirely to blame for everything that had, or rather had not, happened to Shirley since their marriage.

The voices were quiet now. Ruth was sure she heard a faint giggle: that must mean that Shirley had won and that Dad had been forced to agree to whatever it was she wanted, presumably going into business as a newsagent, whether he wanted to or not. She heard their footsteps on the staircase. The row was over, and they were going to bed, whispering to each other and stumbling in the dark. At last Ruth relaxed her guard, for the only sounds to reach her room from behind their closed door were the normal muffled noises of the night. She turned her face to the wall, yawned and closed her eyes. Maybe it would not be too bad, she thought drowsily; it might even be an improvement on their present circumstances. Shirley was right: their house was very small and pokey, hemmed in on all sides by other houses and other people.

The paper shop was on the main road, on the Broadway by the zebra crossing next to the post office. It looked more like a house that had once, a long time ago, been made into a shop with a large flat upstairs, and out at the back it overlooked a garden and the park at the rear. That much she knew because she saw it whenever she went to the park. Sometimes, on a fine day, old Mr Farjeon would stand at his back gate surveying the park and having a quiet smoke, while in the shop his wife grudgingly served the penny bull's-eyes and liquorice sticks from the sweet counter to homeward-bound schoolchildren.

Drifting into a reassured state of half-sleep, clutching a ragged old teddy, she reverted to a less complex world, one where she always felt at ease: the dream world of her early memories, particularly of her closeness to her grandmother and of everything connected with her house, with its enigmatic name, Haydn, engraved on the gate at number 10, Beech Grove. These were the dreams that came floating into her mind just as the last wisps of daylight had wafted into her bedroom hours earlier, and they were the dreams that often gave her refuge from her uncertain home life.

Nan rarely gave the impression of suffering from the unintelligible complications of adulthood that beset Dad and Shirley. Nan's outlook on the past and the future was only very occasionally tarnished with regret or sadness for what had been and might have been; she was sensible and unchanging. Although she lived so far away, her image, now ageing, was ever present and reassured Ruth in times of domestic upheaval.

Inextricably linked with the image of Nan and completely at one with her personality, her house was the source of Ruth's most memorable impressions, impressions which she carried everywhere with her and which in their vividness would for ever condition her whole outlook on life. Dreams of that house offered her a secure haven from all the anxieties occasioned by a home life which was and always had been, by its very nature, uncertain. That house was also the guardian of her greatest secret, one that she shared with Nan, but not with her parents.

Dear Nan: if Ruth had any doubts as to whether Shirley, with her fluffy blonde curls, her green eyes and her neat, oval face, were her real mother, there were no such doubts about her relationship with her grandmother. Nan had the same straight hair – formerly brown, now plaited back in a greying bun – the same large, trusting brown eyes and the same broad face and darkish skin which Ruth saw repeated in her father and which she recognized in herself. Their features were distinctive but undistinguished, frankly not capable of great beauty according to conventional perceptions.

At first glance, most people would have regarded Nan as simply a kind and unassuming elderly lady. Ruth knew better than that. She knew that Nan had hidden powers and possessed a magical capacity for invention, for she told entertaining stories at night as she and Ruth prepared for bed in their shared bedroom on holiday at the guest house by the sea, just as she had done years ago on those occasions when Grandpa was still alive and Ruth was small and went to stay with them. Sometimes the stories were about the fairy folk at the bottom of her garden, who had endless problems with their families. Sometimes they were about Dad when he was a little boy and was constantly getting into scrapes.

Twice he had got stuck up the old oak tree in the Dell down the road, and the fire brigade had had to come and rescue him with their ladders. Once he vanished for a whole night until they discovered him early the following morning, sleeping contentedly in the shed, shut in among his beloved tools – and once, when Nan and Grandpa were out, he decided, thinking he was being helpful, to colour the front door bright orange with some paint he had found on a shelf. The fairies' children indulged in the same sort of pranks, and their parents were forever coming to Nan to ask her advice on how to deal with them. Surprisingly no one was ever cross with their children, neither Nan and Grandpa with Dad, nor the fairies with their offspring. They all credited their children with the best of intentions even if the results of those intentions were not quite as they hoped.

Last summer Ruth had become uncomfortably conscious that she was getting rather too old for these stories. Sadly she foresaw that growing up would spell the end of such childishness. Her school friends would laugh at her if they knew about them, as they would if they knew that she still took her old teddy to bed with her. Nevertheless, she felt an urge to keep the magic alive, so in private she continued to encourage Nan to recount the latest yarn.

"How is poor Mrs Spindleberry and that boy of hers – his name's Tig, isn't it?" she would enquire innocently.

"Well, now you're asking!" Nan would reply with a sigh of exasperation, and then would launch into the story of Tig's latest escapade, so that you might have believed it was only yesterday that poor Mrs Spindleberry had come to plead with her to bring Tig down from the cherry tree, where he had picked all the cherries and then found that the basket – which had been empty and light when he had flown up into the tree with it under his arm – was much too heavy to bring down.

Nan was mildly irritated but not in the least bit angry with Tig because, she said, the fairies, even Tig, were such good company for her that she was happy for them to help themselves to the cherries and anything else they wanted. Ruth smiled to herself, for she knew that Tig was the rogue blackbird that ate all Nan's ripe cherries. When asked why she did not shoo him away or get a cat, Nan would reply simply that the cherries were small payment for his beautiful singing.

The tranquillizing effect of these stories lulled Ruth into a peaceful sleep. In fact, this diversion was a strategy which subconsciously she had adopted from a very early age to protect herself from the upsets of life at home. The pictures she conjured up were as endlessly reassuring as Shirley's moods were disturbing, for they helped her erect a barrier between the two sides of her life: on the one hand, the cramped bleakness of London, which was her home, and on the other, the calm, gentleness and clarity of Norhambury, the city where Nan lived, with its trees and gardens, its castle and cathedral, backstreets and alleyways – and, of course, its market. The differences extended to the people, especially the people in her own family. She herself was unable to reconcile the extremes of personality even among her own relations, nor were there any satisfactory reasons for their obvious incompatibility however much she wondered about them.

At breakfast next morning, apart perhaps from a slightly complacent smile which hovered over her lips, Shirley behaved with complete normality, so that one might be forgiven for thinking that there had been nothing amiss the previous evening. True to form, she clapped two charcoal-covered slices of toast down directly onto the tablecloth and splashed the dark tea over the rims of the cups into the saucers. Dad said nothing, his eyes fixed on the red squares of the tablecloth, apparently trying to decipher some extremely perplexing mathematical pattern contained therein.

Suddenly and as calmly as if she might have been predicting the day's weather, Shirley announced, "Well, it's all settled: we're going to move and I'm going to set up in business as a newsagent."

Ruth raised her eyes from her bowl of cereal. Unable to pretend that she hadn't heard such a loudly broadcast piece of news, all she said was "Oh" for want of anything better.

Untroubled for once by the lack of dramatic impact of her statement because she was too far carried away in her own schemes and plans, Shirley continued: "Your dad will carry on with his work at the Rates Office for the time being. And oh, I nearly forgot: we've decided you'll have to go and spend the summer at Beech Grove while we get on with the moving."

Overcome with joy, Ruth maintained sufficient presence of mind to greet these instructions with another noncommittal "Oh", lest too great a display of enthusiasm might have the wholly perverse but possible effect of changing her mother's mind. The promise of spending the whole of the summer holiday – not simply the occasional weekend – at Nan's filled Ruth with such excitement and anticipation that for the next three weeks, until the end of term, she found it almost impossible to concentrate on anything else, and certainly not her schoolwork.

2

The last time that Ruth had stayed for more than a weekend or at most a few days at Nan's house was several years ago. Consequently the unexpected, unimagined prospect of spending the carefree weeks at the height of summer there filled her with keen anticipation, and that was not simply because she was very fond of her grandmother and loved being with her in her house, in her garden, in the quaint old city of Norhambury and in the surrounding countryside.

There was much more to it than that. For Ruth, Nan's house, over a hundred miles from London, not only held the key to her past, it held the key to her future as well, in that it allowed her the freedom to do whatever she liked without the restraints and pressures of home. That freedom, with Nan's encouragement and guidance, she devoted to the overriding passion which surged from her inner core and which she kept secret from her parents for fear of ridicule, disapproval or, as past experience suggested, a downright ban. In London the opportunities to indulge that yearning passion were limited and hedged about with subterfuge and anxiety, but so intense was it that already she recognized it as the goal to which she would devote her life, come what may. It was like a bright star beckoning her from the depths of darkness, burning with ever-increasing splendour, giving her no choice but to follow wherever it led.

At the end of the usual holiday week by the sea, she always accompanied her father when he took Nan home, but those few days scarcely ever allowed her any chance to do what she wanted, because he was a constant presence in the house. Much though she loved him, she often wished he would leave her in peace and go to join Shirley, who never came to Nan's house but went instead to stay with her Cousin Edith in Birmingham.

As a rule, Shirley would stay away for the following week as well, because, she said, she needed a rest, claiming to be the sole person on whom the burden of the house rested for the other fifty weeks of the year.

Her Birmingham visit would be devoted to shopping sprees with Edith and long hours spent chatting far into the night. It was not the sort of holiday that would appeal to John, and Shirley never suggested that he might like to go with her. She insisted however that in her absence her husband and daughter should return straight away to take care of their inconspicuous little terraced house in London after settling Nan in at home in Norhambury. Shirley's word was law and had to be obeyed, so Ruth and her father had no choice but to return to London together – and that was the end of the matter.

The first week of holiday, the week by the sea, had become a family tradition which Shirley herself had instigated in one of her better, more generous moods several years previously, and in which all were allowed to share, notwithstanding anxieties about burglars and vandals, fires and gas leaks back in London. In fact, that week was a revival of an earlier family tradition, which many years ago had provided the setting for Ruth's very first impressions of her paternal grandparents, Nan and Grandpa Joe.

As she was only two years old at the time, still a baby, Ruth's recollections of that holiday, buried deep in the recesses of her mind, were hazy in most respects, except for her own astonishment at the sight of so much water. That huge blue expanse, strangely salty to the taste, and the vast stretch of yellow sand which looked nice enough to eat and was soft when it ran through your fingers, but rough and gritty if you put it in your mouth, had fixed themselves in her mind almost to the exclusion of the adults around her. Their personalities scarcely impinged upon her, and even less their activities – except, that is to say, for Grandpa Joe's, because he kept building sand pies and castles for her to knock down.

Granddad Reggie, Shirley's father, had come too, though he always came alone as there did not seem to be a corresponding granny in his life. He sat, as was his custom, asleep in a deck-chair with a newspaper or a model-train magazine over his balding head, scarcely talking to anyone, least of all to Ruth, except in monosyllables, but Grandpa was energetic and jolly, and made everyone laugh. He kept little cards with pictures on them in his pocket and would bring them out to entertain his granddaughter. Anywhere they went, if he turned over the picture of a bird or an animal, he would make the appropriate sound – a roar or a bark, a miaow, a whistling or a chirruping; for a house he would cut out the windows and doors and invent lives for the people who, according to him, lived there.

There had been another grown-up present on that holiday, a blurred presence, not someone Ruth could identify in her mind's eye. A mere impression of a pale face with long brown hair and staring eyes was all she recalled. That person seldom came out onto the beach. Occasionally she walked slowly up and down the promenade with Nan, but mostly she stayed in the hotel. Nan was at that time no more than a distant figure, because she also stayed indoors, keeping that other shadowy person company in her room.

Then some weeks before Ruth's third birthday the following spring, Nan and Grandpa came to stay in London. They hardly spoke at all and never smiled. Grandpa did not tell any funny stories: he did not laugh, nor did he try to make anyone else do so. To Ruth's disappointment he also had forgotten to bring his little cards. She sat on Nan's knee sometimes while they thumbed through a picture book together, but Nan was too tired and too listless to want to do anything for very long. Even Shirley was quiet and put flowers in their bedroom, the back room where Ruth normally slept, but when Nan and Grandpa came to stay she moved into the box room, and had to go through their room to reach hers, so she heard Nan sobbing every night.

They said that Evelyn, the pale, thin girl, had gone to live with God, which Ruth supposed meant that she had gone back to the seaside. She thought that must be rather nice for Evelyn, though why she had gone with an unknown person called God and not with Nan and Grandpa she did not understand. It was many years before Nan came on holiday again, and that was only after Grandpa had died, when Shirley thought to revive the tradition.

It was when Ruth was four, nearly five years old, that she went on her first visit to Nan's house. She did not remember exactly how long she stayed, except that she arrived in winter when the trees were bare and white with frost, and stayed till her birthday, well into the spring, when the trees were full of blossom and the dip at the end of Nan's garden, where the fairies lived, was carpeted with primroses. It was easy to remember precisely which year it was, because that Christmas she had had the terrifying nightmare of Father Christmas getting stuck in the chimney.

Dad had come to comfort her in the middle of the night and, holding her on his knee, had confided a big secret, one that he said few people knew. The truth was that he, Dad, was the real Father Christmas. He did not come down the chimney, because Shirley didn't like him getting his clothes dirty, so he came in by the front door instead. There was no need for Ruthie to worry, but she must go back to sleep because he could not work the magic and change into Father Christmas with a sack of toys on his back if she stayed awake. Indeed, the very next morning, to her delight, there, waiting for her under the tree, was a beautiful, blue-painted doll's cot with a shiny pink-and-blue satin coverlet. Inside the cot was a glamorous baby doll with golden hair and big blue eyes. Dad and Shirley had smiled lovingly at each other as they watched her enchanted expression.

Only a couple of weeks later, one dull, wet Saturday or Sunday afternoon – it definitely must have been a weekend, because Dad was at home – Ruth was playing with her doll, while Dad read her a story about a wicked witch and a princess. All of a sudden, Shirley came screaming out of the little bathroom which was tacked on to the end of the kitchen and sat down heavily on a chair, gasping: "The baby, the baby!" Ruth was frightened. There was no sign of any baby, except her doll, and nobody had ever spoken of one. Dad ran out of the house, calling "I'll go and phone!" as he went. He came back a little later, and soon after that an ambulance arrived. While Ruth stood watching, Shirley was carried moaning out of the house, and soon afterwards the vehicle drove off, its bell clanging and its light flashing against the darkening sky.

Indoors Dad paced up and down for a while, looking drawn and anxious. He then went out to the telephone again, this time taking Ruth with him. He made lots of calls, speaking quickly, with uncharacteristic agitation, while Ruth sat on the cold stone floor of the telephone box watching the lamplighter reach up with his long pole to light the gas lamp on the corner of the street. Then patiently she drew patterns on the dirty, steamed-up window panes. At last Dad put the receiver down and attempted to explain. "Shirley is not well, Ruthie, that's why she's gone to hospital; I'm sure she'll be better soon. I'm taking you to stay with Nan and Grandpa. You'll like that, won't you?" Ruth nodded her agreement, since that clearly was what was anticipated, but she didn't know whether she would like it or not.

Although it was clear that the decision had already been taken, it worried her for the rest of the day because, apart from the scant impressions of Nan and Grandpa on that first holiday by the sea, her more recent reminiscences of them were cloaked in gloom and sadness. However, after a long and serious discussion with her soft toys in bed that night, she satisfied herself that it would probably be all right. It was bound to be better than going to Mrs Cox, the childminder across the road, and because Dad had said he would be coming too, she would be safe. Ruth took Shirley's departure perfectly calmly: as long as her dad was there, she did not miss her mother, though she was still mystified as to why she had gone away in an ambulance, crying about a baby.

3

The morning after Shirley's dramatic departure, labouring under the effects of an anxiously wakeful night, John Platt struggled wearily up the road to the Tube station, bearing the still somnolent Ruth and the various indispensable soft toys over his left shoulder while, in his right hand, he held a hastily prepared suitcase containing nightclothes for himself and some random items of Ruth's wardrobe. He carried his burdens into the clanking lift and then, once below ground, along the winding, yellow-tiled Victorian passages to the dingy platform. He clutched them to him in the swaying, clattering Tube train which lulled Ruth into a deeper sleep. She did not wake until they emerged from the escalators onto the platform at Liverpool Street, where he set her down on her feet.

Whimpering at the noise and bustle of the main-line station, she clung to him, immobilizing him, while he scanned the sign-boards. Still clinging to him in the thick smoky atmosphere, she look around at the jostling crowds and then put her hands over her ears to shut out the din of shunting engines, bursts of steam, screeching whistles, rumbling trolleys and the cadaverous voice from above which filled the space with unintelligible announcements.

While her father made yet more phone calls and she began to understand where she was and what was happening, her anxiety gave way to an impatient excitement. She knew that she had travelled by express train before, most likely when she went to the sea, but did not remember it at all distinctly, unlike those short suburban rides with Shirley when they went to visit Granddad Reggie. Many a time as she and Dad had stood watching the trains steaming through the cutting at the end of the street, she had begged him to take her on a proper train on a long journey out to the country. At last it was going to happen!

They boarded the train, installing themselves with their miscellaneous entourage of soft toys in an empty compartment only seconds before a short, sharp whistle blast signalled their departure. The jerking movement of the train easing itself out of its slumber like a waking dragon sent a thrill of adventure coursing through Ruth's small person, though she held her father's hand tightly. This was a step into a new world, the unknown world of grown-ups.

Beyond the end of the station, houses and shops and churches were all moving away from her with increasing speed. And with them went those ugly walls and spires standing alone, like blackened monsters among grass and weeds on bare patches of land, their windows gouged out and blind and their steeples pointing heavenward for no apparent purpose. Whenever she asked what they were, the answer was always the same: "That was the Blitz." "What was the Blitz?" she would ask. "In the War," they said, leaving her none the wiser. Today those monsters and all other signs of the city were being swiftly replaced by fields and trees, cows and horses, as the train followed its inevitable trajectory, cutting a swathe of city hubbub, speed and urgency through the timeless tranquillity of meadows, woods and sleepy villages.

Dad laughed when, pointing at the houses and ruins, she exclaimed, "Look, they are all getting left behind!" He said that it was the train that was moving, not the fields and trees. If she kept her eyes open, he said, sooner or later she would see the farm where he used to go and stay with his cousins. She turned from the window and stared at him in disbelief. It had never occurred to her that he had lived anywhere other than in their little house in London or stayed with anyone other than Shirley, and perhaps Nan and Grandpa, who were, of course, his parents. What's more, it was unbelievable that he had cousins, possibly lots of people whom she had not only not met but never even heard of, and that these unknown people had a farm in the country with fields and animals, where Dad, her dad, had stayed when he was a boy. This unsuspected revelation, so nonchalantly imparted, left Ruth mystified. It took her some time to digest all the implications, not least the idea that Dad had once been a boy. She had never imagined that he had been a boy. What had he been like?

Having pondered this unlikely information for a while, she then began to ply her father with questions. How many cousins did he have? What were their names? Dad scratched his head, trying to remember; there were so many of them: Muriel, Abe (short for Abraham), Eva, Rick, Bartholomew and Freddie. How many cows, pigs, chickens, horses? she then persisted, urgently wanting to find out more and more. She kept her eyes fixed on the window, waiting impatiently for the farm to come into view. "Is it that one?" she would ask at every sighting of a house, barn, shed or pigsty, and then: "I think I can see it over there!" she would announce optimistically, scarcely able to conceal her disappointment when Dad shook his head. He promised to tell her when to expect it, but her impatience knew no bounds as she focused intently on every object that came into view for fear of missing something of such profound significance. "How much longer will it be?" she asked every five minutes until, after an eternity, Dad said that they were very near.

When at last the longed-for farmhouse came into view, she drank in every detail of its thatched roof and black, tar-covered walls. It was old and decrepit, with a pronounced list to the left, but that did not concern Ruth: to her it was beautiful, and the sight of it carried her away with wonder that such a grand property should belong to her relatives, even though she had only just discovered their existence. She registered every cow and horse in the field between the railway and the house, and would have counted every hen in the yard had she been given the chance. She craned her head round to try to look back down the line, watching constantly in the hope that the farm might reappear, while the train sped on through the day, oblivious of the preoccupations of its young passenger.

At the end of the line, Nan and Grandpa were waiting for them on the platform. Grandpa swept his little granddaughter off her feet, whirling her high in the air with a whoop of delight.

Then Nan bent down and enveloped her in a warm, furry hug, smelling of mothballs and a faint, fascinating trace of perfume.

"How's my dear little Ruthie?" she asked with such concern that Ruth discovered, to her intense joy, that here were people, other than Dad and Shirley, to whom she belonged. Grandpa was exactly as she remembered him, funny and bouncy, but Nan was different. Perhaps this was the real Nan, whom she had never yet known properly – gentle, sensible and quietly confident. This was certainly not the distant, anxious person whom she vaguely remembered from those days at the sea, nor the grieving elderly lady with the tear-stained face who had come to stay when Evelyn had gone off to live with God.

As they came out of the station, John drew in a deep breath of the cold, clean air and exhaled it with slow satisfaction. Ruth did the same in imitation. "Tha's a difference, that is!" Dad exclaimed. "Tha's real pure. You don't get air like that in London. It's all fog there, even on a fine day you're breathing in tons of soot." Ruth was struck by the way he spoke: it was unlike his normal London way of speaking. The words came out more slowly; they sounded softer, friendlier, less formal, less correct. He was speaking like Nan and Grandpa, perhaps in recognition of his homecoming. Grandpa regretfully explained that Nan had dissuaded him from bringing the bike and sidecar to meet them as she was afraid that Ruth would be scared of it, so they would have to join the queue for the bus instead. "Bike" and "sidecar" as yet meant nothing to Ruth. For her part, she was happy to stand at the bus stop with her hand in Nan's and watch the changing sky while the adults talked.

"It was a boy..." Dad was saying, and then muttered something about Shirley being very upset and having to stay in hospital for some weeks. Ruth took little notice of their conversation, because she was too absorbed in the radiance of the sunset to bother with it, knowing that she would not understand it in any case. She had never seen such beautiful colours. High above her head the sky was already black, and through it, the twinkling stars, like bright pinpricks of light in a velvet cloth, were beginning to wink and flash their opening eyes at her. As she lowered hcr head, she saw the darkness of advancing night being held at bay by the vibrant colours of sunset as they descended the sky in clear, luminous bands, merging and fusing and melting into each other. Black yielded to purple; purple to a streak of clear bright blue; blue to turquoise and turquoise to emerald green, which was then absorbed in a ribbon of palest yellow. The yellow gained the intensity of ochre as it dropped into a brilliant layer of fiery orange. On the horizon this sank into the bed of rich, glowing crimson on which the entire sky rested.

Against the crimson, the buildings of the old city, its towers, spires and bare trees, were a single fused line of black silhouettes. Ruth was bewitched; all the colours of her paintbox were there, more startling in their brilliance, more striking in their clarity, more elusive in their evanescence. Her paints were so clumsy by comparison.

"What a little dreamer!" a voice said in her ear. She turned round to see Nan's bemused face, lit by the glare of the headlights of the bus, which had drawn up at the stop during her reverie.

It was dark by the time they arrived at Nan and Grandpa's house. Although Ruth had struggled to keep her eyes open on the bus, extreme tiredness overcame her, with the humiliating result that she had to be carried into the house and taken straight up to bed, fighting sleep with tears of angry frustration. She had travelled so far and seen so much, yet there remained so much more that she wanted to see and discover before that remarkable day came to an end. However much they reassured her that there would be time for all that in the morning, she wanted to see it now, at once. In the event she had no choice; she was fighting a losing battle with sleep as her eyes closed, leaving her with lingering impressions of a creaking gate, moist fresh air, a wide doorway and a well-lit hall. Above all, it was the pervasive smell of that house that she carried to bed with her, a fascinating aroma, spicy and fragrant: it was Nan's faint perfume mixed with other unidentifiable smells. Later she recognized them as the traces of wax polish, wood shavings, tobacco and sweet-briar pipe in the special combination which gave that very ordinary house its distinctive character.

4

Grandpa came into the bedroom the next morning, bearing a cup of hot chocolate and singing "Wake up, brown eyes, sleepy head!" to the tune of 'Half a Pound of Tuppenny Rice'. He put the mug down on the bedside table, drew back the heavy threadbare curtains, noisily pulling their brass rings along the rod and revealing a grey, wintry sky. Ruth woke up blinking in the aggressive light which hurt her eyes and inspected the room: beside her bed there stood a wicker chair and the small table bearing her chocolate mug. There was a tall wardrobe at the end of the bed by the window. The only other piece of furniture was a marble washstand with a backing of dark green tiles. Grandpa watched patiently while she found her bearings. "Come on, little Miss Brown Eyes, drink your cocoa and then come downstairs, there's a something waiting for you!"

When he left the room, Ruth's reaction was not to drink her cocoa or to dress, but to rush to the window. There was indeed a great deal waiting for her, though not perhaps what Grandpa intended – waiting for her there, outside the very window, without her even having to set foot on the stairs. She was half expecting to see familiar walls on all sides and the backs of other houses across a tiny patch of yard. She stood on tiptoe to look over the window sill, but overbalanced in amazement at the scene which met her gaze. There was not a house in sight, except in the far distance. She peeped out again. Beneath the window a long lawn sloped away from the house down to a wooden fence, beyond which was a vast ploughed field. The few signs of habitation were so far away on the other side of the field that their rooftops were visible only as splashes of red among the trees on the edge of the field.

Along the line of the garden fence stood a row of tall bushes and trees, now bare and black, and down each side of the lawn ran narrow flower beds, also bare and black but neat and tidy. The border on the right ran up as far as the back wall of the house, but the one on the left came only halfway up the lawn because the space nearer the house was taken up by a small wooden shed, onto which a rather chaotic corrugated lean-to had been appended. In the middle of the lawn there was a strange hump with a wheelbarrow standing by it. Two spades leant against the wheelbarrow, which meant that somebody had already been out working in the garden while she slept.

The cold floor of the unheated room drove her back into bed to sip her cocoa, but from time to time she dashed back to the window to make sure that the view had not by some mischance been magicked away. She dressed in the same intermittent manner. Normally she was proud of her ability to dress herself quickly and correctly, apart from the occasional problem with an awkward button, but today she struggled into her clothes willy-nilly, so that when she appeared in the kitchen doorway having negotiated the steep staircase, the three adults, all sitting round the table, had difficulty in concealing their amusement. Nan rose and came over to greet her with a kiss and a hug.

"Well, my dear little Ruthie," she said with that same warmth of affection that she had shown at the railway station, "aren't you a clever girl to dress yourself all on your own! Let me help you to get these silly clothes the right way round." She swiftly rearranged the errant clothing, tied a small blue apron around Ruth's waist and sat her on a chair at the table where breakfast was laid for her.

Dad, Nan and Grandpa were drinking a sweet-smelling coffee, presumably made from the coffee bottle with its picture on the label of a man by a tent with his servant. Dad and Grandpa must have been out working in the garden, down by the hump that Ruth had seen from the window.

"I'll give you another hour or so, Father," Dad said, "and that should finish it and then I'll be off."

"Good job we had that old shelter, bor, saved our lives a good few times, that did," Grandpa rejoined, "but I shall be glad to see it go. Let's hope we won't ever need another one."

Ruth turned from one to the other. "What was it?" she enquired timidly.

"That was our shelter in the War, little Miss Brown Eyes," Grandpa answered her, "and don't you worry your littl' self about that." Then he changed the subject, adding with a sly wink in her direction, "As soon as your dad and I have finished filling in that old Anderson, I'll show you what I've got for you in my shed."

When the men had gone out, Ruth remembered that Dad had said that he must be off; what did he mean?

"Where are we going?" she asked Nan. "Where are we going today?"

"Nowhere that I know of," Nan replied.

"But Dad said he must be off," Ruth persisted. "And I don't want to go back to London!" she added vehemently.

"Ah, of course," said Nan cautiously. She left the sink where she had been washing up and came to sit beside Ruth, then feeling her way by degrees into the subject, she began tentatively: "Your daddy has got to go back to London, Ruthie; he has to go to work." She fell silent for a moment and then said: "And as your mummy is not well, we hoped, Grandpa and I, you might like to stay here with us for a little while. We'd love that, we would!"

Alarm bells rang loud in Ruth's mind and filled her eyes with prickly tears. Desperately anxious because the rules of Mrs Cox, the childminder, decreed that big girls of nearly five do not cry, and ashamed at the memory of the tantrum she had displayed the previous night, she tried to hold back the hot tears, biting her lip with the effort. Nan and Grandpa were very kind and showed absolutely no sign of holding that tantrum against her. Indeed, she was sure she loved them very much; their house and the garden, yet to be explored, were like a dream, yet although she certainly did not want to go back to London, it was unbearable to think of being separated from her father. It was too much to ask of her, and moreover she could not imagine how he would manage without her. And, after all, how many more changes were going to be sprung on her? No sooner had she adjusted to one new situation than another unsuspected step was announced. The tears plopped forlornly into her bowl of porridge.

Nan put her arm round her. "My dear little Ruthie," she said. "Don't you worry. We'll look after you, and there is such a lot we can do together – you, me and Grandpa. We'll have a lovely time. And don't you worry about your father: he'll be all right. He'll be busy with his work, though, and with looking after that mother of yours." The words "that mother" bore a slight, possibly unintentional, stress which Ruth did not register. On the contrary she was impressed by the comforting tone of Nan's little speech, so stopped crying and considered her words while she ate her toast. From the moment Nan had greeted her at the station, she had been especially touched by being called "My dear little Ruthie".

Dad always called her "Ruthie" – which, of course, showed that he loved her, but no one else did. At weekends he took her for long walks in the park, and every night he read stories to her. Although, like most mothers, Shirley took care of her, and tucked her up in bed and sometimes kissed her goodnight, she rarely spoke to her, except to say impatiently "Do this!" or "Don't do that!" or "Come on!" – occasionally reinforcing the command with a timely slap. Sometimes she would regard Ruth quizzically, almost with palpable hostility, sighing. "What a strange child you are! I really don't know how I came to have a creature like you. What a little duckling!"

She seldom answered any of Ruth's questions, always being far too absorbed in her own world even to listen. She would often study herself in the mirror, arranging her fair curls or putting on powder or lipstick. She would spend hours with her ear to the wireless, humming along to the songs and flicking through magazines while she listened. Frequently she would go out, leaving Ruth with Mrs Cox across the road.

Certainly Mrs Cox never called her "My dear little Ruthie". It would have been surprising if she had so much as called Ruth by her name. Mrs Cox did not appear to know any of the names of the twelve or so children committed to her charge, addressing them, individually and collectively, only as "ducks!" Large and lumbering, she would consign them to the unheated front room, which served as a nursery, while she herself remained aloof in the kitchen preparing enormous meals for her three grown-up sons. She would come padding in from time to time with a tray of watery drinks and hard, plain biscuits. She scarcely said anything except "Toilet, ducks!" at predetermined intervals, in a rasping, bronchial wheeze. This was the cue for an orderly procession to file quietly through the steaming kitchen to queue at the draughty, smelly outside toilet in the yard. Ruth was glad that at home their "toilet" was indoors. Dad said he did not like the word "toilet", so would Ruth please say "lavatory" at home. It was so confusing!

The toys in Mrs Cox's front room were so old and battered there was little competition for them. In any case, squabbles for toys, like crying or clinging to departing parents, were strictly forbidden, since it was well understood that Mrs Cox's nerves would not stand any disturbance. There was only one remedy for such behaviour – and that was immediate expulsion from her establishment, to the inconvenience of the parents who relied on her services. There was therefore considerable motivation for children to be disciplined into acceptable modes of conduct in advance of their admission to and during their stay at Mrs Cox's.

Ruth bore these sessions across the road philosophically, because she had no option; she was fortunate in that she had a friend, Susan, for company there. Susan was forced to spend every day at Mrs Cox's as her mother went out to work in a clothing factory. Every so often the two girls would play with the moth-eaten dolls, inventing improbable escapades to alleviate the monotony of the poor things' existence. Their preferred way of passing the time was to chat, grown-up fashion, about their own families and tell each other stories to enliven the long hours away from home. Susan was an endless source of entertainment as her fifteen-year-old stepbrother, David, was constantly getting into scrapes. Once he had run away from home and had been brought back by the police just as he was on the point of leaving the country. On other occasions he had filled the postbox with bangers in anticipation of Guy Fawkes Night, and had also ridden off in pursuit of Apache warriors on the milkman's old nag, with the milk float scattering its cargo behind him in all directions.

Susan's father was hardly ever at home. Susan said that he worked for a very important orchestra and had met lots of famous people. Ruth was very uncertain as to what he actually did or even what an orchestra was, but there was no doubt that he travelled a great deal, because he never came home without bringing little presents for Susan. Often he would bring her a tiny doll in a pretty dress, and once he brought a pair of little wooden shoes, called clogs he said, from a place named Holland. Another time he brought a small pen which made its own ink and had a tiny ball for a nib. He said it was the latest invention.

Susan, for her part, was intrigued by Shirley and her glamour. When she herself had no more stories to tell, she would ask Ruth all about Shirley's lipsticks, how many she had, what colour they were, how often she used them or if she had bought any new ones lately. This, together with other similar matters, was easy information for Ruth to impart, since she had had plenty of opportunity to observe the minutiae of Shirley's dressing-table arrangements, although she wondered why Susan should be interested.

She herself would much rather have exchanged Susan's mother, older and plump though she was, for her own. Susan's mother, whom she had seen when she came to collect her daughter, had a nice face and a warm smile, despite her permanently worried air. She was never cross or flustered, yet she had none of the luxuries which adorned Shirley's person, graced her dressing table and filled her handbags. Susan was similar to Shirley in appearance – fair-haired, blue-eyed rather than green-eyed, and impulsive – which made Ruth wonder, now and again, if perhaps there had not been a mistake when they were babies, if perhaps they had been given to the wrong mothers.

Sitting in Nan's kitchen, Ruth spared a passing thought for Susan, left behind in London. Susan would be all right, she decided, because she was never shy and would soon find someone else to chatter to. Then she concentrated on her own situation. Staying with Nan and Grandpa, if she let her father go, would definitely be better than going back to Mrs Cox's, for she knew she would be spending all day and every day across the road if, as Nan said, Shirley was ill and Dad was at work. In contrast to this grim prospect, the experience of being called "My dear little Ruthie" by Nan and "Miss Brown Eyes" by Grandpa made her feel like a kitten, soft and warm and much loved. She dried her eyes.

"That's my little Ruthie," said Nan. "Let's go and see what your daddy and Grandpa are a-doing, shall we?"

She produced a grey coat with a red velvet collar, put it over Ruth's shoulders and together they descended the steep stone steps at the side door, their aprons blowing in the chill breeze.

"What a cold wind!" Nan remarked, sharply drawing breath. "Let's see how they're getting on and then we'll hurry back indoors."

The earthworks were nearly completed: apart from a slight ridge in the middle, the lawn was almost flat, and Dad and Grandpa were stamping the turf back into place. Sheets of corrugated iron lay on the lawn, having apparently come from nowhere, and what had been a large mound of earth in the sideway was reduced to a few spadefuls of crumbly dark soil which smelt damp and wholesome, rather like train smoke but cleaner and fresher.

John looked up as Ruth came into the garden and hurriedly announced that he had better go and get ready. Ruth virtually ignored him: there were too many other demands on her attention. Every detail of the garden, which she had seen with such astonishment from her window, captured her interest. The lean-to contained what looked like a very small car, which

Grandpa said was his sidecar. A couple of worn bus seats were stacked against one wall, and against the other there was an old tin bath. She walked on down the garden. Despite the raw wind and the lack of vegetation, she observed every feature with intense fascination.

A white fluttering at ground level at the end of the lawn by the fence caught her eye. She held her breath, grabbed Nan's arm and gasped in a loud whisper: "Look, Nan, fairies!" Nan rose to the occasion with perfect ease, forgetting her earlier fears about the cold wind.

"Well, let's go and have a look," she replied, as if this were the most natural thing in the world. They tiptoed to the end of the lawn and stooped to inspect the snowdrops growing in the lee of the fence. "You're right, Ruth," Nan remarked thoughtfully, "the fairies have been here: these snowdrops are their washing put out to dry, so you can see what pretty frocks they wear. They're always leaving their clothes about the garden." She tut-tutted in disapproval. "Look up there and you can see their winter hats and scarves and mittens hanging on their hatstands." She pointed to a pussy willow in the corner. Indeed, its branches were lined with vertical rows of small furry objects, each hanging on its own peg, and next to it on a hazel bush, catkins swayed in the wind. "But you'll be unlikely to see the fairies themselves: you have to have very sharp eyes for that," Nan added.

Dad came out of the house at that moment, dressed for a journey. He moved towards them, but Nan signalled to him to stay where he was and beckoned to Grandpa who was putting his spades and wheelbarrow away in the lean-to to come over. "And now for the big surprise!" he announced gleefully, picking Ruth up and slinging her over his shoulder as he advanced up the lawn in the direction of the house. Already overwhelmed by so much that was new and delighted by the fairy costumes, Ruth had forgotten about Grandpa's surprise. "Give your dad a kiss," Grandpa instructed, leaning her over towards her father but scarcely allowing time for more than a reciprocal peck on the cheek, "and let's see what we've got in here." Instead of proceeding along the driveway to the side door of the house, he opened the door of his shed. He put Ruth down on the threshold and told her to close her eyes tight. She obeyed fervently for what felt like a very long time, during which she heard him clambering about in the shed: he seemed to be playing a game with empty tin cans in there.

At length he came out. "You can open your eyes, now, little miss," he said. She did as she was told. There, standing in front of her was the most magnificent tricycle she had ever seen in her life. It was shiny and new with a green frame and a red seat. She contemplated it in silent raptures. "Well, come on," said Grandpa, recalling her from her stupor, "get on it, let's see you ride it; it's yours!" Tentatively she stretched a leg over the frame and seated herself at the handlebars. "Feet on the pedals," Grandpa commanded, "then push them!" It was hard at first: the pedals would not move. "Push forward," Grandpa said, tapping her right leg. She pushed. Slowly the pedal moved and, as she pushed it round and round, the machine advanced a little way up the drive. Then the other foot joined in, as if trying to push its pedal over a steep hill.

"Wave goodbye to your daddy!" Nan called, pointing towards the gate, but Ruth was concentrating with such determination on the new exercise that the bus had already passed the gate in a flash of scarlet before she had time to look up. Dad had gone. Unconcerned, she returned to the matter in hand. As the tricycle moved faster and faster, her excitement grew, inspired equally by the amazing present itself, by the increasing speed and by her own achievement.

"I can do it, I can do it!" she called out.

5

Ruth spent the rest of the daylight hours tricycling up and down the driveway with only short breaks for meals. Nan kept bringing out extra layers of clothing, cardigans, hats, scarves, gloves and leggings, none of which belonged to Ruth, although they fitted her neatly and might have been made for her. In the early afternoon the wind dropped as an anaemic sun forced its way through the misty cloud. Only then did Nan stop worrying about the cold and Ruth was allowed to ride to her heart's content.

Sometimes she was the train taking her father back to London. For that Grandpa found her a whistle to blow and Nan managed to produce a square of green material for a flag, so that she was both the engine driver and the guard. Sometimes she was the bus that passed the gate every fifteen minutes, and Grandpa obliged with some old bus tickets. He continued to hammer and chisel in his shed, occasionally issuing station announcements. "The four forty-five for Glasgow is leaving from platform six. Would passengers please board at once!" he boomed in a suitably resonant voice. The four forty-five had no idea where Glasgow was, but dutifully set out on time with a full load of passengers. From time to time, he would also act as the bus conductor, calling, "Tickets please!"

The sole obstacle to Ruth's unalloyed pleasure was a long, bulky object standing in the sideway leaning against the wall of the house. Covered in black tarpaulin, it was ugly and threatening, like a sleeping dragon. She gave it a wide berth, hurrying past it very quietly, either to Grandpa in his shed at one end of the run, or to the open space of the garden and the gate in the other direction. She did not feel safe anywhere near its shapeless mass. As darkness began to fall, Nan called out shrilly from the kitchen door, announcing that it was teatime. Grandpa from the depths of the shed replied that two minutes would finish off whatever it was that he was doing, but Ruth, up by the gate, pretended that she had not heard. She was determined to stay out all night on her precious trike. Nan called again, but Ruth defiantly refused to move or even to answer.

At that moment a distant droning became audible on the still air. The sound quickly gathered a menacing force as it approached, growing in a whining howl to a deafening din which rent the calm winter evening with its piercing vibrations. The terrible noise came closer and closer. It was coming from the sky! For a split second, Ruth froze in terror, then hastily abandoned her tricycle, kicking it over in her panic to get back into the house as fast as her legs would carry her. She ran screaming down the sideway, but her screams were drowned by the screeching roar of the jet engines as a formation of four aircraft flew low overhead.

Trembling from head to foot, she flung herself in at the open kitchen door where Nan was standing and, gasping with fright, she clutched her grandmother. The noise was inside her, all around her, a shrieking demon of a sound, a strident genie which had escaped its bottle and held her thrashing helplessly in its cruel grasp.

Nan put her arms round her. "There there, don't you worry about those old planes: they're just going home to bed, they won't hurt you," she said.

By now, Grandpa had come indoors, drawn by the commotion. "Silly little old mawther!" he commented, shaking his head. "If it hadn't been for planes, we wouldn't be here now, and those new Meteor jets will stop it all happening again!"

Only very gradually did Ruth's fear begin to subside. Still shaking convulsively but unable to resist the temptation any longer, she peeped out from behind Nan's skirts to gaze questioningly, her eyes still red and moist with tears, at Grandpa. What did he mean? Those howling monsters wouldn't protect anybody. To her consternation, he continued a second or two later with a grin, "You know, little Miss Ruth, those planes are friends of mine; I'll have to take you up to the aerodrome to meet them one day!"

"That's enough, Grandpa," Nan reprimanded him sharply. "We all know you're mad about those planes, but we've heard enough of them for the present, thank you. Ruthie will get used to them in time."

He took the rebuke undismayed, winking mischievously at Ruth. She was doubtful that she would ever get used to them – indeed she did not see why she should even try, but Grandpa's chubby round face and the sparkle of his blue eyes were so appealing that she had to respond with a faint flicker of a smile. Nan announced that the tea was ready and that if Grandpa wanted to get to Speedway they had better sit down at once.

The table was laid in the back room. It was officially the dining room, though it also served various other purposes. As well as the solid oak table, it housed dining chairs which competed for space with a long sofa, at present pushed against the wall, a glass-fronted bookcase in one corner, easy chairs by the fire and a highly polished sideboard which was home to an inkstand, plant pots and large photographs of Ruth as a baby, of her father as a little boy, of Shirley and Dad together, and of another child, a girl, who at first sight looked rather like Ruth. It was a warm, comfortable room, despite the brown-stained woodwork, the faded wallpaper and the dingy, gold-framed oil paintings, one of a barren landscape and the other of a sailing ship on the high seas in the depths of night illuminated only by a huge yellow moon. Beneath the high mantelpiece on which stood a clock with an ornate brass face in a heavy wooden case, a coal fire blazed in the grate, its dancing flames reflecting with added brilliance off the polished copper fire irons and coal scuttle.

Grandpa was raising his fork to his mouth but put it down abruptly just as he was about to take a mouthful. Without a word, he reached out to the wireless on a shelf in the corner behind him and turned it on very loud. It was playing dance music.

"Really, Grandpa…" Nan protested, but then she too stopped abruptly.

Before Ruth had time to register any show of alarm, another wave of returning aircraft howled overhead, the sound muffled by the walls of the house and masked by the blaring radio. Ruth slid quickly onto Nan's knee; Nan held her so tight that she managed to stay calm, stifling with a heroic effort the cries of terror which welled up inside her. Only her face, pale and tense, revealed her inner torment. It was not pleasant by any stretch of the imagination, but indoors and on Nan's knee, it was much better than outside.

Outside! She let out a cry of despair. Her shiny new trike was outside, all alone in the dark, doubtless terror-struck at the sound of those planes. How could she have forgotten it? Grandpa dashed out of the house on a mercy mission and came back instantly, bearing the beloved machine. It was unscathed apart from a film of hoar frost on its handlebars, which he wiped off before parking the trike in the hall at the bottom of the stairs.

When the disturbance had abated, he hurriedly finished his meal and left the room. He returned dressed up in a most curious outfit: a heavy black jacket, buckled at the waist, a leather helmet which fitted closely and thick goggles. These were perched on his head, pushed back on top of the helmet. Ruth recognized him only by his voice and his eyes.

"Night, night, Ruthie!" he called as he went out. "Sleep tight, Miss Brown Eyes!"

Seconds later, a horrendous noise came from the sideway. Surely one of those planes had not landed right by the back door, but that was what it sounded like! Ruth felt yet another surge of panic. As she forced back a tell-tale whimper, she realized that it was not one of those planes after all: it was that black monster that had been slumbering in the sideway leaning against the house! It had woken up. She was sure it was going to eat them all for its supper and, worse still, Grandpa had gone out there!

"Quick, save Grandpa!" Ruth pleaded, slipping off Nan's knee and making for the back door, all her anxiety for herself forgotten in her concern for Grandpa. Nan gave a slight shrug of the shoulders, unmoved and apparently indifferent to the danger facing her husband.

"He's all right. That's only his motorbike. He's off to Speedway for the racing. Let's go and wave to him from the front door."

Together they stood watching from the porch as Grandpa charged off, down the driveway, through the gate and out into the lane, mounted fearlessly on the back of the fiery dragon, which snorted impatiently, emitting sparks and smoke as it roared away. Ruth never found out whether Grandpa actually raced his motorbike at Speedway or whether he was simply a spectator. With Grandpa it was impossible to tell.

Nan decided that Ruth should have her bath in the large, stone kitchen sink, because – as she said – her granddaughter had had enough excitement for one day. Ruth was content with this arrangement, not liking even to imagine that there might be yet more dangers in store. As she sank into bed, Nan drew the old curtains against the hard white moon, which forced its harsh, cold light through the whorls and fronds of frost creeping up the windowpane, and then she sat down by the bed to tell her grandchild a calming story. It began as a tale about the snowdrop fairies, but somehow ended as a story about Dad as a little boy, when he decided to chop down the branches of the pussy willow to make himself an Indian wigwam, leaving the fairies no winter coats and hats. Ruth did not hear the end of the story, because she had already fallen asleep.

6

Over the next several days revelations of sight, sound and smell were waiting around every corner, at every window, behind every door, to enchant the small visitor. On the other hand, waiting in ambush to assault her, there was also an armoury of electrifying terrors such as she had never known, even in the grimy squalor of the London backstreet which until then had bounded her existence. In due course, by slow degrees she learnt to reconcile herself to the jet planes screaming overhead as they went out in the morning and came back in the evening. Out of doors, she kept her ears permanently attuned so that at the merest hint of the ominous droning, she could run for the shelter of the house. She declared a tacit truce with the motorbike, which she was forced to acknowledge as an essential part of Grandpa's identity, because he was forever riding away on it.

Of the remaining horrors, the worst was certainly the geyser in the bathroom; it made her grateful that she was small enough to bathe in the kitchen sink or in the old tin bath in front of the fire. The geyser was indisputably an impressive piece of equipment. A tall gleaming cylinder of copper, it stood in one corner of the bathroom with its spout directed over the bath. It was harmless by day when you leant over the side or, if you were brave enough, stood in the tub and saw the funny elongated reflection of yourself stretched thin like a piece of elastic in the burnished mirror of its surface. However, by night, when Grandpa bravely moved a little brass lever in its black mouth with one hand, and with the other fed it a lighted match, it was transformed into another of those tiresome monsters, on a par with the planes or the motorbike. The explosion as it ignited was tremendous, but Grandpa showed not the least sign of alarm at this terrifying spectacle and Nan never even turned a hair – indeed occasionally she lit it herself without a qualm.

Ruth always heard the explosion, even when she was already sinking deep into the feathery cushions of sleep. In spite of, or perhaps because of its fearsome behaviour, the geyser exerted a weird fascination over her. Once lit, the black hollow of its mouth filled up with jagged turquoise tongues of bright-blue flame, like rows of flickering teeth leaping eagerly upwards to devour an invisible prey. Their hungry roar would draw her from her sleep to peer around the bathroom door and watch the fiery furnace from a safe distance through clouds of mounting steam, until Nan or Grandpa discovered her there and sent her scurrying back to bed.

Planes, geysers and motorbikes notwithstanding, Nan's house was in all other respects a haven of tranquillity, shut off from the outside world. Never was it more so than one Sunday in early February when, around lunchtime, after Nan had come home from church, huge flakes of snow began floating softly out of leaden clouds, like so many stars falling gently to earth, too heavy to maintain their hold on the sky. During lunch the snow settled quickly, covering the lawn and drifting up against the side wall of the house.

After lunch Grandpa subsided into his usual nap, while Ruth stood at the window of the garden door with her nose pressed against the glass, entranced by the rapidly changing landscape. Every branch and twig of every bush and tree became festooned with a white ribbon of snow as, without warning, the garden fell silently under a magic spell of white mystery. The snowdrops and the fairies with them were buried completely under its protective cloak. Nan said that they would not come to any harm, since the magic would send them to sleep under the snow until it melted.

All of a sudden, Grandpa sat bolt upright. His irrepressible vitality restored by his forty winks, as he called them, he rubbed his hands with the impatient glee of a small boy and startled Ruth with an unexpected suggestion.

"Come on, then, young lady!" he commanded, expecting that she would be ready and waiting for him. "Hurry up! Put your boots and coat on and we'll go and build a snowman!"

Ruth was taken aback; she had not dared hope that Grandpa would want to go out and play in the snow. Her delight was soon tempered with a momentary suspicion when she began to wonder whether he really meant what he said. He might be teasing her, for he often did that, and she was learning to expect it. Sometimes of an evening he would casually announce: "I'm off to see King George." Ruth would regard him open-mouthed. "You're not, Grandpa, you're teasing me!" she would insist, but he would appeal to Nan. "That's right, isn't it, Nan?" he would demand, his eyes twinkling and a smile hovering on his lips. "Well, if that's what you call it, I suppose so," she would reply with a dubious grin, usually adding: "Mind the King doesn't make you drink too much!" Ruth found that she always knew if he were teasing by looking into his eyes and at his mouth: then his eyes would sparkle and little creases would appear at the corners of his mouth.

This time he meant what he said as his smile and his eyes gave no hint of that mischievous, teasing look, so she fetched her coat from the low peg he had made for her in the hall by the coat rack and her boots from the mat at the kitchen door, and followed him out into the garden. She hesitated on the edge of the lawn. The snow was so perfectly white and pure and smooth she did not want to spoil it with ugly footprints, but there was Grandpa, already marching across the lawn leaving a trail of deep, dark hollows like the tracks of a giant. She tried putting her small boot into one of the hollows and thought how odd it must be to have such large feet. Then she picked up a little ball of snow and put it in her mouth, expecting it to taste like ice cream, but was disappointed for it was cold and watery like Mrs Cox's drinks.

Everywhere was unusually quiet; no sound penetrated the silence, which spread over the ground and filled the air like a thick blanket of cotton wool, deadening all noise and isolating everyone and everything, each in its individual cocoon. Standing in the snow, Grandpa appeared to be much farther away than if he had been standing on grass. His voice rang out, cutting through the dense stillness.

"Don't stand there eating snow and dreaming: you'll get cold, Ruthie, come and help me!"

They set to work vigorously, digging, piling, pushing the heavy snow into a heap which they then shaped till, satisfied with their efforts, they stood back to admire their handiwork. Their bodies were hot with the toil, their hands and feet frozen stiff. Ruth's cheeks glowed pink with cold and with pleasure.

Nan watched them from the window, applauding their hard work with smiles and waves. She beckoned Grandpa to the kitchen door and handed him a brass coal scuttle to fill, declaring that she was lighting the fire in the front room to celebrate all their hard work. He filled the coal scuttle, extracting two small pieces of coal for eyes for their snowman. With the coal for eyes, a carrot for a nose and an old hat of Grandpa's on his head, the snowman acquired a kindly, almost human demeanour. Ruth was certain that he was trying to smile, grateful for the gift of sight, although daylight was fading and he would not have long to enjoy his newfound faculty. She grew anxious about him, but Grandpa allayed her fears by pointing out that he, the snowman, would be much happier out of doors all night than she would, so she might safely leave him out in the snow. Indeed, if he could talk, he would certainly be more anxious about her and would tell her that she ought to be indoors, thawing her fingers and toes in front of Nan's fire.

7

The door to the front room had always been closed. Ruth had never been in there and had been too busy with other things to give it a moment's consideration, but when she came back indoors, that door was wide open. The eerie white light which filled the room wafted out into the hall, replenishing itself in the mirror above the hall stand. From there it mercilessly directed shafts of wintry light at the hidden angles and dark folds in the dusty garments on the hall stand where Ruth hung up her coat on her own low peg.

Inside the room the glare from the snow outside was unreal and ghostly: it pervaded the room with a chill clarity, reflecting icily off the ceiling and spitefully glazing all competing colour with a frosty sheen. Down on her knees Nan was blowing the reluctant flames with a pair of bellows, but the fire was scarcely capable of melting the snowman, let alone thawing fingers and toes. The fingers and toes were, however, taking care of themselves, pleasantly tingling in the general warmth of the house after the freezing temperatures outside. Uncomfortably conscious that her planned treat was not yet coming up to expectations, Nan rose from the hearth to close the curtains and switch on the light. Then at last the fire began to leap in the grate, suffusing the room with a welcoming tawny flush in contrast to its previous deathly pallor.

It was a light, airy room, more spacious, if more formal, than the cosy back room with its dark mahogany woodwork and red carpet. Here the carpet was green and the furniture upholstered in shades of soft cream and beige, matching the wallpaper and the curtains. Brass candlesticks stood evenly spaced on the sill of the bay window complementing the fire irons in the hearth. On a round table by the fire, a remarkable piece of shiny machinery under a glass dome caught Ruth's eye as she scanned the room from the doorway. It was a clock, its moon face mounted on gold pillars, within the confines of which the mechanism swung to and fro, back and forth in an unceasing semicircular movement. While Grandpa sank into an armchair with the evening paper, Ruth settled herself on a small stool by the clock, hypnotized by the perpetual motion of its cogs and wheels, some so small and so intricately connected that they would not have been out of place in a doll's house.

She did not stir until Nan came back into the room, as usual carrying a laden tea tray, and Grandpa hurriedly sprang out of his armchair to find space for the tray. In the general confusion, Ruth's stool tipped over backwards, bringing her head into sharp contact with a substantial solid piece of furniture behind her. When the shock, the pain and the tears had eased, she forgot about the blow in her curiosity to find out what it was that had hit her. She turned round to see an exceptionally large misshapen sideboard with a shelf protruding at the front and ornate, curved legs. It was against one of these that she had fallen.

Perplexed, she asked Nan what it was. By way of reply Nan lifted the shelf at the front to reveal a keyboard. "Haven't you ever seen a piano, our little Ruthie?" she asked. Ruth shook her head. "Well I never," Nan reflected. "That is odd, considering what a good pianist your father used to be." (This was yet more information about Dad which was news to Ruth.)

"We haven't got one," she explained.

"No, of course you haven't," Nan agreed as she lifted the lid, "you haven't got room for one in your house. But still, I wonder why your father has never found one somewhere to play for you." Ruth did not join in Nan's speculation; she already knew that would be useless, because in this, as in so many other grown-up matters, lines of enquiry never led to any satisfactory conclusion. The more you managed to find out, the more questions would arise and remain unanswered.

She was about to ask if she might touch the keys when a framed photograph which stood on top of the piano caught her eye. It bore a slight resemblance to that thin girl who had gone to live with God.

"Who is that?" she asked bluntly.

Nan hesitated, while Grandpa, who had resumed his newspaper as he waited for the tea to cool, lowered it and peered over the top of the sports page. "That's your Aunt Evelyn, your father's sister," he answered calmly. "If you look on the sideboard in the other room, you'll see a photo of her when she was a little girl."

Nan took the photo down as he spoke. She held it for Ruth to see. The photo indeed showed the thin girl Ruth recalled seeing on that first visit to the sea, but here she was looking happier and fuller in the face, very much like Dad in fact, but prettier, with long dark hair parted on one side and held back in a clip. She had large eyes, also dark, and a broad smile.

"That was taken when she won the City Music competition; she played the piano very well, you see," Nan said proudly.

Ruth gazed at the photo again, scrutinizing the inscription underneath the picture. She recognized a familiar grouping of letters. "This is my name!" she exclaimed in astonishment as she deciphered the spelling. "Ruth Platt!"

"Yes," Nan replied, "you were named after her, but your name is Ruth Jean Platt; see, here it says 'Evelyn Ruth Platt'." Ruth sighed enviously. Evelyn Ruth Platt was a lovely long name which flowed like a song, whereas Ruth Jean Platt was so plain, so dull, so abrupt. "Jean is after your mother – well, Shirley Jean, actually," Nan added brusquely, evidently wanting to conclude the subject.

Ruth grasped the photo in her hand, unwilling to let it go, for this was a topic she wanted to pursue. "Where is she now?" she asked. "Evelyn Ruth Platt, where did she go?"

A shadow crossed Nan's face; in it Ruth saw that she had been too brash in her questioning. Nevertheless, after a moment, the shadow passed and Nan began to speak. "Well, you see, Ruthie dear, she d—" she was saying hesitantly when Grandpa interrupted, swiftly coming to her rescue.

"We'll take you one day to see where she is; let's leave that for now, shall we?" he said solemnly. Was he teasing? Ruth decided that he was not: there was no smile on his face or twinkle in his eye. She saw from the expressions on the faces of both her grandparents that the answers to any further questions would not be readily forthcoming and might upset them, so she kept quiet.

"Look, Ruthie, Grandpa made this bench for Evelyn," Nan said as she lifted the seat of the long stool in front of the piano, revealing piles of large thin books. Her tone lightened as she said, "You are wearing Evelyn's clothes, Ruthie, the ones I made for her when she was little, and this is her music; maybe one day you'll play it for us?"

Ruth's heart leapt as she examined the tartan skirt she was wearing, and then the music. "Can I try it now?" she demanded, conscious that she had suddenly gained an unexpected importance, an enhanced identity by association with that girl, Evelyn, who was also called Ruth, who resembled her, who must have been very clever but who had apparently vanished, leaving only her clothes, her music and photos of herself. Nan promised that she should play the piano after tea.

Eating ham sandwiches and cake was a painfully slow business, which for an impatient child was maddening. Today it appeared to take twice as long as usual, frustrating Ruth in her eagerness to clamber onto the piano stool and begin her recital. At last her plate was cleared to Nan's satisfaction, leaving her free to scramble into position, raised up on a thick cushion, and immediately bring all her fingers down onto the keys in a resounding discord.

Grandpa jumped out of his chair, spilling his tea. "Hold on, young lady!" he exclaimed. "What about the neighbours on the other side of that wall, let alone my tea?" Ruth, stunned by the noise that she had produced, turned round to see him pointing to the fireplace wall. It had not occurred to her that there were people living on the other side of that wall.

She had caught glimpses of the people in the house across the driveway – a family with two tall daughters, much older than herself — but had never seen or heard the people on the other side. In fact, much later she discovered that they were a very elderly couple, older even than Nan and Grandpa and, in addition, both were very deaf and very unlikely to be disturbed by the piano. With quiet dignity, she resumed her performance, behaving as though nothing untoward had happened, purposefully picking out each note one by one, using only the index fingers of each hand.

"That's right," said Nan, "play us a nice quiet little tune, but first you must sit with a straight back, head up and shoulders down." She applied a light pressure to Ruth's shoulders and tilted her head up. Try as Ruth would, nothing that she played sounded remotely like a tune. The keys played random sounds which refused to assemble themselves into any sort of order, not even remotely like any of the tunes Shirley listened to on the wireless.

"I need a book," she announced defiantly, confident that this was the solution to the problem, so Nan selected a book and placed it open on the stand in front of her. The pages revealed row upon row of little black dots with an occasional white one thrown in; they wandered in waves up and down sets of closely placed tramlines. Ruth's fingers did not respond automatically to the dots as she had hoped. In fact, they did not make the slightest difference to her performance. "You play something, Nan," she begged in despair. Nan wavered. "Well, I don't know whether I can; I haven't played anything since Evelyn died." She wiped her eyes and her nose.

So that's what it was! Evelyn had died. That was what Nan had been about to say when Grandpa had interrupted her earlier, but which had now escaped spontaneously. That was the truth that grown-ups were so reluctant to admit, though what it signified Ruth did not know, except that people disappeared without trace, possibly going to live with God. Babies were born and people died, yet no one would tell her how these things happened or why or what they signified. She had developed her own theory that babies were found under bushes in hospital gardens, put there by the fairies; perhaps people died under bushes, too, and the fairies took them away to live with God, wherever that was.

Nan took a fatter book with a red cover down off the top of the piano. "I suppose I might try a few hymns," she murmured as she opened it. She sat down beside Ruth and remarked: "As I said, your grandpa made this long stool for us – for Evelyn and me – so that we could play duets together. Isn't he clever?" Ruth took no notice; of course she knew that Grandpa could do anything he chose. Nan started to play, placing all her fingers on the keys but not bringing them down in one crashing chord as Ruth had done. The fingers moved separately over the keyboard, seemingly propelled individually.

As she played, Nan began to sing, in a beautiful voice tremulous with age and with emotion: "Now the day is over, night is drawing nigh, shadows of the evening creep across the sky."

By the fourth verse Ruth had picked up the tune and was humming it with her. "How do you do it, Nan?" she demanded.

Nan shrugged. "Well, dear, you have to learn to do it, of course," she said.

"Please teach me!" Ruth implored.

"I'm not sure I could do that," Nan replied, "but you should start with one finger. See here, put your finger down on that white note and play it twice, then move it onto the next white note, and play that twice, and then one further, and then back to the note where you started. It's not the same as it's written in the hymn book, but we won't bother about that now, because it's easier like this."

Ruth pored over the keys, concentrating hard on each note. She did exactly as she was told and, to her utter joy, discovered that she was playing Nan's hymn. They repeated the exercise till Ruth had learnt it for herself, and together they sang that one line of the hymn over and over again to Ruth's accompaniment. Grandpa quietly picked up his newspaper and removed himself to the back room, and sometime later Nan slipped away to do the washing-up, leaving Ruth to play those six notes of her first piano lesson to her heart's content.

8

Thereafter Ruth was apparently given free rein to use the front room and play the piano: the door was left open permanently and a one-bar electric fire in the grate kept the temperature above freezing when the coal fire was not lit. The problem was that time was so scarce. Every morning before breakfast, she would help Grandpa clear the grate and lay the fire in the back room. After breakfast, in all weathers, she would trudge out to his shed with him, drawn by the irresistible delights of that extraordinary treasure trove. On dark winter mornings the shed was lit by a solitary bulb hanging from a cable above their heads. Adaptations to the same fixture also served an electric fire suspended from a hook in the end wall. The heat it gave out was supplemented by a smelly paraffin stove so that, initially freezing cold, the atmosphere soon became comfortably snug and stuffy and the windows steamed over, shutting out all interference from the outside world.

Grandpa never went straight into the shed. He always knocked three times and commanded "Open sesame!" before entering into his Aladdin's Cave. Its name, painted on the door, was fully justified, because with its bewitching array of nails and hammers, tins of paint and pots of glue, saws, planes, a clamp and an anvil, and its mixed odours of paint, grease and paraffin, it was a truly enchanted den, ruled by Grandpa, the Wonderful Wizard, as he called himself. Inevitably it constituted a strong rival attraction which each morning succeeded in supplanting the charms of the piano.

In his den, Grandpa showed her how to handle a saw, to hammer a nail and to plane a surface, and allowed her to use all of his tools – the chisel, the screwdriver and the nails, as well as the saw and the hammer – always trusting in her own good sense, though lending a discreet helping hand with rough corners or sharp edges. He gave her little pieces of wood from which to construct cots and wardrobes for dolls, or the toy boats and aeroplanes for which he expressed a preference. He let her use any paint she chose, including a very special tin of real gold lacquer, to give her creations the finishing touch. "Abracadabra, hocus-pocus! Hey presto!" he would say. And then the job was done: a miniature piece of furniture or a vehicle, if somewhat basic in design and rough and ready in construction, was miraculously finished, to be added to the collection of others like it on a rack above their heads.

In a drawer he kept a strange little globe on a red stand. He would remove its top to reveal a white ball. Then he would put the top back on and say the magic words while blowing on it and waving his hand over it. When he took the top off again, the ball had vanished. For a couple of seconds he would look worried and scratch his head in disbelief while Ruth waited in suspense for him to find it. "Where has it gone?" he would say, seeming to be as mystified as she was. Then, with great sleight of hand, he would produce it, sometimes from one of the rickety cupboards, sometimes from behind her ear, sometimes from her pocket. He was a real magician.

Nan, on the other hand, needed a great deal of practical help in her efforts to satisfy Grandpa's extraordinarily insatiable appetite for sponge cakes and jam tarts for his tea. Little suspecting that these tasks were assigned to her to divert her from the piano while Grandpa took his afternoon snooze, Ruth enjoyed plunging her arms into the soft, powdery flour and mixing in the little bits of fat, of course tasting the dough to test for quality. The best part of all was rolling out the kneaded pastry until it was as thin as cardboard, and cutting out neat fluted shapes with the pastry cutter.

There were endless pots of jam to choose from for the fillings. Lined up on their shelf in the larder, their colours gleamed transparently in the light from the small window, like the tall glass bottles in chemists' shops, especially when stray rays of reflected sunlight glinted on that side of the house. Ruth chose the pots for their colour rather than their flavour, the bright ruby red of strawberry one day, the deep luxurious purple of blackcurrant or blackberry the next, still leaving green gooseberry and golden plum in reserve. All these fruits came from the garden or from the farm, Nan informed her proudly. Ruth seized on the subject of the farm, which had slipped her mind since that distant day of the train journey, and cajoled Nan into telling her more about it. So Dad had not been making up stories when he had pointed the farm out to her from the train. It did belong to his cousins and their parents, Nan's sister, Aunt Dolly and her husband, Uncle George. Dad's cousins had grown up and now had their own families, all of whom lived close by and helped on the farm when needed.

Over the pastry dough and the fairy-cake mixture, Nan would reminisce, with a faraway look in her eye and a smile on her lips, about holidays on the farm when they all went to help with the fruit-picking and the harvesting. She told of picnics out in the sun-baked fields by day, of dancing in the big barn or in the farmyard under the full moon by night, of how Dad would ride home on the very top of the hay cart at sundown, of how she and Evelyn would feed the chickens and search for the new-laid eggs in the dewy freshness of the early morning. Ruth sighed in wonder at such visions of happiness. "I tell you what, Ruthie, we'll go there in the summer when the weather is warmer, then you can meet the children – there are so many of them, I can't remember all their names, but some of them are about your age. Mind you," she added by way of a proviso, "it can be pretty uncomfortable out there. They don't have a nice bathroom like we do." She surveyed Ruth, who was fitting the last pastry case into the tin, from head to foot. "And, what's more, as they don't have running water like us, we'd have to take you, my dear little Ruthie, and put you under the village pump and give you a tidy wash, the state you're in. That would be cold indeed, you mark my words."

Nan was right. The worst of pastry-making was that it was a messy business. The flour did have an irritating way of getting everywhere. It covered your face and clothes as well as your hands, however hard you tried to keep clean, with the result that by the time Ruth had finished making Grandpa's cakes, not only did she have to wash, but she had to change all her clothes as well.

Such a wealth of activities, all equally compelling and attractive, every morning and every afternoon, left only a frustratingly limited amount of time for the beloved piano, sometimes as little as half an hour before tea. If Grandpa went out to Speedway or stock-car racing, or to the greyhounds or to visit the King, Ruth might be able to squeeze in another half-hour after tea, but if he stayed at home she would sit beside him while he turned the wireless on and got out his pipe or rolled himself a cigarette.

Then, as she waited in expectation, he would pull out a box full of yet more fascinating, irresistible knick-knacks from a drawer in the sideboard. The box overflowed with broken fob watches, their open backs exposing tiny glittering rubies, gold rings that had lost their stones, lengths of gold and silver chain, cigarette lighters in a variety of forms and metals, and a very small case containing two miniature gold pistols. Grandpa showed Ruth the little hole in the wall where her father had once accidentally fired one of the pistols. The hole went right through the wall and came out in the kitchen on the other side. "Good job Nan wasn't in there at the time," he remarked with a grin. "We might have missed our dinner!"

Nan also had boxes of treasures which she too would produce in the evening, boxes full to the brim with sparkling beads, glass beads, painted beads, shiny beads, patterned beads and pearls, all positively begging Ruth to thread them onto strings to make long, varied, colourful necklaces. There were also boxes of buttons – hundreds of them, in all sizes – the surviving remnants of the once cherished and fashionable but now forgotten suits and dresses, jackets and blouses which in their heyday had filled wardrobes and drawers. Once past their prime, they had been cut up into patches used for mending other garments, before ending their useful life ignominiously in the ragbag.

Nor were these, the beads and buttons and knick-knacks, the only forms of entertainment in the long winter evenings. When they began to pall, Nan would bring out from the bookcase in the corner sets of games that were new to Ruth: a Snakes and Ladders board with Ludo on the other side, or packs of cards for Snap or Happy Families. Nan was not in favour of Snakes and Ladders, because – as she said – the snakes, particularly the three nasty ones on the final line of the board right at the end, made people much too tense and excitable before bedtime.

Ruth was inclined to agree with her, because she did not like losing, and that last snake on the board was always lying in wait for her, but Grandpa phlegmatically remarked that, as that was how life was, the sooner she got used to it the better. Often bedtime would arrive and yet another day had passed without any chance of playing the piano at all. Ruth never for one moment suspected that Nan or Grandpa might be deliberately distracting her from the instrument or trying to steer her away from it. Her days were so contentedly filled that it was simply impossible for her to choose between the numerous diversions.

Whenever she did find a few moments to spare, she would tiptoe into the front room to sit at the piano; she could not explain even to herself why she felt surreptitious about it, except that perhaps she felt a faint but perceptible reluctance both from Nan and from Grandpa to refer to the piano or to anything connected with it. However, once settled at the keyboard, she applied herself wholeheartedly to the instrument and to the music, forgetting whatever subconscious reservations she may have felt. She persevered with 'Now the Day Is Over' until she had mastered the whole verse and then called out to Nan to come and help with the chords in the left hand which she herself did not yet begin to attempt.

Nan would come in, wiping her hands on her apron, and together they made their own unique rendering of the hymn – duet fashion but for two hands only, with numerous hesitations, omissions and errors. With each performance the margin of error was gradually reduced. The effect on Ruth was mesmerizing. She could not believe what she was hearing. With Nan's help, she had played a real tune; she had strung those notes and sounds together in a sequence that, discounting the mistakes, was recognizable. She had created the sounds from nothing, simply by using her fingers on the keys. Those sounds had lasted for only as long as it had taken to create them and had now melted into thin air, but they were there to be recreated at will. She was ecstatic at her own success – so was Nan.

Grandpa was interrupted in the middle of repairs to the motorbike to provide an audience for the final version. To avoid smearing the wallpaper with his oily overalls and hands, he stood hovering in the doorway, his head on one side in a reverie, repeatedly muttering "Well I never, well I never" to himself.

At the end of the performance he passed his hand across his eyes, leaving greasy smudges over his face, and, as he applauded, he remarked to Nan: "Takes us back a bit, doesn't it, ole girl?"

Nan nodded, also wiping her eyes. "Yes, it's history repeating itself," she agreed. "And look at those fingers of hers, real pianist's fingers; we'll have to let her play to her heart's content."

"True," he agreed, "it's time to close the door on the past and give the future a chance." Without waiting for more discussion, he went out and hurried back to the motorbike.

These enigmatic references to the past and the future were lost on Ruth, although she did stop to look down at her fingers, stubby little fingers with the nails bitten down to the quick: they certainly did not look particularly special or unusual. But in her mind there was not the least shadow of a doubt: she was going to become a pianist, a pianist like Evelyn Ruth, only she would not leave Nan and Grandpa to go and live with God. She would stay with them always and play for them every day.

The one remaining obstacle to the achievement of this grand scheme lay in the little black dots dancing up and down the tramlines on the pages. She could not understand what they were doing there, and they continued to worry her because she didn't see that they bore any relation to the keys on the keyboard or to the beautiful sounds that she wanted to produce – yet she knew that they were relevant in some mysterious way. At present Nan would play a tune for her until she had learnt to hum it and would then show her where to find the keys. Gradually this latter part of the exercise became unnecessary, as Ruth found the keys almost as quickly as Nan pointed them out. Nan was called upon to play more and more tunes, nursery rhymes and hymns; hardly had she played one tune than Ruth would be demanding the next.

Finally, one Saturday afternoon when the snows had melted and Grandpa had gone to football, Nan, a trifle weary of beating a path from kitchen to living room, abandoned her other pursuits to give Ruth a lesson in piano technique. She explained that if she really wanted to learn to play the piano properly, she would have to learn and begin with five-finger exercises, then learn and practise scales, chords and arpeggios and recognize the black dots on the page, each of which corresponded to a key on the piano. She showed Ruth how to find middle C on the keyboard, though this was not difficult, because Ruth had already been using it in 'Now the Day Is Over', and also how to recognize it on the printed stave. Similarly, she taught her the finger positions and the names of the four notes above and the four notes below middle C, showing her where they appeared in print.

While Ruth painstakingly tried out the five-finger exercises, Nan, preoccupied with thoughts of her own, suddenly said: "Ah! I think I know the very thing. Let's see what we've got in here, shall we?" She lifted her granddaughter down off the piano stool and opened the lid. After rummaging around inside for a minute or so, she produced a yellowed album with green and orange writing on the cover. "I knew it!" she declared triumphantly, like Grandpa when he produced the little white ball from behind Ruth's ear. "I knew Evelyn had these: they're the books she had when she started to learn, and you can begin with 'Off We Go!', because the early pieces use the notes you've just been learning. I think you'll enjoy them. Now, we'll start with 'Buy a Broom'!" She played the two notes up and down in the right hand and then the four down and up again in the left. As she did so, she sang, "Buy a broom, buy a broom, buy a broom and sweep your room!"

When it was Ruth's turn to place her fingers on the keys, she imitated her grandmother with ease. In the same fashion they tried out several more pieces: there was 'The Monkey', who with four notes in the left hand and three in the right was practising a clever trick on a stick, and 'The Cobbler', who had to mend a shoe by half-past two, as well as a piece called 'Currants' – which when they were picked and plucked were put in a pie. There was also 'Little Gossip', who apparently spent her money on shoes to travel about and carry the news. Ruth set to her task with a will, at first guided by Nan, who some time later returned to the kitchen, but not before she had warned Ruth against rushing ahead, because the later pieces in the book used other notes that she had not yet learnt.

Later she found Ruth puzzling over the other collection of easy pieces. It was called 'Scenes at a Farm' and did indeed use all those notes she had been learning and more, higher up and lower down the keyboard, to conjure up visions of life on the farm – the jolly farmer trotting up and down on his dappled grey horse, the little brook murmuring, the milkmaids singing, the peace of the quiet wood. Images of the farmhouse by the railway line together with the tales Nan had told came flooding into the music. Life on a farm must be a blissful round of dancing, singing and tossing hay.

A touch of sadness crept into the music in one piece about a lonely shepherd watching over his sheep and in another which echoed a strangely plaintive bird call. She did not remember ever hearing the call in London and knew it to be a bird only from the drawing that someone had made in the margin beside its music, which consisted simply of two groups of two notes each, played a space apart. When the two-note tune palled, she allowed herself to return once more to tapping out 'Now the Day Is Over'.

From time to time, she thumbed through Nan's hymn book and tried to play the notes of the right hand. Hymn tunes had a quality which even the best of the farm tunes lacked. Some made you feel calm and peaceful, others were lively and vigorous. Others were very sad. Without understanding the words,

Ruth understood the music, which told her that the hymns were describing something very serious. Since she was using her left hand in exercises and in the farm melodies, she tried to use it to accompany the melody of the hymns, but once again she found that putting her fingers down spontaneously on the keys was not an adequate solution: notes chosen at random in the left hand rarely provided the required accompaniment for the notes in the right. They sounded wrong. Disappointed, she limited her left hand to practising the farmyard sounds.

As she was working her way through 'Off We Go!' a couple of days later, she came across yet another unexpected stumbling block. The notes, which mostly until now had simply consisted of single black dots, had grown tails, some pointing upwards, some pointing downwards, and they began to join up, like washing hanging from a line, or flowers growing in a row. She was baffled.

Nan patiently explained that the notes had different lengths. The single black notes with tails were crochets and were held for one beat, while the joined-up notes, called quavers, were shorter and the white ones, called minims, which had been there from the very beginning, were longer. They all had to fit into bars of regular length – here she pointed to the vertical bar lines – so you had to count up to four, or three, or two, depending on how many beats there were in each bar. Ruth let her hands drop onto her knees in dismay: it was so hard to follow what Nan was saying. It was bad enough that sums, which Dad had begun to teach her and which she definitely did not like, should somehow be involved with the beautiful sounds she was trying to make. All in all, playing the piano was not going to be nearly as simple as she had at first imagined.

"Don't worry," said Nan, "let me put my thinking cap on."

Only a day later, Nan's thinking cap produced the required result. She came into the front room, where Ruth was seated at the piano, bearing a small toy drum.

"Now Ruthie," she announced, "it's time we learnt about rhythm properly. It's not an easy word to say, and even worse to spell, but if we work on it together, you'll find it's not too difficult to do, and it'll help your playing a lot." Ruth looked gravely suspicious at this newest addition to the problems to be mastered, but Nan went on: "I'm going to play some tunes, marching and dancing tunes, on the piano, and you are going to beat time on this little drum." That sounded fairly easy, so Ruth yielded her place on the piano stool to Nan and took hold of the drum, putting its cord round her neck. "Now," said Nan, "I'm going to show you what two beats in a bar sounds like, and you can beat your drum and march round the room like a soldier."

Nan played and Ruth beat "One, two, one, two..." That was fairly straightforward. Then Nan showed her the music on the page; there were only two separate black notes in a bar. "But," Nan said, "there's one more thing: you must make the first beat stronger in each bar." They progressed to three notes in a bar; at first Ruth beat her drum, but then, caught up in the music, she dropped it and skipped round the room instead. "There you are, you see!" Nan declared. "You can do it; we'll take it gently, one step at a time." Later she introduced quavers and semiquavers as little hops and running steps, and semibreves and minims as long strides, all of which explained rhythm in a playful way, since it involved dancing – and Ruth knew about dancing, because sometimes in London Shirley danced round her room when there was music on the wireless.

9

One afternoon, when mastering the little joined-up black notes was proving to be a particularly frustrating and fruitless exercise, Nan placed her arm protectively round her granddaughter to shield her from any more disappointment and closed the piano lid firmly. "Time for a change, my little Ruthie," she said gently. "Let's get that trike of yours out and you can take a message to Grandpa. He's up by the gate, chopping two old trees down, one on our side of the fence and one next door. Ask him to get the sewing machine out for me, will you, dear?" She fetched Ruth's coat and a woolly hat and deposited her and the tricycle by the back door. Ruth cycled up the driveway to give Grandpa the message and then sat looking through the bars of the gate by the stump of the tree which Grandpa had felled.

Through the gaps in the hedge on the other side of the road, a green haze of sprouting barley was already visible. Elsewhere the city was expanding, sending voracious tentacles out into the countryside, but the lane of twelve modest, red-brick, semi-detached houses where Nan and Grandpa had lived since long before Ruth was born was no more than a solitary, forgotten arm of development languidly reaching out into the fields. Far from threatening the country with the menace of further development, it appeared to be detaching itself from the city, disowning its urban identity, preferring to be absorbed into the fields and pastures that surrounded it. Very little traffic passed along the road which led out into the country, apart from the bus service, which had taken upon itself the responsibility of keeping this wayward arm of lapsed modernity in touch with the central authorities which had spawned it.

Ruth was listening to the larks twittering high above the fields across the road when a bus drew up, briefly disrupting the quietness and drowning the piercing song of the birds with its throbbing engine. As the bus pulled away, the two girls from next door crossed the road, swinging their bulky satchels by their straps and laughing and talking in clear, confident voices. "Oh good, look!" one of them called out. "Mr Platt has chopped that old tree down. Mother said it was rotten; she will be pleased!"

As they opened their own front gate, the taller of the two noticed Ruth, sitting inside the gate next door. "Hello!" she exclaimed and stopped as she peered round the gatepost. "What's your name?" she asked, looking Ruth directly in the eye. Ruth was overcome with shyness, which the girl pretended not to notice. She then introduced herself and her sister, who also stepped fully into view. "I'm Ann," the older girl said. "I'm fifteen, and this is my sister, Valerie. She's twelve. So who are you, and how old are you?" Emboldened, Ruth whispered, "I'm Ruth. I'm nearly five."

Both girls were tall and thin. They were very much alike, with short, fair, curly hair, broad, open faces and lively hazel eyes.

They smiled at Ruth. "Ah! Mother said there was a little girl staying with Mrs Platt," Valerie, the younger girl, said, "and we wanted to see you, but the weather has been so bad and we are at school all day and we have so much homework."

"And there's games," the older girl added with a groan, swinging a long curved stick in one hand. "It'll soon be the holidays, though, and then you can come round to our house, if you like. Would you like that?" she enquired, smiling down at Ruth, who nodded, too embarrassed to reply.

"Bye then!" both girls called as they ran down the driveway behind the wooden palings which divided the two properties. She heard them laughing as they ran. "How sweet!" she heard one of them say, without in the least understanding what they meant. "What lovely big brown eyes!" the other joined in. She sat for a moment or two longer by the gate and then cycled back to the house absorbed in contemplation.

Grandpa had set up the sewing machine for Nan on the dining table. She was wearing her glasses and was seated at the machine, her head bent closely over a line of stitching that her steady hand was guiding through the whirring mechanism, while he stood with his hand on the door handle, about to go and clear away the remains of the old trees. They were talking as Ruth came into the house; Grandpa stopped when he saw her, but Nan, who was sitting with her back to Ruth and had not noticed that she had come into the room, carried on speaking. "She's too little to be so serious; we must take her out more." Grandpa coughed and Nan glanced up from her work to find Ruth in the doorway beside him.

Ruth was too full of her own news to take much interest in their discussion. "Nan," she exclaimed, her eyes shining, "those girls from next door spoke to me! They asked me to go and play!"

"Well, there, isn't that nice!" Nan responded. "Now you've made some new friends!" She shot Grandpa a significant look, which seemed to say "She'll be all right – no need to worry, after all", and came to the end of a seam. Grandpa went out to finish his job and Ruth sneaked away into the front room.

As she was about to sit down again at the piano in the front room, Nan called her back and asked if she would like to do some sewing. The shirt she was making for Grandpa was finished, and there were a few scraps of material left which with luck would be sufficient for a tunic for Teddy. Nan laid out the material and showed Ruth how to cut it, using a very small pair of scissors. When they had pinned the pieces, Ruth was shown how to tack them together. This she did loosely and erratically, for it was the first time she had ever handled a needle or done any sewing at all, while Nan inserted a new spool of thread into a hole in the base of the machine.

Ruth was expecting to watch Nan doing the stitching, so was thrilled when she piled cushions onto the chair where she had been sitting and said: "There you are! Now you try the machine, very carefully and very slowly, mind." Nan clamped the garment into position and lifted Ruth onto the chair in front of the machine. Cautiously she placed her hands on the material as Nan had done, her eyes fixed on the area beneath the light bulb where the needle hung poised for action, and Nan applied a slight pressure to the foot. The machine hummed as the needle slowly started to move of its own accord, piercing the material, vanishing from sight and then jumping up again ready for the next insertion and leaving a neat white stitch in its path as it set out along the seam of Teddy's tunic.

Nan applied more pressure, and the needle hopped faster and faster on its one leg, still depositing a neat trail of even stitches in its wake. All Ruth had to do was to guide the material underneath the leg in a straight line. It was so clever. "Is it magic?" she asked. Nan replied that it worked by a sort of magic, called electricity, the same as the light and the vacuum cleaner, but that was as much as she knew about it. Doubtless Grandpa could explain it, because he was an engineer and knew all there was to know about these things, but she would rather not ask him, because he would take it all to pieces to show them how it worked, and then it would never be the same again.

When Teddy's tunic, consisting simply of two rectangles of material stitched together with gaps for his arms and head, was finished, Nan let Ruth experiment with other bits of material. She did not particularly want to make anything else; she liked to watch in fascination as the rows of stitches formed themselves up and down each scrap of material. The curious thing was that the thread came up from below as well as down from above. The cotton reel moved round and round on the upper spool releasing the thread, but it was impossible to see what went on down below. Nevertheless, the underside of each piece of sewing also had its rows of neat, firm stitches exactly like the upper side. She liked the sound of the machine too: it whirred and hummed with a rhythmical beat like the miniature hammer of the elfin shoemaker in one of her story books. When the sewing was finished, she went to try out that hammering beat on the piano.

That evening Nan announced that, as it was Pancake Day, she would like Ruth to help her make the batter and fry the pancakes. The batter had to be just so, according to Nan, neither too thick nor too runny, so although Ruth was given the task of mixing the eggs and the flour, Nan poured the milk in, promising Ruth that the best part was yet to come – as indeed it was. Ruth watched patiently as Nan sliced some lemons and poured sugar into a small bowl.

Then she fried the pancakes, while Ruth waited patiently to find out what was going to happen next.

"What is the best part, Nan?" she asked, as her patience began to wear thin.

"Well, eating them, of course, as you must know," Nan replied, "but we have to toss them first, and that's fun! Once Grandpa tossed his so high it hit the ceiling."

"Oh," said Ruth uncertainly, not knowing whether to believe Nan.

"Surely you do this at home? Don't you?" Nan asked, as she eased a pancake away from the edge of the pan.

"No, I don't think so," Ruth replied.

"Gracious me, whatever next!" Nan exclaimed, but did not pursue the matter. Instead, she called Grandpa to come and help out, and true to form he tossed his pancake so high that it hit the ceiling. Then, putting his big hands over Ruth's, he helped her toss a pancake high in the air, high enough for it to turn a somersault and land back in the pan, the other side up!

10

Before long there was another sewing session when Ruth said that Teddy would like a new pair of trousers. Nan was only too happy to oblige and set up the sewing machine one cold, wet afternoon. The session, which might have lasted indefinitely, was interrupted by Grandpa, who came in jubilantly waving the evening paper. "Would you believe it!" he exclaimed. "Here we have it, a ready-made outing. Why didn't I think of that sooner? Tha's a rum 'un, that is, don't ask me how I came to forget; the boys told me about it weeks ago, and it must hev gone clean outa my mind." He spread out the paper for Nan to see, in among the scissors and pins, cottons and ends of material, and pointed to an advertisement.

Nan followed his pointing finger in the light from the sewing machine and, adjusting her glasses, read aloud: "Open day at Corton St Chad's Aerodrome, all our gallant fighters on display..." She searched down the page for the date and the time. "Saturday, all day from ten o'clock." She mulled over the information, her eyes still wandering up and down the newspaper columns. "Yes, I see... very well, Grandpa, but I wonder if that's the right sort of outing for us. For our little Ruth as well, I mean."

The sombre shadow of doubt in her voice, expressing Ruth's unspoken reactions all too eloquently, hovered in the darkening room, lit only by the coals in the grate and the light of the machine. Grandpa shifted from one foot to the other uneasily, disappointed by the chilly reception given to his enthusiastic suggestion. Nan's tone changed dramatically, however, when another advertisement caught her eye. "Well now, here's something really special, and I think it's what we want for a birthday outing for all of us – wouldn't you agree, Grandpa?"

"Oh, birthday? Who's having a birthday?" he grinned, winking at Ruth. She had an impression that her fifth birthday was not far off, but was not sure exactly when.

"Now, now, Grandpa, don't tease the poor child: you know full well her birthday's on Easter Monday," Nan scolded him, adjusting her glasses yet again. "This sounds like just the thing!"

"What's that then? Come on, tell us! Don't keep us in the dark!" he joked as he switched the main light on and squinted over her shoulder. She read slowly, savouring every syllable. "It says here that the ballet's coming to the Queen's Theatre three weeks on Saturday to perform 'The Sleeping Beauty' by Tchaikovsky." She regarded Ruth questioningly. "How about that, Ruthie? Would you like to go to the ballet?"

Ruth had been listening in miserable silence. Mere talk of a visit to the aerodrome to meet Grandpa's so-called friends, those aeroplanes, filled her with dread. She could well do without that and took some small comfort from Nan's cautious reaction. On the other hand, the ballet might be something she would like, so first she nodded slowly in answer to Nan's question and then enquired, "What is the ballet?"

Nan was bewildered, for this was not the answer she had anticipated. "Hasn't Shirley ever taken you to the ballet in London?" she asked, as lines appeared in her forehead. "Well, the ballet is a story told in dancing, set to music, with beautiful costumes and scenery. We'll read the story of 'The Sleeping Beauty' tonight when you go to bed. It's in that pile of story books of Evelyn's down by your bed. What do you think, Grandpa?"

"Fine," he agreed, "I'll take you and I'll even go up into the city to get the tickets on my way to football tomorrow, so long as you both promise to come with me to the aerodrome and meet my friends next Saturday." The bargain was struck; there was no escaping from the commitment, no two ways about it: the acquaintance of Grandpa's noisy, nerve-racking friends was the price that had to be paid for the ballet.

There was more to it than that. The acquaintance of Grandpa's friends on the aerodrome would only be made by first coming into closer contact with the monster in the sideway. On the morning of the football match, from which he later returned armed with three tickets for the ballet, he stayed out of doors for some time. First he pushed the small car, rather like a large pram, with a clear glass top, out of the lean-to beside the shed, up the lawn and into the sideway. Ruth observed this operation, from the safety, as she presumed, of her tricycle.

Next he attached the contraption to the motorbike, and when that was fixed, he folded back the top and revealed two seats inside, one in front of the other. "There we are," he declared with pride. "Now for a treat, we are going to try it for size!" Before Ruth had time to protest, he had picked her up and dropped her into the front seat. "There, how's that?" he asked with one of his mischievous grins forming in the corner of his mouth and a twinkle in his eye. She was forced to admit that it was all right so far. Nan was called to get into the back seat, because Grandpa had decided that it was time for a trial run. He pulled the top down, shutting Ruth and Nan into their box on wheels. The top was not made of glass after all; the window panels, instead of being clear and hard, like the windows in a car or a train, were opaque and yellowing, so that it was not easy to see out as they flapped in the breeze.

A recognizable roar assaulted Ruth's left ear. She twisted her neck round and saw Grandpa's dark shape sitting up above her on the bike. She twisted round farther to make sure that Nan was still there in the seat behind her. Fortunately she was there, unperturbed as usual, and placed a comforting hand on Ruth's shoulder. The vehicle started to move. Spluttering and shuddering, it accelerated out of the gate onto the road and then, as it settled to a constant speed, the initial roar subsided into a perpetual snarling growl, still deafening but more tolerable than at first. The wind was almost as loud, whistling through the flapping window panels, drowning whatever it was that Nan was trying to say to reassure Ruth.

The ride was bumpy too, like being bounced along the road inside a rubber ball. They turned right and left, swaying from side to side, and gaining speed followed a road out into the country. Open fields, some woods, a church and some houses dimly glimpsed shot past. Grandpa swung round several more turns and, just as Ruth feared that she was going to be sick, the machine suddenly came to a standstill and the engine stopped. Grandpa lifted the top and there they were, back home in the driveway. "So how about it, little miss?" he asked, tossing her up in the air.

"All right," was all that she was prepared to concede.

Although her tummy was a little queasy and her head was swimming, she did not want Grandpa to think her a real baby, in case he never took her out again. The ride was certainly not what she expected from a "treat", but it might have been much worse, noisier, bumpier and more frightening. The great advantage was that suddenly the monster had lost its power. She now rode past it on her trike without having to give it a wide berth. If she chose, she would stop right beside it and pat it – or even, privately, stick her tongue out at it, as the children sometimes did at Mrs Cox's. However much it snarled and snorted and roared, she could afford to laugh at it, because it no longer frightened her. Indeed, it had to obey her. She could ask Grandpa to take her out for a ride, and it was up to her to decide where to go. The monster would have to do as it was told.

Early the next Saturday morning, Nan sent Ruth out in the garden to pick a small bunch of flowers; it was a dull, cold day enlivened only by the clumps of primroses, violets and starry blue flowers that had sprung up in the border at the end of the lawn in place of the snowdrops. As she carefully picked a handful of mixed colours, Ruth wondered why Nan should be intending to take flowers to Grandpa's aeroplanes. She brought the flowers into the house and asked Nan what they were for. Nan pretended not to hear. Ruth repeated her question but did not receive a very helpful reply. "They're for somebody special, dear," was all Nan said. She wrapped the flowers in a piece of tissue paper, inserting a small card between the stems.

The ride to the aerodrome was hardly any worse or any longer than Grandpa's trial run of the previous Saturday, over almost as soon as it had begun, and the aerodrome was nothing more than a vast open field, exposed to all four winds, with a several huge sheds and some huts at one end. Motorbikes, cars and bicycles were strewn all over the grass verges by the side of the road, and crowds of people, mostly men and boys, were milling over the airfield, especially around the planes, some of which were large, some small, some painted green and brown, some silvery grey, all quietly lined up in a deceptively docile row. Ruth took Nan's hand on one side and Grandpa's on the other and, thus safely protected, walked between them. Perhaps the planes were no worse than the monster, but they were menacing even when they were quiet. Until she was sure of them, she was going to keep very close to her grandparents.

As they strolled with the crowds along the lines of parked planes, men in uniform or in overalls would accost Grandpa. "Hello, Joe!" they would call out to him and then would come over to talk to him. "Good to see you!" they would say, before asking, "Have you seen your old friend?" pointing down the line to an old plane with two sets of wings, or, "You must have a look at our new Meteors over there!" or, "Good line-up of Defiants, Blenheims and Hawker Hurricanes today, quite like old times!" They would nod to Nan and, gesturing towards Ruth, would enquire, "So this is your John's littl'un, is it?" Grandpa would nod in smiling acquiescence.

Holding Ruth by the hand, Nan waited with a placid stoicism acquired over years of practice, while he became immersed in endless technical discussions about the merits of this or that engine, this or that wingspan, this or that undercarriage mechanism. He and his companions would wander over to each exhibit, walk round it, run their hands over it, scan it all over and generally analyse every aspect of its manufacture and performance. "You can't beat those Merlin PV12 engines," Grandpa would announce sagely to a murmur of general agreement. "We should be real proud of those. Rolls and Royce and I, we knew they would be a winner."

The two Spitfires on display naturally took up a great deal of their time and attention, but the plane that received the most affectionate greeting was the old biplane at the end of the line-up. Lighting his pipe, Grandpa leant against the fuselage and drew a deep breath of satisfaction. His audience had by now expanded and included some important-looking people in uniform. "Ah!" he reminisced nostalgically. "Many's the time I went out over the North Sea in the Great War, sitting on the wing of this old girl, putting her through her paces, seeing how much she could take. I'd do it all again tomorrow, given the chance. Although, I have to say, it were mighty cold up there!"

A tall man dressed in blue stepped forward and patted Grandpa on the back. "It's good to have you with us, Joe," he said. "We owe a great deal to you, your knowledge, your skill and your bravery. You must come and dine in the Officers' Mess. I'll get something arranged and let you know." The Commander then addressed Nan. "And how nice to have you here, Mrs Platt! Your husband is a remarkable man. I hope you are enjoying retirement?"

Although these questions were purely formal, Nan spoke hesitantly, searching for a suitable reply. "Yes, sir, thank you, sir." The man smiled at Ruth, but shyness overcame her and she hid behind Nan's skirts.

Ruth sensed that here, at the aerodrome, Grandpa was a very important person, though, as with so many matters, she did not know why. There was another intriguing question preying on her mind as a result of his conversation with the man in blue, but this undoubtedly was not the place to ask for an explanation. People might laugh. The gathering dispersed, and Ruth and her grandparents resumed their tour of inspection. Grandpa hoisted Ruth onto his shoulders, encouraging her to put her hand out and touch each plane as they ambled past. "You won't ever be frightened of them again once you've touched them," Grandpa assured her. "Give that old Meteor a good slap for upsetting you." She did as she was told: the surface of the Meteor was cold, smooth and hard, and stood passively, unmoved by her act of aggression, but she felt better for it.

Across the airfield, far enough away not to be frightening, planes were taking off and landing, and performing acrobatics, rolling high in the sky. They were fun to watch, and Ruth was at last beginning to relax and enjoy herself when suddenly a raging wind whipped up her hair. Nan held on to her hat, while other bystanders went chasing theirs in all directions. Like a mammoth bird beating its wings and creating an infernal din, a black-and-yellow helicopter swooped down from the sky and came to rest in the space right in front of them. Ruth screamed her whole body rigid with terror. Grandpa took her down from his shoulders, held her close and ran, carrying her back to the motorbike. Nan stumbled along behind, producing a comforting piece of chocolate from her handbag.

"Oh dear, that was a pity, just as we were having such a nice time, too," she commiserated, stroking Ruth's hair in an attempt to calm her trembling body and quieten her convulsive sobbing.

"I'll take you both home and I'll come back after lunch," Grandpa offered, as he lifted Ruth into the sidecar. Nan caught his arm and pleadingly murmured something in his ear, indicating the posy which still lay on her seat. "Oh, of course, tha's so like me to have forgotten. I'm sorry, my dear," he said. A shadow crossed his normally cheerful face. "Do you think she'll be all right?" he murmured, gesturing towards Ruth, who was recovering her composure sufficiently to take an interest again in what was happening, to ask: "Where are we going, Grandpa?"

"Well, as we are near, we are going to the church to show you where Evelyn is," he replied sharply.

"Ah," she said.

They drove to the church that Nan attended on Sunday mornings. By comparison with the helicopter, the motorbike had become an old friend. Grandpa parked it and lifted Ruth out of the sidecar, announcing, "Well, here we are," while Nan straightened herself up. They led Ruth through the gate and down the path, but did not go into the church. Instead, walking onto the grass, they wended their way among the primroses and stopped at a long flat stone. It was whiter and cleaner than the others around it. Beside it stood a small tree with a few tiny shoots at the end of its branches.

"This is it, Ruth dear," said Nan in a subdued voice. "This is Evelyn's rose tree."

Ruth gazed at the tree and the inscription. She read the bit that said "Evelyn Ruth Platt", but that was followed by something else and some numbers which she could not read.

"What do the numbers say, Nan?" she asked.

"5th June 1921 to 27th March 1948," Nan replied, bending down to put the posy under the bush. Ruth watched, without daring to ask any more of the nagging questions which were forming in confusion in her mind. Instead, she drew her own conclusions. Anyhow, there was no doubt about it. She had been right all along. People were born under bushes and people died under bushes, and the fairies – or God or whoever he was – put them there in the first place and then came to take them away.

Both Nan and Grandpa had become forlorn and distant, old and sad, so she took their hands in hers and walked in silence with them back to the motorbike. She then remembered the question she had wanted to ask earlier.

"What's a mess, Grandpa? Why did that man ask you to go and eat in a mess?" This innocent enquiry brought the smile back to Grandpa's face.

11

As the motorbike drew into the sideway, the back door of the neighbouring house opened and the mother of the two girls Ruth had met by the gate came out onto the doorstep. "Hello, Mrs Platt!" she called to Nan, who was easing herself out of the sidecar. "How did it go?"

Nan grimaced ruefully. "It would have been fine if a great helicopter had not landed right in front of us, so of course we had to run for it. But Joe can go back this afternoon and see the rest of the displays."

"That's a pity," the lady next door remarked sympathetically, surveying them from the other side of the fence. She was tall, with a round, healthy face, short, curly grey hair and kind, light-brown eyes. She looked at Ruth, hesitantly. "Do you think Ruth would like to come and spend the afternoon with us?" she asked a couple of seconds later, "then you would both be able to go back to the air show. The girls break up next week, so they don't have any homework."

Nan and Grandpa glanced at Ruth uncertainly. "Well, I don't know..." Nan began, unprepared for the decision that Ruth had already made.

"Yes, please!" she butted in impulsively, forestalling Nan's reply.

"She knows her own mind, doesn't she?" the neighbour commented.

"She's beginning to," Grandpa conceded, "but she's still very nervous; who knows what goes on in that little head of hers."

Ruth had been longing for the promised invitation to go and play with the big girls next door, and she already liked the friendly, grey-haired lady, whom she had often seen over the fence. Once, when they had been busily nailing some pieces of wood together in the shed, Ruth had asked Grandpa why there was no dad next door. Sucking his pipe, Grandpa had shaken his head. "Lost in the War..." was all he said, without elaborating further.

That afternoon was the first of many that Ruth was to spend next door. Although externally the house was a mirror image of Nan's, inside it could not have been more dissimilar. Everywhere the woodwork was painted cream instead of stained brown, and the furniture was newer and more modern. Even though it was so very unlike the house she was used to, Ruth was made to feel at home there from the moment the mother of the family opened the door to her.

"Come in, Ruth! You must call me Carrie like everyone else," she laughed, and continued: "I've got such a funny name. You see, my name is Caroline, but then I married Mr Carrington, so instead of calling myself Caroline Carrington, which would be really stupid, I call myself Carrie."

The frankness of this introduction was not at all off-putting. On the contrary, Ruth was flattered to be treated like a grown-up: that encouraged her to be open with Carrie in return. An adult who laughed at herself inspired trust. Nan and Grandpa she trusted and loved, of course, but there were so many subjects it was impossible to talk about with them, so perhaps here was someone who would answer her questions truthfully, without evasion. It would be a relief to have proper answers for some of those questions which spun round endlessly, trapped in a dizzy whirl in her head.

The girls had competed with each other in their preparations for their young visitor. As Ann was going to be a schoolteacher, like her mother, her boundless enthusiasm suited her very well to the profession. She had selected an armful of books and a collection of toys to keep Ruth constructively occupied for the whole afternoon, while on the other hand Valerie, the twelve-year-old, suspended in the limbo between childhood and adolescence, was less sure of herself. At one moment she would adopt adult mannerisms and attitudes, and the next she would behave like a five-year-old herself. On this occasion she took the opportunity to revert to her childhood ways and got out all her old toys. She had blown the dust off her dolls and was busy polishing their furniture when Ruth was delivered at the door. She leapt up to greet her ahead of her sister and shepherded Ruth in the direction of her doll's house.

Carrie stayed with them to put Ruth at ease. "Well, Ruth," she asked casually, "how do you like being back in your nan's house?"

Ruth was so floored by the question that, hastening to correct Carrie, she exclaimed, "I've never been here before!"

"But you were born here!" Carrie cried. Ruth let the doll she was playing with fall to the floor. "Hasn't anyone ever told you that you were born in your nan's house?" Carrie asked, as her face reddened with confusion.

Ruth was as confused as Carrie. She was no longer surprised to discover stories about Dad's childhood, but she was unwilling to believe that there were things about her own life that she did not know. She stared blankly at Carrie. "No, no one ever told me," was her limp reply. Carrie hastily escaped to the kitchen sink, where she scrubbed a burnt pan energetically.

However, Ruth was not prepared to let her go so easily; she would not allow Carrie to disappoint her. The adults in her life, however loving most of them were, formed conspiracies from which she had always been excluded. At last, having begun to penetrate a tiny chink in that wall of secrecy and half-truths, she would not let this precious moment slip. She must seize the chance to learn about her own past, about facts which apparently no one else had bothered to tell her.

"Was I born in Nan's house?" she asked, following Carrie and challenging her. "Were my dad and Shirley there too?"

"Of course Shirley was there," Carrie laughed uneasily, "but your dad was away in the War.

In acute embarrassment, Carrie found herself obliged to reveal the circumstances of Ruth's early life as one question led to another. She explained how Shirley had come to live with Nan and Grandpa because it was too dangerous for her to stay in London while her husband was away in the War. Not that it was much safer where they were, but there was nowhere else to go. Shirley had not really wanted to leave London and, after Ruth's birth, had become very ill – not with any pain or sickness, but with an illness which made her very unhappy and unable to look after the new baby. She had gone to a hospital somewhere out in the country and was there for a long time. Meanwhile Nan had cared for Ruth.

"Do you mean that Nan was my mummy?" Ruth enquired.

"No, no, that's not what I mean," Carrie replied, "but she looked after you while your mummy was ill. We all helped a bit. Evelyn, your dad's sister, too – you do remember Evelyn, don't you?"

Ruth nodded. "Yes," she said, "we went to see her today, but there was only a white stone and a rose tree."

This remark baffled Carrie, and she fell silent. It was some while before she picked up the thread of her tale again. "Evelyn adored you and used to take you for walks, and I used to babysit sometimes – for your grandparents, so they could go to Evelyn's concerts," Carrie reminisced. "She was so beautiful and so clever, your Aunt Evelyn, and the way she played the piano! It brought tears to my eyes. It was such a pity your mummy didn't ever go to hear her play. Who knows, it might have done her good, stopped her getting into such a low state."

Ruth kept quiet. There was so much she wanted to ask, yet she was afraid of overstepping the boundaries of what Carrie was prepared to tell her. She allowed herself one more logical question. "Why do I live in London then?"

"Long after the end of the War, when Shirley came out of hospital, she wanted to go straight back to London, which was where she came from, so off you all went. I think your father got a job with the borough council when finally he came home some time later," Carrie explained briefly, anxious to extricate herself from further interrogation.

"I see," said Ruth, not seeing at all, and rejoined the girls in the living room, where Ann had set up a toy post office.

When Nan came to collect Ruth, Carrie drew her aside. "I am so sorry. I'm afraid I've put my foot in it. It didn't occur to me that she didn't know she was born here." Ruth pricked up her ears on hearing Carrie's profuse apologies.

"No, no, don't worry," said Nan. "It's better for her to know – not that there's much to tell, but sometimes Joe and I don't know where to begin. You see, some things, like Shirley's illness, are so difficult to explain, and she's such a serious little mite, we're afraid of upsetting her. And, anyhow, with your experience, you are so good with children…" Nan's customary quiet confidence had deserted her; in its place a nervous anxiety reduced her speech to an incoherent whisper which tailed away into silence.

12

Ruth dawdled back home behind Nan. As the creaking gate swung open, she stopped to study the detail of the rusty red-brick façade of that dear, plain house, nestling among the hedges and bushes of the front garden. Now she found it even lovelier, for it was not just Nan's house, Grandpa's house: it was her house as well, because she had been born there. In that very garden the fairies must have left her under a bush to be discovered by her mother! This information about her origins provided the missing piece of a jigsaw puzzle. This, not London, was her true home: here was where she belonged, and here was the centre of the puzzle. Nan and Grandpa had been part of her life since the very beginning – and they were there, too, at the centre. That was why she loved them so much. But why did it all have to be so secret? Why did adults make such a big mystery out of everything?

She fetched her tricycle and rode up and down for a while, contemplating these new perspectives. There were certain strange shapes and forms, though, which refused to fit into the spaces in the puzzle. How did Shirley fit into it? The connection between her and Ruth began to seem rather faint if, as Carrie had said, Shirley had gone away for a long time as soon as she was born. Was she really her mother? Real mothers did not go away and leave their new babies. And if Shirley was not her mother, how did Dad come into it? Was he really her father? And what about Evelyn, who had loved her so much and had helped Nan care for her when she was a baby?

She stopped at the back door, parked her trike and entered the house. She went straight into the front room and sat down at the piano. She did not touch the keys. Instead, she gave her whole attention to the photograph of Evelyn. She searched the face for help and inspiration, and there she found the seeds of an idea which began to implant themselves in her mind, offering potential solutions to some of the problems which were tormenting her. The portrait of Evelyn, flush with success, beaming down at her, resembled her so closely with her dark hair and eyes – and she was clever, beautiful and, from what she had heard, kind. This was the same Evelyn who had adored her so much when she was little. Evelyn had been a brilliant pianist, and she too was going to be a pianist, just like her. Perhaps it was Evelyn – the lovely, famous, clever Evelyn – and not hard, cold Shirley, who was her mother. It must have been Evelyn who had found her one spring morning down the garden, safely hidden who knows where, perhaps among the primroses under the pussy willow.

The delight Ruth felt at this idea bred a succession of further questions, like weeds invading a flower bed. "Why did she live in London with Shirley, who did not seem to care for her very much?" But there was no easy answer to this question. Try as she might, she was not able to discover an explanation. She could only suppose that Evelyn had given her away to her brother, known as Dad, when she knew that she was going to die. Ruth's one surviving memory of Evelyn gave her a twinge of deep regret. It consisted of no more than that faint recollection of her first holiday by the sea when Evelyn, pale and thin, had stayed in the hotel all the time and had taken such scant notice of her. Although she searched her memory for happier scenes, scenes of Evelyn taking her for walks, talking to her, playing the piano for her, cuddling her, these were only teasing spectres which cruelly evaded her grasp. Anything more substantial was buried and forgotten.

The troublesome doubts surrounding Evelyn were eclipsed by one certainty: whatever had happened in the past, it was not possible for Shirley to be her mother. Ruth had often doubted that she was, and now she was convinced. This would explain why Shirley did not want to be called "Mummy". Therefore it simply did not matter after all that she did not have fair curly hair and green eyes like Shirley. In fact, it was exciting, because her story was like a fairy tale, like 'Cinderella' or 'Snow White', and she was an orphan, left in the care of a wicked stepmother. In contrast, Evelyn, her real mother, had the air of a fairy-tale princess, guarding a secret under a magic spell. The secret must be kept at all costs. All things considered, it was better not to mention these things even to Nan and Grandpa, because they were old and would be upset. It was enough that Ruth had discovered the truth for herself.

That evening Nan brought out a shabby box from the sideboard and set it on the table. "These will amuse you, Ruthie," she said, tipping out the top layer of contents. Bundles of small photos, falling like autumn leaves out of the hardened rubber bands which held them in place, came to rest scattered over the table. Their edges were brown and curling. Some were faded, others were blurred. Ruth seized them avidly, scrutinizing each one and assaulting Nan with a barrage of questions about the identities of the people depicted in them. Some were obvious enough: there were Nan and Grandpa, several years younger. There was her father in his army uniform and there were photos of him and Shirley: in one, Dad was in uniform and Shirley was dressed in a fur coat and a lacy hat, her fair curls prettily bobbing round her face, with a rose in her buttonhole. "That's their wedding photo," Nan explained tersely with a marked lack of enthusiasm.

She pushed the wedding photo out of the way and rummaged through the pile until she found pictures of the family at the farm: these enchanted her granddaughter, particularly because they had been taken by her father with the camera that Nan had given him for his twenty-first birthday. There were photos of all the cousins, grinning and making faces, lined up with Aunt Dolly and Uncle George against the background of the old farmhouse, and there were also a few snapshots of individual cousins clutching their favourite animals. "I never knew how he could get so close to that dreadful thing!" Nan exclaimed at the sight of her nephew Barty, with his arms round the neck of a goose.

Dad had also taken photos of them all on day trips to the sea – sitting on the beach in deckchairs right by the shoreline with waves lapping their feet or chasing each other into the sea or crunching long sticks of rock. There were, too, photos of Nan and Aunt Dolly holding hands, looking very much alike. In another they were supporting a diminutive old lady, dressed in black, whose face was screwed up against the sunlight. "That's our mother," Nan explained, "your great-grandmother. Your father took this on her eightieth birthday. She was a lovely person," Nan sighed. "If only you had known her, Ruth, you would have loved her."

In the middle of the box lay a set of formal, professional portraits of Dad and Evelyn as children. In a sepia-tinted study, Evelyn, aged about seven, sat on a high stool, straight-backed, her hands crossed in her lap, a half-smile playing on her lips. Her hair was short with a heavy fringe covering her forehead. Ruth imagined herself there in the portrait, standing between Evelyn and the towering plant which overshadowed the sitter. In another set portrait, a tubby four-year-old Dad, wearing a sailor suit, leant anxiously over the rug on which his little sister was lying in a long flowing robe.

Ruth laughed. "Is this Dad? He does look silly!" Nan shrugged with a faint smile. Then there was Dad aged eight, dressed for a party in another sailor suit, but obscured by the yards of organza of Evelyn's party frock.

All these photographs conjured up an idyllic, unknown past, one that was beginning to illuminate Ruth's own present. She was related to all the people in these photos, yet she did not know many of them – some indeed she would never know, because they had died, and they did not know her.

Finally, Nan unearthed the most fascinating and, she said, the most precious set of the entire captivating collection, from the very bottom of the box. These photos were concealed from the damaging effects of light by the formal portraits lying on top of them, and all were photos of Ruth as a baby: Ruth when she was newborn, held tightly by someone whose face was not visible because the camera was focusing on the tiny, feature-less face, embedded in a mass of white shawl, and Ruth with a mass of dark hair, equally small, held nonchalantly aloft by Grandpa above his head.

"I can't think how we ever let you do that," Nan remarked, nodding in his direction.

"Just teaching her to fly," he replied.

There were photos of Ruth in Nan's arms and there were also ones of Shirley looking miserable, giving the impression that summoning a smile was too difficult, with her fingers splayed on the handle of a cumbersome pram. Dad did not appear in the photos until Ruth was already nine months old. He was still wearing uniform and looked directly at the camera while Ruth pulled his hair.

All these people came and went. However, throughout the photos, from the time of her birth until those few snaps with Dad, Ruth had one truly constant companion, either in the background or in the foreground, and that was Evelyn: Evelyn holding Ruth, Evelyn sitting on the lawn beside Ruth, Evelyn with Nan and Ruth, Evelyn with Grandpa and Ruth, and the very last one of all, Evelyn at the piano with Ruth on her knee, placing her tiny fingers on the keys. Ruth was agitated at the sight of these particular photos: they confirmed so much of what she already suspected. She wanted to snatch the last one for herself. Impetuously she asked Nan if she might keep it, and Nan agreed. She took it up to bed with her and leant it against the green tiles of the washstand until she could think of a safe place to hide it. Later she hid it in her coat pocket

13

During the Easter holidays when the girls were at home, Ruth became a frequent visitor to the house on the other side of the fence. Nan and Grandpa were relieved that, of her own accord, she was coming out of her shell and making friends.

"I'm going to call on Ann and Val," she would call out to Grandpa airily as she slipped out of the shed whenever she heard voices in the neighbouring garden. For their part, the girls welcomed her in their games – or, if their activities were too advanced, would invent games especially for her. Ann taught her to catch a ball, to hold a small racket and to recognize flowers and plants. They fed the goldfish in the pond and checked up on Ann's hibernating tortoise, tucked away in straw in his box in the garden shed. All three of them went for walks down to the Dell at the end of the road in search of the wild flowers, the celandines and violets that were hiding in the copse but beginning to open, and there Ruth learnt to listen for the songs of different birds.

Ann told her that in summer they always heard the most beautiful birdsong, that of the nightingale in the wood. It was too early for the nightingale, but one day in early April Ruth identified a bird call with only two notes herself.

"Listen!" she shouted excitedly to the others. "That's a cuckoo!"

"Yes, you're right! That's early for the cuckoo," Ann remarked, and explained that the call of the cuckoo was a warning to other birds that there was a raider in the area who would come and throw their babies out of their nests and then substitute its own eggs. Ruth was dismayed to learn that her musical friend was so wicked.

On their return from these excursions, they would show Carrie their finds while drinking squash and eating biscuits. One morning, as they were telling her that they had seen a squirrel leaping among the high treetops, a large wasp flew buzzing venomously into the kitchen where they were standing. Val was allergic to wasp stings and squealed in terror. Carrie pushed her out of the way, closed the door and told Ruth and Ann not to move.

"I don't like to do this," she muttered grimly, "but if the choice is between that early queen wasp or Val, then off with its head!" She grabbed a fly swat and crushed the intruder, still drowsily emerging from hibernation in the warmth of the sun, against the window. "There, that's finished it off," she declared.

From the hall, Val called out: "Is it dead? Can I come back in?"

"Yes, well and truly dead," Carrie replied.

Ruth inspected the crushed body of the wasp oozing a sticky mess. It no longer moved. She reflected for a while, trying to assemble her ideas. "Is that dead?" she asked, emphasizing "dead".

"Yes, of course," Ann said in a matter-of-fact fashion, but Carrie glanced sharply at Ruth, suspecting that there was more to come. "Evelyn's dead, isn't she?" Ruth continued.

Carrie motioned to Ann to keep silent and gently answered, "Yes, dear, but that's not how she died, of course."

"What's dying?" came the inevitable question.

Carrie wiped her hands methodically, playing for time. "I think we had better go and sit down," she decreed, taking Ruth by the hand and leading her into the sitting room while Val burst into giggles, which she stifled quickly when her sister glared at her. The girls followed, curious to witness the scene and inquisitive to know how their mother would resolve a delicate situation. They had not reckoned with Carrie's long experience as a primary-school teacher, which now stood her in good stead. She sat down in an armchair, drawing up a low stool at her feet for Ruth, as though she were about to embark on a story. She addressed Ruth as an adult, which she always did when talking to a child.

"You see, Ruth," she began, "we all have to die some day. Some people die accidentally or violently, like that wasp; some people die when they get very old; others die when they become very ill." She discreetly allowed time for her words to sink in. "Their bodies get too worn out or too damaged for them to go on living. The life goes out of them, and all that is left is an empty shell, like that wasp." She waited again, carefully watching Ruth's face, before continuing. "The empty shell is not a person, or a wasp, any longer; it can't eat or sleep or fly or think or talk or play. It was only the outer shell of the person inside anyhow, and when the person doesn't need it any more, it falls apart and rots away, so we have to bury it in the earth. We'll go and bury that wasp in a minute."

"Shall we bury it in the garden under a tree?" Ruth asked after she had considered the situation.

"Yes, if you like," Carrie replied.

If she were uncertain of the significance of the tree, Ruth soon enlightened her. "Evelyn died under a tree," she explained.

"I see," said Carrie, appearing to take her seriously, but then added gently, by way of correction: "I think you mean she was buried under a tree, the rose tree by her grave in the churchyard, when she died."

"Yes, I think so," Ruth replied doubtfully.

So far all her deductions had been more or less right, but Carrie's account still did not explain where Evelyn was now. If her body had been buried under that rose tree, where was the rest of her, the lovely, clever, piano-playing Evelyn?

"Did she go to live with God?" she asked anxiously.

"You might put it like that," Carrie agreed, preparing to encounter the next major topic, which loomed predictably. "People have different ideas though as to what that means." Ruth waited for her to continue. Carrie gazed out of the window as the changing reflections of the spring sky drifted across her eyes, which clouded over wistfully as she spoke. She was no longer addressing Ruth or her daughters: she was talking to herself, and her voice grew unusually quiet as she spoke, "My own view, rightly or wrongly, is that we each of us have a little spark inside us, a little spark of goodness, and as we lead our lives, that little spark grows or shrinks, depending on how we behave. Then when we die the spark, or what is left of it, goes to join itself up with God, because the word 'God' means goodness."

"What about the wasp, Mum?" Val butted in, destroying the calm, contemplative atmosphere.

Carrie sighed at the interruption. "Well, I don't know, dear, but I expect that all animals, even wasps, have a tiny spark of God's creation somewhere inside them, but perhaps it's a spark which they hold jointly, regardless of their shape or form. The difference is that people, unlike animals, can think and make choices. They can choose whether to ignore that spark and let it shrink away, so that there is nothing left for God to take back, or encourage it to grow until it sparkles with the brilliance of a large diamond."

"You mean by being good and kind?" said Ann, enlarging upon Carrie's train of thought.

"Yes, I suppose so; that is the only way to happiness, though not many people understand it. Perhaps considering what happened in the War, that's not surprising. I suppose those of us who do realize it ought to encourage and forgive all those bad, cruel people who are in danger of losing their own spark of goodness, even the criminals and the dictators – though I must say, I find that hard."

Ruth felt that the conversation, which had been crystal-clear, was getting too deep for her, and she foresaw that it was going to develop into a complicated discussion between Carrie and Ann – and Val as well. Sometimes Carrie and her daughters became involved in long and earnest conversations, in the course of which words like "health", "education", "welfare" and "politics" kept cropping up. Ruth would listen for a while and then, tired of so many long words, would slink away to play with the doll's house.

Rather than lose the thread of this very important discussion completely, however, she interrupted with a question of great personal significance. "Did Evelyn have a large spark?" she asked.

"Oh yes, a huge one, like a diamond," came the certain reply. Recovering her normal vivacity, Carrie gave her a broad smile. "No one was ever better."

This remark provoked a sudden afterthought in Ruth. "And what about Shirley, has she died in hospital?"

"No, no, what ideas you are getting into your head, little Ruth! Ask your nan, she told me that your mother is getting better. Come on, let's bury that wasp."

That afternoon Ruth shut herself in the front room. She wanted to be alone to try to understand some of the things that Carrie had said. She played the piano sporadically, tapping out the occasional tune absent-mindedly with one finger. She glanced from time to time at Evelyn's smiling portrait. The goodness in her face was there for all to see: all that goodness must have gone straight back to God, sparkling like the stone in the ring that Nan always wore. Carrie's idea of the spark of goodness conjured up a lovely picture, but it was still very bewildering. Carrie had talked about God, who was often mentioned in Nan's hymns with the baby Jesus, yet she had not so much as mentioned the fairies. Where did they come into it? And what about other people? There was no question about Nan's goodness or Grandpa's. Dad was a good person too, but what about Shirley? Where was her essential spark? Did she have one, or had it shrunk away to nothing?

Ruth sat deep in confusion, until Nan put her head round the door. "Why have you shut yourself in, Ruthie?" she asked. "Are you all right?"

"Yes, Nan," she replied.

"Grandpa is looking for you; he's got something else for you! You'd better come and see," Nan said. Ruth did not need to be asked twice. She slid off the stool, grateful to escape from the complexity of her own thoughts.

Nan led her out into the garden, where Grandpa's latest scheme was nearing completion. He had removed the sidecar from the lean-to behind the shed and was sweeping the floor, which was made up of old strips of lino. The bus seats had been cleaned, and in one corner stood the tin bath, now dry and full of sand.

"Here you are then!" he exclaimed as Ruth came running down the lawn. "Welcome to Ruth's Cabin!" Ruth stood open-mouthed while he explained. "Nan and I think you should have somewhere out of doors to play even if it's raining. You can keep your trike in here, and here's your sand. It'll have to be builders' sand for the moment, but in the summer we can bring some nice clean sand back from the seaside."

Ruth peeped into the tin bath; there, lying on the sand ready for her immediate use, was a collection of Nan's old baking tins and pastry cutters.

"You can make tea for us out here and invite us to come and join you," Nan suggested.

Grandpa reached up and unhooked a length of rope dangling from the roof of the lean-to. "And here's your swing, specially made for you this morning; let's see if it's the right size."

Gasping with joy, Ruth eased herself onto the seat, and Grandpa gave her a gentle push from behind, saying, "There she goes!"

"Swing your legs out as you go forward, and under you as you come back," said Nan.

Grandpa continued to push until Ruth had captured the rhythm for herself. As the swing went higher and higher, she recovered her voice, squealing with happiness as the breeze fanned her face and caught her hair, sending it streaming out behind her. Her grandparents stood to one side, revelling in the spectacle of such innocent pleasure.

14

Nan came into Ruth's room early, as she was waking up one morning. "Saturday today!" Nan's voice sang out loudly in her ear as she yawned sleepily. "Have you forgotten? Today's the day for the ballet, your birthday treat!" This announcement woke her, and she sat up. At last, the great day had arrived! She certainly had not forgotten, but she never knew which day was which, nor when things like the ballet and birthdays were going to happen. Nan opened the door of the wardrobe at the foot of the bed. "Come and choose one of Evelyn's best frocks," she said. "There are plenty here; there must be something you'd like."

She pulled out piles of neatly folded dresses in all colours – some cotton, some woollen, some plain, some floral, some pleated, some smocked. Ruth dived down to the end of the bed to examine the mounting pile. The choice would have been impossible had Nan not produced what was certainly the best of the bunch: the velvet dress that Evelyn wore in one of her early photos. It was a deep burgundy red with a white satin collar, so the choice was made without a moment's hesitation. Nan promised to search out a matching ribbon to tie back Ruth's thick, glossy hair, which now reached down to her shoulders. Nan advised her to take the morning gently, as the afternoon was going to be rather tiring, and she would not want to go to sleep in the ballet.

It was well-nigh impossible to take the morning gently. Time dragged with a leaden sluggishness, crawling along at the pace of Ann's tortoise – which, to Ruth's astonishment, was slowly beginning to stir and come back to life, after being buried in a box all through the harsh winter months. The tortoise had not eaten or moved in that time but, inexplicably, his body had not rotted or fallen to pieces, nor had whatever little spark he held inside him flown away. Ruth called next door hoping that she might be able to make time pass by watching him emerge from his shell and lumber across the lawn, but there was no one at home.

She went back to Nan's house and sat at the end of the garden under the cherry tree for a while, watching its clouds of blossom wave in the breeze against the azure sky above her head. Although it was a heavenly sight, it failed to hold her attention for long, so she went indoors and took up her customary position on the piano stool. Unusually for her, there was nothing that she wanted to play. She went out of doors again and sat on her swing idly twisting and turning for ages, but, according to Nan's watch, only five minutes had passed. She then leant against Grandpa's chair while he tried to mend a cigarette lighter. It was a finicky business, demanding his full concentration, so he was not in the mood for conversation.

Finally, she was reduced to following Nan's recommendation and retired to her room to look at the pictures in 'The Sleeping Beauty' story book. She lay on her bed flicking through the pages of the familiar story. There was the baby Princess in her cradle attended by her parents and their courtiers; then the fairies came flying in to present their gifts – of beauty, kindness, happiness and so on – to the baby at her christening. Ruth hesitated before moving on to the next page: she knew what was coming, and although she would have preferred to skip past that particular image altogether, it gripped her with a fearful, inescapable fascination. The whole page was taken up by the portrait of the thirteenth fairy, the one whom the King and Queen had omitted to invite to their daughter's christening. Her black wings were open wide, like thunderclouds behind her head of silvery-blonde hair, which stood on end in a tapering mane; her slanting green eyes narrowed to vicious slits as, with sharply pointing fingers, she directed a glittering wand out of the picture, out of the page, at the reader. Ruth shivered, but then when she heard Nan calling her down to lunch she quickly closed the book.

Unlike the morning, the afternoon came and went in a flash, as though time itself had speeded up. It began with a ride on the bus. Self-consciously resplendent in the red velvet dress with a ribbon in her dark hair, Ruth clambered up the steep steps to the top deck. It was going to be a longish journey, Grandpa said, so it was worth struggling up the steps for the view. In any case, he needed some compensation for the discomfort of having to wear a stiff white collar and a brown suit which was too tight for him, and for leaving the motorbike at home. He insisted on wearing his old cloth cap, because otherwise – he said – he would not know himself. On his necktie he wore a shiny brass propeller mounted on a pin. He allowed Ruth to twirl the propeller, and as she did so he made the noise of an engine starting up. The faster she twirled, the louder the noise of the engine grew, until finally Nan nudged Grandpa and said, "Hey, you two, you're disturbing the other passengers!"

The bus trundled along tree-lined roads where rows of ordinary houses and gardens gave way without warning to patches of waste ground over which Nature was hastily invoking all the powers of spring to cover up piles of broken bricks, tiles and twisted pieces of metal with weeds, grass and fast-growing saplings. They passed the shops where Nan stretched the coupons in her ration book to the limit to place her weekly orders for quarter-pounds of tea, blue-bagged pounds of sugar and slices of spam, and then they crossed the river bridge into the heart of the city, making their way bumpily along cobbled medieval streets and across squares bearing peculiar names – Graveland, Queens' Walk, St Radegund's Street.

On the left, the tall white spire of the cathedral soared heavenwards on the wings of its gilded weather-vane cockerel. The road bore to the right, bringing into view the solid, impregnable mass of the castle, defiantly looming above them on its mound. At its base, on the other side of the road, lay a grisly wreckage, as of defeated invaders repelled from the keep: blackened ruins, burnt-out shells of buildings, hollow sightless walls, tumbling over each other in their haste to escape the inferno unleashed upon them from above.

"What's that?" asked Ruth, recalling similar nightmarish scenes in London, no more able to disregard them than she had been able to ignore the picture of the thirteenth fairy.

"Bombed in the War, dear," came the reply, which told her nothing.

At a signal from Grandpa, they descended the stairs and got off the bus by the entrance to a narrow, tunnel-like alleyway, which led between tall dark buildings and brought them out in an open, sunlit space, covered with rows of market stalls. The market had a permanently festive air, for each stall was laden with colourful displays of fruit and early spring flowers, and was roofed with gaily striped awnings. Mesmerized and forgetting the forthcoming ballet, Ruth imagined how lovely it would be to run up and down the aisles inspecting the multicoloured and multifarious produce on sale. Unexpectedly her wish was granted, for Grandpa steered his party across the road and then into one of the rows, marching through the very heart of the market, where daylight scarcely penetrated and the stallholders had to rely on oil lamps to ply their trade.

They passed stalls straining under the weight of fruit and vegetables, while others were devoted to a single commodity – eggs, cheese or sweets – each with its own particular aroma and each with its jovial, good-natured stallholder.

"Come along then, my littl' ole dear," the sweet-seller said to Ruth when they stopped at her stall. "What are you a-goin' to choose?"

She would have chosen the shiny, pungent red bull's-eyes, but Nan said they were too large for her mouth, so she had to settle for a quarter of dolly mixture instead. Towards the far end of the row, Ruth found the goods less enticing – not so Nan. Grandpa had to hustle her past the rolls of dress materials over which she would have lingered, permitting himself the merest sidelong glance at the boxes of tools and mechanical equipment on the opposite row of stalls. Even here he was well known.

"Hello, Joe!" the stallholders called out to him. "Didn't recognize you, all dressed up like that. Where are you off to?"

"I'm not a-goin to tell, and you don't want to know!" he replied enigmatically, with a rueful grin.

They came out at the back of the market into the fading sunlight by the steps of the City Hall, where they stopped briefly to admire the view from above: a sea of coloured canvases billowed slightly in the breeze allowing no hint of the bustle of activity beneath. Grandpa said he was dying of thirst and would not survive the performance if he did not have a drink. Nan said she knew of a "nice little tea shop" and advised them to follow her. Grandpa winked at Ruth, clicked his heels, saluted Nan and said something which Ruth did not quite grasp, but which sounded like "Hail!" in a funny voice.

Nan led the way up the hill to an imposing, elegant building around three sides of a courtyard, set back from the street behind high iron railings. A "nice little tea shop" it certainly was not. The lawn in the forecourt was criss-crossed into triangular shapes by neat gravel paths and protected by low hedges which ran round each wedge of grass. People were coming in and out of the wrought-iron gate on the street and out of the main front door at the far end of the central gravel path. Nan set off down the central path with Grandpa and Ruth in tow.

"Be lucky to get anything here, I bet," Grandpa grumbled.

"You wait and see," Nan replied over her shoulder.

"Not what I'd call a drink anyhow," he muttered with a grimace.

Ruth was inclined to agree with Grandpa that it was a very improbable tea shop, but she was curious to see where Nan was taking them.

Nan marched down the central path and went in at the open door. She waited in the lobby for her companions to catch her up and then, with a flourish, flung open the inner glass-panelled door. Ruth gasped: Nan had opened the door into a glittering fairy palace. In the hall in front of her there hung from a long, gilded chain a massive ball of diamonds – sparkling, twinkling, reflecting every hue under the sun – a million golden raindrops shimmering with all the colours of the rainbow, a sky full of stars glinting in the sunset, the stone in Nan's ring magnified and repeated hundreds of times.

"Is this the ballet?" she whispered in awe, all thoughts of tea and ice cream brushed aside.

"No, no," Nan laughed, "these are the Regency Rooms, and that's a chandelier. They've just opened a tearoom here. The ballet doesn't start for another half an hour; the theatre's only next door."

Ruth would happily have stayed in the Regency Rooms all afternoon, not for the tea or the ice creams, but for the sheer pleasure of running from room to room comparing the size, the style, the brilliance and the radiance of the three chandeliers: the one in the hall, huge, round and uniform, another in the high-ceilinged tearoom, more silvery and elongated, less scintillating but with the ethereal mystery of bubbles floating on air, and a third, the smallest, in a side room, the brightest of all in its incandescent splendour, composed of an interlacing myriad of minute crystal droplets.

In none of the chandeliers was it possible to identify the central source of light: that was hidden from view. On the other hand, each crystal bead contained its own natural spark of iridescence, which it projected onto its neighbours in an endlessly reciprocal game of reflecting spectra. No one spark of light would have been sufficient on its own to create any very significant effect. The overall magnificence derived from the combination of all the component parts, from the largest to the smallest, regardless of shape or position. It was with the greatest reluctance that Ruth agreed to leave this dazzling spectacle. Nothing else that she might imagine could compete with it in flawless beauty. She was content to leave only when Nan promised that they would come back another day.

Although the chandeliers had held Ruth utterly spellbound and given her to wonder whether these were the sparks that Carrie had told her about, within minutes their effect was eclipsed by the ballet. From the moment they took their seats in the circle she was enraptured by the secret life of the theatre. When Nan pointed to the members of the orchestra taking their places in the pit, she suddenly remembered Susan, far away in London, and Susan's father who worked in an orchestra. She felt a sharp pang of envy, the more so when the lights dimmed and the orchestra struck the first chord, sending a thrill through her small person. "Orchestra" meant music on a grand scale, she discovered. She wished that her father worked in an orchestra, but then she recalled with pride that Evelyn had played the piano, sometimes with an orchestra. This realization made her even more susceptible to the power of the music as it rose and fell, intoxicating her with its charms, transporting her to uncharted realms of the imagination. When the curtain went up, the music had already carried her far away into her own fantasy world.

The rising of the curtain brought her back to the reality of the theatre. There on the stage everything was happening just as in the story book. There was the court scene complete with cradle, king, queen and courtiers, all sumptuously dressed in a palace of fairy-tale dimensions. In accord with the music, the people of the court walked majestically about the stage bowing and curtseying, and communicating with each other by means of expansive gestures. What followed however was even more miraculous: the fairies who danced in to bring the baby her christening gifts swayed from side to side, twirled and spun round in their exquisite flowing gauze dresses, all on the very tips of their toes!

It was unbelievable that any normal person, with flattish feet and five squat toes on each foot, should ever rise to the very tips of their toes and dance on them with such grace and speed and ease. It simply was not possible. Perhaps they were suspended from wires hanging from the roof. But then the wires would get all tangled up because the dancers wove in and out, circling each other, passing each other and making complicated patterns with their movements on the stage. She searched for traces of wire coming down from above, but there were none, which simply confirmed her suspicions that these were no ordinary dancers. They were real fairies, like the ones whom she had never yet succeeded in seeing at the end of the lawn and whose existence she had half begun to doubt. Here they were, after all, on the stage in the theatre, living proof that fairies did exist!

She could not take her eyes off them but then, out of nowhere, in a dreadful frenzy of clashing brass, the thirteenth fairy burst into the centre of the stage, petrifying the King and the Queen and all their attendants. They clutched each other in fright while the fairies grouped themselves protectively round the cradle of the sleeping Princess Aurora. Here the thunderous black-winged fairy of the book was transformed into none other than a hideous, snarling, black-cloaked old witch. Scared out of her wits, Ruth slid to the floor and hid under her seat.

15

In London, apart from imagining herself to be the fairy on the Christmas tree or fearing that Father Christmas was stuck in the chimney, Ruth frequently used to dream a horrible nightmare in which walls and buildings were collapsing on top of her. Since coming to stay at Beech Grove, she had rarely been beset by any sort of nightmare, for here in Nan and Grandpa's house she had scarcely registered any of her dreams, until the night of the ballet. That night she dreamt that she was a fairy dancer tiptoeing through blackened ruins inhabited by a wicked witch. She had to get through the ruins to rescue something or someone without disturbing the witch. Alas, she gave a little cry when she trod on a thorn, and that cry alerted the witch, who appeared before her in a towering rage. She had white hair, pale, cold eyes and long fingers which were reaching out to catch her. Choking with fright she started to run but woke up. Daylight flooded her bedroom and gleamed off the smooth top of the washstand. Grandpa had already drawn the curtains and left her early-morning drink at her bedside. She was still very scared and lay for a while trying to get the dream out of her mind until she remembered a most important experiment.

Although her head was heavy and her limbs felt very weary, she stood up and went directly over to the washstand as soon as she was fully awake. Tall enough to lean her elbows on its cold marble surface, she pressed down on them with all her might and gradually raised herself onto the tips of her toes. It was very painful. Even with all her weight on her elbows and hands, her toes hurt unbearably, and when she looked down she saw that they did not form themselves into neat rounded points as they should have done: they were uneven, and her big toes stuck out. She lowered herself onto the balls of her feet, which was easier but not correct. The fairies had definitely been dancing on the tips of their toes; she had seen them for herself. In fact, her obsession with their feet had often distracted her from the rest of the performance the previous afternoon – except, of course, when the wicked witch made her dramatically unwelcome entrance and sent her precipitately into hiding on the floor.

Disillusioned with the problems of dancing on tiptoe, she rested for a moment and considered how she would spend the day ahead: first she would go down to the end of the garden in the morning and spy on the fairies to try to find out for certain whether they danced on their toes all the time. Secondly she would try to persuade Nan to teach her some of the ballet music to add to the tunes she already knew, because Evelyn must surely have played some of that spine-chilling music which brought her out in goose pimples even in the warmth of the theatre and which still, the next morning, was waltzing round in her head. Fierce and frightening, calming and soothing, either it brought tears to the eyes or created strange sensations of excitement and pleasure, not altogether unlike Nan's hymn tunes, though on a much grander scale. A third plan came to mind, and she was sorry it had not occurred to her sooner, because it was more urgent than all the rest: she must call next door and tell Carrie, Ann and Val about all the amazing things that had happened yesterday. She would do this straight away, after she had tried standing on tiptoe one last time.

She was raising herself up onto her toes, leaning on the washstand, when one foot was seized with an agonizing spasm which sent her moaning back onto the bed. As she cried out, Grandpa came hurrying in to see what was wrong. She was afraid that he would laugh at her if she told the truth, so she made up a story about catching her foot on the leg of the bed. The pain in her foot was compounded by the embarrassment of telling him a lie, something that proved to be most unpleasant – more unpleasant than being laughed at, especially as Grandpa very kindly insisted on rubbing the hurt until it was better. As the muscle in her foot began to ease, she noticed that he was wearing his brown suit and starched collar again. All that was missing was the old cloth cap. She wondered whether he had not yet been to bed or whether there was to be another visit to the ballet. He read her mind and explained: "Orders is orders, little Miss Ruth. We can't have our Easter eggs till we've been to church, so out with your Easter bonnet and make haste."

Ruth had frequently waved Nan goodbye as she set off to walk to the church in the village outside the city boundary every Sunday come wind, come rain – even in the February snow. Nobody questioned that she, Ruth, would stay at home with Grandpa, pottering about in his shed. This, then, was the normal routine, and it had never occurred to her to ask why Nan went to church every week, because she was mostly too preoccupied, initially with the activities in the shed and then later, when she tired of those, with music. She experienced a sensation almost of illicit pleasure at being alone in the empty house having left Grandpa at his workbench in the shed, and having the freedom to sing as she played and make as much noise as she liked. With no audience within earshot, she would experiment on the keyboard without being tied down to the nasty little notes on the printed page – or, if she chose, she would interpret them as she pleased, sometimes playing the black notes on the page slowly and the white ones much faster.

She had seen the church, a grey building with a round tower, set back from the road in among dark, spreading trees in the heart of the village, when she had gone with Nan and Grandpa to see where Evelyn was buried, and again when she had been out on the motorbike with Grandpa to collect Nan from the church hall close by. The church hall was a gloomy place with large, resonant rooms, banging doors and a grimy, stale-smelling kitchen where they usually found Nan doing the washing-up, if she wasn't playing hymns on one of the two pianos for the Mothers' Union or the Young Wives in the main hall.

Ruth simply did not understand why Nan went there, especially when you saw the people she went to meet. In the Mothers' Union they were all extremely bent and old – ancient in fact, much, much older than Nan herself, with walking sticks, baggy eyes and yellowish, sagging skin. They exuded an unpleasant, musty smell. Grandpa joked about them, saying: "What a fine lot of mothers they are; most of them are old enough to be my grandmother!" He called them the Mothballs. Ruth disliked having to go into the hall to meet them, because they all wanted to cuddle her and wanted her to kiss them. She would try to smile politely, but found it nauseating. If at all possible, she would blow a kiss at a moth-eaten fur sleeve or a wisp of whitish hair rather than touch those decaying, flabby complexions with her lips. As for the Young Wives, they certainly were nearer Nan's age and generally smarter, livelier and more active but, as Grandpa said, since the Mothers were a hundred if they were a day, it went without saying that the Young Wives were all in their seventies.

Even though she had seen plenty of the church hall, Ruth had never been inside the church. If church was at all like the church hall, she was certain that she would not like it – and, in any case, she had made other plans, Easter eggs or no Easter eggs. Nan was dressed ready to go out in her hat and coat when Ruth came downstairs, but typically she showed no signs of impatience as her granddaughter hovered with deliberate reluctance over her cereal. On the other hand, a simmering resentment began to bubble up inside Ruth at the imminent disruption of her plans. Seething with irritation, she blurted out in a tearful show of rebellion, "I don't want to go to church: I want to go and see Carrie and Ann and Val!"

Although Nan was startled at this eruption of temper, all she said was, "I don't think that will be much good, Ruthie: they've gone away for the weekend to Carrie's brother at the sea. You remember they had already gone when you went round there yesterday morning? They'll be back for your birthday tea tomorrow, though."

This cool, unflustered response had the paradoxically negative effect of bringing Ruth's anger to boiling point, and the mention of her eagerly awaited birthday did nothing to prevent it from spilling over in Nan's direction. Really, Nan was so infuriating at times. She had an answer for everything. She was always calm, always good-natured, never cross. Ruth felt crosser and crosser, so cross that, glaring furiously at Nan, she stamped her foot on the floor.

"I won't to go to church."

"Well, that's awkward, because Grandpa is coming and there won't be anyone at home," Nan replied in a very matter-of-fact tone. "Anyhow, the fresh air will do you good. It'll wake you up a bit and calm that temper of yours." So saying, she fetched Ruth's coat.

Grandpa came in. "Trouble?" he asked.

"Not really," Nan replied. "She's tired, poor little thing. Like mother, like daughter, though, that's for certain," she added, giving Grandpa a knowing look.

"Right enough there!" he responded, raising his eyebrows in agreement. Oblivious of their comments, Ruth meanwhile had sat defiantly down on the floor; Grandpa scooped her up and carried her straight out of the house. "Come on, missy, you'll make us late," he said abruptly. He strode down the road out towards the country and, when they had passed the last house in the Grove, set her down on her own two feet. "Now it's your turn to carry me," he announced, breathing heavily.

Nan regarded him anxiously. "Are you all right Joe?" she enquired.

"Yes, fine," he assured her, "but I can't carry that young lady all the way to church: she's getting too heavy for me; you feed her too well, Nan."

It was useless to resist. Ruth walked between Nan and Grandpa, dragging her feet and scuffing her shoes on the gravel path. She refused to hold hands by keeping hers in her pockets – thereby, she supposed, eloquently registering her silent protest. She fingered the photo of Evelyn, hidden deep in one pocket, but that did not bring her any consolation: quite the contrary, it made her feel more isolated and more discontented. She was very tired, and her legs ached.

Meanwhile, Nan kept cheerfully pointing out calves and lambs in the meadow across the road, and on their side, primroses on the bank bordering the footpath. She even wondered aloud whether there were tadpoles in the stream that ran through the meadow, but her wonderings fell on deaf ears. Ruth kept her eyes steadfastly fixed on the path at her feet, refusing to look at anything that Nan tried to show her. It was such a long way to the village. How she wished they had taken the motorbike! Why did Grandpa have to wear his best suit again?

During the walk to the church, Ruth decided that she was not going to show the least flicker of interest or take part in anything that was happening there. By the time they arrived, the service had begun, so they had to creep quietly in and sit in an empty side aisle. Her resolution faltered however the very minute they stepped through the heavy oak door because, to her amazement, the hymn that was being sung was one from her own repertoire and she knew both the words and the music so well that the temptation to join in was far too great. It was one of the sadder hymns, about a green hill outside a city wall, and was one that she mused over often, having no idea what the strange words meant. It was overwhelming to find so many people singing it.

Then, when the hymn was over, even from the side aisle there was a great deal to capture her attention. The Mothballs, still wrapped in their fur coats, were out in force in the central pews and glanced across at her, but she ignored their smiles. Her eyes were directed beyond them, over their heads, at the bright, quivering patterns, projected onto the high arch of the chancel by the shafts of sunlight pouring through the tiny fragments of stained glass which made up the upper section of one of the windows on the other side of the church. She shifted along the pew to get a better view of the rich, elusive rainbow colours dancing on the mellow old stone. Then, when the sun clouded over, the colours faded away, and she saw that Nan and Grandpa and everyone else were on their knees, their faces hidden in their hands while a distant man's voice intoned a long speech about God. She too fell to her knees but, as she did not understand what the man was saying, she continued to cast her eyes around her.

Although it smelt old and dank, the church with its high roof, tall pillars and large windows was very pretty, much lighter and nicer than the oppressive church hall. Along every window ledge and at the base of every pillar, there were masses of yellow daffodils trumpeting the joys of spring, echoing the strains of the well-known hymns, which grew more triumphant as the service progressed. At the end of the aisle where she and her grandparents were sitting, a youngish man was playing the hymn tunes on an instrument like a huge piano. It had two keyboards and, above the keyboards, encased in a large box, were rows and rows of metal pipes. A fat boy stood beside the instrument pushing a long wooden lever up and down as the young man played.

Grandpa whispered to her that the boy was working the bellows to pump air through the pipes of the organ. She watched the boy as he puffed and blew with the effort. In contrast the organist, although he remained seated, moved with remarkable agility, as if dancing on the spot, using all his limbs, hands, arms, feet, and even toes at once. At the beginning of each hymn he would pull out a few knobs on panels on either side of the keyboards, and then his fingers would skim over the keys with lightning speed, much faster than Nan played the piano, and his feet moved too, across some wooden bars under the instrument.

At the end of one of the hymns a very odd thing happened. Having bent down to pick up some music, the organist then, without changing his position on the bench, craned his neck round to survey the congregation. He noticed Nan and Grandpa in the pew very close to him and gave them a nod of recognition. He then noticed Ruth. He did not smile at her, but stared at her in a manner which bothered her. She was conscious of not paying attention to the service and of not behaving very well – indeed she knew to her shame that she had behaved very badly earlier – but she did not see how he could have known any of that, because he had been concentrating on the music all the time. She lowered her gaze, wishing that he would do the same.

At last the man who had been reciting the prayers about God and had been hidden behind a wooden screen came into view. Ruth was astounded as she watched him climb into the pulpit. He was very old and bent, as old as the mothers in the Mothers' Union, with white hair and gold-rimmed glasses like some of the old men in the congregation, but unlike them he was wearing a gown, a plain white gown which reached nearly to the floor.

"Is that God? Why is he wearing a dress?" she asked Grandpa in a loud whisper.

He spluttered and nudged Nan. "Tell you later," he replied.

The old man began to talk. His opening words were sensational and caught Ruth's attention. "Today Jesus rose from the dead," he said.

Unfortunately he did not explain what he meant by that extraordinary statement, but went on to use words, long words, which Ruth did not understand, like "fulfilment of the Scriptures" and "Resurrection" and "the unbroken line of Christian tradition", so that she lost track of his pronouncements. Leaning against Grandpa, she yawned and let her mind wander off to the chandeliers and the ballet.

When, after a very long time, the old man finished speaking, the service came to an end quickly with one final jubilant hymn and a few short prayers. Ruth stood up to leave, but Nan and Grandpa stayed seated in their pew, beckoning her to sit down again. She sat down, happy to see all the elderly ladies leaving the church without accosting her, but it took her a little while to realize that Nan and Grandpa, who seemed to be rooted to the pew, were listening to the music from the organ. As the last chord died away, they stood up and applauded discreetly.

"Well done, Charles!" said Nan, congratulating the organist. "Bach, wasn't it?"

"That's right, Mrs Platt, the 'St Anne' Prelude. I hoped it would go down well today. Thank you for staying to listen: not many people bother to do that." In fact, Nan, Grandpa, Ruth and the boy were the only people left in the church.

The organist nodded to the boy and slipped something into his hand. "You can go now, Jeff," he said to him as he collected up his music and put it into a case. He then came over to Nan and Grandpa and walked out of the church with them, though Ruth was troubled by the way that he seemed to be staring at her. His stare, however, was not rude, rather it was penetrating and enquiring, as though he were asking himself a question about her but without finding the answer. As they reached Evelyn's grave with its rose tree, he addressed the question that was troubling him to Nan, hoarsely, the words almost failing him. "And who is this little girl, Mrs Platt?"

"Why, Charles, don't you remember? This is Ruth, John's little girl!" she answered. "Don't you remember taking those photos of her when she was a baby?"

"Yes, of course," he stammered, "it's just that she is so like Evelyn I could hardly believe my eyes."

He turned away, embarrassed at his own mistake and at his own distress. Ruth felt so sorry for him that she would have liked to give him the photo she had in her pocket, which he perhaps had taken nearly five years ago, but the opportunity did not arise, because he took his leave of them and, nearly running, went off round the back of the church.

"That was Mr Stannard, Charles Stannard, Evelyn's best friend – well, her fiancé," Nan explained, gazing despairingly at the spot where he had been standing before going over to the grave, where she and Grandpa stood in silence for a couple of minutes.

Ruth was overcome with contrition. Intuitively, she sensed that this scene demonstrated the interplay of deepest human emotions. The sadness in Nan's face, as though in reflection of Charles Stannard's, made her regret her earlier behaviour. Nan's self-assurance had vanished, leaving her hurt and vulnerable. Now it was her opportunity to try and to cheer Nan up. She forgot about her tiredness and her aching legs and, on the way home, endeavoured to point out to Nan all the things that Nan had been trying to interest her in on the way out. Nan brightened considerably at Ruth's change of heart, and a flicker of amusement crossed her face when Ruth repeated the question about the old man in the white dress that she had asked Grandpa in church. "What was he talking about?" she then wanted to know, satisfied that his white dress was in fact a type of uniform.

Nan's explanation was shocking: she said that Jesus, who was the kindest man who had ever lived, had been killed on the Cross by people who had cast him out.

"They shouldn't have done that, should they?" Ruth said, searching Nan's face for her reaction, and was taken aback by her reply, for Nan agreed that they should not, but added, "I suppose they were ordinary people like us, easily swayed, easily influenced. They didn't know what they were doing."

Grandpa nodded in tactful agreement. Nan went on to explain that on Easter Day, three days later, Jesus came alive again to prove to people that, if they believed in him, they would go to live with God when they died.

"Like those sparkling lights in the tearoom?" Ruth asked.

Nan was mystified but replied, "Maybe that's how it is."

16

Early the next morning a faint, chill breeze wafted inquisitively up the staircase, bringing in its wake an enthusiastic multitude of the tingling fresh perfumes and sounds of spring, the scents of new grass and pale, delicate flowers opening in the morning dew, together with the sound of birds, great and small, singing their ecstatic hymns of praise from the blossoming treetops to the warm, reviving sun. Even before she reached the top of the stairs Ruth knew that, downstairs, the garden door was open. She tiptoed down, anxious not to draw attention to herself in her keen desire to confirm these expectations undisturbed. Nan and Grandpa were talking behind the closed door of the kitchen as she slipped silently into the back room where, as she had suspected, the door was flung wide and the sun was pouring in. There was a cleansing, rain-washed chill in the air which invigorated the atmosphere and chased away the stale, tobacco-laden odours of winter – yet, for all its newness and its freshness, it had already taken up residence in the house. Ruth ran to the open doorway and stood there motionless, absorbing every detail of the bewitching scene which was unfolding before her eyes as a special greeting for her on her fifth birthday.

Every blade of grass in the sunlit lawn and every gossamer spider's web bore its own sparkling array of jewels, shimmering in the light of the sun and reflecting every imaginable hue. The lawn had become a carpet of intertwining diamond necklaces which stretched across the garden and hung festooned from the windows of the old shed and from the beams of the old lean-to, now "Ruth's Cabin". It was fairy magic, of that she was certain, as if the fairies were proving to her that they were equal to, even better than the splendour of the crystal chandeliers in the Regency Rooms that had held her spellbound only the day before yesterday.

Enthralled by a vision of such wonder, she was breathing in the sweet fresh air when a voice behind her gently brought her back to the pressing reality of her birthday.

"I don't know, I really don't, little Miss Ruth," said Grandpa. "Here you are on your birthday with all your presents waiting for you and you haven't even noticed them... standing there in the doorway a-dreaming, as usual... what are we going to do with you?"

She turned to see him with Nan beside him, smiling the perplexed smile they wore when they did not fully understand what she was thinking. She returned their smiles somewhat sheepishly, not knowing how to explain her preoccupation, and only then did she notice that alongside the Easter eggs which she had begun to eat the previous day the table bore a large square object under a cloth and various parcels wrapped in coloured tissue paper.

"Happy birthday, our little Ruthie! Come and have your presents, then," said Nan, handing her a soft, flat parcel. Grandpa stood holding a box, also wrapped. Entranced, she sat down on the floor to open her presents. Nan's parcel contained a dress, in a light fabric patterned with tiny blue-and-cream flowers and green leaves. It had long sleeves, and across the chest the material was gathered into tight little pleats over which Nan had embroidered a criss-cross design.

"It's called smocking," Nan explained.

Out of the parcel there also fell a length of turquoise velvet ribbon.

Ruth laughed with pleasure. "Oh! It's lovely, Nan, can I wear it now?"

"Of course," said Nan. "After all, it's your birthday, and that's what I made it for."

Ruth raced upstairs, followed by Nan, to change quickly out of her pyjamas into the new dress. Then Nan tied the ribbon in her hair.

"How long your hair is, Ruthie," she observed. "Nearly long enough for plaits." She gave her a hug. "And what a pretty girl you are in your new dress! Let's go down and show Grandpa."

Ruth peeped into the mirror on the washstand to inspect the new dress and the ribbon holding her hair back from her face. There she saw to her satisfaction that her hair had grown long and thick, and as a result she was almost as pretty as ringleted, blonde, blue-eyed Susan, so far away in London. How lucky she was to be here, on the edge of the country, with Nan and Grandpa! She was never going back to London.

"I won't ever have to go back to London, will I Nan?" she asked anxiously as they descended the stairs.

Nan stopped halfway down and turned to look up at Ruth on the stair above her. "What a funny question to ask!" she exclaimed. "Whyever do you ask that now, Ruthie?" She did not wait for a reply, but continued in a matter-of-fact tone of voice, "Of course, I expect you'll have to go back to London one day, because that's where your mummy and daddy live, and you'll have to go to school – but not yet. I can promise you that."

Reassured, though still worried by the intrusion of such unwelcome thoughts, Ruth returned to the important business of opening her presents. She pirouetted for Grandpa for him to admire the dress, and then eagerly unwrapped the present that he had given her. Out in his Aladdin's Cave he had made her a toolkit, consisting of a miniature hammer, a screwdriver, a chisel and a small saw, all in a smooth shiny wooden box with brass fastenings and extra compartments for screws and nails. Attached to it was a note, which said: "For the Sorcerer's Apprentice". Grandpa promised he would tell the story of what that was all about another day, when they were working out in the shed together using the new tools and she was wearing her dungarees again, not her new dress. There were still other presents: a story book with coloured pictures, about a family of rabbits moving out to the fields in the summer and building a pretty new house for themselves, helped by mice and squirrels.

Lastly, at the bottom of the pile lay a thin edition of music entitled *Easy Piano Pieces for Young Beginners*. The pieces themselves looked impossibly difficult, but the mischievous fairies and grinning pixies prancing along the lines of notes compelled Ruth to take the book straight to the piano to find out what they were doing and why they had such naughty faces. Nan read one of the titles for her: 'Stealing the Witch's Broomstick!' it said. There were long, heavy-looking notes in the left hand and lots of little notes running up and down the scales in the right hand. Nan played some of them and promised she would help with the rest after lunch.

Grandpa, left alone in the back room, unexpectedly started uttering the magic words, slowly in a magisterial voice which summoned his wife and granddaughter to his presence at once. "Abracadabra, hey presto!" he proclaimed and, with a flourish, he whisked away the cloth over the large box. Beneath it there was the most beautiful cake imaginable, decorated in white icing with bunches of purple sugared violets at each corner. In the middle someone had inscribed "Happy Birthday, Ruth" in fine pink writing. The cake, Nan said, was for later, when Carrie and the girls next door would be home and would be coming to tea. There were three cards by the cake, one from Nan and Grandpa and one from Carrie and the girls. The third card had come through the post. It was addressed to Miss Ruth Platt. Ruth picked it up and turned it over before opening it. Nan read the inscription: "Darling Ruth, We hope you have a lovely birthday. We are so sorry not to be with you. Lots of love, Daddy and Mummy." Ruth put the card down; then, when Nan had left the room, she pushed it under the cake plate out of sight.

After a hasty breakfast, Ruth was faced with a problem. It was lovely having a birthday and looking pretty, wearing ribbons and a new dress, but it did stop her doing all those things, other than playing the piano, that normally she would like to be doing, like helping Grandpa, who had made a beeline off into his shed with the tools and the oil, or Nan, who was busy in the kitchen with the flour and the pastry – or even riding her trike. She sat on the garden doorstep for a while, relishing the sharp spring air, and then, at Nan's suggestion, she took a cushion and her new book and went to sit on her swing, as Nan said, to have a little rest from all the excitement. She swung gently to and fro, looking out at the clumps of sweet-smelling violets nestling beneath their broad, glossy leaves, and the primroses raising their wide, pale faces to the peerless blue sky. She rested her book on her knee, but did not open it. There was too much to contemplate all around her.

Daffodils, lulling her with their strong, dusty perfume, nodded their trumpets while the clouds of cherry blossom, a softer, pinker white than the winter snow, fluttered as light as swansdown in the breeze. High at the top of the tree, his dark feathers hidden by the blossom, a blackbird poured out his heart in song to the brilliant, unseeing depths of the sky. Ruth held her breath, overcome by the beauty of it all. This was fairyland; whether or not they were visible, there must be fairies in this garden. Quietly she slipped off her swing and lifted a violet leaf in the hope of catching sight of an unsuspecting fairy. Then, as she carefully took hold of a primrose leaf between her index finger and thumb, she was startled to hear her name being called from the other end of the lawn. She glanced up in the direction of the voice, but quickly looked away, not wanting to acknowledge what she had seen. Her heart began to pound as she kept her eyes firmly fixed on the leaf, no longer remembering why she was holding it or what she was searching for beneath it.

"Ruth!" the man's voice called again. She refused to answer. Why was he there? Why had he come? She did not want to see him or be reminded of that life she had left behind. After all, if they had forgotten her, as they apparently had, why should she have to remember them? They had not visited her, and the only contact she had had with them was the occasional little note or drawing scrawled at the end of the letters to Nan; in reply, she had done little drawings at the end of the letters which Nan was sending. And then this morning there had been that annoying card which she would rather not have seen.

"Ruth!" he called again. She heard his footsteps approaching. She wanted to run away, but there was nowhere to run to. She was trapped. He came close. "Ruthie dear, don't you know me? Won't you say hello? I've come to wish you a happy birthday!" He was standing above her. Then she had no choice but to glance up, and what she saw made her sorry, very sorry that she had ignored him and sorry at the sight of him. His face was tired and haggard, and he was very thin.

"Hello Daddy," she said gravely and stood up, holding her arms out to him.

17

Nan and Grandpa were of course delighted, if astonished, to see their son. He had tried to get in touch with them to warn them of his arrival by ringing Carrie the previous evening, but there had been no reply, he explained, as they stood in the kitchen, celebrating with a glass of sherry. He had not let go of Ruth's hand since they had walked up to the house from the end of the garden together, and still he kept her close by him, suggesting that he needed her there for comfort. Although she would have liked to wriggle free and return to the flowers, the blossoms and the blackbird, she was chastened by guilt at her earlier show of hostility towards him and was afraid of hurting his feelings again.

John bent down to his daughter's level, but addressed himself to his parents, echoing their warm, lilting accents. "Doesn't she look lovely?" He stroked her hair. "She's hardly the same child. You have taken such good care of her! Thank you so much, Mother and Father. I can't get over how grown up and how pretty she is with her long hair and pink cheeks – and her new dress! I hardly dare say it, but she's just like Evelyn…"

There ensued a long silence, interrupted only by the roar of a formation of jet engines flying low overhead. Ruth did not flinch at the noise. In her impassive stillness, Grandpa found his cue for reopening the conversation. "Funny littl' mawther when you first brought her – so frightened of everything, she were," he said, then added with his usual twinkle: "she's better now. She fair likes them aeroplanes and the old bike – don't you, little miss?"

Nan, having recovered her composure, smiled benevolently. "Yes," she said, "but that's not all. You know you're right about her taking after Evelyn, because I do believe she's inherited

Evelyn's musical talent. You should hear her playing that piano! We'll give you a concert after lunch, won't we Ruthie?" Ruth beamed in agreement, too shy to find words to express her pride at being grown up and pretty, resembling Evelyn and being able to play the piano. Her pride was lamentably short-lived, however. She was basking in the full flush of it when, to her disbelief, she heard her father saying gently but firmly: "I'm afraid that will have to wait for another time. We must be off straight after lunch."

The warmth generated by the flush of pride instantly subsided, replaced by a chill foreboding which rooted Ruth to the spot. Why had he said "we"? The reason became clear all too soon when her father launched into his explanation. "You see, I promised Shirley we'd be back before dark and, as she has only just come out of hospital, I don't want to leave her alone for too long."

"We?" Nan queried.

"Well, me, of course, and Ruth," he replied.

Ruth started to whimper. "I want to stay here with Nan and Grandpa!" she cried, the tears already running down her cheeks.

He spoke sharply to her. "Come on, Ruth, you're a big girl now, what are you crying for? You want to come home to Mummy and Daddy, don't you?"

Nan intervened firmly, her voice calm but tense through pursed lips. "You can't go back to London tonight, John; what about Ruthie's little party? We've got a lovely cake for her, and Carrie and the girls are coming to tea when they get back from her brother's." She looked severely at her son, then compassionately at Ruth's tear-stained face and then at John again. "Poor little mite, have a heart, she don't want to spend her birthday on the train! Don't you be so cruel," she said, upbraiding him forcefully.

John's voice rose in indignation, abandoning the gentle accents of his native speech, "Really, Mother, that's not fair! You have been very kind to Ruth, but you don't seem to be showing any consideration to poor Shirley. She's just out of hospital and she wants to see her daughter on her birthday.

Surely it's not too much to ask!" Staring blankly out of the window with tear-filled eyes, Nan bit her lip and said nothing while repeatedly applying smelling salts to her nostrils.

Grandpa laid his hand gently on Ruth's shoulder; trembling visibly, he steered her towards the kitchen door. "Well, well, my little miss," he said, "we'll have to go and put away our tools for the time being, only till you come back the next time."

He propelled Ruth out into the hall where, unobserved by his son, he took her in his arms and hugged her to his chest. She buried her face in his neck, giving vent to the great suppressed sob that had been welling up from tiny beginnings deep inside, ever since she had had that first glimpse of her father's tall, lanky figure hailing her from the edge of the lawn.

Chivvied by her son to produce the lunch early, Nan was flustered. The lunch would be ready when it was ready, she said firmly, trying to stand by her opinion that it was more important to comfort her unhappy, confused granddaughter and pack her small suitcase, the while attempting to conceal her own distress. Nevertheless, so many sudden and conflicting demands put Nan, usually so calm and meticulous, under an unaccustomed pressure which she was not able to sustain. Consequently, to her embarrassment, the steak-and-kidney pudding, the high point of her culinary arts, was undercooked, the meat tough and the pastry soggy, and Ruth's bag was packed with a motley assortment of disparate clothes, mismatching socks and gloves, and pyjamas with the wrong trousers or top.

The sole new item of clothing that she was allowed to take back to London was the dress which she was wearing. Only the clothes with which she had arrived three months earlier and which she was fast outgrowing were packed in the bag, because, Dad maintained, for reasons which he chose not to elaborate, it would not be a good idea for Ruth to be seen wearing Evelyn's clothes in London, especially not the crimson velvet party frock. He insisted that all those lovely clothes – dungarees, blouses and cardigans – as well as the dresses, which fitted Ruth perfectly, should be left out of the luggage.

Nan was even more upset at this unreasonable stricture and, again losing her customary self-control, started muttering to herself under her breath. Ruth caught the odd word and phrase. "Stupid nonsense!" – "Hussy!" – "Running rings round him!" Back in the kitchen, believing Ruth to be out of earshot, Nan was heard to plead with Grandpa. "Why don't you tell him to stand up to her for once?" she begged. But Grandpa only shrugged his shoulders and sighed.

The birthday presents were an unfortunate casualty in the rush to have everything prepared in time for the two o'clock bus and were left behind. As Dad was later to reason with Ruth, there would not have been much use in London for her toolkit without a workbench and her music without a piano. The sole concession that he did allow was a brief celebration after lunch when, without much enthusiasm, Ruth blew out her candles while Nan played 'Happy Birthday' and Grandpa and Dad sang. The cake was cut: a portion was wrapped hurriedly and put in a bag, and the rest was abandoned for Nan and Grandpa, Carrie and the girls to eat their way through later in pensive commiseration.

Stunned by the speed of events, Ruth hardly had time to register what was happening before she found herself striving to locate a comfortable perch on Dad's knee in a stuffy compartment crowded with returning holidaymakers. She still had not settled properly when the train started to pull away, responding to the invisible thread which, with increasing rapidity, drew it inexorably back to the capital whence it had come. The window was steamed up with a fog of condensation, so there was no chance of catching a comforting glimpse of the family farm, even had it been possible to get anywhere near the window. All she detected was a glimmer of an ever-darkening sky and the raindrops that were beginning to streak the dirty glass. The air was thick with cigarette smoke.

Rather than stare at each other face to face, most of the passengers had their eyes closed. Some were even snoring already. Dad also closed his eyes. Tears trickled from the corners of Ruth's, not because they were smarting from the smoke, but because only now, to the monotonous accompaniment of the clanking wheels, the heaving engine and the sudden April shower lashing the window in furious gusts, did she begin to contemplate the shattering change in her circumstances. It hurt too much to think of Nan and Grandpa; they were already a long way behind her, in the past. They belonged to a past which, until it was so rudely interrupted, had been a blissfully happy present, gliding into an unknown but confident future, that future that Nan and Grandpa had talked about when they were admiring her pianist's hands.

All the things that she treasured most and in which her best hopes lay, were left behind, without any warning, there in the past: the fairy-tale garden, the piano and the shed, her cabin and her swing, her beloved trike and many more, all were nothing but a memory. The tears flowed faster when she remembered that she had not had time to say goodbye to any of them. She might even have felt emboldened to give Grandpa's motorbike – for which in retrospect she felt a surge of affection – a parting pat.

The abruptness of their departure meant, too, that she had come away without seeing Carrie and the girls. They had been real friends, the first true friends she had ever had, despite the difference in ages, and she had felt confident in their company, because she knew that they were people she could trust, people who respected her and did not laugh at her questions. There had been so much she wanted to tell them. As a wave of anguish swept over her, she hung her head to hide her tears. When, much later, the anguish began to subside, she wondered what lay ahead. Today, this very afternoon, she saw the forthcoming days, weeks and months in a completely different light – a cold, bleak light, different from yesterday or this morning. She knew for a fact that there would be no more piano – no music, no garden, no flowers or birds or trees.

She looked at her sleeping father. Why had he treated her so cruelly? Perhaps he had not meant to; perhaps it was because he, too, was very unhappy, for even in sleep there were deep furrows in his forehead. She felt twinges of sympathy for him in spite of the way he had treated her. As for Shirley, she had virtually forgotten about her. After all, with her she had never done any of those hundreds of exciting things that Nan and Grandpa had devised for her, nor could she imagine that she ever would. Was Shirley so keen to see her? It was hard to believe.

She recalled the ballet and all those stories about princes and princesses being cruelly treated or whisked away from their real parents by witches or by wicked stepmothers: Snow White, Sleeping Beauty, Cinderella – there were lots of them. With a mixture of fear and wonder, she saw herself as one of those fairy-tale princesses who had been magicked away to live with a cruel stepmother. And maybe Evelyn was a princess who had been put under a spell by a wicked witch. Whatever Carrie might say about her dying of an illness, she might as well have been put to sleep for a hundred years. It was possible, for she herself had seen it happening with her own eyes in the ballet. And another thing: like Evelyn, the Sleeping Beauty had rose bushes all round her to protect her in her sleep. Well, Evelyn had only one rose bush, but that was enough.

She put her hand into her coat pocket to reach for a hand-kerchief to wipe her eyes and nose. Instead of the handker-chief, her fingers grasped a small piece of card. It was bent and worn, but smooth and slippery to the touch on one side. What was it? She pulled it out. To her immense joy, she found it was the little photo of herself and Evelyn sitting at the piano, which Nan had given her and which in all probability Charles Stannard had taken. She smiled at it through her tears. At least one of her most private treasures had come with her! She put it back, placing it carefully in the very depths of the pocket. Not letting go of her precious talisman, she too fell asleep for the rest of the journey.

18

When the train reached London, it was impossible to tell whether it was day or night. The black tunnels and grimy passages of the Underground engulfed the returning travellers instantly, so that it was not until Ruth and her father surfaced from its murky depths and stepped out of the lift at the dilapidated Northern Line station that they saw the sky again. Although the rain had stopped, heavy clouds still lowered above their heads, leaving space on the horizon only for a sickly band of bright-yellow light that muddied the red tiles of the station façade, gleamed menacingly across the grey slate roofs and glistened malevolently in the wet, greasy pavements.

John set off striding straight down the road, splashing through the oily puddles, without noticing that his little daughter was having to run to keep up with him. Her shoes were already full of water and her socks were wet through.

"Wait for me, Daddy!" she called.

He stopped at once, apologizing for his haste. "I'm sorry, Ruth," he said, taking her hand and slowing his step. "I should have known better; after all, when we set out for Nan's only three months ago, I had to carry you all the way to the train. Now you're so grown up, I'm forgetting that your legs are not as long as mine!"

He laughed and then, talking to her properly for the first time since they had left Nan's, continued in a much more serious tone which Ruth found upsetting, because she anticipated that she was going to be made party to some information which she did not want to hear.

"You see," he said, "we must get home to Shirley." He hesitated: words failed him, and he said no more.

As they turned into the backstreets where the lamplighter was vainly trying to ward off the blackening effects of night, he took up the thread again. "I'm so pleased you have had such a good time with Nan and Grandpa." He did sound really pleased for a moment, but the note of pleasure faded rapidly. "All the time you've been away, poor Shirley has been in hospital." He made an effort to appear more cheerful. "She's a lot better and has come out now, but we still have to take great care of her." His voice faltered. "It may be difficult at times, and I shall need your help. You do understand, don't you?"

Conscious that she was being appealed to as an adult, Ruth tried to respond as an adult. She nodded gravely, trying to think what sort of help she might be able to give. Nan had taught her to cook – well, jam tarts at least. That might be some help. A reply was not required, however, because Dad was still talking. "I'm so sorry I had to interrupt your birthday," he was saying. "There was no other way, because Shirley is not well enough to travel, and she does want to see you on your birthday so badly. You are our only child," he added rather sadly.

Ruth was overwhelmed with remorse. She had indeed been having a fine time with Nan and Grandpa, and had scarcely spared a thought for Dad and Shirley. Moreover, she blushed to recall that the thoughts that she had entertained had not been kind at all. In fact, they had been downright wicked. She remained silent, indistinctly remembering something the man in the white dress in the church had said about punishment for our sins and wondering whether the spark of light which Carrie said she held inside herself had gone out altogether. She cringed in the dark at her own selfishness and decided that she would try very hard to be kind and helpful to Dad and to Shirley, who according to Dad really did love her after all.

The house was shrouded in darkness when they arrived. No light came from within. John fumbled with the keys in his haste to open the front door and then called into the black space of the hallway with an unconvincing cheerfulness which rang false. "Here we are, dear! We're home!" He went in and, having switched the hall light on, ran down the narrow passage to the back room. Ruth followed more hesitantly some steps behind. She heard him ask, "Are you all right, dear?" – but there came no answer. Her father beckoned to her to join him in the doorway of the back room. "Look, dear, here's Ruth," he announced with the same forced joviality. Nothing stirred. Ruth, peeping out from behind her father, stared across the room at the figure seated by the fireplace, where dying embers wanly struggled for survival. By their glimmering light, she made out Shirley's unmoving figure; she sat upright, her blonde hair drawn back from her thin face in a headscarf tied at the back, her eyes fixed on the floor. Her right hand, resting on her knee, held a cigarette, which had become an extension of her long tapering fingers. Her only movement was to flick the ash occasionally into the hearth. She did not look up. Contrite and well intentioned, Ruth was on the point of running across the room to hug and kiss her mother, but the impassive figure exerted a strongly deterrent power which halted her in her tracks.

Dad switched the light on and again said: "Look, dear, here's our Ruth. She's come home on her birthday to see you!" There was no response. Dad pushed Ruth into the centre of the room, adding, as he ran his fingers affectionately through her long glossy hair, "Look how lovely and grown up she is – and she's five today! She has come home for her birthday, aren't you glad to see her?" This did provoke a response. Shirley surveyed Ruth searchingly from head to foot. Her eyes met Ruth's, sending a shiver down the child's spine; they were very pale and cold, with barely a spark of life in them. Ruth shuddered involuntarily, realizing that she had seen them somewhere before.

"Her hair is too long," was Shirley's only pronouncement before she fixed her gaze once again on the floor. Ruth shrank away in confusion, for this was not what she had been led to expect from all the talk of how pleased Shirley would be to see her on her birthday. Backing out into the hall, she checked that her precious photo was still in her coat pocket. Leaving it there – as there was no safer place for it – she took her coat off and ran upstairs to her own room.

Upstairs nothing had changed. Her dolls and soft toys lolled in their cot at the end of her bed, grinning stupidly. This, however fatuous, was more welcoming than the reception she had been given downstairs, so she picked them out of their cot and lined them up against the wall by her bed. Encouraged by their stupid smiles, she began to recount her adventures to them, since no one else was the least bit interested in finding out what she had been doing in the course of her long absence. A little while later Dad called her down for supper. There were two parcels for her on the table by her place, presents from Dad and Shirley. These at least were a passing reminder of her birthday, and they were not a disappointment.

Opening them at once, she discovered two books, one of which was a Rupert Bear Annual. She took heart from the friendly face of the little bear in his red pullover and yellow checked trousers playing with his animal friends under the trees, in surroundings which were not unlike the country round Nan's house. Rupert's parents stood watching from a distance. They too were warm and cuddly; his father was smoking a pipe like Grandpa's. The second book was sheer magic: it was full of enchanting pictures of all the fairies, sitting and dancing among the flowers; they were those very fairies that Ruth had been searching for in Nan's garden that same morning! She did not believe what she saw in front of her, and was thrilled.

"Shirley chose the 'Flower Fairies' for you, Ruth," Dad said, prompting Ruth to thank her mother.

"Oh, it's lovely, thank you! I was looking for those fairies this morning!" Ruth beamed at Shirley, but Shirley took no notice of her daughter's gratitude.

They ate sandwiches and the portion of birthday cake in chill silence. It was a poor substitute for the birthday tea that Nan had prepared. In spite of her pleasure at the books, the obstinate tears pricking the backs of her eyelids would not be stifled. Shirley did not look up from her plate, thus dampening all attempts at conversation while Dad tried valiantly to regain the cheerful exterior he had assumed on their arrival. "Well, now, Ruth, tell us what you have been doing with…"

He was about to say "Nan and Grandpa" but stopped suddenly; instead, he said, "...while you have been away." At last someone was showing some interest!

Ruth drew in a deep breath and eagerly launched into a description of her activities. "I can make aeroplanes," she announced excitedly, "and jam tarts!" She hoped that the tarts would indicate her willingness to help even if the aeroplanes were not of obvious use. "Oh, and I can play the piano!"

"Very good!" said Dad with hesitant appreciation, but Shirley, who had by now raised her head slightly, poured a gaze full of such withering scorn in Ruth's direction that all the other wonderful experiences she had intended to describe – the market, the chandeliers, the ballet – shrivelled away to naught under that scrutiny.

It was a relief when Dad sent her up to bed. She was glad to discover that Teddy was already asleep under the covers and her old hot-water bottle, a shaggy grey rubber dog with a cocked ear and a red tongue, was already warming the bed for her. Not only did he comfort her with his warmth, but he also gave a sympathetic ear to her troubles and provided a captive and more responsive audience than the silly dolls for her traveller's tales. Dad came up to say goodnight. He read her a Rupert story and then, as he bent down to kiss her, he said: "You can see, can't you, that Shirley has been very ill?"

Ruth could not honestly say that she saw anything except that Shirley was very bad-tempered, like the wicked witch in Nan's story book and in the ballet. However, she simply nodded since, as usual, that was what he expected.

"I'm sure everything will be all right," he added without any great display of conviction. He hesitated and cleared his throat, as if finding his next piece of information difficult to divulge. "Er... tomorrow I have to go back to work. I'll get your breakfast, then I suggest you come and play with your toys up here. I'll try to come home at lunchtime to check that all is well, and I'll see if Mrs Cox can take you for a few days until you start school."

He switched the light off and went out hurriedly, leaving Ruth to survey the wreckage of the day and to anticipate the next with foreboding. She closed her eyes to force back the tears. The blissful happiness to which she had grown accustomed with Nan and Grandpa was without any warning lost, prob- ably for ever. Why had everything changed so suddenly? Shirley showed no signs at all of wanting her or of loving her. All the signs she had shown were of chilling hostility: the mere sight of her daughter was enough to enrage her for no good reason that Ruth could ascertain.

Next, she wondered what would happen tomorrow, when Dad was away at work. She hated the prospect of going back to Mrs Cox's, the more so because now she knew that she was so much happier with Nan and Grandpa. In the darkness, hor- rible images began to fill her mind, images of those terrifying, solitary, blackened walls with hollow blank spaces, like empty eyes where their windows should have been. Flying in and out of the hollows, scooping up babies from under rose bushes on the ground were witches on broomsticks.

When Ruth woke the next morning she felt terrible: her head ached and her body was hot and itched all over. Dad came up to say goodbye hurriedly before he went to work, but when he saw her flushed face on opening the curtains, he stopped in his tracks. "Oh dear, Ruth, what is the matter with you?" he asked with alarm.

"I don't know," was Ruth's tearful reply.

"Let me take a look at you," said Dad, helping her to ease herself out of her pyjama top. Her chest was covered with angry red spots. "You stay there, Ruth. Well, that is after you've had a wash, and I'll call in at the doctor's on my way to work. I'll bring you a drink first, though." He shepherded Ruth down to the bathroom, gave her a wash and helped her clean her teeth. There was no sign of Shirley anywhere. "Do you want anything to eat?" Dad enquired.

"No, thank you," Ruth stammered miserably as she strug- gled to climb the stairs.

Her father tucked her back into bed and placed a glass of water beside her. He then went into the front bedroom where, she gathered from the voices she heard, Shirley was still in bed. Her father was doing most of the talking. Dad's voice was low and strong. Shirley's was faint and weak. He came back into Ruth's room. "Well, I'm off now, but I'll run home at lunchtime. The doctor should come to see you. Shirley says she will let him in. Is there anything more I can get for you?"

"No," said Ruth in a sleepy haze, and as soon as her dad left, she fell into a slumber.

She woke with a start to find a strange, elderly man standing over her. "Don't worry, little one," he said reassuringly. "I'm Dr Williams, and I've come to make you better." Then he added: "Your mother let me in, but as she is feeling poorly too: I've sent her back to bed." Dr Williams inspected Ruth's tummy and examined her mouth. "Well, little miss," he said, just like Grandpa, "I'm afraid this is a severe case of the measles. You must stay in bed with the curtains closed and sleep as much as you can. I'll write a prescription and leave it for your father downstairs. Now I'll go and talk to your mother." He pulled the covers over Ruth and went out. There was an audible babble of conversation from Shirley's room as she drifted back into sleep.

Dad came home as promised at lunchtime, but Ruth hardly noticed that he was there. She slept for long periods for days on end and did not see Shirley at all, though she did find that the glass of water on her bedside table was always full, even if she had emptied it in her waking moments, and as she regained her appetite, sandwiches would appear beside the water glass. Whenever she went to the bathroom, the house seemed deserted. There was no one downstairs, and not a sound came from any of the rooms, except when Dad came home. Then, bringing her medicine, he would always come into her room to see how she was, and as she slowly recovered, he would shower her with new picture books and comics, and colouring books with crayons. Nan and Grandpa sent lovely letters every other day with pictures drawn by Grandpa of the garden and the shed and the trike and the blackbird, and even of the motorbike. Ruth would pore over these longingly and wistfully, trying to pretend that she was with them and not at home in London. Often the sweetness of those letters would tear at her heartstrings.

Her dad's next port of call would be the front bedroom, from where Ruth heard him talking to Shirley, also asking her, "How are you, love?" But Ruth never heard any reply. Dad cooked the evening meal and served it on a tray until Dr Williams decreed that Ruth was well enough to get out of bed, in the evenings for supper at first, then gradually more and more during the day, until he pronounced her fully fit. In all this time Ruth scarcely saw Shirley.

19

Now that Ruth was much better, her father resumed his normal routine in the household before dashing off to work. This consisted of having breakfast ready for her when he woke her and, while she ate it, preparing her lunch. He also brushed her hair, inspected her teeth and, despite her protests, fed her a spoonful of cod-liver oil before allowing her to escape upstairs to put her clothes on. Under Nan and Grandpa's lax regime, she had been glad to find herself exempt from these unwelcome early-morning ministrations, having supposed them to be common to every household. On discovering that this was not necessarily the case and things might be done differently, she resented their resumption, particularly the cod-liver oil with its clinging, viscous fishiness.

"I don't like it! Take it away!" she demanded, turning her head defiantly to one side.

Dad was amused. "So, in spite of the measles, we've discovered a mind of our own, have we, young lady?" Laughing good-naturedly, he placed his hand firmly on the top of her head, pulled her face towards him and poured the oil into her open mouth, making her splutter. He found it so funny that she had to laugh with him, although in truth she did not think it very amusing. She laughed because that was better than crying, and in the past three weeks since smelling the fresh spring breeze from the top of Nan's staircase on her birthday, she had been crying rather a lot.

After breakfast Ruth obediently went back up to her room. Dad always came upstairs to say goodbye to her before leaving. "Be a good girl and stay up here with your toys until I come back at lunchtime, if I can manage it, or this evening – unless you need to go to the bathroom or fetch your lunch," he said today as on all other days, as he straightened the covers over the bed. Ruth sat on the floor imitating her father's routine with the dolls; she gave them breakfast, combed their hair and brushed their teeth. She brooked no protests, pouring vast quantities of imaginary cod-liver oil into each one of them. She heard someone – probably Shirley – moving about elsewhere in the house, but took little notice as she was happily concentrating on her game. When she heard her mother calling her name, however, she found herself in a quandary, not knowing what to do.

"Ruth, Ruth! Come down, Ruth!" she called, pleasantly enough. What was Ruth to do? Dad had told her to stay upstairs in her room. He had not told her what to do if Shirley summoned her downstairs. Cautiously she stood up and peeped round the door.

"I'm up here!" she called in reply and ventured out to the landing.

Shirley came to the bottom of the stairs. She was not threatening at all, and gave Ruth a lovely smile. "Time for your elevenses, Ruth! Come down, do! Look, I've peeled an apple for you! And you can have a piece of your birthday cake." She held out a plate bearing an apple, peeled and quartered, and a rather ancient slice of birthday cake.

Unsure of what to do next, Ruth slowly went down the stairs, trusting that Shirley was at last better. She seemed much more cheerful than she had been since Ruth's return home, as she stood waiting with one hand behind her back, so Ruth began to hope that they might have a nice day together. Shirley pointed to the plate. "Come and sit down and eat your apple while I have a coffee. I want to know what you did with your grandparents before you fell ill. Poor Ruth, what a horrible illness measles is!"

Ruth sat down unsuspectingly and, as Shirley pushed her chair in, picked up a piece of the apple. Shirley stroked her hair from behind. "Lovely long hair," she cooed, "it's like your Aunt Evelyn's, isn't it?" Then her tone changed rapidly to one of angry bitterness and she yelled, "But it's too long, and it's grown very ragged since you fell ill. It needs cutting!" She grabbed a handful of hair and, jerking Ruth's head backwards with one hand and producing a pair of scissors from behind her back with the other, cut off the lock that she was holding.

"No! No! Let me go!" Ruth screamed, spitting out the apple and struggling to free herself from the iron grasp which held her down.

"Keep still, you silly little thing, or it won't be level!" Shirley shouted furiously, cutting through another handful of chestnut tresses. Then one more snip and all Ruth's hair was on the floor, strewn around the base of her chair. She glanced down at it and then ran, her chest heaving, up to her room, where she flung herself on the bed and wept into her pillow.

Dad came home at lunchtime that day and was delighted to find Shirley apparently herself again – indeed she seemed jubilant. Greatly encouraged, he called Ruth, but met with no answer. He called again and then, with a sinking heart, mounted the stairs three at a time. Ruth was there on her bed alive and well, but one glance was sufficient to tell him what had happened. She turned a sorrowful face towards him as he knelt by the bed, reproaching himself for leaving her. Over his shoulder, she caught sight of herself in the mirror. What a sight she was! Her eyes were red and swollen from crying, and her hair, her lovely hair, cut short above the ears, was sticking out in all directions like a scarecrow's. Dad said nothing; there was nothing to be said. He raced downstairs again and, for the first time, Ruth heard him raise his voice. He shouted loudly, and Shirley yelled back at him. There were thumps and scuffles from below.

"No! No! Let me go!" Shirley screamed, just as Ruth had screamed earlier. And then there was silence.

"You can come down now, Ruth!" Dad called out several minutes later. She obeyed. There, on the back-room floor, was an astonishing sight. Where her brown locks had been earlier, there were now masses of blonde curls. Dad had cut Shirley's hair! Shirley was seated with her head in her hands. Dad stood with his hand on her shoulders.

"Shirley has something to say to you, Ruth," he said.

Shirley let out a big sigh and then, curtly, without looking at Ruth, muttered, "I'm sorry, Ruth." Raising her eyes to John, she appealed to him through her sobs. "I had to do it. It hurt so much. You do understand, don't you?"

To Ruth's uncomprehending horror, Dad said, "Yes, I think I understand."

Ruth was indignant at such injustice. Why should he try to understand such a cruel act? She was the one who had been hurt, not Shirley. To add insult to injury, with her hair cropped short, curling round her fine features, Shirley was even prettier than before.

It was obvious that, in the exceptional circumstances, Dad would have to take the afternoon off, thereby sacrificing a precious half day's holiday. This he did with good grace, promising to make a special occasion of it by taking his womenfolk, as he called them, out to tea.

Shirley jumped at the idea. "Marvellous!" she cooed, kissing him on the forehead and running her fingers through his hair. "We don't need coupons any more, so we might go to Gowlands', have tea and look at the spring dresses," she suggested gleefully, her eyes lighting up at the realization of how easy it was to cajole her husband into spending money.

She scrutinized her daughter for a couple of seconds and then burst into laughter. "Oh, poor, sad little Ruth!" she laughed with barely a hint of sympathy. "You do look a mess!" Her laughter implied that the aforesaid mess was Ruth's fault. "Well," she added, "at least you've already got your spring wardrobe. That was such a pretty dress your nan made you!" She contemplated her daughter for a moment. "I know!" she exclaimed. Wide-eyed at her own cleverness, she sprang on them her novel solution to Ruth's problem. "I know – we'll take Ruth to the hairdresser's for a perm! That will make her look so much prettier!"

"What?" said Dad, aghast at such a preposterous notion. "Perm a five-year-old's hair?"

"Why not?" Shirley retorted, innocently defiant.

The hairdresser grinned at the sight of Ruth as the three of them walked through the door. "Oh dear! Been playing with the scissors, have we?" she asked, hardly able to conceal her mirth.

Ruth kept her eyes on the floor of the whitewashed salon with its glaring lights and its magazine cut-outs of ladies modelling extravagant hairstyles stuck on the walls. Dad and Shirley did not actually tell a lie, but they said nothing to disabuse the hairdresser of her mistake. "We hoped you would give her a light perm. It's such a shame, but these things do happen, you know!"

With the utmost delicacy, Shirley, the consummate actress, volunteered a possible solution to a domestic disaster which had so patently caused her, the child's mother, great distress and great amusement at one and the same time. The hairdresser eyed Ruth carefully. "Well, I've never done one on such a small child before, and it'll take some time. Can she sit still for a couple of hours?"

"Oh yes, of course she can. You can Ruth, can't you?" Shirley settled the matter in a trice, so Ruth was swiftly lifted into a large chair in front of a washbasin and cushions were packed around and under her. She already had her head in the basin with warm water streaming down her face when she heard Shirley say: "Bye, Ruth, we'll be back in a little while. We're going to have a look round Gowlands' while you're having your hair done."

The hairdresser began by plying Ruth with questions which, although friendly in intent, were acutely embarrassing. "How did you get hold of the scissors then?" she asked. "Lucky not to cut your ear off, weren't you?" and when she elicited no response, she shrugged her shoulders, deciding that Ruth was a sullen brat who should have known better and did not deserve her sympathy. Thereupon she began to chat idly to her colleagues and the other customers instead, scarcely bothering to say anything to Ruth for the rest of the afternoon.

The perm took an awful long time, and Dad and Shirley were away for ages. Ruth sat stock still, mute and fearful, not daring to move while the hairdresser washed her hair, plastered strands of it with an acrid-smelling liquid, rolled them in curlers and then left her to dry under a domed machine. The process was repeated endless times in one form or another until, finally, when Ruth was on the point of crying out that she couldn't stand it any longer, the door opened and her parents came in. Shirley was carrying a large carrier bag and several smaller ones.

The hairdresser greeted Shirley and Dad like long-lost friends, pretending that throughout their absence, she had been amusing her sweet little customer with an endless flow of witty and interesting conversation. "Well, here they are then! Aren't we pleased to see them! Ooh, look at all Mummy's parcels! They've come at just the right moment, we're almost finished here." She glanced at Shirley's carrier bags. "Bought something nice, have you?" she enquired enviously. "Must have cost a lot – good job you didn't need coupons."

"Mm, they were rather expensive," Shirley informed her grandly, allowing her to glimpse the contents of the bags, "but then, I haven't had anything new for a long time, have I, John?" She smiled winsomely at her husband for corroboration of this statement. He acquiesced with only a slight nod, unwilling to be drawn into a conversation about domestic matters, financial or otherwise, but in so doing he put his arm round her waist.

"Lovely material, lovely colour," the hairdresser whistled through partly closed lips, peering into the bags and lavishing praise on the articles at the same time as doing a quick mental review of what they must have cost.

She was removing the latest set of rollers, which, Ruth saw with relief, was also the last, and, as the calculations reached astronomical heights, the hairdresser tugged harder and harder at the roots of each lock of hair. Though the sharp stabs of discomfort made her wince, Ruth watched eagerly as curl after tight curl sprang from the rollers, astonished that her hair had lent itself to such a radical transformation. The hairdresser ran a comb through it and the curls bounced back into place like Shirley's. Strangely enough, Ruth saw instantly that she now bore a slight resemblance to her mother who patted her shoulder.

"Oh, you do look nice!" she said, giving her affectionate approval. "Aren't you pleased? With your new dress you'll look lovely!"

Ruth was certainly pleased that she no longer looked such a fright but, in her unspoken opinion, the mass of tight curls, like so many little brown knots all over her head, was rather ridiculous, not a recognizable or familiar version of herself. She would have preferred to keep her long, shiny, straight locks. Moreover, her resemblance to Evelyn was sadly much diminished. "Can we go and have tea now?" she asked, anxious to reap at least some reward for the tedious ordeal she had so patiently endured.

"Oh, it's too late for that!" came the caustic reply. "We've had tea, and the shops are closing. You'll have to have tea when we get home."

Staring at herself in the mirror, Ruth experimented with an angry scowl. "Tut-tut," said the hairdresser. "Proper little madam, isn't she? Got your hands full there, haven't you?" she remarked sympathetically to Shirley, leaving any listeners in no doubt how she would have handled such a rebellious spirit.

Tactfully disregarding this unhelpful observation, Dad took Ruth's hand, helped her down from her throne, put her coat over her shoulders, paid the bill and ushered her and her mother out of the salon. Shirley clung to Dad's arm on the way home while, with the other hand, she clasped her parcels. Because there were so many of them and because they were so bulky, Dad had to help her carry them, which meant that he did not have a free hand for Ruth, who trotted along behind her parents.

"Are you happier now, love?" she heard her father whisper to Shirley.

"Yes, much better," she replied.

As they approached the telephone box, Dad tentatively asked Shirley what she would like to do the next day. The trouble was, he explained, that with all the rates coming into the office, he could not take any more time off at present. Because they were so badly understaffed, he would feel very guilty about leaving his colleagues in the lurch.

"I wonder," he suggested, "whether you feel well enough to take Ruth to your father's for the day tomorrow? Then, of course, on Thursday Ruth will be starting school. That was when the doctor said she could start, wasn't it?"

Shirley had no idea when Ruth was supposed to start school, but she agreed willingly to her husband's suggestion for the next day. She herself had been thinking along the same lines. A visit to her father and her brother, Ted, would be a lovely trip down memory lane, even with Ruth in tow.

"Right, then," said Dad, relieved to have found a solution to the problem of how to cope with the following day, "why don't we give them a ring straight away?"

It was only when Shirley had gone into the phone box that Dad consulted Ruth, but she was happy enough with the proposal, especially because she knew it would involve a ride on the tram.

20

The red-and-yellow tram, always so noisy yet so smooth, glided to a halt in the middle of the road with its bell clanging. Wearing her winter coat over the new dress that had been Nan's birthday present to her, Ruth clambered excitedly on board, followed by Shirley, demure in her new pale-turquoise suit and the matching hat with a tiny bit of sparkling gauze for a veil which, perched rakishly to one side of her head, allowed the short blonde curls to appear to full effect on the other.

"You look so pretty!" Dad had complimented her before he left for work.

"And Ruth looks lovely too, doesn't she, with her curls and her new dress?" was Shirley's surprising reply.

Ruth ran to the front of the tram, claiming the plush patterned seats directly behind the driver. From this position she would watch him moving the lever, guiding the majestic vehicle along its rails as it towered above the other, lesser forms of transport – for, infinitely superior to the common trolleybuses, the tram was the undisputed king of the road. At the clang of its bell, everything else precipitately yielded pride of place until, mysteriously, it deserted the deafening chaos of the streets and was swallowed up in the darkness of its silent underground cavern, where all was night. It was much more entertaining than the Tube. Blue lights winked mischievously from time to time in the blackness, and occasionally people would get on or off at dimly lit stops. Why, Ruth wondered, did people get off in the dark, leaving the bright safety of their rumbling fortress on wheels? Where were they going? There might be witches or monsters out there waiting to gobble them up in this twilight world where only the driver knew the way ahead. It was no use asking Shirley these questions: she was too preoccupied with her handbag mirror, and all she ever said in reply was, "How should I know?"

Ruth fingered the photo in her pocket in silent communication with Evelyn, her unseen companion. Shirley, of course, was smartening herself up, as she would be doing on and off, on tram and train, for the next hour, in preparation for her arrival at Granddad Reggie's. There, from the moment she walked into the newsagent's, she would be greeted like a returning heroine. Granddad's double chin would merge with his chest in a gaping smile, although he didn't say much, whereas Ted, her brother, who always kept the sleeve of one arm folded into his jacket pocket, would come round from his cycle shop on the ground floor of the premises next door as soon as she arrived and fall on her neck saying, "Hello, sis, our heroine!" She would reciprocate saying, "How's our hero, then?" Unaccountably they would proceed to communicate in a strange tongue which Ruth did not understand, so she would hang back, mystified by the gobbledegook they spoke. Perhaps this was how brothers and sisters normally communicated: she didn't know, as she had none herself.

Then Tilly Morgan would emerge from among the piles of newspapers at the back of the shop and would practically prostrate herself at Shirley's feet.

"Miss Shirley, Miss Shirley!" was all this short, stout person was able to say until she recovered her breath. Straightway she would send out messages for her nine-year-old son Albert and her husband to come at once. Albert would be fetched from school, and together they would obey the command, presenting themselves in no time at all, dressed as for a royal parade.

"Now, Albert," Tilly would instruct her son, "say 'How do you do' and 'Thank you' to Miss Shirley." Albert would do as he was told, blushing with the shyness of a child meeting royalty.

Shirley had not brought any presents for him, so it was not clear to Ruth why he had to thank her. For her part, Shirley behaved with regal dignity, bestowing gracious smiles on her subjects and enquiring after their health and well-being, in cutglass accents which she assumed for the occasion, and which bore little relation to theirs. The arrival of Tilly's family would be followed by the appearance of two elderly ladies – the one tall, austere and dressed in black, who spoke to Shirley in the same sort of gibberish that she and Ted used when talking together, and the other shrunken and white-haired, who said little but would keep patting Ruth on the head, which she did not enjoy. Then a small red-cheeked man, similar to a gnome, would come into the shop and sit himself down on a chair in a corner. "Well, hello, Shirley dear!" he would exclaim cheerfully as he came in. "You will go and call on Eileen, won't you?"

Shirley hugged him briefly. "Cousin Archie! How are you? Yes, of course I will!"

When the visitors had left and the formalities were completed, Shirley would then follow her father up the steep, soot-blackened staircase to Granddad Reggie's flat.

Granddad Reggie, overcome, after all the excitement and the climb up the stairs, would fall into a battered leather armchair and light a cigarette.

"Our Shirl!" he would splutter gruffly, coughing bronchially through the clouds of smoke which ascended both from his own cigarettes and from the trains that constantly shunted back and forth on the railway line at the back of the house. The effort involved in uttering "Our Shirl!" exhausted his powers of speech. With a grunt in Ruth's direction which might at last have been "Hello, young'un", he subsided into his armchair in front of the gas fire, not to stir for the rest of the day, and there he would resume his perusal of the huge pile of motor-racing magazines stacked beside his chair. With a nod of his bald head, he would indicate other piles in the corner and on every piece of furniture. Some of these contained well-thumbed back copies of *Dandy* and *Beano*, with which Ruth would keep herself amused for as long as was necessary. There was a piano in the flat, but since it too was covered in magazines as well as dust, she decided it would be best not to ask if she might open it. In any case, she doubted that it would be very nice to play – not like Evelyn's.

From the comics she had begun to teach herself to read, but as her skills were still very elementary, the cartoons rather than the text filled the long hours while Shirley was elsewhere, preparing a meal in the bare, draughty kitchen, still talking incomprehensibly to Ted, or after lunch, helping down in the shop, chatting to Tilly and any of her old friends who happened to pass by, or simply sitting on the arm of Granddad Reggie's chair and stroking his shiny pate.

"Well, how are you, Pa?" she would ask him several times for want of anything else to say to him, and he would always reply, "Mustn't grumble. Not too bad, not too bad, when Tilly gives me an afternoon off, like today! You should come more often, then I would have more time off, Shirl!"

"Go on, Pa!" Shirley would exclaim. "It's your business, so you can do what you like!"

To Ruth's consternation there was no sign in the house of a nan or a granny or a grandma to do the cooking or shopping or washing for Granddad Reggie or for Ted, which was why the flat was so dirty and the food, consisting only and always of baked beans on toast, so awful. Then, of course, the question arose where was Shirley's mother – and, for that matter, if Ted were Shirley's brother, Ted's mother too. They did indeed always walk round the corner to visit Uncle Archie's wife, Eileen, a sweet old lady who, although she was as thin as a rod, always served freshly made scones and cake for tea from an immaculate kitchen in her large house – but because she was married to Cousin Archie, she clearly wasn't Shirley's mother or Granddad's wife, although she and Shirley were fond of each other and talked a great deal.

Back in the flat, Ruth continued to scour the low mantelpiece and the shelves in Granddad's flat, where yet more old papers and magazines were stored, searching for photos of the absent grandmother. There were one or two photos of babies in their cots or prams and a couple more of small children: one was of Shirley as a tiny girl in a pretty dress with her fair curls dancing round her neat face, and another of Ted, dressed in a velvet suit. These children had no mother, because nowhere was there a photo of Granddad Reggie with any lady who might qualify as his wife or the mother of the children. Overcome by curiosity, she asked Shirley on the way home after one of these visits where was the nan in that establishment. Glaring at her, Shirley left her in no doubt that she should never have asked. "Don't you dare ask that question again!" she snapped and did not speak to Ruth for the rest of the way home.

The journey to Granddad Reggie's in south London was a long one, though much shorter than the journey to Nan's. The best part was the tram ride, which ended when the tram came out of the tunnel into daylight down by the river. After the tram ride, there was the walk over the bridge to the railway station, followed by twenty minutes on the train. Shirley looked at her watch as she and Ruth got off the tram. "Ah, we're going miss the eleven o'clock train," she said. "Never mind, there's no point in running for it. We can watch the boats on the river for a bit and then catch the twelve o'clock. Would you like that?" Shirley was responding happily to the spring sunshine, her new clothes and the prospect of seeing her family and friends.

These visits always put Shirley in a good humour; fortunately, in spite of yesterday's upset, today was no exception. They crossed the road and walked along the riverbank to the bridge. Holding Ruth by the hand, Shirley hummed one of her favourite tunes to herself while they watched the ships on the water. They were halfway across the bridge when she stopped and leaned over the parapet. "See the boats, Ruth! Aren't they lovely!" she exclaimed, "Wouldn't it be fun to go on one of those!"

"I can't see!" Ruth complained, her view obscured by the stone balustrade. Shirley lifted her up and sat her on the parapet, from where her legs dangled over the edge. Since Shirley's arm was round her, she felt secure.

The scene was fascinating, for the river was alive with traffic: cargo boats, tugboats, sailing boats, pleasure boats and fishing boats. They all, large and small, carried flags which fluttered in the breeze while their movement and colour made her briefly call to mind Nan's cherry tree and the market stalls so far away. Beneath her, the water fast flowing under her feet, was a muddy brown with streaked patches of oil which gleamed like rainbows floating on the surface or like the bubbles that came from those little pots when you blew through a small ring. It seemed that even dirty water shimmered in the sunlight, but looking down made her dizzy. She was about to raise her head when a barge came through the bridge.

The bargeman was lolling against the side of his cabin, idly smoking a cigarette.

"Wave to him, Ruth," said Shirley.

He looked up as Ruth waved, but he did not wave back. His face registering alarm, he grabbed a net and a lifebelt and shouted to someone in the wheelhouse to slow the engine. At that very moment, Ruth was seized from behind and dragged from her perch high above the river. Shirley screamed and Ruth scarcely had time to notice the dark-blue uniform before she found herself hoisted onto the shoulders of a policeman. With his free hand, he was gripping Shirley by the arm and marching her across the bridge to the police station on the other side.

Ruth might not have been so alarmed had they not also been pursued by a shouting, indignant army of elderly ladies, layabouts, drunks, women with pushchairs and military gentlemen, all of whom were vociferously presenting their versions of an event which, as far as Ruth was concerned, had never happened. When they shouted "Lock her up, lock her up!", she had no idea what they were talking about – nor whether the "her" referred to herself or to Shirley. There was no reason why it should refer to either of them.

The policeman, all too aware of the avenging horde at his back, shouted at them over his shoulder, "Now, now, ladies and gents, keep calm. I know what I saw and justice will be done."

Precipitately the whole gathering tumbled into the police station, causing pandemonium in the front office, where another policeman stood in shirtsleeves behind a counter and a telephonist sat at a switchboard. Ruth was deposited on the ground and left in the charge of the telephonist, while Shirley, sobbing uncontrollably and crying "No, no, please, no!" was marched by the policeman who had arrested her straight through the office and was then whisked away out of sight behind swing doors at the back.

The telephonist put Ruth on a chair in the corner and left her there while she went to help the duty policeman attend to the clamorous demands of the crowd of self-appointed witnesses, each of whom was absolutely sure that his or her version of the attempted crime was the most accurate and therefore the one which should have priority. Ruth overheard plenty of loudly voiced opinions from the assembled company, few of which she understood.

"Quite obvious, isn't it?" said a thin, hard-faced elderly woman, poking her walking stick at the swing doors. "You can see she's no better than she should be and doesn't want any encumbrances. Disgraceful, I say!"

There was a general murmur of assent, but it did not impress the policeman behind the counter. "Please, please, ladies and gentlemen," he implored. "Tell me one by one exactly what you saw, not what you think might have been happening."

The elderly woman was offended. "I know what I saw, and I know what I think and I speak as I find. Don't let anyone tell me I don't!" she announced huffily, prodding her stick into the floor. "Anyhow," she added, pointing at Ruth, "why don't you ask her, the poor child? What a tragic ordeal for one so young, poor little creature! Is no one looking after her?" she asked imperiously.

The telephonist glanced anxiously at Ruth. "Are you all right?" she was about to enquire when she was interrupted by a loud banging of the main door and an accompanying gust of wind which scattered all the papers on the counter. The barge-man swept into the centre of the police station, commanding the attention of all the onlookers on account of his size, his ugliness and his manner.

"Saw it all wiv me own eyes!" he asserted, thumping the counter. "An' I've seed a fing or two in me time, but never anyfink loik it." He ignored the pleas of the policeman to join the queue and continued regardless. "Not loikely," he said, "if you wants me statement, you better 'ave it quick. I moored me barge speshally an' I gotta get me load down them docks before the pubs open." The duty officer grimaced in exasperation; nevertheless, he began to write as the bargeman dictated his version of events. "Well, wot did oi see? Oi seed this fancy bit of fluff, loik, wiv this nippa."

At close quarters the bargeman was horrible. His arms were too long for his body and his massive shoulders were too broad. His face was red and twisted and his eyes bulged frighteningly beneath his flat blue cap. Ruth wished she had never waved to him. Luckily, puffed up with self-importance, he had not yet noticed her in a corner of the office; nonetheless, nervously sensing that he was referring to her, she tried to make herself invisible, curling her legs up, hunching her shoulders and lowering her head. "The nippa," he was saying, "she 'ad 'er legs roight over the worta, roight on the edge o' that bridge. An' that tart, she was gonna shove 'er inter the drink. Oi tell you" – he included the whole assembly, not just the policeman and the telephonist in his address – "oi tell you, if oi 'adna come up wiv me barge jus' then, she'da bin in the worta, drownded, loik as not."

If he had been expecting to receive a medal for heroism, he was disappointed, because each of the listeners then indignantly stated his or her claim to equal heroism. Someone had seen the woman acting suspiciously and had warned someone else who had sent someone else to fetch a policeman, and so on. Too scared and shocked to cry, Ruth sat snivelling in the corner; she was completely at a loss to understand what was going on, and everything that was said sounded to her like so much nonsense. Why was it that whenever she was enjoying herself, things had a habit of going so badly wrong? She remembered her birthday only a little while ago. How happy she had been until Dad's arrival! And how very unhappy she had been afterwards!

Yesterday had been a terrible day. On the other hand, today she and Shirley had been enjoying their day out. Sitting on the bridge watching the river had almost been as good as sitting in Nan's garden, watching the flowers and the trees without a care in the world – until, that is, it had all been spoilt by that policeman and these horrid, interfering people. And that was not all: when Shirley had cut her hair, Ruth had hated her and would have welcomed outside interference, but today they had begun to get on rather well. Shirley had been relaxed and happy. She had even said how sweet Ruth was, and had talked to her affectionately, as if she wanted to make up for her violent fury of the day before.

Then suddenly she had gone sobbing through that door. Where was she now? Had she had been magicked away by these nasty people? Who knew what might be happening to her? They might be putting her to sleep like Evelyn. The old woman with the stick might well be a witch and, as for the bargeman, he was certainly a hobgoblin or a troll, one of those creatures that jumped out at people in stories and ate them up. Doubtless they had their accomplices through those swing doors.

She was very anxious. She put her hand in her pocket and searched for the photo, longing for reassurance. As she touched the shiny, cracked surface, she felt a surge of strength, which gave her the courage to get to her feet and to announce in a loud voice, "I want my daddy!"

The policeman stopped writing in mid-sentence, his pen poised in the air. All faces turned to look at Ruth in amazement. "Your daddy? Have you got a daddy?" an elderly man with a large moustache boomed, taking up the challenge, because everyone else was momentarily struck dumb. The others laughed. Ruth flushed angrily. What a stupid question! Everyone had a daddy. "Yes, I've got a daddy!" she replied indignantly. "Where is he? I want him!"

If there had been bad magic at work, there was good magic as well. Grandpa the Wonderful Wizard, somewhere a long way away, must have been waving his magic wand and saying "Abracadabra, hey presto!" – for, no sooner had Ruth risen to her feet than, lo and behold, the door opened and in walked her father. Never had she been so pleased to see him.

"Ruth!" he shouted across the crowded office. The crowd dispersed to let him through and slowly drifted away as their evil power dissolved into thin air. Dad's intensely worried frown relaxed slightly as, heaving a deep sigh, he clasped his daughter in his arms. "Ruthie, Ruthie, are you all right? What on earth has been happening? Where is Mummy?" The questions came thick and fast.

Ruth pointed to the swing doors. "She's through there," she told him; as she spoke, she noticed another man, wearing a raincoat and carrying a briefcase, standing behind her father.

"What happened?" Dad asked again.

She tried hard to think whether anything had happened that she ought to tell him.

"Nothing," she said.

He made her retrace every step that she and Shirley had taken that morning, but still there had been nothing untoward or upsetting that she remembered, quite the opposite, and unlike yesterday.

Finally, he addressed the policeman. "Look here, officer, this is ridiculous. You and your colleague have subjected my wife and my child to terrible suffering for no reason at all. My daughter says that nothing happened."

The man in the raincoat placed a restraining arm on Dad's sleeve. "Keep calm, old chap," he muttered under his breath.

"I'm sorry sir," the policeman replied curtly, "but we have witnesses who think differently, and we have to consider their statements. Anyhow," he eyed Ruth critically, "she's too young to know what was happening, and a statement from her wouldn't be admissible evidence – not one that would be of any use."

Politely but firmly the man who was with Dad demanded to see someone he called his "client", and they were both taken through the swing doors. When finally they returned, long past lunchtime, Ruth was hungry and thirsty, but she knew instinctively that the affair was not yet over. With Dad there was now another man who was ordinary in appearance: he had grey hair and was wearing a suit. All three men pulled up chairs and sat down beside her.

"This is Mr Miller, Ruth. He wants to ask you a few questions."

Mr Miller smiled at Ruth. "Well, so this is Ruth!" he exclaimed. "How old are you, Ruth?" Why did adults always ask how old you were? They also said, "How you've grown!" It was very tiresome. She was tempted to do what Grandpa did and invent an age. Sometimes he would say he was a hundred and sometimes twenty-one. However, a sidelong glance at Dad's face told her that, despite Mr Miller's smile, this was no time for joking.

"I've just turned five," she said, trying to answer with precision, but she found that her voice stuck nervously in her throat and she had to cough to make the words come out.

Mr Miller was evidently impressed. "Bright child," he remarked to Dad, and then continued: "Well, Ruth, let's go into my office and then you can take your time and tell me everything you have done today." Ruth suddenly detected a troublesome difficulty. Her sixth sense, reinforced by the way her father had framed his earlier question, warned her not to refer to Shirley by her name, but it was unnatural to call her "Mummy" or "Mum", so in her lengthy account of the tram ride and the walk by the river, she simply said, "We did this" and "We did that".

When she had finished, Mr Miller gently asked if, at any point, she had been frightened.

"No," she replied candidly, tempted to ask why she might have been frightened.

Then Dad quietly asked Mr Miller's permission to interrupt. "What Mr Miller means, Ruthie, is whether Mummy was holding on to you when you sat on the bridge."

Ruth was struck by his use of the word "Mummy" again: her sixth sense had been justified. "Oh, yes," she said, "she had her arm tight round me."

Dad's face lit up with satisfaction, and the man in the raincoat spoke to Mr Miller. "There, you see; no case to answer!" he said, savouring the scent of victory.

Mr Miller only raised his eyebrows and said, "Thank you, Ruth."

There was more discussion, which did not involve Ruth; then Dad went to visit Shirley again. He wore a grim expression when he came back, alone, through the swing doors. "Off we go, Ruth. Let's get something to eat, then I'll take you home," he sighed.

"Where's Mummy?" Ruth asked deliberately with genuine anxiety.

He brushed her question off. "Oh, they're keeping her till they've finished their enquiries. Completely unnecessary, of course, and I shall make sure they let her come home tomorrow."

21

Shirley did not come home the next day, or the next week. In her absence, Ruth did not, as before, go to Norhambury to stay, since, now that she was five, she had to start school. Every morning she ran by her father's side as he strode purposefully up the main road to the quaint, slate-grey Victorian school-house, which lay in the shadow of St Luke's, the gaunt Victorian church. The church stood squarely, authoritatively, alongside the arterial road, while the school, bearing an unpleasant resemblance to a witch's cottage, with its steeply pointing gables and arched Gothic windows, hid coyly away round the corner at the side, almost out of sight, ashamed at its own sinister intrusion into such a holy setting.

On that first morning, Susan and her mother came out of their front door just as Ruth and her father were passing. Although the two girls had often played together at Mrs Cox's, their parents had rarely exchanged more than a polite greeting out in the street. Now that they were all going in the same direction, communication was unavoidable, so it was not long before Susan's mother, on hearing of Shirley's illness, was offering to bring Ruth home from school every afternoon.

Susan's mother, who during Ruth's absence in the winter had become unaccountably fat, no longer worked in the factory but at home, sewing and hemming garments at fourpence a hem, and was free to collect both girls at the end of the day. Delighted at this unexpected solution to a major problem, Dad delivered Ruth to the classroom and, like all the other parents, waited in the queue to introduce himself and his daughter to the elderly teacher, Miss Dunstan. On subsequent mornings, in his haste to get to work on time, he waved Ruth and Susan goodbye at the school gate. Thereafter, according to the mutually convenient arrangement with Susan's mother, Dad took both girls to school in the morning and she fetched them later in the day.

Ruth had been inside Susan's house before, but now, every afternoon, she had tea there, played games or watched the television until her father collected her. Sometimes he would come immediately after work; at others he would arrive much later in the evening, looking drained and hollow-eyed. On those occasions, Susan's mother would take pity on him. Putting a plate of supper in front of him, she would persuade him to eat it and tell her the latest news. When Susan's father was at home, and not away with the orchestra, he too would join in, and the three of them would put their heads together, talking in whispers so that Ruth could not hear what was being said, even if she were in the same room. As a rule she was not in the same room, for in Susan's house there were no restrictions on movement – that is to say, the front room was not out of bounds, since it did not belong to anybody in particular, but housed the television, an old sofa and Susan's toys and doll's house, not the dangerously fragile glass ornaments and china figurines of Shirley's private domain.

There too stood a piano. It was permanently closed, its role usurped by the new arrival, the walnut-encased television with its small flickering screen, which had become the focal point of Susan's attention. Ruth would dearly have loved to open the lid of the piano and run her fingers over the keys but, because of the constant intrusion of the television, there was never any opportunity – and anyhow she was too shy to ask. She did venture to drop a hint to Susan, saying, "I can play the piano," but Susan took no notice, being too intent on Muffin the Mule on television. Later Susan remarked that she hated the piano, because "they" – meaning her parents – wanted her to learn to play it and it was much too hard.

Like Nan, Susan's mother spent long hours in the kitchen, preparing meals for her family. Her cooking, however, was very unfamiliar, because she used a lot of fish and cabbage but never ham or bacon, and when she used the beef ration she often made it into delicate little parcels, wrapping thin slices round a filling of egg, onion, carrots and gherkins, or stuffing a mash of bread and potato with mince and rolling it into balls which she then dropped into boiling water. She even made bread rolls by dropping the dough into boiling water and then baking them in the oven. They tasted soft and chewy, a bit like Nan's dumplings. Ruth would watch in fascination, perched on the kitchen stool, although Susan showed no interest in baking whatsoever, preferring to play at dressing-up in her bedroom, where she had a collection of her mother's old clothes and hats.

Susan's father worked unusual hours. Sometimes he was at home when all other fathers were at work, and sometimes he was away at night when other fathers would be coming home. Ruth would always slip off her stool and go to find Susan if he came home during the cookery sessions, because it was rather embarrassing to be there in the kitchen with him and his wife. He was small and dark, with a thin, rather gaunt face. Whenever he came home, the tears would roll down his cheeks as he fell into his wife's arms, gasping, in thick guttural tones which were difficult to understand: "Rachel, my Rachel, *oy vey*, Rachel, and are you still here?"

Rachel always was there, of course, but she never chided him or laughed at him for this seemingly ridiculous question. Taking his violin case out of his trembling hand and stroking his sleeve, she would calmly reply, "Yes, yes, Jacob, you know I'm here and always will be."

Of late, on arrival, he had also begun to ask, "And how is our Benjamin?"

"Fine, fine," Rachel would reply, smiling.

This exchange was meaningless to Ruth, because Susan's stepbrother had now left home altogether. They said he had gone to work as a cadet in the Merchant Navy. Anyhow, his name was David, not Benjamin, and there was no one else, apart from Susan.

One evening, after a particularly emotional display when Susan's father had arrived home from a long tour, Ruth slunk off to join Susan, who was sitting on the floor in the front room, dressing her dolls.

"Susan," she asked, "who is Benjamin?"

Caught out by the question, Susan put her doll down as an unusually thoughtful expression swept across her face. Her forehead puckered in a frown as she began searching how to explain what she herself had been told.

"I *think*" – she stressed "think" as if not sure – "I think he was my grandpa. He lived in some place a long way off; I think it's called Bearling or something."

She stared at Ruth, and her face assumed such an uncharacteristically grave air that she seemed much older than her five and a half years. It was hard to believe that this was Susan talking. Her story was not one that she had told Ruth during their time together at Mrs Cox's nursery establishment.

"And, do you know," she continued, "one night, Poppa came home late from a concert and found that they had all vanished – all of them, Grandpa Benjamin, Granny Sara and Davy's momma."

"You don't mean your brother, David?" Ruth enquired incredulously, anxious to make absolutely sure that she had all the facts properly in her possession.

"Yes, that's right. His momma was Poppa's wife then, but she was taken away too, then she got shot when she tried to escape. That's why Poppa cries when he comes home. He's afraid we might disappear too."

"What do you mean, 'disappear'?" Ruth asked as a horrible, shivery feeling ran down her spine. "Do you mean magicked away by a witch?"

"Don't be so silly, Ruth," Susan retorted sharply. "All you ever think of is fairy stories. You are such a baby! I mean some very nasty people – I think they were called Nasties – came and took them away and burned them up in a gas oven!"

Ruth gasped in horror. "What! Like the gingerbread house in Hansel and Gretel?"

"No, stupid, that's only a fairy story. This was *real*." Susan placed a terrible emphasis on "real".

She was exasperated now, so Ruth was careful to try to ask only sensible questions. "Why didn't they take David?" she ventured cautiously.

"Oh, he had already come here with lots of other children," Susan explained, and then she added, "and Poppa managed to escape in the night. He was nearly caught lots of times."

Ruth fell silent. For the rest of that day and for the whole of the following night the terrifying story would not leave her in peace. It haunted her in her wakefulness and in her attempts to sleep. Sudden, irreconcilable images flashed unpredictably through her mind. For instance, she recalled the story Nan had once told her about Dad's canary, Tweet, when he fell off his perch and lay on the bottom of his cage. Nan had put him into the oven, but he had come out alive and flown off. And then, countering this positive tale, there was the image of the horrible bargeman and the old lady with the stick, both accusing Shirley of something that she had not done. Not only that, but also there was the image of lovely Evelyn lying under that stone, and too of the man they killed on a cross. It was terrible to think that people could be as wicked – perhaps even more wicked – than witches, but there was no escaping the truth of what Susan had told her, because that was not a story that she would have made up. The expression on Susan's face had been proof enough of that. It was far worse than anything in the story books.

She was so scared that the next morning she refused to go into the kitchen in case some evil person came and pushed her into the oven. Dad noticed her standing anxiously in the doorway and saw the frightened look on her face.

"What's the matter, Ruthie?" he asked.

The kindness and concern in his voice reduced her to tears. He came over and bent down, putting his arm around her to comfort her. "Tell me what's wrong," he said sitting down and gently taking her onto his knee.

Overcome with the emotional strain, she recited the whole tale exactly as Susan had told it, secretly hoping that perhaps he would say that it was not true after all, that it was all just a dreadful story. But he did not. His face grew solemn and he sighed. "It's horrific, isn't it?" he said. "It's almost too horrendous to believe, but it did happen. It happened to Jacob's family and to lots and lots of other families. He came home one night and was told by the neighbours that his wife had been taken out and shot as she tried to run away, and his parents were sent off to the camps, where they died. Jacob fled into the night with only his violin and, after a long struggle, goodness knows how, he got to this country, where he was reunited with David."

There was little comfort in these words. The truth was stark and terrifying. So often Ruth had wished that adults would tell her the truth and, now that she was hearing it from her own father, it was far more troubling than any fairy story. It was not unlike that time when Nan had told her what had happened to Jesus and had the same effect on her. She sat in a numbed silence on her father's knee, staring at the oven.

"But" – hardly daring to raise her voice above a whisper, she struggled to get the words out – "what about the oven? Were they burnt up in an oven?"

Her father was bemused at first, but once he had collected up his thoughts, he said: "Ruthie, Ruthie, where do you get these strange ideas from? Those poor people weren't burnt, they were gassed!"

Fearing that he had been too blunt, he adopted a lighter tone. "Well, that's all over now, thank goodness, and Jacob has David and, since marrying Rachel, he has a new life and a new family."

"What about Tweet?" Ruth persevered, returning to the original subject. "Nan put him in the oven and he came out alive."

Dad laughed. "Oh, that was different. Tweet wasn't dead, he was only stunned, and the warmth of the oven woke him up."

"Ah," Ruth replied, hopelessly lost in a tangled web of conflicting theories, accounts, experiences and observations. "What about Val's tortoise, and the Sleeping Beauty, and Jesus – he woke up again, didn't he?"

"Hold on, hold on!" Dad exclaimed. "These are very complicated questions, and if we start discussing them now we shall be here all day. You'll be late for school and I'll be late for work, and that would never do." He looked at his watch. "Come on, old girl. Susan will wonder what has happened to us."

That morning Ruth regarded Susan through new eyes. In her estimation, Susan had become a heroine by association with her family history. Ruth stood by her protectively in the playground while the children waited for the headmaster to ring the bell to order them into line, and she kept glancing across the classroom at her to check that she was happy. Sitting at her desk, intent on her reading book, Susan was scowling but otherwise was unperturbed by the drama that she had recounted the previous evening. At playtime she announced sullenly, "I hate reading: it's too difficult."

"I'll help you," Ruth offered, anxious to do anything to please her.

"There's a word I don't know and I've got to read to Miss Dunstan after playtime," Susan wailed.

"All right, show me what it is when we go back indoors," Ruth volunteered.

Susan agreed, but at the end of playtime she spent so long in the girls' cloakroom arranging her hair for her performance that there was no time for Ruth to help her.

Susan stood at Miss Dunstan's desk for the rest of the morning, puzzling over the stumbling block until finally Miss Dunstan wrote the word on the blackboard and asked the class to tell Susan what it was.

"Pony!" they all shouted.

Susan sat down at her desk, flinging the reading primer onto the lid. She sulked throughout the lunch hour, impervious to Ruth's well-intentioned efforts to cheer her up. All she said was, "I shall run away like Davy. He hated reading too. But I shall run away and become a ballet dancer."

Ruth was about to agree that the idea appealed to her too when Susan forestalled her by exclaiming, "Ballet! It's today, I think." Urgently she asked, "What day is it today, Ruth?"

"Wednesday, I think," Ruth replied.

"Oh, goodie, goodie! It's my ballet lesson today! You can come and watch!"

Ruth was completely taken aback. The mere notion of Susan having ballet lessons filled her with envy, and the idea of having to watch while Susan danced was very frustrating. She supposed she might learn something from going with her, but the only possible consolation was that finally she might find out whether the dancers she had seen at the theatre were real fairies or people pretending to be fairies. After her experiences of the past days, the whole notion of fairyland and fairy tales was beginning to appear more and more remote, because fairies and witches and magic spells were apparently nothing more than an adult excuse for things they were unable or did not want to explain properly.

"I've been to the ballet," she informed Susan, trying to gain the upper hand, "I know all about it."

"But you can't dance: you're not having lessons, I am," Susan replied.

22

Susan was right about the day: it was Wednesday. That afternoon, when her mother met the two girls, they did not go straight home, down the busy main road, but crossed the road outside the school and took a side street. Outside, the dance centre was a tall, grey, double-fronted terraced house like all the others in the street. Inside, through the open doors, both the identical ground-floor rooms on either side of the entrance hall were bare of furniture, apart from a line of chairs placed against one of the pink-painted side walls. In each room the other side wall had a *barre* all the way along it, while the end wall was covered by a huge mirror. A piano stood in the bay window.

The cloakroom where the girls were changing was a mass of bodies. The small girls of Susan's class were shedding their bulky skirts and cardigans and squeezing their feet into little black shoes which were held in place by an elastic strap. Meanwhile, the older girls from the other class were tying their hair into neat buns and were pulling on close-fitting black costumes, which transformed them from ordinary schoolgirls into slender, elegant beings, proud of their own superiority. Truly some magic must have been at work for, bewitched by their new apparel, their movements changed, becoming slower, more studied and more graceful, as the costumes introduced them into a more beautiful, more delicate dimension than the humdrum world of their north-London lives. Feeling clumsy and out of place in her outdoor shoes and socks, Ruth gazed with envious wonder as they slipped their feet into real ballet shoes, pink satin shoes with satin laces that they criss-crossed round their legs. Thus apparelled, they waltzed into the room on the left and the door closed behind them.

Hiding behind Susan's mother, Ruth followed her into the room on the right, dragging her feet in a most unballetic manner, and sat down, slouching on a chair at the side of the room. There was nothing for it but to watch the proceedings. Perhaps she would learn something by observing. The class began with toe-pointing exercises, which she mimicked from her chair. Then the large ginger-haired teacher, who did not look at all like a ballet dancer, took the class through a series of positions, both for the feet and for the arms. They were easy, so easy that Ruth decided that she would try them herself at home. Afterwards there was a period of dancing in which she would have loved to participate. It was sheer torment to have to sit watching instead of joining in, while the class was invited to listen to the music played by the enormous man seated at the piano and invent appropriate dances.

Although he was so huge that the folds of his body spilled over the edges of the piano stool, the pianist played nimbly and imaginatively. Ruth would have felt happier if she might at least have stood beside him watching his fingers instead of the dancers' feet. Some of the music was for witches, some for fairies, some for kings and queens and some for giants, but Susan was hopeless whatever role she tried to interpret. She had no idea of how to respond and no understanding of the rhythm of the music. Moreover, however pretty she might be, dressed only in her pants and vest without her outer garments, Susan was rather podgy and ungainly. Her feet did not move delicately at all. At the end of the class she came puffing up to her mother, beaming all over her face and demanding, "Did you watch me? Wasn't I good? Did you see me being a horse?"

Ruth pretended not to hear in case Susan asked for her opinion. She knew that she might say something rude which would upset not only Susan but her kind mother as well and, because she was ever conscious of the horrific story she had been told the previous day, she was anxious to avoid hurting any member of that family. Having benevolently satisfied her daughter's demands, Susan's mother took Ruth by the hand as Susan was getting dressed, and quietly made a startling suggestion. "Why don't you ask your daddy if you can join the class, Ruth? It only started a week ago, so you haven't missed much. It would be much nicer for you than just sitting with me." Ruth could have hugged her; it was a perfect idea. Dad would surely let her join the class. There was no reason for him to refuse. She spent the rest of the afternoon in a glow of hopeful expectation.

Afraid that Ruth might still be brooding on the horrendous facts which he had found himself obliged to tell her that morning before school, her father collected her on time from Susan's house in the evening. He was pleased at her apparent lightness of spirit as she skipped along beside him, no longer burdened by the weight of recent human history. She, for her part, found it hard to contain her eagerness to ask him the all-important question about ballet lessons; only shyness restrained her, because she was afraid he might not take her seriously, and then it would all be in vain. So, until she plucked up the courage to overcome the shyness, she chattered about school and the reading lesson instead. She permitted herself a touch of derision at Susan's literary incompetence, because Susan had a rather high opinion of herself in other respects.

The house was chilly after being closed up all day, so Dad decided to light a fire before supper. It was time to wash Ruth's hair, he said, as he stood holding opened sheets of newspaper across the fireplace to draw the fire up. It was indeed time to wash her hair, as more than a week had elapsed since the hair-cutting episode and Shirley's subsequent disappearance. Fortunately, in all that time no one had commented on her permed curls – except Susan, who had said, "Oh, Ruth, I didn't know you had curly hair!", and Susan's mother, who had remarked, "What lovely curls, Ruth dear." Luckily neither of these remarks had required a reply or any explanation.

After supper, John set to work to wash his daughter's hair under the Ascot in the kitchen sink and then sat down by the fire while she sat on a stool beside him; she leant her head on his knee while he rubbed her hair vigorously with a large towel. The moment for the big question had arrived. Ruth felt emboldened to speak out since, from under the towel, her father's face was not visible, and that made it easier because, if the idea of it made him frown, she would not know.

"I went to Susan's ballet lesson today," she began, feeling her way into the subject.

"Did you, Ruthie? Was it fun?" he replied.

"It was lovely. The big girls all wore pointed pink satin shoes." She remembered her admiration, tinged with envy, of the older girls. "And Susan wears little black shoes because she is learning the steps."

This, she expected, would be his cue for asking her if she would like to dance too, but, although she waited hopefully, the question was not forthcoming.

"The steps were easy. I can do them. And then you have to dance to the music, like witches or fairies or giants," she persevered. Another unproductive lull followed. Finally, in desperation, she blurted out: "I'd like to have ballet lessons, too." She had said it! She held her breath, waiting for a positive response. Dad stopped rubbing her hair and sat with his hand resting on her head. He did not answer, so supposing that he hadn't heard, she said imploringly: "Can I join in the ballet class – please, Dad!" She sat up and, turning round on her stool, looked him straight in the eye. He was wrapt up in his own preoccupations, impervious to her pleading expression. "Please, Dad, please!" she persisted.

He hesitated, took a deep breath and then embarked on a lengthy explanation, which, with every word, grew more and more depressing. His tone of voice made her heart sink even as he started to speak. "I don't know how to explain this, Ruthie," he began, "but you see, I'm very sorry, I don't think we can afford ballet lessons for you. The trouble is, I don't have what is called 'capital'. Well, that means a lot of money in savings. I only have what I earn, it's called income, and that isn't very much." He stopped, as likely as not hoping that Ruth would be satisfied with his explanation, but had not reckoned on the determined streak in her nature, which asserted itself when, at long last and after much inner hesitancy, she plucked up courage to voice her opinions. "Susan has lessons, and I don't think they have got a lot of money," she argued with resolute fierceness.

"No, no, I understand that," he replied, "but you see, I have expenses that the Meyers don't have…" His voice petered out, as he considered how to proceed. Ruth's firmly set jawline gave him scant option but to proceed somehow. Stammering slightly, he picked up the thread of his explanation. "You see, Ruthie, I have to spend a lot of money on Shirley. She has to be properly cared for, and that costs practically all the money I earn." As an afterthought he added: "And, in any case, I'm not sure that Shirley would want you to have ballet lessons. She might be unhappy about that."

For a second, Ruth was dumbstruck, then her ferocious sense of injustice overcame her – that same sense of injustice which had been fermenting inside her ever since she had been so summarily dragged out of her blissful existence at Nan's house on her birthday and brought home to please Shirley. She jumped to her feet; her eyes, which had previously shone with hope, now blazing with anger. She stamped her foot. "I hate Shirley!" she exploded in a furious rage. "I hate her! She spoils everything!"

"Stop it, Ruth!" Dad shouted back at her, also jumping to his feet. "How dare you behave like that! That is no way to talk about your mother!" His voice grew quieter, gradually petering out as he muttered unconvincingly, "You should show more love and concern for her."

He sank back onto his chair by the fire and buried his head in his hands – a lonely, pathetic figure. Pity for him outweighed the indignation which only a moment ago had been so over-powering. Ruth sat down on the stool at his feet and put her head on his knee once again. He spoke softly. "There are things I have to try and explain to you, Ruthie. They are hard to understand and I am very sorry, very sorry, that I can't let you have and do whatever you want. Of course I understand that you would like to go to the ballet class, and I wish I had the money to pay for it – even though, as I said, I'm not sure how Shirley would feel about it."

He took a slow breath inward before continuing. "Last week's upset down by the river, at that police station where everyone was so nasty, you remember, don't you?" Ruth nodded. "Well, that had a very bad effect on Shirley. The shock of it made her very ill, all over again. Every bit as bad as she was last winter, and she had to go back to hospital – to a different one this time – where they are trying to make her well again. But the hospital is such an awful place, so depressing, that I have to pay for her to have a private room so she can have peace and quiet away from all the other patients. And I'm afraid that it costs a lot of money. There's not much left for anything else." He saw from the expression on Ruth's face that she hadn't the slightest idea of what he was talking about. To press the point home, he made a suggestion. "I know it's hard for you to understand, but if you were to come and see for yourself, it might be easier. The rule is, of course, that children are not allowed to visit, but I daresay we might persuade the matron to let you in just once, as an exception, if we say that you are missing your mummy. What do you think?"

23

Ruth had given her father's suggestion her tacit, if reluctant, approval, which was how she came to be accompanying him to the hospital the following Sunday afternoon. Standing in isolation, a massive block of dirty red-brick, towering above an intricate wasteland of railway sidings, marshalling yards, goods depots and gasometers at the back of one of the main railway termini, the hospital would not have been more frightening had it actually been one of those hollowed-out bomb sites which still figured so prominently in Ruth's dreams.

Leaning against the cavernous arch of the doorway was an ugly creature, with a hunched back, a gnarled body, bandy legs and a lopsided face which looked as if it had been hurriedly stuck together from ill-matching cardboard cut-outs. A cigarette dangled from his twisted lips as he stepped out to bar their way. Ruth clutched her father's hand in fright. She wished that she had been left at the Sunday school where she had had to spend the previous Sunday afternoon while her father visited Shirley, even though on that occasion she had been indignant at being sent back to school. At this moment she would have given anything to be sitting quietly in the church, on the hard pew, kicking her heels and inattentively minding her own business, while the vicar's wife harped on and on about the importance of being good. It was very unfair: all week, adults told children to be good or asked them if they had been good, and then, on Sundays, those same children were told to remember all the bad things they must have done. No credit was given for trying to be good. Church was a joyless affair, but by comparison with this, the mental hospital, it was a friendly, welcoming place. Dad looked as if he was affected by a similar apprehension, for his tall frame shrank visibly as he approached the entrance;

his shoulders stooped, and he bowed his head in apparent anticipation of some unpleasantness.

The hunchback did not launch into the expected attack, but began to speak quietly with respect. He had a pleasant, apologetic voice which belied his ghoulish appearance. "Sorry, sir," he began, "yer does know, don't yer, that children ain't allowed in this 'ere institution?"

Equally unexpectedly, Dad was neither perturbed nor unduly cowed by this prohibition, and in fact, despite his dejected air, he replied with an assertive jollity. "It's all right, Bob, I talked to Matron when I was here on Thursday, and she gave me permission to bring Ruth to see her mother."

"Ah, your littl' gowl, is she?" Bob replied, reaching out a nicotine-stained finger to chuck Ruth under the chin. Ruth gritted her teeth, gripping her father's arm tightly to avoid showing her distaste at this frighteningly close contact with such a foul fiend. Bob leered into her face. "Pretty littl' fing, ain't she? Sad for her, ain't it?" he remarked, then he sighed a sigh which disclaimed responsibility in advance for what he was about to say. "Matron ain't said nuffink to me, sir, an' it's more than me job's worf to let yer in wivout 'er permission, if yer see what I mean."

Dad gave vent to his exasperation in a wry grimace. "Well, perhaps I might have a word with Matron?" he suggested patiently.

"No luck, sir, it's 'er afternoon awff."

"The assistant matron then, perhaps?" Dad persevered, ever a model of courtesy and patience.

"Well, we'll give it a try, but I don't 'old out much 'ope wiv 'er, pers'nally speaking, if yer gets me meaning." Bob hobbled away in search of the assistant matron.

Ruth waited until Bob had passed through the inner doors into a long corridor, before pulling on her father's sleeve and whispering, "Dad, I don't like him, I want to go home!"

Dad knelt down to her level. "Oh, Ruthie, Ruthie, how could you talk like that!" he said. There was no anger in his voice, only a disappointment which made her uncomfortably guilty. She would almost have preferred him to have screamed and shouted at her, because then she would have shouted back without feeling guilty at all. She regretted confiding her fears to him.

"You must learn not to judge people by their appearances," he went on, "it's very important to respect people for what they are, not for what they appear to be. Bob has been very unfortunate. He was abandoned by his parents and brought up in an orphanage, where he was bullied by the other children because of his deformities, but he has a heart of gold. A better person you will never find. There are lots of people like him – some deformed, some wounded, some," he hesitated, "some have skins of different colours – but it's the way they are, not the way they look, that tells you whether they are good or bad people. And of course, not all beautiful people are good people." Ruth was duly chastised and said no more.

Bob soon returned, bringing with him a thin elderly woman with a sharply pointed chin. Her dark-blue uniform and her starched white cap did nothing to alleviate the intimidating severity of her presence. She snorted as she surveyed Ruth. "Och, so this is the wee bairn who's missing her mam?" she asked, stretching her lips taut in an unsuccessful attempt at a smile, for Bob must have painted a sufficiently harrowing picture of Ruth's distress to encourage her to make an effort to soften the contours of her features. Ruth perceived that here was the living proof that Dad was wrong – that you could guess what people were like from their appearance – but this was not the time to mention it. She kept her eyes shyly on the ground, snivelling for effect and leaving her dad to do the talking. Again he repeated the conversation he had had with the matron the previous Thursday, while the assistant matron constantly shook her head, asserting the impossibility of allowing a child onto the premises.

They were interrupted by the ringing of the telephone in Bob's cubbyhole. He answered it and called out: "It's Matron for you, ma'am, she's remembered somefink she forgot ter tell yer." Bob handed her the phone, the while grinning at Dad. They all waited. The assistant matron emerged unsmiling from the porter's office. "Most irregular, most irregular," she muttered, rolling her Rs and then closing her mouth until the roll ceased. "Matron says you may take the bairn to see her mother – but not for longer than five minutes, mind." Flinging both inner doors apart, she marched away, head held high, with never a backward glance.

Bob watched her go and, turning to Dad, wheezed apologetically: "Sorry abowt that, sir. Pity Matron forgot ter tell me afore she went awff duty. She's a good sort, Matron is. Not like that old cow... a real pain, she is. Yer can see it in 'er face, can't yer? Well, now..." He gave Ruth a crooked grin, and she tried her hardest to muster a smile. "Well, now, we don't want ter frighten this little kiddie, do we? So I'd better come along wiv yer." He held out a bony hand for Ruth to take; at first she recoiled, then, realizing that her father was watching, put one hand limply, with extreme caution, into Bob's palm, clinging ever more ferociously to her father's hand with the other. In subdued silence, the trio abandoned the warm sunny afternoon and pushed their way through the inner swing doors into the dark, damp corridor which stretched endlessly before them.

Every so often, loosing his hand from Ruth's, Bob would stop, on one or other side of the corridor, to close an open door from which weird wailings issued, or he would lead an errant pyjama-clad figure, flitting among the shadows, back through one of those same doors. A bevy of uniformed nurses clustering round a trolley in the middle of the corridor took no notice either of the patients or of the visitors, leaving Bob to attend to the wandering wraiths supposedly in their charge. Occasionally an ashen face, drained of all comprehension, with eyes sunk deep in their sockets, would appear, gawping round a doorpost. With a calm gesture of his free hand, Bob would dismiss it back to where it belonged.

A corpulent woman dressed in black, her head covered in a bright-orange shawl, slowly crossed their path. With her mouth wide open and her chin resting on folds of flesh, she swayed unsteadily from side to side, repeatedly warbling one single strain of music, regaling the whole corridor with her full, rich voice. "When I am lai-aid, am lai-ai-ai-ai-aid in earth, may my wro-o-ongs create no trou-ouble, no trou-ouble in-in thy breast." She ceased as they passed and inclined her substantial frame in a low, extravagant bow.

Bob again loosed his hand from Ruth's and leant confidentially towards Dad. "Applaud, sir, if yer would be so kind. Poor soul, 'asn't been able to do anyfink else since the featre she were in was bombed. Finks she's Kafleen Ferrier. It's the demon drink, yer know."

He and Dad applauded politely. Ruth gazed at the ageing diva, repelled by her bloated features and her overblown proportions, yet drawn by the haunting beauty of her song. She was too scared to bring herself to clap with Dad and Bob, though afterwards she was ashamed of her recalcitrance.

"Luvely, Kaffy dear, luvely." Bob was lavish in his praise before abruptly opening a door which swallowed her up exactly like all the other apparitions they had seen.

At the end of the corridor as they mounted a cold, stone staircase, lit by the steely reflections of the all-encompassing railway lines outside, Bob let go of Ruth's hand and edged closer to Dad. "A word in yer ear, sir" – he lowered his voice to a whisper – "I fink I oughta warn yer, cos no one else will, that yer missus ain't very well. They've given 'er that new treatment, the shock ferapy, they calls it, an' she took it real bad. I knows cos I were there – 'ad to 'elp 'old 'er down. They say it'll 'elp 'er get better quick, but I dunno, meself. Come out o' them Nazi camps, they say. Blimey, wot them poor people 'ad ter suffer. Makes yer fink, dunnit?" He shook his head, and Ruth suspected that she saw a tear glistening in the corner of his eye. He wiped it away with the back of his hand as they reached the top of the staircase.

On that floor another corridor, identical to the one below, peopled with a similar motley collection of stiffly starched nurses and macabre scarecrows, stretched ahead of them. Bob knocked on the first door on the left, however, and, on opening it for Dad and Ruth to enter, announced that he had to be getting back to his porter's lodge in case his absence was discovered by the powers that be. Ruth followed Dad into the bare, high-ceilinged room, illuminated by the same steely reflections as the staircase. It contained only a single chair, a small table, placed beneath the tall window, and a bed.

Wearing a white overall, Shirley lay motionless on the bed, her eyes closed. On a metal chair in the corner, in sympathy with its owner, the new turquoise suit lay in a crumpled heap with the new hat forlornly askew on top of it, its little veil torn and missing many of its sequins. "Is that you John?" she murmured before bursting into floods of tears. Dad sat on the bed, enfolding her in his arms, while Ruth waited in the doorway. "It was terrible, terrible, you can't imagine; I can't do it again, never, never. It was like being struck by lightning." Shirley was convulsed with sobs, shaking uncontrollably in Dad's arms.

He stroked her hair and kissed her forehead. "There, there, love, it'll be all right, it'll be all right. Open your eyes; look who's come to see you." Shirley resisted his efforts to comfort her until her sobs abated and then she opened her eyes and turned her pale face enquiringly towards the door.

At first her expression registered sheer amazement on seeing Ruth, who was not sure whether this reaction implied pleasure or annoyance. Nor was she sure from the tears welling up in Shirley's eyes. It was only when she finally held out her arms, laughed and said, "Ruth, Ruth, so they've let you come and see me, at last!" that it dawned on her that her mother was pleased to see her. She ran to the bed, where Shirley kissed and hugged her as never before. "Ruth, Ruth, I was never going to hurt you!" she cried. Ruth was at a loss for words. She had never supposed that Shirley was going to hurt her, despite the shock of the hair-cutting episode.

"There, you see," said Dad to Shirley, "you are getting better already."

Shirley slowly eased herself into a sitting position. At first, thin and frail, delicate and vulnerable, holding her head in her hands, she moaned in pain. When after some anxious minutes she began to recover, she put her arm round Ruth again and asked her about her school. "What's it like?" she enquired enthusiastically, apparently recovering some of her old energy. "What's your teacher's name? What are the other children like?" She was as impatient for the answers as Ruth was impatient to provide them.

Since this fragile creature on the bed was fully and gladly acknowledging the relationship between them, Ruth was eager to respond with good grace. "Well," she said, taking a deep breath, "my teacher's name is Miss Dunstan. She's very old and she's very cross. She smacks your hand if you can't do your sums."

"Oh, dear!" Dismay spread across Shirley's face, implying that she would never dream of smacking Ruth. "Has she ever smacked you?" she asked with grave, almost shocked, concern.

"Oh yes, lots of times," Ruth replied airily, "because I can't do sums. I hate sums. But that's better than not being able to read, because then you have to stand at the front and all the other children laugh at you afterwards in the playground."

Shirley nodded sympathetically. "I used to hate sums too," she said. "Not like your dad: he's very good at sums – aren't you, darling?" Dad nodded modestly. "But you know," she added, "I did get better at them, so don't you worry!"

"I can read," Ruth added reassuringly.

"Good, but what about the other children?" Shirley asked. "Are they nice?"

Her interest in Ruth's activities appeared to be real. Keen to respond to this unprecedented show of concern, Ruth reflected for a moment, trying to recall all the details of the past ten days that would entertain her mother. "They're all right – there's Susan, you know her; she lives on the corner. She can't read, but she can do sums. We sit together on the steps at playtime. There is a stupid boy, his name's Simon, Simple Simon. He's fat and says silly things. He calls me 'golliwog' and all the children laugh."

Shirley and Dad glanced at each other uneasily. "I expect it's because of your dark curls that he calls you that," Dad suggested.

Ruth nodded. "But he's nasty to Susan too; he calls her 'Jewy'."

Dad drew breath sharply. Shirley did not say anything. "What does Susan say to that?" Dad asked seriously, with no hint of amusement in his voice.

Unperturbed, Ruth continued in the same nonchalant fashion: "Oh Susan doesn't take any notice, she just says 'Go away goy boy, you're stupid!' and he goes."

She broke off her narration, remembering how only a couple of days previously she had asked Susan if she knew why Simple Simon called her "Jewy". Susan had shrugged. She supposed it was because she did not go to prayers in the church with the rest of the school – and that, she said, was because she did not believe in Jesus. Ruth was appalled. "That's terrible," she said, "because if you don't believe in Jesus, you can't have Christmas!" Susan had turned on her scornfully. "Why not?" she asked. "You told me you don't believe in Father Christmas, but you still have Christmas, so why can't I?" While having to admit that Susan was right in that particular respect, Ruth was conscious of an elusive flaw in her reasoning without being able to pinpoint exactly what it was.

She awoke from her reverie to find Dad and Shirley involved in a discussion. Shirley was saying, "It's not right. I think you ought to go and talk to the Headmaster."

Dad on the other hand simply shrugged, as Susan had done, saying, "I don't think it would do much good. The boy is retarded, and wouldn't understand anyhow – nor, I suspect, would his family."

Shirley turned her attention back to Ruth. "What else do you do in school, Ruth? Do you do painting?"

"Oh yes! I love painting: we go into Miss Bevan's class for that," Ruth replied, and began to describe the picture she had embarked upon, a painting of the sun made up of all the colours on the palette.

"Ruth, Ruth, you are funny!" Shirley laughed fondly. "You know the sun is yellow!"

Ruth wanted to explain that the sun she was painting was going to be like those huge crystal balls, sparkling with every imaginable colour, that she had seen when she and Nan and Grandpa went out to tea before the ballet – or like the spiders' webs in Nan's garden on the morning of her birthday – but she suspected that Shirley would not understand, so she reverted to the original subject. "Miss Lake comes into our class sometimes for singing and, do you know, we sing a song about the HP Sauce bottle!"

"Not really?" Dad exclaimed. "How does it go?"

As Ruth started to sing "I am H-A-P-P-Y, I am H-A-P-P-Y", Shirley and Dad gazed at each other, holding their hands to their mouths, trying to keep a straight face. "Oh, you are such a sweet little girl!" Shirley gave Ruth her most lovely smile and hugged her once again. Ruth was carried away in her elation. She would scarcely have believed that it was possible to be so happy in such squalid surroundings, but the fact was that, here, together, the family group had found perfect harmony, like a lovely piece of music or the dancers weaving in and out on the stage.

Having seen for herself, she fully understood why Shirley needed her own room in that horrible place, and she was glad that Dad was paying for it. Anyhow, the sooner Shirley was better – and already she was getting much better – the sooner she would come home; then there might be money for ballet lessons after all – except, of course, Dad had said that Shirley might not like that, so she asked herself whether it would be wise to tell Shirley about Susan's ballet class. She decided in the end that it would be safer to tell her more about school.

"And," Ruth commanded the attention of her audience once more, "and Miss Lake comes into our class to take the band on Friday afternoons." Although Dad and Shirley were still giggling about the HP song, she carried on, warming to her subject. "And Miss Lake told us to put our hands up to choose the instruments we wanted to play."

"What instruments are there?" Dad asked.

"There are drums and triangles and tangerines and pipes and canstanets – well I think that's what they are called,"

Ruth replied, seriously trying to remember the range of possibilities.

"So what did you choose?" Shirley asked.

"I said I would like to play the piano," Ruth answered candidly, recalling the astonishment on Miss Lake's face at her request. Miss Lake had asked her to come out and play something for the class, so she had played Nan's favourite hymn, 'Now the Day Is Over'. The class had applauded rapturously and Miss Lake had said that she was very clever and would she please stand beside her at the piano and help her to play the accompaniments for the band? Miss Lake played the tunes while Ruth elaborated on them at the end of the keyboard, sometimes in the treble end, sometimes in the bass. Miss Lake was so impressed she had even offered to give her lessons occasionally in playtime.

Ruth was not prepared for the dramatic effect that this revelation would have in the hospital room that Sunday afternoon. Shirley's arm fell away from Ruth's shoulders, nearly pushing her off the bed. In alarm Ruth glanced at her mother's face and saw that the little wrinkles around her eyes and mouth, so recently of pleasure and amusement, had hardened instantly into set lines of dour resentment and sullen displeasure. Ruth was shocked at the sudden change and shrank away from the bed to position herself behind her father.

"Give me a fag, will you?" Shirley demanded of Dad coarsely, through clenched teeth, without looking at him.

"Of course, love." Reaching into his pocket, he pulled out his cigarette case and opened it for her. She snatched it out of his hand and feverishly put the cigarette to the flame of the lighter, which he held out to her. He then took Ruth's hand and led her towards the door.

"Ruthie, wait outside for a minute, will you? I'll say goodbye to Shirley then we must be going home." Shirley was silent.

He pushed Ruth out into the corridor and then went back inside, closing the door. As things had gone so badly wrong, for unfathomable reasons, she was glad to be out of that room. Her relief was cut short, however, when she discovered that the upstairs corridor was just as nightmarish as the one downstairs. She stood stock still, pressing herself into the wall in a futile attempt to make herself invisible to the hideous, half-dressed forms which loomed out of the gloom and then vanished. Spine-chilling noises echoed off the walls and grisly faces peered inquisitively out of doorways before snarling dismissively and disappearing. Directly opposite Shirley's room an open door revealed a vast room with beds lining the walls. Disjointed figures lolled on the beds, gesticulating and performing ill-coordinated antics with their arms and legs as they emitted blood-curdling cries to empty space. In the distance, at the other end of the corridor, she made out a tall, gangling figure, all awry, its arms and legs disconnected from its body. It was coming towards her shouting something at the top of its voice. The bevy of nurses ignored it completely, but she was terrified.

If only Bob would reappear! What was she to do? Dad was taking such a long time. She could not go back into Shirley's room. Shaking like a leaf, she was about to force her way headlong through the door onto the staircase when Shirley's door opened and, straightening his tie and flattening his hair with the back of his hand, Dad came out. Hurriedly he picked Ruth up and stood aside to allow the advancing figure to pass.

With wide staring eyes, the inmate lumbered past them. He wore a placard on his front which announced a simple message which Ruth read easily. "THE END" it said, in roughly painted capitals. The message was reinforced by his cry, which resounded off the walls: "Repent ye! Repent ye!" he yelled, oblivious to the fact that, for once, he had an audience. He passed them without registering their presence and, reaching the end of the corridor, began to retrace his steps.

24

Although there were so many questions concerning the hospital and their visit that Ruth would have liked to put to her father, he was disinclined to talk about it, except for a passing comment which he made on the way home as they were sitting side by side on the Tube train rumbling along deep under the streets and buildings of north London. "I think, Ruthie," he said quietly, "I think it would be better not to mention the piano to your mother ever again. It seems to upset her and set her back, which is not what we want, is it?"

It was self-evident that the mention of the piano upset Shirley, but Ruth would have liked to know why. Her tale about the school band and the piano had been told in all innocence, with the intention of entertaining her parents. How was she to know that Shirley would react so badly to it? It was clear that she was unlikely to receive any answers, let alone satisfactory ones, if she pressed these questions. So, as usual, she kept quiet. Naturally she was also puzzled as to why it was that her mother detested the piano so vehemently, while Evelyn – her beautiful, talented godmother whose photo she still kept in her pocket – had loved it so much.

Her father's stricture posed problems for Ruth later that week. In the band sessions, Miss Lake now regularly invited her to come out to the front to help with accompanying the band on the piano. She had complimented Ruth on how quickly she was learning and how competently she played at her end of the keyboard. This week she summoned her to the front as usual. Ruth leapt to her feet eagerly and played with her accustomed assurance and bravado. It was only when she sat down again that she was beset by pangs of conscience. When Dad had told her not to mention the piano, perhaps he also meant that she was not to play it. What should she say if he asked her whether she had been playing the piano in school?

That very evening he confronted her with the dreaded question: had she been playing in the band? With burning cheeks, she admitted that she had been playing the piano. He had not scolded her; he had simply said, "Ah," but the unease conveyed by that "Ah" made Ruth feel so guilty that thereafter, although Miss Lake continued to invite her to play the piano, she expressed a preference for the triangle and, when Miss Lake offered, as she frequently did, to help her with some scales, she mumbled an excuse about having to go to Miss Dunstan to do extra sums. Miss Lake frowned, because she was unwilling to believe that Ruth had so indifferently given up her favourite instrument, but she did not try to change her mind. She did however ask if there were something wrong with the piano.

"No, I don't know," was the enigmatic reply she received from her pupil.

The sacrifice proved to be beneficial in that it quietened Ruth's conscience, and when Dad asked her, as he did regularly, what instrument she had been playing in the band, she answered truthfully, "The triangle." On the other hand, from her point of view the situation was most unsatisfactory. It was grossly unfair that the two things that she wanted to do most, the ballet and the piano, were forbidden, both on account of Shirley.

Although Ruth never visited the hospital again, she found herself thinking about Shirley often. Such musings punctually aroused conflicting emotions. The restrictions placed on Ruth by Shirley's unseen presence were infuriatingly unjust: in that respect Shirley was every bit as wicked as all the witches in all the fairy stories that Ruth had ever read – and, indeed, she was capable of looking as evil as them. Yet the memory of Shirley, pale and helpless, lying weeping on her bed in that monstrously frightening place never ceased to haunt her, for then she became every bit as much of a princess as Evelyn – a princess suffering under a wicked spell, who had the indisputable right to demand the love and the loyalty of all the other characters in the story, a love and a loyalty which were to be put to the test in unforeseen circumstances.

Every morning Simple Simon, who came to school on his own, stood on the corner by the church, waiting to join a group of boys whom he was anxious to regard as his friends. With his upper lip curled in a sneer, he would watch as Ruth and Susan, one on each side of John, came hurrying up the main road. As they turned the corner he would look away, never answering the bright "Hello there, Simon!" which, to Ruth's annoyance, Dad always insisted on giving him. In the first couple of weeks of school, Simon was little more than an irritating nuisance – a bothersome, buzzing fly which would not go away. As he grew keener to assert himself in the group, he adapted his tactics and began bullying other less confident children. Not only would he run off with the girls' skipping rope. he would actually whip other children with it. Frequently he would stick out his large foot to trip people up, both in the classroom in the narrow aisles between desks and out in the playground.

He had first teased Ruth with the "golliwog" taunt in her third week at the school, but that had not disturbed her unduly, especially since Dad had found a plausible and amusing explanation for it, saying that it was on account of her lovely little dark curls. With increasing anxiety, however, she perceived that he had his eye trained on her as a target for more sinister activities. Sitting on the steps in the playground with Susan in break times, she would watch his moves warily, expecting him to come in her direction. Susan still adopted the same bored superior tone when Simon addressed her as "Jewy", but even she refrained from calling him "Simple Simon" any more.

The attack that Ruth anticipated was a little while longer in coming: it did not materialize until the Wednesday of the fourth week of the term, when summer was fast becoming a reality and playtimes were longer. Simon was having trouble maintaining his position in the boys' corner of the yard. Some of the boys were jeering at him. "Simple Simon, Simple Simon met a pieman!" they shouted, pushing him out of their circle. He stood alone, disoriented in the centre of the playground, searching for a victim on whom to vent his frustration. His gaze settled on Ruth, who was watching him nervously from the steps where she and Susan were sitting. Susan was chattering about her cousin, Samuel, whose bar mitzvah she had been to the previous Saturday. Samuel lived in a big house with two bathrooms and two gardens, front and back, and his mother, Susan's aunt on her mother's side, was very rich and wore rings, huge rings, on every finger of both hands.

Ruth was less impressed than she should have been by this information, for she was concentrating on Simon's movements. As she suspected, he started coming towards her with a malicious grin. "Golliwog, golliwog," he yelled, "your dad's a wog! Wog, wog, your dad's a wog!"

Susan stopped in mid-sentence, indignant at having her account of Samuel's party interrupted, and called out: "Do go away, goy boy! Leave us alone!"

For her part, Ruth was aghast at Simon's stupidity. Why did he call her dad a wog? Dad had sleek black hair, not curly, permed hair like hers. She might look like a golliwog, although her curls were now getting looser, but Dad in no way resembled her black doll with his red and white stripy trousers and blue jacket. She laughed at Simon, thinking that, after all, he was not pursuing her with malicious intent but was joking in a way best known to himself.

Deflated at his lack of success, Simon slunk away. Susan was about to take up the thread of her account again when Ruth asked her: "Why did he call my dad a wog? Do you know why?"

Susan shrugged her shoulders with a knowledgeable air. "I expect it's because your poppa has black hair and a dark skin and looks like he comes from somewhere else."

This answer was most unsatisfactory, because it was so wrong. "My dad comes from here," Ruth asserted defiantly. "Well, I mean he comes from Nan's house, not anywhere else. Anyhow, what about your poppa?" She visualized Jacob's appearance, so unlike Susan's or Susan's mother's. "He has dark skin and black hair and a black beard, too."

Susan had a ready answer, "Yes, but Simon already calls me 'Jewy', so he can't call me 'wog' as well, and anyhow he hasn't ever seen my poppa."

Ruth was still watching Simon. He had gone back to the group of boys and was whispering to them, his head lowered in the centre of their group. They looked round and surveyed Ruth from the far corner of the schoolyard. Ruth wished that the bell would ring.

"What do you think they are doing?" she asked Susan.

"I don't know," Susan replied apprehensively. "Let's go in: we can say we need to go to the cloakroom."

Too late the two girls stood up to go indoors. Simon and his gang were already halfway across the yard, chanting a phrase, parrot fashion, at Ruth under Simon's direction. "Your mum's a tart and she's in prison! Your mum's a tart and she's in prison! Ruth's mum's a tart and she's in prison!" they mocked, coming closer and forming a semicircle around the bottom of the steps.

There was nothing funny about this: it was not a joke, and was not intended to be one. Images of Shirley, slender and forlorn, lying on her bed, the enchanted princess, not the wicked witch, rushed through Ruth's mind. Anger and indignation boiled inside her, stifling her breath and sending tingling sensations to the tips of her fingers. In a split second, she jumped off the bottom step, put her head down and charged into Simon's midriff, catching him completely off guard. He screamed and toppled over backwards, hitting his head on the ground. The boys laughed scornfully at him as he picked himself up. Clutching his stomach with one hand and rubbing the back of his head with the other, he went off bawling in search of a teacher.

The boys dispersed with respectful glances at Ruth. Her head in a whirl and startled at her own audacity, she was on the point of resuming her seat on the steps when she caught sight of Mr Green, the Headmaster, who was looking out of his office window on the right of the entrance. She did not like the way he was observing her, for there was no doubt that he had been a witness to the scene which had just taken place. The bell rang. Ruth crept back into school, trying to hide behind Susan, but, as she had feared, Mr Green was waiting for her in the doorway of his office.

He addressed her fiercely, "You, child, what's your name?"

"Ruth Platt," she replied meekly.

"Well, Ruth Platt, step into my study, please. I want a word with you."

Ruth obeyed, quaking with fright.

"Right," he said in a business-like manner when he had closed the door, "what do you think you were doing just now in the playground, head-butting that poor boy? I saw you, you know, so don't pretend you didn't do it."

"He said my—" Ruth began, searching for the appropriate words to describe the ignominy to which Simon had subjected her, her father and her mother. She was interrupted brusquely before she had even completed the first sentence.

"I don't want to hear any tales," Mr Green interjected. "Just explain what sort of demon it was that made you do such a terrible thing to Simon. I won't have children behaving like that in my school."

He waited for her to reply, but there was nothing she was able to bring to her own defence, since he had refused to listen to the insults that Simon had flung at her. "Right then. If you've nothing to say to explain your behaviour, I shall have to teach you a lesson." He picked up a newspaper from his desk, folded it methodically lengthwise and then, without speaking, took hold of Ruth's right hand, palm facing upwards, and straightened out the fingers. "This is for hitting Simon," he declared as he brought the newspaper down onto the palm of her hand. "This is for telling tales," he said as he brought it down for the second time, "and this is to remind you not to do it again. And you can come and apologize to that boy at lunchtime."

The smart from the final blow brought tears of pain to Ruth's eyes, but it was not until she was left standing in the empty corridor outside the Headmaster's office that hot tears of anger at the injustice and humiliation began to flow. She tried to soothe the burning palm by holding it against the cool wall while wondering what to do next. Should she go back to her classroom and then await the additional indignity of being summoned to the Headmaster's study in the lunch hour, as he had instructed, to say sorry to Simon? Or should she run away? Where would she go? She was not sure of the way to Dad's office, since she had only been there twice, on the two previous Wednesday afternoons when he had collected her from school and taken her back there for the rest of the day so that she would not have to go to Susan's ballet lesson. Home would be locked up.

She was staring at the blank, cream-painted wall, still pressing her hand against it wherever she could find a cool patch, when she heard her name spoken.

"Ruth, whatever are you doing here out of your classroom?" Recognizing the voice she turned a tear stained face to Miss Lake, the music teacher, who was looking at her in puzzlement. "Oh, poor little Ruth!" Miss Lake exclaimed on seeing her tears. Bending down to Ruth's level, she asked solicitously: "Tell me what has happened." Afraid of voicing the true explanation, Ruth simply held out the palm of her right hand. Miss Lake was shocked. Although she was fairly short, she had to bend down further and take her glasses off to peer at the outstretched palm. Gently she ran her cool fingers over it. "Come on, we'll go to the cloakroom and run it under the cold tap, then you can tell me what happened."

In the pungent atmosphere of the cloakroom, Miss Lake produced a clean, sweet-smelling handkerchief to wipe Ruth's eyes, before holding her hand under cold running water. The water eased the pain of the hand, but the inner hurt was less easily assuaged. "Now, tell me all about it," Miss Lake urged, sitting down on a narrow bench beneath the coat pegs. At first Ruth said nothing, fearful that to confide in Miss Lake would be telling tales, which might incur further punishment. However, Miss Lake was so kind and so persuasive that at last the words came gushing out in a torrent of despair.

"Mr Green hit me with the newspaper – three times."

"Why?" Miss Lake frowned at the unlikelihood of such a thing.

"Because I knocked Simon over," Ruth confessed.

"What? A tiny little girl like you knocked that enormous boy over? I don't believe it!" said Miss Lake stifling an inappropriate grin.

Ruth nodded. "With my head," she added, in an attempt to confirm the truth of her story.

"Good gracious me!" Miss Lake exclaimed. "But I don't understand why. It's not like you to be violent. He must have done something to you first. What did he do to you?"

Ruth took time to consider her answer. It was plain to her by now that the "golliwog" and "wog" taunts had been as malicious as the reference to Shirley's whereabouts. "He called me a 'golliwog' and my daddy a 'wog', and he said my mummy was a 'jam tart' and she was in prison," she replied in a whisper.

"Heavens above!" Miss Lake's threw up her hands and shook her head, tossing her frizzy hair from side to side. "Didn't you tell Mr Green what he said?"

"He wouldn't let me; he said that was telling tales," Ruth replied, sniffing.

"I see," Miss Lake said pensively. "Well, I think I had better take you back to your class, if you're all right now, and then I'll see what I can do to sort it out."

She steered Ruth in the direction of the classroom, where a hush greeted her arrival as the other children, especially the boys, craned their heads round to look at her and followed her passage to her desk with awed expressions. One of the boys, cheerful and round-faced, who sat at the back of the class, even whispered to her as she passed his desk. "You were terrific!" Unbeknown to Ruth, Miss Lake then returned to the Headmaster's study; she knocked on the door and with a determined step went straight in.

Apart from a persistent soreness in her right hand, there were no apparent further adverse repercussions for Ruth, although she was awaiting them on tenterhooks. She was not summoned to the Headmaster's study in the lunch hour after all. Thereafter, not only did Simon give her a wide berth: he ceased to bother Susan as well. Among the children, the incident raised Ruth's status to that of a heroine. It became a passport to any playground game she chose to join, and she was showered with so many promises of invitations to birthday parties that Susan became quite jealous.

In that same lunch hour, the round-faced boy from the back of the class came up to her and introduced himself.

"Hello," he said, "I'm Jimmy, I live round the corner from you. I am going to marry you."

Ruth found this mode of introduction perfectly acceptable, for she liked Jimmy's friendly face and his openness of manner.

"What's your name?" she asked.

"I've already told you, I'm Jimmy," he replied.

"No, no, I mean your other name, what is it?"

"Oh, that, it's Evans, Jimmy Evans." He watched her closely, not sure what particular significance should be attached to his surname.

"That's all right. I shall be Mrs Evans, Ruth Evans. I like that."

Ruth smiled approvingly, and Jimmy put his arm round her. "I'll tell my mummy and then you can come to tea," he announced confidently.

It was quickly arranged at the end of the school day: Jimmy told his mother that he wanted to invite Ruth home to tea because he was going to marry her, and she raised no objection. Jimmy's mother then conferred with Ruth's father, who was waiting to take her back to his office for the rest of the afternoon while Susan went to her ballet class, and he readily agreed, grateful for the unexpected offer of help.

"So I must call you Mrs Evans then?" Jimmy's mother said playfully to Ruth in her sing-song voice. "Jimmy tells me he's going to marry you." Embarrassed that a private agreement should so quickly be made public, Ruth grinned sheepishly in reply.

The new arrangement, which soon became permanent on Wednesday afternoons, worked to everyone's advantage. Ruth no longer had to go either to Susan's ballet class or to Dad's office, where she had had to make herself as inconspicuous as possible for a long time, sitting very quietly in a corner with a book on her knees. Her father was relieved of the responsibility of meeting her from school and occupying her for two hours in his office, and Jimmy apparently had his heart's desire, a girlfriend of heroic stature, admired by all, whom he was going to marry. On that first Wednesday afternoon, Ruth was so delighted to have a new friend, especially one who had such a vast selection of unfamiliar toys, that, although her hand was still very sore, the shock of the brutal experience of earlier that day began to wear off.

In Jimmy's house, the front room was given over to his toys, many of them new. There were piles of red-and-blue bricks, with which they set about building themselves a house to live in. There were clockwork cars and buses, and a clockwork railway which, Jimmy said, his Uncle Frank had sent him from America. Often Jimmy's mother would come and sit cross-legged on the floor to join in their games. Short and stocky, she was scarcely more than a child herself. Her face, like Jimmy's, was as round as the full moon and just as pale, with the features of a sparrow, a hooked beak for a nose and beady, brown eyes, framed by a mop of straight brown hair.

Her bird-like resemblance did not end with her appearance for, standing at the stove in her tiny kitchen, she sang with the ease and the lyricism of a lark soaring above the fields on a fine spring morning. Her voice transported Ruth back to Nan's house and the fields at the end of the garden where, before her departure, the germinating wheat had been sending a fine green haze over the ploughed earth, blessed by the trill of the ascending larks. She marvelled at the endless variety and versatility of Mrs Evan's repertoire, preferring her to stay in the kitchen and sing because, whenever she joined in their games, her rhapsodic outbursts of song were replaced by an endless, irrepressible running commentary on every move on the Snakes and Ladders board, or whatever game they happened to be playing. "Look out Jimmy, boyo! There's a snake waiting to gobble you up if you throw a three!" she would yell with uncontrolled excitement, or, "Well done, the new Mrs

Evans" – meaning Ruth – "you've hit the long ladder with that five!" When she herself happened to fall on a snake or a ladder, Jimmy's mother would scream with such terror or delight that you might have believed that her very existence depended on the next move.

For such a small person she was capable of making an excessive amount of noise, yet Ruth was fascinated by her and, at the same time, not a little scared, because she never knew what sort of sound might issue forth from her next. One minute she would be apparently carried away high on the crest of a sweet-sounding melody, but the next she would be giving Jimmy a hard slap and reprimanding him in an unknown tongue for picking his nose or biting his nails.

Scowling, Jimmy would refrain from the offending exercise and then would beam at Ruth, saying in language she could understand, "It's all right, you can bite your nails if you like, she won't hit you!"

Ruth was not taking any chances. She hid her hands behind her back to hide her already severely bitten nails. Jimmy would reply to his mother in her own language, and whatever he said usually had the effect of making her grab the rolling pin and chase him round the room until they both ended up in a giggling on the floor. Ruth would watch these antics mistrustfully, not knowing how to interpret them or whom to support. It was even worse when Jimmy's father was at home, because he would join in and the three of them would roll on the floor, laughing hysterically and shouting in their unintelligible language at the tops of their voices. Then she would count the minutes till her own father arrived and she could escape.

When Dad called for her on the first evening, she had so much to tell him about Jimmy's house and his toys that the Simple Simon episode was all but forgotten. It was not until later, when she was having her bath and he was washing her with the flannel that he noticed the red weals on the palm of her right hand.

A look of horror crossed his face. "Ruthie, what have you done to your hand?" he asked.

"That's where Mr Green hit me," she replied.

"What do you mean?" he asked in bafflement.

She tried to explain. "Mr Green hit me because I knocked Simple Simon over. He had been nasty to me." She knew as she told the tale that she was not doing herself justice, but she was by now so tired and agitated by everything that had occurred that day that she wanted to put the whole sorry business out of her mind.

"Poor Ruth!" Dad exclaimed, bending down to kiss the bruised hand. "I'm so sorry!"

As she feared, he then wanted more details – details that she was unwilling to give. For instance, he wanted to know precisely why she had knocked Simon over – itself, admittedly, an improbable achievement. She would not provide the answers he insisted upon, because she loved him too much to repeat to him, even at second-hand, the words that Simon had flung at her, since by now she had fully realized that "wog" was a very ugly word, one which would hurt Dad if she were so much as to pronounce it in his hearing. She tried to fob him off with vague answers such as "Simon was rude to me" and "Simon is a bully".

Dissatisfied but unable to extract a more convincing account from her, Dad became less sympathetic. "The fact that Simon's a bully is no excuse for you to behave badly. We expect better things of you," he remarked critically.

Ruth smarted under the sting of this reprimand on account of the injustice of it, mild though it was by comparison with Mr Green's. If only Dad knew how loyally she had been defending him and Shirley, he would not scold her in this way, but would praise her instead.

"You must remember," Dad was saying, "that if you behave badly, there's always a price to pay. You may have to pay it yourself or you may find that other people suffer as a result of your behaviour."

Ruth did not know what he was talking about; she had suffered enough for one day and had paid a very heavy price for defending other people who did not appreciate what she had done for them. She yawned deliberately to indicate to her father that she was too tired to listen to any more of his moralizing, but was gratified to hear him say, "Still, I don't like the way you've been treated at all. I think we'd better leave early tomorrow morning so that I can come and have a word with Mr Green."

25

Their special efforts to leave home early the following morning and all Dad's good intentions about "having a word with Mr Green" came to an untimely end on Susan's front doorstep. They rang the bell and stood waiting for Susan, who was always ready to leave even when they arrived early. Ruth pushed open the flap of the letter box and peered through, calling Susan by name. In the silent passage there was no sign of movement.

"Try shouting more loudly," Dad suggested, for by now he was growing impatient.

After a further interval, there were stirrings upstairs, as of feet padding across the landing; then Ruth's call to Susan was echoed urgently by a deep male voice, easily recognizable as Jacob's. Through the letter box, Ruth saw Jacob stampeding down the stairs, battling to pull on his dressing gown as he came, followed at a snail's pace by Susan, who was rubbing her eyes and yawning. Jacob hurried to the front door. With an expansive gesture, he put his arms first around Dad and then around Ruth. "Come in, my friends, come in!" he exclaimed, his accents even more guttural than usual, as both tears and smiles fought for domination of his facial muscles. "Come in and celebrate! This is a very special day! It is a boy! I have a new son, an English son, and we are calling him Benjamin!"

Dad shook his hand warmly. "Congratulations, Jacob! We're very pleased for you – aren't we, Ruth?"

Ruth assented but did not speak; she was too staggered at the news. Susan stood in the passage behind Jacob, wearing a very sulky expression, and there was no sign of Rachel. Jacob sent Susan back upstairs to get dressed while he recounted how Rachel had gone by ambulance to the nursing home in the early hours, and he had spent most of the rest of the night in the phone box, which fortunately was close to his front door, ringing for news every half-hour or so until they told him that the baby had arrived safely. This of course was why he was still asleep at eight-thirty in the morning. As Jacob was having the day off, he told them not to wait for Susan: he would bring her to school later and would collect the two girls that afternoon. Thereafter his mother-in-law would be coming to stay, so the household and all other arrangements would run normally.

As a result of so much delightful if perplexing news, far from being early as planned, Ruth was late for school. As she and Dad ran up the road, there was no time to discuss the advent of the new baby or for Dad to go in for the promised word with Mr Green. Out of breath, Ruth sank thankfully into her seat in the classroom, but her concentration kept straying from her work, because the mystery of the unforeseen event constantly surged through her mind. It was very odd that the baby had arrived so suddenly without anyone appearing to have known that he was coming. Indeed, Susan had not so much as mentioned the fact that she was going to have a little brother. As for Rachel, Ruth was speculating why it was that she had had to go to a nursing home to collect him, when it struck her that Susan's house, like her own, had no garden – so, naturally, there was nowhere for the fairies to leave a baby. Perhaps nursing homes, like hospitals, had large gardens with lots of flowers and bushes where people who did not have gardens of their own went to collect their babies.

These questions occupied her fully, diverting her attention from her sums to the extent that when Susan arrived late in school with her father, Miss Dunstan was standing over Ruth's desk, eyeing her efforts with a sharply critical eye. "This is not very good, Ruth," she was saying. "What have you been doing all this time? You haven't had Susan here to distract you, but you've only done two sums. I think you deserve a slap on the hand." The ruler was poised to come down onto Ruth's hand when Miss Dunstan suddenly withdrew it. She explained her restraint by pointing it at Ruth's hand and saying, "On second thoughts, I gather that hand of yours has suffered enough lately.

When I have had a word with Susan's father, you can come out to the front and do your sums at my desk."

Though Ruth was thankful for the special dispensation, this alternative punishment of standing out at the front beside Miss Dunstan's desk meant that it was not possible to whisper to Susan, whose desk was next to her own. Then, at playtime, by a twist of fate, on the very day when Ruth would have preferred to sit quietly on the steps with Susan, discussing the circumstances of Benjamin's birth, all the other children wanted Ruth, the class heroine, to participate in their games. Susan, however, was not inclined to be at all communicative in the first playtime, so Ruth allowed herself to be pulled away – first by Jimmy, who prevailed upon her to play catch with his gang of boys, and secondly, when she was tired of so much running, by Judy Fitch, one of the girls who had been at Mrs Cox's. Judy with a gaggle of girls was playing skipping games and insisted that Ruth should be the leader of the group. Simon stood alone, throwing stones at the tree in the corner of the yard.

In the lunch hour, when it was too hot to play energetic games and all the children were lolling lethargically round the edge of the playground, Susan began to unburden herself. She did not mention the baby. Her whole attention was focused irritably on the arrival of Baba, her grandmother, later that day.

"She's horrible, she's cross all the time," Susan grumbled. "You're so lucky, Ruth, your nan sounds so nice." She sighed. "When Baba comes, I'm not allowed to eat what I want and I can't come out to play on Saturdays; I have to stay indoors doing nothing. And she's going to have my room and I've got to sleep in the box room where Davy's got all his things. It's not fair!"

Susan's description made her grandmother sound like a terrifying witch, contrary to Ruth's belief that all grandmothers must be as kind and gentle as Nan. "How long is she coming for?" she enquired, and then added helpfully: "I sometimes sleep in the box room, you know."

Susan ignored this last remark, preferring to dwell on the horrors of life with her grandmother. "Oh, ages," she sighed.

"Poppa says Momma will be away in the nursing home for two weeks, and then Baba will stay to look after her when she comes home."

Ruth frowned. "Why does it take two weeks to bring the baby home?" she asked.

"Well," said Susan with her knowing air, "it takes a long time for the mummy to recover from having the baby; it's very painful, you know, pushing him out of your tummy." Ruth drew in a sharp breath, startling Susan. "You do know, don't you, that babies come out of their mummies' tummies?" she asked, casting a suspicious glance at Ruth's stunned expression.

"Yes, of course I do – well, no, not really – I'm not sure," Ruth stammered, thrown into confusion by what she had just heard.

"Babies grow in their mummies' tummies," Susan announced authoritatively, "that's why Momma was so fat, didn't you notice?"

"Yes I did notice, but I didn't know why," Ruth admitted in embarrassment. A sudden inspiration prompted her to catch Susan off guard. "And you didn't know either, did you?"

Susan had to confess that she did not, and that it was only that morning, when her poppa had told her the news about the baby and had explained how it had happened, that she herself had found out why her momma had become so fat.

Reeling from the death blow dealt to the precious fantasy world of her own construction, Ruth managed to summon the presence of mind to formulate one logical question. If babies were not brought by the fairies and placed in lovely gardens, how did they get into the mummies' tummies? Susan had suddenly become very well versed in all the answers, and this one was no exception. "The daddies put them there."

Ruth screwed up her face. "They can't, you're teasing," she said. "How can they?"

"Poppa said that when you get married, the daddy plants a little seed in the mummy's tummy."

Ruth was appalled. "I don't believe you," she replied defiantly, but Susan simply said: "It's true."

Susan's story disturbed Ruth deeply, yet there was no one with whom she might discuss it, as it was not a subject about which she wished to challenge her father. She suspected that he would be inclined to brush it off, as he always did when faced with an awkward question, so she was reduced to debating it in her customary fashion, at night in bed with only her dolls for company. The implications for herself extended beyond the physical reality, because, if she were no longer to believe that the fairies had left her in Nan's garden, neither could she believe that they had intended Evelyn to find her. The stark truth, if Susan was to be trusted, was that she had grown from a little seed planted by Dad in Shirley's tummy, so Shirley was her mother and always had been. One thing was absolutely certain: she was never going to marry Jimmy Evans if that was what marriage was all about. She confided as much to Susan. "I don't think I want to marry Jimmy Evans," she said. "I might have to push a baby out of my tummy and that would be horrible!"

Whatever the truth about the facts of life, Susan was right about one thing: her grandmother, Baba, was a formidable person. It was not that she was particularly unkind; indeed, when she met the girls from school every afternoon, she would take them for a stroll in the park or buy them sweets before taking them home for tea, and she always enquired with interest about their day in school. She was, however, such a stickler for cleanliness, tidiness, correct posture, politeness and propriety in every form that she ruled the house with a rod of iron, with the result that Susan did not have a minute's respite from her attentions, unless somehow she and Ruth escaped out into the street to play.

Small and wiry, dynamic and fine-boned, Baba held forceful opinions on everything under the sun, especially on the upbringing of children, and had no compunction about voicing those opinions wherever she went. To Susan's overwhelming embarrassment, she would accost mothers in the street to point out that their children were walking with hunched shoulders, or with their hands in their pockets, or that their babies were not properly protected against the sun. While Susan turned her back, trying to pretend that Baba was nothing to do with her, Baba exerted such charm over her victims that, although taken aback, the mothers always expressed gratitude for her concern.

"Why is your Baba so fierce?" Ruth asked Susan after one of these episodes.

"Well, Momma says she came from a place called 'Rusha' a long time ago, and the people there are very fierce, much fiercer than Baba," Susan replied.

"Why do you call her Baba?" Ruth persevered.

"It's Rushan, short for Babushka, I think it means granny."

Although Susan was pleased with herself at being the purveyor of such exotic information, she was less pleased when she discovered that Baba regarded herself as an authority on the ballet – particularly the Russian ballet – and, after attending Susan's ballet class for the first time, was so shocked by her granddaughter's incompetence that she set herself the task of improving her balletic technique, with practice sessions every day in the narrow confines of the front room. She would reprimand Susan in her own tongue, which sounded like a bag of marbles rattling in her mouth. "*Niet, niet, dievushka!*" she would complain, shaking both her head and her finger at Susan. "You must hold your head up and your back straight, then arch your arms and point your toe, using all the muscles in your leg!" Susan glowered angrily, not daring to complain.

Baba's next ploy was to encourage Ruth to practise with Susan. Not realizing that she was simply being used as a stooge, Ruth was thrilled and then flattered when Baba liberally praised the speed and agility with which she picked up the movements that Susan had been learning in class. Baba's ploy was short-lived because, wily though she was, she was no match for her young granddaughter, who detested these sessions. As as she heard Baba moving the furniture aside for a Susan would grab Ruth's arm and drag her out Only when she already had her hand on the front door would she call out to tell Baba out to play, without saying where. Then, ta advantage of Ruth's friendship with Jimmy Evans, she would race off with Ruth in tow to his house round the corner, leaving Baba to mutter peevishly at the disobedience and utter lack of discipline of the younger generation.

Susan continued to make herself scarce, disappearing to Jimmy's house even when Rachel came home, though not on account of Baba's threats of ballet practice, for they had receded now that Baba had other more important concerns, namely the care of her new grandson. Baba's interest in Susan's prowess as a ballet dancer diminished as rapidly as her solicitude for the new baby's upbringing increased. "*Niet, niet, dievushka!*" she now chided her daughter instead of her granddaughter. "You must sit him on the potty, *dievushka*," she commanded, producing a minute blue pot, large enough for only the smallest of behinds. "If he doesn't start now, he will never learn, and you will always have problems with him."

Rachel took her mother's fussing patiently, in good part, quietly keeping her own counsel. Politely disregarding most of the advice, she left the two-week-old infant to perform his business as and when he chose, in the privacy of his towelling nappies. Her experience with Susan, with whom she had scrupulously followed her mother's dictates, had convinced Rachel that no amount of training at however premature an age would ever suffice to counteract the force of the highly individual grandmaternal genes which her daughter must have inherited. Predicting a hopeless fate for the new baby, doomed already to a life of dissipation and profligacy, Baba marched off to the kitchen, where she battled noisily against the odds in an effort to maintain her kosher principles – already, she declared, sadly undermined in this degenerate age – in the diminutive space and the imperfect conditions.

One effect of the individuality of Susan's genes was that they brooked no rivalry, least of all the rivalry of a new sibling. David, ten years her senior, had been more like a third parent ɔ her than a half-brother, and since independence, which ɔrded with his natural wanderlust, had been forced on him a very early age, he did not claim any proprietorial rights over the second home and family which his refugee father had established in England. On the contrary, his aim had always been to leave home as soon as possible, and after a number of false starts he was fulfilling that aim successfully in the Merchant Navy. He came home on leave from time to time, but always found the small terraced house so unbearably cramped that he habitually invented some excuse to cut his leave short and make again for the open seas.

Fiercely possessive by nature, Susan had only to take one look at Benjamin and hear him howl to be convinced that he was likely to cause irreparable disruption to her pampered way of life. She resolved, there and then, that she would have as little to do with him as possible, and she was as good as her resolve. To put it into practice, she regularly took herself off to Jimmy's. She lost no time in telling Jimmy of Ruth's change of heart over the question of their marriage, whereupon he automatically transferred his affections to her, so that his house became a natural place for her to seek asylum. Jimmy made no attempt to disguise the fact that Susan had usurped Ruth's place in his esteem and said so to Ruth one day when Susan had allowed him to kiss her, a privilege which Ruth had not yet accorded him.

"I'm not going to marry you any more," he told Ruth bluntly. "I'm going to marry Susan, but you can still come to tea on Wednesdays."

Far from being hurt by this candid pronouncement, Ruth was rather relieved by it, for she had no regrets about her decision not to marry Jimmy, and she was finding her visits to his house less and less agreeable. When they were together, he would keep running his hands all over her body, rumpling her clothes and pinching her in a way that caused her acute embarrassment. Susan might well like that sort of behaviour, but Ruth preferred to play out in the street with the gang of local children rather than alone with him in his house. She endured the prospect of spending Wednesday afternoons in his company because there was no alternative. Otherwise, when Susan was playing at Jimmy's, Ruth was happy to be left behind, for she had another, much more engaging interest.

When Benjamin came home from the nursing home, Ruth was enchanted by him. Never had she seen such perfection on such a miniature scale. It scarcely mattered where he came from, because he himself was a miracle in human form. His eyes, as bright as two stars in his smoothly sculpted face, bewitched her; his tiny fingers with their powerful grasp and even smaller fingernails, all present and correct, enchanted her. She wanted nothing more than to hold the minute, fragile body close to her own – and this, since Susan was never at home, she was allowed to do to her heart's content.

"What should I do without you, Ruth? You are such a help," Rachel declared as Ruth willingly rushed up- and downstairs, fetching and carrying tiny garments, bottles and nappies, cotton wool and ointment. While Susan played with Jimmy or lounged with him on a settee elsewhere, Ruth would stand watching as Rachel changed Benjamin's nappies, fascinated that his anatomy was so different from her own.

"I wish I had a little brother," Ruth sighed on one of these occasions.

"Well, who knows, perhaps one day you will have a little brother too, and what a good sister you will be for him," Rachel remarked encouragingly.

For weeks Ruth thought of little else. She longed for a baby, she said prayers at school assembly, begging for a little brother, and finally she asked her father.

"Do you think we could have a baby brother one day?" she enquired one evening a couple of weeks later as he was leaning over to tuck her up in.

"It would be nice," he said, brushing his hair away from his face as he bent over her, "but I don't think it will be possible. Don't say anything about it to Shirley, will you, Ruthie darling?" he continued, "it would make her very unhappy. We don't want to upset her, do we, as soon as she comes home? And she will be coming home soon, I hope."

Her hopes dashed, Ruth did not respond.

He added, "Oh, and perhaps when she comes home you shouldn't talk about Benjamin. He's lovely, I know, but it would be better not to talk about him: it would upset Shirley. In frustration and bitter disappointment at the ever-growing litany of forbidden topics, Ruth shunned his goodnight kiss.

Unlike her father, she wasn't at all sure that she was hoping for Shirley's early return home, nor had she had any desire to repeat the terrifying experience of that one and only visit to see her in hospital, so she was quite happy when, on Sunday afternoons, her father arranged for her to go and play with Susan. While he cooked the lunch, she would spend the morning colouring a picture for him to take to her mother, then after lunch, protesting his gratitude to the Meyers, he would leave her with Rachel.

"You mustn't worry," Rachel insisted on the first occasion. "We love having her, she's no trouble – in fact she is a great help to me with the baby, and she is helping Susan come to terms with his existence." She added, "It hasn't been easy, you know, John – Susan resents little Ben. I suppose she's held centre stage for too long."

None of this was very intelligible to Ruth, except for the bit about helping Susan become fond of her little brother, so she nodded happily when her father said, "Now, Ruth, make sure you let Susan play with Benjamin too, won't you?"

As she closed the front door, Rachel asked, "Ruth, Ben needs changing, would you go and get a clean romper for him, there's a good girl?" Ruth scampered upstairs and found Susan sitting on the top step. Susan was pleased to see her, but declared sullenly, "I'm really cross. Baba is in the sitting room having her nap, and if I go in there, she'll start bossing me about, wanting me to practise the piano or ballet steps, and Momma keeps wanting me to do things for the baby, and Poppa is away working. I don't think I want to be a ballet dancer any more."

"Well, why don't you help your momma?" replied Ruth. "Then you'd be too busy when Baba wakes up to do anything else." Susan admitted that this was a good idea, and followed Ruth into the bedroom, where she gingerly picked up a romper from the clean pile on the chest of drawers before going downstairs into the kitchen, where Rachel was leaning over Ben, who lay on a towel on the table.

Joy spread across Rachel's face, "Ah, Susan," she said, sounding as matter-of-fact as possible, when she had mastered her expression. "So you've come to help. Ben will be pleased." The baby gurgled and smiled in such a winning fashion that, without even noticing what she was doing, Susan smiled too and put out a finger for him to grasp. Thereafter there was no going back: from that moment she too was captivated by her younger brother.

"I think we might go to the park, as it's a sunny afternoon, don't you?" said Rachel. "We can leave Baba asleep: she's tired after all the cooking and washing she's done today."

Susan was the first to agree and hastily went to put her sandals on, lest Baba should wake up before she slid out of the door. Ruth straightened out the sheets in the pram while Rachel wrapped Ben in a blanket. Baba still dozed as the party slipped quietly away to the park, where they fed the ducks, ate ice creams and listened to the band playing.

This became the accepted routine of most Sunday afternoons that summer. Susan grew to love her small brother, and Ruth felt secure and happy with their family. Her father was sometimes late calling for her, but nobody seemed to mind: Rachel was so grateful for the beneficial effect Ruth was having on Susan that she never complained, and Susan valued Ruth's presence as a deterrent to Baba's interference. While Susan was busily employed attending to her brother, Baba did not feel the need to occupy her in other more demanding pursuits and, in any case, she herself was beginning to tire of all the chores in the household and was keen to escape to her own home.

26

At the end of her first term at school, which was also the end of the school year, Dad asked Ruth, out of the blue, if she would like to spend the summer holidays with Nan and Grandpa. He said that Shirley would not be coming home for a long time after all, and he wasn't sure what she, Ruth, would do on her own in London while he was at work, except perhaps go to Mrs Cox's. He didn't think it was fair to ask Rachel to take her in every day.

After her abrupt and traumatic departure from Beech Grove in the spring, Ruth had hardly dared hope that she would ever be allowed to go there again and she certainly dared not ask. Sometimes she lay awake at night also wondering if she would ever see Nan and Grandpa again. Visions of their remarkable house and its dear occupants brought tears to her eyes, prolonging the misery. When her dad wrote to his parents every Sunday, she always spelt out her name in a large, careful script at the end of the letter and then went out with him to post it. On Tuesday mornings a blue envelope containing letters from Nan and Grandpa would regularly fall onto the doormat. Dad would read the letters while Ruth waited to find out if there were any messages for her. Without fail Nan or Grandpa or both would enclose a scrap of paper with a note and a drawing for her. The note would usually consist of one line that she could read, letting her know that the blackbird was high in the cherry tree, singing to his heart's content, or that Grandpa had had to spend the whole weekend repairing two punctured tyres on his motorbike, or that he and Nan had been on a visit to the seaside and eaten ice creams on the pier. These messages would be illustrated by little pictures, sometimes in black and white, sometimes coloured. There was never any mention of the possibility of a further visit by Ruth, so when her father made his suggestion she jumped at the idea, afraid that if she wavered for even one moment, the offer might not be repeated.

She need not have worried, for one Sunday morning at the beginning of the holidays she and her Dad boarded the train at Liverpool Street; he carried a small suitcase for her, but unaccountably had no luggage for himself.

"Where's your case, Dad?" she asked as he flung hers up onto the rack.

"Oh, I'm not staying in Norhambury," he said, "I must get back to London, so I'll leave you with your Nan and Grandpa. I'll say goodbye to you on the station and catch the next train to be back in time to visit Shirley."

Ruth was not unduly concerned, because she knew that Nan and Grandpa would be at the other end of the line to meet her, and it didn't matter if her father wanted to return to London. He could do what he liked. Adults always did.

He sat down and closed his eyes while she looked out for all those features that he had pointed out to her on her first journey the previous winter, and kept her eyes glued to the window, searching for the farm where Dad had said his cousins lived, but she was not at all sure that she would be able to identify it: there were so many farms and so many farmhouses. He slept for the whole journey, so she had to keep quiet and not ask him which one it was.

Nan and Grandpa were indeed waiting at the station for their son and granddaughter. Grinning with excitement, Grandpa said he had a surprise in store for them. "You won't believe what we've got!" he announced as he swung his granddaughter up in the air at the ticket barrier by way of greeting.

"What is it? Tell me Grandpa!" she begged impatiently.

John watched in silence, biding his time before announcing, "Well, I'm sorry, but I can't hang around to see any surprises, because I have to be on the next train back to London."

His parents' pleasure rapidly changed to dismay, and their faces clouded over. "What! You're not going to stay even for one night?" his mother exclaimed in disbelief. Grandpa was speechless.

"No, I have my ticket here, so I'll leave you to show Ruth the surprise, and I'll get back on the train now. I'll stay for a few days when I come to collect her, though," John added to ease their disappointment. He turned hurriedly on his heel and retraced his steps down the platform with never a backward glance.

Forlornly his parents watched him go.

"What's the surprise Nan?" Ruth piped up, interrupting their sad contemplation of the much-loved receding figure.

"Three guesses," said Nan turning to her and beaming again.

"Have you got a kitten?" asked Ruth hopefully.

"No," came the reply with a shake of the head, and this was also the answer when she asked if they had a puppy. She had run out of questions, but was even more mystified when she saw that they were not walking over to the bus stop outside the station yard, nor was Grandpa's motorbike waiting for them outside the entrance. Instead, they crossed the forecourt and came to a halt beside a small black car.

"Here we are! This is it!" said Grandpa as he unlocked the door.

"Yes, Ruthie," added Nan. "This is it! It's our car. Think what fun we shall have! No more bumping along in that old sidecar. We can go out every day – to the sea, to the city, to the farm, whenever we like. Mind you," she added by way of a warning, to herself rather than to Ruth, "Grandpa won't part with that old bike of his, and he still goes out to Speedway on it." Ruth wasn't bothered that the motorbike stood in its usual position up against the wall in the sideway, for she now regarded it as a friend, even more so since she had been parted from it.

Grandpa did indeed go out to Speedway on the bike, but throughout the weeks of the summer holidays he was so obsessed with his car that he jumped at any opportunity to take it out, to tinker with its engine or to clean and polish it. Ruth as his willing assistant would stand every morning holding a spanner from her very own toolbox – the one she had had to leave behind on her birthday – at the ready while the mechanic himself, with his head under the bonnet, fine-tuned the engine, or she would wring out her cloth in a bucket of soapy water and carefully wipe the slightest trace of mud or grime from the bodywork of his new toy. Then, with his eyes sparkling, Grandpa would declare that a little run to get some petrol and try out the fine-tuning was in order, preparatory to the afternoon's excursion. Ruth would jump into the car and off they would go, not necessarily to the nearest garage for petrol, because, as Grandpa said, the engine had to warm up before he could take it out to test it properly. He was of course well known at whichever garage he went to.

"Two shots and five gallons, is it, Mr Platt?" the attendant would enquire deferentially, although most certainly he already knew the answer.

"That's right," Grandpa would reply with relish, "taking her out this afternoon, down to the sea, most likely, so the little mawther" – here he would gesture to Ruth, patiently sitting in the back – "can fill her lungs with some good sea air and get rid of that smut she breathes in London."

Although lunch would always be waiting for them, Grandpa inevitably needed to open up the bonnet again and make further adjustments after their brief outing. On the way home he would listen keenly to every little sound the engine made. "Mmm," he would say, "tha' sounds a bit rough," or, "Tha's not bad, not bad at all, but I think we can make it even smoother."

Nan would leave him to his own devices out in the driveway, but insisted on calling Ruth in. "Come on, my little Ruthie, it's time you had your lunch: you must be real hungry." She would glance out to where Grandpa was hidden beneath the bonnet and shake her head. "Well, I can't believe it, I've never known Grandpa be late for a meal in all the years we've been married – and why he should start now just for the sake of an old car beats me."

She and Ruth sat down together, and Grandpa's lunch was left to grow cold on the side. Not that that mattered. When he came indoors, he was always too preoccupied to notice that his food was lukewarm and that the gravy had congealed. "Why don't we go to Haverswick this afternoon?"

he might propose, "that road rises up onto the cliffs, and it'll be a good test of the horsepower." Or he might equally express a preference for the east coast to try out the speed on the straight road across the marshes. He was even prepared to take his precious acquisition out in the rain to see how watertight the engine was.

In fact, it proved not to be watertight at all. After they had driven through many deep puddles, they came to rest in a field entrance, where they had to wait hours for it to dry out. But nobody minded. When the windows steamed up, Ruth contented herself with drawing patterns on the misty panes, and Nan and Grandpa snoozed over a cup of tea poured from the thermos flask while the rain poured down outside.

Such waterlogging was rare. The excursions to the sea were usually sun-soaked and trouble-free. Ruth and Grandpa played on the sand building castles, tossed a ball about and paddled in the sea, while Nan walked along the seafront, then watched them play and read a magazine, comfortably settled in a deckchair.

At weekends, at last fulfilling Nan's promise of the previous winter, they went to the farm – not once, but often. When first she saw the house, Ruth was disconcerted, for it was painted black, having forgotten that early glimpse of it from the train when anything new had assumed a wondrous aura in her eyes.

"Why is it black, Grandpa?" she asked, the disappointment audible in her voice.

"Ah," Grandpa explained with a laugh. "Tha's not paint – tha's tar to keep 'em warm and dry."

The house didn't matter, however, for what was important was the farmyard, teeming with all shapes and sizes of feathered life. Around it were the barns where the cows were milked, and the stables, home to a couple of old shire horses and a bright new tractor.

Aunt Dolly was busy in the kitchen churning butter, while her second daughter Eva sat in a corner knitting, when they arrived unannounced one Saturday afternoon. Dolly proved to be a larger and rather more expansive version of Nan.

"Welcome, my dears, to Glebe Farm!" she greeted them all as they stood in the sunlit doorway. "This is a treat! I was hoping you'd come and pay us a visit." Then, when she saw Ruth, she exclaimed loudly, "What a lovely little girl! Isn't she like your Evelyn?" Nan and Grandpa silently registered their agreement. Dolly went on: "Oh, would you believe it? She's wearing that little yellow dress you made for Evelyn, isn't she?" Nan nodded again, probably wishing that she had not unloaded even more of Evelyn's clothes from the wardrobe for Ruth.

Next Dolly addressed Ruth. "And do you play the piano too, littl'un? Your Aunt Evelyn, she were a truly gifted pianist, you should'a heard her!" She turned to Nan. "Don't you remember that concert she gave with that orchestra – in the City Hall, wasn't it? It brought tears to my eyes, it did."

Nan nodded but, otherwise ignoring the question, she answered for Ruth. "Yes, our Ruthie, she's beginning to play the piano. In fact, when she's not out of doors helping Joe, she can't be dragged away from it. My heart alive, you should hear her play! Mozart at six was not a patch on her! I tell you, Dolly, anything you put before her she can play: all those pieces Evelyn was playing at the same age, any of them. And she learns so fast. You should see her little fingers skimming up and down the keys! It's a pity she doesn't have a piano in London, but there you are, there's not much we can do about that." She stressed the "that", and Dolly nodded knowingly. Eva ignored them, but Dolly seemed to regard that as normal.

Uncle George was thin and angular, as quiet as Aunt Dolly was plump and talkative. He and Grandpa were old friends and went off to smoke their pipes together. As for the rest of the family, Ruth was overwhelmed to find how many of them there were. All her dad's six cousins were there with their wives and children. Once Grandpa had proudly demonstrated the new car to all present and gone into a long discussion with Uncle George over which was the best brand of petrol, the younger cousins of her own generation took Ruth to see the latest additions to the farmyard – the chicks, the ducklings and the goslings. Ruth held back while her cousins shooed the parent geese away.

"They are the stupidest things," said Andy, the eldest. "You don't need to be afraid of them, Ruth." Ruth wasn't so sure; she did not want to find herself embattled with one of those honking, squawking monsters.

She preferred to go with Wizzie, who was a year older than her, to look for eggs hidden in the straw in the hen coop. The eggs, some a rich brown, some white, were like buried treasure. Sometimes there would even be a few scattered in odd corners out in the run. Then they would all – a dozen or more children – go down to the meadow to see the fast-growing lambs and the doe-eyed calves. They would linger at the fence by the railway line, hoping that an express would come past and shroud them in its grey smoke.

After the first impromptu visit, Ruth and her grandparents were expected at the farm every Saturday afternoon. The next weekend Dad's cousin, Abe, greeted Grandpa with a hearty wave.

"You've come at just the right moment, Uncle Joe. It's our go with that new combine harvester, but cor blast me if it's not giving us a real headache! When it works, it's a miracle, but jus' now there's a problem with the transmission: it's stuck and we can't get it to move. We can't afford to waste time while the fine weather's here."

Grandpa did not have to be asked twice. "Don't you worry your head about tha', ole bor," was all he said, and quickly brought out his toolbox from the boot of the car. In a trice he was down in the field, struggling into dungarees as he went. He had a good look round the mighty machine before selecting a handful of tools and setting to work.

The children crowded round to watch, but he shooed the little ones away, telling them they were blocking his light and only allowing the older boys to help in his task. A couple of hours later, he stood back, wiping his hands on a rag and panting with a rasping cough, while beads of sweat rolled down his face. "There you are, Abe," he croaked, "it's only temp'ry, but

I think it'll see you through. You try starting the ole girl up."
He coughed hard to clear his throat as Abe clambered into
the cab, and moments later the engine began to roar. Then the
ungainly apparatus, a great red hunk of a machine, lumbered
away down the field, emitting clouds of dust and husks as it
scythed through the tall, yellow stalks.

Ruth ran to the edge of the field in fright, although, taking no
notice of her, the other children ran after the harvester, spluttering in its dusty wake. Grandpa came and took her hand in
his oily one. "Don't you worry, my sugarplum," he reassured
her, "that ole machine is eating up the corn, not the children.
You go and play with the others; I'm going to be driving it
soon, and then you can come into the cab with me."

The children took turns to ride in the cab, but after a while,
when Grandpa clambered up into the driving seat, Ruth climbed
up into the cab beside him. It was hot, noisy and cramped, but
also awe-inspiring as the blades gathered up the corn in front
of them in great swathes. Feeling proud and important and
hoping that Nan was watching, she wished her dad was there
to see her; surely he would not stop her doing that. Afterwards
she was given a drink of sharp, fresh lemonade and was sent to
sit in the orchard to take a break from the hot, dusty exercise.

A week later it was fun to watch the baler trundling up and
down the fields behind the tractor, scooping up the straw and
packing it into rectangular blocks. This was the prelude to a
great effort the week after that, when all those bales had to be
heaved up onto the cart by the most able-bodied members of
the family, both young and old – men, women and children.
Grandpa was out there with the workers, while Ruth sat up on
the top of the cart, climbing up as the bales grew higher and
higher around her. Then, with all the younger children, she
rode back to the farm, high above the fields, the people and
the animals. Grandpa did not ride on the wagon. He said, as
he scratched a sore place on his arm, that he'd had enough sun
for one day, so went straight back to the house.

27

The following weekend at the farm after the harvest was in, Nan was picking fruit with Aunt Dolly out in the orchard up a ladder.

"I do hope these will bottle as well as last year's," she observed, rotating a greengage between her fingers: the bloom wore away, leaving a gleaming surface.

"Should do," said Dolly. "It's a good crop, and they've had plenty of sun and rain."

"The gooseberries have come out lovely," Nan added. "Some more currants wouldn't come amiss too so, if there are any left, I'll make another batch of jam and let you have some more pots. Oh, and by the way, how are the raspberries doing this year?"

"Well, they're a bit on the dry side; really they're over now, but you can try them if you like," Aunt Dolly replied.

There was a gap in their conversation while Nan came down her ladder and went to test the raspberries.

"You're right," she said when she came back. "I don't think they'd make a good jam. She moved her ladder to another part of the tree, and as the sisters resumed their discussion, Dolly changed the subject from fruit and jam-making. "And how's your poor John? It sounds to me from your letters like he's got his hands full there."

"You can say that again, Dolly," Nan replied with a sigh. "I just wish he hadn't a-been so silly in the first place. I wish he'd a-gone to the university instead of signing up straight away. Things might hev been different then."

"Well, it was the War, wasn't it?" Dolly sighed. "Mind you, a lot of mistakes were made then."

They both mused on the mistakes for a while, before Dolly broke the silence. "As for her, you can't blame him for that:

she's such a pretty girl." She fell silent again and then continued: "You know Abe saw her when he was on leave once. He said he saw her in a show, and she was a beautiful dancer. Poor thing, she has suffered a lot with that depression of hers and losing a baby too. You hev to feel sorry for her."

"I know," said Nan, "but that's not what we wanted for John. If it hadn't a-been for her, just think of what he might hev done after the War, instead of struggling to get his diploma in night school at the same time as holding down a job. Poor boy, breaks my heart to see him struggle so, it does."

Dolly nodded sagely but remarked, "Well, I doubt he'd hev been able to study after the War, he'd hev been too old. But that dear littl' Ruth, not much of a life for her, is it?"

"No, that's right, that is," Nan agreed. She deftly changed the subject, throwing the ball into Dolly's court. "And what about your boy, Barty, and his wife? Hev they sorted out their problems?"

"Well," answered Dolly, "with five children they had to, didn't they? Though I must say that little one with her blonde hair and her fancy ways, you can see she's not really one of us. But we hev to do our best, and Barty, well, he's very good with her: he insists she's one of his family, and in any case we don't want her to feel she's not wanted. There you are, you see, that was the War again, wasn't it? If he hadn't a-been a prisoner o' war for so long, who knows how different things might hev been."

Ruth had taken a break from the heat out in the fields and had wanted to get away from Wizzie, who was always asking questions about London – for which she, Ruth, didn't have answers, since it had occurred to her that only Shirley would be able to provide those. For instance, she would be able to tell Wizzie where the best dress shops were or where they sold diamonds, but these were not topics that interested Ruth, so Wizzie was left disappointed. Ruth happened to be resting in the shade of a tree in the orchard unbeknown to Nan and Dolly as they carried on their conversation. She listened in fascination and then slipped away on tiptoe back to the field, with the awkward sensation that she had heard things not intended for her ears. As ever she was at a loss to understand the meaning of those enigmatic observations.

Although they spent their afternoons chatting endlessly while picking and sampling the ripe fruit, Aunt Dolly and Nan always had a huge tea ready for all the workers when they came in from the fields. There was bacon and ham from their own pigs, the eggs Ruth and Wizzie had collected earlier, fresh milk, salads from the garden, home-made bread and every imaginable shade of jam, and Aunt Muriel came to join them laden with delicious cakes.

"That's your nan's jam," Aunt Dolly told Ruth. "She always makes our jam for us, and it lasts all year."

Ruth remembered the jars gleaming on the shelf in Nan's pantry and helped herself to a copious spoonful of strawberry jam. While ever silent though seemingly in communion with her clicking needles, Eva continued to knit in her corner, one of the cousins took her a tray of food and drink, and the rest of them sat round the massive farmhouse table with the August sun still streaming in through the open door and the massive black iron range giving out a gentle warmth in the cool of the evening. Ruth and her cousins drank the rich, warm milk while Grandpa helped himself to liberal quantities of Uncle George's home-made cider.

It was over high tea that Ruth gradually came to know her aunts and uncles and army of second cousins. Each week she learnt more names and recognized more faces. Lively Aunt Muriel, the one who brought lots of cakes from her own cottage up the road, was always laughing rather too loudly, and quiet Aunt Eva sat knitting, winter and summer, without saying a word to anyone. Wizzie confided in Ruth that she had heard that Eva had been dropped on her head as a baby and had never recovered. Of the uncles, Abe and Rick shared the running of the farm with their father, while Barty – as they called him – and Freddie had bought their own smaller farms, coming home to help out when required. Some of the cousins were old – Andy was fifteen and Dan his brother was only a year younger. Amy, at twelve, was the eldest of a family of five girls, whom she was well used to marshalling while her parents, Rick and his wife, worked on the farm. Wizzie was the youngest of that family. No one knew why she was called Wizzie – least of all Wizzie herself – but the nickname suited her well: small, bright, blue-eyed and fair, she moved like quicksilver but had a very fierce voice and a commanding personality.

Then there were the twins, Ralph and Peter, who were twelve, and their sister, eight-year-old Elizabeth, known as Lisa. There were several small boys of about Ruth's age, but she and they did not have much to say to each other – and anyway, Wizzie told her that they were a nuisance, because all they wanted to do was to kick a football. She, Wizzie, felt it was her duty to keep them in order, so she bossed them about mercilessly. It was impossible to match up all these children with their parents, but that did not matter, because all the parents looked after all the children and naturally included Ruth in their care. Everyone was friendly; everyone smiled, almost no one regretted not having bathrooms, running water or electricity.

"They say we're going to have running water soon," said Uncle George over supper, "but I doubt it'll be in my lifetime."

"You're wrong there, Father," said Uncle Rick. "And I reckon you might see the electricity installed as well – and that'll be the end of the old oil lamps!"

"Do you have a bathroom at home?" Wizzie enquired of Ruth.

"Well, yes," said Ruth, who had already experienced the quaint little hut down the garden which served as a rather smelly but scrupulously clean lavatory.

"Oh you are lucky, Ruth, I wish we had a bathroom! Can I come to your house?" Wizzie begged.

"Oh, Wizzie, do stop it!" Peter laughed, and quickly made a suggestion relieving Ruth of the need to reply. "Come on, let's show Ruth where we get our water from!"

All the children jumped up and marched off into an outhouse to collect buckets.

"Have you ever seen a pump before, Ruth?" Ralph asked.

She had not, and had no idea what to expect, so she joined in, traipsing down the lane to the village green, carrying a small pail, like everyone else. They made a long, orderly line on the green, queuing up to fill their pails as Ralph and Peter worked the pump.

"You don't want to be a-doing this in the middle of winter, Ruth," Ralph declared. "Sometimes it's so cold the water freezes and won't come up, and then we have to break the ice on our water butts in the garden to get at the water in there. The animals are lucky; we can give them water from the pond, and that doesn't usually freeze over, though sometimes it does and then we have problems."

Because even the smallest children carried their full pails back to the farm, Ruth felt obliged to do the same. The pail was heavy and she struggled under its weight, losing some of the precious liquid as she went. The water was distributed among the families, leaving several buckets at the farmhouse for Uncle George and Aunt Dolly.

Aunt Dolly's resemblance to Nan fascinated Ruth, who had trouble taking her eyes off the pair of them: Dolly was larger certainly, but had the same dark skin and hair, now greying, and the same deep-brown eyes. They were so alike they might be twins. She was on the point of asking when Nan announced, "Well, my dears, we've had a lovely time, but we ought to be going. Our Ruthie gets very tired and needs to go to bed early. It's getting late for her already."

Ruth wished that Nan wouldn't say things like that. It was the cue for Wizzie to turn to her in scorn. "Oh, you do go to bed early, don't you! I wouldn't like that. I don't go to bed till ten o'clock!" she said. Although Ruth had no idea exactly when she went to bed, she was glad after all that Nan was pushing her towards the door, so she ignored Wizzie's comments. As usual, arrangements were made for the following Saturday before Grandpa went out to start the car.

"I know I say it every time we go there, but thank goodness we don't have to get our water from a pump!" Nan observed as they sped home that evening.

Grandpa was so well supplied with farmhouse cider and drove so fast that one might have thought he had filled his petrol tank with it. Accordingly, they arrived home in record time and, because it was still fairly early in the evening, Nan insisted on sorting and washing the fruit as Grandpa unloaded it, ready for the jamming and bottling processes the next day, but as if in apology for embarrassing Ruth in front of Wizzie, did not insist on sending her to bed immediately on their arrival home, tired though she was. Instead, she let her stay up until well past nine o'clock, so that she practised her scales and played a dozen pieces or so, while the fruit was being weighed in the kitchen.

The next morning Nan went to church, leaving Ruth to play the piano while Grandpa worked on his car. "You can pray for the lame and the lazy," he called cheerfully after her as she went out of the front door. Almost as soon as Nan came home, the jam factory started up and, in between spells at the piano, the rest of Ruth's day was spent in the kitchen, stirring the various mixtures of ripe fruit and sugar, and watching Nan pour the green, red and gold liquids into warm jars. Ruth was delighted with the results. Grandpa was less so as the kitchen failed to produce any hot food that day and he had to help himself to slices of cold ham and tomato whenever he felt the pangs of hunger.

Ruth was at her happiest. There was comparatively little time for the piano, but the simple glories of that summer began to dispel the distress of the preceding months and compensated somewhat for that rude interruption to her birthday celebrations when her dad had come to snatch her away so cruelly. The nagging fear that she might never see Nan and Grandpa again diminished as the days wore on and she grew in self-confidence. Nan had frowned on first seeing her curls and was heard to mutter "Whatever next?", but her hair was now growing back to its earlier length, and the curls were unwinding into the wavy locks Ruth had always wanted.

As her hair grew, the memory of all the problems with Shirley began to fade. When she thought about her, which was not very often, she felt a twinge of sympathy for her, there in that horrible hospital place, all alone. She missed her dad, it was true, but she understood that he had to go to work and he had to visit Shirley. He had promised to come for a week at the end of the holiday if Shirley agreed, though Nan insisted that this time Ruth should be informed well in advance of what was happening, to avoid a repetition of the disturbance on her birthday. She pointed out the weeks of the month of August on the calendar, so that Ruth might see how long she would be staying and when her dad would be coming for her; then she turned over the page to September to show when the new school term would begin. Towards the end of the holiday, before her son's arrival, she made Ruth a birthday cake and invited the Carringtons to tea, "to lay the ghost", she said, "of that earlier unfortunate interruption".

Nan was visibly shocked when John did arrive. He was sallow and tired, and said little. She tried to draw him out by kindly asking questions such as how was Shirley now? Was she getting better? When would she be coming out of hospital? She even offered to accompany him and Ruth back to London and keep house for the three of them.

"After all," she remarked, "if I know you, you will be doing everything – the shopping, the cooking, the cleaning and the washing. I don't know how you'll manage. Grandpa can cope for a few days without me – or he can go and stay with Dolly."

John gave a wan smile. "No, no thanks, Mother, it'll be all right, you don't need to come. It'll be fine. I'll do the shopping in my lunch hour, and Ruth and I will go to the market on Saturday mornings. And the cooking is not difficult, because we eat very simply. As for the washing, I must admit, I'll hand that over to Mrs Cox across the road. She's given up her childminding and says she'll be happy to earn a bit of extra cash."

Nan had to be content with this, because for the first couple of days John slept in an armchair or in a deckchair in the garden, without even enough energy to express more than a polite, passing interest in Grandpa's new toy. By the Tuesday, though, he had recovered sufficiently to join them in a daytrip to the sea. He admired the car, inside and out, and was allowed to drive it. Once down on the beach his spirits revived and he played with Ruth, taking her into the sea to paddle while he swam far out.

Nan was worried. "I hope he's not going too far," she said, screwing up her eyes to watch the dark head bobbing in the water.

"Oh, he'll be all right; the tide's coming in anyhow, so it'll bring him back," Grandpa reassured her.

At the weekend, on the Saturday before the return to London, they went to the farm. There John was in his element, joking with all his cousins, kicking a ball about with the smaller boys, touring the fields, picking apples in the orchard and helping to dig early potatoes. Finally, he joined the queue at the pump for water.

"There you are, Aunt Dolly, two extra buckets this week to keep you going."

"Oh, thank you, John dear," Aunt Dolly replied. "Now you make sure and bring your Shirley to see us some time. It'd do her good."

John smiled but said nothing.

On the Sunday morning he ran Ruth's hair through his fingers thoughtfully.

"I think maybe Ruth's hair is getting a bit too long," he said. "Do you think you could trim it a little, Mother?"

Nan regarded him with suspicion but said nothing. She took out a pair of longish, fine scissors from the kitchen drawer.

"You remember these, don't you, John?" she said with a laugh. "These are my old hair-cutting scissors. See, I've still got them. I used to trim your dad's hair with these, Ruthie," she said. "I'm not going to take too much off, mind, a little tidy-up will do." She sat Ruth at the kitchen table and began to snip carefully at the glossy dark curls while Ruth, who was content to let Nan cut and trim, sat patiently without moving. It was so much better like that than her last hair-cutting experience.

As Nan wiped the nape of her neck with a damp cloth, she declared, "There, that'll have to do for her ladyship."

John simply said, "Thank you, Mother."

Casting a worried glance at the curls lying on the kitchen floor, Ruth ran off to look at herself in the long wardrobe mirror, and was pleased to see that she was recognizably herself. Her hair was neither long nor short, and there remained a pleasing trace of a wave, the residue of those tight curls.

She did not go near the piano at any time during the week of her father's visit. All too keenly she remembered the sharp reprimand he had given her after she had mentioned her piano-playing in school and the dramatic effect it had had on Shirley as she lay in hospital. She had decided that silence on that topic was the best policy.

She said as much to Nan. "Dad says Shirley doesn't like the piano, so I mustn't talk about it."

"That is a pity!" Nan replied. "I'd have imagined they would have been so proud of you. But if they don't want to know, then we'll close the door on the piano while he's here and we won't talk about it. A little rest from it will do you good, anyhow. You'll come back to it refreshed; you see if you don't."

28

Although Shirley came out of hospital in the early autumn days after the start of the new school year, Ruth's way of life back in London was much the same as it had been in the summer: Dad took her and Susan to school in the morning and Rachel, pushing Ben in his pram, collected the girls in the afternoon. Ruth then stayed to play with Susan until her father came home. Although Susan was relieved that Baba had gone home, Ruth was disappointed to be deprived of Baba's ballet tuition, especially because during the holidays Jimmy and his parents had moved back to Wales. His mother had often declared that the London soot was getting into her lungs and she was losing her ability to sing – which was true, because she coughed often and had already lost her childish sparkle and energy. On Wednesday afternoons she would lie on the sofa sadly watching Jimmy and Ruth at play, but no longer joined in. To return to Wales was her dream, and finally, when her husband found a job there, her dream was fulfilled.

This change meant that once again Ruth had to sit through Susan's dance classes as tea at Jimmy Evans's on a Wednesday afternoon was no longer an option. Nowadays, however, she found it was not as agonizing as before since, with the knowledge she had already gained from Baba, she knew what to look for. She paid careful attention to the lessons and then practised the steps and moves at home, which was easily done, because at first Shirley stayed in bed all day, every day, and when Dad was at home, he was busy in the kitchen, so she would slip into the front room and cautiously, ever wary of all the china models, try out her steps in there.

Shirley appeared only on the rare occasions when she felt well enough to come downstairs in the evening; even then she scarcely ever took any notice of Ruth, and if she had observed her hair, she said nothing at all about it. She simply sat silently in an armchair, absent-mindedly gazing into the fire, while at the table Ruth ate the supper that her dad had cooked for her. These occasions were awkward. She kept quiet for fear of provoking Shirley, although there was so much she wanted to say to her father, and she judged that conversation would be unwelcome, unlike those evenings when Shirley stayed in bed and she was alone with her father. Then he would quiz her on every aspect of her school day, apart from music, and she would respond spontaneously and enthusiastically, especially now that the bullying had ceased and she was regarded with respect by her schoolmates. Often there were little details from her long summer holidays as yet unsaid that she wanted to share with her dad, but she knew better than to voice them when Shirley was present. And, too, she was bursting to tell him all about the new school term – there was so much to recount.

Not sorry to leave fierce Miss Dunstan behind after only one term in her class, Ruth was positively glad to move up into Miss Lake's class. Miss Lake, the music teacher who had come to her rescue over the head-butting incident, had a bright, airy room which was full of instruments. Her pupils were the envy of the school, because in wet playtimes they were allowed to stay in the classroom and make music. There was the school band, in which Ruth played the triangle, but there was also a Class Two band, which was definitely superior, because the instrumentalists had the benefit of Miss Lake's undivided attention. Each child was permitted to choose his or her preferred instrument, and when Ruth, having recovered her confidence, found the temptation to choose the piano irresistible, Miss Lake did not object. "Why yes, of course, Ruth, I'm glad!" she said encouragingly. "We can play together at first, and then, when you have learnt a little more, you can play on your own. You can come in here and practise when it rains in playtime, though it might be rather noisy with all the other instruments!"

Ruth was delighted, but was careful not to announce this development at home, because she knew for certain that any mention of the piano would spell the end of her playing. Nonetheless, her pleasure at the sight of rain caused her father some puzzlement.

"Oh, good, it's raining!" she would exclaim as Dad drew back the curtains to reveal a dank, drear London sky.

"You are funny, Ruth," he said with the little light laugh that was so typical of him, "but you like the sunshine best, don't you?" This, in Ruth's opinion, was a question which did not require an answer.

Occasionally, even in fine weather, Miss Lake would show her a short exercise, or would tap out a tune, just as Nan had done, and would allow her to stay in to practise it. Although Ruth felt shy at being singled out from the other children, no problems arose from her special position. Not only was there no bullying, but there was not even any teasing as she sat at the piano in the corner of the classroom to do her practising.

Susan was generous in her praise. "You are clever, Ruth, you can always do things I can't." Then, one fine autumn day, as they were sitting on the steps at playtime, she asked, "Don't you have a piano in your house?"

"No," said Ruth, unsure of what was coming next.

"Why not?" asked Susan. "Doesn't everyone have a piano? Poppa makes me practise every day, but I'm no good at it." Ruth hoped she would not have to answer Susan's questions, but Susan persevered: "Why don't you have a piano, then?"

Ruth tried to frame an acceptable answer out of the jumble of uncertainties that revolved in her mind. "I don't know," she said, "I think Shirley doesn't like the piano and doesn't want me to have one. She gets very upset if anyone talks about it. Anyhow, we can't afford it. We are very poor."

Although Shirley's reactions were inexplicable, this was the sum total of what she had been able to fathom about them. She certainly had intimations that these reactions somehow involved her Aunt Evelyn and even her own appearance. As for the financial aspect, she was in no doubt that although her father worked hard, there was no money to spare in their household, except for

Shirley's cigarettes and clothes and perfume. Susan nodded and, when asked, promised that she would never talk about Ruth's piano-playing at home. Unexpectedly, even she understood that Ruth was in a difficult situation and said no more.

As the day was chilly despite the sun, Ruth was again wearing the winter coat that had accompanied her on her travels earlier in the year, but was now too short and too tight for her. The association between the piano, dark hair and Evelyn suddenly reminded her of something that had been in one of the coat pockets. She plunged her hand deep into the right pocket but there was nothing there. She tried again on the left-hand side and, to her relief, felt what she was looking for. Without thinking she pulled the photo out and, of course, Susan was immediately curious to know what she had in her hand.

"Oh, it's nothing," Ruth said, trying to brush her off.

"What is it? I want to see!" cried Susan.

Ruth hesitated before relenting. "Oh, all right then. It's my Aunt Evelyn; she played the piano."

Susan studied the photo. "Ooh!" she exclaimed. "She's so much like you, Ruth. I expect my poppa knows her. Where does she live?"

Ruth wrinkled her nose. "They said she's gone to live with God, but I don't understand that. I supposed they meant she'd gone to the seaside, but I went with Nan and Grandpa to the church and we left flowers in the garden; they said that was where she was. I think they meant she had died and that's why we don't see her any more."

Susan was baffled, but said she would ask her poppa what he knew. The bell rang, and that was the end of their discussion. Ruth stored the photo away in her coat pocket again, as that was definitely the safest place for it.

The next morning, when Ruth and her father called for Susan, Jacob Meyer came to the door. He was beaming all over his face, almost as much as he had when Ben was born. "John, my friend – you will let me call you John, won't you? I am so thrilled to meet the brother of Evelyn Platt! She was my musical idol. After they released me from internment, I once played in the orchestra when she was the soloist. I shall never forget her Rachmaninov – that D-minor concerto, so full of foreboding! My mother adored her! How thrilled she will be to hear this news, and how silly of me not to have made the connection before! I mean, on account of the name and little Ruth's appearance, her dark eyes and hair. And, of course, Susan tells me she is already a good pianist."

Dad was startled and had to steady himself against the doorpost as Jacob's outpouring was unstoppable. "It was all so tragic," Jacob went on. "Fate was so unkind to her, a beautiful girl like that who had so much to live for."

"Yes, yes, Jacob, thank you, that's so kind," was all that Dad managed to say. "Perhaps we should talk about it some other time." Whereupon he took Ruth and Susan smartly by the hand and led them away.

That evening, though Shirley stayed in bed, Dad was quiet and subdued. After supper, he asked Ruth to come and sit by the fire as he said he wanted to talk to her.

"Ruth," he began awkwardly, "you remember, don't you, that I asked you not to mention the piano in front of your mother?"

Ruth held her breath, terrified of a scolding, or even worse of being told that she should not play the piano any more in school. No such rebuke or injunction was forthcoming, so Susan had not let her down. "Yes," was the only word needed.

"Well, whatever happens, please remember that, will you? Do what you like in school, but don't talk about it at home!"

"Yes," she said again, but was unprepared for what he said next. "You see, Ruthie, your mother and Evelyn didn't get on very well together. Evelyn was a wonderful pianist and was famous, and Shirley wanted to be famous too, but it didn't work out like that for her, and then Evelyn died and we were all very sad…" His voice trailed away, having lost track of what he wanted to say. Ruth waited. "It's very hard to explain, and I expect you'll understand one day, but for the moment, be careful, will you? And if you do want to play the piano, as I said before, don't talk about it in front of Shirley."

He hugged her and then suggested a game of Ludo until bedtime. Weighed down by his own worries, he had no conception of how important the piano was to Ruth, nor did he make the connection between his sister's talent and his daughter's, so in all likelihood he imagined that it was simply a passing fancy. Ruth however lay awake puzzling over his speech, which was supposed to be some sort of a warning; she still did not understand how anyone could not like the piano – nor why, if Evelyn was famous, Shirley should be so jealous of her, especially because Evelyn had died a long time ago.

The following morning it was Rachel who came to the door when they called for Susan. Dad asked to see Jacob, but he was still asleep because he had been playing in a concert the night before.

"I wondered if I might drop in for a word with you both," Dad asked cautiously.

"Why yes, of course, John," Rachel replied in her warm, kindly way. "Come in for a cup of tea when you collect Ruth. Jacob's not playing tonight and will be so pleased to see you. Susan told us about your sister."

Dad nodded. "Thanks, I'll see you then."

Later that day, he sat for a long time talking with Jacob and Rachel in the Meyers' front room, while Susan and Ruth played with Ben at the back of the house. When the three adults emerged, they were all very quiet and solemn.

Rachel put her hand on Dad's arm. "Don't worry, John, but let us know what we can do to help," she said.

"Oh, you're helping so much already with Ruth, and I'm so grateful for that," he replied.

"No, no, that's a pleasure, you know it is, I've already told you that," she answered. "What I mean is, you must ask if you'd like me to come round and help at home for a bit."

Dad shuffled from foot to foot as though this was too much kindness, and he did not know how to respond to it, or how Shirley would react to it. Finally, he said: "That's very kind, but I don't think I should let you do that." Realizing that Rachel was about to propose some other very kind scheme, he added with obvious embarrassment: "You see, the problem as far as that's concerned is little Ben." Then in case he had given offence, he felt bound to attempt some sort of explanation. "He is a beautiful baby, but things are very delicate at the moment, and that might be too much of a challenge." Ruth would have loved to have Ben at home in her own house, and still dreamt of having a baby brother. For her it was unthinkable that any baby would present a problem. This was just one more of those inexplicable adult mysteries.

By the time Ruth and her father arrived home, it was already getting dark, and they did not expect to find the light on in the hall. "Surely I didn't leave the light on this morning, did I?" Dad asked, more to himself than to Ruth. The door opened just as he was unlocking it, and there on the threshold was Shirley, dressed in a skirt and jumper.

She flung her arms around Dad's neck. "Oh, there you are, I was afraid you were never coming. Look at me! I'm better! I've been sorting out my wardrobe. There's not much I can wear, but this is all right, isn't it?" She smoothed the pleats in her skirt.

"You look lovely, darling," Dad replied, giving his wife a hug. "I'm so pleased to see you looking so well – and Ruth is too, aren't you, Ruth?" Ruth tried to appear pleased.

Shirley smiled at her and said. "Well, Ruth, how are you? Your hair does shine nicely! I don't think I've seen you in such a long time. Come here, give me a kiss." Ruth kissed the soft cheek, her face brushing against the blonde curls, and inhaled a warm, enveloping scent which had very little to do with the gaslit London backstreet where they lived. Gratified by Ruth's reaction, Shirley laughingly explained to her husband: "And I treated myself to a dab of that Chanel No. 5 you bought me for my birthday!"

Shirley's sudden recovery was sustained, though she did not get up till the afternoon, so Ruth still went to the Meyers' after school, and she did not participate in the running of the household to any great extent, so John still did the shopping and the cooking. She did however get out the vacuum cleaner and a duster and set to work on the front room, her domain.

There she would retire for a quiet smoke, and there she would entertain the friends she had not seen for so long. She washed and rearranged all her china ornaments on the mantelpiece, and instructed John to light a fire in the grate. Although this was yet another chore for him in the morning, he willingly complied. As winter was approaching, he had to light two fires – one in the front room and one in the back – before taking Ruth and Susan to school and going to work himself. He piled both fires high with coal and logs and closed the grate.

"There, that should last," he said to himself each morning as he swept up the coal dust on the hearth.

His wife sent out notes to all her friends, asking them to come and see her: some of them lived close by, others were scattered all over London. Soon the steady stream of visitors to the front door resumed on most afternoons, and soon clouds of cigarette smoke filtered once more from that room into all the other rooms in the house, blending with the smoke from the railway line at the end of the road.

The last of the guests would be on the point of departure as John and Ruth arrived home, and often Shirley would be excited. "Guess who came this afternoon?" She would ply John with questions for which he had no answers, because they were mostly about people he had never met, but today an answer was not expected. "I'll tell you, because you'll never guess," Shirley would continue. "Well, it was Cynthia Curtis – I haven't seen her for years – and, do you know, she's auditioning for the Sadler's Wells ballet!"

John tried to show an appropriate amount of astonishment.

"Of course, she'll never get in, she's put on far too much weight, and she's too old. I bet they'll cast her as the thirteenth fairy, if at all," was Shirley's scathing verdict on Cynthia's chances.

Other visitors were more local; they were the ones who had been conspicuous by their absence during Shirley's illness, but were now only too flattered to be invited to share in her glamour, the more so when she would also introduce them to aspiring companions from the world of the stage, if not the screen. There was a tacit understanding that no reference would ever be made to the events of the past months, and these occasions certainly gave Shirley's morale a boost.

After her "tea and a smoke" parties as she called them, she would busily don an apron and, pushing John out of the way, say, "I'll do the supper tonight, if you'll just give me what you've bought." She would hum as she worked in the kitchen, now and then calling John to tell him a piece of gossip that she had picked up that afternoon. The front room was now out of bounds to Ruth, who found that she had nowhere to practise her ballet steps except in the confined space of her bedroom. She preferred to be upstairs anyhow, out of the way of the cigarette smoke, which made her cough, so once she had practised those steps that inevitably had given Susan a great deal of trouble in the ballet class, she would lie down on her bed with a book until she was called down for supper.

A calmer, less tense atmosphere gradually descended on the house as Shirley advanced along the road to recovery. When she was well, her *joie de vivre* was infectious. She it was who suggested a Guy Fawkes party.

"Surely you don't mean here in our backyard?" was Dad's startled reply.

"No, silly, of course not! I mean in the park. We wouldn't be allowed to have a bonfire, but supposing we buy some fireworks and invite a few friends? Afterwards we might go and get fish and chips. You'd like that, wouldn't you, Ruth?" Ruth had only ever seen other people's fireworks from a distance, so clapped her hands in glee.

The following Saturday the three of them went to the market for the usual greengrocery shopping, and then, on the way home, called in at the paper shop, where Mr Farjeon had rearranged his display cabinet. Usually reserved for boxes of chocolates, it now sported an assortment of fireworks, large and small, many with intriguing names. Ruth was allowed to choose the ones she liked and those with the most appealing names – Golden Rain, Silver Fountain, Crackpot, Chrysanthemum Spray, Mount Vesuvius, Catherine Wheel. Dad added a few rockets and Roman Candles and Shirley insisted on a handful of bangers and Jumping Jacks.

"Are you sure about those, love?" Dad asked anxiously. "I don't think Ruth will like them."

"Oh, we must have a bit of excitement," was Shirley's curt retort. She invited her local friends, and Ruth was permitted to invite Susan.

The friends who assembled in the park that 5th November were a noisy bunch. Apart from Jacob, who brought Susan, they laughed and shouted a lot, calling to each other and pushing each other about. Ruth was timid with them and wanted to stay with her dad, but he was busy setting off the fireworks. They were spellbinding indeed with all their dazzling, sparkling colours, hissing, crackling and whooshing until they died away, so it would have been great fun, had Shirley not insisted on giving the bangers and Jumping Jacks to one of her friends. His name was Bert. Burly and loud, he dominated the party with his raucous laughter and brash manner.

Just as Dad might be letting off a Roman Candle or a Mount Vesuvius, Bert would call out, "Come on then, let's have a bit of a bang!" and let off a nasty little banger or, even worse, a Jumping Jack. While the adults laughed and screamed at the explosions and the bangs around their feet, Ruth stayed close to Susan and Jacob. Susan was enjoying herself thoroughly and was not perturbed by the bangs, but Jacob was silent. He took Ruth's hand, sensing her anxiety, and drew her towards him; she felt him wince with every loud noise. A banger went off right behind them, and then a Jumping Jack started to sputter close by. Ruth moved even closer to Jacob, while Susan danced up and down in delight. Shirley, in the midst of her friends, was doing the same.

Before the grand finale, which was a large rocket already set up in a milk bottle, Dad went over to a tree where he had pinned a Catherine Wheel. On the way, a banger that Bert had flung exploded right in front of him. Ruth was distraught; forgetting her own fears, she ran over to him. "Daddy! Oh, Daddy, are you all right?" she cried.

Shirley laughed. "Of course he's all right, you ninny! It was only a little banger!" Saying nothing, John wiped his face with his hand and continued on his way over to the tree. He lit the Catherine Wheel, which ignited and flared for a moment as it started to revolve unsurely, as though pitting itself against the whole weight of the tree; then it came to a standstill, sending its white flame and sparks, like a blowtorch, into the ground beneath. Dad with Ruth in tow marched back to the rocket, set it off and firmly announced, "Well, that's that then. Home we go."

The gathering dispersed in silence, simply nodding a mute thank you to John and Shirley as they went. John picked up the spent fireworks and the milk bottle, then taking Ruth by the hand joined Jacob and Susan, leaving Shirley, in her high heels, to clatter along behind.

"What about the fish and chips?" she called from over their shoulders.

"They will have to wait for another time," John shouted firmly. "What did you like best Ruth?" he asked on the way home.

"Oh, the Roman Candles," she replied after a little reflection.

"I like the bangs!" Susan interrupted.

"No, no, not the bangs," said Jacob with anguish in his voice. "They remind me too much of the War."

Shirley had caught them up by now. "Wasn't that nice?" she beamed. Susan was the only one who agreed wholeheartedly with her.

Back home, when John switched the hall light on, Ruth was shocked at the sight of his face. It was covered in soot and pockmarked with little black holes and red smears all over it.

"Oh, Daddy, you're hurt," she cried.

"No, it's all right, I'll go and have a wash, then I'll be fine," he answered. A minute or two later he came back from the bathroom and indeed he did look better. His face was now clean, the black holes were now no more than red pimples, and the bloodstains were washed away.

Shirley laughed. "You've got chickenpox!" she declared, laughing uncontrollably. "You shouldn't have walked in the way of that banger!"

Dad suddenly became fiercely angry. "It was that stupid Bert: you shouldn't have invited him to come; you know I detest him!" Ruth was astonished. Only once had she heard her dad raise his voice to Shirley ever before, and that was over the hair-cutting episode, and now he was furious.

Shirley shouted back at him, "Am I not allowed to have friends then?" Working herself up to a fury, she raised her voice even louder. "You are so boring, just like a policeman! I wish I'd never married you!"

Dad was still angry, but he kept calm. "Right, if that's how you feel, the door's over there," he replied, pointing in the direction of the front door.

Shirley suddenly changed her tone, as for once she knew that she had gone too far. "I'm sorry," she said meekly, but also coyly. "Let me put some ointment on for you, then I'll go and fetch the fish and chips." She led him upstairs to the bathroom. Wondering if Nan and Grandpa ever had fireworks, Ruth fetched her crayons and some colouring paper and started to make a picture for them. She did not notice how long her parents were away, but when they came down from the bathroom, Dad was smiling and said: "I'm fine now. I'll go for the fish and chips."

29

Despite the ill-fated firework party, a comforting air of normality began to envelope the family. Ruth was unquestioningly content, if only because her home life had become calmer and less unpredictable. She demanded nothing more. Her dad was much less haggard and more relaxed, and Shirley was irrepressible, attacking life with boundless enthusiasm. Though tired by the end of the day, she devoted herself to creating constant activity and excitement around her, so much so that at the beginning of December she decided that it was time for a shopping expedition.

"After all, look at Ruth's coat," she urged John. "She must have had that for at least two years, and see how she's grown! It hardly covers her knees. Let's buy her a new coat for Christmas!"

Ruth did not want a new coat for Christmas: she would have much preferred a toy post office, or a shop from where to serve her dolls, but she was not asked what she would like, and her father was already agreeing with Shirley's proposal.

"Yes, that's a good idea, why don't I take my two girls Christmas shopping on Saturday – well, that's tomorrow, isn't it? But that suits me. Let's have a day out in the West End!"

Shirley's eyes shone. "They'll have the lights up by now! Oh, that will be lovely!" She hugged her husband and left a bright-red trace of lipstick on his cheek.

The day went well, though it had its tedious moments. Ruth was nervous that the plan might include leaving her at the hairdresser's while her parents went shopping, but as this did not happen she gradually dropped her guard and allowed herself to be carried away by the twinkling lights, the brightly lit shops, the Christmas tree in Trafalgar Square, tea and cake in a smart restaurant and, above all, her visit to Santa's grotto in one of the big department stores. Long ago, she recalled, Dad had tried to comfort her by saying that Father Christmas did not exist, but she wanted to keep her options open in case he was wrong, so she confided in Santa that she would like a toy post office for Christmas and he promised that he would see what he could do. However, there were no visits to toyshops. In fact, they walked straight past a very large toyshop, and Ruth had to be satisfied with a quick glance in the window, where dolls and teddy bears vied for space with train sets, cars, doll's houses, toy shops and toy post offices.

She was walking between her parents at the time and dragged on their hands as she craned round to look at that window, but they did not stop.

"Come, on, Ruth," Shirley said sharply, "we're not looking in there today. We've got to get you a coat, remember?" Shirley steered them into the children's clothing department of a large store and selected a navy-blue mackintosh. "Try this one on," she commanded, "you'll need this for school." Ruth tried it on and looked at herself in the mirror. All she saw was a forlorn little figure – herself – trying hard, oh, so hard, to hide her disappointment. Was this what Shirley meant by a new coat for Christmas?

"Don't worry, Ruthie," Dad said, alert to her dismay, "that's not your Christmas present; that's something you need for school." Shirley, who had gone off on an errand while Ruth was trying on the mackintosh, came back with an assistant who was carrying a pile of coats over her arm.

"This is lovely," Shirley said, "try this one." She handed Ruth a blue coat with a collar in navy velvet.

This time Ruth was pleased with the effect as she surveyed herself in the mirror. "I like it," she said.

"Well, that's good, it's a nice colour, good quality and it fits all right. We'll take that one," Shirley said to the assistant, who was hovering close by. Ruth took off the blue coat for the assistant to take away and wrap. Shirley followed her, saying something that Ruth did not catch. After an inordinately long wait, they both came back, the assistant carrying a parcel, which she put on the counter while Dad got out his wallet.

Shirley meanwhile was edging towards the ladies' clothing department and beckoned to Dad to follow her, "I think they have some nice things here," she said, suggesting that she already had foreknowledge of what was in "there". Ruth sat watching in silence on a chair while Shirley tried on a whole range of dresses, some in silk, some in velvet, some red, some blue, some green. She, of course, looked beautiful in all the clothes she tried on, whatever their style, colour or fabric. At long last, after much parading up and down and twisting round to survey herself in the mirror, she settled on a long red velvet gown.

"Really," she said playfully, "I never expected we would buy anything for me. I hope if we buy this, we'll go to a dance somewhere so I can wear it."

Dad laughed. "We'll have to make sure we do," he answered cheerfully. "Of course, I'll have to have a pair of shoes to go with it," Shirley demanded grandly as if money were no object.

"Of course," Dad agreed without the slightest hesitation, so their next stop was the shoe department, where Shirley tried on every available pair in her size and Ruth sat yawning in silence.

"Oh, you are tired, Ruth," Shirley exclaimed when finally she had made her selection, "I think we'd better go home now. Anyhow," she added, winking mischievously at Dad, "I've spent far too much of Dad's money!"

Dad smiled. They took a trolleybus home and got off outside the fish shop. "Fish and chips again?" Dad enquired.

"Yes, please!" Shirley beamed. "That would a perfect ending to a lovely day!"

While they were eating supper there was a ring at the doorbell. Dad went to answer it and came back saying, "It's the church Christmas bazaar: they're having a second-hand-clothes stall and wonder if we've got anything for it."

"Mm," said Shirley putting her chin in her hand as she considered the request. "Well, it's a bit awkward to find things as we're in the middle of supper, but I'll let them have the turquoise suit you bought me last spring, I don't think I'll wear that again," she said with a decisive nod. Her features contracted, but briskly she pulled herself together, declaring, "I'll go and get it. Ask them to wait a minute, will you?"

She hurried upstairs. When she came down, Ruth heard her talking to the people on the doorstep. They were apologizing for interrupting the meal, explaining that they had called that afternoon by way of advance warning, but there had been no one at home. "I see," said Shirley pleasantly, "and I'm sure there must be other things you could have, but I can't think what they are at present. Then a variety of old coats and mackintoshes hanging on pegs in the hall caught her eye. "Why don't you take these?" she said, offering them an old mackintosh of her husband's, one of her own old coats and the coat that Ruth had outgrown. There was another exchange of pleasantries before Shirley closed the front door.

She did not come straight back but went upstairs first. When she came down, she had an unusually pensive air, and did not speak for a minute or two, but then remarked, "No point in hanging on to old clothes that we aren't going to wear again. We certainly don't need them for gardening!" She sighed. "Oh, how nice it would be to have a garden one day, wouldn't it?" she continued, addressing the question to no one in particular.

Ruth had the feeling that something was wrong, but it was not until she was tucked up in bed and was recounting the day's events to her soft toys that the terrible truth dawned on her. In the pocket of her old coat, the one that Shirley had given to the church bazaar, she had kept the treasured little photo of her Aunt Evelyn. She felt faint with despair: the precious picture that Nan had given her was lost and gone for ever. Never again would she have the comfort of pulling it out of her pocket to scrutinize in a quiet moment. Even if Evelyn were not her mother, the knowledge that she, Ruth, was so much like her and might one day play the piano as she had, had given her great comfort among all the perplexities and anxieties of her young life.

She tried not to sob aloud to avoid attracting attention, and pulled the sheet and blanket over her head to muffle any audible signs of her misery. When at last she sank into sleep, her dreams came fitfully and chaotically. Her teddy was sitting at Nan's piano playing beautiful tunes, while Nan sang hymns to him, then fairy lights came down and danced around him, and Shirley, wearing her turquoise suit, sat weeping on a sofa. When, in addition to all this, Father Christmas, whether or not he really existed, came charging into the room on his sleigh, pulled by a team of reindeer, she awoke with a start and screamed. Both Dad and Shirley came running to her bedside.

"What's the matter, Ruth?" Dad asked.

"There, there," said Shirley gently.

They both sat on her bed until she was calmer. Dad felt her forehead. "She's hot: I hope she's not sickening for something," he remarked.

The next morning Ruth was not ill, but nor did she feel well. During the day an unpleasant sensation in her mouth began to develop into a dull ache which throbbed unremittingly until by the evening it had become a stabbing pain. Sobbing with the discomfort at least gave her the opportunity of venting some of her anguish at the loss of the photo. Both her parents were generous with their sympathy.

"She'll have to go to the dentist's tomorrow," Shirley decreed.

"Yes, of course," Dad said, "but the only problem is that I have meetings all morning. I doubt I can be free before three."

"Never mind," Shirley replied, "I can take her. I'll ring my pals in the morning and tell them not to come in the afternoon."

"Do you think that would be all right?" Dad asked cautiously. "You haven't been out on your own yet, you know."

"Oh, come on! I'm fine, and she is my daughter! It's not far up the road. We'll be all right, won't we, Ruth?" Shirley insisted. She crushed an aspirin in some jam and gave it to Ruth on a teaspoon. "Here, take this, it'll make you feel better," she said, patting Ruth's tousled hair and putting an arm round her shoulders. The aspirin had the desired effect in calming the pain and sending Ruth into a deep sleep.

All morning she stayed in bed. Her dad went out to the phone box to call the dental surgery before he left for work and took the only available appointment – at two o'clock in the afternoon.

"You are sure you'll be all right?" he asked Shirley more than once.

"Well of course, silly," she laughed. "What can possibly go wrong between here and the dentist's?" Shirley came upstairs regularly to bring Ruth drinks and renew a cold compress that she had prepared. "Poor little thing!" she said, gazing down at Ruth as she applied the pad to the side of her face. "This will take some of the heat out of the pain; the dentist will make it better. Don't you worry, I'll look after you." With this glimmer of maternal concern, she sought to reassure Ruth, and then as the maternal spark flared into a warm flame, she stayed to read her a story.

There was a hitch when Shirley realized that because she had given Ruth's old coat away, her daughter would have to wear either her Christmas present, the smart new coat, or the mackintosh, which was too long for her. She decided on the mackintosh. Ruth cut a sorry figure indeed with her red swollen face, her bleary eyes and the long navy mackintosh which came down to her heels. The nagging pain of the tooth drained all her energy, and she found the short walk to the dentist's – along the street to the corner and then a hundred yards up the road – a struggle. Someone lifted her into the dentist's chair without her noticing – and in any case, she was too exhausted to protest as the round brown rubber mask was fitted right over her face.

She drifted quickly into sleep and, when she awoke, she heard the dentist, a youngish man with bright-red hair, talking to Shirley.

"She'll be fine," he was saying, "but I am worried about her teeth. They are not in good shape. I reckon she eats too many sweets."

"No, no," Shirley replied, "she hardly has any at all. We only give her one to suck when she goes to bed at night."

The dentist's mouth fell open in astonishment, then he whistled between his teeth. "That is the very worst thing you can do!" he exploded in Shirley's face. "Don't you know that all that sugar is clinging to her teeth and rotting them right through the night!"

Shirley was taken aback. "Well, my husband cleans her teeth at night while she is having a bath and again in the morning." She gave a sullen little pout, which did not endear her to the dentist.

"My advice to you" – the dentist was becoming authoritative – "my advice to you," he repeated harshly, "is never to give that child a sweet ever again, otherwise she will have constant toothache and will lose all her teeth!"

"Oh, thanks!" Shirley retorted in great agitation, as she swiftly put Ruth's mac round her shoulders and ushered her smartly to the door. Once outside, she stopped for breath. "What a horrible man!" she exclaimed indignantly. "We'll have to find another dentist!"

She marched with a very strange gait, purposeful yet limping, back down the road with Ruth running along beside to keep up with her. It was not until they reached the greengrocer's on the corner that Shirley slowed down a little and remembered that not only had Ruth just undergone a searing experience, but had not eaten for more than twenty-four hours.

"Poor Ruth!" she said with a catch in her voice. "There, I'm not looking after you at all well, am I? That dentist upset me so much. How are you, lovey?" Ruth was feeling too faint to answer. "I know, let's buy some bananas. They are soft and easy to eat, so maybe you could manage one now. That'll help you get home. Oh, and look, they've got some tangerines! Let's have some of them as a special treat! Your dad will like those too." She pointed to the fruit on the display outside the shop and beckoned to the greengrocer to come to serve her.

Shirley was following the greengrocer back into the shop to pay for her purchases when Ruth, who was waiting outside, saw Rachel coming round the corner pushing Ben in his pram, on her way to meet Susan from school. Alarm bells clanged loudly in Ruth's befuddled brain, for she knew there was some reason why it would not be a good thing for Shirley to meet Rachel and little Ben, but it was too late, and even worse, Rachel stopped when she saw Ruth. She had heard about the toothache from John that morning and was naturally concerned to see Ruth standing alone outside the greengrocer's.

"Are you all right Ruth?" Rachel enquired.

"Yes, yes," Ruth replied urgently but unconvincingly. She hoped against all hope that Rachel would move on before Shirley came out of the shop, but she did not.

"What are you doing here?" Rachel persisted.

"I've been to the dentist and we are buying bananas," was the limit of Ruth's conversation. The door of the shop opened, and Shirley emerged.

"I've bought some dates as well," she was saying before she saw Rachel. Then she blanched an instant before recovering her self-control. She stepped forward, smiling her most gracious of smiles. "Oh, it's Mrs Meyer, isn't it?" she asked with the utmost charm. "John has told me so much about you and how kind you've been to Ruth over the past months when I've been out of action."

"Don't mention it; it's been a pleasure, as I have said many times to your husband. Ruth has been such a help with the baby," said Rachel, who now was very anxious to be going.

With unconcealed amazement Shirley peered into the pram. "And who is this little person?" she asked. "I didn't know you had a new baby."

"Well, he's six months old now," Rachel said almost apologetically, as if Ben no longer qualified as a new baby. "His name is Ben – Benjamin," she added, rather superfluously.

"Oh! Isn't he beautiful?" said Shirley, still peering into the pram, which Rachel had turned to reveal its occupant. "Oh, you are so lucky, a girl and a boy! I do love babies!"

She groped in her handbag and pulled out half a crown. "Ruth," she whispered, while Rachel pulled the blankets over Benjamin again, "I want you to put this on the cover of the pram." Ruth slunk back behind her mother: she was far too shy to make such a public gesture. Shirley gripped her arm, but Ruth refused to take the coin, so Shirley had to place it herself.

"That's so kind! There's no need," said Rachel, before thanking her and adding, "Do come round and have a cup of tea some time if you like. I should be so pleased to see you." Shirley nodded without releasing her grip on Ruth's arm. "We must be getting on," Rachel remarked, manoeuvring the pram to face up the hill. "Susan will be coming out of school, and I don't like to be late. I hope you'll be better soon, Ruth."

"Oh, she'll be fine tomorrow," was Shirley's parting and very determined shot.

She steered Ruth round the corner, changing her grip from her arm to her shoulder once Rachel was out of sight. Her nails were sharp even through the mackintosh. "You knew about that baby, didn't you?" she asked angrily. Ruth had no option but to answer, "Yes." She said it softly in the hope of averting further questioning, but in vain.

"Why didn't you tell me?" Shirley asked, hardly bothering to suppress her fury.

"I don't know," Ruth said.

She felt so miserable. Hungry and thirsty, tired and confused from the anaesthetic, in pain and bleeding from the extraction which had left a gaping hole, worried by the encounter with Rachel and Ben and, above all, terrified of Shirley's temper, she longed for her dad and she dreaded arriving home.

They had almost reached the front door when the sound of running footsteps behind them made Shirley stop instantly. A familiar voice called, "Hey, you two, wait for me!" Ruth breathed a deep sigh of relief. It was her dad's voice! He caught up with them and asked cheerfully, "How did it go? Are you all right, Ruthie? The meetings finished earlier than expected so I reckoned I'd take the rest of the afternoon off and come home to see how you are." By now he had noticed the stony glare that Shirley was casting upon him and his voice faltered. "Let's go in and make a cup of tea; I expect you are both exhausted," he suggested.

Ruth could have wept for him in his innocence and his ignorance of the storm that was about to burst over his head. He opened the door and stood aside for them to pass. Shirley sailed into the house, her head held high. Released from her iron grip, Ruth took her father by the hand and led him indoors. She stood firmly by his side as Shirley, like a cat about to pounce, waited for him to hang up his coat.

At first she spoke quietly: "I'm shocked you didn't tell me that the Meyers have a new baby."

With the horror-struck expression of a man standing on thin ice which he knows is about to crack, Dad searched his wife's face for a clue that might save him. There was no clue, no branch to hang on to, and the ice gave way beneath him. Too late he saw how it had happened and stammered cautiously, "Ah, so you've seen Rachel Meyer and little Ben, have you? I saw them myself as I came down the road."

"Oh, we've seen them all right," said Shirley, raising her voice slightly. "Why did nobody bother to tell me they've got a new baby?"

"We were afraid it might upset you," John replied gently.

Shirley's voice rose louder. "What do you think I am? Some sort of idiot? I've already had that from the dentist today. He made me out to be some sort of fool for giving Ruth a sweet when she goes to bed, and now I find you're worse! You're making me out to be a moron!"

She was already screaming so loudly and clenching her fists so tightly that Ruth was afraid she was going to attack her father. John however was much taller and stronger than her, so that when the attack came, pummelling her fists into his chest, he grasped hold of her arms above the wrists and immobilized her. He pulled her down the hall into the dining room and pushed her into the armchair by the fire.

"Sit there and calm down, I'll be with you in a minute, but now I must make some tea and get Ruth something to eat. Look at the poor child, she's starving!" He then said gently, "Ruthie, dear, I haven't done the shopping yet, but we have got some eggs. What about scrambled eggs?" Shirley had quietened down. Sitting in the armchair she stared vacantly into space, trapped in her own concerns, oblivious to her husband and daughter.

Dad did not extract any more information from her about the visit to the dentist's, so left to his own devices he ran a warm bath for Ruth, rinsed her mouth with mild disinfectant, gave her half an aspirin instead of a sweet and put her to bed, even though it was still light. Ruth drifted in and out of sleep for the rest of that afternoon and evening. Voices ascended the stairs and mingled with her dreams, so that she did not know whether it was in her dreams or in reality that she heard a woman screaming, "I hate you, I hate you! Look at the mess you've got me into." Later she was disturbed by hysterical sobbing. "My life is a complete disaster," the same voice lamented, "nothing has ever worked out well for me! I want to end it!" The words came out in a broken series of hiccups. A deeper, calmer voice spoke for a long time. Then there was silence, then another sob, plaintively offering some sort of excuse for the disturbance at the firework party. "As for Bert, that was nothing; you were away so long and I was lonely, that's all." The deeper voice spoke again, and for a while all was quiet until it all started up again and again throughout the night.

There was no sign of Shirley in the morning, though that was not unusual. Ruth was barely well enough to go to school, nevertheless she was roused early by her father, who was in a world of his own. Yawning a lot, as she did while she ate her breakfast, he said very little, and then asked if she would mind if he went out for a minute, as he wanted to see Mrs Cox. He was back before Ruth had time to finish her cereal, and Mrs Cox trailed heavily in behind him.

"Hallo, ducks," she said to Ruth, who tried to ignore her.

"Mrs Cox is going to keep an eye on Shirley while I take you to school," Dad explained to Ruth.

She nodded, shooting a sidelong glance at Mrs Cox. She did not imagine that Shirley would enjoy being cared for by her, for she herself certainly would not, and was thankful that Mrs Cox had not been summoned for her benefit. Her mouth suddenly felt much better, and she was anxious to be off to school.

Dad took Mrs Cox upstairs, having prepared a tray with some food and a drink on it, which he carried up with him.

At last he put his coat on and helped Ruth into her mackintosh. She did not care that it was too long, because she simply wanted to get out of the house. They called as usual for Susan, and when Rachel opened the door, the first thing she said was, "Oh, John, is everything all right? I'm so sorry, I didn't know what to do when I saw Ruth standing alone outside the greengrocer's – and then Shirley came out. I knew she was upset."

Dad stood talking to Rachel while Susan searched for her school bag. "Don't worry, Rachel, it wasn't your fault," he said. "I fear she'll have to go into hospital again, though. She is in a bad way, and I don't like to leave her. Mrs Cox is there at present, and I'll phone the doctor once the girls are in school. Then I'll call in at work to tell them the situation and be back soon."

Susan and Ruth had to run to keep up with him. Even so they were late for school, but fortunately he did remember to come in and apologize to Miss Lake, who said that she was sorry and understood, so the day passed without further incident for Ruth. There were a few sniggers at playtime at the length of her mackintosh, but she laughed them off. "I know, it's horrid and I don't like it," she said, thus disarming any potential adversaries.

After school Ruth played with Susan and helped with Ben as usual, but was taken aback when Rachel cheerfully announced, "You are staying for supper with us tonight, Ruth, because your daddy will be late coming home." This worried Ruth. She had not expected that the trouble with Shirley would affect Dad that much. Suppose he had to go to hospital as well? What would she do on her own?

"Don't worry," said Rachel, putting her motherly arm round her, "he'll be back, he's all right."

Ruth did not eat much supper. The gap in her mouth was healing, but it was still sore, so that she had not been able to eat her lunch, and she even found it hard to eat the goulash soup that Rachel put in front of her. In any case, the additional worry about her dad took away all appetite.

She helped put Ben to bed, then Susan went to bed and Ruth was left sitting in the kitchen with Rachel, who said that Jacob was out playing in a concert.

"Cheer up, Ruth!" said Rachel breezily. "Your daddy will be here soon. Let's see, what time is it?" She looked at the clock. "It's now half-past eight, and he said he would be no later than nine."

How Ruth wished she could tell the time! "How do you know?" she asked Rachel, whereupon Rachel kindly filled in the next half-hour by teaching her to read the time on the clock.

When Dad arrived, he was unsmiling. "They've taken her in again," he told Rachel with a sigh. "I think she'll be there for several weeks. They said they might try a new treatment, sedating her to give the brain a rest. At least it won't be that electric-shock therapy that she is so frightened of." Rachel made sympathetic noises and as always offered more help. "Thanks, but I'm hoping that won't be necessary too often," John replied. "You see, I've telegraphed my parents."

30

Nan and Grandpa arrived two days later. They had not come by car, but had taken the train and then the Underground, having refused to let John meet them because, as they said, they did not want him to take any more time off work than was necessary. When they arrived, they both were understandably weary, but in Ruth's eyes, as soon as she saw him, Grandpa appeared very odd and desperately tired, more tired than she had ever seen him before. He walked slowly, leaning on Nan, who was carrying their small suitcase, and his face was covered in blotches. He tried to smile at her, but that bright beam of blue light was gone from his eyes, and he coughed frequently. Nan was her usual cheerful self and drew Ruth into the folds of her old scented fur coat to hug her.

"Well, how's my little Ruth, then?" she asked, as gently and as warmly as ever. "Dear me, I shan't be picking you up any more, you are much too big now! How you've grown!"

Ruth laughed excitedly, taking Nan by the hand to lead her to what passed for a dining room, where she had helped her father set out the tea. "Come with me, Nan," she said, "it's all ready for you; Dad and I made a cake for you last night before I went to bed!"

"Sorry, dear, what did you say?" Nan asked, putting her hand to one ear. Ruth repeated her invitation and guided Nan to her chair. John did not follow. Dumbstruck, he stood in the hallway looking at his father. Eventually he pulled himself together and, finding his tongue, he slipped quickly into his native accents: "Well, Father, it seems to me you need a helping hand."

"No, no, ole bor, I'm fine, you go ahead and I'll follow you," his father replied with a note of defiance. John went ahead cautiously with many a backward glance and saw that his father was steadying himself against the wall and feeling his way along the narrow passageway down to the back room.

Nan took charge. "My, what a lovely tea you have laid out for us!" she exclaimed. "Shall I be mother and pour out?"

"Yes, please do," said John, stationing himself anxiously behind his father, who was easing himself onto a chair. Satisfied that all was well, at least for the moment, he too sat down and tried to raise a smile. "It's so good of you to come! I'm sorry to have brought you all this way but—" he began when Nan interrupted him.

"Don't you think that we jump at any opportunity to come and see you?" she laughed. "It's no problem at all. We may be getting a bit old, but we can still get to London to see our son and granddaughter, especially when they need us badly!" Although she didn't include the absent Shirley in her list of welcome faces, she did enquire, "And how is Shirley? I do hope she'll recover quickly this time. It must be so horrible for her as well as difficult for you."

John sighed. "I'm hoping this episode is only a brief relapse, because she was doing so well and was almost back to normal." He turned from one to the other of them as they began to help themselves to ham and salad and bread and butter. "And now, tell me, how are you?" he enquired meaningfully, fixing his gaze on his father.

"Oh, we're fine, aren't we, Grandpa?" Nan asserted, answering for them both a touch too quickly to be convincing.

Grandpa nodded his agreement. "Yes, that's right, we're fine. Never been better!" His voice gave the lie to this brave assertion, sounding hoarse and faint, and he constantly needed to cough. He cleared his throat, trying to make his speech sound stronger. "We're just a little tired from the journey, that's all," he added by way of a not very credible explanation as he struggled to wield his knife and fork.

After supper, although Ruth was not at all tired and had hoped to stay up playing Ludo or Snakes and Ladders with Grandpa and Nan, she saw from her dad's expression that he needed to talk seriously to his parents about grown-up things, and it would be easier if she were out of the way. So when he announced, with as much joviality as he could muster, "Now Ruth, time for bed," she made only a token protest, pausing only to ask if Nan would come and kiss her goodnight. She washed and cleaned her teeth in the little bathroom beyond the kitchen and then went upstairs.

When Nan came to tuck her up as promised, she enquired, "Are you and Grandpa sleeping up here too, next to me?"

At this Nan hesitated. "No, I don't think so, dear. You see, Grandpa is not so good on his feet these days. He manages at home, but he's not used to these stairs, so I think your dad is going to make up his old camp bed in the front room for Grandpa, and I'll sleep on the sofa. It's nearer the bathroom anyhow."

Ruth lay awake listening to the sounds from downstairs. At first there was the hum of conversation, mostly dominated by Dad's voice, slightly raised because of Nan's incipient deafness. By the sounds of it, he was asking lots of questions without getting any answers. Then she heard the tea things being cleared away and washed up, almost certainly by Nan in the kitchen beneath her bedroom, while, with some clattering, Dad took the old camp bed out from the cupboard under the stairs and set it up in the front room. A little later he came up to collect the bedclothes from the back bedroom, where earlier, on his return from work, Ruth had helped him make up the twin beds.

He popped his head round the door to her little room. "Night night, sweetheart. Are you all right?"

"Yes, I'm nearly asleep," she lied, and then saw her chance to ask, "What's wrong with Grandpa?"

John came into the bedroom. "I don't know, love, but I think he is rather ill. We shall have to look after him and Nan. But don't you worry."

"What if they break one of Shirley's china dolls?" she enquired, afraid that her grandparents might incur the absent Shirley's wrath, as she herself had done more than once.

"Don't you worry. I'm going to clear all those things away and put them in a box for safety!" He kissed her goodnight and went out.

Early the next morning the sound of voices from below woke Ruth. It seemed as if Nan and Dad had been talking all night. She dressed and went downstairs and, indeed, found them dressed and in the kitchen. Grandpa was not with them. They were so intent on talking to each other they did not notice Ruth helping herself to cornflakes and milk in the back room.

"No, no," Nan was saying, "he would never agree to see a doctor. He hates the very idea of going into hospital."

"But mother, he is ill, he can't even get out of bed this morning; he needs to see a doctor and have treatment urgently," John insisted. "I'm going to call at the surgery on my way to work and ask the doctor to call. He's a nice man and will know what to do for the best." As he left his mother to fetch his coat, he saw Ruth watching him. "Good, well done, Ruth," he remarked briskly. "We'll be off to school in ten minutes."

Rachel collected Ruth from school that afternoon, though Ruth had been expecting to see Nan, if not Grandpa, at the school gate, and when she asked where her grandparents were, Rachel simply answered, "I don't know, dear, I expect they'll be along later." Dad called for Ruth at his normal time, but Nan and Grandpa were not at home. Nan came back in the early evening, not long before Dad had to go to visit Shirley, but Ruth never saw Grandpa again.

The funeral, attended by John, Nan, Ruth and Rachel, took place at the crematorium one bright, frosty morning a week before Christmas. Ruth was overwhelmed by the solemnity of the occasion. Somewhere someone was playing slow, soothing music that moved her to the core. Otherwise she did not fully understand what was happening, except that Grandpa had died, so she would not see him again, yet without a doubt he was there with her and Nan and Dad, standing, albeit invisibly, with them chuckling and commenting wryly on the proceedings, doubtless complaining that this was all too much just for him, and they should not have bothered. Dad was stifling tears, but Nan did not weep. She kept very quiet and held Ruth's hand tightly.

At home over tea she hesitantly observed, "You've all been so kind, and I don't want to make a fuss, but what worries me is that he will be so unhappy at being buried here in London. He always hoped he would be buried with Evelyn."

"Of course," said Dad, putting his cup down, "I'm sure we can arrange that. I'm sure it's not too late. I'll get in touch with them in the morning." Ruth wondered who "they" were.

Nan stayed over Christmas. She shopped and cooked, declaring, "Now then, Grandpa told me I had to look after you two and make sure you had a good Christmas, and that's what I am going to do."

So in a way they did have a good Christmas: they ate well and had their presents, but a heavy pall of sadness hung over the household. Only four days later Dad brought Shirley home in a taxi. No sooner had she stepped through the front door than she went up to Nan and put her arms round her in a long embrace.

"I'm so sorry," she whispered. "He was such a good man; I loved him."

At this Nan wept for the first time. Shirley drew Ruth towards her and included her in the embrace. "And you loved Grandpa Joe, didn't you, Ruth?" Ruth nodded, and her tears began to flow too. "You must stay with us until you feel better," Shirley persisted.

"Thank you, dear," Nan replied, "but I shall be fine; I shall need to get back home to make sure the pipes don't freeze."

Towards the end of the Christmas holiday, Shirley went to stay with her father in south London for the weekend, while Dad took a Friday off work and, with a small wooden box packed in his bag, guided Nan and Ruth to the station, where they caught the train to Norhambury. Ruth sat by the window, hoping to see the farm and all the cousins, but there was only the gaunt black outline of bare trees looming out of the mist.

Nan's house was bitterly cold and drear on their arrival. They kept their coats on while Dad brought in coal, lit the fire and put hot-water bottles in the beds and Nan went across the road and over the patch of wasteland known as the Green to a row of shops consisting of a post office, a fish-and-chip shop and a local store, which sold an array of odds and ends and a few provisions. There were only the most basic provisions available so soon after Christmas, so she was expecting to do her shopping in next to no time, but when she appeared half an hour later, she explained apologetically that so many people had stopped her to ask about Grandpa that she was afraid she would never get home. Somehow word of his passing had come through, perhaps travelling on the train with them.

On the Saturday, Grandpa's ashes were laid to rest near Evelyn's grave amid a throng of his admirers – from his workplace, from the airbase, from the Speedway racetrack, from the football and from among the neighbours, including Carrie and the girls. There were many more people than had attended his funeral in London, thus fully justifying his wish to be buried in his home city. A trumpeter, resplendent in uniform and brandishing his shiny brass instrument, sounded the last post, sending a thrill of pride as well as sorrow down Ruth's spine, as the small wooden box was lowered into the grave and the mourners threw handfuls of fresh earth over it. A man whom Ruth thought she recognized stood over on the other side of the grave with a young woman. When he came over to express his condolences to Nan, she remembered that he was the organist, Charles Stannard, Evelyn's former fiancé, whom she had met in the spring. Nan smiled bleakly at him and shook hands with the young woman. The following day Ruth and her dad set off for London again, having had only scant opportunity to talk to Carrie and her daughters. Shirley welcomed them with smiles and had supper ready for them.

PART TWO

31

Soon after Grandpa's death, on her homecoming from the last of her long stays in hospital, Shirley had proposed the week by the sea in the summer holidays which had become a fairly regular institution. One bleak evening that winter after John and Ruth's return from Norhambury, where Grandpa's ashes had been laid to rest next to Evelyn's gravestone, Shirley bestowed one of her winsome smiles on her husband and declared, "You know, I've been thinking. I hate to imagine your poor mother all on her own in this horrible weather. Poor soul, she could do with a proper holiday. Why don't we all go to the sea next summer and take her with us? Like we did when Ruth was little... Can you believe it, she's nearly six now! That would give your mother something to look forward to, wouldn't it?"

John was delighted, and Ruth scarcely believed what she was hearing. Shirley went on, "Then you and Ruth could take her home and stay for a weekend or so before coming back to London." She fell silent, considering the situation from all angles. "Obviously we can't leave the house unattended for longer than that, but I might go and visit Cousin Edith in Birmingham for a week or two after the week at the sea, like I sometimes did in the old days. Anyhow, I need a longer break from the housekeeping."

"That's an excellent idea!" was John's quick response.

It was in Shirley's nature to be impulsively happy to do anything that she herself had first thought of, however contrary that might appear to her previous attitudes and opinions. It might also on occasion, if she were feeling low, appear contrary to her later attitudes and opinions, because she might then forget that she had ever made the suggestion in the first place, and would resent any intrusion into her lifestyle. She grumbled from time to time, saying, "Why, oh why, do we have to take your mother on holiday with us? Whose idea was that?" but these phases passed quickly. Naturally Nan was very pleased when the idea was put to her in a letter from her son before Shirley had had time to change her mind.

On the whole Shirley was undoubtedly much better, although there were still days when she sat motionless or retired to bed, overcome by a crushing tiredness, and then John would become quietly anxious and Ruth would slink up to her room to keep out of harm's way, but such days were fairly rare. Occasionally Shirley would buzz with an intensity of enthusiasm and activity that was liable to explode in violent and vicious outbursts of temper, which were mostly directed at her husband for no apparent reason other than that he was an easy target, but if Ruth happened to be in the firing line, she too would suffer. Usually these episodes passed like storms on sultry afternoons; later the air would clear and life would resume its normal pattern, as usual giving the impression that nothing untoward had occurred. Sometimes, as Shirley appeared to be heading for a bout of nervous excitability, she would take herself off for a day in town or go to help out in her father's newsagent's shop for a couple of days, and come home defused, calmer and more in control of her own personality.

Generally though, after the humiliation at the dentist's and the discovery of Ben's birth, which together on the same day all those years ago had provoked her catastrophic relapse, she had benefited from her hospital treatment and had begun to attain a unwonted state of mental equilibrium. She called on her doctor regularly, and sometimes had to go for hospital appointments, but only infrequently did she have to stay there for any length of time. Then, as she said, it was only because her medical team wanted to moderate her drugs – especially the recently introduced lithium, which seemed to be instrumental in controlling her moods. The more she grew accustomed to them, the more she liked these sessions, which placed her at the centre of an admiring audience of doctors and students.

Once, after one of these episodes, she said proudly, "They say I am their prize patient, and they like to show me off!"

In all those years Ruth's routine had not changed much: Dad still took her and Susan to school on his way to work, and she came home in the afternoon with Rachel and Susan. Ben graduated from pram to pushchair and greeted the two girls with such whoops of joy every day when they emerged from school that one might have believed that this was the first time in his short life he had ever seen them. Before long he too ran up the road alongside Ruth and Susan and waved goodbye to John at the school gate. Now that he was well past babyhood, Shirley had no objection to seeing him, even extending her tolerance to inviting him with his mother and sister to come in for tea from time to time.

With Rachel, Shirley was always more sensible and down-to-earth than with the friends who came to her "court". She did not bother to dress up, nor to plaster her face with make-up or her nails with bright-red varnish, but would come to the door wearing her overall with her head tied in a scarf. With mutual compassion and without any attempt at rivalry, she and Rachel would chat quietly about the neighbours, about the school and about times past, or their memories of the War. Meanwhile Ruth and Susan would play games and Ben would try to help by moving the pieces around the board.

From time to time, Ruth would pick up a word or two of the adults' conversation. "We left Russia when I was a baby," she heard Rachel confiding to Shirley, "so I don't remember much about it, except a long train journey with endless stops, crowds of people pushing and shoving and not much to eat or drink." She pondered the history that she scarcely remembered, and then shrugged, saying, "Still, imagine how glad we were to be here, not there, in the War! Jacob had a much harder time in Berlin than we did here. Luckily David had already come here on the Kindertransport, but Jacob lost his first wife, Ute, David's mother, and his parents while he himself escaped only by the skin of his teeth. And then, to think of it! He was interned when he arrived here!"

Shirley did not volunteer much information, but listened attentively before asking, "Were you caught in the Blitz?"

"No, we were fortunate: my parents lived outside London, and my mother still does," Rachel replied, and then tentatively enquired, "But what about you?"

Shirley sighed. "Yes, yes, we were... well, that is me and my family and..." She stopped and was lowering her voice when Ben started to cry, having hit his head on a sharp corner, so Ruth did not hear what her mother was saying. Rachel reached out a hand to Ben, but continued to listen to Shirley. She leant over and put her other arm round Shirley's shoulders.

"I am so sorry," Ruth heard her saying. "I am so sorry, it must have been dreadful for you; I never realized."

Shirley nodded wistfully. "Yes, it was terrible," she said, "but I try to forget." She lowered her voice. "And of course, John doesn't know anything about all that," she whispered.

After these relaxed little tea parties, which became more frequent and which she liked, Shirley would be pensive for a couple of days until she took up her usual routine of receiving her friends in "her" front room again. Gradually she took over the running of the house and did do some of the shopping and even some of the cooking, not always to a very high or appetizing standard, but neither John nor Ruth complained. Both knew better than even to think of doing that.

The food available was in any case more varied now that rationing was coming to an end, and they valued the peace and relative harmony of their home life too much to want to jeopardize it. Washing and housework were in principle shared by the three of them at weekends, though more often than not John, helped by Ruth, saw to those chores. At least a way of life, neither particularly happy nor unhappy, but somewhat monotonous, evolved in the household, leaving Ruth free to read books, write letters to Nan and sit with her dad listening to music on the Third Programme of an evening, while at school she pursued her music, her friendships and other new interests discovered through her lessons. How she longed to play some of those entrancing piano pieces she heard on the wireless!

She sensibly refrained from talking much about what she did in school, and was still careful to avoid all mention of the band and the piano which she loved as much as ever. She lived in hope that Miss Lake had not told Dad about her piano-playing since that time long ago when she had surreptitiously reverted to it instead of the triangle for the band. If Dad did know about her music, which was unlikely, he never referred to it, so she assumed that Miss Lake had not betrayed her secret. As she was so important to the band, she was allowed to practise whenever she liked, and the occasional lesson with Miss Lake at break time had become a regular weekly, or even twice-weekly fixture. Naturally she longed to have a piano at home, but knew, for reasons that remained frustratingly obscure, that that was impossible, even had there been room for one, which there certainly was not, except perhaps in Shirley's front room.

* * *

It had been as astonishing for Ruth as it was for her dad when Shirley, who had not of late been showing any significant signs of mounting tension, came up with the idea of the move to the newsagent's. A day or two after the violent dispute with John over the plans had subsided, she became submissive and almost apologetic, for perhaps she knew that she had over-stepped the mark in demanding too much of him too suddenly. To Ruth she tried to rationalize her behaviour. "I don't want to make life difficult for you and your dad," she began with uncharacteristic bashfulness one afternoon as she sat down beside Ruth, who was listening to a dramatization of *Nicholas Nickleby* on the wireless.

Speaking as one who was not used to apologizing for any-thing, let alone her own behaviour, she was having trouble expressing herself. Ruth wished she would go away and stop interrupting the broadcast, but felt obliged to listen. Shirley went on, disregarding the wireless. "The thing is, you see, I don't have much to do and there is so much I know I might do. You are growing up – I can't believe that you are ten already – and soon you won't need me any more." There was silence before, with an apparent effort, she whispered, "You are my only child, after all." A tiny hint of a sob crept into her voice here, and she moved over to the window. Ruth did not respond but, with one ear tuned to the wireless, waited with the other for her mother to continue.

"You see, Ruth, there was so much that I hoped I would be able to do, but the War came and messed all that up." She took a deep breath, before adding inexplicably, "I suppose it was in the War that I came into my own, but not for long." Lost in her own thoughts, she left Ruth free to attend to Nicholas's escape with Smike from Dotheboys Hall. Shirley went out into the kitchen as the spellbinding signature tune played itself out at the end of the programme, returning some minutes later with a tea tray. As she poured the tea, she delivered what sounded like a speech she had been preparing out in the kitchen. "At last, you see, I have a golden opportunity to do something I know I would do well and earn more money for all of us." She waxed lyrical as all the possibilities came to mind, "We might have a car one day and a television. And the flat above the shop is huge; it's like a whole house up there. There would be room for anything and everything there." Room for a piano? Ruth wondered, but did not dare ask.

She did not fully appreciate her mother's reasoning, but with pleasure remembered the little garden at the back of the shop and the view over the park. Perhaps, she surmised, there were various and differing reasons why it might be good for each of them: Shirley would have her television, even a car one day; Dad wouldn't have to work so hard to earn the money for them, and she herself would be nearer school in a nicer place. As if reading her mind, Shirley went on, "And of course you'll be going to the grammar school or even the high school next year. If you go to the high school, of course, you can walk, but if it's the grammar school, well then, the bus stop is right outside the door!"

It was by no means a foregone conclusion that Ruth would be going to any particular school in fourteen months' time, because there was still the hurdle of the Eleven Plus to be surmounted, but she was reluctant to raise that spectre either for herself or for Shirley at present. The immediate issue was whether she would in fact be going to spend the summer holidays at Nan's.

"Oh, yes, certainly," said Shirley, "though I'm afraid we won't be going to the sea this year, there won't be time. Your father won't be visiting your Nan either, because we will have such a lot to do with the move and setting up our own shop, so you'll have to stay with your nan for the whole of the holiday. You don't mind, do you?" she asked, casting a cautious glance in Ruth's direction. As nonchalantly as possible, Ruth reassured her mother that she didn't mind. She did not say that she was counting the days, the hours, the minutes and the seconds to the summer holidays, which were only three weeks away.

32

Unusually, this time it was Shirley who took Ruth to the station and put her on the train in the care of the guard, giving him money with which to buy lunch for her daughter. She helped Ruth lift her suitcase onto the rack, settled her in her seat and gave her a quick peck on the cheek, saying, "Bye, Ruth, have a lovely time, give my love to your nan. I must rush; I have so much to do." Ruth opened her bag to get out a book and some coloured pencils and paper ready to keep herself occupied, while Shirley exchanged a few words with the guard before running off, her high heels clattering on the platform.

The guard watched her go, shaking his head and grinning to himself. He came into Ruth's compartment. "Hello, young lady," he began, "you'll be fine here, won't you? I'll come back in half an hour or so to take you to the restaurant car for your lunch." He was a kindly man, so she responded with a smile.

She was proud to be travelling on her own again on a journey that was familiar to her, so familiar that she didn't think she needed to be put in the charge of the guard any longer, but out of politeness she refrained from saying so. In fact, she did not once open her book or her tin of pencils, because as usual she spent the whole journey, apart from the mealtime, looking out of the window. Even though the train did not pass through the cutting at the end of her street, she had learnt to detect well-known sights on the route – church spires, shabby streets glimpsed from bridges and clean new buildings growing out of blackened patches of earth. As the train gathered speed and emerged from the soot and the grime of north-east London, smoke blew past the window, obscuring the view though the day was fine, and leaving dirty specks on the glass. She smelt the smoke with relish, remembering that Grandpa had once said that that smell, together with the similar smell of his yellow soap, was what he liked best – which was why he used to lather himself all over with the soap and carried the odour of it with him all day.

Although it was now a long time since his death, his bright eyes and his funny little jokes were still fresh in her mind. Sometimes she felt that he was never far away, and she still heard his voice. Since neither her dad nor Shirley ever went to church in London and avoided discussion of matters like illness and death, she did not dare to broach the topic with her mother, and when once she had asked her father what it was like to die, he had simply replied, "I expect it's like falling into a very deep sleep," before walking off, so that there was no chance of plying him with any further questions. Of course, she had long since ceased to imagine that people went to live with God at the seaside when they died, any more than she believed that God lived on a cloud up in the sky, but she had found no satisfactory substitute for that childish notion. The barren, sad truth was that when people died you didn't see them again and you missed them a lot.

She pondered over the years that had passed since Grandpa died. That Christmas she had been in Miss Lake's class, and the next year there was Mr Brown, who was not unlike Grandpa – funny, always making jokes and showing off his strange accomplishments, like balancing a pencil on the end of his finger and twirling it around while he stood on one foot; then there followed the thoroughly enjoyable but rather chaotic year with Miss Bevan, the art teacher. Instead of books, chalks and pencils on her desk, she kept pots of paint and brushes, which were always falling over, to the great amusement of her pupils. Lately schoolwork had become more serious and more arduous, and last year Mr Green, the headmaster, had taken her class.

Even though so many years had passed since the Simple Simon episode, Mr Green had treated her guardedly, often asking anxiously, "Are you all right, Ruth? How are you getting on?" as though he was scared of her. He was a good teacher nonetheless, and despite the distress of her first encounter with him, she enjoyed his lessons, particularly his history lessons, which mostly concentrated on the history of London.

Playtimes might have been dull, because some of her friends had moved away, but there was always Ben to be cared for and protected from pushier children. Last winter Susan had announced petulantly, "Poppa says we're going to move house in the summer holidays – to the country, somewhere a long way off. He says he's found a nice house for us, and I'll have to go to school there." She made a face. "I don't want to move, I like it here."

Tears were welling up in her eyes, so Ruth tried not to show how dismayed she was too, but at that stage she did not know that she also would be moving house. Sometimes Susan annoyed her, sometimes they didn't speak to each other for a couple of days, but she knew that she would miss her – not only her, but Rachel and Ben as well, and Jacob too, though she seldom saw him. She would even miss Babushka, who recently on one of her visits had said to her, "You know, Ruth, you should be a dancer. You've grown tall, but you are still neat and light, and you hold yourself so well. Show me, can you do *pliés* in all positions?" Ruth had practised *pliés* in private ever since she had seen some of the older girls learning them in Susan's ballet class, so she easily executed the sequence. "*Ochin harashò*! Very nice," Babushka observed admiringly.

Ruth regretted that she was very unlikely to see Babushka again, although it transpired that the Meyers' move was only to somewhere south of London. Shirley's first reaction to the news had been pragmatic: "It won't matter," she said, because you are old enough to come home alone now." She did not mention Rachel or their growing friendship, though after she had reconsidered the news her delayed reaction conveyed a hint of disappointment. "It's a pity," she added, "They're a nice family. I like them. Rachel and I have become good friends."

As the countryside vanished before her eyes, Ruth was lost in a reverie, conjuring up the image of grandpa, who would not be at the station to meet her, either with his old motor-bike or his car. Sadness and amusement mingled equally in her thoughts as she smiled nostalgically to herself, wondering if he were looking down on her, watching her as she travelled alone with confidence and eager with anticipation. The guard, commissioned by Shirley, came at lunchtime to take her to sit in the restaurant car among older people. They smiled at her, but she did not need their interest or sympathy, because she knew what she was doing and where she was going, perhaps better than they did. The only drawback was sitting on the wrong side of the train for the farm.

At the end of the line she was impatient to get off and dash to Nan, who would be waiting by the barrier, but her impatience was frustrated when the guard, kind though he was, said, "No, no, miss, I'm afraid you'll have to wait for me. I can't let you get off alone, and I have to see all the passengers off the train before I can take you to meet your granny."

Ruth forced herself to suppress her indignation at being treated like a small child, having discovered long ago that displays of temper, however successfully her mother might manipulate hers to advantage, simply were counterproductive and always ended in trouble. Happily, since the other passengers were as keen to be off the train as she was, the carriages were soon cleared, and there was Nan, warm and welcoming as ever, waiting for her as expected. They hadn't met since last Christmas, when Nan had come to London for the festive season, giving Ruth the odd feeling that she had been away at boarding school all that time and was now coming home.

She glanced down at Ruth's suitcase. "Ah, that's good," she remarked, "you've only brought a small case. Come on, give that to me." Ruth did as she was bidden, but then was embarrassed to find that Nan intended to carry the case. She tried to take it back. "No, no," Nan insisted, "I'll carry the suitcase: you look after your bag. We are going to go and have tea in the city. Would you like that? It's such a long time since I last saw you, I'm going to start spoiling you right away – and have a little treat myself!"

Of course Ruth wanted to go into the city for tea. They sat looking out over the coloured awnings of the market, eating scones and cakes and ice cream, while in answer to Nan's question Ruth considered what she would like to do for the next six weeks. "I'd like to see the castle and the cathedral," she ventured tentatively. Then, without thinking of the practicalities, she quickly added: "And shall we go to the sea and to the farm?"

"Sorry, dear?" Nan replied, throwing Ruth into confusion. She was afraid she had asked for too much because, before she left home, Dad had said seriously, "Now Ruth, you mustn't forget that Nan is not as young as she was, so don't expect too much of her." However, Nan put a hand to her ear and said, "You'll have to shout, Ruthie, I'm getting so very deaf." With relief Ruth repeated her requests more loudly and more slowly, and Nan laughed. "Yes, certainly, we can do all those things. Mark my words, we shall be busy, but remember to speak up!"

They were indeed busy and achieved everything that Ruth wanted. Nan showed her the sights of the city, leading her along a warren of little cobbled streets and back alleys lined with bookshops, toyshops, antique shops and the occasional café, not to mention churches and museums. Each day held a new discovery and a new delight in store. One day it was the treasures inside the Norman keep, which somewhat mitigated the gloomy terrors of the dungeons; another it was the soaring glory of the cathedral with its high embossed roof and its reaching spire. They went to tea in the Regency Rooms, though Ruth confessed to being slightly disappointed that the chandeliers did not seem to sparkle as brightly as they did years ago.

"Yes, it's a pity. They need cleaning, dear," said Nan. "I don't know when they'll get round to doing that. It's a very difficult job. Goodness only knows how they do it."

Grandpa's car had been sold after his death. Nan had offered it to her son, but though grateful, he had declined the offer, saying that they had nowhere to keep it in London. His refusal had provoked, understandably, a particularly thunderous response from Shirley. "You knew I always wanted to have a car, and your mother offered it to you! Why on earth didn't you accept? We could have gone on holiday in it and taken her with us! That would have been so much easier than trudging off to the station with all the luggage. And think of the nice times we would have had on days out in the country!" She ranted on and on about it for several days, but John stubbornly stood his ground until finally she gave up when his argument that his mother needed the money from the sale of the vehicle, because her pension was not adequate, hit home.

Ruth and her grandmother travelled everywhere by train and by bus; they went to the sea several times and to the farm once. At the seaside Nan would paddle briefly and then as usual sit in a deckchair on the beach, watching while Ruth tried to swim in the chill, grey waters of the North Sea. In London both her parents forbade her to go to the swimming pool for fear of some terrible illness, so she had not learnt to swim, and here, as she was beginning to float, waves would crash over her head, filling her nose and ears with salt water. After their day on the beach, Nan treated her to fish and chips on the pier before the train ride home. It did not matter that the sea was very cold and she was shivering, her ears were blocked and her eyes were stinging, for the sun shone and Ruth was sublimely happy.

One weekend they took a bus to the station nearest to the farm. There Uncle Rick was waiting for them in his truck and, as soon as they had clambered on board, he sped off down winding lanes to get back to the harvesting, which was in full progress. The cousins, enveloped in a cloud of dust as they followed the harvester, waved and shouted through the din, beckoning Ruth to come and join them in the field.

"You'll need boots for that," Nan observed.

In no time Aunt Muriel produced an old pair of wellingtons, which Ruth donned hastily before rushing off to work alongside the family.

"Would you like a ride on the old harvester?" asked Uncle Abe. Without a second's delay, she climbed up into the cab and sat high above the golden field, watching the corn disappear before her, remembering an earlier occasion long ago when she had sat next to her grandpa as he drove the mighty machine.

"I don't know why you like it so much," her Cousin Wizzie said as she climbed out of the cab, "it's so hot and dirty! I'd

much rather live in a city like you!" Wizzie was still good fun
when they went searching for eggs together, but Ruth began
to prefer the company of the boys, although they made fun of
her, calling her "little townie". Their teasing was good-natured,
and she had to admire their hard work. She particularly liked
her eldest cousin, Andy. He was tall and dark, rather like her
father, and he worked harder than any of them, but there
was also an engaging gentleness about him which she found
appealing when he looked at her, as he often did with a rather
mischievous smile.

In the evening the whole family sat at supper, laughing and
talking, their faces glistening with the exertion and satisfaction. The farm did now have both mains electricity and running
water, which Aunt Dolly was proud to point out, and which
Uncle George demonstrated by turning the taps above the sink
on and switching the light on and off.

That night Ruth stayed at the farm and slept soundly in a
camp bed beside Nan's. Although the bed was hard and the
sheets stiff, she fell asleep as soon as her head touched the
pillow, without noticing how dark it was outside, nor how
quiet, for not a sound was heard, until suddenly at dawn the
cock crowed loudly, right beneath the window, and all the
animals and cockerels in the village sprang to life, joining in
a vigorous chorus. There was a clanking of pails in the yard
and the sound of Cousin Andy's voice, muttering as he slapped
something hard, "Come on, you silly old girl, get a move on!
You're holding us all up!"

These excursions were in themselves the stuff of dreams,
yet there was also so much to do in Nan's house and garden
without ever going outside the front gate. The only disappointment was that Carrie and the girls were away. "They've gone
camping for a whole month to Scotland!" said Nan sceptically
as she mused on the folly of leaving one's comfortable home
and sleeping out of doors, without electricity or running
water, in distant parts where no doubt it rained most of the
time. Nonetheless, there was little time to miss them as there
was so much to keep Ruth occupied for the garden constantly

needed weeding and the lawns, front and back, had to be mown every week.

At the end of the lawn Nan had made a small vegetable patch where she grew beans and peas, lettuces, tomatoes and a pound or two of potatoes. Every day some of these had to be picked or dug up and then washed, shelled or chopped for their meals. In less active moments Ruth would repair to the lean-to, her old cabin, with its tin bath full of sand. There the old bus seats still leant against the side, rather the worse for wear, and her swing, dangling from its hooks in the beam above, silently awaited her. It was rather too near the ground for Ruth these days, but she liked to sit on it and sing to herself while swaying to and fro, letting her feet graze against the hard earth on the floor and wondering what had become of Nan's fairy stories. Much as part of her would have liked to revive that tradition, by the age of ten she was keen to put such silliness behind her.

Grandpa's shed, which stood there next to the lean-to, was another matter, for she would never be too old for that. Although Nan had said she herself didn't go in there, Ruth did not believe a word of what she said, because everything was in such good order with not a cobweb or a speck of dust in sight. When it rained outside, the shed as ever could be relied upon to be an Aladdin's den of treasures. Taking out Grandpa's tools, she sawed one end off a thin piece of wood which she had fastened to the clamp. Then, not being altogether sure what to make with it, she did the same to another, and another until finally she decided that she had enough pieces of wood to make a star. All that was needed was to file down the ends to a point, hammer them together with a couple of small nails and then paint them with the gold paint which was still there in its old tin. This kept her occupied for the best part of a morning, so that at lunchtime she was able to present Nan with a large gold star.

"That's splendid!" said Nan admiringly, as she hung the star on a hook on the wall. "There," she remarked, "I knew Grandpa had some good reason for putting that hook up there – and look, your star covers up the hole your dad made with that tiny pistol! Would you make me some more of those for my stall at the Christmas bazaar, if you'd be so kind?"

On another rainy day Ruth helped Nan set up her jam factory, since the plums were falling off the trees faster than they could eat them. As ever the jars were lined up, joining those of an earlier vintage, glinting reds and golds and greens on the shelf by the window in the larder.

"What are you going to do with all that jam, Nan?" Ruth asked. After all, Grandpa was not there to eat it, and there was too much for Nan to bring on the train to London or take out to the farm to share with the cousins.

"Well, let me see," Nan replied as she made a mental reckoning of the various uses her jam would be put to. "I shall give some to my friends at the Mothers' Union" – Ruth remembered with a shudder of distaste the ancient ladies with their hairy chins, who would insist on kissing and hugging her – "some to Carrie and the girls, and so on, and then there's the Harvest Festival in September, when you've gone back to school, and then there'll be the Christmas bazaar. And of course Abe will come and collect some for Dolly. So there won't be much left, but enough to last me through the winter, and enough for you and your father next time you come to stay. And maybe you might manage to take a jar or two back to London with you."

Above all, whatever the weather, there was the piano. On her previous brief summer visits with her dad, Ruth had worked her way through the intermediate books in the piano stool and then had embarked on some more difficult pieces, as and when he went out, but the time available had always been too short for her, and his absences were always unpredictable. He might spend a whole morning out in the city, roaming the old streets or looking up historical documents in the library or browsing in the museum, or he might return quite soon, armed with a book or a newspaper which he would then settle down to read for the rest of the day.

"Won't you come with me to the Castle Museum?" he had once asked Ruth. "No, I'll stay with Nan," she replied without offering any other explanation in her impatience to sit down at the piano.

Longing to play anything from Evelyn's collection fluently, she began to take out large works from an old case which stood beside the piano; from among those, she selected the ones that had Evelyn's name written inside the cover. This summer she revelled in the time and freedom to practise as much as she liked, and to discover new melodies and new composers. Nan was impressed by her progress and kept coming in with comments.

"Well, that's beautiful, Ruthie!" she would exclaim with satisfaction. Similarly, Nan might be delighted at her own ability to identify a set of pieces: "Now, I recognize that. It's Schumann's 'Papillons'. I love that!" Then she declared with evident pleasure, "How quickly you've come on since you first arrived and you were playing his 'Kinderszenen'!" Then she added a suggestion, "And since you're playing Schumann, why not try his 'Arabesque'? It is delightful, one of my favourite pieces." Ruth followed this suggestion, becoming intoxicated with 'Arabesque' herself. Had she not been seated at the piano, she would certainly have wanted to dance to it.

Relishing in the old friends that Ruth was bringing back to life at Evelyn's piano, Nan kept interrupting to give her opinions on other works once Ruth had mastered 'Arabesque' to her satisfaction.

"I love that Mozart C major Sonata – that's right, isn't it?" or "That Ravel 'Pavane' is enchanting!" she would exclaim, her face shining with delight. Later she suggested that Ruth might begin to learn some Bach. "I think you would enjoy the 'Two-Part Inventions', but maybe you should start with the 'Anna Magdalena Notebook': she was Bach's first wife, you know. Let me look for a moment in that pile over there – I think that's where they are. With the 'Two-Part Inventions' you'll discover contrapuntal music – that is, music in two equal parts."

Nan was overjoyed at her granddaughter's progress, but some embarrassment arose when she asked how it was that Ruth had learnt to play so well.

"Oh, I do it in school," Ruth replied evasively. "Miss Lake teaches me sometimes when she has time, usually about once or twice a week."

"I see!" said Nan, though she didn't really see at all. "Your dad must be very happy that you can play so well." She went on to ask cautiously, "It's not a secret any more, is it?" There was a touch of caution in her voice. "Your parents do know about it, don't they? It's years since you told me that your father was afraid it might make Shirley ill – and she's much better now, isn't she?" She searched Ruth's face for an answer.

"Well, he doesn't know about it yet," Ruth replied. "I haven't told him, because a long time ago he was so serious and strict when he asked me not to mention the piano, I haven't dared talk about it since. He was very worried it might upset Shirley then, and I don't know how she would take it now."

"I understand. Perhaps he's right," Nan reflected. "I can't say I'm happy about it, but we had better keep it a secret still, hadn't we? It's our secret. At least for the time being." Ruth was relieved, grateful that Nan had not scolded her or insisted on telling her parents. "It's a pity, even so," Nan observed as she went back to the kitchen to put labels on yet more jars of jam.

In the early part of the holiday, when the weather was fine, they ate their meals out of doors, but towards the middle of August the evenings grew chilly and Nan decided that the time had come to eat supper indoors.

She declared, "It's too cold out here with that north wind blowing. Let's take our plates inside, and I think I'll light a fire." Once the flames were flickering in the grate, she turned the wireless on to the Third Programme to catch the Prom. "Friday night, it must be Beethoven night!" She thumbed through the *Radio Times* to see what was on. "Oh, good!" she exclaimed. "It's going to be the 'Emperor' Concerto! You'll love this, Ruth! Evelyn was going to play it at the Proms once, but when it came to it she was too ill. But we have got those old gramophone records of when she played it with the City Orchestra." She sighed and urged Ruth to listen for the slow movement. "It's one of the most beautiful pieces of music ever written." They listened together and both fell silent.

The slow movement overwhelmed Ruth: it brought together all the sorrow she had ever known, flooding over her in such a great wave of pathos that she almost wept, except that the feeling penetrated deep within her, beyond the level of tears. The wave carried on infinitely rolling, washing the sadness away, leaving her enveloped in an indescribable sensation of light and beauty. Perhaps that was what dying was like, she thought.

At last she spoke quietly. "I'd like to play that one day, Nan."

Nan nodded. "I don't see why you shouldn't, if you keep on practising; Evelyn's score of it is somewhere on the piano or in the stool," she said. "And one of these days, when you have space for it, you shall have Evelyn's piano. But," she added, "maybe we had better keep quiet about that for the moment."

"Yes, certainly," agreed Ruth, "that's right."

"But I don't see why you shouldn't have Evelyn's music, her piano score for it, then you can begin to study it whenever you want and you can listen to her recordings," Nan declared firmly.

33

Ruth did not look forward to going back to London. On the one hand she had no idea what the move to the shop might involve, and on the other she longed to live with Nan in that house where she was so happy. She saw no reason why she should not go to school in the city – in which case of course she would also be able to play the piano every day. By now she knew the bus route well and was fairly confident that she could make her own way to the school that both the girls next door attended. All things considered, she would not be any trouble to Nan, she reasoned, and would help her and keep her company on those dark winter evenings. When she put the idea to Nan, she considered it for long enough to imply that she was taking it seriously, before remarking, "Well, Ruthie, it's a lovely idea and, of course, I'd like to have you here with me all the time, but think how much your dad would miss you!" Ruth hadn't thought of that and was abashed that she had not taken her father into consideration. It did not matter that she hadn't thought of Shirley, because she doubted that Shirley would be bothered.

At the beginning of September she closed her suitcase with a heavy heart and hauled it downstairs to where Nan was waiting by the door with her coat and hat already on. "The bus will be here soon, and if we don't catch it you'll miss your train, and your dad will be worried if you don't arrive," she announced with an urgency which left Ruth no option but to follow her out of the house.

Once on the bus, Nan, who seemed to be weighing up the various possibilities, addressed the topic again. "You know I'd love to have you here, Ruthie, but as there's still so much fruit down on the farm, I'm going back there next week for ten days or so to make their jam and do some bottling for them. So I wouldn't be here to keep house for you." Ruth had no choice but to accept Nan's argument, though the image of the farm and the orchard tugged at her heartstrings, simply increasing her reluctance to catch the train.

It was cheering therefore to discover that being back in London was not as bad as she had feared. As Dad explained when he met her at Liverpool Street, the newsagent's shop had, like all the other shops on the Broadway, been converted out of a rather fine Edwardian house by previous owners.

"I think you'll like it," he said encouragingly as they emerged from the Underground and set off down the road. Although it was unbelievable, he was right: she did like it. The large front room of the former house was big enough to serve not only as the shop with its own entrance, but also towards the back, behind a newly erected partition wall, as an office. Like the post office next door, the shop had been extended at the front, where once there had been a large bay window, and there it had its own entrance and display window. This left the rest of the house for the family.

The original front door next to the shop entrance opened onto a hallway which led to a high-ceilinged room on the left behind the shop, looking out over a small garden. Although it was not as big as the shop, the room was nevertheless a good size and made all the old furniture seem rather small, shabby and insignificant. Shirley had designated it as the living room, where sooner or later she intended to install a television. At the end of the hallway, down a couple of steps, was a small dining room with a kitchen and, beyond the kitchen, side by side, a cloakroom, scullery and larder extended the building even farther out into the garden. Under the stairs, a door opened onto steep steps which led down to a huge cellar covering the whole extent of the house: this served as the stockroom, its shelves stacked with every known brand of cigarette, from Black Cat and Players to the very expensive Sobranie Black Russian, which Shirley smoked from time to time.

At the top of a steep flight of stairs leading up from the hall near the front door were two large rooms: the one above the shop had become Shirley's reception room, where not a single ornament was on display, and behind it was the double bedroom. Ruth was at first given a little room at the front next to the reception room, which she did not much like, since it gave onto the street and was noisy. Shirley however was remarkably obliging when, the morning after her arrival, Ruth complained that the noise from the main road had kept her awake, and offered her instead one or other of the two small rooms right at the very back of the house, above the outhouses, down a short but steep staircase. These rooms were quiet; their small windows overlooked not only the garden, where clouds of blue Michaelmas daisies were coming into flower, but also the park with its tall spreading trees and green open spaces.

Granddad Reggie, who had come to give a hand with the business during the takeover, was lodged in the other of those two rooms. The bathroom was at the top of yet another flight of stairs which led up from the landing. He complained frequently about the stairs. "Stairs everywhere in this house!" he grumbled, as he heaved his lumbering form up to the bathroom last thing at night.

"Well, Pa, you're a fine one to grumble. You've as many if not more stairs at home, but we can move you to the little bedroom at the front as Ruth doesn't want it any more, if you like. It will be noisier with the traffic, but you're used to the railway, so that won't matter," said Shirley agreeably, as she set to work changing the bed linen. "Now you'll only have two flights of stairs instead of three," she remarked on finishing that chore, "and anyhow you only need to go up there at night because, remember, we've got two lavatories, one downstairs as well as the one up at the top."

Granddad Reggie retorted in an extremely long and wheezy utterance that he knew the stairs at home, whereas these were different, and he didn't feel safe on them – and what's more climbing those stairs several times in the dead of night was no joke. Having voiced his objections, however, he made the adjustment without further ado.

Although Shirley had not exactly given Ruth a hug on her arrival, she had smiled and put an arm round her shoulder. "Look at this, Ruth!" she exclaimed excitedly. "You never imagined you'd come back to find us living in a house this big, did you?"

Ruth had to admit that she certainly had not, as she was led from room to room, and each detail of brand-new carpeting and curtains, new counters and glass cases in the shop, where there was even the unheard-of luxury of a telephone, was pointed out to her. The smell of paint pervaded every space, especially the large upstairs room at the front, which had been the last to be redecorated.

Shirley laughed. "I may have to give up smoking: it does spoil the paint and the furnishings so!" she announced cheerfully.

Ruth was amazed, for she had never seen Shirley on such good form or so relaxed. In her absence her mother had undergone an extraordinary transformation into a different person – one she might warm to. If this was what was needed to change Shirley's personality and consequently their home life, she had no objection whatsoever.

When she had shown her daughter over the whole property, Shirley asked expectantly, "Well, what do you think of your new home? Isn't it fabulous?"

"Oh, yes," Ruth agreed, laughing with enthusiasm, "It's lovely!"

Shirley was so thrilled by her reply that finally she hugged her daughter. "I'm so glad you like it," she said. "Oh, and what's more, did your dad tell you he's been promoted?" she added as an afterthought as she turned on her heel and fled back into the shop through a newly installed connecting door in the hallway.

It was not all plain sailing, naturally enough. One evening, soon after Ruth had gone back to school, Granddad Reggie left, having been given his marching orders by his confident daughter.

"It's all right, Pa," Shirley had commanded, briskly, "I can cope on my own now, thank you. You go off home: Ted will be pleased to see you." However, in a matter of hours she had collapsed and become agitated. "It's too much for me on my own," she moaned. "I should never have taken all this on." John tried to comfort her, offering to give whatever help he could when not at work. "It's your fault," she complained, "you should have stopped me. You should have put your foot down and said 'no'."

Taking a deep breath he succeeded in keeping calm. "It'll be fine," he said soothingly, putting his arm round her prostrate frame. "You're doing very well. You need time to adjust, that's all. Perhaps you were too quick to send your father home."

Shirley did not appreciate these observations, but started to raise her voice, the recognizable danger signal indicating a mounting head of steam.

"Wait a moment! I've got an idea," John interrupted quickly. "We have a telephone now, so why don't we use it? I'll ring your father and ask him to come back. He won't mind. After all, he said he liked helping you with your new business, in spite of the stairs, so if Tilly and Cousin Archie can take over his shop again, which I'm sure they can, he'll want to stay as long as he's needed."

So Granddad Reggie came back from south London and was compelled to struggle up the stairs to the bathroom at the top of the house several times in the night, grumbling loudly enough to wake the whole household as he went. Nonetheless, he was content to share with his daughter his profound knowledge of the sale of newspapers, magazines, tobacco, cigarettes, sweets, stationery – and fireworks, since the 5th of November was approaching. Shirley devoted herself entirely to the business, working in the shop all day and in the office and stockroom for much of the night, rising early to instruct the paperboys and send them on their rounds. She took only one hour off after supper for her husband to give her some instruction in accountancy.

Meanwhile Ruth and her father did the shopping and the cooking in their spare time, and Granddad Reggie bought them a washing machine, which they operated on Saturday afternoons.

Dad had muttered, "No, that's going too far when you've done so much for us already" to Granddad Reggie when the machine was delivered, but as usual the latter grunted something unintelligible and settled himself down in an armchair by the fire in the back room with one of his model-train magazines. He stayed for a week to help Shirley with the books before departing once again for his home territory. By the time he left, she had everything under control and felt truly confident about running the business herself.

One by one modern appliances made their appearance in the house. First it was the washing machine, and then one afternoon Shirley greeted her daughter in great excitement. "Come and see what we've got now!" she cried, leading Ruth into the kitchen. There in a corner stood a gleaming-white, brand-new fridge.

"Oh, this will make the whole business of shopping and cooking so much easier!" she exclaimed.

Ruth inspected the acquisition approvingly inside and out. "Yes, yes," she agreed, "it certainly will." She was not sure how much Shirley understood the difference it would make to her life and her father's, but was grateful that they, the kitchen staff, had been considered. Or perhaps they had not. Perhaps the fridge was simply an indication of the material wealth with which Shirley would seek to impress her friends. Truth to tell, though, Shirley did not entertain as she used to: she was far too busy and preoccupied with her business to want to waste time on people she now regarded as idlers.

However, when a television arrived and was installed in the living room, she insisted on having a party to celebrate. "Yes," she said to her admiring friends one Sunday evening as they assembled, "it's what we've always wanted and now the shop is going so well we can afford it!"

They all sat round intent on the flickering screen as it came to life. Ruth watched the ensuing programme, 'What's My Line', with the rest of them, since she was as fascinated as they were, particularly because several of her friends at school had televisions, so now she would know what they were talking about in playtime. She still listened to the radio with her father and she read books, but the television would allow her to see some of those stories and other more modern dramas, about the police and detectives for instance, enacted before her own eyes.

Shirley, though immensely proud of her television, never had time to watch it, being far too busy making money. Rather, she gave the impression of being determined to make up for lost time, all the time she had spent in hospital being ill and all the time she had spent in domesticity – or what she regarded as domesticity – and the most satisfactory way of doing that was by making money. In that endeavour she was prepared to deprive herself of many a pleasure and many an opportunity for relaxation, the television being but one example.

Bonfire night was another case in point. Ruth and her father were allowed a handful of leftover, unsold fireworks – a rocket, a couple of Golden Rains, a Roman Candle, two Jumping George and a Mount Vesuvius, plus a packet of sparklers – to let off in the back garden while Shirley retreated to her office to tot up the takings from the firework sales, which were considerable – "an unexpected bonus" was how she described them. She had considered cancelling the orders, given the amount of work her other merchandise generated, together with the trouble of having to set aside a counter to house the fireworks, but had decided in the end that she would give them a try, for the first year at least. In the event the sales had been as spectacular as the goods themselves, so she vowed to continue selling them.

Out in the garden after supper on 5th November, the rain poured down from an overcast sky that had been deceptively clear until about five o'clock, and many of the fireworks fizzled out. It would have been a rather sad occasion had Dad not produced from under his coat a dozen more that he must have bought elsewhere on his way home from work without telling Shirley. He put his finger to his lips when he showed them to Ruth, and went back indoors to fetch his big, black umbrella. Holding it over the illicit fireworks with one hand, he set about lighting them, one by one, with the other. When he came to the last rocket, he stood it upright in a milk bottle before lighting the blue touchpaper, but he was not prepared for the speed with which the rocket ignited. It shot into the air with a whoosh, piercing a hole through his umbrella. Though taken off guard, Dad was unscathed if somewhat sooty.

"Well! Would you believe it?" he asked. "I've never known that to happen before!" Ruth laughed out loud. They both heard Shirley approaching and hastened to clear away the debris before she discovered their pyrotechnic disloyalty.

"What's going on out here?" she asked, suspecting that she might have missed out on some fun.

"Nothing, dear," Dad said innocently. "We're clearing up now. The rocket shot through my umbrella!"

"Not to worry," she replied sympathetically, wiping the soot from his face, unaware that her sympathy was uncalled for. "I'll buy you a new one for Christmas."

34

Even though the distance to school was shorter by ten minutes as a result of the move, Ruth left home at the same time as before to walk up the road with her father. His office was only ten minutes beyond the school, but since his recent promotion, he liked to arrive earlier than the rest of the staff, attacking his new duties as Manager of the Rates Office with his customary seriousness of purpose. The arrangement gave Ruth, by special dispensation, a welcome clear fifteen minutes of piano practice before the bell rang. Her class teacher for the year, the assistant Head, raised no objection to her arriving early for her music practice, and although her father may have wondered why she ran off into school so eagerly while the other children still played in the playground, his mind by this stage would be focusing on his own day ahead and he never stopped to enquire. By the end of the day he would have forgotten about it anyway.

In the companionship of the piano and her music, Ruth found some compensation for the absence of Susan and Ben. Simple Simon had also gone, but no one knew where. Rumours were rife: some said that he had been caught stealing, others that he had attacked his younger sister. The only certain fact was that he was not in school. Ruth did have friends with whom she played skipping games or jacks or pick-a-stick in break time, but none were as close as Susan had been, so it was no great sacrifice to relinquish their company in favour of Chopin or Mozart.

In any case a general air of gloom and apprehension hung over that class of children in this, the year of the Eleven Plus exams, upon which the rest of their lives depended. The whole course of their lives might be determined by the results. If successful, they would go to the grammar school, or even to the high school on an assisted place, with opportunities for higher education. Otherwise the Secondary Modern would mop up the failures and destine them to a life as second-class citizens. Although, like all the others, Ruth hoped for a place at the grammar school, she was sure that her maths would let her down.

Shirley had reacted brusquely one evening when over supper Ruth had complained that she simply didn't understand how to do subtraction with pounds, shillings and pence.

"I don't believe it," she remarked cuttingly. "I expected you were going to be a mathematician like your father. After all, it's obvious that you take after him, not me." She went on more encouragingly after a minute or two, in which time she may have considered her remarks rather unfair. "As I've said before, it wasn't my best subject either, but you can learn if you try – I did, and look at me now, doing sums all day behind the counter and much of the night as well! I'm sure your father would teach you." She considered the matter and then concluded, "Anyhow, there are no two ways about it: you've got to learn. We have to do a lot of sums in the business, and we might need you to help out sometimes."

She looked to her husband for his agreement, while Ruth sought clarification by scanning her parents' expressions. Dad said nothing, and Shirley went off to do something else. It was news to Ruth that one day she might be required to play a part in the business, but she let it pass for the time being, although in the longer term that was not the plan that she had begun to formulate for herself.

Dad was always tired at the end of his day at work. It wasn't the calculations involved, he used to say: they were no problem at all. The trouble lay in the staff. One could never rely on them to turn up. If they didn't, he would have to do their work as well as his own.

He gave Ruth a weary smile. "Yes, of course, I'll see what I can do. Anything for our Ruth! Let's start after supper, but that means that you" – here he addressed Shirley – "will have to go without your accountancy lesson for the time being."

"That's all right," she replied. "I'm fine with the bookkeeping, and that's what matters at the moment. Anyway, when I've finished with my stocktaking, I think I'll watch the telly for a bit."

So for half an hour, often longer, after supper every evening for the rest of that term, Ruth was guided by her dad through the intricacies of Eleven Plus maths, through division, fractions and decimals, shapes, measurements, percentages, graphs and averages. Money was indeed a huge problem. "If Paul had half a crown and Jack had one shilling and sevenpence ha'penny, how much more money did Paul have?" was the question posed in the book that Ruth had brought home from school for homework. Dad toyed with the problem and regarded Ruth seriously, as if the sum were insoluble. "Well, I'll tell you a secret when we've done it the correct way first." He wrote out the sum for her and helped her work laboriously through the subtraction. Then he said, "Now for the easy way. Imagine you've got one shilling and sevenpence ha'penny in your pocket. Then count up from one shilling and sevenpence ha'penny to two shillings. You can use your fingers. How much is that?"

"Fourpence ha'penny?" Ruth suggested uncertainly.

"Yes, that's right, now you've got to two shillings. How much more do you need to make it half a crown?"

"Oh, I see!" exclaimed Ruth, as light burst in on dark corners of her mathematical understanding. "Only another sixpence! So it's…" – she counted slowly– "it's tenpence ha'penny!"

"Well done," Dad smiled. "You see, it's not so bad after all! But you must remember to write out the sum in the exam, otherwise they might think you're a mathematical genius!"

Ruth laughed. Dad was so funny when he wasn't too tired, because he had a knack of bringing numbers to life and making them understandable, sometimes lampooning the questions. "Goodness," he said, pushing his glasses back over his temples, where his previously thick dark hair was thinning with grey streaks showing in it, "whoever in their right mind would want to know how many more carrots one rabbit ate than another in three hours?" This question involved something called "algebra", which Ruth hated even more than subtraction and division and money.

Some questions involving bags of sweets and the amount of time children were taking over their homework were fairly easy by comparison, though Dad made them more entertaining by pointing out how preposterous they were. He remarked that the person who ate three-fifths of a bag of three hundred sweets in one hour must have awful toothache and would be terribly sick, and when it came to calculating how long it took poor Keith to do his homework when he spent three times as long as Judy did over hers, he sighed, "Poor boy, if it takes Judy two hours and forty-five minutes to do hers, he'll be up all night!" The lessons went quickly under his tuition, and Ruth enjoyed them; they awoke memories of learning to play the piano under Nan's guidance.

"You're wasted in that office, John," Shirley observed over supper a week or two later.

He sighed, "Maybe. I would have liked to be a teacher, but it's too late for that now."

"That's true," Shirley agreed, "but it was all because of the War, wasn't it? Perhaps there's something else you could take up now."

John shook his head ruefully. "I don't think so, dear. I'll have to make the best of it."

"Well, for a start would you like to help me in the shop?" Shirley proposed. "Why not give it a try on Saturday mornings?" While John considered that proposition, another idea occurred to her. "Why doesn't Ruth come and help too? She can practise all those sums she's learning in real life! She can manage the sweet counter and measure out the sweets and take the money and give out the correct change just as you've shown her!" Shirley's ideas were put into practice without delay the next weekend and, before she knew it, Ruth found herself installed behind the counter measuring out quarters and halves of boiled sweets and liquorice allsorts, lollipops and sherbets, sweet cigarettes and jelly babies.

Though nervous at first, she soon grew more confident and began to enjoy her position. Most of her customers were children spending their pocket money, many of them from her school, so they did not mind waiting while she counted up the change on her fingers. Indeed, they were impressed and not a little envious.

"You're not allowed to eat them yourself, are you, Ruth?" they all asked, and when she said that she was allowed to eat one if she had sold a lot, they sighed and whistled enviously. She refrained from telling them that her mother had banned the night-time sweet long ago, and had strictly rationed how many she was allowed to eat during the week for the sake of her teeth.

Some children also enquired, "And are you allowed to read the comics too?"

"Oh yes," Ruth would reply airily, reciting the list of publications available to her, "*Eagle, Girl, Robin, Beano*... when I'm not serving."

That gave rise to a hopeful chorus pleading, "Can we stay and read comics too?" Whereupon Shirley would come over from the tobacco counter and hustle the young customers away, saying generously, "If we have any leftovers we can't return, Ruth will bring them to school for you on Monday morning."

This was not such a satisfactory arrangement for Ruth, because it meant that on Monday mornings she no longer ran straight into school and sat down at the piano after the deprivation of the weekend, but had to distribute a pile of remaindered comics to the excited crowd awaiting her arrival at the school gate. Her father's presence helping her in this task kept the crowd in order, but it took a long time, usually until the bell rang. In fact, it was Dad who sorted out the old comics, for he too worked in the shop, not only on Saturdays but on Sunday mornings as well. When she discovered how efficient he was on Saturday mornings, Shirley offered to do the washing on Sundays, if he wouldn't mind sorting out the bulk delivery of newspapers, opening the shop and sending the paperboys on their way.

Naturally he agreed, so Shirley stayed in bed till ten, and then got up to do the washing and cook the lunch. Although Ruth, ever protective, viewed this arrangement as exploitation of her father, in fact it worked reasonably well. John was naturally an early riser, however tired he had been the night before, so getting up on a Sunday morning was no hardship for him, and the advantage of it was that Shirley was content. She worked hard, slept well, and on Sundays had time to recover from her exertions of the past week.

Nan arrived a week before Christmas and as usual helped out tirelessly. Though slightly lame in her right leg and slightly harder of hearing, she took over the kitchen from the moment of her arrival. Slowly but methodically she shopped and cooked, served and did the washing-up, darned socks and mended clothing, refusing all offers of help, because, as she said, Ruth and John had far too many other things to think about in the evenings. She encouraged them to work on the Eleven Plus questions while she made puddings and mince pies, and marvelled at the usefulness of the new refrigerator.

"Well, that's beautiful!" she remarked admiringly. "Mind you, I wouldn't have any need for one of those; my larder is quite cold enough, thank you!"

As for the television, she found it captivating at first and stood in the doorway watching it, saying "Goodness gracious me!", but decided that she preferred the wireless, even though she had to turn up the sound and sit close to it, because she said she liked to create her own pictures in her mind – and in any case the wireless was better for music. Nonetheless, she was impressed with the house and the business, and told Shirley so. Gratified at Nan's approval but wanting to leave her in no doubt as to how hard she worked, Shirley joined the family for meal-times and then sidled off back into the office or the stockroom to count out the day's takings or check supplies for the next day.

Nan was less pleased to discover how hard her son was work-ing, not simply at his weekday job, but at the weekends as well, especially in the pre-Christmas rush, when the shelves had to be kept stocked and customers queued up to buy the goods.

"I'm worried about your father," Nan confided in Ruth. "I think he's got far too much to do."

"Don't worry, Nan," Ruth replied, trying to comfort her. "It's so much easier now that you are here! And I think Dad likes working in the shop."

Nan shook her head, unconvinced. She was relieved though that Ruth, because of the complications involved in multiple purchases, was not required in the shop in the run-up to Christmas: she certainly did not approve of her granddaughter being put to work as well as her son. This release left Ruth free to spend most of the weekend with Nan, and together they baked, made decorations and sang carols. During the week, the last week of term, Nan attended the school carol service in the church to Ruth's joy, the more so because neither her dad nor her mother were there through pressure of work. Both Ruth and her nan avoided all mention of the piano or piano music.

On Christmas Day Granddad Reggie and Ted came over from south London bearing gifts of crackers, flowers and some cut-out books and a paint box for Ruth.

"Ooh, crackers!" Shirley exclaimed. "Why didn't I think of those? We must stock them next year!"

Even on Christmas Day she insisted on going back to work after dinner, still wearing her paper hat, as apparently that was her ideal opportunity, the first she had had since taking over the business, of fully catching up with her accounts. She thanked her mother-in-law for the delicious dinner, saying that she would never have had time to cook it herself and then, taking her brother into the office with her, left Nan and the rest of them to do the clearing-away and washing-up. Granddad Reggie fell asleep in his armchair while Nan listened to the Queen's Christmas broadcast on the wireless.

A new umbrella for her husband was not the only present Shirley bought at Christmas. She was lavish in her generosity and showered presents on the whole family.

"It's thanks to the business," she explained to Nan as she handed her a parcel containing a pair of fluffy pink slippers. Nan was fulsome in her gratitude, although anyone who knew her at all well would have guessed that fluffy pink slippers were not her style. In addition to his umbrella, Dad received a pullover and some socks, and Ruth was given a new skirt, a cardigan and, out of the blue, a book about the ballet.

Both overawed and saddened when she opened this, the last of her presents, Ruth wished she might have been given such a book years ago. She took it upstairs and put it down by her bedside. When later she had time to look at it, she was reminded of Susan's ballet class and Baba's frustrated attempts to teach her granddaughter. She also remembered that one and only early visit to the ballet with Nan and Grandpa, which had made such an overwhelming impression on her. If only Shirley had given her a book like that in those far-off days, then perhaps she, Ruth, might have dared tell her that she too wanted to dance like the dancers in the book, and perhaps she might have gone to the ballet class as well and become a ballerina. It was already too late for that.

She consoled herself when she caught sight of her hands, for with their lengthening slender fingers, no longer those stubby ones with the bitten nails of her early childhood, they held the promise that one day, she would fulfil her other passion, even if at present she had to keep it a secret for fear of Shirley's displeasure or worse. Certainly it was not her ambition to "go into the business", as Shirley had suggested.

Nan left after Boxing Day, expressing her usual concerns about her pipes freezing as the cold weather set in, although Ruth wanted her to stay for the whole winter. "No, Ruthie, that would never do." She shook her head. "My poor house needs me and, anyhow, lovely though this new home of yours is, there are too many stairs for my old bones. But you'll come and see me soon, won't you?" Ruth promised that she would, though she didn't know when, because that looming prospect of the Eleven Plus blotted out all pleasanter possibilities.

Indeed, soon after the beginning of the new term, the top class were all ushered into the hall, where desks, each of them bearing sheets of paper, were lined up. The first of the papers was maths, which a couple of months ago would have terrified

Ruth in rather the same way as Nan's old copper geyser, or Grandpa's motorbike, or the planes screaming overhead used to terrify her as a small child. Nevertheless, thanks to Dad's help and all those Saturdays in the shop, she took the paper in her stride, and was quietly jubilant that by using his easy method and counting on her fingers she was able to master the money sums. The other tests were less of a battle, though she regretted that there was no music test, for then she knew she would easily have given her best.

The results came out in early March. One evening at supper, Dad opened a fat, official-looking envelope which had been lying on the cupboard in the hall. He read through the letter and then put it to one side, saying nothing. Ruth waited in suspense.

"Well, young lady," he finally said in sober tones, "you're not going to the grammar school after all." Ruth was utterly crestfallen and hardly registered what came next. "No, it's not to be a place at the grammar school, but an assisted place at the high school if you pass their entrance exam in two weeks' time!" he exclaimed.

"Is that better or worse?" Ruth enquired cautiously.

"Why," he exclaimed with evident delight, "it's very special, better than we dared hope! You've done very well!"

A couple of days after the Eleven Plus announcement, Shirley came up from the stockroom one night when a late snow was forecast, radiating warmth and excitement.

"What do you think?" she questioned her audience of two. Ruth looked up from the book she was reading, and her father tore his attention from the television. "I've some good news for you!"

The audience waited, not daring to guess what that news might be in case it involved another major undertaking, or even perhaps another move, because recently Shirley had begun to hint that one day she would like to move out of London altogether.

Ruth did her best to appear eager. "What is it, Shirley?" she asked.

"Well, let me see," Shirley replied, looking down at a piece of paper on which she had jotted down some sums. "You'd better have a look at these, John," she said, handing it to her husband, "but at twenty pounds a week for the four of us, I think we will be able to afford to go to the sea for two weeks, not one, next summer – and take your mother with us of course!"

Having studied the paper closely, John approved the calculations and declared, "Well done! This is excellent. The business is doing well. I think you're right! You clever old girl!"

Shirley basked in the glory of his praise. "You see, this was the best thing we could have done. I was right, wasn't I?"

All she needed was her husband's confirmation of her foresight and effort, and this she received in abundant quantities. "I think we should celebrate the success of Mrs John Platt's enterprise!" he announced. "And to show my faith in her business I shall open a box of chocolates, but first of all I shall buy one from her shop! And at the same time we can celebrate our daughter's success in her exams! Now Ruth, come and help me choose something nice – but mark you, it had better be an expensive box!" As they opened the chocolates, Dad too revealed modestly that he had "a little something to celebrate", which he had forgotten to tell them earlier. He had been given a pay rise in token of his new position in the Rates Office.

35

The summer term passed in an aura both of nostalgia that those long years of primary school were soon to be consigned to the past and of apprehension at the prospect of a new and untried experience. There were some preparatory classes for the grammar and high-school entrants, as if the teachers had suddenly realized that there were subjects that they should have taught and had omitted; but these were given only a cursory airing, and their treatment was so relaxed that schoolwork became unexpectedly enjoyable after all, leaving some of the pupils wondering why it was only now that they were discovering the pleasures of learning.

The special lessons were supplemented with extra art classes and games. There were leavers' parties and fancy-dress competitions, and even a day out to the Tower of London to see the Crown Jewels, which evoked "oohs" and "aahs" from the class. Ruth was reminded of the Coronation, which she and her parents had watched one wet summer day on the Meyers' television. It had been like the ballet, but without the dancing. The spectacle was magnificent and the finery sumptuous, but she had found it hard to believe that it was real. On the trip to the Tower she had the proof before her eyes in the heavy, glittering crowns, the diamonds, the rubies, the emeralds, the sapphires and the amethysts – all magnified versions of the dewdrops glistening in the early-morning sun on the spiders' webs in Nan's garden. The display certainly brought a certain sparkle to history lessons, which until then had been little more than a succession of dates, kings and queens and battles. She wondered how one came to be queen, and it occurred to her that Shirley should have been a queen. How she would have loved the paraphernalia and the palaces and, above all, the attention!

Later that day, when she emerged from the shop, Shirley was indeed keen to hear about the visit. Her eyes shone at Ruth's description of the jewels. "Ooh, they must be lovely!" she exclaimed, clapping her hands. "I'd love to wear that crown, but maybe it would be too heavy for me." She removed her overall, its pockets bulging with pens, pencils, rubbers and paper clips, to reveal her slight form, and held her head high, her back erect. "Imagine being the Queen and living in all those palaces! We wouldn't have to worry about anything then, would we John?"

Switching his attention from the pan he was stirring on the stove, Dad said: "I think we'd have plenty to worry about. Uneasy lies the head that wears a crown, you know."

Shirley sighed. "Well, it's nice to think about it for a minute or two."

She sat down slowly, her thoughts abruptly moving else-where. "I've had an idea!" she then announced brightly. "I don't know whether I've told you, Ruth, but my Cousin Edith from Birmingham is coming to stay for ten days or so at the beginning of your holiday – her boys are going camping, so she'll be free. We should take her to the Tower; she'd love that!" She laughed the laugh which meant that she was pleased with herself. "Isn't that a good idea? You can explain all the different jewels to us. We should go together on early-closing day. I'll take the afternoon off from accounts and stocktaking and I'll be able to come too – won't that be nice? Then on the other days you can go with her to see the other sights, the zoo and so on. You'll like that, and so will she."

Ruth was busy laying the table. The knives and forks clattered onto the hard surface and one fell to the floor. She bent down to pick it up, glad to have a moment to hide her dismay. "No, I didn't know that Cousin Edith was coming," she stammered as she stood up again, red in the face. Cousin Edith's impending visit was news to her – and unwelcome news at that. She had hoped that she might be packed off to stay with Nan for the early part of the holiday before the week – or was it two? – by the sea. Instead it had been decided that she was going to have to stay in London to entertain Cousin Edith, whom she had never met. Nan would be coming to the sea, it was true, but at the end of that holiday there would be no chance of going to stay with her, because the final week before the new term was already earmarked by Shirley for buying school uniform and generally preparing to dive into the big pond of second-ary education.

Anxious to find out precisely what was planned for her, she asked, "Won't I be going to stay with Nan, then?"

"No, no, of course not, there won't be time! Anyhow, you'll be seeing your nan at the sea," said Shirley, dismissing the question scornfully.

Though two weeks with Nan by the sea would certainly be welcome, that from Ruth's point of view was by no means the whole story. She was also counting on playing Nan's piano and practising to her heart's content for as long as possible. There was so much music that she wanted to play well, having discovered a veritable host of composers all competing for the attention of her agile fingers. In their company she felt like a queen, and their compositions were her crown jewels. Nan's piano – or, failing that, any other piano – provided her with her own kingdom in which, with help from Nan and Miss Lake, she ruled supreme. Practising after school had been a good solution in the weeks of term in London, but that arrangement was certain to come to an end when she changed schools. The fear that she might never have access to a piano in London again made her tense and pensive.

"What's the matter, Ruthie?" Dad asked kindly as he served the meal.

"Nothing, tired, that's all," she replied.

With the end of term came the goodbyes to her classmates, all of whom were going to other schools, and to the teachers. On the last day, Miss Lake, the only one Ruth regretted leav-ing behind, came up to her as she was clearing her desk and packing her satchel.

"Ruth," she said, "I've been thinking. How will you be able to continue with your music when you've left this school? I know I haven't taught you very much – there hasn't been enough time

– but you are good, clever and dedicated. You've made such progress just by practising in playtimes and in the lunch hour." She radiated pride at the achievements of her eleven-year-old part-time pupil. "It has been a pleasure to help you. It worries me, though, that you might not have the same opportunities at the high school. Music lessons are given privately there – you have to pay for them."

Ruth sighed despondently. "Yes, I've thought about it a lot too. But I don't know what to do."

"Well, I do think the time has come, after all these years, to tell your parents about your piano-playing, and perhaps your father would pay for you to have proper lessons," Miss Lake went on, her smile disappearing to be replaced by a very serious expression.

"No, no, please don't do that!" Ruth implored her.

"Can you tell me why not? Is it still the same problem?" Miss Lake persisted gently.

Yet again Ruth tried to assemble her arguments in explanation of an intractable problem. "Yes, it seems my mother hates the piano, and it makes her ill." The words tumbled out of her mouth as if they had been lying in wait for Miss Lake for years.

She shook her head. "That's peculiar!" she remarked. "I don't understand it at all!"

"No, nor do I," Ruth said sadly. As ever, Ruth wondered how far she should go in attempting a further explanation of family matters, and then, sensing that she had nothing to lose, confided her own long-considered assessment of the situation to her teacher. "You see, my aunt was a concert pianist, but she died…" Her voice trailed away, because she was not sure how to continue.

Miss Lake soon filled the silence. "Your aunt?" she queried, frowning before light dawned. "Oh, I don't believe it! Of course, I should have known from the name! How stupid of me! Your aunt was Evelyn Platt!" Ruth nodded. "And you look so much like her! I might have guessed! I used to go to her concerts when I was a student. And during the War she sometimes gave lunchtime recitals in the National Gallery. She was wonderful yet so young!" Miss Lake was overwhelmed by the revelation. "But I don't understand why your mother should hate the piano..." Ruth preferred not to answer. She shrugged, sighed again and shook her head.

Fortunately Miss Lake did not press her with more questions. She stood deep in thought, regarding Ruth intently for a minute or two, before smiling quizzically and adopting a matter-of-fact tone. "I see," she declared. "Well, we can't let that sort of talent go to waste, can we?" Ruth waited, hanging on her every word. "I won't tell anyone about the problem, but look, if you can come here after school on weekdays for half an hour or so next term, I'll give you a lesson once a week. I'm always here till five, and on the other days you can practise. I'll tell the caretakers, Mr and Mrs Burns; you know them, don't you? I don't think there'll be any problem. They know you already and are such kind people. It'll be up to you to decide how to explain your lateness to your parents." The latter recommendation was the least of Ruth's worries; Shirley was always in the shop till six or seven, and hardly noticed Ruth's return home. "And," Miss Lake concluded, "one of these days you'll have to tell your parents, because you too are going to be famous!" She added, "Oh, and if you get the chance, play anything new that you can find over the holidays. Good luck!"

Though much relieved by Miss Lake's generous offer, Ruth was still worried by the difficulty of finding a piano to play in secret over the summer. Because she had been able to practise at school in term time and last summer at Nan's throughout the holiday, she had not been unduly bothered if, for a week or two here and there, she found herself without a piano. Now she was desperate to practise regularly, especially as there were certain pieces in which she found herself obsessing over tiny musical details. They revolved in her head all day until she fell asleep at night, only to reappear as soon as she awoke the next morning. Resigned to six weeks or more without a piano, she drummed her fingers on any surface in her bedroom, usually her small chest of drawers, pretending that it was a hidden, silent keyboard.

There was also the problem of her sheet music, some of it given to her by Nan and secreted away in her luggage out of Shirley's sight, and some of it lent by Miss Lake. Hitherto she had kept the latter in the piano stool at school, smuggling the music Nan had given her out of the house in her satchel at the beginning of term. What was she to do with it now that she had officially left the school? Could she still leave it safely in the piano stool? She decided to give Miss Lake's music back to her and take the rest home in her satchel to hide away under her bed in her suitcase.

Cousin Edith arrived from Birmingham in a flurry of feathers and perfume. She was large and noisy, given to extravagant gestures and loud, constant chatter in her strong Brummie accent. Dad politely took himself off elsewhere whenever she came into the room, claiming that he had had to bring work home from the office and must be getting on with it. Shirley revelled in her company and glowed in the praise that Edith heaped upon her as she showed her over the house and the business.

"Oh, that's amazing, Shirl! You have done well! I always said you were a very talented girl. So many talents too! What lovely colours! It's such an enormous house – ooh, and look out there! A nice little garden as well! And what a lovely view over the park! Ooh, you are lucky!"

She inspected every inch of the property so closely that Ruth was afraid that she was going to look under her bed and pull out the suitcase when she came into her bedroom. However, she gave Ruth's room only a cursory glance in much the same way as she had surveyed Ruth herself on arrival.

"Oh, so you're Ruth," she had said without much enthusiasm. "Yes, I've heard a lot about you." It wasn't clear what she had heard, but from her tone of voice whatever it was did not sound at all complimentary.

Ruth decided to follow her father's example and make herself scarce, so she often went out into the park to lie on the grass under the sweet, honey-scented lime trees and listen to the buzzing of hundreds of bees. She smiled to herself as she recalled how once she had asked Grandpa what music he had liked best, and to her amusement he had answered, "'The Flight of the Bumble Bee'" – but after some reflection had changed his choice to 'The Galloping Major', always with a twinkle in his eye. Or, to evade Edith's overpowering presence, she would shut herself away in her bedroom, claiming that she had schoolwork to do in preparation for the next term.

"Ooh, a little swot, are we, then?" Cousin Edith asked, not expecting a reply, but Dad came to the rescue, caustically putting Edith in her place, so that thereafter she refrained from commenting on Ruth's evasive action.

"We are very proud of Ruth, aren't we, dear?" he said, turning to Shirley, who nodded her assent.

"She's the only pupil in her class to have won an assisted place to the high school," she said.

"Hmm, very clever, I'm sure," Edith retorted. "I expect she takes after you, John, with all your book learning. Though I hope she's got some of her mother's talents as well!"

"I'm sure she has," was Dad's impassive reply.

Cousin Edith was not interested in seeing the sights of London; she said she was much happier working in the shop and helping Shirley out with the business. The consequence of this for Ruth was that she was not obliged to spend all day and every day in her company, although she was still frustrated that Edith's much-trumpeted visit had deprived her of her stay at Nan's. She retreated to her room to read books, and then went for walks in the park or traipsed off to the library for another batch of reading material. She wished that her old school were open, but it was firmly closed. Sometimes she came across some of her primary-school friends, and with borrowed rackets they tried to teach themselves to play tennis on the municipal court in the park – or, when the weather was hot, they went to the municipal swimming pool. At last Ruth found to her delight that she could swim. Proud of her achievement she told her parents about it over supper.

"What?" questioned Edith loudly. "You've only just learnt to swim? My boys were swimming by the time they were six years old!"

This time Shirley came to the rescue. In a sudden reversal of her affection for Edith, she glared at her and said pointedly, "John wouldn't allow her to go to the public pool before the polio vaccine came in – and nor would I – so she hasn't had much opportunity till this year, and I must say I don't know why you let your boys go to the public pool, considering what happened to your sister!"

"Ah," was all that Edith said in response to this outburst, since for once she was silenced, but she did permit herself a smirk and a sniff which may simply have confirmed her low opinion of Shirley's husband, or expressed a reaction to that caustic reminder of a family tragedy.

The rest of the meal was eaten in silence, and afterwards nothing more was said about swimming pools or Edith's boys' swimming ability, and a veil was drawn over the fate of Edith's sister, though Ruth would have liked to know more. The evening was spent on neutral ground in front of the television, and the next day Shirley took the afternoon off to go sightseeing with Edith, but to Ruth's relief they did not press her to go too. On the following Saturday they left John and Ruth in charge of the shop, while they went to the West End sales on a shopping spree. The Cousin Edith episode drew to a close, not before time as far as Ruth and her father were concerned, but at least it made Shirley happy and put her in a good mood for the holiday.

No sooner had Cousin Edith left than Granddad Reggie arrived to take over the business. He wrinkled his nose when he came into the hallway, where Edith's pervasive perfume lingered on after her departure. "She's not still here, is she, littl'un?" were his first words to Ruth, who opened the door to him.

"Who do you mean, Granddad?" Ruth enquired innocently, though knowing perfectly well what he meant.

"That woman," he replied gruffly, making no attempt to conceal the fact that Edith, his sister's daughter, was not a relative whose company he relished.

Once he was satisfied that Edith was no longer on the premises, he stumbled farther into the house and then into the shop, where Shirley gave him a rapturous welcome. "Now will you be all right, Pa?" she asked solicitously.

"Yes, yes, of course I will. You know me, I can run this business with my eyes shut, and Ted's coming over on Sunday to bring me some shopping, so off you go and have a good time." This was such a long speech for Granddad Reggie that he collapsed exhausted with the effort onto a stool behind the counter, waving Shirley and Ruth away as he did so.

Mother and daughter travelled directly to the coast, while John took the longer route to enable him to collect his own mother and take care of her on the journey. As planned, they all met in the evening at the guest house. On arrival, to her great joy, Ruth spotted an upright piano in the dining room. Nan saw it too. Although her increasing lameness made her slow and her advancing deafness impeded easy conversation, there was no doubt that she had kept her wits about her.

"You saw that piano in the dining room, didn't you?" she asked Ruth later that evening as they were preparing for bed in their shared room.

"Yes, I did, but how on earth am I going to be able to play it?" Ruth replied anxiously.

"Oh, don't you worry about that! I'll think of something," Nan reassured her.

She was as good as her promise, managing to engineer free practice time for Ruth by sending Shirley and John out in the evening for a walk or a show on the pier or a film, and arranging with the proprietors for Ruth to use the piano after the diners had left the room. "It's a secret," she impressed both upon them and upon anyone among the guests who happened to be listening. "It's a treat for her parents!" It proved an unnecessary precaution, as no one else was at all interested in Ruth's piano-playing, and in any case all the other guests went out in the evening, like John and Shirley.

The problem was that it took some time to clear the dining room, and even then Dad was reluctant to tear himself away from the wireless, which broadcast regular commentaries and reports on the state of affairs in Hungary, where the democratic uprising was being suppressed by Russian tanks. At last, when the coast was clear, Ruth seated herself at the piano and practised her scales, while Nan settled herself close to the instrument in order to hear the performance and watch Ruth's fingers on the keyboard, at the same time offering useful advice on the interpretation of one of the Chopin Preludes or a Schubert Impromptu, or any other of the pieces of music that she had brought with her from Norhambury in the hope that there might be a piano in the guest house.

"Watch out for the fingering there, Ruth! You'll get in a muddle if you're not careful, and either you will run out of fingers or they'll trip each other up!" Then she herself would try out a few fingering patterns until she found the best way through a tricky passage. "I like the phrasing, but I think you need to vary the dynamic rather more," she would observe as Ruth proceeded to run her fingers over the keys. "Try a subito piano there and then a gradual crescendo," she would suggest, "and perhaps a bit of rubato in that very moving phrase where there's a diminuendo. What do you think?" Ruth agreed and tried out her instructions, which she found usually produced precisely the effects she was searching for.

Unaccountably, Nan knew a great deal more about playing the piano than she liked to admit. Her advice was always pertinent, and her encouragement always helpful, particularly now that, infected by Ruth's enthusiasm and talent, she herself had taken up the piano again.

"You know, Ruthie," she confessed happily one evening as she applied her own fingers to the keys, "since you've been playing, I've grown to love the piano again. Not that my poor old bent fingers are as agile as they used to be, but it does give me great pleasure! And sometimes I play in the church when the organist is away."

No more was said, but Ruth suspected that she had abandoned the piano a long time ago, because it was too poignant a reminder of Evelyn. Nan must have been no mean pianist in her day and was most undoubtedly the source of Evelyn's talent.

Ruth grew more relaxed as she consigned Beethoven or Mozart or Schumann, as well as Chopin and Schubert, to the piano keys, and relieved her brain of the burden of their constant company. They ceased to be pitiless taskmasters and resumed their role as guardian angels instead. Their music was always there in her head, but rather than being at the forefront of her mind as an inescapable pressure, it receded into the background as a gentle accompaniment to her activities.

As a precaution Nan made sure to ascertain how long Dad and Shirley would be out in the evenings. If they were only going for a walk, she knew that Ruth might have only a quarter of an hour at the piano, but if they were going to a show, the chances were that there might be a couple of hours free. To be absolutely certain that they would do as agreed, she insisted on buying their tickets for them.

Only once were teacher and pupil nearly caught out. They had settled themselves at the piano and Ruth had begun her scales when they heard a key turning in the front door. Quickly Ruth slid off the stool and Nan, with an unaccustomed agility, took her place and began to play scales, while Ruth grabbed a magazine.

"Oh, there you are!" Dad announced as he came into the room. "So you're playing the piano again, are you, Mother? That's good!"

He explained that he had come back for his umbrella, because they had felt one or two ominous drops of rain, and he was afraid that it might be pouring by the time they came out of the cinema. Two minutes later he closed the front door behind him. Thereafter Nan insisted on taking a pack of playing cards downstairs after supper and spreading out hands to make it appear that she and Ruth were engaged in a game of rummy.

"Just in case we are interrupted again," she said.

Shirley was in a positive frame of mind, especially as she and her husband were free to enjoy unaccustomed evenings out. She assumed that Ruth and her grandmother were content in each other's company, and it never crossed her mind to wonder how they passed their time. She was appreciative, patient and friendly towards Nan, who often paid for coffees and teas, lunches and other treats as well as the tickets for the evening entertainments. During the day Nan was content to sit on the beach in a deckchair, while the rest of them played games on the sand or swam in the sea; then she would go for a walk on the promenade while they played crazy golf – so, as Shirley benevolently observed, she gave them no trouble at all.

Not only did Ruth have plenty of opportunity to improve her swimming, she also practised her tennis, playing with her father on a nearby court. Although she enjoyed herself every day in the sun and the sea, secretly she was anticipating the evening sessions at the piano. Towards the end of the fortnight, Shirley began to get restless. She said that as she would not be going to Birmingham to Edith's this year, it was time to be returning to London; she had been away from the business for long enough and, despite many reassurances about her father's competence, she wanted to be sure all was well. She it was who suggested, contrary to her earlier pronouncement, that Ruth should in fact travel with her father as usual and return to London via Nan's house, as that would give her, Shirley, more time to reorganize the shop and settle in without having to bother about anyone else. This suited Ruth perfectly well, for she longed to spend even a couple of days at Nan's, and she also wanted to put off being in London again with all uncertainties of a new school.

36

The High School for Girls was only a couple of hundred yards beyond the primary school, in the same street where the church stood on the corner. On Ruth's first day the route was reassuringly familiar, though the imposing, grey-faced building with its black-painted front door hardly spelt out a warm welcome. As she and her dad approached, the door which was ajar was flung wide by an unsmiling grey-haired woman, who beckoned Ruth inside.

"May I come in too?" Dad asked anxiously.

"No, no, that won't be necessary," said the woman as she searched down a list for Ruth's name. "Ah, yes, a new girl. You'll have to go and line up outside the headmistress's study with the other new girls. Elspeth will take you." She gestured to a tall girl in uniform standing beside her. The tall girl ushered Ruth away before she had time to say goodbye to her father, and the door closed in his face.

The girl led the way down a wide corridor, where the lower half of the walls was covered in brown panelling and the upper half in cream paint. On one side were classrooms and on the other offices and rooms with closed doors. There was a bustle of activity, but silence reigned except for the sound of footsteps and the orders given out by some older girls who stood guard every few yards, telling the younger ones not to run, not to talk, to keep in line, to straighten their navy-blue uniforms and to put their bags in the cloakroom at the end of the corridor.

A line of fifteen or so girls, all about Ruth's age, stood waiting outside one of the closed doors. "This is the Head's study, so I'll leave you here," the tall girl announced and then walked off. Ruth remembered waiting outside that same door when she had come with her father for an interview after the entrance exam the previous spring, some six months ago.

At that interview the Headmistress, a dumpy, unsmiling woman in a brown tweed suit, the colour of which matched the brown panelling in the corridor, had asked her about her hobbies. She had simply replied, "reading and listening to music, helping in the garden..." her voice trailing away at the impossibility of confiding her true passion. "I see you are good at maths," the Head had gone on, rifling through some papers, presumably a report on Ruth's Eleven Plus results, together with the results of the school entrance exam. She had kept her eyes down, fixed on the paperwork, while Ruth wished that her dad had been permitted to accompany her to the interview. On that occasion he had been allowed to enter the school, but no further than the lobby, where he was made to wait with other anxious parents.

"Yes, yes, my maths is not too bad," she had replied a touch uncertainly and knowing that she was not really telling the truth, but unexpectedly that had been enough to win her a place. She hadn't much liked what little she had seen of the school then and, indeed, had much preferred the Girls' Grammar School with its airy, modern buildings and its friendly Headmistress. However, she was given no say in the matter, and it was all decided for her by powers unseen.

The Head, wearing the same brown tweed suit, came out of her office and held the door open for the line of new girls. "You may all come in," she said without so much as a smile. "Move over into the far corner to make room," she said sitting down at her desk and briefly surveying the newcomers. "I am Miss Dent, the Headmistress of this school, as you doubtless know. You are all new here, so I must check your details and then I will send you to your allotted form rooms. As I read out your names say 'Yes, Miss Dent'; then pick up this list of school rules from my desk and go to stand where I tell you." She opened a file from which she started to read through the names. "Claire Atkins?" The girl answering to that name registered her presence with a scarcely audible "Yes, Miss Dent" and a shy smile which Miss Dent did not reciprocate. "You are a fee-paying pupil and you will be in form Lower Four B, so stand here in front of the fireplace." Claire Atkins duly advanced to a space on the right of Miss Dent's desk. "Sarah Banham? Ah, yes, fee-paying, in form Lower Four B. Stand here on my right also." Miss Dent waved a hand over to where Claire Atkins was standing, and so it went on and on until Ruth's legs ached, with the pupils allotted to Form Lower Four C being told to stay where they were.

It was not until Miss Dent reached the letter M that at last an assisted-place pupil came to light. Ruth had begun to wonder whether she was the only one in that category in the ever-diminishing group.

"Elizabeth Mair?"

"Yes, Miss Dent," said a short, fair-haired girl who stood beside her.

"Assisted place, Miss Jenkins's form, Lower Four A. Over here." She pointed to her left. Ruth waited for her name to be called, but there were yet more to come.

"Alison Newman?"

"Yes, Miss Dent."

"Assisted place, form Lower Four A. Over here on the left."

"Janet Otway?"

"Yes, Miss Dent."

"Assisted place, form Lower Four A to the left."

Then the moment came: "Ruth Platt?"

"Yes, Miss Dent."

"Assisted place, form Lower Four A. Over here to the left."

The six feet across Miss Dent's red-and-blue carpet seemed an immeasurable distance as Ruth tiptoed across it to take her place with the form Lower Four A pupils, collecting a copy of the school rules as she went. Four more girls from the nether reaches of the alphabet were allotted forms, whereupon Miss Dent rose abruptly to her feet and made for the door with the strict injunction that the girls were not to move but to read the school rules in her absence.

CHAPTER 36

Nobody dared speak. According to the rules, anything that might be described as normal activity was suppressed in the school: no talking in corridors or between lessons, no untidiness, no slouching in school uniform – whatever that meant – no loitering after school, no this, no that, no the other. Miss Dent came back with three sixth-formers, into whose care she delivered the three groups. Before they filed out of her office, she sternly recommended that they memorize and obey the rules. The sixth formers led the way silently through the school, opened the doors of the respective classrooms and showed their groups in.

The form to which Ruth had been allotted sat in total silence: here there was no sign of the usual cheerful early-morning hubbub that she was used to in primary school. The other girls in her group were also visibly taken aback, not only by the silence, but also by the sight of the form teacher – a tall, wiry person with short black hair, a sharply pointed chin and an icy stare.

"Ah, so these are the new girls. Mostly on assisted places, I see." There was a sneer in her voice. "Well, you had better come in. You're late already. It's nearly time for the bell."

The sixth-former did not attempt to explain that the girls had been delayed in the Head's study, but quietly and quickly edged out of the room. The group shrank back, afraid to advance farther.

"Well, come in! Don't keep us all waiting again!" shrieked the woman, whom the headmistress had called Miss Jenkins. "I have a very busy schedule, and I do not expect any trouble from the Lower Fourth! Now tell me your names in alphabetical order, then pick up a timetable sheet and take your places in that row of desks by the wall."

One by one the girls gave their names. When it came to Ruth, Miss Jenkins surveyed her up and down, and asked, "So where do you come from, Ruth Platt?"

"I live down the road on the Broadway," Ruth answered correctly.

"No, no, I mean where were you born."

"Oh, at my nan's house in Nor—"

Miss Jenkins was becoming dangerously exasperated at not receiving the answer she expected. "I can't believe that you have an assisted place if you can't answer a simple question like that! Go and sit down at once, you idiot!"

Meekly and nonplussed Ruth went to sit at her desk, convinced that her form teacher was yet another of those witches who had escaped from the pages of a story book. Some of the class cautiously lifted their heads from their desks and surreptitiously glanced at her, while Miss Jenkins carried on down the list.

At that moment the bell rang and, as of one mind, the class stood up. "Come on, Janet Otway! Come out to the front!" came the stentorian command. Poor Janet Otway, who had only just sat down, had no idea where she was supposed to lead to. Nervously she stepped forward, and Ruth followed her. "Come on, come on!" Miss Jenkins shouted impatiently. "We shall all be late for assembly at this rate."

"I'm sorry, Miss Jenkins, I don't know where to go," Janet Otway stammered nervously.

Tight-lipped, Miss Jenkins snapped, "I know that. I'm not stupid. I shall lead the way when everyone is standing in line, and then you follow me. Pick up a hymn book from this shelf by the door as you go." Janet Otway was near to tears; Ruth longed to put out a comforting hand and touch her on the shoulder, but did not dare.

Assembly took place in the hall at the top of the stairs. The girls stood, sat and kneeled on the dusty floor while Miss Dent announced a hymn, read a passage from the Bible and finally intoned some prayers, all in a monotone. Before dismissing the assembly, she made a short speech, urging the girls again to memorize the school rules, to work hard, to beat every other school in the area at hockey, lacrosse, netball, swimming and cricket in the course of the year – and, with a mere flicker of a smile, to improve on the otherwise excellent examination results of last year. There was nothing to inspire in her dull, brown persona, or in her dull, leaden delivery, or in her dull, grey outlook. Ruth despaired anticipating this as her way of life for the next seven years or so.

It was one thing to be unpleasant to people if, like Shirley, you had been very ill and had had to undergo terrible treatment. She had never forgotten visiting Shirley in hospital as a small child, and although Shirley was often demanding and occasionally even downright nasty, Ruth had always borne in mind the shock of seeing her lying trembling and crying on that bare white bed. That was an image that recurred. But these people were not ill, they were not suffering, they merely enjoyed terrifying the girls in their charge, as though, inexplicably, the girls were to blame for all that was wrong either with them or in their lives. She was not sure how she would tolerate this regime for very long.

"Right, so we are going to work on timetables," Miss Jenkins decreed after the school assembly, and proceeded to run through all the hours of all the classes in all the different rooms on all of the schooldays of the week. It was difficult to follow her rapid review of the timetable, but putting it into effect was easier than Ruth feared, because form Lower Four A was the top set, so all that she and her fellow newcomers, the assisted-place pupils, had to do was to follow the other girls who already knew the layout of the school, wherever they went: this rule applied to all subjects except French, in which the new girls were to be taught separately, as none of them had ever learnt a foreign language before, whilst the girls already in the school had learnt French in the junior house.

Timetabling and book distribution occupied the rest of the morning. The latter gave Ruth some cause for concern. She gathered from the other girls that their parents were going to have to buy the books and would be sent a bill for them at half-term. For each subject there were two piles of books: one was a pile of new textbooks with colourful, shiny covers, clear print on the spines and blocks of unopened clean pages, while the other pile was of second-hand books; the covers were scuffed and faded, their titles illegible and their pages discoloured.

Much as she would have liked to have new books, Ruth, not daring to state her preference for them, was directed by Miss

Jenkins to the second-hand pile. Although the form mistress smirked each time she went up to collect yet another battered copy, Ruth noticed that the other assisted-place girls had no choice in the matter and also were told to take their books from the second-hand pile.

The advantage of Miss Jenkins's behaviour was that it united her class against her from the outset. When at last break time came, Ruth followed the other girls through the rabbit warren of corridors to the milk bar to collect their daily third of a pint – and there, out of Miss Jenkins's earshot and out of reach of the school rules, they all began to talk at once. "Isn't she horrible?" they grumbled. They were unanimously sympathetic to Ruth and to Janet Otway because of the harsh treatment they had already received, and Ruth found herself surrounded by a crowd of potential new friends. They spilled out of the school into the yard, which also served as a netball court, devising plans for getting the better of Miss Jenkins. The plans never came to anything, but they made the girls feel less miserable about their shared misfortune.

Lunch was inedible: a couple of slices of tough, leathery meat lay submerged in congealed gravy alongside grey cabbage. Ruth was pushing it all to one side when she saw Miss Jenkins hastily advancing in her direction, so in a panic she tried to appear to be relishing the plateful. Luckily Miss Jenkins had some other unfortunate miscreant in her sights and passed on, leaving Ruth free to clear her plate away and empty the contents into the waste bucket.

The afternoon was less of a disaster. Lessons began in the science labs across the playground, where a young chemistry teacher was setting up experiments using Bunsen burners and test tubes, litmus paper and a handful of crystals. She was lively and interesting, working as she did well out of the way of the rest of the school, and ran a very different establishment, which operated on its own principles of friendliness, discovery and enlightenment. French also proved to be an unexpected pleasure, because the teacher, Madame Delplace, an elegant Frenchwoman, was in fact a real human being, unlike many of her colleagues. She laughed frequently, and taught her pupils the language simply by telling them about her own life, in a lively blend of French and English.

She was in England because that was where her husband was working, she explained; she had a family of three sons and lived in Paris when not in England. Her description of her home city was so vivid that the girls were transported in their imaginations to the banks of the Seine and to the top of the Eiffel Tower, unsuspecting that at the same time they were learning the language.

"I want zat you enjoy French," Madame Delplace insisted, rolling the "r" in "French", "and zat you go in France on your 'olidays."

Nobody objected to this highly effective attitude to tuition and, despite her eccentric English, nobody even for one second considered misbehaving in her class.

Music did not feature on the timetable for that first day, though it did appear later in the week, but only for half an hour on Thursday afternoons. The real black spots in the week were Monday and Friday afternoons, when Miss Jenkins, the head of games, presided over the extensive games field on the right-hand side of the school. The Lower Fourth formers spent the long hours on the sidelines being initiated by the assistant games mistress into the method of holding the ball in the basket on a lacrosse stick and running with it, while on the hockey pitch Miss Jenkins bawled at any Upper Fourth former who missed the ball or did not run fast enough or accidentally hit the ball into her own goal.

After school on that first day Ruth made her way hurriedly down the road into her old school. Miss Lake was there waiting for her, as were Mr and Mrs Burns.

"Well, how was it?" they enquired eagerly.

"It was horrible," Ruth replied; then, wondering whether she might have been unjust to the science and the French teachers, she added, "Most of the teachers are horrible, but some are all right."

"That's life," Mrs Burns observed, as so many other people had observed to Ruth. "You have to take the rough with the smooth, dearie – but look, I've brought you some buns for tea, and here's some orange squash."

Ruth fell upon the buns gratefully and, as a great wave of relief swept over her, sat down at the piano and started to play.

"That's good, Ruth!" Miss Lake exclaimed. "So you've done some practice during the holidays?" Transported into the world where she felt secure, Ruth told her all about the piano in the guest house, about Nan's clever ruses for getting her parents out of the way in the evenings, and about those last days of the holiday when she and her dad had taken Nan home.

Even then Nan had not been short of ideas to keep Dad occupied to allow Ruth to sit at the piano for at least half an hour at a time. As soon as they arrived at 10 Beech Grove, she sent him out shopping, keeping Ruth with her, she said, so that she could help her unpack. On the Sunday morning she asked him to accompany her to church in the village, insisting that Ruth should be allowed to enjoy a long lie-in as she was going to find the coming weeks very taxing. On the Monday morning before the departure to London in the afternoon, she went so far as to suggest that her son might be interested in a quick trip up into the city to see some of the new monstrosities which were being built on the old bomb sites. He would never have guessed that during these absences, as soon as he left the house, his daughter would quickly sit down at the piano, practise her scales and exercises and run through her repertoire, which was now extensive and ever expanding.

"You are learning to play very well, Ruthie," Nan remarked on the Monday morning. "I'm very proud of you, but I don't think we can keep up this charade – you are going to have to let your parents know how clever you are. Don't you think it's rather deceitful not to let them know?"

"Not yet, please, Nan," Ruth insisted.

"And another thing," Nan persisted, "this Miss Lake – who pays her for the lessons she gives you?"

Ruth was embarrassed, not having a convincing answer to Nan's question. "Well, no one… she's always taught me for free. She says it's a pleasure."

"That's not right, she must need the money," Nan said, frowning at such a perceived injustice. "Pass me my bag, will you, dear? Oh, and there's some writing paper and envelopes in the drawer beside my fountain pen." Nan reached into her bag and brought out her cheque book. She wrote a brief letter, then put it and a cheque in an envelope, which she handed to Ruth. "Now run upstairs and put this in your suitcase. Keep it safe, and when you next see Miss Lake, please give it to her with my compliments."

At the end of that first session of the new term, Ruth pulled the envelope out of the depths of her satchel where she had hidden it and handed it over to a mystified Miss Lake.

"What's this, Ruth?" she asked as she opened the envelope.

"It's from my nan with her compliments and thanks for teaching me to play."

Miss Lake's mouth opened wide as she saw the cheque and read the letter. "Heavens! That's very, very kind," she said quietly. "I'll write and thank her very much."

Uncharacteristically, Shirley was waiting for Ruth when she came home. She emerged from the shop asking, "How was it?"

"Some of the teachers are nice, some are horrible," Ruth replied. Then in a flash she saw an opportunity to anticipate any trouble without having to tell lies. "But I called in on Mr and Mrs Burns on the way home – you know, the caretakers at St Luke's. They were so pleased to see me and had a lovely tea ready for me."

"Oh that is nice," Shirley smiled. "How kind of them! I wondered where you were. So long as you're not too late coming home, you can call on them as often as you like."

Shirley's blessing on this half-truth was a timely godsend. On the Wednesday afternoon of the following week, as Ruth emerged from St Luke's having had tea and played the piano, she saw one of the teachers from the high school watching her from the other side of the road. Ruth recognized her as Miss Price, the history teacher, who found it impossible to keep control in any of her classes and had become something of a laughing stock among the girls; they were released from the daunting strictures of other members of staff – not least Miss Jenkins – and played her up mercilessly. Nevertheless, the older girls warned Ruth to watch out for her, as she was reputed to share a house with Miss Jenkins. "She won't admit that she can't keep discipline in class," they said, "but she likes to pick on us one by one if she gets the chance."

Ruth smiled across the road at this sad apparition, who quickly turned on her heel and walked off. The next morning Miss Jenkins greeted Ruth with a grin and instructed her to go straight to Miss Dent's study. Ruth stood outside the Head's door speculating why she had been summoned.

Miss Dent did not beat about the bush: "Ruth Platt?"

"Yes, Miss Dent," Ruth replied.

"You were seen coming out of St Luke's primary school yesterday afternoon. What were you doing there?"

"I went to call on my friends, the caretakers," was Ruth's confident reply.

"Don't you know that the school rules forbid you to go anywhere other than straight home after school?"

Ruth did not respond straight away: she had not fully digested the school rules, but she knew that for once she had an ally in this battle. "My mother knows I go there, and she doesn't mind."

Miss Dent's facial expression registered shock; drily she said: "You had better ask your mother to write two letters, one to me and one to Miss Jenkins, giving her permission for you to go to St Luke's after school."

Shirley was indignant when Ruth conveyed the command from on high that evening. She had already felt personally insulted when, at the beginning of the term she saw that Ruth's bag was full of scuffed second-hand books – "I won't have you going to that school looking like a beggar," she let it be known. "We will buy the new ones! We can afford them after all!"

It was also abundantly clear from her reaction to Miss Dent's message that she had an aversion to elderly women schoolteachers. "Silly baggage!" Shirley exclaimed. "I'll write her a letter, indeed I will, and I'll write one to that awful form teacher of yours as well! Who do they think they are? Ordering me to write letters to give permission for my own daughter to go and visit her friends?" She scribbled furiously, signing her name on each letter with a flourish. She gave the two letters in sealed envelopes to Ruth to take to school the next day.

Ruth rather enjoyed delivering the letters, one to Miss Dent's letter box outside her study and the other to Miss Jenkins as she sat at her desk scrutinizing the girls for faults in the dress code as they came into the form room.

Ruth waited while Miss Jenkins read the letter. She peered at it. "What's this all about, Ruth Platt?" she asked, taking her glasses off and then putting them on again. "What dreadful writing! I can't make it out at all! Who's it from?" Coolly, Ruth replied, "It's from my mother."

"Ah, I see, well, you can read it out for me."

She took the letter, with difficulty suppressing a giggle like the rest of the class in their amused anticipation of drama ahead. The handwriting certainly revealed Shirley at her most tempestuous.

"It says," Ruth began aloud for all the class to hear, "'I am deeply offended that my daughter, Ruth Platt, has not been allowed to choose new text books but only shabby second-hand ones. What's more, she tells me that I need to write to you to give my permission for her to visit her friends in St Luke's school on the way home in the afternoons. I have already given Ruth my permission and I don't expect my authority to be called into question by anyone else. I trust there will be no further discussion on this matter and you will not prevent Ruth from visiting St Luke's after school. Yours faithfully, Shirley Platt.' That's all it says," Ruth added for good measure.

There was silence as she handed the letter back to Miss Jenkins and resumed her seat. The class waited with bated breath for her reaction, but she said nothing. She folded the letter and put it in a drawer, before smartly commanding, "Register!" One morning a week later a pile of new textbooks was standing on Ruth's desk.

On weekdays her reward for suffering all the indignities and harshness of the high school was the sheer joy of being able to practise to her heart's content after school hours for as long as Mr and Mrs Burns were busy at their cleaning. Miss Lake stayed a little longer than usual on Tuesday afternoons to give her a half-hour lesson, and this system prevailed for the whole of the autumn term right through to Christmas. As the nights drew longer and the days shorter, the Burns accompanied Ruth home because, they said, the shop was on their way, only one bus stop down the road, and they were happy to walk that first stretch with her, as they would not be happy to think of her out in the dark on her own. Although she knew that she ought to invite them into the shop to meet Shirley, she was afraid that they might mention her music-making, so she said goodbye rather gauchely, leaving them at the bus stop.

She settled into the school regime, resigned to hating games and history, liking French and science and tolerating the other subjects: maths, Latin, English and geography in between. The class music lesson on Thursday afternoons was the gravest disappointment. The teacher, the only man in the school – apart from the vicar, who came in once a week to teach divinity – usually limited his efforts to placing a record on the turntable of the gramophone, and then ignored the class for the rest of the period while he marked and corrected papers on his desk, or sometimes read a book. There was never any discussion or tuition about the music or the performance unless another adult, a teacher or very occasionally an inspector, happened to be present; then he would talk about the sonata form or symphonic structure animatedly as an eloquent indication that this was his customary method of teaching.

Mr Barkley, known throughout the school for good reason as "Barking Barkley", was an ugly man, burly and overweight, with pale, bulging eyes and a few reddish wisps of hair on his balding scalp. Despite his inadequacy as a teacher, he nevertheless maintained silence in his classroom, even during those frequent unexplained absences, when he would leave the room for five or ten minutes at a time. The worst of it was that his room housed an upright piano, not a very special instrument, but Ruth ached to be able to play it for want of anything better. It was out of bounds for fourth formers and was available for pupils higher up the school only if they were learning an instrument on a fee-paying basis. Admission to the choir worked on a similar basis: pupils were admitted only if they were learning an instrument.

Shortly before the end of term, Nan arrived. She moved more slowly than ever and had to complete her journey by taxi, because it was too difficult for her to manage the Underground, and everything moved so fast – although it hadn't been a problem getting to the station at home, she explained, because the bus driver and conductor were always patient and helpful.

Scarcely had she arrived than she told Ruth in a quiet moment that she wanted to meet Miss Lake, while Ruth, for her part, had long wanted to arrange such a meeting and had been wondering how to make it happen. Nan insisted that she was perfectly able to walk the shortish distance up the road to the primary school. She had no interest whatsoever in seeing the high school, for, as she said, she had heard quite enough of that already from Ruth's letters. So one afternoon, shortly before the end of term, she slowly made her way up the road leaning on her stick and met Ruth at the gates of St Luke's.

"I told your mother I was coming to meet you, and she very kindly gave me this big box of chocolates for the caretakers. She said, 'Ruth will want to introduce you to the Burns, so please take them these chocolates with my thanks for all those lovely teas they give her.'"

Ruth was pleased, but regretted not having anything to show her appreciation for Miss Lake.

"Don't worry," Nan reassured her, "I'll take care of that."

That afternoon Nan delivered the chocolates to the grateful Burns, who produced buns and cups of tea, and she met Miss Lake, with whom she established an instant rapport. Ruth played some of Schumann's 'Waldszenen' and a Beethoven Bagatelle for them all, and was gratified by their applause. Discreetly Nan pulled an envelope out of her handbag and passed it to Miss Lake, who accepted it with some embarrassment.

On the way home, Nan once again brought up that subject that Ruth was happy to forget. "You must tell your parents about your music. Miss Lake says, as if I didn't know already, that you are going to be a performer one day. Think how proud your dad would be of you, and how sorry he would be if he knew that you were depriving him of all your talent!"

"No, Nan, you know I can't do that!" Ruth contended obstinately, but she promised that she would consider it, although for the present she saw no reason to change an arrangement that worked perfectly well and gave her a certain cherished independence. In any case, as there was no piano at home, there was no chance of her practising there.

That evening, while Ruth worked on her last homework of the term, she overheard a conversation between Nan and her parents in the sitting room. She listened, afraid that Nan might be giving her secret away, but what she heard intrigued her.

"She hates that school, you know," Nan was remarking, "Couldn't she go somewhere else?"

"Yes, I agree with you," Shirley concurred. "That's what I say to John; she would be much happier at the grammar school, but he won't hear of it."

"No, it's not that," Dad interrupted. "She won a place at the high school, and it is the best school in the area. Just look at their results, excellent at GCE Ordinary Level, excellent at Advanced Level and lots of university places. I don't want her to waste that opportunity. Anyhow, I'm not sure she would be able to change. It's unlikely there are any spare places at the grammar school."

Such a discussion was a welcome distraction from Latin verbs. Ruth was grateful that Nan should be concerned about her, but it was unexpected that Shirley should be in such close agreement. On the other hand, Ruth understood her father's reasoning. She herself didn't mind, because she had become used to the high school, for all its faults; she had made friends and had to admit that the teaching was mostly good. It was ironic though that at last her home scene had become relatively calm and happy, while school was fraught with tensions of one sort or another. Evidently life would never be straightforward. Nonetheless, everything faded into insignificance by comparison with the neat arrangement for playing the piano at St Luke's after school. Above all, she didn't want that to change.

37

The arrangement with Miss Lake and the Burns did not change, but persisted throughout the next term and, as far as Ruth knew, would be permanent. As Easter approached, Shirley persuaded Granddad Reggie to come over and hold the fort to allow her go to Birmingham to stay with her Cousin Edith for a couple of days' rest. Consequently Ruth and her father were allowed to go to visit Nan for the bank-holiday week-end. Nan was as buoyant as ever but, however hard she tried to conceal her discomfort, her leg was giving her a great deal of pain, making all movement difficult. On the afternoon of their arrival, Dad persuaded her to sit still while he and Ruth fetched and carried for her. He lit the fire in the front room and wrapped a rug around her, saying, "Now Mother, you must rest while we're here, then you'll be fine when we leave on Monday."

Ruth tried not to show her mounting frustration at the impossibility of playing the piano both on account of her dad's constant presence and also because she did not want to disturb Nan, who spent much of her time asleep. Only when he went out shopping did an opportunity present itself.

"Are you coming down to the shops with me, Ruthie?" he asked as he put his coat on. "I think if I go now, I'll just catch the bus."

"No, I'll stay and keep Nan company," Ruth replied.

Nan, who was dozing, opened her eyes as soon as her son left the house and said, "Quick, Ruth, I've had my nap, now's your chance to climb onto that piano stool!" Ruth glanced out of the window, and when she was sure that her dad had gone out, closing the creaking gate behind him, she opened the lid and sat down, grabbing the first pieces of music she found on top of the piano. There were two collections, one of Chopin's 'Polonaises' and the other of waltzes by various composers.

"These look rather difficult to sight-read," she murmured as she thumbed through the volume of the 'Polonaises'. "I've only played some of the Mazurkas and a few of the Preludes before."

"Don't be ridiculous! You can play those!" Nan asserted with a confidence that Ruth did not share. She kept watch and applauded while the pianist tentatively sight-read a selection of the waltzes, leaving the 'Polonaises' for another occasion.

Nan's legs might have been infirm and her hearing unreliable, but her eyesight was as sharp as ever, so that when she saw her son approaching the gate three quarters of an hour or so later, she said urgently: "You'd better stop now, here he comes!" This was the cue for Ruth to slide off the stool without question, put the music away and close the piano lid.

"I do think we ought at least to tell your father, if not your mother, about your playing," Nan muttered while Dad unloaded his shopping in the kitchen, but Ruth whispered in her ear: "No, please don't! I don't want them to know about it yet. It's my secret, and if I tell anyone, it might go wrong."

Nan nodded wisely. "All right, but not for much longer," she agreed.

When Dad came in carrying the tea tray he remarked, "I must put some oil on that gate."

"No, no," said Nan, "it's so noisy it's one of the few things I can hear clearly, and it warns me if someone is coming in, even in the dark or if I have my eyes closed."

Once her dad had come home, Ruth preferred to get away from the temptation of the piano. Donning her coat and boots, she went out into the garden, leaving him to bring Nan news of the people he had encountered on his foray to the shops. A chill wind blew down from the north, cleansing the sky and lending it a luminescent, turquoise clarity.

Outside, the wind blew far too keenly for her to sit on the swing even in the shelter of her cabin, nor did she feel like going into Grandpa's shed. She was standing alone on the ridge at the top of the lawn, wondering what to do next, when she heard a voice calling her name. She turned round and saw Carrie waving from her open kitchen window.

"Ruth, Ruth! Do come and say hello to us!" she called.

Ruth smiled at the familiar figure. "Oh yes, let me tell Dad and Nan!" she replied. She ran indoors and left a note, since both Nan and her dad were nodding off comfortably in front of the fire, and then dashed round to the neighbouring house.

Carrie was standing on the step holding the door open to let her in. "Come on in and let's close the door against this wind!" she said, ushering her into the hall.

Ruth was delighted to find Carrie and her daughters at home for once. So often they were away in Scotland, and there was never any chance of predicting whether they would be at home or not when she and her father paid their brief summer visits at the end of the usual week by the sea. Even Nan did not seem to have any very precise idea of their movements. The friendship, which had been very close when Ruth was a small child, was still vibrant, so that with Carrie, Anne and Val she felt few inhibitions. Nonetheless, she kept her musical secret even from them, afraid that its blossoming bud might be nipped off for reasons that were still vague.

Their house was strangely bare and uninviting after Nan's warm sitting room with its cheerful fire in the grate. Boxes lay everywhere, in every room and on every surface, and were apparently being filled with the contents of the drawers and cupboards, which had spilt out all over the floor. The girls were on their knees in the front room retrieving the best china from the glass-fronted cabinet and carefully packing each piece in sheets of newspaper.

They looked up as Carrie ushered Ruth into the room. "Look who's here, girls! We have a visitor!"

"Ruth!" they both exclaimed with evident pleasure.

"Oh, good! Can we stop for tea now?" Val asked.

"Yes, of course," Carrie agreed. "Come into the kitchen all of you and we'll have a chat."

Ruth was bewildered by the chaos in that house, which was usually so well ordered. At first it was impossible to make out what was happening. She was sure she would have remembered if Nan had mentioned anything particular about Carrie and her family that weekend, or at Christmas, or in her letters, other than that they were fine, though upset because the old tortoise had died. She certainly hadn't said anything about packing cases and boxes, which Ruth knew from her own experience implied a move, so her suspicions were aroused when she saw what was happening here.

All too soon those suspicions were confirmed. "We're moving, Ruth!" Val announced. "But you'll never guess where to!"

"Now, now," Anne interposed. "Give Ruth a chance! We haven't seen her for ages, and all you want to do is burst our news upon her!" She added: "Tell me, Ruth, how do you like the high school? I gather you did very well in the Eleven Plus last year."

School and the Eleven Plus were the last things Ruth wanted to talk about: she had left all that behind her in London. She was curious to find out what was going on, so she simply said, "Oh, all right," in as bored and off-putting a fashion as possible.

Anne, ever the schoolmistress, was not content with that, but persisted with her questions. "Come on, tell us more! What about the maths? I seem to remember you told me when we last met that you hated maths."

Although that had been true once, so much had changed in the meantime that Ruth felt obliged to offer at least some sort of explanation. "Well, Dad taught me, and so I help out in the shop on Saturdays," she said, keeping the information to a minimum.

"Goodness! Your arithmetic must have improved if you can serve in the shop!" came Anne's response. "What do you do there?"

"Oh, I sell sweets on Saturday afternoons," Ruth informed her nonchalantly.

Carrie then wanted to know all about the shop. What was it like? Was the house nice? Was Shirley happy running her business? Ruth provided all the answers, although of course

Nan must have already told them all about it ages ago. At last, after tea, as Ruth cast her eyes round the bare kitchen, Carrie started to explain the reasons for the turmoil.

"I expect you're wondering what's happening here?" she began.

"Um, yes," Ruth admitted, at a loss to know what else to say, prompting Carrie to launch into a halting explanation.

"Well, as Val said, we're moving!"

Ruth nodded: Val had said as much and that was obvious, but she wondered what was coming next.

"We're moving to Australia!" Val chipped in. "And you can come and see us!"

Ruth reeled at this bolt from the blue. Because only that past term she had been studying Australia in geography, she knew that it was on the other side of the world, about as far away as was possible. Had the family been intending to move out into the country, say, or to the coast, or even perhaps to another city, that would have been understandable – but Australia!

"We are emigrating, Ruth," Carrie said rather more gently. "My brother has moved out there on the immigration scheme: he's in Sydney, and he says it's heavenly, so we are going out to join him. It is too good an opportunity to miss; it only costs ten pounds for each of us. We shall be leaving in early July. It's a good time for us to go, as Anne wants to find a job teaching and Val will be going to college when we get there."

"Oh," said Ruth for want of anything better.

"There's just one problem," Carrie continued. "We don't like to tell your nan, as we know she will be very upset, so we haven't said anything to her yet."

Naturally Ruth was upset for her grandmother as much as for herself, but she was also shocked. Although she guarded her own most precious secret closely for good reasons, she did not understand why adults were so secretive about things that were not secrets at all, and would come to light in the long run. Why did Carrie, of all people, conceal this most terrible piece of news from Nan? By implication she too was expected to conceal it from dear Nan who, though fiercely independent, had long drawn comfort from her kind, reliable neighbours and regarded them as part of her family.

"I'll show you a map of Australia," Anne volunteered, and went to fetch it from one of the piles of books and papers that Ruth had already noticed in the living room. She wasn't interested in the map of Australia, because she had drawn it many times in outline in the past year, and had memorized every possible fact about it, for instance that the coastal areas, particularly in the east and south, were the most densely inhabited, that the rest of the continent consisted of deserts and the tropics, and that Canberra had been built as a new capital to avoid the rivalry between Sydney and Melbourne. All that had come up in the end-of-term geography exam.

What she wanted to do was to go next door to Nan and hug her in a vain attempt to protect her from the news that was bound to break before very long. Having attended politely but without enthusiasm to Anne's geography lesson, she slipped away as soon as she could politely do so, with the excuse that she had to help her dad prepare the supper. Despite the cold wind, she dawdled outside for a while, contemplating what to say, but came to no very satisfactory resolution of the problem. At least, as Carrie had kissed her goodbye, she had said that by all accounts the new neighbours, an elderly couple, were very nice people.

Dad was cooking an omelette when she came back into the house.

"All right, Ruth?" he asked, without looking at her, because he was busy cracking eggs into a bowl. She did not answer, and at supper she was very quiet.

Nan cast an eye over her, shrewdly asking, "What's the matter, Ruthie? Didn't you enjoy your time next door?"

"Oh yes," Ruth replied with feigned indifference.

"Are you sad about the tortoise then?" Nan persisted.

"No, not really – well, yes a bit."

Ruth was beginning to squirm under Nan's searching spotlight. Dad didn't know about the tortoise, so he asked when it had died, and then he and Nan started a discussion about tortoises, where they came from, how long they lived and so on, while Ruth ate her plate of omelette, toast and salad in silence.

"Would you like salad cream on your lettuce, dear?" Nan asked cheerily, the bottle poised in one hand, ready to pour the thick creamy liquid onto Ruth's plate.

"No, thank you," Ruth replied gloomily.

"Have a look in the encyclopedia, John," Nan instructed Dad, "and see what they say about tortoises."

He stood up, fetched the encyclopedia and began to read, balancing the book on his knee.

"It says here," he began, "that tortoises belong to the order of Testudines." He took his glasses off and peered more closely at the text, then continued reading, "They can live for hundreds of years in the right conditions. There is one alive today that was given to the Tongan royal family by Captain Cook in 1777!"

"Oh, well I never! That is interesting! The tortoise next door must have been one of the unlucky ones, then. Perhaps it didn't like living here. Too cold for it, I expect," Nan observed.

Dad put the book down saying, "Do you realize – that tortoise in Tonga must be at least one hundred and seventy-nine years old, if not more?"

"Gracious," said Nan, "that makes it a hundred years older than me – and I thought I was ancient!"

Then, in the same cheerful tone of voice, she continued, "I suppose, Ruthie, they told you next door that they're moving to Australia? It will be lovely for them, won't it?"

Ruth was so astounded that it was a while before she found the words to reply. "Yes, yes," she stammered. "They're packing up now." How had Nan found out, she wondered.

Nan herself soon answered the unspoken question. "It was Mrs Baker at church who told me. Her son, Bob, works for Picton's, the removal firm, and he delivered the packing cases ten days ago. I saw his lorry arriving." She mused for a moment. "All the way to Australia! What a long way to go! Mind you, I suspected they might go one day. Carrie's brother went last year, and he kept writing to say how easy life was there, and sending postcards with lovely pictures, so don't worry. I've had time to adjust to it." She paused. "I hope it works out for them, that's all," she said. Ruth sat still in silent amazement. "Oh, and I do hope I have some nice new neighbours," Nan added wistfully. Ruth was happy to reassure her on that point.

Leaning on her son's arm, Nan insisted on walking to church on Easter Day. Although she would have liked to spend the morning at the piano, Ruth went with them, for she was conscious that Nan needed some moral support. Charles Stannard was seated as usual at the organ bench, though the pew nearest to the organ was now taken up by his wife and two small children. He glanced at Nan as she came in with her son and granddaughter, and stared at Ruth unnervingly as he had done years ago, before hastily turning back to the keyboard. The sunlight streamed through the stained-glass windows and made its patterns on the pillars as the service took its habitual course.

On the way home, after a brief exchange of greetings with the Stannard family and a more spontaneous one with some of Nan's friends from the Mothers' Union, including Mrs Baker, Nan said to her son, "When I go, you'll know where I want to be, won't you, John?"

"Of course, Mother," he replied, "but please don't talk like that. It won't happen for a long time."

Ruth, who had overheard the exchange, understood what Nan meant, but tried to forget what she had heard, though that snippet of conversation continued to prey on her mind. Life without Nan was unthinkable, and if Nan died, so much that was important and valuable in her own life would come to an end. She didn't like to contemplate how much, but she knew that inevitably her life would change for ever. The next afternoon Dad brought enough coal indoors to keep Nan going for a week or two before he and Ruth left for London.

Shirley had arrived home before them and greeted them in a buzz of excitement. As she took her coat off, Ruth feared that this simple action might lead to some sort of explosion as had happened two years ago over Shirley's plans for the move to the Broadway, but this time Dad was ready: he was actually anticipating something of the sort, so when Shirley said

"Guess what? You'll never believe this!", instead of taking his coat off in his usual methodical way and politely asking after Edith or requesting a cup of tea, he replied: "No, tell me! I can't possibly guess."

"Well," Shirley went on animatedly, "you know Rita next door?" Dad nodded; he knew that Rita ran the post office, because he often went in there to buy stamps or post a parcel or a magazine to his mother, but he did not know Rita at all well. Nevertheless, he refrained from saying so for fear of interrupting Shirley's flow. "Can you believe it? She was in Birmingham with Sam – he's her husband, in case you didn't know – visiting relatives this weekend, and we bumped into each other in New Street! What a coincidence! So, because we're too busy to have time to meet for a coffee here, we went into a café and sat down for a chat. As it happens, her sister lives near Cousin Edith, so they got on well while we talked about our businesses."

At last she stopped for breath, thus allowing Dad and Ruth to proceed down the hall to the kitchen and put the kettle on. Shirley followed them, undisturbed by this interruption, for she was sailing high on a cloud. "The thing is, you see," she continued, "they are thinking of selling up and moving to Canada, where their son lives."

Now Dad was truly stumped and had to interrupt. "Just a minute, who are 'they'? Edith or Rita's sister?"

"No, stupid!" Shirley took up the thread again with good-humoured tolerance. "No, I mean Rita and Sam!"

"Oh, I see," said Dad. "Carry on, then."

"Right, well, they are moving, so of course their business is coming up for sale."

Dad was alarmed. "You're not suggesting we should sell up and move to Canada too, are you? Mother said that the Carringtons are moving to Australia and now you say that Rita and Sam are moving to Canada – there won't be anybody left here!" he exclaimed.

"No, that's not what I mean." Shirley persevered patiently, as though talking to an elderly customer or a small child. "I'm saying, why don't we take over the post office?"

Unexpectedly she gave Dad time to sip his tea. "Where would we get the money for that?" he asked. "We can't buy their house as well as this one!"

"No, listen, you don't understand" – there was a dangerous tinge of impatience in Shirley's voice – "we don't buy their house at all, we buy the franchise for the post office – I think we can afford it, and I know Pa would help – and incorporate it into our business here instead!"

Dad sat down, still in his overcoat, and said, "All right, I'm listening. So tell me how we are going to do that."

Ruth was proud of him: however hungry he might be, he had at last learnt the all-important lesson of attending first and foremost – disregarding all other distractions, particularly the rumblings in his stomach – to what Shirley had to say. She hovered in the doorway, not wanting to be sent away while yet another life-changing decision was hammered out in the kitchen, and listened to Shirley's plans. She of course had it all worked out without reference to anybody else; indeed the likelihood was that she had not talked of anything else after the chance meeting with Rita and Sam in Birmingham, as was confirmed by her next sentence, "Edith and I talked it over and she thinks it's a very sensible idea."

What, Ruth wondered, did Cousin Edith know about it? She worked in the hospital as some sort of ward orderly, though to hear her talk you might have believed that she was a consultant.

"Edith's very practical, you know," Shirley went on. "She remembered the whole layout of the shop and suggested we should convert our present office into the post office, and make a counter in there; we'd have to cut into the partition wall to put up a screen, of course, but that's no problem. Then, you see, we would convert the back room – which we don't use much – into the new business office with shelves and desks for you and me."

"You and me?" Dad queried.

"Oh, yes, I forgot to say, silly me! The whole point of this is that you can give up the Rates Office and become the postmaster!"

No one spoke while Dad gulped on his tea and restrained himself. "I see," he said with due care and consideration. "Yes, that is an idea! But do you think I'd be any good at it?"

"Any good at it? Why, without a doubt you would be good at it, my darling! You're precisely the sort of person that's needed – honest and upright and good with figures. Rita agreed when I told her about you – we met again on the train home," she explained. "She would help you out with a bit of training before she goes, and we would have to do the conversion in the summer before they leave, but I think it would be perfect for you!"

"Well," said Dad, "you may be right! But what about your television?"

"Oh," said Shirley, without wavering for a second, "that's not a problem: we'll take it upstairs and make the room up there into a sitting room – well, that is, when we have time."

Shirley then made a show of giving Ruth her full and apologetic attention. "Oh! Poor Ruth!" she cried. "I was forgetting you! The summer holidays without the weeks by the sea! Would you mind terribly spending the whole summer holiday at Nan's again?"

"No, no, of course not," Ruth replied at once. Not only was there nowhere else that she would rather be, but she and her father had come away feeling very apprehensive at leaving Nan on her own, especially as Carrie and her daughters would be moving far away very soon.

"Are you sure, Ruth?" Dad enquired. "Your nan might need a lot of help by then."

"Well then, I can be there to look after her!" Ruth announced firmly. "I know what to do and I can shop and cook for us; I've done it before occasionally, so it's no trouble. Dad, don't worry! We'll be fine together."

Gazing at her lovingly, he said. "Ruth, I'm proud of you. You are such a good, kind girl!"

"There, you see!" Shirley exclaimed. "It's all arranged, just like that!" She performed a little dance, spinning round the kitchen with not a trace of a limp, while her husband watched in admiration. Ruth was amazed by her agility and grace.

38

One evening before Ruth set out for the summer at Beech Grove, her father raised the subject of Nan's disability yet again, in the way that adults do when they think they have something extremely important to say.

"Ruthie, you know, don't you, that I am very worried about Nan?" he confided. "She is so deaf and so lame, I can't imagine how she copes."

Ruth was irritated: she too had been worried about Nan ever since Easter, and they had talked and wondered about her often, so there was no reason for her dad to bring the subject up again. Nonetheless she nodded in agreement.

"I don't like to worry you, as well," Dad continued, "but you might have to help Nan out more than you expect when you're there. The problem is this wretched hip of hers; it's giving her a great deal of pain, and she has to take a lot of aspirin, which are making her very sleepy. Well, as you know she doesn't say as much in her letters, but that's what I suspect. She hardly goes out at all, and I'm afraid she's not eating properly. It's such a pity the Carringtons had to emigrate just at this moment..." His voice tailed off, signalling his anxiety.

Understanding how worried and helpless he felt, Ruth's irritation subsided as he went on. "I wish she would allow me to have a phone installed for her, but she refuses. She says you never know who might ring up, so it would be worse than not having one, and in any case she wouldn't be able to hear the person at the other end."

Ruth put her hand on Dad's arm: "Don't worry, Dad, I'll look after her. I've told you before – I can do everything that needs doing. I can cut the grass and clean the house, and do the shopping, even if it's only for eggs and bacon from down the road – and there's the fish shop, so we can live on fish and chips! Don't forget, I am twelve, after all!"

"Ruth, where would I be without you?" Dad declared with a sigh as he gave her a hug. "You're growing up into such a lovely person! I shall miss you – and," he added, "I'm sure that Shirley will miss you too."

Dad was right to be anxious. Nan came to meet Ruth at the station, though from the steps of the train she was hardly recognizable, so shrunken was her frame and so white her hair as she stood leaning on her stick at the barrier. Ruth tried not to show her concern, but greeted her with her customary show of excitement, and Nan responded similarly, if in a somewhat muted fashion.

"My dear Ruthie!" she began. "How good of you to come and spend your holidays with me! Though I can't think why you should want to do that: I'm just an old bag of bones and no good to anyone!"

"Don't say that, Nan!" Ruth exclaimed. "You know there's nowhere else I'd rather be! We'll have a lovely time!"

"Well, at least I can hear better with this thing, and that's something to be grateful for!" said Nan as she pointed to a large pink contraption in her ear.

They made slow progress to the bus stop, where Nan had to be helped onto the bus by the conductor. However, since he travelled that route frequently, he knew her well and was not bothered by any delay to the schedule.

"Come you along there, Mrs Platt," he said in the kindest manner possible. "Didn' I tell you that it'd be my bus comin' back just as you come out o' the station wi' your gran'daughter?"

Nan nodded as he helped her to a seat. "Well, there you are then, my ole darlin', it shows I was right, doesn' it?" Nan dropped gratefully into the nearest seat, and Ruth sat down behind her.

Despite the assurances she had given her father, she began to wonder how they would cope. There was no question of going into the city for tea, for it would be remarkable if they ever managed to venture outside the gate. Nor would there be visits to the farm or to the sea: that much was plain. Nevertheless, once inside the gate, after the conductor had helped them off the bus, Nan moved more confidently, glad to be home in her familiar surroundings, and eagerly accelerated her pace up the driveway to the front door, doubtless keen to prove that she was not as pathetic as people, including her granddaughter, might think.

Ruth had been expecting to get the lawn mower out from her cabin as soon as she arrived, so was astonished to find that the grass was neatly trimmed and the hedge clipped. "Who cut the lawn for you, Nan?" she asked.

Nan glanced at her, a little indignantly. "What do you mean, Ruthie? I cut it myself, of course!" she said. "It's easier if I have something like the lawn mower to lean on! And I can do a little gardening if I have the rake or the hoe to lean against too. So it's not too bad at all. Don't you worry, I'm all right!"

There was no doubt that Nan was "all right" in a manner of speaking and according to her own terms, though goodness knows how: the house was like a new pin, and everywhere smelt of lavender polish. Upstairs Ruth's bed was made, and the bathroom was spotless. How did Nan even get to the top of those treacherous stairs? Ruth wondered.

"You must let me help, Nan," she announced when she came back downstairs after depositing her suitcase and having a quick wash.

"I said you mustn't worry!" Nan insisted firmly, as she buttered some bread. "I've worked out my systems, so don't you worry about me. I want you to play the piano to your heart's content and enjoy yourself while you're here. I know you help out a lot at home, and I want you to have a good holiday after all your hard work at that high school!" There was a hint of contempt in her reference to Ruth's school. She added: "We might not be able to get to the sea or the farm, but I'm determined you're going to have a good time. So you go and play the piano while I wait for the kettle to boil."

This then was an order, which Ruth fulfilled with a pang of guilty pleasure as she ran her fingers over the keys, practising her scales and selecting her favourite pieces. "It's lovely to hear you play, Ruthie!" Nan called from the kitchen. "I've had the piano tuned. Charles Stannard sent me his tuner, and I've found some more Schubert and some Beethoven Sonatas for you. Perhaps you might like to try them over the summer?"

With her tea Nan took two tablets, explaining, "The doctor says I should take these at teatime to help me sleep at night, but you don't have to go to bed when I do, Ruthie. And don't worry about playing the piano or listening to the Proms, you won't disturb me; when I take my hearing aid out, I'm as deaf as a post! Anyhow, these pills won't work for an hour or two, so we can have a nice chat first." Reluctantly Nan allowed Ruth to clear away the tea things and wash up, but only because Ruth was quicker on her feet. She had decided while she was practising the piano that the only way she could help Nan was to get on with the chores quickly before Nan had time to stop her. Nan protested, of course, but her protests were in vain.

It was a fine, warm evening, so they sat chatting by the open garden door. Nan particularly wanted to know about her son, regretting that he would be deprived of a summer holiday yet again. "On the other hand," she remarked, "I have to hand it to your mother. She's full of energy and ideas, isn't she?" Ruth agreed and Nan went on. "I must admit I think it's a very clever idea of hers to set up a post office in the shop and make your father the postmaster. He'll be good at that, and maybe he won't get so tired."

With this observation she began to feel the effects of her tablets and judged that the time had come to retire to bed before she fell asleep in her chair. It had happened once, she said, and she had awoken next morning to find the early sun streaming in through the open door. "Beautiful but rather chilly," she added. It was bedtime for Ruth too, and, after carefully closing the garden door, she followed Nan, who was heaving herself slowly up the stairs.

"What a nuisance I am, Ruthie," Nan tut-tutted, as she pulled herself up on the banister. "I shall be all right when I get to the top."

Once on the landing, she hobbled into the bathroom and lit the geyser. "There," she commented, as steaming-hot water gushed from the spout. "You can have a nice hot bath. Don't mind that old strip of wood I put behind the taps. It's lucky for me that there are two tall old taps, even if the hot one doesn't work! That piece of wood is there for me to lower myself into the bath and pull myself up again. You'll find the bottom of the bath is rather rough: I rubbed it with some of Grandpa's old glass paper so I wouldn't slip. If you don't like it, you can put a towel in and sit on that. Oh, and you can move that little stool out of the way, I stand on that to get in." Nan's ingenuity and spirit were admirable: plainly she was not intending to allow her disability to beat her.

Ruth rose early and went down to prepare the breakfast before Nan woke. She put the kettle on and sliced some bread for toast, then opened the back door to let the warmth of summer into the house. As she stepped out onto the back doorstep to enjoy the clean fresh air and the scent of the pink rose tumbling over Grandpa's shed, she was astonished by the sight of a large but old car standing in Carrie's driveway on the other side of the dividing fence. Recalling that Carrie and the girls had left at least a month ago, she surmised that the car must belong to the new neighbours, and was wondering who they were when Nan came into the kitchen. "Oh, Ruthie! What's all this? What are you a-doin' down here? It's only half-past seven! I was a-goin' to bring you breakfast in bed!" she cried.

How on earth was Nan going to do that, Ruth asked herself, but simply replied: "No Nan, I've put the kettle on and the bread's ready for toasting. I've found the butter and marmalade, so sit down and let me get the breakfast ready."

Without further protest, Nan sat down while Ruth prepared the tea and toast. "Whose car is that next door, Nan?" she enquired.

"Oh, didn't I tell you last night?" Nan replied. "That belongs to my new neighbours. They are ever so nice – Mr and Mrs Hardy, they're called. At least, I think that's what they said, but I can never be quite sure I've caught exactly what people are saying. Mr Hardy – well, I should say the Reverend Hardy – he was a clergyman and he's now retired, so they've come to live here. Real nice it is, they say, to have a modern house instead of a cold, draughty barn of a rectory, but I wouldn't call these houses modern myself. Why, Grandpa and I bought this one when it was new, and that was when your dad was a little boy!" She reminisced happily about times which were prehistoric to Ruth. "I'll show you some photos, Ruthie, if you like, this evening after tea," she offered. Ruth loved old photos: the very mention of them stirred the depths of her memory, bringing back the images of Evelyn and her dad as tiny children and those of herself as a baby that Nan had shown her long ago when she had stayed with her and Grandpa throughout that very cold winter. It was the winter when she had first encountered the piano.

Ruth had been allowed to prepare the breakfast and clear it away, but then Nan shooed her out of the kitchen. "Well, Miss Ruth," she said, "out you go. You need to fill your lungs with fresh air, and I have things to do here!" There was no arguing with Nan. "Having things to do" meant that she wanted to assume control of her domain, so Ruth diplomatically slipped away to see if there was any gardening to be done. She took some tools out of the lean-to and set to work weeding in Nan's vegetable patch, where the lettuces were struggling for survival against rampant speedwell. She staked and tied up the tomato plants, which were bending over under a good crop of ripe fruit, and she fetched a bowl for the abundant raspberries and loganberries. Nan came to the back door to take delivery of the salads and the berries, exclaiming in delight, "Well, I didn't need to buy lettuces and tomatoes, did I?" What she didn't say was that the bottom of the garden was now too far away and the ground too uneven for her uncertain steps, but Ruth guessed, because although the lawn had been mown, it was rough in places and not as neatly trimmed as the front lawn, where the ground was level – and not only the vegetable patch, but also the flower beds were unkempt and running to seed.

As Ruth stood on the back doorstep handing the produce over to Nan, Carrie's back door opened and a plump, grey-haired lady came out. "Hello, Mrs Platt!" she called over the fence. "Is that your granddaughter?"

Nan was momentarily unsure of what she had said, and gave an answer which, though appropriate, was an approximate reply, despite her hearing aid. "Hello, Mrs Hardy," she replied. "My granddaughter, Ruth, was admiring your car a little while ago and wondering who had moved in next door."

Mrs Hardy waved to Ruth, saying cheerily, "Hello, Ruth, nice to meet you! I see you are helping your granny, good girl! Ask her, will you, if there is anything she needs today, and let her know that we shall be away for a few days?"

Ruth relayed the message to Nan, who said no, thank you: she had everything they needed, because Ruth had found plenty to eat in the garden. The new neighbour then explained that she and her husband were going to meet their grandsons, who were coming to stay, and she hoped that Ruth and the boys, as she called them, would get on well together.

After her efforts in the garden, Ruth went indoors to play the piano, while Nan set to work to prepare a cooked lunch in the kitchen. "I may be lame and deaf, but don't let anybody tell me I can't cook," she declared. Ruth understood this, especially as Nan did most of her preparations seated on a stool at the kitchen table, from where she easily twisted round and stretched across to the gas stove or to the sink without having to put a foot on the ground.

She listened while she worked, calling out suggestions and encouraging remarks, "Try the slow movement of that Schubert B flat Sonata, Ruth: you'll find it in the stool. That's one of my favourites." Then, after Ruth's first trial run at sight-reading, she called out, satisfied with her granddaughter's efforts: "Yes, you see, you're getting the idea of that one. It'll get easier the more you practise it." As Ruth sketched in the whole sonata, she discovered how beautiful its stirring melody was, and almost believed that her Aunt Evelyn was talking to her, advising her, teaching her, through those haunting sounds that came out of the piano. She did not allow herself to practise it for very long, because it carried her away to another sphere beyond her comprehension to an ethereal place where there was an infinite peace, far removed from her present, very practical reality of having to learn the notes. Nan came in, interrupting her daydreaming. "I am so lucky!" she declared as a youthful smile spread across her face, "I was afraid I might not be able to hear your playing, but with this thing in my ear, I can! Praise be for modern inventions!"

Buoyed up by her discovery, Nan made a suggestion over lunch, in the hope that the advantages of her hearing aid extended further than simply allowing her to listen to music. "Would you like to go up to the city this afternoon, Ruthie?" she asked.

Ruth was about to say "Yes, please, do let's!" but quickly changed her mind when she wondered what her father would say to that. Although she would have loved to go on the bus to the city, she answered: "No, not today, thank you, Nan. It's so nice here I'd rather stay put, then I can play the piano and go out in the garden."

While Ruth sat on her swing for a while and then weeded the flower bed, Nan slept, the mere fact of which confirmed that a trip to the city would have been too much of a strain for her.

Ruth brought her a cup of tea when she woke up. "Oh dear!" said Nan as she saw the time on the clock on the mantelpiece. "I never intended to sleep that long! You must wake me, Ruthie: five minutes is more than enough!" Ruth then alternated piano and gardening for the rest of the afternoon until it was time for her to be helping Nan with the supper, but, lo and behold, it was already prepared when she came in from clearing away the piles of weeds.

"You said you would show me some photos, Nan," Ruth reminded her as they finished the meal. "Can we look at them this evening?"

"Yes, of course, dear," Nan replied. "I hadn't forgotten, but let me clear the tea things away. Nothing like fresh tomatoes and lettuce, is there? I'm so glad you found them this morning!"

Ruth jumped to her feet. "No, I'll clear the tea things and you can look out the photos," she announced, not giving Nan any option, because she had already stacked the tea plates and cutlery and was carrying them into the kitchen.

They listened to the Prom while Nan unveiled the contents of her box of photos, the one with the false bottom, from which she extracted in random order the evocative pictures that Ruth had seen once long ago, the photos of her parents at their wedding, the photos of herself as a baby, the photo of her father as a child leaning over his baby sister, the photo of her father in uniform. Ruth pored over them, fascinated by the past history of her own family. There was, too, the photo of the little old lady standing between Nan and Aunt Dolly.

There was also a photo she must have missed before, in which ladies were wearing long dresses and gentlemen wore white suits with round white helmets on their heads. Tables were laden with food in a large garden in front of a huge white house, and dark-haired servants carried trays of drinks.

"Who are these people, Nan?" Ruth asked.

"Those are the people your great-grandmother, my mother, worked for," Nan replied.

"Where are they?" Ruth persisted.

"They're in India, dear," Nan answered shortly, as if steeling herself for the questions that were bound to follow.

"India?" Ruth queried in amazement.

Nan reached out to turn the wireless down and began to speak quietly, telling a story that she herself seemed to regard as a mystery. "Have you ever wondered, Ruthie, why we – that is you, your dad and I, and Aunt Dolly, and most, though not all, of the cousins – have this dark skin? She pointed with a brown finger to her own brown arm.

"Yes, I have," said Ruth, as she realized that this was the beginning of the all-important explanation of why her skin was darker than her friends', even perhaps of why, long ago, Simple Simon had called her dad a "wog".

"What I'm going to tell you," Nan said as she deliberately embarked on her tale to the elegiac accompaniment of the Brahms Violin Concerto on the Third Programme, "is a sad, strange story which began when my mother was born a hundred years ago."

Although she punctuated her story with a good few "ums" and "ers", essentially it flowed coherently from start to finish, suggesting that she had considered the material often, even perhaps reciting it to herself and pondering its content.

"My grandparents had a poultry farm out in the country, not far from where Uncle George's farm is now. Clara, their daughter, my dear mother, was the apple of their eye, a clever girl, and went to a good school for local girls in Martlesham, where she even learnt French and music and all that sort of thing. She told me once that her parents had been very proud of her and had high hopes for her, but she feared that she had sadly disappointed them.

"Well, you see, there was a big house on a country estate near the family farm, and that was owned by a Lord Dellamore. He and his family lived in London for most of the year, but when they came home to their estate, my grandmother used to go and help out in the house. She was a born organizer, my grandmother, and would go up there to help the housekeeper engage new staff and keep them in order. Sometimes she would take my mother with her, and Lady Dellamore grew to like Clara. She didn't have a daughter of her own, only sons, so when Clara left school, Lady Dellamore asked my grandparents if she might engage Clara as her lady's maid. Clara wasn't sure that she wanted to be a lady's maid, because she was hoping for a position as a governess, but, as nothing had come up, she agreed to go and work for the Dellamores for the time being.

"At first she worked at the big house, and then the family moved to London for the winter." Nan came to a halt to allow herself to recall the precise details and sequence of her story, but Ruth, who was listening with bated breath, urged her to go on. "Well, so my mother, Clara, went to London with the family, and that was fine: that was how they lived for the next two or three years, the summers here and the winters in London. Clara liked that, because it meant she would see her family in the summertime and enjoy London in the winter, and that was certainly more comfortable than life on the farm!

"Lord Dellamore, it seems, had some position high up in the government, and one winter he was posted to India. Lady Dellamore didn't want to stay in England without him, so once he had settled into his new job, she and her little boys sailed out to join him, taking Clara with them to act more as governess to the boys than lady's maid to their mother. She was very well treated and regarded as a companion rather than a servant by Lady Dellamore. And that was even more the case when they got to India because, there, they had so many servants that there was nothing for the English staff to do. But Clara got on with her job as governess, and sometimes as lady's maid as well when there was an important function, because Lady Dellamore said that no one had the ability to dress her hair like my mother."

Here Nan broke off to search through the box of photos and found a picture of a slim young woman dressed in white; she had a mass of fair hair piled on her head.

"Oh!" exclaimed Ruth. "Is that Lady Dellamore? She's beautiful!"

"No, no," Nan replied. "That's my mother when she was a young governess in India."

Ruth gasped. "Oh, but she's lovely! I wish I had hair like that! So was she my great-grandmother?"

"Yes, that's right, and you do have hair like hers, except that yours is dark and hers was fair," said Nan, before taking up the thread of her story again. "The household was a very large one and, as I said, there were servants everywhere. So many that even Clara had her own servants to fetch and carry for her, to take care of her clothes and bring her whatever she asked for. In fact, she was treated like a lady herself. All she had to do, apart from arranging Lady Dellamore's hair, was teach the two boys in the morning – they went riding in the afternoon, you see – and keep her ladyship company when she was bored, as she often was.

"Lord Dellamore was a very busy man, and he not only had a procession of servants wherever he went, he also had a team of secretaries in his office and an assistant, the most important of the secretaries, who was his right-hand man and organized everything for him. Now this man was young, clever and good-looking. He was Indian, with dark hair and an olive skin; his name was Rohan Arya. Arya – that was my surname and Dolly's until we married." Nan stopped her narration here, sighed and, rising from her chair, said she could do with a cup of tea. Ruth hastened ahead of her into the kitchen to put the kettle on and prepare a tray. Nan did not follow her, and when Ruth came back into the dining room where they had been sitting, she found Nan wiping her eyes.

"Are you all right, Nan?" Ruth asked.

"Yes, yes, dear, only a speck of dust in my eye, that's all." She took the teacup that Ruth offered her and sipped it slowly. "Look, Ruthie, here is a picture of Rohan Arya." She handed Ruth a very faded sepia photo, ragged at the edges, of a handsome young man. Ruth was astonished to see that he bore a close resemblance to her dad. She frowned in suspense but kept quiet, waiting for Nan to continue.

Nan drank her tea and then, carefully putting the cup back on the saucer, said, "I expect you can see that that young man was my father!" Ruth was so overcome that she didn't know what to say. "What happened," said Nan with another sigh, "was that Clara and that young man fell in love – they saw each other every day and they knew that they wanted to get married. If you ask me, it wasn't at all surprising. He was handsome and intelligent – oh, did I say that he dealt with all the accounts and had a very good head for figures? And Clara, well, as you can see, she was beautiful and intelligent too. Clara daren't ask Lady Dellamore for her permission, because she was afraid that milady might not give it, so they were married anyhow. They didn't live together of course, but friends – his and hers – helped them meet until Clara found out that she was expecting a baby. This was something that was impossible to hide, so she knew that she would have to tell Lady Dellamore after all. She trusted that because she had always been such a kind person – and not only that, but had had a variety of gentleman friends – milady would understand. But she didn't understand at all. On the contrary she flew into a rage, screamed at my mother, called her all sorts of terrible names and sent her out of her sight. And Lord Dellamore, when he found out, had my father whipped, and dismissed him from his service at once."

"Why did they behave like that – those Dellamore people, I mean?" Ruth interrupted in disbelief at the cruelty of the English aristocracy.

"I don't really know dear, except that ladies' maids always had to ask permission to get married, and then they were expected to leave service. And, too, English girls were not supposed to marry the natives, something to do with the colour of their skin," said Nan, shaking her head and pausing to blow her nose before taking up her narrative again. "In next to no time, before my mother knew what was happening, she found herself being taken down to the docks and put on the first ship back to England, below deck in steerage, the cheapest part of the ship. It was terrible, hot and airless, with lots of people crowded in together. The smell was awful, the food was dreadful, the sea was rough, and there was not enough fresh drinking water. My poor mother was sick all the way to England and feared that she was going to lose her baby. Of course she was also very unhappy. She had not even been allowed to say goodbye to her husband and had no idea where he was. The only hope she clung to was that he might find her one day, because she had given him her address in England when they were married, in case they were separated.

"Fortunately for her there was a group of very kind, I mean truly kind, people on board: they were missionaries on their way home on leave, and they took pity on my mother. They saw how unhappy and ill she was, and that she was expecting a baby; they did their best to care for her and brought her the best food and water available on board. At last there were people she trusted, so she told them the whole sad story. Funnily enough, she said later, they showed no signs whatsoever of being scandalized, unlike the Dellamores and the rest of the English society she had encountered. Apparently the missionaries had heard gossip of a secret marriage between a handsome young Indian secretary and a beautiful English servant girl, who had then been sent packing.

"When the boat reached Southampton, one of the missionary couples, a middle-aged couple, took her under their wing and brought her all the way home. As you can imagine, her parents, my grandparents, were shocked at first, thinking she was having an illegitimate child – that means a child who hasn't got a father – and they were on the point of sending her to the workhouse, but the kind missionary couple assured them that that was not the case. They explained that the marriage had been properly conducted, from what they had heard, and went on to explain how Clara and her husband had been treated by, they said, 'people who ought to have known better'. After that, my grandparents needed no further persuading to take Clara in and care for her after her dreadful ordeal. Clara produced a copy of the Indian marriage certificate – and that certainly helped, if help were needed.

"Of course, my grandmother was very glad to have Clara back, despite the unfortunate circumstances, because she had missed her so badly, and my grandfather went along with his wife's wishes, particularly because Clara was his favourite child. At home with her parents she recovered from the shock and the hardship, though not from the separation from her husband. So that was how she came home, and several months later she gave birth, not to one baby but to two, two little girls."

"I see!" Ruth exclaimed. "You mean Aunt Dolly and you, Nan!"

"Yes, didn't you know we are twins? I can't believe that no one told you that! Dolly is my big sister, because she is older than me by ten minutes."

Nan yawned as she put the photos back in their box. "I'm really tired Ruthie, I think I'll have to go to bed now. We'll talk more about this another time. Can you close up the garden door, please?"

"Yes, of course," Ruth replied, even though she herself was not at all tired and was desperate to learn much more about this extraordinary story. She thumbed through the photos once again after Nan had gone to bed and studied the picture of her great-grandmother. Mulling over the unjust treatment she had received, she felt deeply sorry for her and angry with the people who had inflicted so much suffering on her. She was impatient to know what had happened next, yet she decided that it would be wise to be cautious and not press Nan for more details, since the tears that Nan had kept dabbing away had shown how haunted she still was by her parents' story, even as she had been relating it.

She put the box back in the drawer, then stood in the garden doorway for a while, gazing out over the tranquil lawn and the circling bats squeaking in the twilit sky. The Prom had come to an end, so she turned the wireless off and finally she locked the garden door. Feeling unaccountably nervous, she went to check both the front and back doors before going up to bed, but slept badly that night, so perturbed and fascinated was she by Nan's narration. When at last she did succeed in falling asleep, she dreamt that she was in the bowels of a ship which tossed from side to side, among weird, ghoulish shapes, ladies and gentlemen dressed in white who floated above her, pointing fingers, sneering at her and whispering "Wog, wog, wog".

39

Nan did not revert to the subject for several days. Meanwhile, as ever, to Ruth's exasperation, her house had yet again become a hive of jam-making, which, entrenched in her routine since the early days of her marriage, had assumed manic proportions in her later life.

"I may be good for nothing, but don't let anybody tell me I can't make jam," she declared, as if she had to be seen to be making jam to justify her existence, even perhaps to prove to herself that she was still in the land of the living. "What you can do for me is help me pick the gooseberries as well as the plums," she informed Ruth one morning. "Then we can eat some, bottle some and make jam. I think the greengages should be getting ripe by now." She stopped to consider the practicalities of the project for a moment. "It's a pity the Hardys are still away," she remarked, looking out of the kitchen window to the empty driveway on the other side of the fence. "Perhaps they're staying the whole week with their daughter; I think she lives somewhere near London." The reason for this train of thought then became clear as she went on, "I believe Carrie left them her ladder; it was new, much better than ours, and I'm sure they wouldn't mind lending it to us, especially if we let them have some fruit."

The car was certainly not in the driveway next door and had not been there since Ruth had first met Mrs Hardy the day after her arrival. "Not to worry, Nan," she said, "I'll get out the old ladder, it's in my cabin."

"Be careful, now!" Nan warned her. Grandpa's old ladder was heavy and, truth to tell, rather rickety, but that did not trouble Ruth unduly. She faltered under its weight, but it was only a short distance from her cabin to the tree, where she leant it carefully against the trunk and climbed up to the lower branches. It was more difficult to balance on the ladder and carry the basket as she filled it up with ripe greengages. There was also the annoying problem of the wasps as they busily asserted their right to the fruit, constantly getting in the way and buzzing around her head. She gingerly fingered each luscious greengage before picking it to make sure that there were no vicious marauders lurking inside.

Nan came hobbling down to the end of the garden to check on her progress and was unnerved to see her wobbling on the ladder. Equally Ruth was not happy to see her nan endeavouring to stay upright on the uneven patch of lawn under the tree.

"You'd better come down, miss," said Nan. "I don't want you breaking an arm or a leg."

"No, nor do I – and I certainly don't want to get stung by those wasps! They're horrible!" Ruth replied as she descended the ladder. "And I don't think you should be out here either, Nan."

"What do you mean, Ruthie?" Nan said huffily. "I was a-goin' to mow the lawn."

"I'll do that," Ruth said firmly. "Why don't you start work on these greengages? Look, I think I've picked enough for at least one batch of jam or bottling. I'll pick the gooseberries next and then I'll cut the grass."

Nan agreed to the pact, so Ruth took the half-filled basket to the door while Nan followed her up the lawn to the kitchen. Then Ruth spent the rest of the morning quietly out of doors, picking the gooseberries and mowing both lawns.

When she came in at lunchtime, Nan gestured to the six pots of gleaming greengage jam on the shelves and the gooseberries bubbling away in the preserving pan. "You see, I'm not finished yet!" she declared proudly. Spurred on by the tangible proof of her success, she decided that they should spend the afternoon in the city, come what may. "If I can make jam, I can get on the bus," she insisted. Ruth was not so sure of the logic of that statement, but knew that there was no way of dissuading Nan from something she had set her heart on doing.

Confirming Ruth's misgivings, the outing proved to be a considerable struggle for them both. The bus conductor, kind and helpful as ever, kept the bus waiting while he virtually lifted Nan on at one end of the journey and off at the other, but the walk through the city to the market was painfully slow, so when at last they found an empty table awaiting them in the corner of the restaurant overlooking the market, they lingered long over their substantial tea.

"Why don't I go and do the shopping on the market, Nan, while you wait here?" Ruth suggested, hoping that her grandmother would be prepared to sit and enjoy the view for half an hour while she bought enough provisions to last for the next week, but Nan would have none of it.

"No, no, I won't have you doing that all on your own," she protested, hastily pulling herself up onto her feet and holding out the payment to the waitress. Ruth sighed, inwardly none too pleased that dear Nan was proving so obstinate. "Anyhow," said Nan, "now I'm here, I might as well go and call on Grandpa's old friends."

They wended their way along the rows of market stalls, buying produce and a bunch of dahlias, until they came to a stall where the friendly proprietor had rolls and rolls of material on display, satins and silks, cottons and linens in all colours.

"Ruthie, you choose a piece of material, and then we'll make you something nice with it," Nan decreed.

Ruth pored over the display for a long time, trying to make up her mind. At last she settled on a length of white cotton with large green cabbage roses all over it.

"That's a very good choice," the lady said. "It's very fashionable this year." She wrapped it up in a brown-paper bag and Nan paid for it, but not before having a chat with the stallholder, who then searched under her counter and put something else in the bag. Ruth's attention meanwhile was elsewhere: she was watching and listening to the endless babble of conversation going on all around her.

"You wouldn't hev believed what a cussed ole bor he was," the lady on the opposite stall was saying to a passer-by.

"O' course I would," came the reply. "You forget they used ter live next door ter me. I know how he treated her, but she got the betta o' him in the end, di'n't she?" They both laughed, leaving Ruth mystified as to what had happened "in the end".

When Nan was ready, they proceeded to the very back of the market, where the sight of tools and machinery suddenly brought to Ruth's mind memories of that earlier visit with Grandpa when she was a small child. It must have been that memorable day of her only visit to the ballet because, as she recalled, Grandpa was very unhappy in his best suit and was being teased by the stallholders. Indeed, she recognized some of the same people who were still there manning their stalls, but there was no jolly bantering this time.

Instead they regarded Nan with concern as she approached their stalls, limping along the alley.

"Well, hello there, my ole darlin'!" one of them said. "How are you a-doin', then? We don't see you up here very often these days!"

"No, that's right, Alf," Nan replied, "but I'm here with Ruth, so I've come to say hello."

"It's lucky you've come jus' now," said Grandpa's friend, Alf. "I was about to close up and go home." Then he asked, "But how did you get here? I see you are havin' a bit o' trouble there with that leg o' yours" – he gestured in the general direction of Nan's stick. Nan did not answer, but Ruth chipped in: "We came on the bus."

"I see," said the stallholder, on a sharp intake of breath.

He fell silent before making a suggestion that was music to Ruth's ears, and probably to Nan's as well, though she did not allow herself to show it. "If you don't mind my dirty ole van, I'll take you home, right to your door, if you like."

"Oh, yes, please!" Ruth almost shouted with joy, for this was indeed an answer to prayer.

On the bumpy ride home, Nan was comfortable in the passenger seat, but Ruth had to squeeze in among Alf's spiky merchandise of screws and nails, spanners and hammers, stored in open boxes in the back of his van. Nonetheless she was so grateful for the lift for herself with the shopping, and especially for Nan with her bad leg, that grumbling was out of the question.

After their ample tea in the city, neither of them wanted supper, so Ruth opened up the garden door and pulled Nan's armchair and a smaller chair for herself into the opening from where they watched the golden rays of the evening sun slanting across the lawn through the gap between the houses. Massive clouds were appearing above the treetops, darkening as they advanced.

"If you ask me, we're going to have to close that door in a minute," Nan observed. Indeed, only a minute or two later, large raindrops began to patter loudly on the tin roof of the lean-to while grandmother and granddaughter sat together reminiscing quietly about their trip to the city.

"My goodness! Weren't we lucky that Alf brought us home?" said Nan, for once dropping her stoicism and allowing herself to show her relief. Ruth agreed, reminding her that not only had Alf brought them home, but he had brought the shopping as well. "Yes, that is good," said Nan, "I wasn't sure how much longer our crops down the garden would last, so now we're well supplied."

Shifting her weight in her chair, she enquired: "So, is there anything you'd like to do this evening, Ruthie – apart from listening to the Prom, I mean?"

Ruth jumped at the chance. "Well, Nan, if you're not too tired, I would like to have a look at the photos again."

"Of course," said Nan, "but I don't think I shall be able to get out of this chair, so you'll have to search them out in the drawer of the sideboard. Oh, look at that rain! Close the door, dear, would you, please? And let's have the wireless on."

Ruth turned the Third Programme on, though it was too early for the Prom, before going over to the sideboard and opening the drawer. She picked up the box, but underneath it discovered a collection of loose photos that Nan must have missed.

"Look at these, Nan!" she exclaimed, gathering them up in a bundle. "There are a lot more photos under the box!"

"Well I never!" Nan mused. "How did they get left out of their box? Let me have a look. Can you bring that little table over here?" She took up a wad of photos and put them down on the small table that Ruth had placed beside her. "Well, well, well," she remarked, "I wonder how long they have been there. How did I miss them?"

"The box is very full: I expect they must have slipped out, or perhaps they were taken out to make room for new ones some time ago," said Ruth, offering plausible explanations.

Nan smiled as she examined each picture. "Look, here's Evelyn when she was about ten or eleven. She's wearing that yellow dress you wore two summers ago! Do you remember? You're so tall, you'll have outgrown that by now!" Ruth smiled too and picked up another photo: it showed her father captured at about the same time as Evelyn, wearing his school uniform – a cap, blazer and long trousers – and carrying a satchel on his back. Nan laughed. "That one was taken on the day he started at the grammar school. He was glad to get into them long trousers! He hated those short ones he had to wear when he was little! He was always scraping his knees, and it was so cold in winter!"

More photos came to light: the deeper Ruth dipped into the pile, the older they were. "Oh, Nan, look at this!" she exclaimed as she picked up an old brown photo of two babies in long white ruched dresses lying on large velvet cushions.

Nan studied the photo and rubbed her eyes. "Well, do you know, I haven't seen that one in years! That's me and Dolly on the day of our christening."

"Your christening?" Ruth echoed.

"Yes, of course, why not?" Nan shot her an injured glance. "We were christened like everybody else!"

Taken aback, Ruth stammered, "Yes, of course."

Nan went on, "And do you remember, I told you the other day about those kind missionaries who helped our mother? Well, they were our godparents, the Reverend and Mrs Hales. What good, kind people they were! They went back to India soon after our baptism. I don't remember that we ever met them again, though every time they wrote to Mother, they wrote to us as well, one letter for me and one for Dolly, with little pictures of palm trees and strange buildings, sometimes even a tiger! They wrote to Mother from time to time, so we had a good collection of pictures, but I don't think any of them have survived."

Here she rummaged further down the pile until she found what she was hoping for. She pulled out a tiny drawing of a fierce-looking tiger on a scrap of paper.

"Oh, here is one of them!" she exclaimed in delight. "Look, Ruth! What does it say? I can't read the writing."

Ruth obliged and read out: "Here is a picture of the tiger we saw yesterday. He was very frightening, so we kept away from him!" The picture was signed "From your loving godparents, M. and E. Hales".

The Prom had begun, so Ruth went to turn up the sound. "Beethoven night," said Nan absent-mindedly, for she was not actually listening to the music: her whole attention was absorbed by another photo she had just uncovered. She leant nearer to the window in the hope of viewing it in brighter light, but the sky had become so black that the detail of the picture eluded her. "Can you switch the light on, dear? It's so dark I can't see who's in this photo."

When the light came on, Nan gasped with pleasure. "You'll like to see this one, Ruthie!" she said at last, handing another very old photo to Ruth when she herself had fully digested its image. It did not show Dad or Evelyn, but it did show two little girls, presumably the ones in the christening photo, though here they were both older and much larger: Ruth guessed that they were about three or four years old. They were in the arms, one on each side, of a tall, black-haired man with a dark skin. "There, I knew there was another photo of my father! That's your great-grandfather here with us in England." Nan announced quietly, plunging Ruth into confusion.

"Oh, didn't Clara have to leave him in India and never see him again? You mean he came to England?" she asked in astonishment.

Nan's reply simply increased her astonishment. "Yes, yes, the Reverend and Mrs Hales traced his whereabouts and helped him get to England. He hadn't any money, because after Lord Dellamore had sacked him – and threatened him with prison – he was banned from getting another job, so it was very hard for him, but the Haleses raised some money to pay for his passage as far as a place called Porto, or something like that, in Portugal, and then he walked from there. It was a long, long way, but one summer afternoon there was a knock on the door of the farm. Mother went to the door – and there he was! He was weary and footsore and very thin. He had scarcely eaten in weeks. My mother was ecstatic, and so were my grandparents, and we were too when we understood who he was. We must have been about three at the time.

"We all cared for him, and after a month or so of good food and rest, he recovered sufficiently to set to work, which he did with a will. He worked in the fields by day with my Uncle Billy and helped Grandfather with his accounts at night, so nobody ever dared say he was a layabout. He was treated well enough by the other workers on the farm, because they knew he was the boss's son-in-law, but other people elsewhere were rude to him and called him all sorts of names."

Ruth shuddered, recalling yet again the names she had heard in the primary-school playground. "What sort of names, Nan?" she asked.

"Don't you worry about that, Ruthie, you don't want to know," said Nan. "I'll tell you one thing though: those Dellamores, when they came home from India, weren't at all pleased to find that my mother and father were living happily together with their family on the farm, and they did their best to make life hard for them." Watching Nan shake her head, Ruth understood that the cruelty and wickedness of the human race were as much, if not more, a cause of pain to Nan as to herself. "They had dogs," said Nan picking up the thread again, "which they let loose to roam about the countryside, and they always came onto our land. I think they were meant to attack us, but they never did. My father would pat them and give them some water or a bone, and then they would lie down as docile as newborn lambs! One afternoon my father was hoeing and tidying up the edge of a field by the road when his lordship came by on horseback. Lord Dellamore raised his whip, but my father saw what was coming and lifted his hoe just in time to protect his face from the blow. It struck hard against the handle of the hoe and lashed Father's arm, but he wasn't too bothered about that, although the wound was a nasty one. And when those Dellamores went out hunting, they did as much damage to our land as possible.

"Of course in church they sailed past us, their heads held high, ignoring us completely. You might have thought we weren't there. My grandmother said they were fine ones to behave like that: if she told all that she had heard when she worked up at the Hall, the name of Dellamore would sink to the depths of the ocean! She didn't tell what she knew, but when Lady Dellamore ignored her, she looked the other way as haughty as milady. In the end they tried to have Father arrested, declaring that he didn't have proper papers – but he did: the Haleses had seen to that. By this stage my grandfather had had enough. He went to see an old school friend of his from days gone by when they were small children together in the village school, and had a chat with him. After that there was no more trouble and we were left in peace, because Grandfather's old friend happened to have become the Lord High Sheriff of the county!"

Ruth had never heard of the Lord High Sheriff, but she supposed that if he were as powerful as the sheriffs in the cowboy films the boys used to talk about in school, he had the authority to put the Dellamores themselves in prison.

"What happened next, Nan?" she asked eagerly.

"Well, I don't rightly know, but some say that even the old Queen got to hear of it, and she wasn't at all pleased – but that might simply be a rumour. Anyhow, the Dellamores went back to India and were never seen again. I don't know what happened to them. The Hall was sold, and we lived in peace."

She paused in her narration to listen to the remaining minutes of the Prom, but dozed off in her chair instead. Ruth tiptoed out into the kitchen to make a plate of sandwiches and two cups of cocoa, which she brought back with Nan's tablets. She woke up with a start when Ruth put the tray down beside her and exclaimed. "Whatever next, Ruthie! Here I am falling asleep while you're getting us a little bit to eat. Oh, that is nice! A sandwich would suit me nicely; it's a long time since we had tea." The rain pelted down outside from a dark sky while they ate and drank in contemplative silence.

Even though Ruth refrained diplomatically from asking any more questions, Nan didn't seem to consider the matter closed. "Let's hope those days are well and truly gone," she observed. "Terrible, isn't it, to treat people like that just because they happen to have a different colour skin?" Ruth nodded in quiet agreement and was then completely taken aback by Nan's next revelation. "Of course," she said, "I know what it's like myself. It was all right for Dolly, because she married our Cousin George – he was Uncle Billy's youngest son, and he inherited Glebe Farm, where they all still live. He and Dolly had known each other since we were born, so he wasn't worried by the colour of her skin. He called her 'My nut-brown maid'." She smiled at the memory.

"So what about you, Nan?" Ruth blurted out, interrupting Nan's reverie.

"Me – well, it was different for me," Nan said rather sadly. "I didn't have George to protect me, and I didn't have many friends except my cousins in the country. It was all right at school, because Dolly and I went to the board school together and Dolly always made friends. Between school and home, we were well educated, and I learnt to play the piano like a young lady, but it was when I came to the city to work as a seamstress. I was all on my own with no friends and none of the comforts of home life. The other girls in the workshop and in the boarding house regarded me as odd – not that they said so, but they avoided me and laughed at me if I made a mistake. Sometimes I heard them whispering about me: among themselves they called me 'coffee face'. Yes, that was hard, real hard. I didn't have any friends at all." She wiped her nose and gave herself a minute's respite in which to reminisce. "I was so glad to get home to the farm at the weekend, you can't imagine!"

"But you met Grandpa, didn't you?" Ruth asked, as she reflected on the extraordinary story of Nan's background.

"Oh, not for a long time, not till after the Great War," came Nan's wistful reply.

Then there was a lull when neither of them spoke. Ruth guessed that Nan had something on the tip of her tongue, so she waited in patient suspense until her grandmother decided to confide the whole story to her.

"But I did have one good friend. That was before I met your grandfather, and it happened one day as I was about to get on the tram – what they called 'the electric tram' in those days," she said. "Though the conductor saw I had one foot on the step, he rang the bell anyhow. Deliberately, I believed. I missed my footing and fell backwards off the tram. Fortunately for me there was someone standing right behind me, and he caught me. 'Caught me in his arms,' he said later, 'as though it was intended!'" Ruth was spellbound again. "That young man, his name was Samuel – he was dark, though not as dark-skinned as me, and he had a fine bushy beard. He took me to a seat and sat me down. He shocked me when he seized my wrist and looked into my eyes. 'Don't worry,' he said, 'I'm a doctor, and I want to make sure you are all right before I let you go to work, so let me look into your eyes and take your pulse.' He saw me onto the next tram and told the conductor to take good care of me.

"We met almost every morning at the tram stop after that, and then often we met after work as well. He said he hadn't any friends either, probably because he was Jewish, even though like me he had lived all his life in this country, so he understood how I felt. Then we met to do things together. In the winter we went roller-skating in the Agricultural Hall, and in the summer we went on the river or we took the train to the coast for an evening by the sea. Yes, we got on very well."

"Oh, my friend Susan is Jewish!" Ruth exclaimed, suddenly recalling her own connection with a Jewish family.

"She's fair, but her father, Jacob, he has dark hair and a dark skin."

Nan nodded, but was not listening to Ruth. "When the Great War began," she said, "Samuel enlisted at once in the medical corps. Unlike everyone else he was certain that the War would be long and that there would be many casualties – and he was right. He was one of the casualties himself..." Nan brought her tale to an abrupt close and shut her eyes.

"Time for bed, Nan!" Ruth urged, trying to conclude the evening on a lighter note.

"Don't you worry about these old stories, my dear," Nan reassured her. "That's all they are: old stories. Remember, later on I did meet your grandpa, and we couldn't have been happier!"

Ruth mused for a little while after Nan had gone to bed on the strange and upsetting history of her own family that she had just heard. The bedtime fantasies of her childhood had yielded place to the much more absorbing tragedies of real life as lived by real people to whom she was related. It seemed that matters which once upon a time had been closely guarded secrets might in the course of time, even over generations, come to light and be revealed. She wondered how many more such surprises she might discover.

40

Rain poured down from leaden skies for days on end, interrupting the gathering of fruit for Nan's jam factory. On the first wet afternoon Nan, never short of ideas, suggested making Ruth a new summer skirt with the length of material they had bought on the market. Ruth lifted the heavy sewing machine onto the dining table and then climbed up to fix the flex into the overhead light fitting. The little lamp on the machine lit up at once, and after she had followed Nan's instructions for cutting out and tacking the garment, she was allowed to clamp the foot down and run the material through the mechanism, depressing the pedal on the floor. The machine made its comforting whirring noise as the needle speedily hopped up and down. By the end of the afternoon, as she was admiring her handiwork – a lovely skirt of white material patterned with large green roses – Nan presented her with a small parcel, inside which was a short-sleeved green blouse with a white trim which matched the skirt perfectly.

"There, now you've got a nice, new summer outfit," Nan commented with evident satisfaction.

On another wet afternoon Ruth practised a Beethoven Sonata until Nan said that Evelyn could not have played it better. Then she helped in the kitchen, where Nan was busy baking cakes and buns: some, she said, were for the Mothers' Union, whereupon Ruth fervently hoped that she would not be required to deliver them. The others, Nan said, she was making in case any visitors came to call. No visitors came that day, but the next, to Ruth's relief, a lady came with her husband by car to collect the cakes for the Mothballs, and they both stayed for tea, so Nan's forethought proved well justified on both counts.

The lady's husband kindly offered to come for Nan and take her to the Mothers' Union the following Tuesday, while Ruth prayed a silent prayer that she would not be expected to go too. Nan naturally voiced doubts about leaving her on her own, but these were quickly dispelled by Ruth herself, who reminded her grandmother that she would be thirteen at her next birthday, and that she was old enough to remain alone for a couple of hours.

"I have to admit," Nan said to her visitors, "she's right! These days it's my Ruthie who's looking after me rather than the other way round!"

After doing so much baking, Nan was alarmed to find that her stocks were running low. "Oh, I hadn't noticed I had already used up so many eggs and the butter and the flour!" she exclaimed ruefully when she examined the contents of the larder. "I'll have to catch the bus and go down to Mr Carter with a long order, because we need things they don't sell in the shop over the Green. You don't have to come, Ruthie, you can stay here and play the piano." Nan gazed out of the window, "And it's still raining hard," she lamented.

"Don't worry," Ruth reassured her. "I'll take the order to Mr Carter. Don't you come out in the rain; it looks muddy and slippery out there. I'll get on the bus and go down to the shops. It won't take a minute. Just give me the list. Shall I get some bread, as well?"

Armed with the grocery list, and also a list for the butcher, whose shop was next door to the grocer's, a shopping bag, a few shillings and some pennies, Ruth climbed onto the bus and requested a penny-ha'penny fare from the conductor. She delivered the order at the grocer's and, while doing so, decided that it would be nice to take a bar of chocolate home to Nan; similarly at the baker's she added two doughnuts at tuppence each to her purchase of a loaf of bread, forgetting that there were still plenty of buns left from Nan's baking session.

She often shopped with her father in London and was used to buying bread and groceries with him on Saturday mornings, so shopping for Nan was well within her capabilities.

Sometimes her mother, who was far too busy behind the counter to attend to such mundane matters, would send her out for extra supplies, allowing her that enjoyable sensation of adult responsibility that came with an errand and with the money to pay for it jingling in her pocket. As usual Nan had included two sixpences for Ruth to buy "something nice", and normally the little treats that she added to the list – doughnuts or flapjacks, or a bar of chocolate – were appreciated, but today was to prove rather different.

In no time at all, she was back on the bus heading home. The showers were easing off, and patches of clear blue were beginning to appear in the rain-cleansed sky. As she stood waiting to cross the road after alighting from the bus, she noticed that both the neighbouring front gate and Nan's were wide open. She stopped outside the neighbours' gateway and glimpsed inside. The car was back, parked fairly near the road, and farther down the driveway beyond the car, a boy was throwing a ball against the side wall of the house. Ruth guessed he was about her own age and height. The ball bounced off a drain pipe instead of the wall, flying off in her direction. The boy ran after it and suddenly spotted her. Ruth was embarrassed that he had witnessed her curiosity, so she ran quickly into her own drive.

A battered truck was parked in Nan's driveway: Ruth remembered seeing it before, but was not absolutely sure where, until she went into the house and heard the familiar voices of Uncle Rick and Aunt Dolly.

"Well, Ruth, come and see who's here!" Nan exclaimed as she came into the living room. "I knew all that baking was for some good purpose."

Uncle Rick explained that because of all the rain they hadn't been able to get on with the harvesting, so he had come up into the city, bringing his mother with him, to buy various spare parts that were needed for the bailer.

"So," said Aunt Dolly, "we thought we'd come and call on your nan. We didn't know you were here as well, Ruth, so it's lovely for us too!"

After hugs all round and the customary remarks about how tall she had grown, Uncle Rick and Aunt Dolly settled back into their armchairs and resumed their tea, while Ruth took her purchases into the kitchen and stored them away in the larder. She wondered rather regretfully what to do with the doughnuts. All the way home she had been looking forward to sharing them with Nan, but as there were only two, not enough for the present company, she put them in the pantry with the rest of the shopping. She glanced out of the kitchen window to see if the boy was still in the sideway, but there was no one there and the neighbouring house was quiet again.

Uncle Rick reclined in his armchair with his eyes closed while Nan and Aunt Dolly chatted, exchanging news and catching up on family gossip. Ruth sat down with them and helped herself to tea and cake. Gazing out of the window, she wondered who the boy next door was, and then remembered that Mrs Hardy had said that she and her husband were going to collect their grandsons. The boy must be one of them. Her attention elsewhere, she listened with only half an ear to the adults' conversation until she heard a suggestion Aunt Dolly was making to Nan.

"Now, as we're here with the truck, why don't you and Ruth come down to the farm for the weekend? Let's hope the weather will improve, though they won't be doing the harvesting till the corn has dried out. Rick would bring you back on Monday, I daresay."

In other circumstances Ruth would have been overjoyed with an invitation to stay at the farm, but at the moment three considerations preoccupied her: the first was the problem of the doughnuts which, she knew, would be hard and dry if not eaten fresh, and the second was a reluctance to be parted from the piano, and the third concerned the boy next door. She wanted to meet him, for though she loved Nan and was passionate about the piano, she was beginning to feel the lack of a companion of her own age. However, since Nan jumped at the invitation to go to the farm, assuming that her granddaughter would share her delight, Ruth went upstairs to pack some clothes for herself in one of the small bags that Nan held in reserve for such eventualities.

Nan's own bag was always kept ready, so that if an offer materialized, as it did from time to time, she would simply have to send someone upstairs to collect it for her.

"There, Rick, you see," she said, "You don't have to fetch my bag for me this time, because Ruthie will do it for me."

Somehow the four of them squeezed onto the front seat of the truck. "You and your nan are skinny, so you won't be taking up much room, Ruth," Uncle Rick remarked. "You get in first, then Mother next to you, and then I'll lift Auntie in last."

Since Aunt Dolly was more rotund than Nan and Uncle Rick was also rather corpulent, Ruth – who was sitting between them – felt that she was being crushed like a hazelnut in a nutcracker, and she supposed that Nan, seated between Aunt Dolly and the door, must have felt the same.

The pleasure of arrival at the farm outweighed any discomfort on the journey. Soon she was sent out with Wizzie to search for eggs for supper. Her cousin was fretful at getting her smart clothes dirty in the muddy farmyard and inveigled Ruth back indoors, even though they had uncovered only a half a dozen eggs. Wizzie was already thirteen and tried to appear at least two years older. She showed Ruth her little make-up bag, which contained a small bottle of scent, a powder puff and a lipstick; these were her proudest possessions, though Ruth didn't understand why she needed them. Wizzie with her fair hair and blue eyes was by far the prettiest of the cousins, the rest of whom resembled Ruth more closely, with their dark brown hair and dark eyes. But when Ruth asked why she used make-up, Wizzie startled her with her reply. "Oh, it's all right for you Ruth, you are beautiful anyway with your long dark hair and your lovely skin. You don't need any make-up, but I'm so pale, I need some colour." Never before had anyone suggested that Ruth might be beautiful, but when she studied herself in the mirror that night, she saw deep chocolate-brown eyes gazing out of a tanned face with pinkish cheeks. The face was framed by long brown locks, and she thought perhaps she didn't look too bad after all. In her opinion, though, Wizzie was prettier – in the same glamorous way as Shirley.

Andy, Ruth's favourite cousin, had married since last year. He and his wife Joan lived in a nearby cottage, and together they ran the farm, which had expanded greatly over the years, with Abe and Rick, since Uncle George had retired from active work. Andy's brother Dan had joined the army, and two of Wizzie's older sisters, Amy and Ellen, were training to become nurses. Wizzie's two other sisters worked in shops in the neighbouring town, one in the chemist's and the other in the grocer's. That still left a large contingent of cousins, including Ralph and his twin Peter, and their sister Lisa, plus the crowd of boys whom Wizzie had despised when they were small, but who were now competing for her attentions. She was forever going off to meet one or other of them.

"Do you have a boyfriend?" she asked Ruth that evening.

"No," said Ruth, not ever having dreamt of boyfriends.

"Oh, I do," Wizzie asserted confidently, "I've got lots, but I don't love any of them and I'm certainly never going to marry any of them – they are so stupid! I'm going to marry a millionaire!"

Ruth wondered why Wizzie was so certain. Where was she going to meet a millionaire, and how did she know that she would fall in love with him? In fact, Ruth had no idea what falling in love was all about and was sure she hadn't fallen in love with any of her cousins – certainly not any of those younger cousins. Andy was nice, but he was married now, and anyhow if love meant kissing, that was boring.

The wet weather meant that fewer members of the family were at supper, since their help with the harvest was not yet required: some were waiting in their own homes for the corn to dry out, others who had bought neighbouring farms were watching the weather apprehensively, fearful for their own crops. Ruth was sent down to the cornfield to summon Andy indoors for supper. She half expected to see a golden haze swaying in the breeze, but was disappointed. The corn was brown, damp and beaten down by the winds that had accompanied the rain.

Andy was testing an ear of corn between his fingers. Gazing up anxiously at the overcast sky and shaking his head, he said, "It'll be all right if it dries out this weekend, but if we have more rain, this field will sprout and be no good at all." Preoccupied with his crop, he might have been addressing his farm workers and scarcely noticed Ruth at all. At supper he, his father, his Uncle Rick and his grandfather discussed all possibilities and likely outcomes, concluding that the harvest was going to be a poor one – but in that case the price of such corn as they could sell would go up, so they might not be too badly off after all.

Ruth half listened to their conversation, but was also listening to and watching Aunt Dolly, who was trying to persuade Nan to move to the farm.

"Look, my dear, with that hip of yours you need to be with your own people: you need to be here with us so as we can help you. You don't want to be there all by yourself. Come and live with us. There's room for you here in the house or in one of the cottages. There's that empty cottage next door to Andy; he was thinking of putting a proper bathroom in there now that it's got running water. And anyhow," she went on, gesturing to her daughter sitting in her usual corner with her knitting, "I'd be glad of the company; the girls are all busy now and, well, you know, Eva's a good girl, but she doesn't hev much to say for herself."

"That's real kind of you," Nan replied, resisting stubbornly, "but I don't want to be a nuisance to you, and I get along just fine in my own house."

Impressed by Aunt Dolly's generosity, Ruth scrutinized her kindly features. She and Nan were certainly very similar. It was possible for Ruth to tell them apart primarily because of their difference in size, but it was also obvious that they were twins, and identical twins at that. Part of her wished that Nan would accept Dolly's invitation, but another part understood why she declined it. She would do the same herself, because Nan's house was so very special and so different from anywhere else that she knew. It held an aura of magic which had always – and was still – throwing up new experiences and even adventures.

Those experiences and adventures might take place out of doors – a trip into the city or an unexpected visit to the farm such as this one, perhaps – but equally they might take place not only indoors but in the depths of the mind, revealing hidden histories and arousing feelings through a handful of old photos or a piece of music which brought her in touch not only with the composer's way of thinking, but also with his innermost emotional being, penetrating in fact right into his heart.

As Ruth surveyed herself in the mirror in the dimly lit bedroom that evening, Nan asked her what she was looking at.

"Just wondering, Nan," she replied. "I was wondering why Wizzie said she needed to wear make-up. She said she didn't have as much colour in her face as I do, but I think she's very pretty."

"Yes, she's pretty, but she's a silly girl too," said Nan. "Don't you take too much notice of her."

"But why does she have fair hair and blue eyes when we all have dark hair?" Ruth persisted.

"I can't answer that," Nan replied brusquely, "and don't you go asking questions!"

Duly chastened, Ruth climbed into bed, but before she fell asleep she reflected that unanswered questions always implied some sort of mystery – and there were so many of them!

41

The two days at the farm were blissful – not only for Ruth, who spent the weekend searching for warm, brown eggs, wandering round the farmyard, watching Joan milk the cows and roaming through the fields once the sun had begun to shine and the ground to dry out, but also for Nan. Well rested in her sister's care and the beneficiary of a pot of home-made ointment which Dolly assured her would ease the pain in her leg, she recovered some of her former enthusiasm and started to make plans for the coming days and weeks ahead.

"We must borrow the ladder from next door so as I can make more jam!" she announced almost as soon as they had arrived home.

Ruth despaired, wondering how much more jam could be accommodated in the larder. "Don't you think we've made enough already?" she enquired plaintively.

"No, no, I can't bear to see all that good fruit going to waste," Nan insisted blithely, her spirits and her vitality restored. "And anyhow, we can share some of it with the neighbours, and as you know, whenever I go to the farm, I like to have something to take with me. I don't have to tell you that Dolly doesn't have time to make jam."

Ruth had been glad for Nan when she overheard Aunt Dolly issuing an invitation to her to come to the farm for the harvest supper in September, assuring her that either Rick or Abe would come to collect her and take her home again after a week or so in the country. "Yes, thank you my dear, that would suit me nicely," Nan had replied, to which Ruth heaved a thankful sigh.

Since Nan, encouraged by the promise of yet another visit to her sister's, was happy to resume her reign over the kitchen for the time being, Ruth went to sit at the piano, but found it hard to decide what to play. She played through all her scales and then a Beethoven Bagatelle, but that did not satisfy her. She felt edgy and restless, not knowing what to choose next. Inevitably she resorted to the andante movement of the Schubert B flat Sonata, but found that her brain had wandered off because her hearing was elsewhere. Her ears were not listening to the music she was trying to play, but to Nan's voice calling out from the back door to someone on the other side of the fence, presumably Mrs Hardy; then, a few minutes later, there was a commotion in the driveway. She went to the window to see what was happening, and there was the boy who had been throwing a ball against the house some three days earlier, carrying one end of a ladder while a distinguished-looking older man, who must have been his grandfather, manhandled the other.

Ruth was faced with a dilemma: although she wanted to meet the boy, she was too shy to go out to say hello to him. Feeling trapped, she sat down at the piano again, without touching the keys, because she didn't want him to hear her playing – as he certainly would have done, since all the outer doors were open – so she sat motionless waiting for the activity to come to an end. She heard voices and laughter from the back garden, where undoubtedly the neighbours were picking plums. "Yet more plums," she sighed peevishly. The boy must have climbed the ladder while his grandfather held it steady, and Nan was giving instructions from the top of the lawn.

After a while she heard Nan exclaiming, "That must be plenty by now! Thank you so much!" Then she must have turned back towards the house, because she was calling out, "Ruthie, Ruthie, where are you? Come and meet Julian!" Ruth slunk quietly away up to her bedroom. Surreptitiously she peeped over the window sill, from where she saw Nan standing outside, leaning on her stick, in animated conversation with the retired clergyman from next door and the boy. They all appeared pleased with their efforts, and for one moment Ruth feared that Nan was going to ask the neighbours in for tea, but they picked up their ladder and carried it away.

Nan came back into the house calling, "Ruthie, Ruthie, where are you?" Emerging from her hiding place, Ruth descended the stairs rather sheepishly. "Oh, there you are!" Nan exclaimed. "I wanted you to meet Julian from next door; he's such a nice boy. He's the younger of their two grandsons. I didn't meet the older one – I forget what his name is… something foreign-sounding, I think."

Ruth was spared cross-examination on her earlier, rather rude, disappearance by a sudden flash of memory. "Oh, Nan, I forgot to tell you, I bought doughnuts for us the other day, but then we went to the farm and they went quite out of my mind. I put them in the breadbin."

Distracted by this news, Nan opened the bread bin. "Oh, that was a nice idea, and it was so kind of you to do the shopping and place the orders! I expect the doughnuts will be fine. Let's try them now, shall we?"

In fact, although the doughnuts were not at their best, as Ruth had anticipated, Nan was most appreciative. "Do you know, I've remembered something too!" she exclaimed. "Tomorrow I'm supposed to be going to the Mothers' Union meeting; is that all right with you, Ruthie? Come with me if you like."

Ruth had her answer ready: "I think I'd better stay here, Nan, because Mr Carter said he would be coming with the groceries tomorrow afternoon, and I think the butcher said he would be coming then as well."

Not long after Nan had left with her friends the following afternoon, Ruth took delivery of the meat and the groceries. She sat at the piano for a little while, savouring her freedom from the Mothballs, but as the sun shone from a clear sky, the lure of the garden proved irresistible, so she went out intending to mow both lawns. The back lawn was hard work, since the grass had quickly grown lush and tufted in the recent rain. After pushing the lawn mower up and down the slope for a good half-hour, she was hot and weary and decided that she needed a drink, so helping herself to a glass of Nan's lemonade, she went to sit on the front doorstep in the afternoon sun. This was one of her favourite places. She stretched out her long legs, basking in the solar warmth like a lizard.

Before long, however, the peace was broken by the sound of the ball – the same ball, as it repeatedly hit the wall of the neighbouring house. "Oh, that boy, what's his name? He's out there again," she thought, half irritated by the constant pounding of the ball against the wall, but half glad that he was there, though she was too shy to approach him. She hid herself in the recess of the porch and kept still. Several minutes later, the noise of the ball was joined by another extraordinary and much more agreeable sound, the sound of a piano. The windows of the front room next door were open, and someone was playing a piano in there! This meant that the new neighbours had a piano in their front room, just like Nan!

As her ears grew accustomed to the rising and falling melodies, she felt like weeping in joy and also in sorrow, for the pianist was playing none other than the andante movement of her beloved Schubert sonata. It was one she had been trying to play, the one that she was currently practising. Nan had encouraged her by saying that she would play it as well as Evelyn one day, though now she knew that was unlikely, because the sounds emitting from next door were so much more poignant than anything she might aspire to. Had it not been for the irritating ball, she would have drowned in the depths of that music, so profoundly did it reach her inner being. Above all, she wanted to know who was playing, who was playing with such passion and yet such lightness of touch. Was it Mrs Hardy or her husband? It wasn't the boy with the ball, for he was impervious to the beguiling sounds that came from the house. Perhaps indeed he was trying to obliterate them.

Absorbed in contemplation, she was startled when a small yellow ball bounced across her field of vision and came to rest in the flower bed on the far side of the lawn. It took her a second or two to register that the ball had come over the fence from next door. She was wondering what to do about it when she heard someone shouting, "Hello, hello! Is there anyone there?"

She stood up and, peeking round the porch, saw the boy who had come to help with the ladder earlier, and who had been throwing his ball against the wall. She was perplexed to find that he was much taller than she expected. She stared at him for a moment, not knowing what to say. At last she found her voice. "Yes, yes, is that your ball?"

"Hey, yes, would you mind throwing it back to me, please?"

This was not a request that she could ignore, but even before she answered, the boy vanished from sight with a yelp. "Ouch!" she heard him cry.

"Are you all right?" she called out: the reason he had seemed so tall was because he must have been standing on the old tree stump by the fence next door, from which he had then fallen off. She remembered that Grandpa had offered to cut a tree down for Carrie many years ago when he was felling its companion on his own side of the fence. The two stumps still stood there separated by the faded wooden palings.

"Yes, I'm all right, just twisted my ankle a bit," the boy answered, reappearing up on the stump again.

Forgetting her shyness, Ruth climbed up onto the companion stump and came face to face with him. He had a round, friendly face with a mop of curly brown hair and hazel eyes.

"Be careful," he urged her.

"Oh, I'm fine, I like to be tall, don't you?" she laughed.

"Yes, it's good to be taller than my brother," he replied. Forgetting about the ball, he introduced himself. "I'm Julian Robinson, and I'm staying with my grandparents. What's your name? Do you live here?"

"No," she said, "I'm staying with my nan. My name is Ruth."

The boy smiled, "I was going to ask for my ball back, but would you like to play with the ball or French cricket or something?"

In the background the pianist had come to the end of the piece, and the music had stopped.

"Yes, that would be nice!" Ruth replied.

"Well, come round then!" Julian said.

Ruth hesitated for a moment, "No, I think I had better stay here. Nan's out, so I mustn't leave the house." There was an awkward pause, then she said. "But why don't you come round here – that is if you like." She had been about to add "Or why don't we throw the ball to each other over the fence?" but didn't have time to get the words out because the boy had already run off into the house saying, "I'll get my cricket bat!" – apparently having forgotten his twisted ankle.

They had a fine time. They began by throwing the ball to each other, sometimes high, sometimes low, trying to catch each other out. When that game palled, the boy picked up his bat and showed Ruth how to hold it for French cricket, and taught her the rules. When they had had enough of that, Ruth demonstrated one of the favourite solitary games that as an only child she had invented for herself. It involved running fast across the lawn from the porch and leaping over the fuchsia bush in the middle. The fuchsia had grown from year to year just as Ruth had grown too, and was now large, but Ruth's legs were long and had kept pace with it. The aim was to jump clear of the bush and avoid damaging any of those delicate red and purple flowers, so much like ballerinas, on the topmost branches or indeed lower down. You scored a point if you cleared the bush, but you lost a point if you so much as touched a leaf, and you were out if you inflicted any damage on the bush.

Julian enjoyed the game. "I say, you do run fast and jump high!" he exclaimed admiringly.

"I've practised this a lot," she admitted, "but I've never had anyone else to do it with."

"Are you on your own, then? Don't you have any brothers and sisters?" Julian asked.

"Yes, I am on my own and no, I don't have any brothers and sisters, but that's all right; it's only that Nan is getting rather old and has a bad leg, so we can't go out as much as we used to."

Julian nodded, "Well, you're lucky not to have any brothers. I have one, but he's no use. I haven't got anyone to play with either," he said. "My brother's very clever, of course," he continued. "He won a scholarship to Eton College, and he has to work very hard there, so he's indoors studying all the time. He never comes out."

Ruth had only a hazy notion of what Eton College was, but gathered from the way that Julian spoke about it that it was a rather special school.

"I go to the high school, on an assisted place," she volunteered.

"Oh, do you? You must be a bit older than me then," said Julian. "I'm eleven, twelve next term though, and I'm going to the grammar school in September, but I know I shan't ever go to Eton: I'm not clever enough." Then he added defiantly, "Anyhow I don't want to. I'd lose all my friends." A car drew up at the gate, and Nan's friends helped her out.

"Oh, Ruthie, you've met Julian!" she called on seeing them together. "I'm so pleased! Now you'll have someone to play with."

Ruth liked Julian: he was open, lively and talkative. He told her about his parents, who didn't come on holiday because his father ran his own business in London, and he told her about his home out in the country, south of London. He said he wasn't terribly good at schoolwork, but he loved games and art. "But you must have passed the Eleven Plus if you're going to the grammar school," Ruth remarked encouragingly.

"Oh, that... that wasn't a problem: any idiot could do that," he announced blandly.

"I found it difficult," Ruth countered.

"I expect it is more difficult for girls," he answered with a provocative grin, deliberately moving away from her and shielding his face with his arm in an evasive gesture. Ruth rose to the occasion, as no doubt he was hoping she would, and ran after him in mock fury. He ran round and round the fuchsia bush and then headed off down to the back lawn with Ruth in hot pursuit.

The pursuit developed into a game of chase until they both collapsed in a giggling heap, tumbling and rolling on the damp grass. Nan, who had been watching from the garden door, beckoned them to come in for a drink to cool themselves down.

"What fun you're having, you two!" she commented with a benevolent smile as they beamed at each other.

"Julian says girls are no good at the Eleven Plus, Nan!" Ruth protested.

"Shame on you, Julian!" Nan exclaimed, joining in the fun.

"Oh, I didn't mean it!" said Julian unconvincingly.

From that day, Ruth and Julian began to enjoy each other's company, climbing trees together down in the Dell, working in Grandpa's shed together, chatting about nothing in particular in Ruth's Cabin, and they even went down to the shops on the bus together to deliver Nan's orders and buy bread and doughnuts. Although she loved having a friend, a real friend of her own, Ruth had qualms of conscience, especially because she was not spending as much time with Nan as she should and feared that she might be feeling lonely. Nonetheless, Nan was resolutely positive about their growing friendship: she said how much she enjoyed hearing the shouts of glee and the laughter out in the garden. Inwardly she was truly pleased that her granddaughter was being taken out of the introspection which she, Nan, considered unhealthy for a twelve-year-old.

If Nan's protestations salved her conscience, Ruth's other profound regret was less easily resolved, because the open piano lay untouched for hours if not days on end, since usually, by the time she came indoors in the evening, it was supper time, and that night's Prom was already being announced on the wireless. Sometimes she also found Julian rather too boisterous and wished he would calm down: he was becoming so noisy and excitable in their games that it was impossible to hear the piano-playing next door. She distinguished only snatches of Mozart or Schubert, Brahms or Schumann, and occasionally longed to be able to resume her seat alone on the front doorstep, immersing herself in those ravishing melodies.

42

At last one afternoon, having told Julian firmly that he was not to come round to play when Nan was asleep, Ruth sat on the front step alone while her grandmother had her nap. In a dream world she listened to the music streaming from the open window next door, trying to make out what the pianist was playing. The work was slow, but not ponderous. It had a familiar ring – she was sure she had heard it more than once before, yet she was unable to identify it, nonplussed by its strange form. The pianist would play a few bars of the powerful but gentle, all-enveloping melody and then stop for some time before taking it up again. She promised herself that she would not play with Julian that afternoon, but would return to the sorely neglected piano. Her concentration, fully absorbed by the music, was suddenly shattered by a yell from the gate: it was Julian.

"Hey, Ruth, let's go for a walk round the village!"

She was annoyed, and her impulse was to shout back at him, telling him to go away, but because she did not want to disturb her nan, who was still comfortably drowsy in the sunlit front room, she put one finger to her lips and with the other pointed to the window.

Absorbed in the music, she stood up and walked to the gate, anxious to grasp the moment. "Nan's asleep," she told Julian with quiet determination, before broaching the question she had been longing to ask. "Who's that playing the piano in your front room?"

Julian grimaced. "Oh, that's my brother, Piers; he's such a bore: he can't think about anything else."

"But what's he playing?" Ruth persisted. "I know that music, but it sounds strange with all the stops and starts."

"That's some old Beethoven piano concerto," Julian replied laconically. "He's going to perform it in a concert at half-term, because they've given him a music scholarship, you see."

He shrugged, clearly regarding the whole subject as too tedious for words – and then, unprovoked, he offered the clarification that Ruth was hoping for. "When he stops, he's counting out the bars' rests while the orchestra plays – well, that's what I think he's doing, though he says he's registering the rests, not actually counting them out."

"Ah, I see... of course!" said Ruth. It was astounding that in that very house, only next door, Julian's brother was playing the bewitching slow movement of that piano concerto, the 'Emperor', the one that her Aunt Evelyn used to play and of which they had a much-loved and much-worn recording. Above all else Ruth wanted to meet Julian's invisible though audible brother. "I'd like to meet Piers: he plays so beautifully," she said, amazed at her own audacity.

"Oh, that's possible, but you wouldn't want to," Julian retorted. "He's so tiresome... all he talks about is his work and music. He won't ever come out and play."

"I see," said Ruth. The music had ceased, so she changed her tone: "Well, let's go for that walk round the village, shall we?" She went to tell Nan – who by now had woken up – where she was going and then joined Julian on an oft-repeated walk.

They walked in silence. Julian kicked at the grass verge, in annoyance at Ruth's interest in his brother, while she was deep in her own thoughts. She was desperately keen to meet the pianist, whilst she also was envious that anyone of more or less her own age could play so much better than her. She broke the silence, having decided that Julian deserved some explanation. "I play the piano too, though not like your brother," she confided. "The trouble is I don't have a piano at home and my parents won't let me play. That's why I would like to meet your brother."

Julian turned to her in astonishment, "Your parents won't let you play! Why ever not?"

Ruth shrugged, "I don't understand why, except that it's got something to do with my mother being in hospital a lot – and she doesn't like it," she answered with such an obvious hint of despair in her voice that Julian quickly altered his tone and stopped scuffing his shoes on the grass. "Well, that's bad luck! I don't understand that either. My parents are mad about music. But if you're sure you want to meet Piers, come and have tea with us: I'm sure Granny won't mind. I don't think you'll like him, but after you've met him we can play cricket." Satisfied with a plan that would keep everybody happy, he added with a laugh: "I think it would be better to do that in our garden than yours, in case we break a window!" They ambled back to the row of houses, and Julian went indoors to ask if Ruth might be invited to tea. He came out again to say that not only Ruth but her granny was invited as well.

Ruth had intended to run back next door straight away after delivering the message to Nan. However, when she caught sight of herself in the hall mirror, she decided that she ought to brush her hair – and then, for no particular reason, she also decided to change out of her shorts and top into a skirt, the one that she and Nan had made during the rainy spell, and the green top that Nan had given her.

"You look a real picture, Ruth, very grown up," Nan observed when she came downstairs again, and then she wondered whether she too should change into smarter clothes.

"No, no, Nan, you're fine. Let's be going." Ruth urged her impatiently as she glanced at herself in the mirror again, patting a loose strand of hair back into place. Nan was not in such a hurry and insisted on putting two jars of plum jam into a basket, which she gave to Ruth to carry.

They made their way out of their own gate and into the neighbouring driveway to the final bars of the famous Mozart C major Sonata wafting from the open windows. The unseen pianist was hard at work again, and she felt more and more intimidated as they approached the house. He then launched into a waltz of bewitching power and grace.

Ruth held Nan's stick for her as she stood still to adjust her hearing aid. "Goodness me! Just listen to that!" Nan exclaimed, as her hearing aid picked up the sounds of the piano. "It's the 'Valse Noble' from 'Carnaval'! Who can that be?"

"Julian says it's his brother," Ruth informed her, "but I haven't met him yet."

"He plays beautifully! I've no doubt he'll be a professional like you one day," Nan observed as she took charge of her stick and set off again down the driveway. Ruth laughed: trust Nan to have so much more confidence in her than she had in herself!

Mrs Hardy was busy setting out the tea in the garden while Mr Hardy and Julian brought chairs from their garden shed.

"How nice to see you both! We should have done this long ago!" Mrs Hardy greeted them warmly. "Do come and sit down!" Then she called out to her husband. "We need one more chair for Piers, dear." Turning to Nan she explained: "Of course, that's if he comes to join us; he's working so hard, we can't get him out of the front room!"

"Now, Ruth," said Nan, "give Mrs Hardy the jam!"

Ruth handed over the basket.

"Oh, that looks delicious! What a lovely colour, and such a good set! That's Piers's favourite jam!" Mrs Hardy exclaimed admiringly, holding a jar up to the light. "Julian," she commanded her younger grandson, "go and tell Piers that we've got plum jam for tea, please!" She turned to Nan with a laugh. "Let's see if that will bring him out to join us!"

Julian was not keen to carry the message to his brother and sulkily complained: "Oh, Gran, it's always me! I'm always having to go and call him. You know he never takes any notice of me and he never comes!"

"I'm sorry, dear," Mrs Hardy sighed. "I know it's a nuisance for you, but we can't have him wasting away."

"I'll go!" Ruth piped up, as much to her own amazement as anyone else's. As an embarrassing blush suffused her cheeks, she felt obliged to offer some reason for her outburst. "I know where he is, because your house is the same as ours but the other way round, and we heard the piano as we came along the drive."

"Of course, dear, that is kind of you, if you don't mind. Go in at the back door," Mrs Hardy replied, smilingly unperturbed, and Ruth stood up as composedly as she could.

In fact, her heart was beating fast, and she felt even redder in the face and light-headed as well. Clumsily she offered a further effusive though unnecessary attempt at explanation. "My friends, Carrie and Anne and Valerie, lived here, and I used to come and see them often."

"So you know our house well, young lady!" Mr Hardy joked, but Ruth did not wait to continue the discussion for fear of betraying her embarrassment even more.

She hurried away, and once round the corner of the house, out of view of the adults, she stopped for a few seconds to draw breath and let the redness in her face subside before opening the kitchen door. "Why had she been so stupid?" she wondered, but then decided that she was only helping Mrs Hardy by fetching Piers, and there was nothing to be ashamed of. Anyway, why shouldn't she meet the hidden pianist? What was wrong with that?

The house was largely unchanged from the Carringtons' occupancy. The cream paintwork was still fresh and clean in the kitchen, where the equipment was more modern than Nan's old gas stove and simple water heater over the sink. In one corner there stood a bright new refrigerator. All was quiet. She wondered if the pianist had gone out or upstairs, for then she would never be able to find him. How she wished she had not offered to undertake the errand after all! With a sinking heart she ventured out into the silent hall.

The door to the front room, which here was on the right whereas in Nan's house it was on the left, was open. She looked in, but could not see anyone there. Sunbeams danced on the opposite wall, and sheets of music stood on the desk of the open piano, but there was no sign of any living being. She stepped inside; on the floor was a pile of books, not unlike all those books that Carrie's daughters had been sorting out the year before, but these books were placed carefully beside a high-backed armchair which had been turned towards the sun, facing the open window. She hesitated on the threshold and then tiptoed into the room, where she saw wavy curls, framed by the sunlight, above the chair back. She walked on tiptoe through the shaft of sunbeams and stepped quietly round the chair. Coughing gently, she found herself standing in front of a boy, almost a young man, who raised his head from his book in astonishment and gazed at her.

Their eyes met, and she held his gaze as a golden thread of silence hung on the air between them. Neither of them spoke. Ruth was mesmerized. Although she knew that she shouldn't be staring at him, her eyes were fixed on him and her tongue seemed to be paralysed. He was so beautiful – the most beautiful boy she had ever seen. She didn't know that it was possible for boys to be as beautiful as this. The beauty was all in his eyes. Those eyes were so bright that they sparkled, but they were also gentle and sensitive.

He smiled at her, and eventually he spoke in a deeper, calmer voice than Julian's, "Ah, hello, what can I do for you?... Who are you?"

"I'm Ruth," she stuttered. "I... I live next door. Well, that is, my grandmother lives next door."

Still lost for words, she could not recall why she was there. "I'm pleased to meet you, Ruth. I'm Piers," he said very slowly, for he too seemed to have lost the power of speech.

Remembering her mission Ruth hurriedly said: "I've come to tell you it's teatime," and moved towards the door.

"Ah, good, how very kind of you, I'll come right away!" he replied swiftly. He put his book down on the floor and followed her out of the room.

"Well done, Ruth!" Mrs Hardy exclaimed when she saw her eldest grandson behind Ruth. "It must have been the plum jam; I knew it would bring him out!" Ruth had completely forgotten to tell Piers about the plum jam and was flustered, fearing that her omission might come to light. Piers, however, was quick off the mark; perhaps he was reading her mind. "I can't resist plum jam!" he laughed, beaming at Ruth.

"You'll have to come round here and summon him for every mealtime, Ruth, if you can be that successful!" Mr Hardy quipped jovially.

"Only if there's plum jam at every meal, Grandfather!" Piers retorted immediately as if on cue, to Ruth's immense relief.

"Can we play cricket after tea?" Julian begged somewhat peevishly. "You never come out to play cricket, Piers, and now that you're here, we should have a game!"

"Yes, go on, Piers," their grandfather said encouragingly.

"I'll play too! We've almost got a team now. You'll play, won't you Ruth?" Piers smiled another of his irresistible smiles at Ruth, who in a daze said yes, she would, but she didn't know how to play.

Her ignorance of the game was no obstacle. Julian kept shouting instructions to her, but Piers demonstrated how to hold the bat properly and bowled so carefully that there was no way she could miss every ball. Mr Hardy did likewise, but when it was Julian's turn to bowl, he took a professional stance and bowled hard, knocking the wicket down and jubilantly calling: "Ruth's out!"

She was glad to be out: being the centre of attention, particularly under Piers's concerned gaze, was too intimidating. She was happy to hand the bat to Julian and retire to the midfield. From there she overheard the conversation of the two elderly ladies, who were still sitting outside.

"Wouldn't it be nice to go to the sea tomorrow?" Mrs Hardy was saying. "Would you and Ruth like to come with us? I think there would be room in the car." If Nan was delighted, Ruth was secretly overjoyed. "That would be so kind of you! We've been to my sister's farm, but otherwise we haven't been able to get out much because of my poor old leg, and I know Ruth would love that!" was Nan's ready response.

43

That night sleep evaded her. She lay wide awake, wondering why she was so happy. It was obvious that her happiness had something to do with Piers – but what? Everything else in her life faded into insignificance: her father, Nan, Nan's house, the farm, the cousins, even the piano: nothing and no one, however much she loved them, could compare with Piers. She wanted to see his face – his beautiful face – and his eyes over and over again. And she was going to see them again tomorrow! The suspense and the anticipation both excited her and calmed her till she fell asleep, only to dream of trying unsuccessfully to play the slow movement of the 'Emperor' Concerto in the presence of a full orchestra and an audience.

The piano was open when she went downstairs in the morning. Usually she would practise scales for a quarter of an hour before breakfast, but today she simply closed the lid.

"No piano practice, Ruth?" Nan enquired as she buttered the toast.

"No, no time, Nan, we're going to the sea, aren't we? We must be ready!" she insisted.

"Wait a minute!" Nan exclaimed. "Surely you're not going to the seaside in your new skirt and blouse, are you? Wouldn't shorts be better for the beach?"

"Ah, all right," Ruth agreed meekly, and while Nan made sandwiches she went back upstairs to change.

In truth she hadn't known what to wear. Normally of course, without even thinking, she would don shorts for the seaside, but this visit was special, so special that she feared that perhaps shorts not only wouldn't be smart enough, but also would make her look like a child – and, for some unfathomable reason, she didn't want to appear childish. She put her skirt and blouse away in the wardrobe, exchanging them for her old navy shorts and a pale-blue top, and instantly felt more at ease physically, though emotionally very uncertain.

The Hardys were loading provisions, rugs and cricket bats and balls into the boot of their car when Nan and Ruth came out with baskets full of sandwiches, cake, thermos flasks of coffee and bottles of lemonade. With a show of reluctance, Julian was helping his grandparents. Piers was nowhere to be seen, but he was audible in the waves of Liszt that emanated through the kitchen doorway.

"Piers came to help, but we sent him away to practise, though why he chose something as demanding as 'Liebestraum' this morning I can't imagine," said Mrs Hardy to Nan.

"It's a magnificent piece," said Nan, adding: "My daughter used to play that, you know."

"Your daughter?" Mrs Hardy's face registered incredulity.

"Yes," said Ruth, coming to Nan's rescue, for Nan's remark had certainly been inadvertent. "Yes," she continued, "My aunt was Evelyn Platt."

Mrs Hardy nearly dropped the bag she was carrying. With her free hand she took Nan gently by the arm. "Oh, my dear! I had no idea! I'm so sorry! I do know," she added, briefly falling pensive, "how traumatic this must have been – and still is – for you."

"That's all right," said Nan. "I shouldn't have said anything: it came out when I heard that young man playing. I was carried away! Usually I don't hear so much these days, but I certainly heard that!"

"She was a great pianist – what talent!" said Mrs Hardy. "Oh, wait till Piers hears about this!"

Ruth didn't want Piers to hear about anything, including – or perhaps above all – about Evelyn. She dreaded complications, for complications had a way of creating distances and difficulties between people, and at present there were no complications, only the wooden fence between Nan's house and next door – and that was of little significance.

Piers emerged to a round of applause. Nan said she was most impressed with his playing; Mrs Hardy said she had no idea that he had learnt that difficult piece; Mr Hardy said: "Well done, my boy!" and Julian said, "Can we go now?"

Ruth kept quiet, but when he had modestly acknowledged the applause, Piers looked her straight in the eye. "Hello, Ruth," he said softly. "Oh, I see you're dressed for the beach!" He glanced down at his neatly pressed slacks and said: "One minute, please, I must go and change into my shorts."

Ruth had scarcely been able to breathe since Piers came out of the house. When he had gone indoors, she took a deep breath; then, feeling dizzy, she slipped away back to Nan's house with the excuse of fetching a bag of plums they had left in the kitchen. There she drank a glass of water and sat down for ten seconds. She returned next door to find that the assembled company, including Piers – who was looking much more relaxed in khaki shorts and a white top – were trying to decide who should sit where in the car. Mrs Hardy settled the matter by announcing: "The two boys can sit in the middle, Piers on the bench seat in the front between Grandfather and me, and Julian in the back between Ruth and her granny. Thus it was decided, with the result that Ruth spent the whole journey trying not to listen to Julian, who prattled on and on about cricket, the while keeping her eyes fixed on the back of Piers's head.

The day was a mixture of ordinary seaside activities suddenly transformed into a blissful sequence of unforgettable images: sea-bathing, digging in the sand to make a hollow to sit in, burying a willing Julian, eating Nan's sandwiches – now gritty – for lunch and drinking home-made lemonade, playing cricket and French cricket, and soaking up the sun and salt air while the two grannies talked incessantly and Mr Hardy read, first the newspaper and then a leather-bound book. Nan offered to buy fish and chips for everyone when they came off the beach in the early evening, but Mrs Hardy said that her husband was officiating at church in the village in the morning, and he still had his sermon to write, so maybe they should be setting out for home.

"Well, then," said Nan, "let me buy fish and chips from across the Green when we get home. They're nearly as good as the ones here at the sea." It was agreed in advance that the grandchildren should go and collect the fish and chips.

As Mr Hardy unlocked the car door, Julian began to protest loudly at having to sit in the back on the way home as well as on the way out. In a flash Piers offered to change places with him, which meant that he would be sitting between Nan and Ruth on the back seat. Nan dozed off in her corner, while Ruth and Piers sat very still, very close together. She trembled slightly when their bare knees touched. Her legs were golden brown, the fair hairs glistening in the slanting sunlight; his were white, and pink just above the knee where they had caught the sun. He glanced at her and smiled. With her heart beating fast, she smiled nervously back at him.

Nan paid for the fish and chips, which the boys went to collect from the shop across the Green, and they all ate out of doors in the Hardys' garden. It was easier that way, Mrs Hardy decreed, because their garden furniture was outside already. What's more, Mr Hardy could eat and write his sermon by the open window, and still participate in the party. Ruth was thankful, since Nan had only a few old pieces of garden furniture, a couple of chairs and a rickety table, just enough for herself and Ruth. Like Nan, Mrs Hardy turned the wireless on at seven-thirty prompt for the Prom, which that evening featured the Elgar Cello Concerto.

"It's so good for Piers to listen to something other than piano music," she said. Piers nodded in a display of apparent agreement, which might also have been indifference.

Although the concert was playing on the wireless, Julian insisted on a few overs of cricket, and Piers and Ruth obliged. After he had finished his sermon, Mr Hardy came out to join them. A few overs became many as they played on and on, until the sun went down and a magnificent full moon came up over the field at the bottom of the garden. Nan watched, still chatting to her new friend, until a sudden breeze made her shiver.

"I don't want to break up such a lovely party, but I think I'll be going in now," she said, struggling to her feet. "I'll become welded to your chair if I sit here any longer!"

"Would you like a lift to church in the morning, Mrs Platt?" asked Mrs Hardy. "We'll have to go early, as my husband is officiating, but we would be happy to take you."

"Thank you very much, I'd love that," Nan replied without hesitation. "It's a long time since I've been able to walk to church, and I can only go if someone offers me a lift." She called out to Ruth. "Stay a little longer if you like, Ruthie: it's getting too chilly for me!"

Mrs Hardy called Julian, saying: "You had better come and have a good soak, and wash all that sand out of your hair and eyes and everywhere else!"

Julian obeyed with less reluctance than usual at such commands. Of all the party, he had been the most active during the day and was ready to drop.

Ruth and Piers were left outside. They sat down on the grass halfway down the garden. The full moon shone over them, out of a deep, clear sky, bathing them in its white light. Everything – the lawn, the flower beds, the trees – gleamed silver, as though with the shimmer of an unseasonal frost. They sat in silence for several minutes, until Piers murmured: "Ruthie, what a sweet name! Do they all call you that?"

"Oh, just Nan and my dad," she replied.

"Not your mother?" he asked.

"No, she doesn't like to be called 'Mother' or 'Mummy', and she doesn't call me Ruthie either. I have to call her Shirley, and she calls me Ruth," she answered.

"That's odd," Piers observed. "Don't you mind?"

"That's how she is, but she has been ill, so we have to be careful," Ruth replied as phlegmatically as possible. In the same way as when she had been talking to Julian, she decided yet again that the best way to account for Shirley's behaviour was to say that she had been ill, even though if pressed she could not define the illness. Not that Shirley was as volatile these days as she used to be in the past, but it still paid to be careful.

"How long have you been playing the piano?" she asked when she summoned the courage to ask Piers a couple of questions.

"Oh," he replied, drawing in breath, "since I was about four years old, I suppose."

Ruth laughed quietly.

"Why do you laugh?" he asked.

"I was four when I started to play," she said, forgetting that she had divulged one of her closest secrets.

"You play too, Ruthie?" There was surprise but also joy in his question. "What do you like playing best?"

At first she could not think of the titles of any of the pieces in her repertoire; it was only after an embarrassing silence that she stammered: "I like some of those pieces I've heard you playing, the Chopin and the Mozart, and I love the Schubert B flat Sonata." Piers was listening intently, so she went on, "There are some of the Beethoven Sonatas I like as well, but I'm not very good at them yet; perhaps they're too difficult for me, but I'd like to play all of them one day, the 'Appassionata', the 'Pathétique' and a bit of the 'Waldstein'. I think you play those, don't you?"

"You are learning them?" he asked, a touch incredulously.

"Yes, I can nearly play the 'Pathétique', but I've only just begun the others. Oh, and there's opus 31 no. 3, and I am also trying to play the Mozart Rondo 'Alla Turca', but it's so hard to get it up to speed."

"Not surprising," Piers countered, taking in a deep breath between his teeth and blowing it, "that's Grade Seven or Eight at least! What grade are you doing now?"

"I'm not doing any grades. I don't have those sort of lessons, you see. Well, only sometimes," she replied in confusion, afraid that Piers would not take her seriously on discovering that she was only a part-time pianist. "I would like to one day, of course," she added with a sigh. "And there's so much music I want to play, like that beautiful waltz you were playing as we came up the drive yesterday."

He pondered for a moment, then laughed, "Ah, that was the 'Valse Noble' from 'Carnaval' – that's Schumann," he said.

"Yes, yes, of course, Nan recognized it, and that's what she said," Ruth remarked, desperately trying to appear knowledgeable. She went on, "I should love to play that too! And then there's the slow movement from the 'Emperor' Concerto you were practising; I do want to play that – I mean the whole thing, the outer movements as well. Julian told me you are going to play it in a concert."

He shrugged off the mention of his concert, preferring to concentrate on her repertoire. "That's incredible!" he exclaimed. "The 'Valse Noble' is not difficult: give it a try – you'll find it easy; but you must be extraordinarily gifted if you are learning all those pieces, yet you don't have lessons! You must be a prodigy!"

She tried to recount the stop-start nature of her musicianship: how Nan had helped and encouraged her in the past when she was little, and still did so nowadays, and how Miss Lake continued to give her lessons if she had time once or twice a week. Although she had told Julian about some of her problems in their walks round the village, she refrained from saying that she didn't have a piano at home and that any mention of the piano was a taboo subject, bound to cause problems in London, because she felt that enough had been said and that to elaborate further might break the spell of this magical evening. She fervently hoped that Piers would not ask any more questions, and to deflect such a possibility she added in a moment of inspiration, which would not have been so far from the truth had Nan not financed the lessons with Miss Lake: "The trouble is that my parents are too poor to pay for real lessons."

"That is a pity," he sympathized.

They sat very close, silently gazing at the moon. Piers began to whisper, "The moon shines bright: in such a night as this, when the sweet wind did gently kiss the trees and they did make no noise." Ruth listened enthralled. Smiling at her, he went on: "How sweet the moonlight sleeps upon this bank! Here we will sit and let the sounds of music creep in our ears; soft stillness and the night become the touches of sweet harmony. Sit, Ruthie, look how the floor of heaven is thick inlaid with patines of bright gold. There's not the smallest orb which thou behold'st but in his motion like an angel sings, still choiring to the young-eyed cherubins; such harmony is in immortal souls." He fell silent.

"That was beautiful," she murmured. "Shakespeare."

"Yes, that's right. So you recognized it?"

"Oh, we did *The Merchant of Venice* in school last year. I remember that speech."

Instantly she regretted mentioning school in such a crass manner. School and whatever she had learnt there had nothing whatsoever to do with this unforgettable night. In an effort to restore the enchantment, she added: "I think that passage is as beautiful as music."

"Yes," he replied, "almost; it speaks from the heart, but don't forget: music is the food of love."

They sat together in silence, watching the pale white moon until Nan's voice rang out into the night air: "Ruthie, Ruthie, time to come in!"

44

Some weeks later Ruth found herself seated on the train on the journey to London for the start of the new school year. The Hardys, who looked very tired and wan, had brought her and Nan to the station with their grandsons, who were not leaving till the weekend, and together they had all given her a rousing send-off – that is to say, the send-off from Julian and his grandparents was rousing, with many encouraging shouts of "See you again soon!" – "Work hard, practise hard!" – "Look after yourself!" Nan was more restrained. Patting her eyes behind her glasses, she gave Ruth a long hug and whispered: "My Ruthie! Come and see me soon!"

Meanwhile, Piers stood pale and unsmiling, slightly apart from his family, behind his brother and grandparents. He did not join in the shouting, but from his position he was able to keep his eyes firmly fixed on Ruth unbeknown to the others. She had eyes only for him, yet was bound to respond to all the attention from the rest of the onlookers. Smiling half-heartedly and waving limply from her compartment window, she hoped – rightly – that the adults and Julian would simply interpret her sad pallor as reluctance to leave the holiday scene in exchange for the return to the humdrum routine of school and homework, autumnal rain and fog. In truth, she was not much bothered about school, or even London and her parents. She was certainly concerned for her nan, but her deepest distress lay in the parting from Piers. Their planned reunion at half-term was not for another six weeks or more.

The train pulled out, enveloping the carriages in clouds of smoke and steam, while rain beat against the windows making any last glimpse of the party on the platform impossible. Once Piers was no longer visible, the tears flowed. How she regretted refusing to give him her address! He had asked her for it repeatedly, and though she wanted nothing more than to be in constant contact with him, to continue their talks by letter, to scrutinize his handwriting and see his face in it, she foresaw the impracticability of receiving letters from him at home. Shirley, with her lynx-like eyes, would immediately notice unfamiliar handwriting on an envelope, especially one addressed to Ruth, because nobody other than Nan ever wrote to Ruth. She would want to know the identity of this correspondent, would quiz her for details, might even open the letters, and would undoubtedly tease her about their contents and provenance. "Oh, look at this! A letter from Eton! I say, Ruth, you are in with the toffs, aren't you? And what's all this about Schubert and Brahms?"

In truth, it might not be quite like that, because Ruth doubted that Shirley had ever heard of Schubert or Brahms, but the humiliation of such a scenario would be unbearable; without question it was to be avoided at all costs. Although her father might possibly understand and might be trusted to be discreet, it was by no means certain that he would pick up the letters in the morning. In any case, presumably henceforth the mail would be delivered to the new post office, not to the front door of the house, and it would be impossible for Ruth to venture in there to search for anything with her name on it without arousing suspicion.

Lurking at the back of her mind there was also a consideration that she scarcely liked to admit even to herself, let alone to anyone else: it was the rather shameful feeling that if Piers were to come and visit her at home, he would see where she lived and she would have to introduce him to her parents – which might well compromise any further contact between them. Not that she would have any qualms about introducing him to her dad, but Shirley was different, and it was easy to imagine her reaction. Without a doubt, she would fawn over him, chattering incessantly, because he was so handsome and well educated. Ignoring Ruth, she would monopolize him, insisting on giving him a guided tour of the shop, the post office and the house. Ruth was in no doubt that he would be desperately bored and ill at ease, though he would be too polite and well mannered to show it. Afterwards, however, he would be unlikely ever to want to see her again, which would be worse than not being able to keep in touch with him at present.

Seeing her mother and Cousin Edith together a year ago had made Ruth realize – to her embarrassment – that, like Edith, Shirley had become rather vulgar and common with her brassy hair and her thickly applied bright lipstick, especially now that she was not as pretty as she used to be. It was not that Shirley had a cockney accent – or a Birmingham accent like Edith's – but, if Julian were to be believed with his talk of Eton School, Piers's background was very different, vastly superior to her own, and he would certainly find Shirley's appearance and manner very off-putting. At Beech Grove they had been on more or less equal terms and on equal ground. The only solution was to write all her news to Nan and ask Nan to pass it on to the Hardys – who, hopefully, would pass it on to Piers. This was the best system that she could devise, though it was miserably inadequate.

Alone in the compartment, she closed her eyes and cast her mind back to those final weeks of the holiday: the recollection of them was exquisite in its pain and its joy. Intoxicated with happiness after the day by the sea and that evening alone with Piers under the full moon in the garden, she had slept soundly and woken late. She had assumed that Nan had gone to church with the Hardys, and expected that she could invite him to come round to give her some advice on those Beethoven Sonatas she was attempting to play. As she had told him the previous evening, she could almost play the Pathétique, of which she had given a credible performance for Nan after a great deal of practice – but it was hard. The task she had set herself of learning the 'Appassionata' proved even more demanding, more dramatic and potentially more satisfying if only there was someone to help her with the fingering, which Nan had said was beyond her.

With this plan in mind, she went downstairs and looked out of the kitchen window. There was no sign of life next door. She opened the back door, hoping to hear the sound of the piano; all was still and quiet. She went outside and looked over the fence. The house was closed up. There were no windows open downstairs, though upstairs a couple of bedroom windows and the bathroom window were open, but no music flowed out of them. As she made herself some toast, she noticed a scrap of paper bearing Nan's handwriting on the dresser. Nan said that she was going to church, but wanted Ruth to have a good rest and sleep in, so had not woken her. She should help herself to whatever she liked. Disconsolately she went back upstairs, taking her toast with her. She sat on her bed, unable to concentrate on her book, unable to do anything except wonder where Piers was, then lay down and fell asleep. She did not wake until she heard Nan calling from the bottom of the stairs: "Ruth, Ruthie, are you up there? Come down and have some coffee. I've such a lot to tell you!"

Sleepily she dragged herself out of bed, dressed and went downstairs. Nan was still wearing her coat and hat, although she was pouring the thick brown liquid out of that thin square bottle with the strange man on the label into two cups. She then filled them with hot milk from a pan on the stove. She faced Ruth with sparkling eyes, brimming with excitement like a small child. "Ah! Here you are, Ruthie! Let's sit down." Nan sat down and beckoned Ruth to the other stool. "Well, I decided to let you sleep in, but how I wish I'd woken you! You missed a treat at church. Mr Hardy gave an exceptionally good sermon – not one person in the congregation nodded off!"

However good Mr Hardy's sermon might have been, Ruth did not regret missing it, and doubted that it had evoked such a rapturous response in Nan, ardent church-goer though she was. "Now let me see, what did he say?" Nan went on, trying to recall the substance of Mr Hardy's sermon – but then, remembering that that was not at the top of her agenda, abruptly changed the subject. "No, no, that can wait: it will come to me later; what I wanted to tell you was something else. You see, Charles Stannard is away on holiday, and usually when he's away someone has to play the piano. I do it from time to time if the hymns are easy ones, but I'm getting too old for that. Anyhow, it's never as good as having the organ. But this morning that young man next door – what's his name?"

"Julian?" Ruth ventured innocently.

"No, no, I know who Julian is; Julian pumped the bellows, because that boy, Jeff, is away on holiday too, but that's not the one I mean. I mean the other one with the unusual name... I can't grasp it; I keep wanting to call him Peter."

"Do you mean Piers?" Ruth felt her cheeks growing hot at the mere mention of his name.

"Yes, that's right, he was superb!"

This news plunged Ruth into turmoil. So Piers had been at church and had been superb while she lazed at home in bed! She was utterly dismayed at her own indolence.

"Why, what did he do?" she asked urgently, impatient to find out what she had missed.

"He played the organ, of course!" came Nan's instant reply. "But he played it as I've never even heard Charles play it. It was a miracle! He played Bach before the service and that Vidor Toccata afterwards. The Church resounded! And do you know the whole congregation stayed to listen? They were all as quiet as mice instead of chattering like rooks or starlings as they usually do after the service – and they clapped at the end! I've never heard anything like it! And, do you know," she went on, "he's only fifteen! Well, fifteen and a half, his granny tells me." Ruth simply nodded. No response was adequate to convey her chaotic reactions and emotions. "Oh, and another thing," Nan continued. "Their grandparents have to go hospital-visiting on Sunday afternoons: there's a relative they have to go and see – Mrs Hardy didn't say much about it, so I don't know who it is. Anyhow, those boys are coming to tea. We had better look sharp and start making a cake for them!"

That afternoon Julian scoffed a large share of the chocolate cake, still warm from the oven. Piers ate in a more restrained fashion, but he too devoured at least a quarter of it, leaving not much more than one quarter for Nan and Ruth.

Nan was amused. "I like to see that you boys have a hearty appetite!" she commented.

Julian was abashed. "Oh, that was delicious, Mrs Platt! I'm sorry I've eaten so much. Dear Granny, she's not very good at cake-making. Her best recipe is rock cakes, but honestly everything she makes turns out like a rock cake, so this is a great treat!"

Nan reassured him that she was delighted to see that her baking was so well received. Anxious to make amends for his greed, Julian asked if there was anything he could do to help her.

"Well, as you so kindly ask," Nan said, "I should be glad of someone to clip the hedges for me. I did them before Ruth arrived, and she has trimmed them a bit, but a strong young man like you would do a much better job. And they do need it."

Julian jumped to his feet in readiness to fetch the shears, but he stopped in the doorway on his way out, turning to Ruth and Piers with a disarming plea. "When I've finished cutting hedges, what about a game of cricket?"

"Of course!" Ruth replied willingly. She was thrilled to have Piers to herself without Julian's interruptions, and wanted to take him straight away into the front room, the piano room, but could not think of a way of phrasing the invitation without seeming too brash or too forward.

Nan came to the rescue, for as soon as Julian had gone out of doors she openly suggested: "Why don't you take Piers to the piano, Ruthie? I'm sure he can help you. He's undoubtedly a much better teacher than me."

"No, I'm sure that's not true," Piers replied modestly, but nevertheless he stood up with alacrity, ready to be led to the piano.

"Oh, look!" Piers exclaimed. "That's a long bench! We can sit on it together, and I can turn pages for you."

Although Evelyn's piano stool was long enough to accommodate them both, they had to sit close together, touching at hip and shoulder. The sorrow at the missed treat at church that morning was fully redeemed by having Piers so close that she could feel his warmth and the shape of his body. The sensation was so powerful that she was hardly able to register what he was saying.

"Come on, then, play me something," he urged her.

She forced herself to concentrate; her hand shaking, she took down an edition of Chopin Preludes. "I love these," she said, opening the score at the 'Raindrop'.

"Oh, good, I like that too!" Piers's approval put her more at ease. She took a deep breath as Nan had taught her and began to play. Gradually the music took over, till she almost forgot his presence at her side.

"That's very good!" he exclaimed as she came to the end of the piece. "Now, why don't you show me how you sight-read."

She took down the Chopin Nocturnes and chose no. 3 from opus 15, which she had not played previously. Having checked the key signature and the time signature, she took a minute to glance through the piece, noting the first few bars and the final bar to establish the key, looking out for changes of key and registering the rhythm. Then she started to play, less fluently perhaps than her rendering of the 'Raindrop', but soon she fell in love with the new, wistful melody that was emerging from under her fingers.

Piers was impressed. "How old did you say you were?" he asked. Ruth hadn't actually told him her age, hoping that he wouldn't ask, because she wanted him to believe that she was nearer his age.

"I'm twelve – and a half," she confessed, somewhat inaccurately, hoping that the half would add to her stature.

"Ah!" he said, taken aback. "You are tall for your age, aren't you?" He said no more, and she couldn't think of any response to that. Luckily he relieved the tension with a compliment. "You are very remarkable, Ruth. As I said the other night, I'd reckon that if you were doing exams, you would be at least Grade Eight by now." She was pleased, though 'Grade Eight' still did not mean much to her. He plied her with questions about her technique: "Are you doing all the scales, major and minor, and in contrary motion in four octaves?" To this the answer was firmly a "yes". But when he asked, "Are you doing four-octave scales in thirds and sixths? Has anyone suggested that to you?", with a frown she replied: "Well no, not exactly: four octaves, yes, in thirds, but not in sixths or even fifths."

"I suggest you try in fifths, to give yourself a bit more fluency, not that what you're doing isn't very good – it is – but give them a try. Look, let me show you."

As he lent across her to demonstrate, his hand brushed against hers and a spark flew between them. Ruth felt the blood rising to her face and Piers suddenly jumped off the piano stool, as if he had been stung by a stray wasp.

He stood up. "No, no," he stammered in some confusion. "On second thoughts, I think it's better if you try first, and then I'll show you what I mean."

In fact, it was providential that he had stood up just then, because only a moment later there was a hammering on the window. Julian was peering through the glass and shouting: "I've done that bit of hedge at the back, and there's only this one left to do." He gestured to the front hedge, which fortunately was rather more substantial and wider than the one in the back garden. "And then can we play cricket?"

"Yes, all right," Piers shouted back irritably. "It'll take you at least half an hour, so you'd better get on with it."

Ruth played all scales, major and minor, in thirds and sixths in four octaves under Piers's supervision, and then showed him some of the sonatas that she was working on.

"Awkward, that one," he remarked, referring to opus 31 no. 3, which she was about to embark upon after they had taken it in turns to make passable attempts at the 'Pathétique' and the 'Appassionata'. "The tempo is a problem: you must think it out before you play, because he slows down straight into a ritardando in the third bar, and if you haven't established the speed in advance you'll be hopelessly lost when you have to go back to it." They worked together with intense enjoyment, though Piers did not sit down on the stool again.

Time flew by, and before they knew it there was Julian banging on the window, signalling the end of the hedge trimming. As they left the room, Piers scrutinized the photo of Evelyn on top of the piano. "She was beautiful," he remarked. "You are so like her, Ruth, and you have obviously inherited her talent." That annoying blush suffused Ruth's cheeks again. She had forgotten about the photo on the piano, and also that Mrs Hardy knew about Evelyn and she must have told her grandson. "Strange," Piers went on. "You are so like your aunt, and they say I'm the image of my uncle Alan, though I've never seen him. Granny and Grandpa won't take us with them when they go to visit him in hospital. It seems he was badly injured in the War, but they won't talk about it."

Julian was impatiently banging on the window yet again. He had already set up the cricket stumps on the back lawn, but when Piers saw how he had arranged them, he objected strongly to the layout, saying: "I think the stumps are the wrong way round. The batsman might hit the ball through Mrs Platt's window."

Julian sighed in resignation at his brother's obtuseness. "We can play with a softer ball," he said. "I've got a tennis ball, and anyhow, if we put the stumps the other way round the ball might go over the fence into the field, and then we'd never find it."

"All right," Piers conceded with some reluctance; he had seen how hard his brother had worked on the hedges, so decided not to delay his reward any longer. Nan was happy for them to do as they pleased and struggled down to Ruth's Cabin, from where she sat watching the match in play.

The first overs when Piers was batting were uneventful; he played carefully, rolling the ball as close to the ground as possible. Ruth did the same, as and when she managed to hit the ball at all. When Julian stood in the crease with the bat and Ruth began to bowl, he threw caution to the winds and attacked her easy balls with vigour and glee. Inevitably, one of his shots crashed right through Nan's dining-room window, the one on the left of the garden door. Ruth and Piers stood aghast, rooted to the spot. About to cry, Julian turned bright red.

"Well done, Julian!" Nan applauded.

"I'm so sorry, Mrs Platt!" Julian exclaimed.

"Don't you worry!" Nan reassured him, spluttering between fits of laughter. "That was such fun! I haven't laughed so much in years!"

In the commotion none of them had heard the car drawing into the sideway next door, nor the car doors banging shut, so when Mr and Mrs Hardy with a very dejected air appeared round the corner of the house they all stopped short.

"We heard you all out in the garden..." Mrs Hardy began, but paused when she saw the assembly of faces, all registering different expressions – Julian near to tears, Piers exasperated, Ruth dismayed and Nan leaning on her stick in floods of laughter. "Oh, dear! What has happened here?" she asked.

Nan was still laughing, sniffing into her handkerchief. "Oh, my dear! Nothing that can't be put right!" she spluttered.

Piers gestured towards the window.

"Ah," said Mr Hardy tersely, "I see."

At a glance he quickly understood the disposition of the cricket pitch. "So we have you to thank for that, do we, Julian?" Still holding the offending cricket bat, Julian nodded. "Well, I suggest you get a brush and dustpan, and go and clear up all the broken glass in Mrs Platt's dining room, and then we'll find a board to tack to the window frame." He apologized to Nan, saying: "I'm so very sorry, Mrs Platt, but don't worry, I'll get it mended for you tomorrow."

"It was only an accident, and he's such a nice boy – see how he's cut the hedges for me!" Nan pleaded, coming to Julian's rescue.

The party repaired to the dining room with the hoover, a collection of dustpans and brushes, and a piece of board, hammers and nails from Grandpa's shed. Nan's amusement was so infectious that, after due hesitation, they all joined in her laughter, even Piers and his grandparents, though Julian came in for a fair bit of teasing, which he took in good part. As Nan said, it was a classic situation just waiting to happen, and it was a story she would enjoy telling her friends and her sister again and again for a long, long time. What's more, when she came to think of it, she remembered that Ruth's father had done exactly the same thing when he was a boy.

The incident had fortunate repercussions, because Mr Hardy brought Ronnie Parr, the sexton at the church, to mend the window the following morning. Ronnie was a cheery soul, a garage mechanic who remembered Grandpa well – indeed, he had often been brought in to help at the airfield in emergencies during the War. Nowadays he had retired from the garage but took on extra odd jobs, as well as the day-to-day maintenance of the church and his role as sexton. Of course Nan knew him, if only because he had assisted at many of the burials that she had attended, not least both Evelyn's and Grandpa's: he it was who had dug their graves. Perhaps he reminded her too keenly of those tragic occasions, for she had never asked for his help in difficulties. Possibly too she had never approached him out of that personal pride to which she still clung, and because, by her very nature, she did not want to burden anyone with her problems.

Ronnie was willing to turn his hand to anything, a broken window being the simplest repair in his extensive repertoire. When the new window was in place, he took Nan gently by the arm. "Now, my ole dear, I'm a-goin' ter come and see you a couple of times a week. I can see as you need a bit o' help. I'm not a-goin' ter interfere, but I can do some gardenin' for you and I can bring the coal and the wood in come wintertime, and do any odd jobs you need. Don't you worry, it woon't cost you a penny, except if I hev ter buy anythin', but I reckon I'll find all I need in Joe's ole shed over there."

Nan was about to protest, but Ruth leapt precipitately into the breach. "Thank you very much, Mr Parr," she piped up before Nan could open her mouth, "that will be such a help to Nan in the winter – and I know my dad will be very pleased too." She added: "We live in London, you see, such a long way away." In defeat Nan kept quiet.

Though abruptly terminated on that Sunday afternoon, the first piano session with Piers had set a precedent, so that thereafter there was no shyness or awkwardness about the two of them disappearing into the piano room. It became an accepted routine in the final weeks of the holidays that Piers would practise all morning at home and then join Ruth in the afternoon. She too would practise some Beethoven Sonatas and other pieces, some Schubert and Schumann, especially 'Carnaval'. Mindful of the other demands on her time, she would go out on the bus to do the shopping for Nan when she had finished her practice, and after that would keep her company, sitting with her for a chat at coffee time. While Nan cooked the lunch, she would go for a walk or play a game with Julian, all the while anticipating the joys that she knew the afternoon would bring.

Nan went to church with the Hardys, but never suggested that Ruth should go with her. Content to go with people of her own generation, she left the young free to play the piano or work in the garden as they wished, and since Charles Stannard was back from his holidays, Piers and Julian were no longer required to man the organ. In the sun that summer, Ruth's sensitivity to everything and everyone around her was heightened: the garden was more beautiful, colours were brighter and richer, shapes sharper, personalities better defined, emotions more intense. Nature vibrated in every minute detail of all its glory: the song of the lark echoed high, invisible in the endless blue depths of the sky above the fields; butterflies settling on the purple fronds of the buddleia opened their orange-brown wings splashed with turquoise eyes; the scent of the pink rose that tumbled over Grandpa's shed wafted seductively across the lawn – everything enchanted her and moved her with its beauty and harmony.

Nan, for all her lameness, moved in an aura of light, while the Hardys, kind and generous though they were, were often enveloped in a misty, grey cloud, and Julian reflected a mix of reds and browns; Piers gleamed golden. Often, as she sat on the garden step bathed in the warmth of the morning sunlight, she would experience a delight so ardent, so fervent that it hurt – not at a superficial level, for it did not bring tears to the eyes, but pulsated deeply through her whole body and soul. She wanted to be immortal, for time to stand still, to witness that scene and experience those moments again and again, unchanged to eternity, with Piers if not by her side, at least within easy reach. If only those brief magical instants with him would last for ever – but they were fleeting, gone as soon as a cloud covered the sun. Already their first meeting was in the past.

If music aroused all those same sensations, music-making with Piers magnified them a thousand times more. When one afternoon they were leafing through the two volumes of Beethoven Sonatas that had belonged to Evelyn, he kept the page open at opus 27 no. 2 and, placing the copy on the music desk, he sat down at the piano.

"You must know this one, Ruthie," he said as he began to play. "Beethoven called it 'Sonata, quasi una Fantasia'; it's terribly overdone, of course." He played through the whole work, the famous first movement tenderly, with a gently mounting intensity which then died away, yielding place to the dancing Allegretto. The Presto Agitato conveyed an unbearable inner pathos, its turbulence never resolved, despite the intervening two-bar breathing space of the Adagio. His fingers came to rest after the final chord, and he sat motionless.

Ruth, who had been standing behind him, gently broke the silence. "It's the 'Moonlight', isn't it? I do try to play it – not very well, of course."

"Oh, I'm sure you'll play it superbly before very long," he whispered. "Then it will remind you of that bewitching evening when we sat out together under the full moon. Well, that's to say, I hope it will."

"Yes, I shall always remember that," she said softly. He swung round on the stool. His eyes were red. She wanted to reach out to touch him, but heard Nan's hobbling footsteps advancing from the kitchen, where she had been making scones, so she moved away, and Piers fixed his eyes on the keyboard.

"Let's play something jollier – some Mozart perhaps, shall we?" he asked as Nan came into the room.

"My goodness!" Nan cried. "That was how the 'Moonlight' should be played. I'll remember your playing till the day I die, no crashing and banging, but delicately, as Beethoven wanted, *delicatissimamente*, I think it's marked. You'll play it like that one day for me, Ruthie, won't you, and you'll take that edition of the Beethoven – well, at least one volume – back to London with you."

One afternoon Piers brought piano duets for them to play, although he suggested taking two stools from the kitchen and placing them side by side rather than sitting together on the piano bench. "We don't have enough room for manoeuvre on that one stool," he explained, at which Ruth was confused, suspecting that insufficient space was not the real reason, for she herself would have been happy to sit close, very close, to him.

"Ruthie, I wonder if you would like to have a look at this," he announced later in the week, opening two books of music, one large and the other much smaller. "It's the Beethoven concerto I have to play at school next term. Would you like to play the solo part for the slow movement from this piano score of mine, and I'll sit and read this miniature orchestral reduction? It would help me to read and imagine the lower instrumental parts while you play the piano part. Then I might be able to hear them better in performance." He had brought his copy of the 'Emperor' Concerto.

"Oh yes, I'd love to!" said Ruth, her mouth wide open and her eyes shining at his suggestion.

Evelyn's recording of the 'Emperor' was beginning to wear thin, so often had Ruth put the records onto the turntable of Nan's old wind-up gramophone. The supply of needles was running out, and she feared she might not be able to listen to it much longer, especially because she was afraid of damaging such a treasure beyond repair. She already knew the music – particularly the piano part – by heart. Not only had she listened to Evelyn's recording and read Evelyn's piano score many times from beginning to end, she had also heard Piers practising from the front garden.

"I tell you what we'll do!" Piers suggested. "We'll practise like this at first, and then we might invite your grandmother and my grandparents to come and listen.

"Good idea," Ruth agreed, "though I'm not sure I'll be any good." Piers would hear none of her modest protests. He gave her ten minutes to read through the score, and then she started to play, hesitantly at first and then with more conviction.

As Nan was outside, showing Ronnie Parr round the garden, there were no eavesdroppers, however benevolent. While Piers sketched in the orchestral part, Ruth played the solo, observing Piers's fingering and phrase markings. Thus carried away in their own project, they worked through the whole movement several times. Ruth did not mind how many times she played it: she was in heaven on finding that she was actually playing that most eloquent movement of that most powerful concerto. What's more, she was playing it with Piers so close – guiding her, correcting her occasionally and generally praising her prowess. Soon she found that she did not need to look at the score: her fingers and her brain had absorbed the sublime piano part apparently without any effort at all; as for the rests, they were now so obvious they scarcely needed registering.

Sometimes Piers hummed bits of the orchestral score. "How is it that you seem to know this concerto so well already?" he asked.

"Oh, I've listened to it many times," she replied evasively, "and I love it!"

"I think you are perfectly well able to play the whole thing, you know. You seem to have an inborn feeling for the music, the dynamics, the rhythm – everything. I'm amazed!" he said, and then reflected for a moment. "Have you ever played before an audience before?" he asked.

"No, only my primary-school teacher, Miss Lake, and the caretakers at my old school. Oh, and Nan, of course."

"That's fine," he replied. "A small audience is as good as a large one: it helps you to get used to playing in public and quietens the nerves, and I think you ought to be doing that as soon as possible. Wouldn't it be strange if you gave a concert next term at the same time as me!" Ruth smiled at the unreality of this suggestion: it was preposterous to imagine that anyone would ever ask her to perform on stage, much as she might have wanted to do so.

She was about to protest at the unlikelihood of such a thing ever happening, but Piers's brain was racing ahead to other considerations. "Look, we really need two pianos and the proper piano scores to be able to play the whole concerto – the piano solo and the orchestral part, I mean. Where would we find two pianos?"

"Oh, I know! That's not a problem!" Ruth exclaimed a few seconds later. "Nan has given me my aunt's piano score, you have yours, and there are two pianos in the church hall; I know that because I've been there with Nan to the Mothballs' meetings!"

"The Mothballs?" he queried.

"Yes," she laughed, "that was Grandpa's name for the Mothers' Union."

Piers grinned. "That's a good name for them! I tell you what: I'll ask Grandfather if he can arrange for us to use the church hall, on a couple of days a week perhaps. Is that all right with you?"

Nothing could have been more "all right" with Ruth. The church hall, as Mr Hardy discovered, was used only infrequently on weekday mornings, so there was no objection to the two young pianists availing themselves of the two pianos for as long as they liked. This was how Ruth came to acquire an intensive working knowledge of the whole of the 'Emperor' Concerto, not only the slow movement. With Evelyn's copy of the concerto under her arm, she and Piers glided along on the country walk to the church, talking little, smiling whenever they caught each other's eye, oblivious of other people and the farming activities around them. From time to time he would suggest how he would play a particular passage, and she, carried away on the wings of her great good fortune, would agree with everything he said. After an initial mishap on finding during the course of her warm-up that she had forgotten everything he had said on the walk, she tried to concentrate, though that was hard, given the heady experience of walking alone beside him through the fields in the warmth of the sun.

Once inside the church hall, Piers's attitude was one of total professionalism: he sat at one piano, she at the other, and after the one bar of the introductory orchestral fanfare of the Concerto she was away, her fingers flying nimbly up and down the keyboard in the soloist's opening arpeggios and scales. The experience was intoxicating and exhilarating; she had never believed that she could play with such ease and fluency. Her fingers had assumed a life of their own and knew exactly what to do and where to place themselves as they ran along the keyboard. Then, before she had to play again, there came a long orchestral interlude and the introduction of the first theme, but she concentrated hard and attended to every note emerging from the ancient instrument that Piers was playing.

They played in complete harmony till lunchtime, when Ruth's inner clock told her that Nan, who had willingly agreed to their project, would be cooking lunch. Occasionally after a full performance of the Concerto, Ruth tried her best to give an impression of the orchestral rendering for piano while Piers played the solo. She didn't care what she played for it was all so much like a beautiful dream. Piers became more and more animated on the way home. "I hope you are enjoying this, Ruthie," he enquired, "because I am and it's a great help to me. Your playing is extraordinary! Where does it come from?"

"I couldn't enjoy anything more," she confessed, her cheeks reddening, "but I myself don't know how my fingers do it! But then, you are so clever too, and I don't know how you do it!"

"I'm sure your talent comes from your aunt," he concluded.

As every morning was spent at the church hall, Ruth felt conscience-stricken at leaving Nan on her own and Julian without a companion. What's more, the larder was running out of supplies, so once in a while she suggested a bus ride and a shopping trip to Julian, which meant that not every afternoon was spent at the piano. As if that wasn't enough, Mrs Hardy was keen to take her own family, as well as Ruth and Nan, out on excursions – "to do them good and build up their resistance," she said, "before the winter sets in." She arranged a picnic by an old water mill, where Piers, Julian and Ruth swam in the cool, clear mill pond, a trip to the north coast where they went out in a boat to a sandbank – although the adults were content to stay behind in a café on shore out of the wind – and yet another excursion to their favourite beaches. Nan wondered about inviting them all to the farm, but decided that so many visitors might be too much for Dolly.

Although at first Piers and Ruth were unhappy about any distractions from their music, they soon grew reconciled to them, because on the way home they were sure of sitting together in the back of the car while Nan had her eyes shut in the corner. Their knees always touched as the car swayed from side to side, sending tingling thrills through their bodies. Drowsy from all the fresh air, Piers did not react with the alarm he had shown when their hands had touched on the piano keys, but simply smiled lazily at Ruth, and she smiled back at him, her tanned skin and rosy cheeks glowing in the evening sun.

Piers had been given a small box camera as an early birthday present by his grandparents. He soon used up all the rolls of film that had come with the camera. He was careful to take plenty of group photos, but had made sure that Ruth was in almost every one of them. She felt uncomfortably self-conscious about her posture, her hair, her expression, her clothes. There were more fish-and-chip suppers in the garden and, at the last of them, Piers went round taking individual snapshots of each person, "so that he would have a gallery to remind him of an unforgettable holiday," he said.

By some mischance he found that the camera did not seem to be working properly when he came to Ruth, so he had to take several shots of her. "Let me take one with you in it, Piers," his grandfather volunteered, "and if it doesn't work, I'll take the camera back to the shop on Monday." Piers handed him the camera and went to sit down between Julian and his grandmother. "Camera seems all right to me," said Mr Hardy, "but I'll take it back if you like."

"No, no, Grandfather, I expect I hadn't wound it on far enough," Piers insisted, and the matter was dropped. He took more photos at Julian's request, because he wanted pictures of himself with his cricket bat. When Julian finally went to bed, Piers hovered by Ruth in the garden, but it was too cold to stay outside, and the waning moon denied them the magic of that earlier night when it had bathed them in silver, so they went indoors and played Monopoly with the adults instead.

"I do want to write to you, Ruthie," Piers had declared more than once in quiet moments, either when they were sitting at the piano or when they were out walking by the sea. Ruth had anticipated this and, having already worried about it, had her reluctant answer ready in some form or other.

"I know, I'd like that so much too," she replied, "but it's not easy at home and..." her voice tailed off. She wanted to say: "I don't want anything to separate us ever or come between us, and I don't want to be made fun of, and I don't want you to meet my mother..." – but that did not sound right or proper, so instead she simply told various versions of a white lie, which in truth amounted to the same thing: "My parents are very strict, and I would have to explain everything, where the letters were coming from and who you are, and it would go on and on, and they might tease me, or stop us writing to each other..."

"I see," he said, wrinkling his brow. "Perhaps when we're older, then?"

"Yes, of course, I hope so!" she answered with undisguised feeling, and then to cheer him up added: "In any case we can meet here every half-term and every holiday, can't we?"

His response was less optimistic. "You never know how plans might change," he said.

Every time he repeated his request, as he did frequently on their walks to and from the church hall, it rang more and more plaintively – and each time, despite the most desperate urge to give way, Ruth's answer was the same. "I just don't see how we can manage it at the moment," she said, sounding exactly like her cautious father.

They continued their rehearsals for their recital, but in the event Nan and Julian were the only members of the audience that evening before Ruth's departure for London. Piers had told his grandparents little about his sessions with Ruth, and they did not ask. They assumed that he was giving her a few elementary piano lessons out of the goodness of his heart, and that consequently they would be treated to a performance of elementary pieces. Nan knew better of course, but refrained from giving the game away before the concert; as for Julian, predictably he wasn't at all interested.

Ruth arranged the armchairs in the living room in anticipation of an audience of five, but when Piers arrived for a warm-up before the recital, he said that his grandparents had been summoned to the hospital just after supper because there had been a crisis: his uncle had had some sort of attack, though whether it was a heart attack or a stroke he did not know. He shook his head sadly, "I so much regret that I've never been allowed to meet him," he lamented.

Although Ruth felt a strong natural urge to hug and comfort him, she drily asked in a perfunctory fashion: "Would you like to call the concert off, then?"

"No," he said. "There's nothing I want to do more. The music will help me, and you need practice in performing."

They decided that, under the circumstances, the 'Emperor' would be too ambitious as, according to Piers, sharing the long stool would not give them enough space for manoeuvre, so Ruth performed the Beethoven Sonata opus 31 no. 3 and the Schumann Waltz from 'Carnaval', while Piers played the 'Moonlight' Sonata among other pieces.

Their performance was impeccable according to Nan, who in the brief interval, with tears in her eyes, said that she never expected to hear Evelyn play again. She thought that Evelyn was there, alive on the piano stool before her very eyes. In the second half, after Ruth had played a couple of Chopin Preludes, Piers played the Schubert B flat Sonata. The unutterable poignancy of his rendering was hard for Ruth to bear. Undoubtedly, though it spoke of his sadness at his uncle's illness, she knew that it was also addressed to her, telling her of his despair, the despair that she shared at their forthcoming parting. To lighten the mood, he concluded the recital with some Mozart.

Nan said that she had not been treated to such a musical feast for a long time. She provided some refreshments, sausage rolls, cheese straws and non-alcoholic cider afterwards, while they waited for Mr and Mrs Hardy's return. As soon as they heard the car advancing along the driveway next door, Piers announced that he and his brother ought to be leaving, as his grandparents might need moral support. Nan wished the boys goodnight, giving them a plateful of cheese straws and sausage rolls to take home, and went into the kitchen to tackle the washing-up. Julian ran on ahead of his brother, and Ruth accompanied Piers down to the gate.

"You played very well," Piers complimented her.

"I'm glad you think so! Thank you for all your help; I couldn't have done it without you," she replied forlornly. There was so much she wanted to say to him, but the courage to do so was not forthcoming.

"You will come to Beech Grove at half-term, won't you?" he pleaded. "I don't think I can bear not to see you and not to be able to write to you."

The light was fading as summer slipped into autumn. Ruth was in torment: she wanted to be with Piers all the time, never to let him out of her sight, but on the other hand, she had the uncomfortable sensation that their friendship was becoming too adult, too serious, perhaps more serious than she could handle, so she just smiled and said, "Yes, I'll certainly be here, but what about you?"

"Certainly I shall come, wild horses won't stop me!" He glanced towards the houses to check that no one was watching, and then bent down and gently pushing her hair aside, kissed her on the forehead, "I love you, Ruthie!" he declared. "And I always will." He walked swiftly into his own gate before she had time to reply, and ran down the drive without looking back. Overwhelmed, Ruth watched him go. She leant on the gate until the sky had darkened fully, and only then did she walk slowly back to Nan's house.

45

There was a reception party waiting on the platform at Liverpool Street Station, though not the one that Ruth was hoping to see. She was expecting her father to be there, having already decided that she would explain away her red eyes and swollen lids with the excuse that she was getting a cold. There would be comfort in his arms. He would hug her and say: "Ruthie! You've been away such a long time. It's good to have you back!" It would be impossible to stop shedding a few tears, but they would help explain her woebegone appearance. She scanned the platform, searching for his tall, familiar shape, but it did not appear among the crowds. Disconcerted, she craned her neck to see if he was waiting at the barrier, but there was no sign of him anywhere.

She was disappointed, yet not unduly worried, because she was certain of finding her way home on the Underground. Besides, the homeward journey would give her time to collect herself up, and carrying the suitcase herself without help from her dad might be a lucky chance, since doubtless he would have wanted to know why it was so heavy. Nan had insisted on giving her Evelyn's copy of the 'Emperor' Concerto, with strict instructions to take it to Miss Lake and to perfect the fine detail of the two outer movements as well as the slow movement. As good as her word, she had also given her one volume of the Beethoven Sonatas, the first, insisting that she was looking forward to hearing the 'Moonlight' at half-term.

As Ruth approached the barrier, she saw two familiar figures. They were not looking in her direction, because they were completely immersed in their own conversation. The one, blonde and slim, was dressed in a smart red suit with a light fur tippet round her neck, and the other, large and blousy, wore a pink dress with a white fluffy bolero over her shoulders. The slim figure was her mother, and the large one Cousin Edith. Ruth was appalled.

She was contemplating evasive action, wondering how to slip past them without their noticing, when Cousin Edith, turning towards her, saw her straight away, prodded Shirley and called out: "Over here, Ruth!"

With sinking heart, blotchy face and bleary eyes, she trudged over to them.

"Goodness, Ruth! You do look a mess! What's happened to you?" her mother exclaimed as she gave her a peck on the cheek. Cousin Edith didn't say anything, but twitched her nose in a disapproving manner, which was meant to say, "I guessed so. What more can you expect of her?"

"I hope you've got some decent clothes in that case of yours," Shirley remarked.

Ruth didn't answer her directly, but made an unconvincing attempt at a sneeze and then, sniffing and pulling out her already sodden handkerchief, asked, "Why? Where's Dad?"

"He's the postmaster now – have you forgotten, you silly girl? So we've left him in charge of the shop and the post office, and we are going to the ballet!" Shirley declared impatiently.

Ruth was stunned. Interpreting her silence as ingratitude, Cousin Edith wasn't going to stay quiet for long. "Well, aren't you pleased? I think this is a great treat! You ought to be grateful. We expected you'd be thrilled!" She pursed her lips. "There's no telling with these teenagers – and she's nearly a teenager, of course. I'm so glad I've got boys! They never give me any trouble."

Shirley coughed, ignoring her cousin and giving the merest of impressions that she was wearying of Cousin Edith's self-righteousness. Instead, she concentrated on her daughter. "Well, as I was saying, I hope you've got something nice in your suitcase. You can't go to the ballet looking like a tramp, you know, so we had better go over to the Ladies' and you can smarten yourself up."

Fortunately Nan had washed and ironed the new skirt and top, which were lying at the top of the suitcase. In the Ladies', Ruth pulled them and a white cardigan out quickly before Shirley had time to delve down further. She also took out her sponge bag, found her flannel and firmly closed the lid of the suitcase; then she washed in cold water and changed in the grimy public convenience.

"You'll just about do – won't she, Edith?" Shirley said, seeking her cousin's support.

"Yes, I suppose so, but maybe a dab of your powder and a touch of lipstick would brighten her up a bit," Edith decreed, nodding dubiously. Shirley applied a pale powder to Ruth's bronzed cheeks and a scarlet lipstick to her mouth.

Ruth surveyed herself in the mirror, and was horrified to see how dreadful she looked – a ghostly white, red-eyed wraith with bright-red lips. Her private reaction was first of all relief that Piers was not there to see her – and nor, for that matter, could he see her mother and Cousin Edith, who were plastering make-up onto their faces in thick layers. Secondly, she was absolutely certain that she had made the right decision in refusing to let him write to her. There was some comfort in knowing that her instincts were correct. Nonetheless, it was strange to think that she knew exactly where he was – in the house next door to Nan's, playing the piano – but he would have no idea of what was happening to her or where she was.

The ballet, *Swan Lake*, was a troubling experience which brought back the frustrated longing to dance that she had known as a child and intensified her present longing for Piers – that inexplicable aching, that new sensation that had so suddenly attacked her only weeks earlier. The sumptuousness of the Opera House recalled the distant memory of her fifth-birthday treat, reminding her of her disbelief that mere mortals could dance on the tips of their toes. Whereas on that previous occasion long ago she had identified with the Princess Aurora, the innocent victim of the wicked witch, now she saw herself centre stage in the story of an impossible thwarted love, where of course Piers was Prince Siegfried and she was Odette, the bewitched swan queen who, waiting for a true love, was allowed to resume her human form only by night.

The music haunted her from the opening chord, sending tingling shivers up and down her spine. Just as when she and Piers had practised together, everything else was forgotten. Here in the Opera House the action, the dancing and the melodies arising from the orchestra captivated her totally, but she did not weep, though her heart was rent by the scenes played out before her.

She shuddered at the appearance of the wicked baron von Rothbart and Odile, the black swan, his daughter. Would anyone ever try to steal Piers from her as Odile stole Prince Siegfried from Odette? How would she ever be able to bear it? Her emotions were so passionately aroused that from time to time she nearly let out a gasp or a little cry, even though her eyes remained dry and were no longer swollen. She was thankful not to be sitting near Edith, who snorted embarrassingly and rustled sweets that she extracted noisily from her handbag. Shirley sat between them, deadening the impact of the interruptions. Occasionally Ruth glanced at her mother. Instead of Shirley's normal pert, self-satisfied expression, tears were streaming down her cheeks.

During the second interval Shirley dived into the Ladies' room. It was her turn to look a mess: her make-up had run, leaving her face as blotchy as Ruth's had been earlier.

Edith naturally was full of sympathy for her, if not for Ruth. "There, there, my love," she cooed as she took Shirley's arm. "I'm here. Come on, dry your eyes and we'll go for a drink. You'll be all right."

She steered Shirley towards the bar and queued up for drinks of some sort or other for the three of them. In the final act, the tragedy was played out as Siegfried, duped by von Rothbart, flung himself into the lake with Odette, for whom the only release from the baron's wicked spell lay in death, since true love had been denied her. Shirley's sobs were pitiful.

After the performance, Shirley limply tidied herself up again before Edith led the way, forcing a path through the outgoing crowds. She waved over their heads to someone standing outside the Opera House. "I can see Jim – he's waiting for us, right on cue, as you might say!"

Edith's husband had obeyed his instructions, though from the smell of his breath it was obvious that he had been out on the town. "You girls had a good time?" he enquired with little interest in the reply.

"Yes, it was lovely," Edith enthused, "though we could all do with a drink."

"Another one wouldn't come amiss for me either; there's a pub across the road," he replied. "But let me carry your case for you, duckie," he added, putting out a hand to relieve Ruth of her suitcase.

She clutched it. "No, no, please don't bother. I can carry it."

"There's no helping some people," Edith observed.

Ruth would have much preferred to be at home than in a hot, stuffy pub. But since she had no choice, she sat in a corner, slightly apart from her relatives, reading the ballet programme, which Cousin Edith had handed over to her. Keeping her head down, yet unpleasantly conscious of some large, beery men leering at her, she then remembered the powder and lipstick on her face, so she pulled her handkerchief out of her pocket and wiped her cheeks and lips clean. She edged nearer to Jim, and the men moved away.

It was only when they left the pub and Shirley and Edith were kissing each other goodnight that it transpired that Cousin Edith and her husband were not staying at the Broadway but had booked into a hotel for a couple of nights.

"I said they would be very welcome to stay with us, but they thought we would be too busy with the post office, so they decided to stay in a hotel," Shirley explained to Ruth, who tried not to show how pleased she was.

"Well, it gives us more chance to see the sights, and it's the first time I've been to London," Jim said. "And, although I say it myself," he added, "the missus was right to bring me here; I didn't know what I was missing!"

"Anyhow," Edith butted in, "we'll meet again tomorrow, won't we, Shirl? Shall we say eleven at Piccadilly?"

"That's fine! John will look after the shop. So goodnight, see you then!" Shirley said as they parted company, having recovered her composure.

Evidently neither Ruth nor her father were to be included in the next day's arrangements, for which she was grateful. A quiet, reflective day would not come amiss, and gladly she looked forward to being with him and helping him out in the shop. Although the ballet had been completely unexpected and not altogether welcome, it had allowed time for the tears to dry and the swellings to subside in the darkness of the theatre before she came face to face with her dad. How relieved she was that she had wiped that horrible make-up of Shirley's off her cheeks and her mouth! Shirley did not notice at all, being preoccupied with her own thoughts all the way home.

Ruth was very pleased to see her dad, even if some hours later than she had hoped. He hugged her, saying how long she had been away and how much he had missed her, and she was pleased to find him in good health. He had not had a real holiday, but apparently he and Shirley had been to Brighton on Sundays after the early-morning paper deliveries, and there he had acquired a tan which had restored his youthful good looks. Then on Thursday afternoons they had taken a bus out into the country, where they had walked and toured old houses and abbeys.

"How's the post office?" she asked.

"I wondered when you were going to ask!" he replied excitedly. "Come and see for yourself!"

He pushed the door and stepped into the newly partitioned post office, with its counter, weighing machine, cash register, its shelves, ledgers, drawers and cupboards, all neatly labelled and corresponding to different areas of business, stamps, postal orders, pensions and so on. The back room, previously the sitting room, was now the office. John was as proud and pleased as Shirley had been when she had taken over the newsagent's. "I'm enjoying this so much! It's like playing at post offices," he declared. "And this has definitely been the easiest time to take it over, though Rita said it will soon get busier and will be frantic in the run-up to Christmas. It's the best thing that could have happened to me, and I have your mother to thank for it!"

He put his arm round Shirley but, in an extraordinary reversal of the roles, Shirley was subdued and scarcely responded.

"I'm tired," she said, "and Ruth must be too! It's time for bed!"

"I'll ask you about Nan in the morning," Dad said to Ruth.

"Oh, apart from her leg, she's doing quite well," his daughter reassured him.

When Ruth came down at nine o'clock after a good night's sleep, her father was already at work, running both the post office and the shop.

"Where's Shirley?" she asked on not finding her mother behind the counter. "Oh, she's gone off to meet her cousin. She said she wanted to get away in good time," he answered.

"That's odd," said Ruth, who was indignant that Shirley was already taking advantage of her father, leaving him to run the entire enterprise.

"What do you mean?" he asked.

"Well, she and Cousin Edith agreed to meet at Piccadilly at eleven."

"I see," Dad said. "Yes, that is odd." His brow furrowed as he considered the discrepancy between what Ruth had told him and Shirley's version. "Tell me, Ruthie, was she all right at the ballet last night?"

"I'm not sure," Ruth replied hesitantly, not wanting to worry her father, but then, deciding that she ought to tell him the truth, she said: "She did cry a bit."

"Oh dear! I was afraid something was wrong when she came in last night," Dad said, as a wave of concern swept across his face. "Ruthie," he asked, "would you just go and look in the kitchen? There should be a piece of paper there with the name of the hotel where Edith and Jim are staying. I think I'll give them a ring to see if your mother is with them."

Ruth fetched the scrap of paper and gave it to her dad, who thumbed quickly through the telephone directory, found the number and dialled the hotel. With audible agitation, he enquired if Edith were there. Although Ruth was serving in the shop, her ears picked up one side of the conversation between her dad and Edith when the latter came to the phone.

"I'm sorry to interrupt you, Edith. I gather you are having breakfast, but do you have Shirley there with you?" Dad asked. Ruth glanced towards the post-office counter and saw his face relaxing on hearing Edith's reply. So Shirley was there in the hotel with Edith and Jim after all.

There was a hiatus while Edith fetched Shirley to the phone. He then had to invent an excuse for tracking her down. "Hello, love, I wanted to let you know, as it's early-closing day and the weather has cleared up, Ruth and I might go out this afternoon. Just in case you get home before us." At the other end of the line, Shirley must have given a somewhat exasperated reply and said that she wouldn't be back till late, because Dad quickly said, "Oh, that's all right then. Have a nice time! See you later," and put the phone down.

Ruth was busy serving a customer with a newspaper but when she finished, her dad leaned over the counter and asked: "What about a trip to the country this afternoon? We can take the Green Line bus from across the road."

Ruth liked the idea, though she was baffled at the way he had suggested it, telling Shirley about it before consulting her. Her only proviso was that she must write a note to Nan first.

"That's fine," Dad replied. "You go and do that straight away, and you'll catch the midday post. We're not busy here."

She escaped to the breakfast room, where she laid out a sheet or two of writing paper and an envelope. Then she searched in her school bag for her fountain pen before sitting down. She savoured a delicious sense of anticipation, since this letter was not only destined for Nan but, secretly, for Piers as well, and she was sure that Nan would convey its contents to the neighbours. Without a doubt Piers would recognize the references that were meant for him. She wrote, choosing her words very carefully: she made light of the journey home, saying merely how sad she had been to leave them all after that splendid holiday. She thanked her nan for the best holiday she had ever had and asked her to thank the Hardys for all those marvellous trips to the seaside, which she would always remember. She hoped that the Hardys' invalid relative was making progress.

Then, referring to the home front, she related that her dad was well and happy, without specifying what he was doing, but wrote that he had been too busy to meet her at Liverpool Street, so her mother had come instead. Omitting all mention of Cousin Edith, she described the visit to the ballet in enthusiastic terms, which made it out to be the happiest occasion imaginable. She reminded her nan of her first visit to the ballet, to *The Sleeping Beauty*, just before her fifth birthday. By comparison, *Swan Lake* had been even more beautiful and powerful, with spellbinding music, and sad – so sad that many people in the audience had to get their handkerchiefs out, and she herself had nearly cried.

She promised that she would practise her music hard as and when the opportunity presented itself, and hoped to play the 'Moonlight' well – as well as Piers had played it and as Beethoven would have wished – the next time they met. She wanted the weeks till half-term to pass quickly. She sent lots of love, put the letter in its envelope, sealed it down before her dad could ask what she had written, then asked him for a stamp and, with satisfaction, popped it into the post box outside.

While her father finished his morning's work, she prepared a light lunch and packed a flask of tea and some biscuits into her father's old army rucksack. He closed the shop at twelve-thirty, changed into more suitable clothes and footwear for walking in the country and ate his lunch quickly. Glancing at his watch, he said: "The bus only comes once an hour, so we mustn't miss it!" But by twelve fifty-five they were waiting at the bus stop on the other side of the road.

Earlier Ruth had been so busy helping in the shop that she was chastened to find that dreams of Piers had been pushed into the background – until, that is, she sat down to write her letter. That attempt to communicate with him had brought his presence to the fore again, so that she felt him to be very close, so real that she almost expected him to appear round a corner at any minute. The reassurance of that feeling and knowing where he was and what he was doing made it almost bearable to live with the pain of his absence.

On the bus, with her dad dozing beside her, she found herself alone with her reminiscences once more, and the trauma of yesterday's parting reasserted itself. She pined for Piers, willing herself to be with him in Nan's front room, practising Beethoven under his auspices or playing piano duets. He was so far away – a long train ride away – and already nearly a whole day had passed since they had last seen each other. She sat on her fingers to stop them getting itchy, so accustomed had they become to regular practice.

By the time the bus came out into open country, she felt thoroughly miserable, and when it dropped them by a huge common on the edge of a small town, Dad, who had woken up, gently probed her: "Hey, Ruthie, what's the matter?"

"Nothing, only a bit queasy after that bus ride."

"The fresh air will help; we'll take the path across the common to the heath, and you can tell me all about your holiday and about Nan," he said, trying to be encouraging.

There was the rub. It would be easy to tell him about Nan, but how was she going to tell him about Piers? On the other hand, there was no harm in letting him at least know who Piers was. He would keep her secret, though it didn't even have to appear to be a secret. There was nothing wrong in telling him what a super time she had had with the Hardys and their grandsons, as well as with Nan.

Nan was the easiest topic of conversation to begin with: there was, of course, plenty to tell about her. She was getting more lame certainly, and often tired, but she was generally in good health and in a very positive frame of mind. John listened attentively to his daughter's account of everything that they had done together, of the trip into the city and the ride back in the van, of the stay at the farm and all the things that Nan had succeeded in taking in her stride, all her baking and jam-making, her outings with her friends and so on. Finally, there was the good news that Ronnie Parr was going to help out with the fires in winter, bringing in the coal and the wood. He had promised to tend the garden and keep an eye on Nan, so there was no need to worry.

Dad was less than convinced. "Mm," he said doubtfully. "I'm not too sure about Ronnie Parr; I don't think your grandpa had much time for him. He wasn't at all reliable."

Ruth was dismayed, even annoyed that her father was shedding cold water on an arrangement that had so many advantages for Nan – and for him too, since it should relieve him of so much anxiety. "He said he would do it out of the goodness of his heart: he didn't want to be paid. And he was a nice man," Ruth insisted, in the face of such seeming ingratitude.

"Well, we'll see," was her dad's disparaging comment. Ruth groaned inwardly, for she had expected him to be very pleased. She had intended to ask him what he knew about the family history on Nan's – and Aunt Dolly's – side, but so irritated was she by his disapproval of Ronnie Parr that she kept her mouth shut.

The tended green grass of the common had given way to rough heathland, where bracken and gorse vied for dominance. A path led through the undergrowth to a clearing where someone had conveniently placed a wooden bench in the full sun.

"Oh, look at that! Just right for tea!" Dad announced. "Let's sit down here. There is something I want to talk to you about, and this is a good opportunity. I expect you must have thought me rather anxious about Shirley this morning, and you may have wondered why," he began. Ruth did not react. "She's missed you such a lot," Dad went on. "I think you are old enough to understand these things, and I think it's time I explained why I'm so worried about Shirley." As ever, overcome with pity for him, Ruth listened, nodding occasionally without interrupting his flow. "I was saying that Shirley missed you a lot while you were away," he said, "but as you know she finds it hard to show it. That's all because she suffers from an illness which these days they call 'depression' or 'nervous breakdown', whichever way you look at it, and it doesn't have a cure. Sometimes she's happy and energetic, and sometimes for no reason at all that I can discover she sinks into a dangerous state of melancholy... Well, that's not quite true, because a long time ago, when you were small, she had a horrible experience, and that certainly was a good and sufficient reason.

"She was expecting a baby, and the baby died before it was born. They call it a 'stillbirth'." The words caught in his throat as he said: "It was a little boy." Ruth remembered that day when Shirley had clutched her stomach, crying "The baby! The baby!" She also recalled that later occasion two years ago when Shirley had wanted to justify the move to the shop and her attempt to confide in Ruth had ended unaccountably in sobs when she had stated the obvious, saying that Ruth was her only child.

Ruth reached out her hand and gently took her father's in hers. "Yes, I remember, that happened when I was four, I think, and then I went to stay with Nan and Grandpa for a long time," she said softly.

He turned to her swiftly, "So you remember that, Ruthie?"

"Yes, of course."

She also recalled keenly how dreadful her welcome home on her fifth birthday had been, but considered it kinder not to mention that.

"I suspect also," Dad continued, "that she had had some terrifying experience during the War before you were born, but she refuses to talk about it." Ruth remembered those hushed chats between Rachel and Shirley, who had willingly talked to Rachel about the War. "After you were born she had to go into hospital with a nervous breakdown." Then he added hastily, "It's not that she wasn't very happy to have you – she was, but apparently it's a condition that affects some new mothers." Ruth remembered Carrie's embarrassment on discovering that she had not known about that episode. She nodded again.

"Of course there was also that terrible business when you and she were watching the boats on the river; the effect of that made her very ill and put her in hospital for a long time," her dad went on. There was a lull while he reviewed the way his explanation was going. "There's not a lot more that I can say, except that there have been other instances when some small thing that we might not notice has been enough to send her into the deepest of depressions. There were several of those during your childhood: she had to go into hospital more than once and undergo dreadful treatment." Ruth was no stranger to this news.

He continued: "She has been so much happier since they put her on that new lithium medication, and also since she opened her own business – so much happier that I was very anxious at how sad she was after the ballet last night, and I was very afraid that she might be sinking into another depression. You see, I have always worried that she might throw herself under a bus. That was why I was so anxious this morning when she went out so much earlier than she had arranged with Edith."

Poor Dad! Ruth hated to think of the burden that he had carried for such a long time, nor could she bear to think how much Shirley, whatever her illness, had, in her opinion, abused his good nature. Although his explanation had confirmed many of her suspicions and assumptions, she wasn't sure that it had reconciled her to Shirley and her waspish character. Only time would tell. For the moment, she forgot about Piers and concentrated on her dad. "Come on, Dad," she encouraged him cheerfully. "It's nearly six. It's time to go home! Let's be getting back to the bus stop."

Her father's expression began to relax, which she took as a sign that he was relieved to have unburdened himself. Recovering his natural good humour, he reverted to more mundane subjects. "What shall we have for supper?" he asked with the eager anticipation of a small boy. "There are some chops in the fridge, and also a steak-and-kidney pie I bought at the butcher's. Which would you like?" Ruth opted for the pie, which they put in the oven as soon as they arrived home.

As they were enjoying the rich flavours, Ruth deemed that this might be a good moment to venture a passing mention of the Hardys and Piers. In an offhand manner she would say: "Nan has such nice new neighbours, Mr and Mrs Hardy. They were so kind to Nan and me. In fact, they took us with their grandsons to the sea several times. It was such fun!" Hopefully Dad would ask more about the Hardys and their grandsons, and also where they went to the seaside and what they did, whereupon she would talk about Piers – not forgetting Julian of course. She was summoning her courage when she heard the front door opening. Shirley was back.

She came bursting into the dining room, laden with shopping. "We've had such a good time, Edith and me! Look what I've bought! Ruth, I've got a lovely new winter dress for you!" No one would have suspected that this was the same person who had been weeping in the Opera House the previous evening. "It's such a shame that Edith and Jim have to go home tomorrow! He has to get back to his shifts, you see. But I've been thinking: it's the bank-holiday weekend. We won't have to work on Sunday afternoon or Monday – maybe Pa would come over and take over tomorrow to do the Saturday and Sunday papers and man the post office, so we would then have the whole weekend off – why don't we go down to Brighton? I think I like the south coast better than the east coast – it's warmer, and anyhow it's where we sometimes used to go on an outing when I was a child." All these ideas, opinions and information came tumbling out in one breath.

John laughed and beamed in relief at his wife. "There's no knowing what you will think of next, is there Shirley?"

She laughed too and flung herself into his arms.

"Pack your suitcase!" Shirley commanded as soon as Ruth came down for breakfast the next day. She had arranged everything over the phone before anyone else was up, having booked a guest house for the three of them for three nights and found out the train timetable. "We're off in twenty minutes! So you'd better be quick!" she warned Ruth, who ran back upstairs, anxious not to give anyone the opportunity to examine the contents of her suitcase. Hastily she took the two Beethoven volumes out of the case, shoved them under the bed, resisting the temptation to open them, and then repacked the bag with the same clothes, sandals and plimsolls, all the things that she had worn when she had been with Piers. Those clothes were like old friends from another age and brought comfort with the recent events they evoked, giving her a real point of contact with him.

"Put something smart in, in case we go to the theatre!" Shirley called up the stairs, so Ruth added her green-and-white floral skirt and the new green blouse to the pile. "Are you ready? Don't forget your toothbrush!" Shirley shouted again from below.

"I'm coming!" Ruth called out and, picking up the case, hurried down to join her parents, who were waiting in the hall with Granddad Reggie. He must have arrived while she was upstairs, so there was no time to greet him, and anyhow he was already moving laboriously towards the connecting door to the shop. He grunted something which might have been "Goodbye!" and took himself off through the opening as John ushered his womenfolk out of the front door.

That early-morning rush was symptomatic of the whole weekend. It was certainly enjoyable, and Shirley saw to it that not a second was wasted, which meant that there was hardly a moment for Ruth to pine for Piers or for a piano. She was certain in any case that with the beginning of the new academic year she would continue to go to St Luke's after school as usual to resume her practice sessions and hopefully, also, her lessons with Miss Lake. Though her fingers twitched with that independent musicality they had acquired, she reckoned that she could just about bear to wait a few days longer for the reunion with her other life and, by extension through music, with Piers.

47

Pleasant though the long weekend in Brighton with her parents had been, school beckoned with an unexpected urgency, not because the school itself had any particular charms to offer, but because like last year Ruth was anticipating going into St Luke's from the first day of term, as had been arranged before the holiday began. There she would be able to practise to her heart's content and have a piano lesson with Miss Lake every week.

As she went out of the house in the morning with the Beethoven works weighing heavy in her satchel, she called out to her mother, who was busy down in the cavernous depths of the stockroom. The inner door to the post office was open, so she was sure that her father, who of course since becoming the postmaster was at home all day, would be able to hear as well.

"Bye, Shirley! Bye Dad!" she called. "I might be late home, as I shall drop in to see Mr and Mrs Burns at St Luke's on the way."

"That's fine – don't be too late, that's all. Have a good day! Bye!" Shirley called up the stairs. Having settled that matter satisfactorily, with luck for the whole of the next academic year, Ruth made her way up the road, smiling as she saw the new entry of tiny children and their nervous mothers going into the primary school for the first time.

School was fairly humdrum, much easier than it had been on the first day last year, with the welcome advantage that Ruth and her classmates were no longer in Miss Jenkins's form. The Upper Fourth was lucky enough to have as its form mistress the chemistry teacher, Miss Neville, who conducted the form business as she did her teaching, with efficiency and good humour; she treated the girls as civilized human beings, and they responded as such. Following the long-established routine, the morning was devoted to administration – the checking of registers, the opening assembly and the giving-out of new books for the year.

Lessons began in the afternoon, but concentration was difficult. Ruth's fingers twitched under the desk, beating out rhythms and trying out fingerings, and her mind was elsewhere, far away communing with Piers and Beethoven. In Brighton on the Monday it had occurred to her that Piers and Julian would be on their way home to somewhere in Surrey, where she would no longer be able to visualize their surroundings, their home life, their parents or their routine – particularly Piers's. This was distressing, making her all the more anxious to begin applying her fingers to the keyboard – when, she hoped, she would be able to establish some imaginary means of contact with him again.

The afternoon dragged on through maths and history, until the bell rang. She gathered up her books for homework, which now made her satchel even heavier, collected her coat from the cloakroom and hurried to the main door.

"Ruth Platt! You're supposed to walk, not run!" an officious prefect yelled, slowing her down. A hundred yards down the road, with great excitement, she pushed open the green gate of her old primary school and hurried into the yard. All was eerily quiet, with none of the usual din of vacuum cleaners at work.

However, as the main door was open, she went in and, looking around for Mr and Mrs Burns, she headed straight for the hall, where the piano stood in its usual position by the stage, but when she sat down at the keyboard and tried to lift the lid, it wouldn't move: it was locked. Her hopes dashed, she sat for a moment with her hands in her lap, wondering how to resolve this untoward situation. Then she heard footsteps approaching and a friendly, familiar voice called her by name. "Ruth! Lovely to see you! Did you have a good holiday?" It was Miss Lake. "Oh, of course! The piano is locked. Don't worry, I've got the key; it's here in my pocket," she exclaimed. "Why don't you warm up for a few minutes while I put the band instruments away in the cupboard?"

While Miss Lake unlocked the piano, raised the lid and arranged the music desk, Ruth took out her copies. Left to her own devices, she began by skimming her fingers up and down the keyboard in the scales that Piers had taught her. Even playing simple scales made her feel more alive, more liberated and more at one with herself than she had been since leaving Norhambury. Because there was also the blissful, imagined sensation that Piers was standing behind her, watching her fingers and listening to the evenness of her playing, in precisely the way that he had at Beech Grove, she concentrated hard, correcting herself when she knew that she was falling short of his standards. Miss Lake, perhaps deliberately leaving her to herself, was away for some time, so she opened the Beethoven Sonatas. Disconcerted to find that the easiest of them – opus 49 no. 2 – was not in volume one, nor was opus 31 no. 3, she resorted to more scales in fifths and sixths, and arpeggios. Then she embarked upon the 'Waldstein'.

She gave a passable performance of the first movement and was so involved in her playing that she did not notice that Miss Lake had tiptoed into the hall through a side door and was standing behind her a little way away. Ruth was startled when she heard her exclaim: "Goodness, you have come on! I'm amazed at what you've done in the holidays! What else have you learnt? Has someone been teaching you?"

Because of the blush rising in her cheeks, Ruth did not turn to face her teacher, as she stammered her cautious answer. "A relative of Nan's neighbours is training to be a concert pianist, and he gave me some help,"

"Gracious! He certainly must be a good teacher as well as a good player!" Miss Lake remarked. "Your nan must be pleased." She peered at the Beethoven score open on the music desk. "Did your nan give you that?"

"Yes, it belonged to my Aunt Evelyn." This was an easier question to answer and did not cause the blood to rush to her cheeks.

"Oh, unbelievable! Can I see, please?" Taking the work from where it stood on the piano, Miss Lake opened it at the frontispiece. "Oh, I say! She has written her name and the date in it! 'Evelyn Platt, 1936'! Ruth, you must keep this carefully. It's very special and, I suspect, very valuable. In fact, you mustn't leave it here. You must take it home with you."

The prospect of having to carry that heavy book of music about with her in her satchel all day and hide it under her bed at night was not only daunting but worrying as well. Someone would be sure to discover it sooner or later, simply by picking up her satchel. Her dad would ask, "What have you got in here, Ruth? This satchel is so heavy!" Then Shirley would say, "Let's have a look! What are you hiding in there?" So she said, "Why can't I leave it here?"

"Well, as I said," Miss Lake went on, "it's certainly valuable, and there's been trouble here over the holiday. Someone broke in and did a lot of damage – not to the piano, thank goodness, but whoever it was ransacked the Head's study and splashed paint all over the Art Room, so we have to be very careful." Then Miss Lake added: "That's why we are keeping the piano locked."

"That's dreadful, but can I still come and practise?" Ruth asked, her concern divided between annoyance that anyone should be so stupid and irritation at the resulting disruption to her own arrangements.

"There's another problem," said Miss Lake. "You see, the Burns are no longer working here. Poor Mr Burns had an accident over the summer. He fell off a ladder while he was trimming a tree and he'll be in hospital for some time. I think he broke a leg and an arm."

"I am sorry!" Ruth cried, for she was very fond of the elderly couple who had been so kind to her.

Miss Lake continued: "And you see, we couldn't get a replacement for the Burns, so some commercial cleaners are coming in to clean the school at the crack of dawn instead."

Ruth held her breath, fearing the worst. Was there to be no more practice time at all? "Not to worry though," Miss Lake continued, with more positive news. "I've been appointed Deputy Head, so I have to be here at the end of the day to check that the school is tidy and properly locked, and I have phone calls to make and correspondence to deal with." Luckily she had anticipated the unspoken question in Ruth's mind. "Of course," she said, "one day a week I shall carry on giving you a lesson, if that's what you'd like, but on the other days I must be away by four-thirty, as I have more private pupils at home." Not at all sure what this implied, Ruth didn't know what to say. "What I mean," Miss Lake went on, "is that if you can get here by, say, five past four, you can practise for twenty minutes or so every day, but I'm afraid that's all, no more than that. And no more tea parties, I'm sorry to say. It might be better if you explained the situation to your parents."

"Not yet," Ruth pleaded. "I know my dad's worried about my mother: he told me so the other day, and I don't want to upset him or her."

"Another thing," said Miss Lake, who must have given much consideration to Ruth's situation. "When it gets dark early towards the end of term, we can walk home together. I would normally take the bus, but I'll walk down the road with you and then catch it at the stop outside your house, like the Burns used to do." Gratitude was the only possible response to such an offer of help, although the curtailment of her practice time was very disappointing. "Oh, and by the way," Miss Lake added, "Thursday would suit me better for your lesson, if that's all right with you. Well, come on, then!" she exclaimed, "let's not waste any more time. What else have you been learning?"

Ruth was about to say "The 'Moonlight' Sonata", but changed her mind, because for her the significance of the 'Moonlight' was much too intimate. "I've tried to learn the Pathétique, and I've also practised the Appassionata and opus 31 no. 3, but those two aren't in this volume that Nan gave me."

"Right," said Miss Lake, trying not to appear too astounded. "So what else have you got, then?"

Ruth took her courage in both hands. "You might think this is silly, but Nan gave me the 'Emperor' Concerto, and I've been working on the slow movement."

"Really? You don't say!" Miss Lake replied, raising her eyebrows in even more astonishment. After some reflection, she nodded, "All right, then, why not? It's very beautiful and moving. Do you have the piano score with you?"

"Yes, I have Evelyn's copy of that too," Ruth replied, pulling the other major work out of her bag and placing it on the music desk.

She proceeded to play the slow movement through, pausing for the rests, as Piers had done on that first afternoon when she had heard him playing through the open window.

When her fingers came to a standstill, Miss Lake did not react immediately. She took a deep breath and declared, "I don't know that there's much that I can teach you, Ruth, but I do have that concerto in a miniature score, so I'll bring mine along and we'll play the whole work together. I'll have to try to sketch in the orchestral part on the violin though, and that won't be easy with so many page turns. You'll have to be patient with me!"

Ruth was gladdened by Miss Lake's encouraging reception of her plans. They would allow her to dream that she was back in the church hall playing the piano solo with Piers playing his piano rendering of the orchestral score on the other piano, only she wouldn't be in the church hall miles away out in the country, but here in a dark Victorian primary school in London, playing to the accompaniment of Miss Lake's violin. However, even that had to be better than nothing.

When she arrived home half an hour later, her dad and Shirley were still in the shop, getting ready to close up for the day. The connecting door was open.

"Hello, is that you Ruth?" Shirley called out. "Have you had a good day?"

"Yes, not too bad," Ruth replied.

"You're rather late, aren't you?" her dad called from behind the post-office counter.

Ruth was contemplating what to say when Shirley butted in. "No, no, John, have you forgotten those letters I had to write last year to those stupid women, giving my permission for her to go and see her friends in St Luke's after school? That's where she's been, haven't you Ruth?" No white lies were needed.

The answer was a straightforward affirmative, but Ruth did not wait for any more questions in case they concerned the well-being of those nice people, Mr and Mrs Burns. She ran upstairs, took her homework out of her satchel, then pushed it with the music still inside it under her bed, well out of sight.

On the chest of drawers which served as a dressing table was a small red booklet. On top was a note from Shirley. It said, "I think it's about time you knew about these things, so please read this booklet, and if you want to talk about it, just ask me." Ruth was mystified; as she picked up the booklet, she read the title: *Growing into Adulthood: The Facts of Life for Young Women.*

She sat down on the edge of the bed and began to read. There was nothing much in the booklet that was new to her. Susan had given her a first lesson in the facts of life all those years ago when Ben was born – Where was Susan now? And little Ben? she wondered. Besides, she had overheard many secret discussions in corners of the playground during the past year, in the course of which these matters had been aired in whispers. Adulthood was so disgustingly horrible, especially the bit about what happened to women once a month, that after worrying about it for a couple of days she had put it to the back of her mind, hoping that it wasn't true. But from reading Shirley's booklet, it sounded to be true after all, and there was no escaping it.

What's more, the booklet had a paragraph headed "Relationships", in which the author warned the young reader that she might find herself drawn to some other person with a strong longing to be with that person all the time. This longing was love-longing, and was to be resisted in young people in case it led to serious trouble. The booklet did not specify what the "trouble" it referred to might be. This was all very shocking, not only on account of the unpleasant information, but also the rejection of all that she felt for Piers, for she certainly had a strong longing for him and wanted to be with him all the time. Altogether she decided that the booklet was inappropriate for her, and she resented the fact that Shirley had left it there.

On the other hand Shirley had better news for her downstairs. "There's a letter for you, Ruth. It looks like your nan's handwriting. Ruth pounced on the blue envelope, but was reluctant to open it in front of her mother, not being at all inclined to share its contents with her. So, putting it in her pocket, she said: "I'll read it later; I came down to see if you need any help with the supper."

"That's kind, but there's nothing to do," Shirley replied, then asked: "Did you see that little book I left on your chest of drawers?"

"Yes, thank you."

"It's a rotten business being a woman," Shirley sighed. "But when it happens, then you won't be a child any more."

Ruth could see little advantage in not being a child in such circumstances, so she slipped away up to her room as her help was not needed in the kitchen. Since Dad had taken on the post office, Shirley had taken it upon herself to cook the evening meal as some sort of reward for him. She closed the door and sat down on the floor to read Nan's letter.

Dear Ruthie – it began in Nan's spidery scrawl – *I was so pleased to receive your letter yesterday so quickly after your arrival in London, and to know that you were safely home. Well done for coping with the journey on your own! You are growing up so fast!*

I gather your dad is enjoying his post office. I am so glad that he is well and happy.

It's very quiet here without you, and the house seems so empty. I miss your piano-playing, and wonder if you are able to take it up again. I do hope so! How is Miss Lake? I hope she can teach you this term. Please tell her to send her bill to me. I am very pleased that you are learning those Beethoven Sonatas, and look forward to hearing them next time you come to stay. Let's hope there will be an opportunity for you to play the 'Emperor' Concerto one of these days, and I hope I shall be there to hear it when you do. I am sure Miss Lake must have been astonished that you were learning that. I know that one day you will play it as well as Evelyn used to.

Ruth scanned this first paragraph searching for some reference to Piers, but there was none. She had to turn over to find any mention of the Hardys. The letter continued:

The Hardys are much relieved, as it seems that their son is rather better, although of course he never will be well and will never come out of hospital.

It is even quieter here now that Piers and Julian have left. They went today after lunch. Their grandparents will miss them – and so shall I. Julian has been so kind to me. He has come round every day after you left to ask if I needed help, and yesterday he worked in the garden. The weeds have begun to grow again after all that rain earlier in the week. I baked a chocolate cake to thank him for all his hard work. He came in for tea yesterday afternoon, and it was very nice for me to have someone to chat with. He likes to talk about you, and said he is missing you a lot. He told me he thought you were "a super girl" and "such a sport" for playing cricket with him and for getting his brother to play cricket as well.

This morning I went to church with the Hardys. Mr Hardy took the service, but did not preach. Charles Stannard said he was sorry he had not seen you, as did my friends in the Mothers' Union. Perhaps we can go to church together next time you come.

I hardly saw Piers at all after you left. His grandmother said he played the piano all day and would not even stop for meals. She left his food out for him, and he grabbed a mouthful from time to time after the rest of the family had eaten. He didn't sleep well at night and wandered about the house in the early hours. Mrs Hardy is worried about him and thinks that next term's concert is putting him under too much strain. She wishes they had a better piano for him. Sadly I didn't hear his playing any more, because since the weather turned much colder soon after you left, the windows were closed.

Mr and Mrs Hardy asked me to say that they too are missing you and what a nice girl you are! I thanked them for taking us out on all those trips. We did have a lovely time,

*didn't we? What a pity the summer is over already! I am
looking forward to my visit to the farm next week. Rick is
going to come and collect me on Friday.*

*Write again soon please, and do come and stay at half-term
if you can bear to spend the week or even just a few days
with your old nan.*

Much love,

Nan

Those last paragraphs of the letter were incomprehensible.
What did they mean? Ruth had fondly imagined that Piers, not
Julian, would call on Nan – that he, not Julian, would offer
to help in the house or garden and would want to sit playing
Evelyn's piano, which was definitely superior to the piano next
door, reminiscing to himself the while about the idyllic time
they had spent together, playing scales, piano duets, individual
pieces, some Beethoven Sonatas and the 'Emperor' Concerto.
How wrong she had been, for this was not the case at all.
Undoubtedly he would be playing the piano whenever Ruth was
able to do so, but apparently he would be immersing himself
completely in the work, never thinking of communicating with
her through it. It sounded, from Nan's letter, that he had no
time for anything other than his performance. Maybe such time
as he had spent with Ruth had merely been a diversion from
what he should have been doing, so he was driving himself hard
to make up for what he had lost. Perhaps he thought of it as
time wasted, frittered away on a twelve-year-old girl who was
too young for him anyhow, when he had far more important
things to think about.

Despite his nervously whispered avowal of love for her, she
could not let herself believe for one instant that his extraordinary present behaviour might indicate any sort of love-longing
– that expression which had only just entered her vocabulary
from the pages of that horrid little red book. She was deeply
hurt and felt rejected, particularly because there was not one
veiled message from him in Nan's letter, in the way that she
had sent veiled messages for him in her letter to Nan. Maybe

he too had been given a little booklet, telling him to keep away from anyone for whom he felt strong feelings.

Dejectedly she let Nan's letter fall onto the floor again. She could suppress her tears of disillusionment, because the disillusionment was tempered with indignation that, unlike Julian, Piers was not bothered even to call on her nan with the tiniest, subtlest of messages for her. If that was what he meant by love, it was not worth having. Perhaps that little book had been right to insist that feelings of love-longing should be ignored: that was what she would try to do henceforth. With the courage of her convictions, she opened her books and set to work on her homework.

Lying on her stomach on the floor with her legs waving in the air, she learnt her French vocabulary and recited some Latin declensions. Tracing outlines in geography was not easy in that position, so she took her books and pens downstairs into the office, formerly the living and television room. It was a useful place in which to do homework, since it was very well ordered, with plenty of work surfaces; there were few distractions, and Shirley had said that she might use it after the shop had closed. Unlike the upstairs sitting room, which was left unheated and unused, it had a three-bar electric fire for use in autumn and a grate already laid with paper, wood and coal, where Dad lit a fire in winter.

She let her gaze wander through the large sash window to the garden outside. The trees were changing colour, already tinged with gold against a deep blue sky. Her earlier resolution forgotten, her mind strayed to Piers, wondering if he too were gazing out at the blue sky wherever he was, most likely back at school by now. Did he have his own piano in school? Would he be practising? These reflections brought on an urge to weep, but then, recalling her earlier wretched disappointment, she pulled herself up short, annoyed that she had allowed old habits to regain power over her. She was about to resume her tracing of the outline of the west coast of Canada when Shirley called her to supper.

The new routine proved more difficult in practice than in Miss Lake's well-intentioned theory. However hard she tried, even on a normal school day, Ruth was hard pressed to reach the primary school by five past four. By the time she had set up her music on the piano, which Miss Lake made sure to unlock for her in advance, she had at most fifteen minutes before she had to leave to let Miss Lake lock up the school. That gave Ruth five minutes for warming-up and scales, and ten for her pieces. On Thursdays in her lesson she had a good half an hour, and that time was mostly devoted to the concerto. The worst of it was that on two afternoons a week games filled the last two periods in school. Games never finished until four – if then – and afterwards it took ages to push through the crush to get into the cloakroom and change before rushing off to St Luke's. On those days she was lucky to have as much as ten minutes at the piano. It was better than nothing, but still frustratingly inadequate.

Then, one wet Saturday afternoon Shirley said: "You know, Ruth, you never tried that new winter dress on – the one I bought for you when Edith was here. There's nothing else to do in this weather, so why don't you go and try it on now?"

Ruth went upstairs to her bedroom and searched in the wardrobe for the new dress. It wasn't hanging on a hanger, but was still in its bag at the bottom of the wardrobe. Pulling it out, she examined the green knitted top above a flared plaid skirt. It was pretty, and she liked it. She tried it on and surveyed herself in the mirror. The colour suited her well, but she didn't like the way the fitted top emphasized her developing figure – not that there was much that could be done about that.

She went down to Shirley, who was thrilled with the purchase. "Ooh, you do look nice! Quite the young lady! Though I must say I don't like those school socks or shoes with that smart dress. We'll need to do something about those." She puckered her nose. "I know! It's too wet to go out to the shops this afternoon, but as soon as you come home on early-closing day, next Thursday, we'll go out and see what we can find." Thursday was the day of her piano lesson, but Ruth was in no position to argue with Shirley on those grounds, so had to agree with a very heavy and frustrated heart.

When Miss Lake heard of the disruption, she was unper-turbed. "Well, Ruth, these things are going to happen from time to time, so don't be upset." She checked her diary. "Ah, see here! One of my private pupils has to go to the dentist on Friday of this week, so I shan't be in such a hurry. Friday is all right for you, isn't it? I know it's a games day, but there will be plenty of time, no rush to get home, so we'll give Thursday a miss this week and have our lesson on Friday instead."

Although a lesson on the Friday was at least a possible solution to the problem, in fact it was only half a solution. By Thursday, Ruth's fingers were so agitated, as they always were in anticipa-tion of her lesson, that she had to sit on them in school. After lunch she went to the cloakroom and plunged her hands into a basin of cold water to see if that would calm them down.

On coming out of the cloakroom, she noticed that the door of the room opposite, the music room, was open. She peeped inside. There, on the other side of the room, gleaming black in the light from the window, stood the beautiful grand piano, bequeathed to the school during the summer holidays in the will of an old girl. Typical of the regimented discipline of the school, only pupils whose parents paid for individual lessons were allowed to use it. The lid was open, issuing an invitation to step into the empty room. Like a sleepwalker, she tiptoed across to the piano and placed her fingers on the smooth ivory keys. It was a heavenly experience. The temptation was too much for her; she sat down at the keyboard and began to play from memory, at first the Mozart Rondo 'alla Turca', then one of the Beethoven Sonatas that she had added to her repertoire.

Fully engrossed and completely happy, she did not hear the bell announcing the beginning of the afternoon lessons, nor did she notice the shadow of a large bulk standing in the doorway. Finally, when she reached the end of the sonata, she came to with a jump as she heard the dreaded Mr Barkley, true to his name, barking at her from the doorway.

"What do you think you are doing in here? What's your name, girl? Don't you know that this piano is out of bounds – it's for private use only?"

Her heart beat fast; she was terrified. Although she had been in his classes for a year already, he had not registered her presence, so she said: "I'm sorry, Mr Barkley. My name's Ruth Platt. I won't do it again."

She stood up quaking, afraid that he was going to hit her as he came into the room, for he was renowned for his bad temper. Against all expectation he smiled and, modifying his tone, said gently: "That's all right, but don't do it again." Ruth scuttled away like a frightened rabbit.

It was almost a pleasure to go home to Shirley at the end of the day. For once, she had had her fill of music and was pleased to be taken out to tea in the local department store. "Let's get on with our shopping first, shall we?" Shirley suggested.

They made for the Ladies' Underwear department, where Shirley bought her a pair of stockings, the first she had ever had, and a belt to hold them up. In the shoe department Shirley insisted that she should have a pair of black patent-leather shoes, "for smart", she said, though Ruth had no idea when she would ever wear them, since her footwear consisted normally of sensible school shoes, boots for games, plimsolls for gym and slippers at home in the evening. To the Opera House she had worn her summer sandals. Black patent-leather shoes demanded a very special occasion. Undeterred, Shirley then led her back to the Ladies' Underwear department, where she was fitted for the proper underwear to go under the new dress – which, to her relief, made her feel less self-conscious and less exposed.

Ruth was impressed by her mother's intuition, impressed that she had known what was needed to make her feel better about the dress. Shirley remarked: "You'll look like a Paris model in your new outfit!"

Ruth laughed. "I think that's going too far!" she exclaimed in delight at having won her mother's approval and thankful that Shirley, of all people, had unwittingly helped her overcome the trauma of her encounter in the music room.

Over tea Shirley showed more interest in Ruth's school than ever before. "So tell me, how do you like French?" she asked.

Shirley spoke with a slight accent and a rolled R, not unlike Mme Delplace's when she pronounced the word "French".

"Oh, it's good, I like it. Did you ever learn French?" Ruth asked, having detected the trace of an authentic accent.

Shirley nodded: "Yes, a bit." That was another revelation.

"Did you ever go to France?" Ruth said, pursuing her line of enquiry.

"Yes, a few times." That was extraordinary.

"Where did you go?" Ruth asked, her curiosity now truly aroused.

"Oh, I don't remember," Shirley said absent-mindedly, and then swiftly changed the subject. "I promised your dad we would have steak for supper, so we'd better get to the butcher's before they close."

"Oh, I know Harold Barkley – he's all right. His bark is worse that his bite!" Miss Lake exclaimed with a laugh when Ruth told her about what had happened in the music room on the Friday afternoon.

"I don't think so," Ruth replied glumly. "I think Mr Barkley has a very nasty bark and bite!"

"Well, perhaps he's simply living up to his name," Miss Lake joked. "Anyhow I'll be seeing him tomorrow at the Union meeting, so I'll talk to him about you then, and I'm sure he'll be pleased to help."

She greeted Ruth when they next met after the weekend with the news that it was all sorted out: Mr Barkley would indeed be pleased to see her and talk to her if she would ask for him at the staff room the following morning at a quarter to nine.

48

At eight forty-five on Tuesday morning it was with some trepidation that Ruth duly presented herself at the staff room door and knocked nervously. She had taken Miss Lake's insistence that Mr Barkley's bark was worse than his bite with a pinch of salt. With a name like that both his bark and his bite were bound to be dreadful.

She was taken aback when the door opened and the very same Mr Barkley came out smiling. "Ah, there you are, Ruth Platt! Elizabeth Lake gave you the message then?"

After all these years, it was as much of a revelation that kind, small, mousy Miss Lake had a Christian name and that it was Elizabeth, regal and sonorous, as it had been to learn that Mr Barkley's first name was Harold.

"Um, yes, she said I should come to the staff room," Ruth answered timidly, unsure of what to expect.

"Right, let's go along to the music room and I'll show you where to find the key."

He led the way smartly down the corridor, opened the music-room door and went over to a cupboard in the corner of the far wall. "This is where all the keys are kept, but they're not labelled, so any malingerer won't know which is which," he said, taking down a small brass key. "This is the one for the grand piano. I don't know why it wasn't locked the other day when you came in here, but anyone who plays that priceless piano has strict instructions to lock it when they've finished, and when I find out who left it unlocked, they'll be in trouble!" Here the more familiar side of his character came to the fore in a threatening growl.

He unlocked the lid and carefully lifted it, saying proudly: "This Model B Steinway is the most magnificent thing about this establishment. As you may have heard, it was left to the school in her will by a former pupil, an old lady who never played it. Whether anyone played it for her, history does not relate. When it came here in August, it was as good as new, and we must keep it that way. It does need a good pianist though; it's been waiting long enough! I'm sorry to say we are lamentably short of pianists at present. Not one good pianist in the school, can you believe it?" He surveyed Ruth keenly. "So you think you'd like to play?" She did not need to answer, because the beaming expression which lit her entire face was more eloquent than any words. "Well, there you go! You've got five minutes before the bell. Sit down and warm up with some scales before assembly. I'll leave you in peace, but lock it up and put the key away when you've finished."

On the point of leaving the room, he looked back and said: "I forgot to say, I've already told Miss Neville that you'll be here practising – and that's fine with her. I've asked her to sign you in on the register. And one other thing, I teach in here in the lunch hour on Fridays and every day after school, but you can come in here every break time and lunchtime, apart from Fridays, for as long as you like, and play to your heart's content." He left the room without another word before Ruth had a chance to thank him. At last luck was on her side!

The piano was a dream to play, with a beautifully smooth action, even touch, smooth pedals and a wide spectrum of tonal colours, even for playing scales and exercises. There were only a couple of minutes left before assembly but that did not matter, because she could come back at break time in the morning and in the lunch hour on Mondays, Tuesdays, Wednesdays and Thursdays. With a warm-up session before school, her practice time might almost amount to an hour a day, even an hour and a quarter, not counting the session at St Luke's.

She played scales in fifths and sixths, then locked the piano, put the key back in its place and, heaving her satchel, joined the lines of girls queuing up to go into the hall for assembly.

"Where were you, Ruth? Miss Neville left your name off the register, so we were wondering what had happened to you," Janet Otway whispered as she sat down with the Upper Fourth.

Given the impossibility of keeping the miraculous change in her fortunes completely secret, she merely replied: "I've been given permission to practise in the music room."

Janet frowned, "I didn't know you played an instrument."

"Well, sort of, I'm learning."

Janet's questions raised a dilemma for Ruth. Janet, also an assisted-place pupil, was her best friend: usually they wandered through the school grounds chatting at break times. What would Janet do now? A bright but shy girl from a poor background who had difficulty making friends with the other girls in the class, many of whom tended to be snobbish, she might well feel abandoned and lonely. Ruth had heard some of the others mimicking Janet's accent behind her back. Though she was not exactly a cockney, she had a long journey to school every day from somewhere in the East End.

A youngish new vicar had come to St Luke's church. Today was his first assembly at the school. "Let us ask God," he prayed, "that in all our doings today, He will help us to treat everyone we meet with kindness and consideration, that we will not hurt anyone and that we will look after those nearest to us."

At that precise moment, Janet was kneeling next to Ruth and bringing her troubling moral dilemma uncomfortably close at hand. "I'll come to the milk bar with you at break," Ruth promised Janet after assembly. "The thing is, I am a long way behind in my practising and I need to catch up." She did not specify the precise problem, but Janet showed no resentment.

At break time they went to the milk bar together and had a brief chat before Ruth dashed off to the music room; again at lunchtime, they talked while they ate and then Ruth swiftly made her way to the piano. She reckoned the price of friendship, including milk and lunch, at about twenty minutes a day. Janet proved to be understanding, undemanding and not overly upset; she said she always brought a book to read in the playground whenever she was on her own, that she was used to being alone and that books were her best companions. Ruth's conscience was assuaged, though Janet's loneliness was saddening.

According to her calculations, the session at St Luke's would with luck bring the total number of daily practice hours up to at least an hour and a half, minus the time she spent with Janet. She did not want to relinquish St Luke's, even though the piano there was rickety and battered, the touch worn and uneven, the action noisy; it was pathetically inferior to the Steinway, but she was fond of it as an old friend. Besides, she told herself, the more opportunities she had to play, the better, and anyhow it would be awkward as, ironically, questions would certainly be asked if she arrived home early.

Later that afternoon Miss Lake listened as, with sheer delight, Ruth recounted the unforeseen turn of events. "There, I told you so! Harold's not a bad old chap. But think, Ruth, what it's like for him in that school surrounded by those women all day – and some of them, by all accounts, very unpleasant!" Ruth's sympathy for Mr Barkley grew at the mention of "those women". Miss Lake then sounded a warning note. "I'm sure he'll want to hear you play before very long, so make sure your repertoire is in good order. I can lend you anything you like. Oh, I suggest some time we might have a look at the outer movements of the 'Emperor' Concerto."

The very next week Mr Barkley invited Ruth to play something for him. He waved to a row of piano music stacked along a high shelf. "Grab a stool to climb on and help yourself to anything from up there. I'll come and listen to you at lunchtime," he said. As she scanned the shelf, her eyes widened at the range of piano music it held. She pulled down a Schumann edition which contained 'Carnaval', with its magnificent 'Valse Noble', then she saw the Chopin Preludes and Nocturnes, the Brahms Intermezzi and the Schubert Sonatas, and so many more that she was hard pressed to choose among them. She felt like a small child let loose in a toyshop. She took her own – that is to say, Evelyn's – edition of the Beethoven Sonatas out of her satchel.

"Don't tell me you're going to play all those!" Harold Barkley exclaimed when he came in after lunch.

"Well, maybe I should try one or two perhaps," Ruth replied modestly. "Would you like to choose first, Mr Barkley?"

Whatever he chose, a piece of Brahms here, Schumann there, she played, concluding with the slow movement from the Beethoven 'Pathétique', which was her own choice. He sat impassively, neither applauding nor frowning, not even commenting, simply placing piece after piece on the music desk. Ruth enjoyed the challenge, for this was a situation she had already encountered with Piers, and that earlier experience had well and truly laid to rest any qualms she might otherwise have felt now.

Piers! No! She must not let herself be distracted by him at the moment. She pushed him to the back of her mind, but still his voice kept reappearing in her head, saying "Careful here, Ruthie, those runs are deceptive: watch out for the accidentals and the fingering" or "Make sure you've established the tempo in your head before you even begin". Weirdly, these instructions were not distractions: they were all relevant and helpful, prodding her to avoid the pitfalls and to make the right choices.

Half an hour later, Mr Barkley stood up. Brusquely announcing that he must be off to his class, he walked out of the room in silence, leaving Ruth to lock the piano. She sat still for a second or two, wondering what he thought of her performance. Did his silence mean that he was not pleased with what he had heard? Was he going to stop her practice sessions because her performance was not worthy of that very special piano?

She replaced the works on the shelf, glancing along to see what else she might play. A bunch of concerto scores caught her eye, among them the 'Emperor'.

"Ah, good!" she said to herself. "I won't need to bring that to school except on Thursdays for the lesson at St Luke's."

The same reasoning applied to the Beethoven Sonatas. Both volumes were on the shelf, whereas she had only the first one, Evelyn's, with her. So not only would she be spared the effort of transporting that and the 'Emperor', she would have the other sonatas readily available – that is if Mr Barkley allowed her to go on playing.

On the Thursday after her audition with Harold Barkley, Elizabeth Lake greeted her at St Luke's with a question. "Have you played for Harold yet?"

"Yes, yesterday. I let him choose, and I played whatever he wanted."

Miss Lake suppressed her astonishment. "I see. Fine. Do you remember, Ruth, I suggested last Thursday we might start playing through the outer movements of the 'Emperor'? You have that sublime slow movement already well mastered from memory, so we can leave that for a bit and work hard on the first and last movements. They're monumental, as you would expect, and very demanding, with lots of arpeggios, scales and trills. The beginning of the first movement is stunning," Miss Lake said, continuing her little lecture. "A majestic opening with piano and full orchestra; it was very unusual in Beethoven's day for the solo piano to come in at the start of a concerto, so you have to make it resound." Ruth nodded; she recalled Piers saying something similar. "With a bit of practice I think you can certainly play both movements, especially if I can sketch in some of the orchestral parts on my fiddle; then, as you know, they won't catch you out. Who knows, at the rate you're going, you might be playing the whole thing in a performance before long!"

Ruth grinned at the impossibility of this, her teacher's preposterous suggestion, but did not divulge that she had practically worn Evelyn's records out on Nan's wind-up gramophone; nor did she let on that she and Piers had often succeeded in playing through the whole concerto together, not without breaks for discussion, but in a fairly concentrated fashion. Mostly in their morning sessions in the church hall, he had played his piano reduction of the orchestral score to allow her to learn the solo piano part, but she had also tried to play bits of the orchestral score to allow him sufficient practice of the solo for his school concert. There was no reason for him or his granny to be concerned about it because he knew every inch of the music intimately, so his excessive anxiety, as recounted by Nan in her letter, was unnecessary. She herself had nearly consigned the entire piece to memory, so there was no reason for him not to do the same.

"It is a big piece for someone as young as you," Miss Lake remarked. "But then, you are lucky to have very long, flexible and strong fingers, and a natural technique, so perhaps you wouldn't find it too much of a strain." Like Harold Barkley, Miss Lake did not comment on her playing, leaving her with the troubling impression that she had acquitted herself badly, so the next day in the mid-morning break in school she practised the runs and the trills from memory to the exclusion of all else.

The door to the music room was open and briefly she had the passing impression of a shadow standing in the doorway, but she didn't take much notice of it, because she was too absorbed in the music. By the time she looked up from the piano, the shadow had melted away. The day was Friday, which meant that there was no chance of practising in the lunch hour, so she went outside with Janet, collecting shiny conkers and shuffling through fallen leaves.

From the moment he came into the classroom the following week, Harold Barkley was unusually animated. "Now, girls, I have something new for you today and for the next couple of weeks! We are going to listen to a piece of music and then analyse it. Any guesses as to what it might be?" Although somehow Ruth already knew what it was going to be, she did not raise her hand. The other girls hazarded a couple of guesses – The 'Blue Danube' Waltz? Fingal's Cave? – both of which were without a doubt off the mark. "I'll have to tell you then," Harold Barkley announced with satisfaction. "No, on second thoughts, I won't do that; I'll let you listen first and then see if any of you can tell me what it is." He switched on the record player and placed an LP on the turntable.

After three minutes or so of the monumental opening *Allegro*, he lifted the needle and surveyed the class. Ruth kept her head down. "Now, who can tell me what that was?" he asked. No one volunteered an answer. "Oh, come on, girls, have a go!"

He was showing signs of exasperation. "Will nobody even tell me who the composer is?" His eyes were burning holes in the top of her head, but still she kept her own eyes down. She glanced up fearfully and saw with some dismay that his earlier enthusiasm was waning. She knew that he was going to ask her.

At last she was about to raise her hand when suddenly, in front of her, Janet's hand shot up. Mr Barkley was startled. "Ah, you, what's your name?"

"Janet Otway, Mr Barkley."

"All right, Janet, who do you think the composer is?"

The question was delivered in a bored tone, conveying the assumption that there was no chance that this girl with the slight cockney accent had any hope of giving the correct answer.

"I think it might be Beethoven," she replied shyly.

"Ah, very good!" The bored tone changed to one of amazement. "Any idea what the work is?"

"I think, sir, it might be a piano concerto."

"Yes, yes, we're getting warmer, any idea which one?"

Janet's voice dropped to a nervous whisper. "Is it number five, the 'Emperor'?"

"Well done!" Mr Barkley heaved a sigh of relief. "At least there's someone in this class who has a grain of musical intelligence and education in her!" he barked.

With the air of a man discouraged by the rebuttal of his best attempts to bring life and enthusiasm into his teaching, he carried on with the lesson, pointing out, exactly as Miss Lake had done, that the introduction of the piano right from the outset was experimental in the 4th and 5th piano concertos and paved the way for other nineteenth-century composers to do the same. He went on to explain the structure of the movement, its simple chords but complex thematic transformations and variations.

The key soon changed from the strong home key of E flat to B major though written in C flat, which involved four extra flats put in as accidentals, with sharps or flats written in beside each individual note rather than in the key signature. This, he said, was a real hazard for an incompetent soloist, because he (he didn't say "she") would have to think himself into that key to be able to cope with it. And if he failed to do that in advance, he would make a mess of the whole thing. (Here he grinned, trying to give the impression that this comment was intended as a joke, since no one in the present class would ever be likely to find herself in that situation.) Then the key changed again rather surprisingly to a more uncertain, questioning key, B minor, before reverting to C flat major in a hesitant passage which itself was resolved more firmly in B flat major before returning to E flat.

Here, he said, the orchestra was full of confidence and was making a big show, while the piano was less assertive, more doubtful. By the time he began to drone on about Beethoven's use of the sonata form in the movement, most of the class were gazing out of the window or surreptitiously doing homework under their desks. Disgruntled, he gave up, put the record back on the turntable and sat down.

Ruth and Janet were without a doubt the only two girls in the class who were giving the music their full attention. Ruth listened intently, following every recurring cadenza-like passage in the piano part and noting the trills and the dynamics, everything in fact that contributed to a performance that was widely divergent from Evelyn's. She wished she had the piano part in front of her to check exactly how this pianist's interpretation differed from the one she knew so well.

"How did you know what that was?" she asked Janet after the class. "We listen to a lot of music at home on the wireless," she replied, "and my father particularly likes Beethoven."

"That's nice. So does mine. Do you mind if I go and practise straight after lunch today? I have such a lot to do." Ruth asked.

"That's fine, but thank you for asking," Janet replied, readily granting her the freedom she so desired.

When her chance came to escape to the music room after lunch, Ruth lifted down the score of the concerto and propped it up on the piano. She had already practised her scales, and intended to study the piano part of the *Allegro*, the first movement, without actually playing it. Nevertheless, her fingers couldn't resist the temptation to experiment a little with those majestic chords, the arpeggios, the trills and the mini-cadenzas. She stopped to reconsider the best way to manage a particular trill. How she wished she might listen to Evelyn's recording to compare it with the one she had just heard! She was wondering if Miss Lake had it among her collection when the door opened.

Mr Barkley strode in, his eyes bulging, looking every bit as terrifying as he had on that first occasion when he had caught her playing the Steinway without his permission. She tried to smile at him without success.

"So you've never heard the 'Emperor' Concerto, then?" he asked, his voice laden with sarcasm. She kept quiet. "Well, what sort of pianist are you if you can't recognize the 'Emperor'? You didn't even know that it was Beethoven, did you?" Still she kept quiet. "Look here, if you're not prepared to help me by showing a little enthusiasm in my classes when I try to get those potato-heads to respond, I'm not sure that I want to help you by allowing you to practise here!"

Ruth regarded those beautiful, beckoning ivory keys with longing. How could she tell him that she didn't want to push herself forward in the class? She did not want to be seen as a show-off. She bit her lip hard, waiting for the storm to pass and wondering: "Why was music so fraught with difficulties? Not the music itself, for that ethereal, wordless communication touched on the divine, but the people who had some sort of involvement with it or reactions to it? They – Shirley, her dad, Piers and now Mr Barkley – always created some sort of trouble, the only exceptions, being Nan and Miss Lake."

Harold Barkley came across to the piano and leant over to see what was on the music desk. "What have you got here? Did I say you were allowed to use this?"

At last Ruth found her tongue. "No, I'm sorry. I saw it there and wanted to have a look at it – after the problems in class, you see."

"Oh, you would, would you? Well, let's see if you can play it, then!"

This was going to be yet another sort of test, not an audition, but a fully fledged examination, and her instinct told her that her life as a musician depended on it. If she acquitted herself well, maybe she would be allowed to continue to practise on the grand piano, but if not, the music room would be for ever closed to her, and without it she stood no chance whatsoever of becoming a professional pianist at this critical stage in her education.

He took a score out of a cupboard marked "Private"; she recognized the piano reduction of the orchestral score, identical to the one Piers played from. "I'll play some of the orchestral part over here on the upright, and you play the piano solo on the grand!" he thundered, seating himself at the old piano on the other side of the room. She anticipated that this was going to become a competition, between piano and orchestra, between herself and Harold Barkley, and she was right. She disliked this approach intensely, but at least she was well prepared, having practised the chords of the first movement before he arrived.

He opened the copy. Without any warning he gave an upbeat and then brought his fingers down on the keys in the massive opening orchestral chord. With fingers poised, Ruth knew exactly what to do, because Piers had trained her for this sort of occurrence. She had been watching Harold Barkley out of the corner of her eye and was ready for the arpeggios, scales, trills and cadenza passages for the piano, exactly as she had practised them, before the next *tutti* chord, in which the piano also participated. She played on for the full two minutes of the introduction, then observed the rests meticulously while following the orchestral part, of which Harold Barkley gave a passable impression.

Scarcely needing to read the score, Ruth's brain and fingers were in control, directed by a voice in her ear: it was Piers's voice, and it was firmly but gently reading the music with her, encouraging her and warning her of what lay ahead. The twenty minutes of the Allegro passed by in a flash, followed by the tranquil simplicity of the Adagio, in which Ruth excelled and at the end of which the short, subtle modulation led into the Rondo, the final movement. The bell rang for afternoon school as they came to the end. Harold Berkley stood up, gruffly muttered something about his next class and walked out. Ruth closed the piano, put the music away and went to her French lesson. She was exhilarated by the music, but dizzy from the tension.

Elizabeth Lake was shocked later that day when she heard how Harold Barkley had treated her. "That's appalling! Do you want to go on practising there if he behaves like that?" she asked anxiously.

"I don't think I've any choice," Ruth replied, "but it does take the pleasure out of the music. You never know what he'll be like. One minute he's fine and the next he's horrible!" She wondered if Mr Barkley was ill, like Shirley, who used to be subject to similar mood swings. "I'll carry on for the time being," she said. "Well, at least till the end of term. Then maybe I'll pluck up the courage to let my parents in on my secret. I think perhaps they might cope with it now. Anyhow, I'm going to Nan's for half-term and I shall practise there all the time, because it'll be winter, so when I come back I shan't be quite so desperate."

Certain that she had acquitted herself extremely well, she was not unduly upset by Mr Barkley's behaviour, although it was unpleasant and had spoilt their rendering of the 'Emperor'. Beethoven was bigger than Harold Barkley, and whatever discomfort she had felt was beginning to wear off, particularly because she had that very day played through the whole Concerto with the orchestral accompaniment in the face of a very critical audience, even if that audience consisted of only one person, Harold Barkley. Or had there been two people present? She felt Piers's influence so strongly that he might have been there in the room with her. Her mind wandered along painful pathways. Where was he? What was he doing? Despite all the disappointment and her resolution not to think about him, she longed to see him more than ever and was counting the days till half-term, only two weeks away.

She woke from her reverie to discover that Miss Lake was talking to her. "If I were you," she suggested, "I'd leave Harold

Barkley to himself for a day or two. Don't go into his room, don't practise there. Come in here as quickly as you can after school, and I'll see if I can squeeze another five minutes out of my timetable for you." Miss Lake was so like Nan – sympathetic, helpful and always ready to put herself out to make life easier for others. Her next remark proved that she even felt sympathy for those who, in Ruth's opinion, did not deserve it. "Of course," Miss Lake said, "Harold has had rather a hard time. Like all of us he imagined he was going to be a famous musician, but that was nothing more than a dream. When you think of all the millions of children in the world who learn to play the piano, how many of them become concert pianists or even professional musicians? Only a few hundred actually become famous. And how many achieve lasting fame? Well, I'd say only a handful – your Aunt Evelyn, Rubinstein, Horowitz, Paderewski. Poor old Harold! Look at him now: a music teacher in a girls' school surrounded by mean-spirited Philistines, and living at home with his elderly mother who won't let him have a life of his own." What she delicately refrained from saying to Ruth was that poor old Harold was also rather too fond of the bottle. "Maybe, too, he was being deliberately cruel to be kind, trying to find out whether you would be able to handle the pressures of being a professional musician."

For the best part of a week, Ruth gave Mr Barkley a wide berth; she steered clear of his room and did not encounter him until the class music lesson the following Thursday which, as usual, took place in the music room. He was agitated and kept mopping his brow and wiping his nose. As soon as he sat down, he stood up and then sat down again. This week's subject was the Grieg Piano Concerto. He contented himself with putting the record on the turntable and sitting back to listen. Afterwards he simply asked the girls whether they had enjoyed the performance. There was a general murmur of appreciation. "That opening is magnificent!" someone commented. "I liked the slow movement: it's so mournful," Janet dared to say on finding the courage to join in the discussion, which continued enthusiastically till the bell rang.

Ruth had not contributed to the discussion, but had sat quietly listening to the others. She hoped to slip out of the room unseen, but Harold Barkley called her, asking if she would spare a moment to help him put the record player and records away. This was a weekly duty that fell to one or other of the girls at random. She agreed, the while trying to suppress her reluctance. She had put the records into their cupboard, ready to beat a hasty retreat, when he addressed her: "Look Ruth, I know I was a bit sharp with you last week. That class was so depressing."

He struggled to get the words out. "I wanted to say I'm sorry. You played superbly!" Ruth began to feel sorry for him, but said nothing. He went on: "I'm arranging the end of-term concert. Usually it's a rather sad affair – the orchestra is hopeless – but I wondered if I were to get a better orchestra together, bringing in some of my colleagues to play, would you like to perform the 'Emperor' for us? You seem to know it extremely well already."

Ruth was overwhelmed at such an unexpected request, and at first her voice stuck in her throat. "Oh! Oh! That would be extraordinary! I… I would l-love to! Thank you very much," she stuttered at last.

He patted her on the back. "Good! That's arranged then. I'm so pleased!"

Elizabeth Lake was the first to hear the news. "This is the start of your professional career, Ruth! I am thrilled for you, and of course I shall be there! I know you'll give an excellent performance." She consulted her indispensable diary, which went everywhere with her. "Did Mr Barkley give you a date for the concert?"

"No, not yet," Ruth replied. "I imagine it will be in the last week of term."

"That's good. We have enough time to polish the details to produce an excellent performance. Let's get started, shall we?"

Ruth was humming to herself when she arrived home after her piano lesson.

"You're cheerful, Ruth," Shirley remarked. "Had a good day?"

"Yes, it was all right, actually."

Dad came out of the post office. "Nice to hear you singing, Ruth," he observed. "I would have sworn that was Beethoven, but maybe I was mistaken."

"Now why would she be humming Beethoven?" Shirley teased him. "You're the only one round here who hums that sort of thing. What was it, Ruth?"

"Oh, I don't know, something I heard on the wireless, I expect," she replied, hoping that would be an end to the discussion.

However, Dad, ever persistent, remarked: "That's odd; it sounded to me like a snatch of the 'Emperor' – and I haven't heard that on the wireless lately. Where did you pick that up?"

"Maybe it was at school I heard it, you know, in the music class; we listen to records," Ruth answered evasively.

To her dismay, Shirley, pursuing her own train of thought, then chipped in, prolonging Ruth's suspenseful agony: "The 'Emperor' – what's that?"

"It's a piano concerto by Beethoven, the most famous one actually," her husband explained.

"Oh, have I heard it?"

"You might have, I don't know; Evelyn performed it, and made a recording of it," John responded nonchalantly, in an effort to gloss over his sister's name in a matter-of-fact manner.

Shirley nodded, "Ah, I see," she said quietly. "I don't expect I have, then. But you know, it's a funny thing: I think I heard something like it on the wireless, on the Light Programme, the other day. It reminds me of something..." And with a pensive frown she fell silent, until after some reflection she added brightly: "But I should like to hear it properly one day – what did you say it was called, the 'Emperor'? – one day, perhaps, when we have a record player, and that won't be so long in coming, because we are doing very, ve-e-ry nicely." She drew out the vowels of "very" as far as they would stretch to prove her point.

Ruth had been waiting on tenterhooks to see how the topic would end. For one dreadful moment she cowered, fearing that the mention of Evelyn and the piano might provoke a cataclysmic storm. The tension passed quickly, so she was able to relax and start on her homework. The one advantage of so much practising in school hours and then in St Luke's after school was that her schoolwork did not suffer: there was plenty of time in the long evenings for homework, even allowing for a walk in the park or a game of tennis on the municipal court with some of her old friends before darkness fell. Doubtless, had there been a piano in the house and had circumstances been different, she would have spent every waking minute at the keyboard, unable to drag herself away. In such circumstances she would have incurred the wrath of her teachers.

When the final bell rang on the Friday, marking the start of half-term, Ruth could hardly wait to get out of school for, in just over twenty-four hours' time, she would be arriving in Norhambury. She still had to pack and secrete her music away in her suitcase without her parents knowing, and this was best done while they were both still at work in the shop. It was too much to expect Nan to be at the station to meet her, but that didn't matter, since she could catch the bus that would take her all the way to the front door of 10 Beech Grove.

As she had written in her weekly letters, she was greatly looking forward to seeing Nan and helping her in any way possible, but – and this she did not write – she was apprehensive about what she might find. The news had not been good lately: Nan, who never complained about anything, had more than once mentioned in her letters that she felt so old and good for nothing on account of her leg. Nonetheless, Ruth was optimistic that at least she would be able to cheer her up, perhaps even take her into the city for tea in the corner of their favourite restaurant looking out over the stalls of the market. Doubtless the Hardys would be willing to help with transport.

Deep down, however, the excitement mounting in her had little to do with Nan. For all his negligence of her – not so much as one carefully phrased message for Nan to pass on – and despite all her efforts to forget him, Piers was still not only constantly at the forefront of her mind in all her waking hours, but in every nook and cranny, every corner of her being. Dreams of him pervaded her existence, sometimes lending it vivacity and sparkle and imbuing all her playing with authority and sensitivity; at others it would cast her down, drowning her in despair at the hopelessness of her situation, at the same time lending her playing a dark foreboding and defeat.

The practice sessions had now developed into rehearsals; Harold Barkley regularly joined her at break times and lunch hours to play as much of the concerto in piano duo as they could fit into the time available. He played the keyboard reduction of the orchestral score and had become almost jovial, appearing to have acquired a new lease of his professional life. He had set with a will to assemble the best possible orchestra from among his friends with a token number of the better players from the school, and his lessons had undergone an extraordinary transformation into lively sessions which the class attended with pleasure and interest.

Elizabeth Lake was also involved in the concert in a more prominent capacity than teacher to the soloist, since she was to be on the concert platform on the night, leading the ranks of the second violins. "Ruth, look what you have let me in for!" she joked. "You know your part better than I know mine, and I shall have to spend the whole of half-term practising the fiddle!"

With her in her role as piano teacher rather than fiddler, Ruth concentrated on technique, strengthening her fingers to avoid cramp in the long runs up and down the keyboard. On those days when a black cloud of despair pervaded her playing, Elizabeth Lake reprimanded her sharply: "Look, Ruth, I know you have problems at home, but you mustn't let them intrude into your playing. Your role is to serve Beethoven, not to use him for your own ends." She added more gently: "It would be much better if we talked about whatever is troubling you rather than let it get in the way of your performance."

Ruth nodded gratefully, but limited herself to saying unconvincingly: "Sometimes I think I'll never manage this performance; there's so much to learn."

As half-term approached, she counted the days till her departure, fidgeting at supper and toying with her food. Her dad had asked, "What's the matter, Ruth? Are you worried about going to Nan's alone? Would you like me to come too?"

"No, no, Dad," she answered at once. The last thing she wanted was to be accompanied by a parent, for then how could she play the piano? Not only was the lure of Piers's presence drawing her to Norhambury but also the sheer delight of unlimited access to the keyboard. "I'll go and check that I've packed everything."

She ran upstairs two at a time and into her bedroom. For the umpteenth time she opened her suitcase, feeling down to the base through her clothes to make doubly, trebly sure that the precious scores were there where she had packed them after school yesterday.

"I hope you've put in enough warm clothes: it will be chilly, you know," was Shirley's practical comment when her daughter returned to her place. "Are you taking your new dress? You haven't worn it much, have you?"

"That's a good idea!" Ruth agreed, and ran upstairs again, thinking how nice it would be to appear in front of Piers in that lovely green dress with her new shoes, looking for all the world like a teenager. That night she struggled to fall asleep, until at last, as a distant clock chimed one in the morning, her eyes closed.

The journey went entirely to plan, even to the extent that the bus drew up at the stop outside the station only five minutes after the train had arrived. It was disconcerting to find that it was already growing dark at five o'clock. In London one barely noticed the changing seasons or the vagaries of the clock: it was light in summer and dark in winter certainly, but with streetlights everywhere, the darkness was not as oppressive as it was here in the provinces.

"Beech Grove!" the conductor finally called out. "I think tha's what you asked for, Miss," he said in the soft accent she loved so well.

"Yes, thank you. I'll get off here."

It took her a little while to find her bearings in the pitch blackness as the bus drove away. There was no silvery moon: the single street lamp had failed, and none of the houses on the other side of the road showed any signs of life. Nor was there any traffic other than the bus to light her path, and that had now drawn away from the stop, heading out into the open country.

She crossed the road, attempting to make out familiar shapes – the high hedge in front of Nan's house for instance, or Grandpa's shed at the end of the driveway – but all was black, except for a distant glow, so faint that she had not seen it from the other side of the road.

"At least there's a light in that house," she said to herself. "But which one is it?" She put out a hand, groping for a gate, and touched cold metal. She pushed it and the gate swung open with that familiar creak which warmed her heart. She had arrived after all, and this was Nan's house! As she stepped into the driveway, she cast her eye over the fence into the darkness towards the Hardys' house. There were no lights on there, but she encouraged herself with the thought that there was nothing unusual in that. They might have gone into the city in the afternoon, possibly staying for a concert in the cathedral in the evening, so of course their house would be sheathed in darkness.

It was odd though that Nan's house was so dark, especially because Nan knew that she was coming. She stood on the step peering through the moulded glass in the front door, trying to detect the source of that single light. Deciding that it must be in the kitchen, she rang the bell. She waited and waited, then rang the bell again. After an age, the hall light was switched on and a shape came slowly towards the door. With the rattling of a chain and much fumbling with a key, it was opened.

"Ruthie! Oh, I'm so sorry! I was sound asleep and completely forgot the time! Come in!"

Ruth was shocked. Was this wizened little person leaning on her stick with her wispy white hair falling about her shoulders really her nan?

"Come in, Ruth! Don't stand there looking as if you've seen a ghost! I know I must look a mess. I washed my hair after lunch and then went to sleep in my chair. I'll go and tidy myself up, but you come in first." The sound of Nan's voice was reassuring; it was definitely her, after all. Ruth stepped inside and gave her a hug. "Well, well, my little Ruthie – you're bigger than me now. Do you remember how I used to pick you up to

hug you when you were little? You'll be picking me up soon!"
Nan slowly climbed the stairs. "Don't you worry about me,
I'm all right!" she called down. "You take your coat off and
warm yourself by the fire."

The house was so cold that Ruth did not feel at all inclined to
take her coat off. In the dining room, where the fire had gone
out, she looked around for the coal scuttle, but it was empty.
Out in the hall, however, buckets, scuttles and hods full of
coal were lined up along the wall. There was also a basket of
logs and a box of wood chippings. She collected a handful of
chippings, a couple of logs and a coal scuttle, and took several
sheets of newspaper from a pile in the kitchen, where a lamp
gave off the glow she had seen from the road. By the time Nan
came downstairs, she had lit the fire which was beginning to
blaze in the grate.

"This is terrible! You come to stay, and the first thing you
have to do after a long journey is light the fire! I am so sorry!"
Nan was mortified, but with her hair in place in a neat bun
she nearly seemed herself again. "Ah, I always have difficulty
standing up straight when I've been asleep for a long time,"
she remarked as she straightened her bent body. "Now, you
see, I'm nearly as tall as you after all!"

Kept at bay by anxiety at the singular nature of her arrival,
sleep was slow in enveloping Ruth into its folds that night. She
had never travelled alone in winter before, nor had she arrived
in the dark, but worse than either of those situations was the
state in which Nan had come to the door – lame, dishevelled
and undeniably old. Her cheerful assertions that she was fine
rang hollow, because it must have slipped her mind that she
should expect to see her granddaughter that evening, despite
the letters from her son to that effect. Even allowing for her
disability, no preparations had been made in advance, and the
high tea which Nan later placed on the spotty tablecloth had
been hastily rustled up with Ruth's help in the kitchen. There,
Nan explained, she kept a lamp switched on, so that there was
always some light in the house if she happened to fall asleep
in her armchair in the afternoon. This meant that she often

fell asleep in the afternoon for long periods. The tea consisted of scrambled eggs on toast followed by bread and butter and jam. There was nothing wrong in this, but it fell far short of Nan's usually high standards.

Ruth made up the bed in her bedroom and, taking her courage in both hands, lit the geyser for the first time in her life; she lit it not for herself, but for her grandmother.

"Yes, that's so kind. I'd like to have a bath; it's a bit difficult for me to reach over to light the gas," Nan explained as she hobbled into the bathroom.

Ruth had placed the little stool by the bath for Nan to climb on, and made sure that the plank of wood was in place behind the taps to enable her to climb out. Ruth went straight to bed, but lay awake until she heard Nan emerging from the bathroom. "Night night, Nan!" she called loudly. Nan reciprocated, adding with a catch in her throat: "I'm so happy you're here, Ruthie!"

Not only did anxiety at the decline in Nan's health keep Ruth awake, but also the lack of any sign of life next door. Before going up to bed she had used the excuse of shaking the crumbs off the tablecloth to open the back door and peep out into the darkness to see if the neighbours had returned from their excursion. It was now long after ten, so one might well expect them to be back. The house was cloaked in darkness as it had been when she arrived, and the car was not in the driveway. The unpalatable truth was that the Reverend and Mrs Hardy were not at home, so despite all her high hopes, Piers and Julian – especially Piers – would not be there either. As her courage, which had borne up so well so far, began to sag, Ruth sobbed silently into her pillow, oppressed by the growing intimation that the longed-for week was not going to live up to her hopes.

She woke late. True to form, she went straight to the end of the bed to look out of the window. A sorry sight met her eyes. The garden, so beautiful when last she had seen it at the end of August, was now brown and bare, dank and bleak. Denuded of their leaves, which covered the emerald lawn in a dark matted carpet, the trees at the bottom of the garden stood out as lank, ghostly skeletons against the pale sky. An untidy mass of sticks, faded flower heads and leaves withered on their stalks had taken the place of the joys of that golden summer: the delphiniums, sunflowers, marigolds, gladioli, geraniums, poppies and lupines had lost all colour, and with it their individual identities, all merging together in an unrecognizable jumble of decaying detritus. The rambler rose had detached itself from the roof of Grandpa's shed and was tumbling onto the lawn.

Where had Ronnie Parr been all this time? she wondered – Ronnie Parr with all his promises of tending the garden, bringing in the coal, keeping an eye on Nan and generally ensuring that all was well? Possibly he had brought in all the coal and wood that was lined up in the hall, but recalling her dad's scepticism when the name of Ronnie Parr had been mentioned, she suspected that he might have been right after all. Without a shadow of a doubt she would have her work cut out to bring order out of all this chaos and still have time to practise for the concert.

Straight away she went to the bathroom, had a quick bath, cleaned the fittings and then inspected Nan's bedroom. It was tidy, but the bed was in need of clean linen, so she changed the sheets and put the greying ones to soak in the bath. Downstairs Nan was attempting to prepare breakfast, hampered by a lack of bread.

"We can have a cup of tea and some cereal instead," Ruth suggested, looking in the larder for milk and cornflakes.

"If you would go over to the post office first, Ruthie, and collect my pension, if the Hardys haven't already brought it to me, then we'll have some money to spend and we'll be able to buy bread. They know you in there: I'll write them a little note," Nan said.

"No, Nan, that won't do; it's Sunday today," Ruth reminded her.

"Oh, goodness, is it? Well, what time is it, dear? We'd better be getting ready for church then." It was ten o'clock. Her concern to be in church on time had quickly erased any anxiety about the empty state of the kitchen cupboard. "Mr and Mrs

Morrison will be here soon. You remember them, don't you, Ruthie? They took me to the Mothers' Union when you were here in the summer." Ruth did indeed remember the kind couple who had collected Nan that Tuesday afternoon, when she had stayed at home on the pretext of taking delivery of the groceries. Nan was flustered, "If I'd known it was Sunday I wouldn't have drunk so much tea! I shall have to go upstairs again."

Poor Nan! She was beset by one problem after another: the pain in her leg was intolerable and slowed her down; her hearing had deteriorated again despite the hearing aid, and now, into the bargain, the fact that she did not know which day of the week it was implied that she was losing her memory as well. Having put the sheets and the towels through the old mangle in Grandpa's shed and then hung them out to dry in the lean-to, now only a sad reminder of her former cabin, Ruth fetched her coat, made up the fire and locked the back door.

The Morrisons rang the bell while Nan was still upstairs.

"Hello, Ruth! – That's your name, isn't it? We met in the summer, didn't we?" said Mrs Morrison, greeting Ruth warmly when she opened the door. "Don't you hurry, Mrs Platt," she shouted up the stairs, "there's plenty of time. We are a bit early."

Mr Morrison followed his wife to the door carrying a basket and a shopping bag and saying: "Here's your nan's shopping, young lady. I know the Hardys usually take an order to the grocer's for her, but it seemed to us that it was easier to do it all in one go. Would you put it in the larder? Let me see..." he said, opening the bags and peering into them, "there's a loaf of bread, a pound of butter, some margarine and six eggs, a bag of flour and a bag of sugar, a tin of peas, a pound of carrots, a cabbage, a few sprouts, tomatoes and a cucumber, some potatoes, six sausages, two lamb chops, half a pound of ham and a piece of stewing beef. Oh, and a couple of tea cakes and some tea. You'll be needing those!"

Ruth was astonished: though this was an answer to prayer, it caused her some embarrassment. "I'm afraid we haven't any money to pay you, because I only arrived yesterday and can't get Nan's pension till tomorrow," she said hesitantly.

"No, no, that's not a problem. Your nan gave us one pound ten shillings last Tuesday, when we took her to the Mothers' Union, and that was more than enough. Look, here's some change." Mrs Morrison handed Ruth nine shillings' change.

"It's very kind of you—" Ruth began, but Mrs Morrison interrupted her: "It's not a problem. We are all very fond of your nan and want to look after her. We are helping out while the Hardys are away."

Ruth's heart dropped like a stone in her chest. She leant against the newel post at the bottom of the stairs hoping that Mrs Morrison would not notice her pallor as the blood drained from her cheeks. Mrs Morrison was not looking at her however: she was watching Nan descending the stairs. She drew breath and whispered, "Dear, dear, she can't go on living here: it's too difficult and too dangerous for her! And see how loose that carpet is!" Ruth did not hear this last observation, because she had taken the shopping into the kitchen and was storing it away in the larder.

She sat in the back of the car on the way to church, staring out of the window at the gaunt landscape, bare trees and brown fields under a threatening sky. It had all been so different in the summer. Would it have looked otherwise if Piers had been here with her? she wondered, and then decided that it most definitely would. His presence would transform any landscape: wherever he was, the sun would shine out of an overcast sky. He would light a wintry landscape and warm her whole being, however chilly and hostile the outside temperatures.

Such fancies persisted throughout the service. She could not remember when she had last been in a church – and how she wished she had been there when Piers had played the organ last summer! Had she been there then, she could imagine him there now, seated on the organ bench, astonishing the congregation with his prodigious voluntaries! That image of him would definitely have brought him closer. She had to accept the miserable, undeniable conclusion that he had not after all come to stay for half-term as he had promised so fervently. And what was worse, she was at an utter loss to know what had kept him away, because there had been no communication between them – and that was her own fault. A light had been extinguished within her, and with it all her enthusiasm for music, the piano – even for life itself.

She tried to listen to the sermon in the hope of finding comfort there, but the Vicar was expatiating at length about the sin of idolatry, which didn't seem to have much relevance to her – until that is she heard him say: "My friends, let us examine our own lives and see whether there might not be some element in them, money perhaps or possessions, or some person which we value and think about more often than we think about God."

Ruth duly examined her own life and quickly concluded that indeed there was both an element and a person therein whom she thought about much more often than God. Music for her enshrined the divine both within her and without. But wasn't music part of God? she asked herself, in which case she thought about Him all the time, except of course when she was thinking about Piers, and she truly believed that Piers had been God's gift to her. If that were the case, though, why had that gift been taken away from her now?

But whatever the other aspects of her attachment to Piers, she was, as a result of knowing him, able to approach that music, that sublime experience which was transforming her life. Music after all might not be so far removed from God, for here in church it was an intrinsic part of the service, played and interpreted with dedication by Charles Stannard, Evelyn's former fiancé. She began to understand the powerful feelings that Charles had held for Evelyn and his devastation when she was no more. How would she feel if she were never to see Piers again?

The Mothers' Union were out in all their mothballed force. She nodded politely to each of them as they enquired of Nan: "So this is your Ruth? Hasn't she grown? She's lovely!" Nan beamed in delight at their approval, whilst Ruth was touched, no longer repulsed, by these elderly ladies. They cared for each other, taking a keen interest in each other's families and each other's welfare. "Well, how are you today, my dear?" "Are you feeling better this week?" "Will you be able to come to the meeting on Tuesday?" "Is there anything I can do for you? Shall I send my son, Ralph, to chop some wood for you?" were the typical questions that circulated among them after the service was over. Whenever these questions were addressed to Nan, she fielded them like someone twenty years younger who had no need of any help whatsoever. She did not of course admit that the Morrisons had just brought her shopping in for her, although it was well known that they gave her a lift because of her infirmity, her reduced mobility being impossible to conceal.

Ruth came out of the church with different attitudes from those she had taken in with her. Her parents were not church-goers, except on those occasions when her dad had accompanied Nan to the village church. Then she had rarely gone with them, preferring to stay at home to practise the piano in her dad's absence. She had attended school assemblies and school services in St Luke's, both when she was in primary school and now at the high school, but had simply regarded those as part of the routine. She had learnt about biblical teachings from divinity lessons, but that was a school subject much like any other.

On this wintry October Sunday, through certain aspects of the service, she discovered a clearer, more personal under-standing of the meaning of those religious observances. The vicar's words had struck home, though perhaps not in the way he had intended: the strength of her feelings for Piers and her passion for music were, in truth, identical. When she was playing the piano, she was in touch both with a higher spiritual element – God perhaps – and also with Piers. Both were unseen, all powerful, the source of all inspiration and well-being. For her they were the fount of all goodness. Then there had been Charles Stannard's playing, which brought a far more persuasive, more moving religious force into the service than the spoken word, though when those spoken words were combined with music, as in the St John Passion that she and her dad had once listened to at Easter on the wireless, the effect was overwhelming in its tragedy.

Last but not least, she had been touched by the kindness and care shown towards Nan by the other members of the congregation, not least the old ladies of the Mothers' Union. Their show of interest in her was loving and generous; it was a heartfelt offer of help from people who were not far short of needing help themselves. She wished that Nan were not so obstinate in refusing their assistance. It transpired that she had only allowed the Morrisons to do her shopping for her because the Hardys had asked them to do so in their absence, and the Hardys had only been allowed to do it because they had taken it on by degrees, buying small items at first when they happened to be in the city or at the grocer's, then progressing to bags full of weekly necessities, or orders for delivery placed with the grocer and the greengrocer when they happened to be passing. This was all paid for out of Nan's pension which, with her agreement, the Hardys usually collected from the post office. Thus by stealth Nan was kept supplied with goods and with money, all the while living under the delusion that she had maintained her independence.

The state of the garden, however, was the clearest indication of that delusion. "I'll go and clear up the garden a bit while the lunch is cooking," Ruth announced decisively later that morning.

"Would you, dear? That is kind. I'll peel the potatoes and some carrots and watch you working," Nan replied, settling herself on her stool in front of the kitchen window. "Would you just light the oven for the chops before you go out?" Having confronted the geyser the previous evening, Ruth was less intimidated by the oven, though she fairly threw the match inside, hoping that it would ignite something when she turned the gas on.

Leaving the chops slowly browning on a low setting, Ruth went out to do battle with the sad graveyard of the summer that the garden had become. She worked hard, raking the leaves into a neat pile, cutting back the dead stems in the flowerbed and trimming the edge of the lawn. Branches had fallen from the trees during an autumn gale, and these she sawed into pieces and collected up for kindling. The work was warming under the cold, drear sky, and by lunchtime she had made a good impression: the garden certainly was tidier and less depressing. Nan knocked on the window summoning her in for lunch.

"That's a good morning's work you've done there, Ruthie!" she exclaimed. "Somewhere I've got some bulbs to plant. Mrs Hardy bought them last week. Do you think you could plant them this afternoon? It would be so nice to have lovely daffs and tulips in the spring!"

"Yes of course, I'll do that," Ruth replied willingly, "but I was wondering if I might play the piano some time too."

"Play the piano?" Nan queried with a blank expression, to all intents and purposes having utterly forgotten Ruth's passion for the instrument.

"Yes, you remember, I played it a lot in the summer, and you gave me some of Evelyn's music."

"Evelyn's music?" Nan mused.

"Yes, yes, the first volume of the Sonatas by Beethoven and the 'Emperor' Concerto."

"Oh, did I? Fancy that! I didn't know we had all of the Beethoven Sonatas and the 'Emperor' Concerto... Did Evelyn really play those?"

Ruth made a great effort to be patient, but was frightened to discover that Nan was having a blank spell: she hoped it simply meant that her grandmother needed a rest. "If you don't mind, Nan, I'll light the fire in the front room, and while you're having your rest, I'll plant the bulbs for you," she said patiently but firmly. "And then when you wake up I'll do some piano practice and you can tell me what you think of my performance."

"Oh that will be good! Nan exclaimed. "Oh, I remember, that nice boy from next door came to help you, didn't he?"

"Yes, that's right! Piers!" Ruth responded with pleasure at the chance to mention his name.

"No, that wasn't his name," Nan insisted. "I'm sure his name was Julian."

Ruth opened the front room, lit the fire, planted the bulbs and brought the damp washing indoors to hang on an airer by the fire while Nan slept. She then fetched the music from her suitcase and ran her fingers over the keys, silently attempting to simulate scales. Next she studied the score of the 'Emperor', trying out the runs of scales, all without making a sound. Nan slept on and on by the fire in the dining room, until the grey sky outside was black.

At about five o'clock, nearly twenty-four hours after her arrival, Ruth decided to take her a cup of tea. "You mustn't keep waiting on me!" Nan protested as she slowly came round from her deep sleep. She had slept for nearly three hours. "Now then," she suddenly announced. "You said you were going to play me some of those Beethoven Sonatas that Evelyn used to play, and you say you've learnt the 'Emperor'! That is exciting! Are you going to perform it somewhere?"

Ruth was mightily relieved to discover that Nan was her old self again, that it was possible to talk sensibly to her and take her into her confidence as in days gone by, to tell her about her most recent lessons with Miss Lake, the developments in school and Harold Barkley, and last of all about the forthcoming concert in which she was to be the soloist.

"That's just as it should be, I'm so pleased!" was Nan's ready reaction. "Mind you, I'll have to come down to London to hear you play!" She shuffled into the front room to listen to her granddaughter's encounter with Beethoven.

"I've rather neglected Schubert this term," Ruth confessed, "because I'm so involved with Beethoven."

"That doesn't matter," Nan observed, "but let's hear what you can make of him."

Ruth warmed up and then moved on to Schubert, to the G major Sonata, which she had been wanting to learn for some time.

"I love this: it's like a song," she remarked.

"Well, of course it is," Nan said with a chuckle. "Don't you know that Schubert wrote over five hundred songs? Anyhow, if you are going to play it, it's a relaxed, flexible hand and finger-work that you need for all those rippling passages which must be absolutely legato, as if they were being sung. As you know, whatever you're playing, if your hand is stiff you won't be able to do that, and it will begin to ache or even go into a cramp, so shake your hands and let your fingers flop before you begin to play." She looked carefully at Ruth's hands and said: "Mm – I have noticed that your fingers are stiffening up, more than they should, so take care of them. Oh, and let me see! I remember Evelyn saying something about 'arm weight', I think she called it. She said you only use arm weight and tension when you want to make a big sound. You will strain your muscles if you use arm weight all the time, so don't do it."

Ruth obeyed, amazed at the transformation in her grandmother. Nan was fully in control, speaking sensibly and with authority too. Each of her teachers, Elizabeth Lake and Harold Barkley – for he now imparted much musical wisdom in their sessions together – each of them had brought different aspects to her playing, but Nan brought an element that neither of them could possibly have accessed. It was undoubtedly an element that had its roots somewhere in her family background, an element to which Ruth related automatically.

The image of Piers standing behind her and influencing her playing had somehow been effaced and replaced by the image of Evelyn, transmitted through Nan's pertinent comments and advice. Nan refused to sit in an armchair, but insisted on having a kitchen stool brought close to the piano to be able to watch Ruth's hands.

"Now, let me see," she pondered as Ruth came to the end of a passage, and then she spoke in an unfamiliar, commanding tone: "I think Evelyn used to play that bar like this. If you just move over I'll demonstrate what I mean." She leant over to the keyboard and ran her aged fingers lightly down the keys. "You see, it is even more legato than you could have imagined."

There appeared to be a third person in the room, directing the activity at the keyboard and voicing her opinions through Nan. Ruth hoped that this was not all a dream which would evaporate as soon as she awoke, but she wasn't asleep, and it wasn't a dream. They worked together for hours, until with a stifled yawn Nan glanced at the clock, still swinging to and fro under its glass dome.

"Goodness! Is that the time?" she exclaimed. "It's nearly time for bed, and we've missed supper."

"Never mind," Ruth replied happily. "We had a good lunch. I'll go and make us some tea and toast. I think there might even be some tea cakes in Mrs Morrison's shopping!"

"No, first I want you to play me the 'Moonlight' Sonata. Don't you remember? You promised me that at the end of the summer holidays!" Nan demanded with pleading eyes.

As always at Nan's, Ruth settled into a routine, though this time it was different from any previous routine. She would help Nan in the house in the morning with the cleaning, washing and cooking, occasionally going out into the garden to sweep up more leaves or tidy another flower bed. Fully prepared for Nan to become vacant and confused just before lunch, she tried to make sure that a substantial meal was ready before the inevitable lapse into incoherence. After lunch Nan always fell asleep by the fire, but said that the piano would not disturb her as her slumbers were so deep. Doubtful at first, Ruth was persuaded to believe that she meant what she said, so she closed the door of the front room and sat down at the piano.

Even when she was alone, there was always the sensation of a benevolent presence in the room, guiding her, leading her fingers, whispering ideas of interpretation and performance practice – and, above all, encouraging her to give of her best. Once, she was sure she heard a voice in her ear saying: "I gave my first public concert when I was twelve, though it was Mozart, Concerto K. 467, not Beethoven. That too has a sublime slow movement. Try it some time!"

When Nan woke up, she asked her: "When did Evelyn give her first public concert?"

Nan wrinkled her brow. "I seem to remember she must have been twelve; it was in the Old Hall, and she played Mozart, though bless me if I can remember which one!" Later that afternoon Nan announced: "I know what it was! It was K. 467!"

Towards the end of the week, since there was still no sign of the Hardys – nor, for that matter, of Ronnie Parr – Ruth decided that she ought to tear herself away from the piano and go out to collect Nan's pension, as she had privately agreed with the Morrisons for the duration of her stay, and do some shopping.

Nan was hesitant about Ronnie Parr. "I'm not sure what's happened to him. I think he might have hurt himself, but I don't really know; I expect he'll be back when he's better," she said, with a singular lack of concern.

Ruth was becoming increasingly agitated, all too conscious that she would be going home to London the following Sunday, and as things stood, she was afraid to leave Nan on her own. The memory of her arrival was uppermost in her mind. Nan was so much better now, so much more alive – it would be dreadful if she sank back into that disoriented, unbalanced state. Yet Ruth did not know what to do for the best. If only Nan had a telephone!

Having collected the pension, she walked the first part of the way to the grocer's with the intention of phoning her dad for advice from the call-box on the corner. She put coins in the slot and dialled the number. The phone rang in the post office, but there was no reply. Oh, of course, it was Thursday, early-closing day! Her dad and Shirley must have gone out for the afternoon. For once she would have been happy to hear Shirley's voice at the other end, but was not granted even that blessing. The bus drew up at the next stop, so she climbed aboard and set off for the grocer's.

As Mr Carter was busy with another customer when she came into his shop, he summoned his assistant, a man of about her dad's age.

"What can I do for you, Miss?" he asked pleasantly.

"I've brought my nan's order for this week," she announced.

"Who is that for, Miss?"

"It's for Mrs Platt at 10 Beech Grove."

A light of recognition shone in the man's eyes. "So you're Mrs Platt's granddaughter, are you?"

"That's right," Ruth replied, anxious not to become involved in the sort of long-winded conversation that Nan used to conduct when ordering her meat or groceries.

"I'm so glad to meet you!" the man said effusively. "Well, I'm Bernie Parr, Ronnie's son, and I've been hoping to meet someone from Mrs Platt's family to explain why my father hasn't been able to help Mrs Platt these past weeks. He had a fall, you see, and hurt his back, and he still can't get out of bed, let alone do any work." The man was thoroughly genuine: this was not an excuse for his father, simply the truth that he was telling. "As you can see, I work here, and I have to go out on deliveries, but when I can I call on your nan and bring in as much coal and wood as there are containers for, and I hope that lasts her for at least a week. She said someone would be coming to stay, so I needn't come this week, but I did fill up all the coal scuttles at the weekend. I didn't know it was you Miss, or I should have come just the same this week. It's too much for a young girl like you."

He was a kind man, and his apologetic manner encouraged Ruth to think better of the Parr family. "I'm very glad to meet you, Mr Parr," she said. "I have to go back to London on Sunday, and I was very worried about leaving Nan, but now that I've met you, I feel happier."

"Don't you worry," he reassured her. "Those nice neighbours of hers will be back soon, and the people at the village church are very good at helping, so between us we can keep her going!" He added: "And tell that father of yours not to worry either, I remember him from primary school. Very clever he was!"

With a lighter step Ruth delivered an order to the butcher, then bought some bread and two doughnuts before catching the homeward bus. It was not yet dark when she got off the bus and crossed the road. She stopped suddenly outside the Hardys' gate, arrested by the sight of their car in the driveway. Piers's absence had been a heart-rending disappointment when she had first arrived: now it was a shock to find that the house was inhabited again. Over the days the initial pain and longing for him had begun to metamorphose into indignation at being cheated by him. His image at the piano had also shrunk under the stronger influence exerted by Evelyn's shadow.

Nonetheless when, on entering the house, she heard voices in the kitchen, her legs felt weak and her hands trembled as she carried the shopping down the hall. Holding her breath, she approached the kitchen door, but heard only three voices – Nan's, Mrs Hardy's and Mr Hardy's – which meant that Julian and Piers were not there. Breathing again, though still feeling weak at the knees, she pushed the door open and went in.

"Ah, Ruth, how nice to see you!" the Hardys both said at once. Mrs Hardy continued: "We were afraid we might miss you, but your nan says you are staying till Sunday. We just came in to let her know that we are back. We are so pleased to find her looking so well. You must have taken very good care of her, Ruth."

"Come on, dear," Mr Hardy said, interrupting what he predicted might develop into an unending discussion. "We must go and unpack and leave these people to have their lunch."

"Yes, of course, but I just wanted to ask if you would like to come and have a cup of coffee tomorrow morning?" Mrs Hardy smiled expectantly at them both. "Then we can tell you all about the concert!" So that was where they had been! At Piers's concert – of course Ruth wanted to hear about it!

"Thank you. That would be lovely!" she replied, before the blood rose to her face and before Nan raised any objections.

"Oh, and we've got some lovely photos to show you as well!" was Mrs Hardy's parting shot.

Although Piers was not with his grandparents, it had been a good day for Ruth. Not only had she met Bernie Parr and was persuaded that Nan was in good hands; not only were the Hardys back and intending to resume their kindly watch over her: even better was their invitation to coffee the following morning, their promise to tell Ruth and her nan about Piers's concert and, better still, the prospect of seeing the photos, presumably those from Piers's box camera taken in August. The only wisp of cloud over Ruth's reviving spirits was the fear that an embarrassing pink flush might rise to her face and suffuse it throughout the morning.

In addition, that afternoon Nan came up with an excellent suggestion, even though she had taken only a very short nap. "Why don't we put Evelyn's records of the 'Emperor' on the old gramophone and you can play along with her?"

"That's a brilliant idea, Nan!" Ruth exclaimed. Having already played her scales and exercises, she brought out the heavy antique gramophone, wound it up, inserted a new needle into the arm and placed the first record on the turntable. Then, while she sat at the piano, Nan lowered the arm onto the record. As the piano had no part in the almighty opening orchestral chord, Ruth had no problem in determining the beat from the invisible conductor's baton and was ready to let her fingers fly at the end of that first bar. She played from memory as she knew that Evelyn must have played. The experience would have been very gratifying had there not been so many stops and starts for turning the record over, putting a new one on the turntable, winding up the mechanism and inserting a new needle, but Nan was transported with delight.

"That's the best treat I could have had!" she exclaimed with tears in her eyes. "My daughter and my granddaughter playing together!"

The coffee morning was also a success. Ruth succeeded in keeping her blushes under control while Mrs Hardy told them how well Piers had played in his concert. Mr Hardy said that he had been completely involved in the music, and played the concerto with a magisterial command. Ruth promised herself that she would look up "magisterial" in the dictionary later.

"Yes, that's true," Mrs Hardy agreed, "but I must say, I am worried about him. He looks so pale and thin. He seems to live in another world. He scarcely spoke to us at all – just to say 'Hello, Granny and Grandpa...' and then, when he was at home with us and his family, for just one day at half-term, he shut himself in his room or in the piano room all day. You remember what he was like in the summer, don't you?" Ruth certainly remembered how he had behaved towards her in the summer. As far as she was concerned, he had been magnificent, but apparently that was not what Mrs Hardy meant. "Well,

Mrs Hardy continued, "he was like that, only much worse. I know he's not satisfied with his piano, and I'd like to be able to buy him a new one, but we can't afford that just at present."

"Let's get the photos out, shall we?" Mr Hardy suggested, changing to a lighter note. The photos were all that Ruth had hoped for. There were group pictures at the sea and in the garden, and photos of the Hardys and Julian with her and Nan, in which Piers was absent because he was behind the camera. The four of them pored over the snaps trying to place the exact location, to decide which beach was in the background, what the weather was like that day, whether there had been a wind or how hot it had been. There were also individual portraits of each of them, including a picture of a shame-faced Julian in Nan's back garden after sending his cricket ball flying through the window, at which they all laughed.

The next photo was a flattering picture of Ruth smiling happily at the photographer. "I think Julian took that one," Mrs Hardy said, pointing to it.

Ruth knew better, but did not disabuse her. She remembered smiling ecstatically at Piers, who had said: "Now, Ruthie, give me one of those lovely smiles of yours!"

"Here's another one that Julian took," Mrs Hardy said, handing her an equally entrancing photo of Piers himself. Again Ruth did not contradict her, although she knew that that one was a photo she herself had taken. She wished she had the courage to ask for a copy of it, along with one or two others of course, but her courage failed her.

"So you're off back to London tomorrow morning, are you, young lady?" Mr Hardy enquired.

"Yes, that's right," Ruth confirmed.

"I'm sorry we can't take you to the station, but my husband is preaching in the morning," Mrs Hardy said. Then, lowering her voice to a whisper, she added: "We think it might be better if we take your nan to church with us after we've seen you off on the bus. She can come to lunch with us, so there'll be plenty to keep her occupied. Oh, and by the way, I nearly forgot, our boys are coming here for Christmas with their parents. Is there any chance you might bring your parents to stay with your nan?" At that a hot flush, impossible to control, rose in Ruth's cheeks.

The wait at the bus stop the next morning was less traumatic for both Nan and Ruth than it might otherwise have been. They had talked the previous evening about the possibility of Christmas at Beech Grove.

"I don't know that your mother will want to come here for Christmas," Nan had remarked dubiously, "but tell her she would be very welcome."

"I'll talk to them both about it, and if they don't want to come, maybe I'll come alone," Ruth suggested. This suggestion was actually more of an assertion, for she was determined to spend Christmas at Nan's, whatever else might happen or whatever plans other people might have. The term had another five or six weeks to run and would end after the concert, ten days more or less before Christmas, so – her heart leaping with unutterable joy – she clung to the hope that she might see Piers after all, even if briefly. According to his grandparents, he had gone away on a music course after only one day at home at half-term, so the same might happen again. Patience would be required, though her time before the end of term would be filled with rehearsals and preparations for the concert, not to mention the usual run of school work.

The bus was coming into view when Mrs Hardy suddenly announced: "Oh, my Goodness, I've forgotten the photos!" She rushed back into her house and emerged as the bus drew up to the stop. She thrust an envelope into Ruth's hands, saying: "The boys wanted you to have these copies of the photos! I should have given them to you yesterday, but it went clean out of my mind!" Ruth stuffed the envelope into a small brown leather handbag that Nan had given her – one which had belonged to Evelyn – thanked Mrs Hardy, hugged Nan and climbed onto the bus.

There had been no time for lingering or fond farewells, simply a hasty shout of "See you at Christmas!" and a wave of the hand as she sat down. Mrs Hardy had her arm comfortingly round Nan's shoulders, and Mr Hardy was already starting his car.

50

After dwelling on every detail of the photo of Piers for much of the train journey, Ruth had put the envelope containing the photos back in her handbag. She would have preferred to store it away in her suitcase with her music, but that had already been lifted onto the rack above her head in the crowded compartment by a helpful fellow passenger. Even though the photos had come as a delightful surprise, the lack of an accompanying note was a disappointment. It might have been Julian, not Piers at all, who had sent her the pictures. Her refusal to allow Piers to write to her she regretted constantly and considered to be even more of an excessive precaution, which hurt her more than it hurt him apparently. There were no two ways about it: her obstinacy had put him off communicating in any way at all, so that she had only her memory of him, her imagination and the sensation of his ethereal presence hovering behind her when she played the piano. She concluded that if the two families were to meet at Beech Grove at Christmas, allowing her to see Piers, however embarrassing Shirley's behaviour might be, it would definitely be better than the intolerable limbo in which she strung out her existence at present.

As the train rumbled through the London suburbs, she began to consider how best to answer the multitude of questions that her dad would want to ask about his mother. Should she tell him of the shocking state of affairs that she encountered on her arrival at Beech Grove, or would it be kinder not to burden him with all that information – which in any case might be rather disloyal to Nan, whose embarrassment about her lapses and moments of confusion had been painful to witness? After considering all the possibilities, she was at least prepared for some of the questions, which she fielded as diplomatically as possible. Dad, of course, did want news of Nan as soon as she arrived.

"How is she? Is she managing, do you think?"

"Well, Nan was rather poorly at first, but she cheered up no end, and we had a good time."

"Did she go out?"

"Not much: the weather wasn't very good, but those kind people, Mr and Mrs Morrison, took us to church, and they took her to the Mothers' Union on Tuesday afternoon." (They had lunched on fish and chips from the shop early on Tuesday in order for Nan to have her nap early, in time for the Morrisons' arrival.)

"So you didn't go into the city?" Ruth shook her head. "That's a pity: she would have liked that," he observed.

"No, no, it was fine; we were happy at home."

"What about her shopping?"

"The Morrisons did it last weekend, because the Hardys, the new neighbours, such kind people, were away. I went down to the shops as well, so she has plenty to eat." The inevitable question followed. "Has Ronnie Parr called to see her? Has he done the garden?"

"Ronnie Parr has hurt his back, so he's out of action, but his son Bernie calls to bring in a week's supply of wood and coal, and he's so nice. I'm sure he'll keep an eye on her too." That answer did not satisfy Dad.

"There, what did I say? I knew Ronnie Parr would think up some excuse!"

Annoyed by this remark, Ruth was about to reprimand her father when she changed her mind. Reassurance was the better policy, so she simply said: "She's managing very well. I cleared the garden, and there are lots of very kind people looking after her – and, as you know, she is very independent."

Shirley came up from the stockroom as Ruth and her dad were about to sit down to tea. "Oh, hello Ruth! We are going to have fireworks after supper!" The ebullience of this welcome gave way to the more serious question which, as Shirley probably knew in her heart of hearts, should have taken priority over the fireworks. "How's your nan?"

This general enquiry presented Ruth with the ideal opportunity to clear up the big question without further ado. "She's all right, as I was telling Dad, but she would like us all to go and spend Christmas with her. The journey here would be too much for her, but we would have a lovely time at Beech Grove."

Ruth tried not to sound over-enthusiastic, because that might well produce the contrary effect, and anyhow she wasn't sure what state Nan's house would be in by Christmas. Astonishingly, Shirley did not reject the idea out of hand, but said: "Well, let's think about that. I suppose just for once it might be possible if we leave here on Christmas Eve; I'll ask Pa to come over and deal with the papers and the post office after Christmas. He's not particularly bothered about Christmas, and business is rather slack afterwards. You know, I think it might be nice to get away to the country even in the middle of winter."

Dad had not been taking any notice of Shirley's reaction, for his thoughts were elsewhere. "I think maybe I ought to go for a weekend fairly soon, just to check up on things and make sure she's all right," he said uneasily, apparently unconvinced by Ruth's carefully prepared report. "Do you think you could cope here, love?"

"Yes, of course," Shirley replied at once. "If you go on a Friday, I can run the post office on the Saturday morning and Ruth will help out in the shop – won't you, Ruth?" As usual, Shirley had it all arranged in the twinkling of an eye. One simply had to agree with her.

Delighted with this quick resolution, Ruth stood up to take her belongings up to her bedroom; in so doing, she brushed against the strap of her handbag hanging from the back of her chair and it fell to the floor. The bag was open, and all its contents, including the photos, which spilled out of their envelope, were scattered across the floor. She bent down to clear them up in the hope that neither of her parents had noticed, but Shirley was quicker off the mark.

"Ooh, look, snaps!" she exclaimed excitedly. "Let's have a look, Ruth! Who are all these people?"

"Oh," said Ruth airily, as she collected up the snapshots, "these are Nan's neighbours; they gave me these photos this morning before I left. They're pictures of the summer holidays," she added with as much apparent indifference as she could summon, though conscious that this might be the providential start of preparations for the Christmas visit to Beech Grove.

"Ooh! So who's that tall gentleman?" asked Shirley, poring over the snap at the top of the pile.

"That's Mr Hardy, and that's his wife next to Nan. He's a clergyman," Ruth replied, searching for all the gratuitous information she could find to keep Shirley satisfied.

"That's nice!" Shirley went on. "And who's that boy with the cricket bat?"

"That's Julian, when he sent the ball through Nan's dining-room window. We all laughed so much..." Ruth replied drily without enthusiasm, as if the laughter had been an inappropriate aberration which she would prefer to overlook. For her part she was not thinking about the broken window at all, but about the irony that at last one of her parents, and the most unlikely one at that, was showing interest in her summer holiday, when in fact she wished Shirley wouldn't. The latter then plied her with questions about the incident: was anyone hurt? Was there a lot of broken glass? Was the window soon mended? and so on, which Ruth fielded while she tussled with the rest of the photos. She tried to assemble them into a neat pile and put them away in the envelope, but Shirley would not let them go so easily.

She still held on to a handful and studied each one with amusement. "So you went to the sea, did you?" she asked, thumbing through them.

"Oh, yes! We had a lovely time," said Ruth cagily.

"Oh, look, here's one of you; you do look happy!" Shirley went on as she picked up one of Piers's portraits of Ruth, who nodded nonchalantly, anxiously anticipating the appearance of the photo of Piers which, she knew, was about to come into view. Shirley picked it up, gazed at it intently, then dropped it and the rest of the photos and ran out of the room, leaving Ruth to collect up the scattered snaps up off the floor for the second time.

Her mother had not gone back into the stockroom but, white as a sheet, had run upstairs, followed by Dad, who had been glancing briefly at the black-and-white pictures over their shoulders. He came down a minute or two later.

"Shirley says she's not feeling very well – a sudden attack of indigestion – so she's gone to bed. She'll be all right. I think I'll just write a note to Mother and let her know I'll go and see her in a couple of weeks' time." The plans for fireworks were shelved indefinitely.

Shirley was still in bed when Ruth left for school the next morning. Dad said he was worried about her and was thinking of calling the doctor, which seemed unnecessary for a simple tummy upset, but when she came home after her piano practice at St Luke's, Shirley was not there and Dad was running the post office and the shop single-handedly.

"Ruth, would you come and help out for a bit, please?" he called. "I do need to make a phone call."

He hurried into the office while Ruth took over selling the evening papers at one counter and stamps and postal orders at the other. Where could Shirley be? Surely not in hospital? Looking flustered, Dad came in several minutes later to serve the lengthening queue at the post office. After the final flurry of last-minute customers, he pulled down the blind promptly and locked the door.

"You mother's in hospital," he announced, "and I'm off to visit her."

"Why, what's the matter?" Ruth asked.

"I don't know," was his only answer as, wearily but urgently, he donned his mackintosh. "Would you make us some supper, Ruthie? I'll be back about eight."

He was more cheerful when he came in at a quarter past eight. "She'll be all right," he said. "They are adjusting her medications; there are some new drugs out now, and this might be a good time to review her situation. They don't know what has caused this relapse, nor do I, nor in fact does she. She was happy enough about going to spend Christmas at Beech Grove, wasn't she?"

"Yes," Ruth agreed, "she liked the idea." Speculating on whether Shirley's condition might have been caused by something she had eaten or some malfunction of her drugs, they ate the simple supper that Ruth had cooked. Nonetheless, although she did not tell her father, Ruth harboured the strong but mysterious suspicion that Shirley's collapse was in some way connected with the photograph of Piers.

For the next week Ruth felt obliged to come home from school early to help her dad run the business. Fortunately for her, Harold Barkley had changed the time of the private lesson he gave on Fridays in the lunch hour, thus freeing up more practice time for her.

"Your playing has entered a new dimension, Ruth," he complimented her when he heard her play on the Monday after half-term. She refrained from telling him either about the sensation of Evelyn's presence in her sessions with Nan, or about playing along to Evelyn's recording.

On the Thursday afternoon she went as usual to her lesson with Elizabeth Lake, only to find that her reaction was similar. "I don't know what you've been doing over half-term," she observed, "but you sound like a solo concert pianist instead of merely a player. We just need to put the finishing touches to your performance, because you'll soon be rehearsing with the orchestra."

Shirley came out of hospital the following week, ostensibly well and anxious to take over the running of her business again. Dad tended to fuss over her, which she did not like. "They've discharged me and said I'm well enough to do whatever I want. I've got my medicines, so I'm coming back to work!" she scolded him in peremptorily warning tones.

Her mother's return and her impatience to take up the reins again proved providential for Ruth, because orchestral rehearsals were about to begin at four o'clock on two afternoons a week. Thanks to Shirley, she was not only able to resume her well-established routine of practising in the primary school in addition to all the practice she was doing in school: she was also able to be present at the rehearsals after school without having to make excuses to anyone.

On those two afternoons, Miss Lake came to the high school to play the violin instead of supervising Ruth's practice at St Luke's. Furthermore, she took it upon herself at the first rehearsal to shield her young protégée from any hostile stares or jealous remarks from the older players. "She's very gifted, but this is her first performance with an orchestra," she explained in an attempt to disarm criticism. However, Ruth was fully confident of her solo part and fully conversant with the orchestral part, so she did not need protecting; indeed, it was the opposite when it came to rehearsing with the orchestra, because various irritating concessions had to be made to the instrumentalists, whose playing was not as fluent as her own and frequently lagged behind the beat.

In her opinion they should have been trying harder to keep in time with Harold Barkley, the conductor, and consequently with her, because after all, she watched him like a hawk. "I'm afraid, Ruth," Mr Barkley said one afternoon after a particularly difficult rehearsal, "we're going to have to slow down the pace to accommodate the orchestra – there's no other way. If we don't, the whole thing will fall apart. I'm sorry, because that's not good practice, and I know it's not how it should be done. I expected better of my colleagues."

To Ruth's astonishment, he continued in the same vein until he went red in the face and sounded heated: "I know it's not how your aunt played, and it annoys me intensely, but in spite of bringing in my professional friends, this is essentially only a part-time amateur orchestra. Some of the players don't appear to know one end of their instrument from the other!"

He wiped his face with his handkerchief as a mark of his own frustration. Miss Lake on the other hand held a more sanguine opinion. "I think Harold is setting too fast a speed from the outset," she said. "If he were to take a more moderate tempo, everyone would be able to cope. It might be slightly problematic for you, because you have learnt to play at a quicker speed. It won't do you any harm to make a few adjustments though, because playing with an orchestra is usually a challenge, and a skill that a concert performer will develop over a lifetime."

Compromise prevailed. Harold reluctantly set a slower tempo, Ruth played at the new tempo and the orchestra speeded up so that they all met somewhere along the way.

Shirley revelled at being back in her shop, which was filling up both with Christmas goods and with customers. Many came in blowing their noses; others coughed and sneezed, handing moist documents, envelopes and money to John across the counter, with the result that as the weekend of his visit to his mother approached, he began to feel feverish and unusually tired, and by the Friday had no choice except to stay in bed.

"Can you send Mother a telegram please, telling her I can't come?" he croaked to Shirley. "I certainly don't feel very well, but more importantly I don't want to give her the flu."

Consequently, instead of going on an inspection tour of Beech Grove, he stayed at home, initially on the Friday in bed, and then by the Sunday wrapped in a blanket by the fire. Tentatively on the Friday morning Ruth asked if Shirley would need her to help in the shop after school. Shirley dismissed the offer with a wave of the hand.

"No, no," she declared, "I'm fine. The queues are never too long. The customers know I'm on my own, so they just have to wait patiently either in the post-office queue or the shop queue. They don't mind."

However, on the Saturday morning, the shop was so busy that Ruth's help was required after all. At the end of the morning Shirley said: "Well done, Ruth! I'm going to take you out to tea this afternoon! You deserve a treat."

"What about Dad?" Ruth asked.

"Oh, he'll be fine. He'll be asleep all afternoon, but we can bring him a nice cake home for tea."

As they took their places at an empty table in a smart new tea shop, fully equipped with potted palms, Shirley jovially remarked. "I like our little tea parties, don't you, Ruth?"

Ruth nodded in partial approval. She had been reflecting on what a strange coincidence it was that she was beginning to go out on such jaunts with her mother at almost the very time that they had ceased to be possible with her nan.

Shirley picked up a menu, "What shall we have? What would you like, Ruth?"

"I fancy a meringue, please," Ruth replied unfolding her napkin.

"Good idea! I'll have that too. I've never been very good at making those." Ruth could not recall, even in the distant depths of her memory, Shirley ever attempting to make meringues, but let that pass as insignificant. "Is there anything else you'd like? What about some sandwiches?"

"No, thanks, just a meringue will be lovely."

"Well, let's treat ourselves to some China tea, shall we? I do like those delicate fragrances," Shirley said.

The waitress came to take the order, which Shirley developed into a veritable charade. She did not simply ask for two meringues and a pot of China tea, but on enquiring how many types of China tea were available, prevaricated over her choice and finally settled for lapsang souchong. She also wanted to know how many types of sandwich were on the menu: the list of fillings, cucumber, ham, cheese, egg and tomato was entirely predictable, despite the excitement attending the recent opening of this new establishment, but then she wrinkled her nose and said: "No, I don't think I want sandwiches; what about you, Ruth?"

"No, nothing more for me, thank you."

Not tempted to change her mind, Ruth was amused rather than irritated by her mother's theatrical pretensions. Shirley would not have been out of place in one of those television dramas that she had taken to watching so regularly of an evening after she had closed the shop and done the accounts.

They sat in silence for a couple of minutes after the waitress had gone away with the order. Shirley wriggled uncomfortably to find a better position on her plush chair, but the discomfort proved not to be connected with the chair, because she then leant across to Ruth, who saw a blush rising in her complexion, not the sort of embarrassing overall redness that suffused her own face whenever Piers was mentioned, but an attractive colouring in her cheeks, so much more attractive than the awful make-up she had worn during Cousin Edith's visit.

"Ruth," she began shyly, like a small child asking for a sweet. Ruth had never known her mother ask her for anything important, let alone in this timid manner, since Shirley normally gave orders in the expectation that they would be promptly obeyed. "Ruth," she began again, "do you remember?…"

Here she was interrupted by the waitress bringing the tea. "Would you like me to pour, madam?" the waitress enquired.

"No, no, thank you," Shirley waved her away impatiently. She herself poured two cups of tea and passed one to Ruth; then she offered her a meringue. "As I was saying," she began for the third time, "do you remember how all those photos fell out of your bag that afternoon you came home?"

Ruth was on her guard. Was she going to be interrogated about the photos? Piers would inevitably feature in the questioning. She felt her own cheeks burning already. But Shirley had her eyes fixed on her meringue, which she was breaking into small fragments, though not eating any of them.

"Um, yes, I do remember. You mean the photos that Mrs Hardy gave me just as I was about to catch the bus?" Ruth answered hesitantly, hoping to fend off awkward questions.

"Yes, yes, I expect that's what they were. And do you remember that photo of a handsome young man?" Ruth gulped but said nothing. "You know, one of those boys, what was his name?"

"Julian?" Ruth queried playing for time.

"No, I don't think that was his name; I mean the tall one with wavy hair."

There was a tremor in her voice, which prevented her from proceeding. Ruth remembered that she had not spoken of Piers to either of her parents when the photos had fallen out of her handbag. Shirley had seen the snapshot of him and inexplicably had run away upstairs without another word; subsequently she had ended up in hospital. "Do you mean Piers?" she asked as calmly as possible. She moved not a muscle, waiting in suspense for Shirley's reaction.

"I expect so," Shirley replied, as if her mind was elsewhere. "What's his surname?" she asked.

"Robinson, I think," Ruth found this factual answer easy to deliver.

"Ah, I see." Shirley's meringue was reduced to crumbs on her plate.

Hoping that this weird inquisition was over, Ruth drank her fragrant tea and ate her meringue. Shirley, however, was not ready to let the matter drop. In the same shy tone she said: "I expect you're wondering why I ask this…" Ruth nodded. "It's just," the words were sticking in Shirley's throat again, and moisture was welling up into the corners of her eyes, "it's just that I knew someone like him during the War."

Ruth had rarely felt sorry for her mother before, so it was an odd sensation when a wave of pity washed over her. She had no idea what had happened, though she had an inkling that Shirley had suffered some sort of traumatic experience, so traumatic that years later the photograph of an unknown boy who bore a passing similarity to that distant friend could arouse intense reactions in her. "He was very good looking, wasn't he?" were Shirley's last whispered words on the subject. Ruth was not sure whether she was talking about Piers or about her long-lost friend. "Why would she have said 'was', not 'is', in relation to Piers?" Ruth frowned, but deemed it best simply to agree with her mother.

Then she had an idea, which she considered carefully before voicing it. Surely there would be no harm in sharing that idea with Shirley, if it would help her? On the other hand, she did not want her friendship with Piers to be jeopardized in any way, even by being made semi-public among their families. She had a horror of hearing Shirley say to all her friends and acquaintances, all the customers in the shop and post office: "Can you believe it! Our Ruth has a boyfriend! He's ever so clever and handsome. He goes to Eton College, you know." That would be too dreadful!

She was silent for a little while, tussling with her conscience and trying to think of the best way of presenting her idea. "If we all go to stay with Nan at Christmas, you might meet Piers. I think he and his brother and parents will be staying with the people next door," she said.

"Really?" Shirley asked eagerly.

"But you'll be lucky to meet Piers; he shuts himself away all the time, practising the piano in the front room," Ruth warned her.

"Oh, why does he do that?"

"He has a music scholarship at his school."

"I see," Shirley said thoughtfully. "Well, perhaps we can liven him up a bit!" she suggested brightly.

In a final coup, perjuring herself into the bargain, Ruth blurted out, "He's such a bore! His brother Julian is much more fun!"

As soon as the words were out of her mouth, she regretted them. She wanted to bite out her tongue. How could she be so disloyal to Piers and so devious? Her duplicity left her feeling very dissatisfied with herself and with the afternoon. The sole consolation was that Shirley was smiling again.

"Not to worry. I think we can have a lovely time with your nan at Christmas!" she said. "I'm looking forward to it already! But what did you say the new neighbours are called?"

"Oh, their name is Hardy," Ruth replied.

Shirley's expression clouded over. "I see," she said with a sigh.

Dad was up and dressed when they brought him a meringue in a special box and a small packet of lapsang souchong. Shirley wandered slowly into the little back room where he was sitting by the fire.

"Have you had a good time, Shirley, been buying new clothes, have you?" he asked, anticipating a hole in his bank account.

"No, not at all – we've had a nice time, haven't we, Ruth?" she replied quietly, putting a brave face on an afternoon which hadn't fully come up to her expectations.

Ruth corroborated this version of the afternoon's expedition: "Yes, it was a lovely tea shop, and we bought packets of tea there as well." She for her part was still trying to come to terms not only with her own treachery, but also with foreboding at what Christmas might have in store for her. Her earlier enthusiasm was waning fast in the face of Shirley's keenness for going to stay at Beech Grove.

In fact, as the latter still kept saying to her husband, there was nothing that she wanted to do more than spend Christmas in Norhambury. She was convinced that it would be lovely; she was going to help with the Christmas dinner and give Nan a good time. She would take some decorations and crackers out of the shop to brighten up the house, and so on and so forth. Her change of mood was amazing; Ruth was very perplexed. It was obvious that Piers, who was born in 1942, was not the person she had known during the War: he was much too young for that, so why was Shirley so intent on meeting him? It was a puzzle for which she had no clues whatsoever, apart from the touching confession about someone she had known during the War that Shirley had made that afternoon in the tea shop, and which, all things considered, hadn't amounted to very much.

Dad on the other hand was pleased at the perceived improvement, however slight, in his wife's condition, and ascribed it to the new drugs. She had been reasonably well when she came out of hospital and certainly fit enough to run the shop again, but he had feared a relapse, believing that, on past experience, her discharge was too soon. Knowing full well that it was not a new medication that had produced any change of attitude in her mother, Ruth was disturbed, labouring under the suspicion that the grounds for Shirley's curiosity about Piers might in some unknown way pose some sort of unidentifiable threat.

She was not able to put her finger on precisely why, for it was absolutely unthinkable that Shirley would run away with Piers, or he with her. That was out of the question, and she did not need to consider it for a second longer than necessary to eliminate it as a possibility. Nevertheless, there was a missing link in this puzzle, and however hard she dug to the depths of the information she had at her disposal, the missing link would not rise to the surface. The War, her mother as a pretty young woman, a friend who must have meant a great deal to her, the photo and Piers, these comprised the sum total of the available pieces in the jigsaw. Somewhere there was another piece, but she had not the least idea where she might find it.

51

Dad had intended to visit Nan the following weekend after recovering from his bout of flu, but tiredness and weakness prevented him from doing more than running the post office, seated on a stool at the counter. Unusually for him, he had to have a short nap at lunchtime when the post office was shut; he went to bed early at night and, on early-closing day, spent the whole afternoon asleep by the fire.

"You're just not well enough, John," Shirley fretted, "and I'm going to make sure you are all right before you go anywhere. Anyhow, when I'm ill you always look after me so well – this is the least I can do. And I'm sure your mother would agree."

Nan wrote to say that they shouldn't worry about her, as she was fine, well cared for by her friends and neighbours, and was already looking forward to Christmas. What she did not say in her letter to Dad and Shirley was that she was intending to come to London for Ruth's concert. She wrote as much to Ruth, though her precise arrangements were not yet finalized. She hoped that Ruth would soon tell her parents about the concert and invite them to come to it, because she was sure that they would be thrilled by her performance. Its tone and the firmness of the script suggested a correspondent in full possession of her senses and determined to carry out her plans.

The forthcoming concert filled all Ruth's waking hours. When she was playing, she devoted herself entirely to the music; when she was not playing, the concerto revolved ceaselessly in her head, both by the day and at night. It was with her and inside her all the time, as she searched for ways of improving even the finest details.

"Ruth, your work is not as good as we expect from you," some of her teachers complained.

"I know, I'm sorry, but I am rather busy at the moment. I'll work in the holidays and make up for it next term," she would reply, hoping to pacify them. The more understanding among them did not put pressure on her, since word had spread that she had a major role in the end-of-term concert, which they had no option but to respect, because it would enhance the reputation of the school if it could claim to have a child prodigy among its pupils.

Harold Barkley, Ruth's keenest advocate in dealing with the other members of staff, especially Miss Jenkins, used this argument to advantage. "I'm not having my star performer catching a cold on your games field," he warned Miss Jenkins. "Think how silly the school would look if we had to cancel the concert!" She retorted that games were compulsory and never did anyone any harm, but he would have none of it. "And what's more," he snorted, warming to his subject and to the opportunity to get the better of a woman whom he detested, "I don't want her performing antics in that gym of yours at present. A fine thing it would be if she broke her wrist just now!"

Miss Jenkins was forced to concede defeat, but exacted from Harold Barkley the concession that Ruth should go for a walk while the others were on the games field. "The girl needs fresh air and exercise if she's to give of her best," she insisted. She gave her permission to Ruth in person, attempting to ingratiate herself with a grin, so unlike her normal grim expression that it became a grotesque leer. "Only walking, mind you! No hopping on and off buses or you'll be in trouble!"

Ruth enjoyed her walks even in the damp, chill winter air. She explored unfamiliar parts of north London, climbing hills, visiting parks and peeping into small shops. At the end of every excursion she had to write a note to Miss Jenkins explaining where she had been and what she had seen.

With only ten days to go, Ruth was becoming agitated – not on account of nerves, because on the contrary she was impatient for the concert day to begin. It was more a case of worrisome complications caused by her home situation.

"I think we will suspend practice sessions from today," Miss Lake decreed one afternoon, mistakenly fearing that Ruth was already suffering from stage fright. "If not, you will be in danger of over-rehearsing. On seeing her pupil's crestfallen expression, she modified her decision. "Suppose you come into St Luke's on Monday to practise after the weekend and on Thursday for your lesson. How would that be? After all you seem to be practising all the time in school." In the lesson Miss Lake introduced some new music. "A change is as good as a rest, they say, so let's have another look at some Brahms. He was a great admirer of Beethoven." She produced a set of Intermezzi from her bag and placed them on the music desk. Ruth was reluctant to interrupt her concentration on Beethoven, but these pieces by Brahms were old friends, and to her relief she discovered an invigorating freedom as her fingers and her brain adapted, returning to a different style. "There, you see!" Miss Lake exclaimed, "Beethoven needed a rest!"

Miss Lake's tone became more serious. "I've had a letter from your nan today with her cheque. In the letter she asks me whether you have told your parents about the concert yet. What am I to say to her?"

"It's all right," Ruth replied. "I am going to tell them about it this weekend."

"Ah, good, and your nan says she is coming to the concert, though she doesn't say how she intends to travel." Nan was still waiting for Ruth to put her parents in the picture before telling them about her visit.

The moment of truth had come at last, though too soon for Ruth's liking, since she had no choice but to reveal all at the weekend. It would undoubtedly be awkward, but she hoped her confession – since that was what it would amount to – would be well received. Shirley was on ebullient form these days; with any luck she would be unlikely to be plunged into depression by the mention of a piano, because she had too much else to occupy her. If Nan came to London as she promised, the secret would inevitably come out. She would have to travel with Dad on his return journey, and he would want to know why she was so keen to leave her home, given her various disabilities. And if Nan came, who knows, maybe she would stay for Christmas in

London after all, and there would be no visit to Beech Grove and no reunion with Piers – which would be terrible.

On the other hand, Ruth reasoned, if Nan did not manage to come for the concert, it would still be impossible to hide her talent from her parents at Christmas: the temptation to play Nan's piano would be too great because, apart from her solo repertoire, she would be playing duets with Piers and she would not be able to rely on their going out for long walks in the depths of winter as they did at the seaside in summer.

She envisaged letting her parents into her secret and imagined scenarios in which they would both jump up in amazement and joy to hug her and congratulate her. Equally they might meet the news with shock and horror; there was still a real possibility that Shirley might collapse in a hysterical state, and Dad would wring his hands in anger and despair at her disobedience.

She wished there were a middle course, a course in which she could trust them to accept her confession without fuss, but with pleasure and encouragement. Nevertheless, she knew that the deed had to be done and should be done quickly. There was now just one week left before the concert. If she told her parents about it on Saturday at lunchtime, they would have time to adjust to the idea by the end of the week without having too much time to fuss. Anyhow, she decided, she would simply tell them that she had a part in the school concert.

Saturday lunch – prepared by Dad, who was beginning to recover some of the energy lost when he had flu – was one of his specialities: his sausage, cabbage and mash were designed to give everyone a boost at the end of the week. He always did the cooking at weekends now that Shirley had taken over the kitchen during the week. Her meals were never the same; sometimes she would set down a wholesome stew complete with potatoes and vegetables, at others it might be no more than scrambled eggs on toast. Dad however always provided a substantial meal, because, as he said, you never knew where your next meal was coming from.

After he had finished serving, he started talking, in between mouthfuls, about getting a rail ticket to go and visit Nan, leaving on Friday. Ruth's appetite disappeared all of a sudden, and she, plunged into turmoil, stopped eating: Friday was none other than the day of the concert. "I know it'll soon be Christmas and we'll be going to stay with her, but I would like to go and check up on her before then. Have you any objection if I go next weekend, dear?" Dad was asking Shirley.

"No, just as long as you are well enough and you promise me to look after yourself, that will be fine. Ruth will help out in the shop, won't you, Ruth?" This was the moment to launch into the startling revelation, for its time had most definitely arrived: it brooked no more delay, though the more she thought about it, the more nervous she became as the perception grew of how shocked her parents would be.

Summoning all her courage, she was on the point of opening her mouth to speak when the telephone rang in the office. "I'll get it," said Shirley, dashing out to pick up the receiver. Ruth's disclosure had to be made when both her parents were present, so she carried on trying to eat her meal while she waited for her mother to reappear. "This is the best meal I've ever had, Dad, apart from Nan's steak-and-kidney pudding," she was saying without great conviction, when Shirley came running back into the room. "It's for you, and it's urgent, but the line is terrible!" she screamed at Dad. He went straight to the phone.

The tears were flowing down Shirley's cheeks as she pushed her plate away and sat back in her chair with her hands folded in her lap. Ruth imagined that perhaps Granddad Reggie had had an accident and needed Dad to help him. Ten minutes later Dad came back, looking white and tense.

"The line crackled throughout the call, but I gathered that that was Mother's next-door neighbour, Mrs Hardy. I could scarcely hear her, but she said that Mother's had a fall; it must have happened yesterday, and they only found her a little while ago. They called earlier to take her out shopping, but when there was no answer, they assumed she was still asleep, as has happened sometimes before, apparently. They rang the bell again on their return, and when there was no answer the second time, they began to worry. Luckily they have a key, so they opened the door." He stopped to wipe his eyes before continuing with an ill-suppressed sob. "They found her in the hall, lying at the bottom of the stairs right by the front door. I think they said she's very badly bruised, but the line was so bad it was impossible to hear what they were saying."

"Oh, no! Please, no!" Ruth cried out. In her mind's eye she saw her darling nan lying in a heap at the bottom of the stairs. With difficulty her dad succeeded in stuttering out short staccato sentences. "Don't worry, Ruth, she is still alive. They called an ambulance. They've taken her to hospital. I must go straight away."

Shirley was very quiet. "I'm very sorry," she said, stroking his arm. "I'll go and pack a bag for you at once and look up the train times while you finish your lunch."

Dad had no appetite for his sausage and mash. Leaving his half-finished plate, he went off to put on his shoes and fetch his mackintosh.

"Shall I come with you?" Ruth offered, oblivious to what the week held in store for her in London.

"No, Ruthie, you stay here, go to school and help your mother when you come home. I'm sure Nan will be fine after a few days in hospital," he stammered, making an effort to be optimistic. "I expect I shall have to find somewhere else for her to live, though. She can't go on living at home. Let's hope she will be well enough to come back here with me." Ruth put her shoes and coat on nonetheless, and both she and Shirley accompanied him to the underground station where, having hugged them both, he hurried off down to the dark depths of the Northern Line.

Mother and daughter walked home in silence, each wrapped in her own concerns. Ruth was plunged into sorrow, too deep for tears. Shirley put an arm round her and led her home. They sat in front of the fire reminiscing about Nan from time to time. Revealing an unusually sensitive side, Shirley spoke gently about the happy holidays they had enjoyed together by the sea, and said how grateful she had been for Nan's help with running the household in that first winter after she had taken over the shop.

"You really loved her, didn't you, Ruth?" she asked. Ruth guessed that there was more to this question than Shirley had actually said. The end of the sentence would have been, "more than me", so she was glad that she had not been required to reply to the unspoken words with more than a nod.

There was plenty of opportunity over the rest of the week-end for Ruth to confide her secret in her mother, but she felt strongly that that would be disloyal to her dad. Either both her parents would attend the concert or neither would. She would just have to invent some other story to explain her absence from home the following Friday evening. It would be easy enough. She might say that there was to be a concert in school and that she had offered to help arrange the chairs, hand out programmes and serve drinks in the interval. Indeed, only last Thursday in assembly, Miss Dent had asked for volunteers for precisely those tasks. Anyhow, Shirley would not be interested in a concert of classical music. She would tell her on Thursday that she was required in school on Friday evening, she decided, but wondered how much help Shirley would need in the shop in the meantime. This was not the best of times for her to have to rush home from school to serve behind the counter.

She need not have worried, for Shirley had already rung her father, and they had agreed that her brother, Ted, would come to help with the post office during John's absence. Tilly would run Granddad Reggie's shop, while he would take over Ted's business, which was not generally overwhelmed with customers before Christmas, the spring and summer being the best time for bicycle sales. Ted arrived early on the Monday morning, and the performance he gave behind the post-office counter with his one arm was an impressive example of bravura, for with extraordinary dexterity he made his one good arm and hand do the work of three.

Ruth watched him work with admiration mingled with amusement, wondering how anyone could come to terms with the loss of an arm and a hand. She herself was so dependent on her two hands and her ten fingers that she dreaded an accident to any of them. To live with one hand loosely and uselessly tucked into a pocket was a ghastly nightmare, if indeed there was a hand and an arm there at all in the sleeve and the pocket.

The first thing Shirley said to her brother was: "Thank you so much for coming at such short notice, Ted." She said it with heartfelt gratitude, and Ted responded with the mysterious refrain that Ruth had heard so often: "Don't you worry, Sis, our heroine!" In the current stressful situation they limited themselves to speaking in plain English.

There had been no news from Dad since his hasty departure on Saturday. Shirley was unconcerned, saying that he would be most unlikely to ring up on the neighbours' phone, as he hated asking for favours. Instead he would have to go down the road to the phone box, and he might not have time for that. How she wished that his mother had agreed to have a phone installed when they suggested it! Communication would be so much easier now, and Ruth agreed with her.

Although she was sure that her father would ring somehow if there were anything to report, she did not cease to worry about Nan. It was dreadful to think of her suffering. "How bad was the fall?" she wondered. "How long had Nan been lying at the bottom of the stairs? Had she slipped on that loose bit of carpet? Had she hit her head or broken her legs or her arms or even her back?" She remembered falling down the stairs as a child several times – but then, she had heard on television that children bounced because their bones were soft, whereas adults and elderly people had brittle bones that broke easily.

On the other hand, there was hope, because her dad had said that Nan was alive, so with luck she hadn't hit her head too badly or broken her back, and surely it was therefore out of the question that she might die? After all, only a few short weeks ago she had been well enough to start planning a trip to London and well enough to advise Ruth on how to play the 'Emperor'. The question was whether she would be well enough to come to the concert or, if she were not able to come herself, whether she would be well enough for Dad to leave her so that he could come. The more she thought about it, the keener Ruth was for him to attend.

Cautious optimism prevailed until she recalled the terrible state in which Nan had come to the door at the beginning of the half-term visit. Of course there was also the question of Nan's mental lapses, which were another worrying factor. Perhaps Nan was not as robust as she had seemed later in that week of recovery under Ruth's watchful eye; perhaps she had relapsed into that forgetful incoherence – in which case there was certainly a possibility that she might not survive. Armed with these arguments, pessimism vanquished optimism, reducing Ruth to inner chaos, drawing her placid features into a tight, tense mask, which was how she appeared in school on the Monday morning.

Harold Barkley was the first to notice. He was alarmed. "What's this, Ruth? You are not yourself, are you? Your playing is all over the place today. What's wrong?" It was true: she was making a hash of everything she tried to play, from Beethoven to Brahms, Schubert to Schumann – even her scales were chaotic. There were no voices guiding her. She could not hear Nan's voice in her ear, nor did Piers seem to be present in her imagination to give her silent encouragement.

Harold Barkley stroked his chin. "I think this is a bad case of over-rehearsal," he declared, "and I think it would be better if you took some time off. No more practising or rehearsing today!" Ruth was appalled at her own incompetence and upset by his diagnosis of it. As she had learnt to trust him well enough, she decided to tell him what had happened during the weekend. "Ah, I see! I'm very sorry," he commiserated. "But look here," he went on, still stroking his chin, though it wasn't obvious what comfort or inspiration he derived from it, "your nan is alive, and she is in hospital. We have hospitals to make people better, not worse, and she's not now lying on the floor at home." This sensible reasoning was only marginally comforting and made no difference to Ruth's playing. Not only was an essential element – her nan's involvement – lacking: her heart was not in it.

Schoolwork was easier in that that was fairly mechanical. One only had to listen to the teachers and answer their questions. It involved memory, but did not demand the coordination of so many faculties – speed of sight, hearing and reaction as the fingers of both hands and her feet acted independently of each other, obeying the notes and markings on the stave. Over and above all that, the player was required to interpret the composer's intentions and communicate the music to the listener, attending to dynamics, from piano to forte with the whole range in between, to crescendos and diminuendos, to accelerandos and ritardandos, to key changes and time-signature changes, as well as to a host of other subtleties unheard of in any other subject, such as the exact timing of special individual notes conveyed in such a way that left the audience hanging on to every one of them. In the present circumstances it was also essential to watch the conductor with an eagle eye and listen to the orchestra with ears strained. Today she felt that she was a beginner all over again, and that was too much.

"Would you like to take the day off school?" Harold Barkley enquired kindly. "I'm sure I could arrange it for you. "His standing in the school had risen to the extent that his advice was now accepted on all matters by the powers that be.

"No, that's all right, thank you," Ruth replied. "It's better to be here doing something than messing about at home." She put her music away, and with drooping shoulders walked out of the room, utterly despondent that, for the first time ever, her ability to make music had let her down.

Although her instructions were to give the piano a rest for a day or two, Ruth's footsteps strayed after school to St Luke's, not intending to play the piano there with any degree of competence, but to have a word with Miss Lake, who by now knew Nan quite well and would be concerned about her. Miss Lake was indeed anxious both for Nan and for Ruth, who demonstrated her state of mind by trying unsuccessfully to play some scales. Her attempts were pathetic, no better than they had been in school earlier in the day. Miss Lake closed the lid of the piano, making no comment on Ruth's ham-fisted endeavour to draw music out of the instrument.

"Your nan wrote to me only last week to say that she was definitely coming to the concert and was already packing her bag," she said. "I'm certain when it comes to it on Friday you'll play beautifully and she will be there. What I suggest for today is that you sit down again at the piano, but don't even open it. See how it feels, and if you want to play then open the lid and try a few scales. You'll see – it will come back."

Ruth sat at the piano, but felt no urge to open it. Nothing happened. She leant her elbows on the closed lid and buried her head in her hands. So much depended on her, yet she couldn't even play a scale or two, or a bar of any of the Beethoven Sonatas that she had been practising for so long.

Miss Lake concluded that it would be kinder to bring the session to an end. She said: "You're very overwrought, Ruth, and this is not doing you any good. I think we had better leave it for today, and I'll walk down the road with you. In any case it's nearly half-past four, and I'll need to be on my way home for my private pupils."

Ruth felt a sudden shiver, though the room was not cold. "Ruthie, don't you worry; come on, now! I want to hear you play. You know you can do it!" Nervously she opened the piano lid. "Take a deep breath – don't hurry, and then begin when you are ready!" said the well-loved voice. Miss Lake had gone to fetch her coat, but came hurrying back when she heard the piano launching into the slow movement of the 'Emperor'.

The communicating door from the house to the post office was open when Ruth arrived home. Uncle Ted called out "Had a good day, Ruth?" as he saw her pass by on her way down the hall from the front door to the kitchen.

"Not too bad, thanks," she called back.

Apparently on cue, Shirley came into the house from the shop and followed Ruth into the back room, where she had stopped to glance at a newspaper. "Oh, there you are, Ruth," she said casually. "Are you all right?"

"Yes, yes, how about you?" said Ruth politely.

"Fair, fair, thanks," Shirley replied. Ruth knew that she was leading up to something, and had little doubt what it might be. "Your dad rang just before you got home…" Shirley began, "He rang to say that your nan died about half an hour ago, at half-past four."

52

A fog of blank incomprehension at the suddenness and the nature of the tragedy that had befallen her nan engulfed Ruth. Overwhelmed though she was with sorrow, tears would not flow, despite the churning, conflicting reactions which kept her awake at night. Everything except music was unreal to her. Music was her only means of expression, her only solace and the only reality in her life since, with Nan's passing, everything else had disappeared, existing only in her individual recollections, never to be restored or reinvented.

The insignificant semi-detached house with its unexceptional garden, Grandpa's shed, her old cabin, the cherry tree and the plum trees – even those quantities of jam, everything that spelt magic for her – all had faded from her life, as well as dear Nan herself with her strange background, her fund of stories, her patience, her courage and her gentle enthusiasm. The past would survive only in memory, and the future, so dependent on Nan and only lately assuming an incipient shape and direction, was now obscured by the shadow of uncertainty and disbelief.

It was inconceivable that she would never see Nan – the real Nan, the flesh-and-blood Nan – again. Yet unaccountably, in the depths of sadness, she began to feel that Nan was very close, there with her in London, ethereally accompanying every movement, every thought, guiding her through the morass of sorrow, doubt and insecurity. The closeness was intensified at the piano: Nan – or was it Evelyn, or Evelyn and Nan together? – were with her whenever and wherever she played, whether at the high school or in St Luke's, in practice sessions or in rehearsals. The strength of their influence released the fountain of music welling up inside her into an even more potent means of expression, enabling her to pierce her way through the mists and recover the motivation, particularly at the keyboard, that she feared lost.

Harold Barkley, though very sympathetic at Nan's death, was immensely relieved at the re-emergence of Ruth's talent, saying: "There, just as I told you, you needed time away from the piano!"

Miss Lake was less assertive; realizing that in the circumstances it was improbable that her well-meant advice had had any effect on Ruth, she limited herself to saying: "I am truly sorry about your nan, Ruth. I am so glad I had the opportunity of meeting her; she was such a lovely person. I know how thrilled she would be to hear you playing now." She regarded Ruth with surprise, implying that she did not understand what had brought about the sudden improvement in her playing; if anything, she would have expected her performance to have deteriorated even more. "I think you shouldn't play Beethoven this week until Friday," she suggested. "Then on Friday brush up tricky passages in the concerto before the rehearsal in the afternoon. I know it will be fine. Why not have a look at some Bach to settle the mind between now and then?"

Bach. In one of their discussions last summer, while they were walking to the village, Piers had talked about Bach. Ruth tried to recall what he had said. She remembered that he regarded Bach with reverence, but insisted that he himself did not play Bach. This of course she knew was not true, because Nan had heard him playing Bach on the organ in church that morning when she herself had stayed in bed. He could be forgiven that untruth, for doubtless it simply indicated his natural modesty. In his opinion one needed to have a mature intelligence to understand the intellectual complexity of the music and appreciate the spirituality of its emotional content. He maintained that very few players could attain the necessary heights of understanding, perception and complexity, and he knew that he himself was not yet ready for Bach. Many players could give a passing performance of the music of the classical, Romantic and even modern periods, but often the profundity of Bach eluded them. He is the father of us all, was what he had said. Mindful of Piers's opinion, she took up Miss Lake's suggestion, doubtful that she could do Bach justice, though memories of playing the 'Two-Part Inventions' soon came flooding back.

On that Tuesday afternoon, as she set her mind and her fingers to work on the C major Prelude that Miss Lake had suggested, she found that Charles Stannard came to mind. It was unlikely that she would ever see him again, or the people in the church and the many others who had shown such concern for Nan – even Ronnie and Bernie Parr. Nor for that matter was she likely to meet the Hardys again, she reasoned, for there would be no more going to Beech Grove, and there was no one there who would be likely to invite her to stay. Her experience of Carrie and her family, of Susan and her family and of Jimmy Evans and his parents, told her that once a connection was broken, people generally did not stay in touch.

It was then that the lightning bolt struck: if she never went to Beech Grove, she reasoned – and there was nowhere there for her to stay – how could she ever hope to meet Piers again? Christmas was no longer on the agenda, since they would not be going to spend it at Nan's, unless Dad left the house exactly as it was and always had been. That was extremely unlikely. People didn't do that sort of thing; when someone died, they sold the house as soon as possible when the legal formalities were over. Closing the piano, she told Miss Lake that she ought to be going home in case there were more messages from her dad.

She did not go straight home, but went to sit in St Luke's Church to contemplate the implications of that dreadful realization which was beginning to assume the proportions of a double bereavement. Nan's death had broken the links with the past, while the unlikelihood of meeting Piers again signified the death of that cherished but unspoken dream. There was some solace to be found in the empty church: it was quiet and not at all forbidding, and gave her the chance to formulate a very brief prayer: "Please look after Nan and please help me," she whispered.

Just then the young vicar came out of a side door. He recognized Ruth from his divinity lessons in the high school. "Hello, Ruth," he said, seemingly unfazed by her woebegone appearance. "Is there anything I can do to help you? I have heard what has happened and I'm very sorry." He sat down beside her and invited her to share her grief with him. She related the whole story as she never had before, the story of her early love of music, of Nan's lessons at the piano, of Shirley's inexplicable aversion to the instrument and her periods of illness. She found the courage to tell him of her devious means for continuing her playing in London. She feared that he might criticize her, but inexplicably he seemed already to have some understanding of what she was saying.

He said gently: "Ruth, don't blame yourself. Your nan was right to help you to learn to play, and you were right to want to fulfil your talent, because that is God-given, and your Nan knew that. She recognized it because she had seen it before. Think how much more frustrated you would be now if you hadn't had the chance to learn and play at all. I met your Nan last Christmas at the carol service, and I could see what a special person she was, but none of us live for ever, and maybe it's easier for her to watch over you now in spirit than if she had struggled to come to London by train in person to attend the concert. You will meet her again one day, when your time has come – but for now she wants you to release that tremendous gift of music that has had to lie silent and hidden to all except a few people for such a long time. Now is your chance to release it and let it ring out to the whole world!" He uttered a short prayer asking for help for Ruth in her sadness and her difficulties, patted her on the back and sent her home saying: "I'm looking forward to Friday, and so is your nan!"

Ruth arrived home with a firmer, lighter step, only to find there was another disturbing message, which Shirley relayed to her over supper. "Your dad rang up again this afternoon – just before you came in, in fact. He sent you his love and wondered if you would go to your nan's funeral. The undertakers had a space on Friday, and of course there was no problem in arranging it at the village church. It's bound to be full." Ruth was dumbfounded. Friday of all days! Why did the funeral have to be on Friday? Of course she wanted to be there, but how could she absent herself from her own concert? On the other hand, how could she absent herself from the funeral? Whatever she did would be wrong. If only she had been able to explain the problem to her dad and discuss it with him herself!

Noticing her distress but ignorant of the full nature of it, Shirley went on: "I told him it would be too much for you. I wish I could come, but I can't, because we're so busy, so you'd be travelling on your own and you'd have to come back on your own, because your dad will be staying on to dispose of the property and settle the legal matters. I know you're capable of making the journey on your own, but this time, I am sure, it would be too much for you, and I said so."

At first Ruth did not know whether to be grateful to or indignant with Shirley for taking the decision for her, yet when she realized that Shirley had spared her the impossible task of deciding what to do and, for once in her life, had actually helped her out of a crisis, she wondered if there had been unseen but sympathetic forces at work while she was in the church with the vicar. Given that there was no fully satisfactory way out of the problem, she accepted Shirley's decision and hoped that her dad would understand.

Bach did indeed bring a spiritual comfort, allowing her to begin the arduous process of coming to terms with her grief. She had to concentrate hard, excluding all other considerations, to master the notes, and found that the notes themselves sympathized and eased her unhappiness, rather than indulging it as Beethoven's tended to do. Whenever she played Bach, she was conscious of Nan's voice advising and encouraging, though Piers was silent, possibly because he didn't think she was ready for it, so there was a blank which might never be filled. Nonetheless, perhaps more importantly, the vicar's extraordinary words had given her strength and confidence, promising her that Nan was with her and affirming her right to be a pianist and to play in public – as well as in that closely guarded privacy where she almost felt herself to be committing a crime against her parents. No longer would her music be silent, though she fervently hoped and prayed that her parents might be converted to it.

53

Heeding Miss Lake's advice, Ruth abandoned Beethoven until the Friday morning of the concert, other than playing for the rehearsal earlier in the week. She had slept well for the first time since the previous Monday, and had already warned Shirley that she would have to go back to school in the evening to help out with the concert, but refrained from saying in precisely what capacity. This was not the time to spring the announcement on her mother, especially not in her father's absence.

Shirley was anxious. "I don't like you going out in the dark," she said. "And what about coming home? What time will you be back?" Ruth wasn't sure. "I think I should come and meet you at least."

"No, there's no need to bother. One of my teachers will meet me outside and we'll walk up the road together, and I'm sure they'll walk back with me afterwards." This was true, because Miss Lake had promised to get off her bus at the stop opposite and wait for her there.

The grand piano had been on the stage in the school hall for several days. Not wanting to practise in public, Ruth sat at the upright piano in the music room and relaxed as the notes of the 'Emperor' rang out under her fingers all in the proper order as Beethoven ordained.

"That's sounding good, Ruth!" Harold Barkley declared as he came into the room. "I think we're all set for this evening! Don't do too much today: take it easy and don't play too hard in the rehearsal this afternoon. We'll deal with the concerto first and then you can go home for a rest and something to eat. Are your parents coming, by the way?"

"No," she said, sorrowfully remembering that today, in another part of the country, Nan's funeral was taking place.

"It's my nan's funeral today, and my dad will still be away."
Enough said. There was no need to explain why Shirley would
not be there.

"I'm sorry your father won't be here to hear you but, remember, you must play for your nan. It's your tribute to her. I gather
from Elizabeth that it's on account of her that you can play
the piano at all." It sounded as if Harold Barkley, for all his
faults, was reinforcing the vicar's words. Ruth nodded and bit
her lip; this was not the time for tears, although what he said
was true: had it not been for Nan, she could never have dreamt
of this golden opportunity, her moment to shine, the first stage
of fulfilment of that extraordinary dream.

Since Ted was living with them, Shirley had taken to preparing a substantial supper every night. Today was no exception,
and she served a stew at six o'clock.

"You'll need something warming inside you if you're going
out on a cold evening," she said to Ruth, who ate quickly
and then went upstairs to dress in her green winter frock, her
new stockings and those shoes which had a purpose after all.
She tied her long hair back with a green ribbon and carefully
applied a dab of Shirley's powder to her nose, but then wiped
it off because it looked so frightful.

When she came down, Shirley and Ted both exclaimed
together: "Ruth, you look lovely!"

Shirley added: "You're wasted just helping out: you ought
to be on the stage – but what about a dab of powder on your
nose? It's rather shiny!"

"No thanks!" Ruth called, grabbing her coat and running
out of the house to meet Elizabeth Lake.

As they walked up the road, she gave Ruth some last-
minute instructions, which were remarkably like Nan's. "Take
your time. There's no rush. Take a deep breath. Check the
position of the piano stool: someone might have moved
it since the rehearsal this afternoon. Align your hands on
the keyboard and only when you really are ready, look up
at the conductor, smile at him and then watch him for all
you're worth."

The vicar stepped out to join them as they passed the church. "Ah, good, Tim, so you are coming too!" Elizabeth Lake exclaimed.

"Well, yes, if that's all right with you, Ruth?" he asked, taking Elizabeth's arm and smiling at Ruth.

"Of course," Ruth replied, amused to find that Elizabeth Lake had secrets too.

They went into the school by a back entrance, out of the way of the crowds milling in through the front door. Miss Lake joined the instrumentalists in a room near the hall, but Ruth went straight to the gym to warm up on the old upright there, which was used for dance classes. It was hopelessly out of tune, but adequate for scales and exercises. An hour later, Elizabeth Lake came across to the gym to bring her a glass of water and a chocolate biscuit and told her that the first half of the concert – an orchestral medley of Mozart and Brahms – was over and that she should prepare for her performance.

"You'll soon hear the bell at the end of the interval, so come across when you're ready. Good luck!" With this she went back to join the throng of players assembling to return to the stage.

When the old school bell rang out announcing her imminent entrance, it sent a tingle down Ruth's spine. She made her way to the main building, stopped at the cloakroom and then approached the hall from the rear. She waited quietly behind the line of chattering instrumentalists. Harold Barkley gave her as reassuring a smile as he was capable of doing and, echoing Elizabeth Lake's advice, said: "Take your time, adjust the piano stool if you need to and then sit very still. Take some deep breaths and wait until not one sound can be heard from the rustling in the audience. When everyone's utmost attention is on you, look up at me. Then play! Oh, and don't forget to take a bow when I bring you on. Good luck!" She waited in the wings, tense not with fright, but with excitement and impatience.

The performance had a dreamlike quality from the moment Harold Barkley led her onto the concert platform: she floated on air as they bowed to the audience and took their places – he

on the conductor's podium and she at the piano, after glancing
at the position of the stool. Nan's voice was strong in her ear.
"Take your time... Move the stool a little, it's not quite right...
Check your hands... are they relaxed? You know the key of
the Concerto – E flat – but remember it's going to go through
many changes, which will only appear as accidentals... Think
yourself into those changes of key... Take a deep breath... And
now look up at the conductor!"

He gave an upbeat, and as his hand came down, the whole
orchestra – strings, wind, brass and timpani as one, struck the
resounding opening chord, daring the soloist to meet the challenge – and she did. After the bar's length of this chord, her
fingers glided effortlessly at speed up and down the keyboard
in the arpeggios, scales and trills. The exchange between soloist
and orchestra continued through two more grandiose chords
and the following cadenza passages, leading to complex variations and virtuosic figurations. The piano made its second
entrance, gently echoing the first theme, introduced earlier very
grandly by the orchestra, but here marked dolce for the piano,
before the hazardous sequence of key changes. At the return
to the home key of E flat, Beethoven allowed the piano to revel
in the virtuosity of its triumphant mood before the final coda.

In a burst of recognition as the coda drew to a close, Ruth
heard in this powerful opening movement an echo of the course
of her own life so far with all its uncertainties, its anxieties, its
sadness, its highs and its lows, its emotional disturbances and the
struggle to fulfil her secret, overwhelming passion: the practice of
music. The final resolution brought a joyous hope and a promise
of success, a success which even now she had already begun to
savour with this, her first public performance. Her passion was
no longer secret, and her music was no longer silent. This realization truly explained the depth of her deeply ingrained love for the
concerto far beyond its associations with Piers or even Evelyn.

Nan's voice had been whispering in her ear throughout the
taxing first movement, but was absent in the second. Ruth was
not perturbed. She knew that here Beethoven himself was telling her that all would be well. In its calm contemplation this

was music from heaven, and the way she played it was enough to melt the hearts of angels. She closed her eyes when it drew to a close with the inspired modulation of a semitone from B to B flat played by the principal bassoonist, providing the link to the third movement, the dancing rondo.

"Careful of the key changes again!" Nan whispered. There were more semiquaver passages in the second part of the rondo, then a longer section presenting the opening theme of the movement in different keys before the penultimate cadenza in the piano, which concluded on a trill. Next, the introductory theme reappeared, first in the piano and then in the orchestra. Finally, that theme underwent a transformation before the concerto entered the cadenza, which the piano shared with the timpani, leading to an almighty flourish of turbulent scales in the piano. To this the orchestra responded in triumph, bringing the concerto and the concert to an end.

Ruth sat still, not knowing what to do next.

The applause rang in her ears, drowning Nan's voice saying: "Well done, Ruthie!"

Harold Barkley came down from his podium to help her up from the piano stool. He held her hand, saying, "Bow! And again, bow! And again, bow! Now we walk off!" They walked into the wings beside the stage. "Come on, back we go!" She stood in the limelight, stupefied, scarcely able to smile at the rapturous audience.

She bowed again as a girl came out of the wings with a bouquet. The girl was Janet Otway. "Well done, Ruth!" she whispered.

Ruth had not expected this, and had no idea how to respond. "Thanks," she said. Taking the bouquet, she looked out over the audience and bowed again. "Were her eyes deceiving her?" she wondered appalled, for there, at the back of the hall, she glimpsed a person with fluffy blonde hair standing on a chair, waving to her. "Surely it wasn't her mother? Oh no!" Her heart sank as she hurried off the stage and took refuge in the performers' room. But there was more applause and she had no choice but to keep reappearing to acknowledge it.

When the orchestra had left the stage and the hubbub in the hall was dying down, members of the audience flooded into the room to join in the congratulations which were coming from all sides, initially from Harold Barkley, from Elizabeth Lake and from the other players, and then from members of staff and parents. It was all more than she could handle; she wanted to run away from the attention and the fuss. The room was hot and stuffy, and she felt faint.

"I think we should let our soloist have a little time to recover. Ladies and gentlemen, would you be so kind as to leave the room, please?" Harold Barkley ordered the crowd, and began ushering them out.

"No, madam, I'm afraid I can't let you in!" Ruth heard him saying to a woman who was trying to push her way into the room against the outgoing flow.

"But she's my daughter!" the well-known voice cried.

Ruth stood up to greet her mother, who embraced her as she had never embraced her before.

"Ruthie, Ruthie, why didn't you tell me? Why didn't you tell me?" she sobbed. "I might have missed it, I had no idea!" Uncle Ted followed his sister into the room and gave Ruth a peck on the cheek. "Some talent you've got there, young lady! If it hadn't been for this arm of mine," he gestured to his pocket, "who knows, I might have been a pianist of sorts myself!"

Ruth slept for the whole weekend. Shirley came into her room on tiptoe bringing her all sorts of treats, stroking her hair as she lay in bed and shedding tears. By Sunday evening, when the exhaustion started to wear off, Ruth dressed and went downstairs. She was afraid that explanations would be demanded and decided it would be better to get them over as soon as possible.

"Why didn't you tell me?" Shirley kept asking.

"A long time ago Dad said you hated the piano and it would make you ill, so Nan taught me on her piano when I stayed with her, and then in primary school Miss Lake taught me and has been teaching me after school ever since," came the reply.

"Who paid her?"

"Well no one at first, but then Nan started sending her cheques."

"Oh dear, I'm so sorry!" Shirley exclaimed mournfully. "It's true I used to hate the piano," she admitted, "but that was long ago, and times have changed. I'm so proud of you! You were tremendous on Friday evening! I knew there was something going on when you hummed that music; I knew I'd heard it before! It was on the radio – some new musical I think! How I wish your dad had been here to hear it."

"Yes, I wish that too," Ruth agreed. "Poor Dad!" Friday's euphoria had evaporated, and the tears flowed copiously.

On the Monday morning everything was back to normal in school: the concerto was a thing of the past, toiled over for so long, performed in less than an hour and forgotten in the space of a weekend. It was not completely forgotten, however. Harold Barkley gruffly acknowledged her in the corridor, and later in the music room said: "I hope you realize, Ruth, how lucky you are. You have a prodigious natural talent and you must never take it for granted! You will go far!"

He said she was welcome to practise at the Steinway as often as she liked, but he recommended a good rest from music over the holiday. That of course was a foregone conclusion, because Ruth would have no access to a piano. Various of the kinder members of staff came up to Ruth in the corridor or the playground to say how much they had enjoyed her playing and how talented she was. Even Miss Jenkins, not customarily regarded as one of the kinder members of staff, congratulated her with a grimace saying that she was pleased to have had such a talented musician in her form the previous year. In assembly, Miss Dent made a scant passing reference to the concert, thanking Mr Barkley for all his efforts in arranging it and all the performers for giving of their time to play in it.

Madame Delplace was the only person to be truly effusive in her praise. "Rut!" she exclaimed, "ze concert was merveilleux, passionnant!" She made an extraordinary comment that Ruth had difficulty in digesting: "I spoke wiz your modder on Friday evening, she spik such good French, n'est-ce pas?"

The reaction among the girls was unexpected. Janet Otway said how thrilled she and her father had been by Ruth's performance. He had said that he hadn't heard the 'Emperor' played like that since he went to a concert given by a young pianist years ago. Coincidentally that young pianist had the same surname as Ruth, but he didn't suppose there was any connection.

Ruth only said "Ah", but was inwardly delighted at the compliment. Janet had been a good and patient friend. She had neglected her badly, but Janet did not seem to hold that against her.

However, the reaction from the other girls was hurtful. They turned their backs on her and ignored her. "Don't worry," Janet advised her. "They're jealous, but they'll boast about you outside school. They don't like to think of anybody being cleverer than they are in any way – they're petty and spiteful – but I think you're brilliant!" This tribute from her one truly faithful friend gave her the courage to disregard the rest.

54

It was some time before Dad came home – not until the week after the concert, the day after the end of term. In the meantime, there were no telephone calls from him.

"It's not like him," Shirley fretted. "Even if he won't ring from the neighbours, there's always the call-box."

He arrived unannounced five days before Christmas, as Shirley was serving the supper. On hearing the front door, she ran to the hall bubbling with excitement. Over the past week she had frequently thought how thrilled he would be to hear about Ruth's concert. She simply couldn't believe it, and that was the first thing she was going to tell him when he came home.

Such was her excitement that she flung herself into his arms before even looking at him. "You'll never guess what's happened!" she exclaimed, pulling away from their long embrace. Only then did she actually look at him, and was shocked by what she saw. In the weeks he had been away, he had grown thin and hollow-eyed, and looked bedraggled and exhausted. Ruth came to join them in the hall; she too was shocked by his appearance. She kissed her father, and he hugged her. "You need a good meal," Shirley said. "Come and sit down, the supper is ready." She helped him off with his coat and, taking him by the hand, led him to the back room. Ruth followed.

Having almost finished his supper, Ted stood up as they came into the room. "Hello, John! I'm so sorry to hear about your mother. You've had a hard time, I gather," he said, as he shook hands with his brother-in-law. "Well, now that you're back, I think I'll be off and leave you people to talk. If I go now, I can catch a train from Waterloo and be home by ten."

"Thank you very much for helping out, Ted," Dad forced himself to say before collapsing onto a chair. Shirley placed a plate of food in front of him, which he ate without speaking while she went to see Ted off.

The news of the concert took second place as mother and daughter waited for him to finish his meal. "We were worried about you; we wondered what had happened to you, as you didn't ring," Shirley said.

"The phone box was out of order, and I didn't like to keep bothering the neighbours: they'd been so good to mother already," was his cursory explanation. Ruth watched him, wondering why he was reduced to this debilitated condition: he was on the point of starvation.

After supper, as they sat by the fire, Shirley asked gently: "Are you going to tell us all about it?"

He sighed. "There's not much to tell. As you know, Mother had a fall and the neighbours found her at the bottom of the stairs. There was a loose bit of carpet, and she must have slipped on it. She was still alive, but was concussed and never fully regained consciousness. Unbelievably though, she was trying to carry her small suitcase down the stairs, so she couldn't hold on to the banister. Goodness knows why she was carrying a suitcase!"

Ruth knew why: she was horrified and blurted out: "She was coming to see us; it was supposed to be a surprise!"

Her dad turned to her aghast. "You knew she was coming?"

"Er, yes."

"Why didn't you tell us?" he asked furiously, but Shirley, putting a protective arm round Ruth's shoulders, intervened.

"There's more to this than you know, John. It's not Ruth's fault. Just tell us your side of the story."

"I sat with her in hospital day and night until she died, as you know, on the Monday afternoon. They decided there was no need for an inquest, and then I managed to organize the funeral for Friday. The church was packed. So many people came to pay their respects. I'm sorry you didn't come," he said pointedly, looking at Ruth.

"She couldn't come; we'll tell you why later, and then you'll understand," Shirley insisted brusquely. "So what did you do next?" He covered his face with his hands for a while. Ruth wanted to go over to him to give him a hug, but after his outburst was afraid that he would push her away.

Dad resumed his account several long minutes later. "As I was there and you had Ted here, I decided to set to work and sort as much out as possible, so I've been clearing the house and Father's old shed. Mrs Hardy from next door has taken Mother's clothes to some charity or other. Funnily enough, it was Ronnie Parr and Bernie, that nice son of his, who offered to help with the clearance; they were very kind and useful, so we did a lot. Apparently probate shouldn't take long to come through, because it's all so straightforward and simple, so I've put the house in the hands of an agent, who will put it on the market as soon as we get the go-ahead from the solicitors. He sipped from the cup of tea that Shirley had put at his side.

"That's why you look so exhausted. And I suppose, you haven't been sleeping or eating properly?" she asked, sounding for all the world like Nan.

"Yes, well, never mind that now," came his guarded reply. "By the way," he went on, "a furniture van from Picton's is coming on Monday with some things I thought you might like. There's the sofa and the armchairs from the front room: they are in good condition and not much used. Maybe we should put them upstairs? We use that big room over the shop for watching television now, and it would be much more comfortable as a sitting room with the good furniture from Norhambury; it might even serve as a dining room as well for special occasions, even though it's so far from the kitchen. You had already put a carpet down in there, so they're bringing the dining table – it's oak, you remember, and the dining chairs and that mahogany sideboard. Oh, and I asked them to bring the glass-fronted bookcase as well. I hope you'll approve?"

Shirley indeed gave her approval. "That is such a good idea! We've never used that room properly, because we didn't have the furniture for it. What else are they bringing?"

"There's not a lot more to bring. Some of Father's tools from the shed that I'd be glad of, and some cutlery, crockery, silverware and suchlike things. Oh, and there's that beautiful bow-fronted chest of drawers from Mother's bedroom for you. I hope you'll like that. And the marble washstand from the little bedroom, where you used to sleep, Ruthie – that's about it, I think." He paused to cast his mind over other arrangements. "I've arranged for Ronnie Parr to dispose of the rest, the old linen, the beds, kitchen utensils and other bits and pieces; he'll clear it after the furniture has gone. It's all labelled, so the removal men can see what to take. They've got the keys and will pass them on to Ronnie for him and his son to go in and empty the house."

Ruth was desperate to know what had become of the piano and the old gramophone with Evelyn's records. During the past week she had told Shirley that she had played the 'Emperor' while listening to Evelyn's performance, and that was how her own interpretation had risen to a higher level. Shirley had even said: "Well, we must make sure that those records and, of course, the piano as well, come to you. I wonder if the piano would go upstairs? It would be just right in that big room!"

"Nan did say that the piano would be mine one day," Ruth admitted modestly.

"But of course! If only your dad would ring, then I would be able to tell him that!" was Shirley's resolute response.

They had put off writing letters to him because from day to day they were living in the expectation of a phone call, or even of his return home. They had never imagined that he would clear the house so soon. Shirley had even speculated about going to stay there at Christmas for one last time. "Then we would meet those kind neighbours and their grandsons at last," she had suggested, though Ruth was in two minds about that proposal. To be in Nan's house without Nan would be a wretchedly miserable experience, even if Piers were next door. In addition, she was beginning to think that perhaps it might be better not to see Piers again: not only would it be too disturbing in itself, but the endless meetings and partings would be much too unsettling and draining.

Shirley must have partially read Ruth's thoughts, because she blurted out: "What about the piano? When is that coming?"

Dad was taken aback, "The piano? I didn't think you'd want the piano! You always hated the piano, especially that one!"

"That was long ago, and there were reasons for it! We must have Evelyn's piano for Ruth!"

"I don't understand, what on earth are you talking about?" he retorted irritably.

"We've been wanting to tell you this all week, but you didn't ring, except to tell us that your mother had died, and then about the arrangements for the funeral," Shirley said, becoming impatient. "We have a star in our midst, and we didn't even know it! Our Ruthie is a concert pianist, a what-do-you-call-it? A prodigy!"

"You're pulling my leg!" Dad replied uncomprehendingly.

"It's such a pity you missed her concert in school!" Shirley continued. "She played the 'Emperor' Concerto by Beethoven like a dream. Look here!" she picked up the *Weekly News* from a pile on a stool. "See, here she is on the front page, on the platform after the performance!"

Ruth cringed in embarrassment at the dreadful photo of her staring like a frightened rabbit into the lights.

"I can't believe my eyes!" her dad declared. "Is this really you, Ruthie?"

"Of course it's her, I was there!" Shirley replied impatiently. "Read what it says." She herself read the caption aloud: "A Star on the Horizon at the High School!" Then she read the accompanying article: "Pianist Ruth Platt, aged twelve, amazed the audience at the high school on Friday with her stunning performance of Beethoven's 'Emperor' Concerto. Ruth, the daughter of Mr and Mrs John Platt of the Broadway Newsagent's and Post Office, has an assisted place at the school. She told the *Weekly News* that this was a dream come true for her. She said she has been learning to play the piano 'on and off' since she was four years old. The school refused to comment on the date of Ruth's next concert."

Dad passed his hand over his eyes. "Oh dear! Oh dear! What have I done?" he groaned quietly, talking to himself.

"Why, what have you done?" Shirley queried sharply.

"I've given the piano to Mr and Mrs Hardy for their grandson. They were very kind to Mother, so it seemed that would be a good way of repaying them. They said their grandson's hoping to be a concert pianist, and they wanted to have a better piano for him when he comes to stay in the holidays. The removal men are going to take it round next door on Monday morning, before they load up the furniture to come here."

"Why did you do that?" Shirley was appalled. "Why didn't you at least try to get in touch with us first?"

Ruth slipped out of the room. She did not want to be party to her parents' argument, for she was overwhelmed with grief and mortification, blaming herself for Nan's fall. The truth was that Nan had fallen down the stairs carrying her suitcase in preparation for her departure to London. She truly had meant it when she said that she was coming to the concert, and she, Ruth, had kept it all a secret. The business with the piano was undoubtedly her punishment for allowing Nan to put her life at risk, and if Piers were to have the piano, that was only right and proper. Evelyn's piano would then have gone to a good home and it would be a tenuous point of contact with him, for she would imagine that she was seeing and hearing him during his holiday at Beech Grove.

She sat halfway up the stairs while her parents argued in the back room. Shirley was fiercely indignant on her behalf, but Dad was tired, weary and tense. "What else was I supposed to do?" he asked tersely. Shirley was insisting that he should ring the neighbours and say that there had been a mistake, that Nan had left the piano to Ruth, that he wanted them to give it back.

He was maintaining angrily that he couldn't and wouldn't do that: he had given the piano away: the neighbours, the Hardys, had been very touched and pleased, and he wouldn't under any circumstances ask for it back.

"What's Ruthie going to do then?" Shirley persisted.

"Well, she seems to have coped so far without telling us, so maybe she has some system worked out and can carry on as things are!"

"That won't do!" Shirley exploded. "Now that we know how brilliant she is, we've got to do all we can to help her! I'll buy her the best piano I can afford, but it won't be the same as Evelyn's! That means so much to her! She's my daughter and I'm very proud of her!"

"You're a fine one to talk!" Dad countered. The row rumbled on for ages.

Ruth went up to bed, but lay awake, half-listening to all the arguments being rehearsed in the distance downstairs. In addition to her guilt about Nan, the discovery that yet again music was the cause of disharmony made her immeasurably sad. That was not all, since now she no longer had a haven to resort to in times of trouble. The prospect of escape to Nan's house and garden was denied her for ever, and the image of Nan herself would become but a shadow. At the age of twelve, nearly thirteen, her reminiscences were all she had left – of Grandpa, of Nan, of the aura of magic that surrounded them. She doubted that she would ever go to the farm again, or even to the east coast. Apart from the few bits of furniture that Dad had selected, there wouldn't even be any mementoes. What had become of the photos and the clock, the gramophone, the records, the music and all the small items that made that house and its atmosphere so special?

Long after she had gone to bed, she heard her parents coming up the stairs. They were still bickering. Shirley was saying bitterly: "There's nothing worse than depriving a child of the means to fulfil his or her talents and ambitions, especially when that child has a real gift. I should know!" Dad muttered something inaudible in reply. Although Ruth was mildly annoyed with both of them – with Shirley for doing precisely that, for having deprived her of the means of fulfilling her talent, and with her father for seemingly colluding with Shirley and consequently suppressing her gift – it was not in her heart to be angry with either of them, with Shirley after the transformation of the past week, or with Dad who was in the depths of mourning.

On the other hand, she knew that she herself was partly to blame for the confusion. Had she not been so very timid as a child, she might have persuaded her parents to let her dance or have piano lessons from an early age. She knew also that she was to blame for keeping it all secret, possibly for much longer than was necessary. But what else could she have done? Had she told them about her music, they might have tried to stop her for their own mysterious, inexplicable reasons. Now, because she hadn't told them, she felt extremely guilty, especially since Nan's fall was indirectly caused by her secrecy. Shirley had said to her after the concert: "Oh, Ruthie, you are a dark horse, aren't you?" She had also said: "Well, of course, we all have our secrets."

Tension reigned over the weekend. Dad was irritable and uncommunicative. Shirley kept on pestering him about the piano. "You must ring the Hardys and ask for the piano. If you don't want to, give me the number and I'll do it!" she declared.

Dad refused to be drawn, but simply glared at both of them until the Sunday evening, when, after Shirley had driven him to distraction, he burst out. "Look, it's not my fault. If Ruth" – now he directed his angry, penetrating gaze at his daughter, deliberately not using his normal term of endearment, but making her sound like a stranger – "if Ruth had not been so devious and secretive, none of this would have happened. Maybe my mother would still be alive, we would all have gone to the concert together and we could all have enjoyed her success!"

Ruth was outraged, stung to the quick, and at last she lashed out, as all her pent-up emotion bubbled to the surface. "What was I supposed to do? You tell me! You" – she glared at both her parents – "you wouldn't let me do anything I was passionate about when I was little." She turned on her father. "Don't you remember all those afternoons when I had to sit through Susan's ballet lessons? It was agony. I was desperate to dance, but you said I couldn't join the ballet class, because you had to spend all your money on her!" She pointed to Shirley, who stared open-mouthed before stuttering: "You, you wanted to d… dance? You never told me! I would have loved it if you had been a dancer!"

"How could I have told you? You never showed any interest in me!" Ruth retorted. Shirley bowed her head. "And what's more" – Ruth turned to her dad again – "Nan told me when I was very little that I was an excellent pianist and that I had a pianist's hands, but you didn't take any interest when I told you I could play the piano, and later, when I was in primary school, you told me never to talk about the piano for fear of upsetting her!" She glowered at Shirley. "Nan was the only person who loved me and understood and wanted to help me fulfil my gift for music, but we all had to keep it secret from you, in case you killed it off in the bud. And that wasn't easy!"

At this point, her anger vented, she began to sob uncontrollably. Shirley came across the room to comfort her, whispering, "I'm sorry, I'm sorry."

Dad took a deep breath. "It seems that we're all to blame. We've made a terrible mess of things," he sighed. "I'm very sorry too. Can we start again?"

55

A removal van drew up outside the shop the following day as Shirley was closing the door at lunchtime. She called John: "Your removal van is here!" Emerging from the post office, he went to open the door to the house.

Two muscular men stood on the step. "Well, well, I'm blowed! It's yew John, isn't it? When they gave me my order for today, I never expected as I'd be a-seeing my ole friends!" said one of them, his familiar accent bringing a whiff of fresh country air into a busy London thoroughfare.

Dad laughed, "Why, Bob! I didn't know they would send you when I booked up Picton's!" Bob Baker, whose mother had attended the village church with Nan, was an old primary-school friend of Dad's.

"This is Alf," Bob said, introducing his colleague. "My ole mother, she were real sad when your mother died. She wanted ter talk ter yew at the funeral, but she said there were too many people all round yew. She were too shy, but she'll be right glad I've seen yew!"

"So you've brought the furniture?" Dad asked, getting down to business.

"Tha's right; yew jus' show us where yew want us ter put it."

"Ah, yes," said Dad, "you'd better come and see." He took Bob and Alf upstairs, saying: "All the furniture goes upstairs, the sofa and armchairs, and the dining table and chairs in here in this big front room; the chest of drawers in the double bedroom" – he motioned towards the main bedroom – "and the washstand in the small bedroom at the back. Can I offer you a cup of tea before you get started?"

"When we've finished tha'll be a treat, thank yew," said Bob, opening the doors and lowering the ramp at the back of the van.

"Here yew are, your boxes of your ole father's tools. I'll bring them in." Dad directed him and Alf to the scullery with them, then Bob called out: "Alf, come yew on, hurry up, bor, and take those two boxes of cutlery and silverware. We'd best not leave them on the van now it's open. Oh, and look over there, there's another box of cutlery, over there beside the crockery."

They brought the semi-precious items into the kitchen, including the clock from Nan's sitting room. Ruth clapped her hands at this unexpected pleasure. "Oh, Dad, I'm so glad you've brought the clock."

"Oh, did I? I'd forgotten that, but if it makes you happy, that's fine by me!"

"That's beautiful!" Shirley breathed in awe. "It will look lovely in the new sitting room!"

Lunch was attended by the sound of furniture being heaved up the stairs and a certain amount of puffing and blowing. Then all fell silent, and there was a light tap on the door. Dad turned round in his chair to see who was there. "I'm sorry to disturb your dinner, ole bor," said Bob.

"Ah, Bob, are you ready for your tea?"

"Noo, not yet, that wasn't what I hev come for. Would yew just like ter come and see where we've put the furniture?" The three of them followed Bob upstairs. Everything was in place where it should be. "We've stored all the cutlery and china away in that sideboard jus' as it was when we collected it."

"Well, that looks fine, thank you, Bob! Now for your tea. The kettle's on the stove."

"Noo," Bob contradicted Dad. "Tha's not what I mean. We hev'nt finished yet. Now yew betta come and see what we've got in that van. I don't know as yew really want it." Mystified, Dad and Shirley followed Bob back downstairs and out to where Alf was waiting by the van.

Ruth stayed behind to open the drawers of the sideboard. She went straight to the right-hand drawer and pulled it open. It had come with all its contents intact – and there, where she hoped they would be, were the boxes of photographs. She picked up a handful, just to check that they were all there, and glanced through them. There were the pictures of Dad and Evelyn as small children, the photos of Dad and Shirley on their wedding day and the ones of herself as a baby. She rummaged further through the drawer and was relieved to find that the photo of Nan and Aunt Dolly with their mother, Clara, was still there. She often wondered how much her dad knew of the extraordinary story that Nan had related to her about their origins. There had never been enough time to talk to him about these things: he was always too busy or too tired at the end of the day, and she always had her homework to do. Anyhow, Shirley wouldn't feel the same fascination as her, and in all likelihood would not appreciate hearing the truth about the family into which she had married.

Dad called up from below. "Ruthie, we're waiting for you to come down!" She ran downstairs and out to where Dad and Shirley were standing at the back of the removal van in time to hear her dad doubtfully saying to Bob and Alf: "Well, do you think you can get it up the stairs?"

"Tha's not a problem," Bob hastily assured him, and Alf concurred.

Ruth interrupted them, "Oh, Dad! I'm so pleased! Nan's photos are in the sideboard!"

"Oh, are they?" he replied absent-mindedly. "I have to admit I didn't look in there, but if you want them, you can have them. It's just as well they've come too." He grinned at Shirley before adding: "Now, Ruthie, there's something in the van for you. Look inside, right at the back."

Ruth squinted into the darkness. In front of her was the gramophone with the case containing Evelyn's records, and also the case that held Evelyn's repertoire of music. Dad was whispering to Shirley: "I hope you won't mind. I couldn't bear to leave them behind."

"Don't be silly," she replied. "I'm thrilled they've come!" Ruth heaved a sigh of relief, then peered farther into the pantechnicon. There, right at the back, was a large, bulky object.

She gasped in amazement at what she saw. "It can't be!" she exclaimed excitedly.

"Oh, yes it is!" Dad confirmed like a pantomime audience.

"It can't be! It's Nan's piano!" cried Ruth, and went hot and cold and dizzy with disbelief and joy.

"Tha's right, Miss," Bob said. "The lady next door, when we went round there this morning to take it to her, she say she don't want it and would we bring it to yew after all. Well, we had space in the van, so there yew are." He turned to Dad, "If you don't mind, John, I'll take up your offer of a cup of tea after all, before we heaves that instrument up those stairs. I should think Alf would be glad of one too!"

Shirley ran indoors to make the tea, followed by John and the removal men. Ruth detached an envelope that was stuck on the piano with a piece of sticky tape. As she slowly walked into the house, she opened it; inside was a letter addressed to her. She read it, lingering over every word:

Dear Ruth,
We were so sorry that your nan died. I know you will miss her greatly. Please accept our deepest sympathy. We were very fond of her too. She was a lovely, special person.

Your father kindly offered us your nan's piano together with all the music, the gramophone and your aunt's recordings. We gratefully accepted his offer, but when Piers heard of it he would have none of it. He said that the piano was yours and he could not possibly accept it, so would we send it with the music, the gramophone and the records to you with all the rest of the furniture. I know that he took the right decision, and I hope you will have much pleasure playing the piano, learning the music and listening to the records.
With love and best wishes,

Alice Harding

Ruth was overwhelmed. In the kitchen she silently handed the letter to her dad, who scanned it and laughed. "That's extraordinary, isn't it? How kind of them – and of their grandson! You'll have to write to him, Ruth!" He handed the letter to Shirley. "Read this, then you'll know what kind people they are! How odd that we've been calling them by the wrong name all this time! Mother must have misheard their name and then it stuck, and they were too polite to correct us. Not much difference between Harding and Hardy, is there?"

Shirley seized the letter and read it through quickly. She gasped and, letting the letter fall to the ground, leant against the sink to steady herself. "What's the matter?" Dad asked apprehensively.

"Oh, nothing, just too much excitement, I expect, and such a moving letter!" she stammered. "A cup of tea will soon put me right. Isn't that an answer to all our prayers? You'll be able to play too, won't you, John? Let's have tea then Bob and Alf can bring the piano in. Ruth, you and your dad can light the fire upstairs before we open the shop again, and you can spend the whole afternoon practising on your piano. We shall expect a concert this evening!" She ran off into the house and shut herself in the bedroom.

Epilogue

Shirley stood in the doorway of her newly refurbished sitting room surveying the disposition of the furniture from Beech Grove. The sofa and armchairs fitted in very nicely, she concluded, and the oak table would be so useful for the drinks parties and the dinner parties they were now in a position to give. There, where the oak table from Norhambury stood in the window bay, was a much more fitting position for fine dining than that of the old gate-leg table downstairs in the small breakfast room. It would have been impossible to invite people to dinner in that cramped space.

The piano stood along the wall opposite the fireplace, and beside it was a bookcase; next to that was the china cupboard, where she now stored her ornaments. Truth to tell, she was not too sure about those ornaments from the past. They were rather cheap, vulgar even, and didn't harmonize at all appropriately with the style that she was seeking to establish in the rest of the room. The immediate question was where might she find suitable homes firstly for the Christmas tree that John and Ruth had just gone out to buy in the lunch hour and, secondly, for the electric record player that she had ordered as a Christmas present for Ruth. She was awaiting delivery of it any day, possibly this very afternoon. She decided that the Christmas tree would fit nicely in the alcove on the right of the fireplace, and the top of the sideboard in the alcove on the left would be perfect for the record player – a clear space in easy reach of an electric socket. There hardly seemed to be room for the television; that would have to go back downstairs, into the office perhaps.

The old wind-up gramophone from Beech Grove which was on the floor by the piano had served very well yesterday evening for playing Evelyn's records of the 'Emperor' Concerto. How thrilled John had been when, to the accompaniment of the orchestra and Evelyn's performance on those old records, Ruth had played the piano solo for him! With all the turning-over of the records and changing the needles, it wasn't nearly as exciting as the real concert before that large audience in the high school, but it had given him a clear enough impression of Ruth's unmistakeable talent.

Of course, she, Shirley, had heard the 'Emperor' Concerto before, and not only in the *West Side Story* version on the radio. Long ago she had encountered it for the first time and then Evelyn had endlessly rehearsed it, to the extent that she had come to know it so well that it had driven her crazy. Since it had suddenly become Ruth's gateway to fame and success, she was determined to reconcile herself to it – though, to tell the truth, when she had seen it on the programme at the school concert, she had seriously wondered whether she should stay in case it brought on one of her attacks. She had stayed – out of curiosity as much as anything, not really expecting anything special – and thank goodness she had! She would not have missed Ruth's performance for anything, whatever piece of music she might have been playing. She was still all of a dither with amazement and the pride of it.

She ran a finger through the dust on the surface of the sideboard: John's mother wouldn't have approved of that, so out of her overall pocket she pulled a cloth and the small tin of polish which she kept about her person for dusting the fittings in the shop, and swept away the specks and particles, revealing the bright mahogany underneath. She stood back to admire the results and felt that her mother-in-law would have been satisfied with her efforts.

Then, bending down, she opened one of the cupboard doors. Inside she found a treasure trove which she did not remember having seen before and which took her breath away, a whole set of Royal Crown Derby china, plates in all sizes, bowls, cups, saucers, tureens and a gravy boat, seemingly intact and unused, but all just waiting to be arrayed in front of those as yet uninvited dinner guests. The blue, red, white and gold patterns, safely delivered and installed by John's school friend, Bob, glinted and gleamed in the fading daylight. The other door in the sideboard opened onto several sets of crystal glasses, again apparently in their pristine condition, and sparkling now that they too were exposed to the light. Undoubtedly they were wedding presents for which Lottie and Joe had not had much use, and had been forgotten, though how they had survived the Blitz was a mystery.

Turning her attention to the drawers above the cupboards, first she opened the one on the left, which was full of silver cutlery: this had definitely been used and was somewhat tarnished, not so badly however that a good polish wouldn't bring back its shine. She expected to find tablecloths and napkins in the right-hand drawer, so was taken aback to find it full of photos. She picked up a handful and sat down on the arm of an armchair to study them. Some were familiar and expected: photos of John and Evelyn as small children, photos of Ruth as a baby, even wedding photos of herself and John, with another one of herself that she was not at all proud of: there she was, resting her hand on the handle of the pram and looking most displeased. She remembered it all too well and placed it at the bottom of the pile.

There was also a curious bundle of very old pictures, probably from the nineteenth century, of parties with lords and ladies in exotic surroundings, and one of a beautiful, aristocratic-looking girl with her fair hair piled on the top of her head. Beneath this one was a photo of a tall, thin, dark man who, in another, was carrying two little children. Shirley looked closely at these pictures. They came from another, distant age. But were those little children Lottie and Dolly? she wondered. She had always speculated why John's skin was so permanently tanned and his hair so dark, like Ruth's in fact, but when once she had asked him about it, he had shrugged and replied that he had no idea. He supposed there might be something foreign in his ancestry, but didn't know what. As she herself well knew what it was like to be of foreign ancestry in this country, she had left it at that and not raised the subject again.

As she put the collection back in the drawer, she remembered something. Leaving the drawer open, she went from the sitting room to the next room, the double bedroom, and opened her own top drawer. In among her handkerchiefs and stockings she found what she was searching for, a small, rather creased and battered photo; picking it out hastily, she fairly ran back into the sitting room to hide it inconspicuously among the other photos in the drawer. She was glad to have relieved herself of that burden which had oppressed her conscience for a very long time, ever since Ruth was little and she had given her old coat away to the church bazaar, but had kept the photo she had found in the pocket without returning it to her daughter.

Rather than close the drawer straight away, she couldn't resist one last glance, thumbing through the photos to see if by any remote chance Lottie had been given copies of the ones that Ruth had brought back at half-term. Ruth had hidden them away somewhere; they were no longer in her shoulder bag: she knew that, because one day, while Ruth was at school, she had rifled through its contents without success.

She longed desperately to see those pictures of that handsome young man again, on a beach on the east coast, or eating fish and chips, or playing cricket with his brother and Ruth. She suspected that Ruth knew him better than she was prepared to admit: certainly her rising blushes at the mention of his name had given that much away when they had gone out to tea together. However, an inner voice warned her against teasing Ruth or pressing her for more information, because then Ruth would clam up, as she always did, and she would be sure to lose the tenuous but certain link with her own past that was so important.

The clues to it were all in that young man's face and in his grandparents' name, which she had only just discovered. Harding was a name she would never forget, yet when she heard it from John's lips as he read the letter attached to the piano, the shock had sent her reeling against the kitchen sink, in the same way as her first sight of the boy in the photo had thrown her into utter confusion and made her ill. How on earth was she going to solve this puzzle that meant so much to her without hurting Ruth or John?

There was one more box on the floor which she had not yet opened. Glancing inside she saw that it contained larger, framed photos. She recognized the first one she pulled out; it showed a beautiful girl with glossy, dark hair and dark eyes. She stared at the face for a couple of seconds, then placed the photo in its frame carefully on top of the piano.

Noises of the front door opening and the sound of familiar voices came up the stairs from the hall, so she closed the drawer and bolted down the stairs to help her husband and daughter bring the Christmas tree indoors, before opening the shop and the post office for the afternoon's business.

Acknowledgements

I am greatly indebted to my dear friend, Mary Taylor, an exemplary pianist and gifted teacher, for her suggestions and help in ensuring the authenticity of the musical elements and references in this novel.

Equally I am profoundly grateful to Alicia Chaffey, a young musician who is embarking on her career as a concert pianist, for sharing her experience and expertise with me.

My thanks go to Sarah Batchelor of the Royal College of Music for helping me find a way through the ill-defined modes of laying out and transcribing musical terminology.

Finally I must thank my publishers, Alex Gallenzi and Elisabetta Minervini of Alma Books, for their faith in me, and to my family for all the encouragement they have given me.

TRAVELLING TO INFINITY

THE TRUE STORY BEHIND THE AWARD-WINNING FILM

THE THEORY OF EVERYTHING

Jane Hawking

THE NUMBER ONE BESTSELLER

ISBN 978-1-84688-366-8 • £7.99

THE INCREDIBLE STORY OF
JANE AND STEPHEN HAWKING

His Mind Changed Our World. Her Love Changed His.

"Stephen Hawking may think in 11 dimensions, but his
first wife has learnt to love in several."
The Sunday Times

"What becomes of time when a marriage unravels?
And what becomes of the woman who has located her
whole self within its sphere? For Jane Hawking, the physics
of love and loss are set in a private universe."
The Guardian

"Jane writes about her former husband with
tenderness, respect and protectiveness."
Sunday Express

 eBook: 978-1-84688-373-6